RETREAT, HELL!

Also by W. E. B. Griffin
in Large Print:

Final Justice
The Fighting Agents
The Investigators
The Secret Warriors
Special Ops

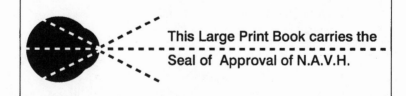

RETREAT, HELL!

W. E. B. Griffin

Thorndike Press • Waterville, Maine

Published in 2004 by arrangement with G. P. Putnam's Sons, a member of Penguin Group (USA) Inc.

Thorndike Press® Large Print Core.

The tree indicium is a trademark of Thorndike Press.

The text of this Large Print edition is unabridged. Other aspects of the book may vary from the original edition.

Set in 16 pt. Plantin by Elena Picard.

Printed in the United States on permanent paper.

Library of Congress Cataloging-in-Publication Data

Griffin, W. E. B.
    Retreat, hell! / W.E.B. Griffin.
       p. cm.
    ISBN 0-7862-6254-0 (lg. print : hc : alk. paper)
    1. United States — History, Military — 20th century — Fiction. 2. United States. Marine Corps — Fiction. 3. Korean War, 1950–1953 — Fiction. 4. Large type books. I. Title.
    PS3557.R489137R48 2004b
    813'.54—dc22   2003070269

*THE CORPS is respectfully dedicated
to the memory of*

*Colonel Drew James Barrett, Jr., USMC
19 April 1919–1 May 2003*

*Second Lieutenant
Drew James Barrett III, USMC
3 April 1945–27 February 1969
Died of wounds, Quang Nam Province,
Republic of Vietnam*

*Major Alfred Lee Butler III, USMC
4 September 1950–8 February 1984
Died as the result of terrorist action,
Beirut, Lebanon*

*Donald L. Schomp
A Marine Fighter Pilot
who became a legendary
U.S. Army Master Aviator
RIP 9 April 1989*

"SEMPER FI!"

As the Founder/CEO of NAVH, the only national health agency solely devoted to those who, although not totally blind, have an eye disease which could lead to serious visual impairment, I am pleased to recognize Thorndike Press* as one of the leading publishers in the large print field.

Founded in 1954 in San Francisco to prepare large print textbooks for partially seeing children, NAVH became the pioneer and standard setting agency in the preparation of large type.

Today, those publishers who meet our standards carry the prestigious "Seal of Approval" indicating high quality large print. We are delighted that Thorndike Press is one of the publishers whose titles meet these standards. We are also pleased to recognize the significant contribution Thorndike Press is making in this important and growing field.

Lorraine H. Marchi, L.H.D.
Founder/CEO
NAVH

* Thorndike Press encompasses the following imprints: Thorndike, Wheeler, Walker and Large Print Press.

KOREAN PENINSULA

Prologue

Until August 1945, when General Order Number One, the protocol for the surrender — and occupation — of Japan was being somewhat hastily drafted in Washington, the 38th Parallel, which runs across the Korean Peninsula, had been just one line on a map of the globe.

At the time, World War II was just about over. Nagasaki and Hiroshima had been obliterated by atomic bombs, and Japan was willing to surrender. The Soviet Union had just — somewhat belatedly — declared war on the Japanese Empire, and had already started to move troops into the Japanese "Protectorates" of Manchuria and Korea.

President Truman, who had already learned not to trust the Soviet Union, realized that to keep the Red Army from occupying all of Korea, a border — "a demarcation line" — between the northern part of the Korean Peninsula and the southern, where the United States planned to station troops, was needed.

If Korea was divided — about equally — at the 38th Parallel, the United States would control Seoul, the capital, and the major ports of Inchon — near Seoul — and Pusan — at the southern tip of the peninsula.

The division at the 38th Parallel was proposed to the Soviets as the demarcation line, and they raised no objections. The seeds for what became the People's Democratic Republic of North Korea and the Republic of South Korea were sown.

Four years and eleven months later, the Inmun Gun — the Soviet-trained North Korean Army — invaded South Korea across the 38th Parallel with the announced intention of "unifying" Korea.

The attack officially — and in fact — came as a "complete surprise" to the United States. United States intelligence agencies at all levels had failed to perform their basic duty to warn of an impending attack on the United States or its allies.

It was hard then — and still is, more than half a century later — to understand why we didn't see the attack coming.

Immediately after World War II, Stalin had managed to establish surrogate governments in East Germany, Poland, Hungary, Czechoslovakia — and North Korea. On 5 March 1946, in a speech at Fulton, Missouri, British Wartime Prime Minister Winston S. Churchill said, "From Stettin in the Baltic to Trieste in the Adriatic, an iron curtain has descended across the Continent."

President Harry S Truman had become very suspicious of Soviet intentions even before he ordered the use of atomic weapons against

Japan, and he had acted to foil them.

For example, Truman had courageously dispatched American advisers — actually the first special forces/operations soldiers, long before anyone even thought of wearing a green beret — to Greece, where they successfully thwarted Soviet intentions to take over the birthplace of democracy.

And when the Soviets tried to force the Americans, French, and English from Berlin, Truman had ordered the Air Lift, which saw U.S. Air Force transports landing round the clock at sixty-second intervals to keep Berlin fed, and the Western Allies in the former German capital.

Many historians now believe that the reason Stalin authorized his surrogate North Korean Army to invade South Korea is that the United States had actually led him to believe we would raise no objections.

On 12 January 1950, Secretary of State Dean Acheson outlined President Truman's Asian policy in a speech at the National Press Club in Washington, D.C. Acheson "drew a line" of countries the United States considered "essential to its national interests," a euphemism everyone understood to mean the United States would go to war to defend.

Acheson placed Japan, Okinawa, and the Philippines within the "American defense perimeter." Taiwan and Korea were not mentioned.

The United States was then "completely surprised" five months later when, in the early morning of 25 June 1950, the North Koreans invaded across the 38th Parallel.

Not that twenty-four hours' — or ten days' or six months' — advance warning of the attack would have been of much real use: The Inmun Gun was well trained, well disciplined, and well armed. The South Korean armed forces were not.

The South Koreans had been denied, for example, heavy artillery because some of Truman's advisers believed they might use it to invade North Korea. South Korea had also been denied modern aircraft, tanks, and other military hardware by the same reasoning. And, of course, for reasons of economy.

There were only several hundred American troops in South Korea on that Sunday morning, assigned to the Korean Military Advisory Group (KMAG), and they were armed only with their individual weapons.

The Eighth United States Army was scattered among the islands of Japan, but it was not prepared to fight a war.

Blame can fairly be laid for this:

The President of the United States, under the Constitution, is Commander-in-Chief of the Armed Forces. The authors of the Constitution wanted to make absolutely sure that the armed forces were firmly under civilian control, and gave that control to the President.

With that authority, of course, came responsibility. It is the responsibility — the duty — of the President to ensure that the armed forces are prepared to wage war when called upon to do so. In practical terms, this means the President ensures that the uniformed officers in command of the armed forces meet their responsibilities to keep their forces in readiness. In turn, that means that the armed forces are trained and equipped to go to war.

There is little question now that the senior American officer in the Pacific, General of the Army Douglas MacArthur, failed in his duty to make sure that the Eighth Army under his command was both trained and equipped to go to war. On 25 June 1950, it was neither.

That it was not adequately *trained* is entirely MacArthur's fault, but to place blame for the literally disgraceful lack of equipment in the Eighth United States Army, it is necessary to go all the way to the top of the chain of command.

United States Forces, Far East, were under the command of the Joint Chiefs of Staff. MacArthur repeatedly advised them of the sorry state of his equipment, and requested to be supplied with what he believed he needed.

The Chairmen of the Joint Chiefs — there were several during this period — repeatedly requested of their superior, the Secretary of Defense, that the U.S. Armed Forces worldwide (not only MacArthur's forces in Japan) be adequately supplied with the necessary equipment.

Truman's Secretary of Defense, Louis Johnson, openly boasted at the time that he had first cut military spending to the bone, and then cut some more.

He had. At Johnson's orders, there were two battalions (instead of the three considered necessary) in most of the U.S. Army's regiments. And there were two regiments (instead of three) in all but one of the divisions.

The Secretary of Defense is, with the advice and consent of the Senate, appointed by the President. Once Louis Johnson had been confirmed, President Truman was responsible for his actions, good or bad.

The blame for the inadequate equipment in the Eighth U.S. Army — and just about everywhere else — has to be laid on the desk of President Harry S Truman, right beside the small sign reading "The Buck Stops Here" that he kept there.

There were, of course, extenuating circumstances.

Congress, for one, was not in the mood to appropriate the billions of dollars it would have cost to bring the armed forces back to the state of preparedness they had been in five years before, when, on 2 September 1945, MacArthur had accepted the unconditional surrender of the Japanese Empire on the battleship USS *Missouri* in Tokyo Harbor.

And Korea was almost at the bottom of the list of problems with which President Truman had to deal on a daily basis. Most of these problems had to do with thwarting Soviet mischief in Europe, the Near East, and even Africa.

The Soviets hadn't done nearly so well in the Far East, and the credit for that unquestionably belongs to Douglas MacArthur, who had flatly refused to permit the Soviets to participate in the occupation of Japan.

MacArthur had also successfully sown the seed of democratic government in the mind of the Japanese people, and taken wide and generally successful steps to get the war-ravaged Japanese economy moving.

As far as the disgraceful condition of the Eighth United States Army in Japan was concerned, one has to remember that all armies are rank conscious.

General of the Army Douglas MacArthur was not only the senior officer on active duty, but he had been Army Chief of Staff when the general officers in the 1950 Pentagon had been captains and majors. In World War II, MacArthur had been a theater commander, commanding more men of all services than there were now in 1950 in all the armed forces of the United States.

There are annual inspections of every organization in the Army, ending with a conference during which the inspectors point out to the commander where he is doing what he should not be doing, or not doing what he should be doing.

It is very difficult to imagine any officer, even one with a galaxy of stars on his epaulets, pointing out to General of the Army Douglas MacArthur, Supreme Commander, Allied Powers, and Commanding General, United States Far East Command (FECOM), where he was doing something wrong, or where he had failed to do something he should have been doing.

And none did.

Because of the International Date Line, when it is Sunday in Korea it is Saturday in New York City and Washington. The first word of the attack reached the Pentagon about eight o'clock Saturday night, and at about the same time, the United Nations Commission in Korea managed to get UN Secretary General Trygve Lie on the telephone at his estate on Long Island.

Lie blurted, "This is war against the United Nations."

President Truman learned of the attack at his home in Independence, Missouri, early Sunday morning and immediately boarded his airplane, the *Independence*, to fly back to Washington.

Lie convened an emergency meeting of the UN Security Council at two o'clock Sunday af-

16

ternoon. The Soviet Union, trying to force the UN into seating Red China — and expelling Chiang Kai-shek's Chinese Nationalists — was refusing to attend Security Council meetings and did not participate.

This was a blunder on their part. Had they attended, the Soviet Union could have vetoed the resolution the UN passed. The resolution stated that the attack constituted a breach of the peace, ordered an immediate cessation of hostilities and the immediate withdrawal of North Korean forces from South Korea, and called upon all UN members to "render every assistance to the UN in the execution of this resolution."

At about six o'clock that evening, in Washington, in Blair House — across Pennsylvania Avenue from the White House, which was being repaired — President Truman met with the more important members of his staff.

They quickly and unanimously agreed with Truman that the interests of the United States demanded that immediate action be taken to stop Communist aggression in Korea.

A little after ten-thirty Sunday evening, two teletype orders from the Chairman of the Joint Chiefs of Staff were sent to the Far East.

The first, to the Commanding General, FECOM — MacArthur — authorized him to send ammunition and military equipment to Korea, to prevent the loss of Seoul; authorized him to provide ships and aircraft to evacuate Amer-

ican citizens from Korea; and directed him to send a "survey party" to Korea to see what was going on.

It is germane to note that until MacArthur got that teletype order he had no official role in Korea. The former Japanese Protectorate of Korea, now the Republic of South Korea, was an independent nation.

The second order went to the United States Seventh Fleet. It was to immediately sail from its several major home ports — the largest were in the Philippines and Okinawa — for the U.S. Navy Base at Sasebo, Japan. On arrival, the warships would come under the operational control of the Commander, U.S. Naval Forces, Far East.

Since Commander, Naval Forces, Far East, was under FECOM, that meant they would be under MacArthur's command.

MacArthur immediately ordered the U.S. Far Eastern Air Force — already under his command — to Korea to protect the evacuation of American civilians and dependents from Inchon and Pusan.

Over Inchon, the American jets were fired upon by three Russian-made YAK fighters, which the Americans promptly shot down.

It was the first American victory in the Korean War, and much time would pass before there was another.

Outnumbered, outgunned, and in many cases poorly led, most of the South Korean

Army simply began to disintegrate in the face of the North Korean attack.

The Survey Party — thirteen officers and two enlisted men under Brigadier General John H. Church — took off from Tokyo as soon as it could be formed. While in the air, they received two messages, the first saying it would probably be wiser not to try to land at Seoul's Kimpo Airfield, and suggested the field at Suwon, thirty miles or so south of Seoul, as an alternate. The second said that the Pentagon had given MacArthur command of all U.S. Forces in Korea, and the Survey Party had been rather grandly redesignated as "GHQ Advance Command and Liaison Group in Korea."

ADCOM landed at Suwon about 1900 27 June. Colonel William H. S. Wright, the KMAG Chief of Staff, who met them, suggested that it probably would be better to wait for morning to drive into Seoul than to try to do so in the hours of darkness.

At 0400 the next day, two KMAG officers drove into Suwon and reported to General Church that the bridges across the Han River had been blown and that Seoul was in the hands of the enemy.

Church radioed MacArthur that U.S. ground troops were going to be necessary if the United States intended to push the North Koreans back across the 38th Parallel. The reply was a query: "Is Suwon safe for a high-ranking officer to land there tomorrow?"

Church replied that it was.

The "high-ranking officer" turned out to be General of the Army Douglas MacArthur, who took a quick look around, then radioed the Pentagon that U.S. troops were going to be necessary.

While this was going on, the United Nations, realizing that the North Koreans had no intention of obeying the UN resolution to cease, desist, and get out of South Korea, issued — on 27 June — another one:

". . . recommends that the members of the UN furnish such assistance to the Republic of Korea as may be necessary to repel the armed attack. . . ."

Resisting the Communist attack would be an action of the United Nations, rather than a unilateral action by the United States.

Just before 0500 30 June, President Truman got MacArthur's assessment of the Korean situation and his request for authorization to use American ground troops. Truman immediately authorized the deployment of one regimental combat team, and after thinking it over for two hours, authorized the deployment of two infantry divisions.

At 0800 1 July "Task Force Smith" — 400 officers and men from the 21st Infantry, 24th Infantry Division, under Lieutenant Colonel Charles B. Smith — boarded USAF C-54 transports at Itazuke Air Force Base in Japan and were flown to Korea.

It was not the regimental combat team Truman had authorized. It was all the men the 24th Division could muster on short notice.

On the morning of 5 July, "Task Force Smith" was in place on the Suwon–Osan Highway, south of Suwon. The "crew-served" weapons with which it was supposed to halt the North Korean Army consisted of two 75-mm recoilless rifles; two 4.2-inch mortars; six 2.36-inch rocket launchers; and four 60-mm mortars. The 52nd Field Artillery — six light 105-mm howitzers — had been assigned to them.

When the North Koreans' Russian-built T-34 tanks attacked, they were engaged by Task Force Smith's 75-mm recoilless rifles. The projectiles bounced off the Russian armor. So did the 2.36-inch rockets. So did the shells from the 105-mm howitzers.

On the morning of 6 July, Colonel Smith *was* able to muster only 248 officers and men of the original 400. The artillery had lost five officers and twenty-six men and most of its cannon.

And they had managed to delay — not stop — the North Koreans for less than seven hours.

More troops were going to be needed, and quickly. The problem was, there were no more troops.

The Marine Corps was ordered to furnish a division. There were two Marine divisions: The

First, in California, was at less than half war-time strength, and the Second, on the East Coast, was in even worse shape. At Head-quarters, USMC, Major Drew J. Barrett, Jr.,* a junior G-1 staff officer, marched into the office of the Commandant of the Marine Corps to report that there was no way the Corps could meet the requirements laid on it by the Commander-in-Chief except by mobilizing the entire reserve. This was done.

The Eighth Army, under General Walton H. "Johnny" Walker, who had served with distinction under Patton in Europe, began a series of delaying actions — in other words, retreated —

---

*Barrett was an infantryman who began his combat service with the Marines as a lieutenant on the beaches of Guadalcanal. "The Corps" is dedicated to his son, Second Lieutenant Drew J. Barrett III, USMC, who was fatally wounded in Vietnam while serving with the 26th Marines, then in combat beside the 9th Marines, which was commanded by his father. While commanding the 9th, Barrett chose a young officer to command one of its companies, making him the first black officer ever to command Marines in combat. In May 2003, as this book was being written, that officer, later Major General and Ambassador Gary Cooper, attended Colonel Barrett's funeral, at which Marines of the 1st Force Recon, in dress blues, rendered full military honors and Barrett's remains were covered with the National Colors he had flown at Khe Sanh.

down the Korean Peninsula.

On 4 August, the Pusan Perimeter was established. This was a small enclave at the tip of the peninsula. The alternative to the perimeter was being pushed into the sea.

Reinforcements began to arrive from Japan, Hawaii, and the continental United States. By gutting the 2nd Marine Division on the East Coast, the Marine Corps was able to form from the 1st Marine Division the First Marine Brigade (Provisional) and send it to Korea.

General Walker immediately made the Marines his "Fire Brigade," moving it around within the perimeter to reinforce whatever Army units seemed most vulnerable to the continuing North Korean attack.

MacArthur, meanwhile — while there was still genuine doubt that Walker could hold the Pusan Perimeter — was planning a counterattack. He was later to claim he'd first thought of it when he'd made his first quick visit to Korea.

It is a matter of record that MacArthur, in early July, had ordered his chief of staff, Major General Edward M. Almond, to plan for a landing on the west coast of the peninsula.

When he finally revealed his plan — to make an amphibious landing at Inchon, the port near Seoul — it was greeted with reactions ranging from "grave doubts" to mutters of "absolute insanity" from just about every senior officer made privy to it.

It was the worst possible place to stage an amphibious landing. There was a long list of things wrong with the plan, primarily the "landing beach" itself.

To get to the "landing beach" the invasion fleet would have to navigate the narrow Flying Fish Channel, which was not navigable except at high tide, and then only for two hours. When the thirty-plus-foot tides receded, the landing area was a sea of mud.

There was no beach. Men would have to climb a seawall when they left their landing barges.

Army Chief of Staff Collins sent General Matthew B. Ridgway, recognized as one of the brightest officers in the Army, to Tokyo to "confer" with MacArthur about the Inchon plan. Everyone understood that Ridgway's mission was to talk MacArthur out of his plan.

He failed to do so.

President Truman was faced with the choice of listening to the senior officers in the Pentagon, who wanted him to forbid the operation, or letting MacArthur have his way.

Political considerations certainly influenced Truman to some degree. It was a given that if Truman supported the Pentagon and forbade the invasion, MacArthur would logically conclude that the President had no faith in him, and retire.

If he did so quietly, fine. But that was unlikely. It was more likely that the "firing" of the legendary national hero would see MacArthur as the Republican candidate in the upcoming presidential election.

Whatever the reasons, Truman decided not to interfere with MacArthur's plan to invade at Inchon on 15 September.

MacArthur gave command of the invasion force — X Corps — to Major General Ned Almond. He did not, however, relieve Almond of his assignment as his chief of staff. While this was perfectly legal, and certainly MacArthur's prerogative, the Pentagon establishment was outraged.

Some of their rage, MacArthur's supporters claimed, was because they could not now give MacArthur a chief of staff who could be counted on to provide them a window into MacArthur's thinking.

Eighth Army Commander Walker bitterly protested the loss of the Marines to X Corps. He said he could not guarantee holding the Pusan Perimeter without them. MacArthur was unmoved. The First Marine Brigade (Provisional) came off the lines in Pusan, boarded the ships of the invasion fleet, and en route to Inchon, reinforced at sea by a third regiment, became the 1st Marine Division.

The invasion was a spectacular success.

At 1200 29 September — two weeks after the landing — MacArthur stood in Seoul's National Assembly Hall and told South Korean President Syngman Rhee,

". . . On behalf of the United Nations Command, I am happy to restore to you, Mr. President, the seat of your government. . . ."

MacArthur then led the assembled dignitaries in recitation of the Lord's Prayer.

The Eighth Army had broken out of the Pusan Perimeter. The North Korean Army was in full retreat.

It was logical to presume that the Korean War was over.

I

[One]
Near Chongju, South Korea
0815 28 September 1950

Major Malcolm S. Pickering, USMCR, whose appearance and physical condition reflected that he had not had a change of clothing — much less the opportunity to bathe with soap or shave — since he had been shot down fifty-eight days before sat between two enormous boulders near the crest of a hill.

He thought — but was by no means sure — that he was about twenty miles north of Taejon and about thirty miles south of Suwon. Where he hoped he was, was in a remote area of South Korea where there were few North Korean soldiers, lessening the chance that he would be spotted until he could attract the attention of an American airplane, and have someone come and pick him up.

Those hopes were of course, after fifty-eight days, fading. Immediately after he had been shot down, there had been a flurry of search activity, but when they hadn't found him the activity had slowed down, and — logic forced him to acknowledge — finally ceased.

He wasn't at all sure that anyone had seen any of the signs he left after the first one, the day after he'd been shot down. What he had done was stamp into the mud of a drained rice paddy with his boots the letters *PP* and an arrow. No one called him "Malcolm." He was called "Pick" and he knew that all the members of his squadron — and other Marine pilots — would make the connection.

The arrow's direction was basically meaningless. If the arrow pointed northward, sometimes he went that way. More often than not, he went east, west, or south. He knew that he couldn't move far enough so that he wouldn't be able to see an airplane searching low and slow for him in the area of the sign left in the mud.

He had left other markers every other — or every third — day since he'd been on the run. The fact that there had been Corsairs flying low over some of the markers — logic forced him to acknowledge — was not proof that they had seen the markers. The Corsairs, when they were not in direct support of the Marines on the ground, went on combined reconnaissance and interdiction flights, which meant that they were flying close to the deck, not that they had seen his markers.

It was too risky to stay in one place, so he had kept moving. He'd gotten his food — and an A-Frame to carry it in — from South Korean peasant farmers, who were anxious to help him, but made it clear they didn't want anyone to know — either the North Korean military or a local Communist — that they had done so. In either case, they would have been shot.

He was, of course, discouraged. Logic forced him to acknowledge that sooner or later, he was going to be spotted by North Koreans, or by someone who would report him to the North Koreans. And if they found him, he would be forced to make a decision that was not at all pleasant to think about.

It wasn't simply a question of becoming a prisoner, although that was an unpleasant prospect in itself. Three times since he had been on the run he had come across bodies — once, more than thirty — of U.S. Army soldiers who, having been captured and after having their hands tied behind them with commo wire, had been summarily executed and left to rot where they had fallen.

If the North Koreans spotted him, and he could not get away, he was going to die. Not with his hands tied behind his back, but very probably by his own hand, unless he was lucky enough to go down with .45 blazing, à la John Wayne. Logic forced him to acknowledge that was wishful thinking, that he couldn't take the risk of going out in a blaze of glory, that he would have to do it himself.

Major Pickering's father was Brigadier General Fleming Pickering, USMCR, who was the Deputy Director of the Central Intelligence Agency for Asia. For obvious reasons, young Pickering could not allow himself to fall into North Korean hands.

It was sort of a moot question anyway. With only five rounds left for the .45, he couldn't put up much of a fight with two North Koreans, much less a platoon of the bastards, or a company.

The hilltop was bathed in bright morning sunlight, the rays of which had finally warmed Major Pickering — it had been as cold as a witch's teat during the night — but had not yet warmed the ground fog in the valley below enough to burn it off.

That meant that Major Pickering could not see what he was looking for, even through the 8 x 35 U.S. Navy binoculars he had somewhat whimsically — if, as it turned out, very fortuitously — "borrowed" from the USS *Badoeng Strait* just before taking off.

The rice paddy in the valley where he had stamped out the last marker in the mud was covered with ground fog.

He set the binoculars down and went into the bag tied to the A-Frame. There was what was left of a roasted chicken carcass and the roasted rib cage of a small pig. Surprising Major Pickering not at all, both were rotten to the point where trying to eat any of it would be gross folly.

After thinking it over carefully, he decided he would bury the rotten meat before breakfast. He dug a small trench with a K-bar knife and did so, and then went back into the A-Frame bag and took from it three balls of cold rice. The smell they gave off was not appealing, but it was not nausea-inducing, and he popped them one at a time into his mouth and forced them down.

That was the end of rations, which meant that he would have to get some food today. That meant tonight. What he would do was come off the hill, very carefully, and look for some Korean farmer's thatch-roofed stone hut. When he found one, he would keep it under surveillance all day and go to it after dark, entering it with .45 drawn and hoping there would be food offered, and that the farmer would not send someone to report the presence of an American the moment he left.

So far, food had been offered and North Korean troops had not come looking for him at first light. So far, he had been lucky. Logic forced him to acknowledge that sooner or later everybody's luck changed, most often for the worse.

When he drank from his canteen — he had two — he drained it, which meant that when he found a Korean farmer's house and more or less threw himself on their mercy, he would have to stick around long enough to boil water to take with him.

He picked up the binoculars and trained them again on the rice paddy below. The fog had burned off somewhat in the area; he could see the dirt path — it didn't deserve to be called a road — leading to it, but not the rice paddy itself.

"Oh, shit," he said aloud.

Two vehicles were just visible on the path.

They had to be North Koreans. It was entirely possible that these were the first two motorized vehicles ever to move down the path used by ox-drawn carts.

"I'm losing my fucking mind," he said softly, but aloud.

The two vehicles were a jeep and a three-quarter-ton weapons carrier. A large American flag was affixed to the tall antenna rising from the rear of the jeep.

He took the binoculars from his eyes, then squinted his eyes and rolled them around, and then raised them again, hooking the eyepieces under the bone at his eye sockets.

The jeep and the flag it had been flying . . .

Jesus Christ, did I really see an American flag?

. . . were no longer in sight in the ground fog, but the rear of the weapons carrier was visible.

There were men holding rifles standing at the back of it, in what looked like U.S. Army uniforms — but he couldn't be sure —

Jesus, they're gooks! What that is, is a captured weapons carrier, with gooks driving it.

And they're right at the paddy when I stomped the signal in the mud!

Jesus Christ, they're looking for me!

How the hell did they know I was here?

Well, if I have trouble seeing them with binoculars, they can't see me, and that's a hell of a distance away.

In what direction did I point the arrow?

South, I pointed it south! I'm north. Maybe they won't even look this way.

And maybe they will.

He took the binoculars from his eyes again and did the eye exercises, and then put the eyepieces back to his eyes.

Another man was now standing at the back of the weapons carrier, a rifle slung from his shoulder. He was at least a foot taller than the others.

Jesus, that's a big gook!

Gook, shit, that's a white man!

Look again. Don't do anything stupid!

He exercised his eyes without removing the binoculars from his face.

When he focused them again there was one more man at the back of the weapons carrier, not quite as tall as the first one but conspicuously larger than the Orientals.

And white. That's a white man.

Those are U.S. Army soldiers.

Or maybe Russians? The Russians would love to grab a downed aviator. And if they are Russians, that would explain the jeep and the weapons carrier.

Shit, those are Americans! I can tell, somehow, by the way they stand.

So what do I do now?

Signal them, obviously. There's no way I can get down this fucking hill in less than thirty minutes. It took me nearly an hour to climb up here.

I could fire the .45.

If they could hear it, which I don't think very likely, they won't be able to tell from which direction the sound came.

If I fire three shots — supposed to be the distress signal — that'll leave me two rounds. And if they can't hear the three shots, they won't be able to recognize the distress signal, and I'm down to two shots.

The signaling mirror!
Where the hell is that?
Jesus, I didn't toss it, lose it, did I?

A frantic search of the bag on the A-Frame turned up the signaling mirror. It was an oblong of polished metal, maybe three by four inches. There was an X-shaped cut in the center of it, presumably to be used as some sort of aiming device — he had never figured out how that worked — to reflect the rays of the sun, and the dots and dashes of the international Morse code were embossed on one side. He had never figured out how you were supposed to be able to send Morse code with the mirror, either.

But the basic idea of the mirror, reflecting the rays of the sun to attract someone's attention, seemed simple enough, and he tried to do that. He was quickly able to focus the reflected light on boulders farther down the hill, and, encouraged by that, tried to direct the light all the way down the hill into the valley, to the rear of the weapons carrier.

He couldn't see the light flashing anywhere in the valley.

He put the binoculars to his eyes again with his left hand and tried to aim the mirror with his right.

He couldn't see a flash of light that way either.

But he saw the two tall guys, the two Americans, vanish from sight, and then the gooks with them . . .

Who the hell are they?

. . . crawled into the bed of the weapons carrier.

And then the weapons carrier backed off the ox path into the edge of the rice paddy. The jeep reappeared . . .

That is an American flag, goddamn it!

. . . and headed the other way down the ox path. The weapons carrier followed it.

In a moment, they were out of sight.

Jesus H. Fucking Christ!

Major Pickering, close to tears, in a frustrated rage, threw the signaling mirror down the hill.

He lay on his back between the rocks for a full minute, and then heaved himself erect.

Then he went down the hill and started looking for the mirror.

[Two]

The jeep — its bumper markings identified it as belonging to Headquarters and Headquarters Company, 7th Infantry Division — had a pedestal-mounted .30-caliber Browning air-cooled machine gun, and the backseat had been replaced with a rack of radios.

There were three men in it, two Americans and a South Korean. One of the Americans was Major Kenneth R. McCoy, USMCR, a lithely muscular, even-featured, fair-skinned thirty-year-old. He was driving. The other American was Master Gunner Ernest W. Zimmerman, USMC — a stocky, round faced, tightly muscled, short, barrel-chested thirty-five-year-old. Zimmerman rode with his right foot resting on the fender extension, the butt of a Thompson .45-ACP-caliber submachine gun resting on his muscular upper leg.

The Korean was a South Korean National Police Sergeant named Kim. He had no place to sit, and had jury-rigged, from web pistol belts, a sort of a harness, and rode standing — or half sitting — in a position to train and fire the machine gun. The rig looked both uncomfortable and precarious, but Sergeant Kim had neither complained nor lost his footing.

Following the jeep was a Dodge three-quarter-ton truck, called a "weapons carrier," that also bore bumper markings identifying it as belonging to the 7th Infantry Division, specifically to the 7th Military Police Company.

It was being driven by another National Police Sergeant, also named Kim. Technical Sergeant Richard C. Jennings, USMC — a long and lanky twenty-six-year-old — rode beside him with an M-1 Garand rifle in his lap. Three sergeants — one Marine and two National Police — rode on the wood-slat seats in the truck bed. Sergeant Alvin C. Cole, USMC, was armed with a Browning automatic rifle (BAR), and there was a .30-caliber air-cooled Browning on a bipod mount on the floor of the truck. The Koreans were armed with M-2 (fully automatic) carbines. Everybody was wearing U.S. Army fatigues without insignia of any kind.

Major McCoy didn't say a word for the next ten minutes, until the ox path came onto a dirt road. He stopped the jeep and took a map from under the cushion.

"Well, at least we know the bastard's still alive," he said. "Your guess is he stamped that out twenty-four hours ago?"

"No more than that. Just before they took the picture," Zimmerman said.

"Well, if he hung around, he would have seen us," McCoy said. "I have no idea where to look for him."

"What do you want to do, Killer?" Zimmerman asked.

Marine master gunners do not ordinarily address Marine majors by anything but their rank — or, of course, as "sir" — but Major McCoy did not seem to either notice or take offense.

"Well, we can't hang around here, can

we, Ernie?" McCoy said. And then he added, bitterly, "If at first you don't succeed, fuck it."

He put the jeep in gear and turned onto the dirt road, heading north.

[Three]
Thirty-eight Miles South of Suwon, South Korea
1205 28 September 1950

The map showed the unnamed road — which ran north from Pyongtaek toward Suwon along the rail line, paralleling Korean National Route 1 — as paved, and surprising both Major McCoy and Gunner Zimmerman, it had been. They had been on it for just over an hour.

There was always the potential threat of mines, but neither the macadam nor the cobblestones with which the road was paved showed signs of having been disturbed. The shoulders, too, had appeared undisturbed, although of course it would have been far easier to conceal the traces of mine-burying in dirt and clay than in macadam or cobblestones.

The thing to do, obviously, was stay off the shoulders, and they had done so. And neither had they driven very fast. They wanted to have plenty of time to stop in case they saw dislodged cobblestones or suspicious-looking disruptions in the macadam.

Major McCoy raised his left arm above his head to catch the attention of Sergeant Kim in the weapons carrier following, then braked.

He pointed to a copse of gnarled pine trees a hundred yards or so down the road.

"I don't think anyone'll see us in there," he said, adding, "I'm hungry."

He slowed to a crawl as he approached the trees. Zimmerman first leaned out the side of the jeep, studying the shoulder, and then held his hand up in a signal to stop.

Then he got out of the jeep and intently studied the shoulder before motioning to McCoy to come ahead. Then he walked carefully across the shoulder and down a slope into a wide ditch. McCoy carefully eased the jeep after him, then Sergeant Kim followed with the weapons carrier.

McCoy took a Thompson from a rack below the windshield, got out of the jeep, and walked carefully southward along the ditch, looking for signs of disturbance in the mud — and for trip wires, booby traps, anything.

Finally, when he was about one hundred yards from the vehicles, he stopped and turned his attention to the grassy slope up to the road. Seeing nothing out of the ordinary, he scurried up the slope. From the road, he looked back to the copse of trees. He could not see anything but the top of the jeep's antenna and maybe eight inches of the flag.

He went back into the ditch and returned to the vehicles. When he got there, Sergeant Cole and two of the Koreans were waiting for him.

"See that they're fed," McCoy ordered, "and then post one up there. You can see where I climbed the slope."

"Aye, aye, sir," Cole said.

"And then post another one a hundred yards north. Watch out for mines and wires."

"Mr. Zimmerman's already been down there, sir."

"Then you really better be careful," McCoy said with a smile.

"Aye, aye, sir," Cole said, smiling back.

McCoy walked to the jeep. The hood was up, and Zimmerman was warming cans on the radiator. McCoy grabbed the antenna, bent it nearly horizontal, and tied it down.

Without really thinking about it, he made sure that no part of the flag was touching the ground.

"I couldn't see anything from the north," Zimmerman said.

"I could see maybe eight inches of the

flag," McCoy replied. "What are we eating?"

"Salisbury Steak and Beans and Franks," Zimmerman said. "Your choice."

McCoy laid the Thompson on the driver's seat, then reached for a ration can.

"I wonder who they think they're fooling when they call hamburger 'Salisbury Steak'?" he asked, not expecting an answer.

He leaned against the side of the jeep, took a fork from the baggy side pocket of the Army fatigues, and began to saw at the Salisbury Steak in the ration can.

He had just about finished raising the final forkful to his mouth when there was a short, shrill whistle, and then a second. He laid the ration can between the rear of the jeep and the back of the radio as he looked toward the sound of the whistle.

Sergeant Cole, who had posted himself with the Korean to the south, made several hand signals, not all of them official, indicating that something of interest was happening and he thought Major McCoy should pay whatever it was his immediate attention.

"Heads up," McCoy ordered as he passed the jeep — picking up the Thompson and a pair of U.S. Navy binoculars as he did — and headed for Cole.

Zimmerman, similarly, made several hand signals to Technical Sergeant

Jennings — these indicating that appropriate defense measures immediately be taken. Jennings indicated his understanding of his orders with a thumbs-up gesture. Zimmerman then trotted after McCoy, toward Sergeant Cole.

There was little doubt in either McCoy's or Zimmerman's mind that what had caught Sergeant Cole's attention were elements of the army of the People's Democratic Republic of North Korea.

The questions were: How large an element and what were they up to? Had McCoy's two-vehicle convoy been spotted, and were the North Koreans in pursuit of them? Or was it a unit trying to get away from the Eighth Army, which had broken out of the Pusan Perimeter and was in hot pursuit of the North Koreans up the peninsula?

Shattered, demoralized, whatever, if it was a company-strength unit — or a single tank, for that matter — McCoy & Company were going to be seriously outnumbered, or outgunned, or both.

"What have you got, Cole?" McCoy asked, handing him the Thompson.

"Looks like a couple of jeeps, sir," Cole said. "Russian jeeps."

McCoy crawled up the slope to the shoulder of the road and looked down it through the binoculars. He then handed them to Zimmerman, who had crawled beside him, and then slid down the slope. A moment later, Zimmerman slid down and returned the binoculars to McCoy.

"Two jeeps, and I make it five Slopes," Zimmerman said. "Moving slow; probably looking for mines."

"The passenger in the second jeep has leather boots — *shiny* leather boots," McCoy said. "I'd really like to talk to him."

"What do we do, Killer?" Zimmerman asked.

"I don't think we could get across the road without being seen," McCoy said. "So, Cole, run down there and tell Jennings what's going on, and to make sure if they get past Mr. Zimmerman and me, they don't get past him."

"Aye, aye, sir," Cole said. "You want me to come back here, sir?"

"No. Your BAR will be more useful there, if they get past us."

Cole nodded and took off at a run.

"How do you want to do this?" Zimmerman asked.

"You shoot out the tires of the first vehicle and watch what happens there. I'll deal with the second jeep." He paused. "I really want to talk to that officer, Ernie."

"Okay," Zimmerman said. "You going to call it?"

44

"I'm going to go another twenty-five yards that way, in case they turn around. When I hear your shots . . ."

Zimmerman nodded.

McCoy moved quickly, but carefully, farther down the ditch, then stopped, examined the slope again, and climbed up it.

Four minutes or so later, McCoy could hear the exhaust of the engines of the Russian jeeps, and the whining crunch of their tires on the road. It grew slowly louder.

When the first vehicle passed McCoy, he began to count. When he reached ten, there were two bursts of fire — one of three shots, followed by a second of two. Then there was the squeal of worn-out brakes, and then a loud thump.

McCoy scrambled onto the road, going over the top of slope on his knees and left hand — he had the Thompson in the right — feeling for a moment a chill of helplessness until he gained his feet and could put his hand on the forestock of the Thompson.

He was very much aware that two hands were necessary to fire a Thompson.

It took him a moment to see and understand what had happened.

The Russian jeep with the North Korean officer in it was stopped, stalled sideward across the road, the driver grinding the starter. The front end of the other jeep was

45

off the road, halfway into the ditch on the near side of the road. The frame had caught on the edge of the road, keeping it from going all the way down into the ditch.

McCoy had just time to wonder — in alarm — if by intention or accident the jeep had run over Zimmerman when he heard Zimmerman order, in Korean, "On your belly, you son of a whore."

McCoy ran toward the stalled jeep.

The officer was trying to work the action of a strange-looking submachine gun.

"I don't want to kill you, Colonel," McCoy called in Korean. "Just drop that and hold your hands over your head."

The North Korean officer complied.

McCoy saw that the look on his face was as much surprise, even astonishment, as fear.

"Yeah, Colonel, I speak Korean," McCoy said.

He walked closer to the jeep and held the Thompson on both of them until Technical Sergeant Jennings ran up the road to them, followed by three South Korean National Policemen.

"See if Mr. Zimmerman needs any help," McCoy said in English, and then switched to Korean as he spoke to one of the National Policemen: "Take the submachine gun from the colonel's lap. Then lay him on the ground and search him."

46

Jennings walked to the edge of the road, where the first jeep was hung up, and looked down.

"Well, just don't stand there with your thumb up your ass, for Christ's sake, Jennings," Zimmerman's impatient voice came up. "Get down here and frisk these Slopes."

"I never saw one like this before," Sergeant Alvin Cole said, holding the submachine gun taken from the North Korean colonel, who was now lying on his stomach, his hands tied behind him.

The other prisoners — a captain, a lieutenant, a sergeant, and a corporal — were being marched, barefoot, their hands tied behind them, down the road toward the copse of trees by Sergeant Jennings and two South Korean National Policemen.

"That's a PPD 1940G," Master Gunner Zimmerman said. "You don't see many of those. Pretty good weapon."

Cole looked at him.

"Proceed, Mr. Zimmerman," McCoy said. "We're fascinated."

Zimmerman looked at McCoy to see if he was serious.

"Okay," he said. "PPD stands for 'Pistolet Pulyemet Degtyarev.' It means machine pistol Degtyarev. Degtyarev being the Russian who stole the idea from the

47

Germans. It's based on the 1928 Bergmann. The Bergmann had a stick magazine. Degtyarev stole a drum magazine design from the Finnish Soumi, chrome-plated the inside parts, including the barrel, put it all together, and got it named after him. But the Russians dumped it because it couldn't be made fast enough for War Two, and went to the crude, easy-to-make PPsh you see all the time. That's why you don't see very many of these."

"I hope you were taking notes, Sergeant Cole," McCoy said. "There will be a written exam at the end of the lecture period."

Master Gunner Zimmerman looked at Major McCoy and said, "You asked, Killer," and gave the major the finger.

"Can I have it?" Sergeant Cole asked.

"You can if you give the pistols you took away from the other officers to the Koreans," McCoy said.

"And the other submachine gun, the PPsh, sir?" Cole asked.

"I think Jennings wants that," McCoy said. "Don't be greedy, Cole."

"Yes, sir."

The weapons carrier crawled back onto the road and headed for them.

McCoy pointed to the half-off-the-road Russian jeep.

"I was thinking about dragging this one down to the trees, but that would tear up the road, and I want to get out of here. Just push it over the side?"

"Yeah," Zimmerman agreed after a moment's thought. "That'd be better."

When the weapons carrier stopped beside him, McCoy, in Korean, ordered the National Police driver to push the Russian jeep into the ditch.

"And when you've done that," McCoy continued in Korean, "we're going to load the colonel in the back, tie him securely to the back of the seat, and put Sergeant Kim in there with him with a carbine. If the colonel even looks as if he's thinking about causing any trouble, Sergeant Kim will shoot him in both feet." He paused. "Did you hear that, Colonel?"

There was no reply from the colonel.

Zimmerman walked to him and nudged him with his boot.

"The major asked if you understood him, Colonel," he said in Korean.

There was no reply. Zimmerman kicked the colonel in the waist.

"I heard," the colonel said.

[Four]
Thirteen Miles South of Suwon,
South Korea
1705 28 September 1950

The sun was low in the sky, and the shadows were long. McCoy, Zimmerman, and Jennings were lying at the crest of a small hill from which they could see a road intersection about five hundred yards away.

Elements — what looked like an infantry platoon reinforced by three tanks — of the United States 7th Infantry Division were manning a hastily erected roadblock on the dirt road paralleling Korean National Route 1.

It had to be elements of the 7th Division. There were only two American divisions in the Seoul area, the 7th and the 1st Marine, and the armed Americans at the roadblock were not Marines.

Gunner Zimmerman took binoculars from his eyes, handed them to Technical Sergeant Jennings, and then turned to Major McCoy.

"Killer," he said conversationally, "if we start down that road, those doggies are going to start shooting at us."

McCoy grunted.

"Especially when they see that Russian jeep," Jennings added.

"Maybe not," McCoy said.

50

Then he pushed himself backward, sliding on his stomach away from the hilltop until he was far enough down the hill so there was no chance of his being seen. There, he rolled over onto his back and then sat up, holding his Thompson erect between his knees.

Zimmerman rolled over on his back, and — holding his Thompson against his chest — slid down after him, and then, when he'd seen all he wanted to, so did Jennings, carrying his Garand.

"I make it three tanks — M4s, Shermans," Jennings said, "plus maybe thirty-five doggies, with two air-cooled .50s, at least that many .30s, and a mortar."

"All of which are going to shoot at whatever they see coming up the road," Zimmerman said. "Like us, for example."

McCoy chuckled.

"What do you suggest we do, Mr. Zimmerman?"

Zimmerman pointed down the slope of the hill toward their small convoy. The Russian light truck, which McCoy had impulsively decided to drive, was at the head. The weapons carrier came next, and the jeep brought up the rear.

The Russian truck looked vaguely like a jeep. It was, McCoy had finally concluded, actually a Chinese-built version of a Russian vehicle, which in turn had been copied from a German vehicle, built on a Volks-wagen chassis, which in turn had been in-spired by the Truck, General Purpose, 1/4 ton, 4 x 4 of the U.S. Army, popularly known as the jeep.

McCoy had found the vehicle very inter-esting, and not just as an example of the enemy's military trucks.

Very few North Korean lieutenant colo-nels had vehicles permanently assigned to them. There were signs that this one was — *had been* — the colonel's personal vehicle. It was extraordinarily well main-tained. The seats, for example, were thickly padded. There had been personal posses-sions in both the glove compartment and under the seats, including three packages of Chesterfield cigarettes.

The dashboard instruments were lettered in the Cyrillic alphabet. Either the Rus-sians had provided the instruments or the Chinese had copied the Russian vehicle slavishly. In any event, calligraphed Can-tonese translations had been prepared and glued to the panel. There were no such Korean calligraphs.

This suggested the possibility that the colonel had acquired the vehicle new from a depot, and had not felt the need for Ko-rean translations from the Russian and Chinese because he spoke one or both of the languages.

Two kinds of North Korean lieutenant colonels would be likely to speak Russian and/or Cantonese: political commissars and intelligence officers.

A political commissar would most likely be at the front, exhorting the troops to give their all, not headed north in an obvious attempt to avoid capture by the now advancing Eighth United States Army. Political commissars are useful even in enemy captivity. Intelligence officers are not. Intelligence officers know a lot of things that should be kept from the enemy. Intelligence officers are taught not to place themselves in positions where they can be captured.

McCoy had a gut feeling their prisoner was an intelligence officer, and probably an important one.

"Untie the skinny Slope, hand him a white flag, and send him over the hill," Zimmerman said.

"That would be a violation of the Geneva Convention," McCoy said. "It's against the rules to endanger a prisoner."

"Shit," Zimmerman said.

"Besides, I really want to talk to him," McCoy said.

"Killer, that Slope sonofabitch isn't going to tell us a goddamn thing," Zimmerman argued.

"I think maybe he will when he sees

we're back in Seoul," McCoy said.

Zimmermann snorted.

"Sergeant Jennings, hoist the colors," McCoy said.

"Sir?"

"Unstrap the antenna on the jeep. Let's get the flag out so our friends at the road-block can see it," McCoy clarified.

"Aye, aye, sir."

"What are you going to do?" Zimmerman asked, as Jennings scurried down the hill.

"Drive the jeep to the crest of the hill, and then — very quickly — get out of it, and the line of fire. Whereupon, the Army will — or will not — fire upon it. If they don't fire on it, I will ask for a volunteer to expose himself. We may get lucky."

"And if we don't?"

"Then I guess you get shot. You were going to volunteer, right?"

"Shit," Zimmerman said, smiling.

"I'll do it, Ernie," Major McCoy said.

Marine majors do not ordinarily address their subordinates by their first names, and certainly not with the affection McCoy had in his voice. But there is always an exception. In this case, the two had been friends since 1940, when both had been in the 4th Marines in Shanghai.

They watched as Jennings untied the whip antenna on the jeep. It sprung erect, but there was no breeze and the flag hung limply.

"We could give Dunston a call in Seoul," Zimmerman said. "He's got somebody sitting on his radio."

"How long would it take, Ernie, for Dunston — even if he was sitting on the radio himself — to get a message to that roadblock?" McCoy asked, patiently. "Hours, anyway."

Zimmerman shrugged, taking McCoy's point.

Jennings got behind the wheel of the jeep, put it in four-wheel drive, and started up the hill.

McCoy got to his feet and waited for him. When he got close, McCoy signaled him to stop.

"I'll take it out there, Major," Jennings said.

McCoy jerked his thumb, ordering Jennings out of the jeep, then got behind the wheel.

Then he put it in gear and drove it slowly to the crest and over.

"Shit!" Zimmerman said when the jeep was out of sight.

Two minutes — two very long minutes — later, McCoy reappeared on foot at the crest of the hill.

"I waved and some doggie waved back at me," he announced. "I think we're all right. I'm going to drive down there. I'll signal you with a flashlight when it's okay to come."

"Permission to speak freely, sir?" Technical Sergeant Jennings said.

McCoy made a *let's have it* gesture with both hands.

"I should drive the jeep, not you."

"He's right," Zimmerman said.

McCoy thought it over, then jerked his thumb for Jennings to come up the hill.

When he came to McCoy, Jennings handed him his rifle. Then he raised his arms over his head and waved to them as he approached the crest, and disappeared over it.

McCoy stood on the crest with his hands on his hips and watched as Jennings eased the jeep down the hill, then onto the dirt road. When Jennings got close to the roadblock, he suddenly stopped the jeep and raised his hands over his head.

McCoy raised his binoculars to his eyes to see what was going on.

Jennings got out of the jeep and walked the last fifty yards to the roadblock, then disappeared from view behind one of the Sherman tanks.

He was out of sight for five minutes, then reappeared, making a nonregulation but clearly understandable sign that it was all right for everybody else to come in.

II

[One]
Thirteen Miles South of Suwon, South Korea
1725 28 September 1950

Captain John C. Allen III, a somewhat plump, pleasant-faced twenty-seven-year-old who was commanding officer of Company C, 1st Battalion, 27th Infantry, 7th Infantry Division, was hesitantly pleased with his current mission, the establishment and operation of a roadblock on a road south of Suwon.

You never knew what the hell was going to happen next in the Army; disappointment, sometimes bitter, was always just around the corner.

He had been told — and he had believed — that it would be days, perhaps weeks, before he actually had to face the enemy. The landing of X Corps (the 1st Marine Division and the 7th Infantry Division) at Inchon had severed the enemy's supply routes to the south. Without supplies, the North Koreans could not maintain their attack on the Pusan Perimeter. The Eighth U.S. Army had already counterattacked, broken out of the perimeter, and was driving the enemy northward.

There was still heavy action around Seoul, but most of that was being fought by the 1st Marine Division. Allen thought that the brass had at least enough sense to realize that the 7th Division really was in no shape to fight anybody.

Any military unit needs training to be effective. It was Captain Allen's professional judgment that none of the platoons in his company had adequate training. Neither had any of the companies in the 1st Battalion, any of the battalions in the 27th Infantry, nor any of the regiments in the 7th Division.

It was also Captain Allen's professional opinion that if the 1st Marine Division hadn't performed so superbly — if it had taken a licking — the 7th Division would have really gotten itself clobbered.

Captain Allen was perfectly happy to form — and to sometimes offer to select individuals, such as First Sergeant Grass — professional opinions about the military, although he was not a career officer, had not graduated from the United States Military Academy at West Point, nor, for that matter, attended the company-grade officers' course at the Infantry School at Fort Benning. He hadn't even gone to Officer Candidate School.

Drafted at twenty during World War II, "Jack" Allen had joined the 26th Infantry of the 1st Infantry Division in North Africa. By the time The Big Red One was training to land on the beaches of Normandy, it was Staff Sergeant Allen. On D–Plus Three, in Normandy, it was twenty-one-year-old Second Lieutenant Allen, holder of the Silver Star and directly commissioned after taking over the company when the officers had all been either blown away or wounded.

When war in Europe was over, Captain Jack Allen, who had added two Bronze Stars and two Purple Hearts to his Silver Star, had been one of the very first officers returned to the United States under the Point System for separation.

At Fort Dix, he had made the mistake of believing the Adjutant General's Corps major, who had told him that if he kept his commission in the reserve, he wouldn't be recalled to active duty unless and until enemy tanks were rolling down Pennsylvania Avenue toward the White House.

Jack Allen, star salesman and heir apparent to the throne of J. C. Allen & Sons Paper Merchants, Inc., Philadelphia, Pennsylvania, had received a telegram from the Adjutant General of the United States Army on 9 July 1950, ordering him to report within seventy-two hours to Camp

Indiantown Gap, Pennsylvania, there to enter upon extended active duty for the duration of the present conflict, plus six months.

At Indiantown Gap, there was just time enough to buy uniforms and have his shot record brought up to date before being loaded on a battered Douglas C-54 and flown to Fort Lewis, Washington. Three days after arriving at Fort Lewis, he boarded a brand-new-looking Lockheed Constellation of Trans-Global Airways and was flown to Tokyo via Honolulu and Wake Island.

At Camp Drake, he was assigned to the 7th Division. When he got there, they didn't seem to know what to do with him. He was given one assignment after another — one of them lasting six hours — but finally he found himself in the 27th Infantry Regiment. There the colonel commanding — who looked smart and competent, if harried — took a sixty-second look at Jack's service record.

Jesus Christ, he thought, *they finally sent me a company commander who's been in combat.*

Then he said: "Congratulations, Captain Allen, you are now commanding officer of Charley Company."

When Allen found his new command, in a battered frame barracks building, the acting first sergeant — a technical sergeant who a week before had been running an NCO club — told him Charley Company's total strength was two officers and twenty-six enlisted men — plus thirteen enlisted men listed as "absent, in confinement." The other officer was Second Lieutenant C. Danton Foster IV, who looked to be about nineteen but who told Allen he had graduated just over a year before from West Point. When Allen looked at Foster's service record, he saw that he was unmarried and listed his next of kin as Major General C. Danton Foster III.

Charley Company's ranks were soon filled out. Among the first "fillers" to arrive the next day was First Sergeant Homer Grass, a beer-bellied regular from West Virginia. It took Captain Allen and Sergeant Grass — who wore the "Bloody Bucket" of the 28th Infantry Division on his right shoulder and the Combat Infantry Badge on his chest — about ninety seconds to judge the other, assess the situation, and conclude that they were both in the deep shit and unless they could fix things in a hurry, they were liable to get killed.

When the next group of fillers appeared — the thirteen just-pardoned malefactors from the Tokyo stockade still wearing fatigues with a large *P* painted on the back — resisting despair had been difficult.

Neither did Charley Company have much in the way of equipment to boast of. They had nowhere near the numbers of individual items prescribed by the Table of Organization & Equipment, and what they did have was in lousy shape — in the case of several bundles of blankets, literally lousy.

Second Lieutenant C. Danton Foster IV — who had immediately become dubbed "Foster Four" — proved far more useful than either Jack Allen or Homer Grass expected. The three other officer fillers, all lieutenants, however, ranged from mediocre to awful, and none had ever heard a shot fired in anger.

Surprising Jack Allen, none of the filler officers ran to the Inspector General when he announced at Officers' Call that seniority regulations be damned, Foster Four was his Exec, and when Foster Four said something, it was to be treated as if he himself had said it.

As the enlisted fillers dribbled in, Jack Allen adopted, with Grass's and Foster Four's approval, a training philosophy of first things first. Everybody fired both his individual weapon and then the .45 pistol, staying on the firing range until they achieved a basic skill. Then they learned to fire — more important, to service — the Browning automatic rifles, the .30- and

.50-caliber machine guns, and the mortars. Soon Grass had them throwing grenades and attacking sandbags with bayonets and entrenching tools.

Some of the fillers were noncoms. Charley Company got a good supply sergeant — a blessing — and an incredibly bad mess sergeant. The company needed three really good platoon sergeants. It got one, with War Two credentials on a par with Grass's, and two who had never heard a shot fired in anger.

Charley Company was almost at authorized strength when they boarded the transport at Sasebo, and before they got into the landing barges at Inchon it was actually overstrength.

Allen thought privately, and more than a little bitterly, that someone knew that poorly trained troops were going to take heavy losses, so they were sending in replacements early.

But after they got ashore, the 1st Battalion went into Division Reserve. They weren't needed and weren't used. It was either the exigencies of the service or the kindness of a merciful God, but Charley Company was not thrown into combat.

It had been, however, subject to personnel levies from division headquarters, ordered to transfer officers and men elsewhere within the division to fill vacancies created by combat. While he hated to lose the men he had trained — it was possible, if not likely, that the reserve would be called to combat — this did provide Allen with the opportunity to get rid of most of the pardoned prisoners, the mess sergeant, and all of the lieutenants except Foster Four.

Before long, Charley Company was down to not many more people than it had had when he assumed command.

Then the battalion was given the mission of setting up roadblocks south of Seoul, and Charley Company and its two officers and fifty-two enlisted men were given the mission of establishing one south of Suwon.

Their mission was to prevent North Korean troops being forced back up the peninsula by the advancing Eighth Army from getting any farther north.

As soon as the trucks dropped them off, Allen had let it be known that they could expect to see the enemy any minute. That had the desired result of energetic position building and foxhole digging.

Then Allen sent First Sergeant Grass and the supply sergeant on a scrounging mission for ammunition of all kinds. When the enemy finally did appear, he wanted his peacetime soldiers to have as much experience in actually firing their weapons as possible. And the chance to replace what weapons that were going to fail.

Then he went to Regiment himself and begged the S-3 for tanks to reinforce the roadblock. He argued that not only was Charley Company way understrength, but that the Shermans of the Regimental Tank Company weren't being used at the moment. He made it clear that he understood that when the enemy finally showed up and the tanks were needed elsewhere, he would have to give them up.

If the Regimental Three believed that, fine. Allen thought it was highly probable that if the enemy showed up and he was using the tanks, and then came a radio message ordering them elsewhere, that message would be garbled beyond his understanding.

The tankers — under the command of a young second lieutenant, a West Point classmate of Foster Four — surprised Jack Allen. They were well trained and welcomed the chance to practice-fire their tubes at maximum range directly down the road. And one of the tank sergeants was a mortar expert and soon had Allen's mortar crews accurately laying their fire on the reverse sides of the slopes lining both sides of the valley.

After a few days, Captain Allen was confident that his men could deliver fire where it probably would be needed — and, as important, that they had the confidence they could.

Allen, Grass, and Foster Four were feeling pretty smug about what they had accomplished when an asshole from division headquarters showed up. He introduced himself as Major Alfred D. Masters and said he was the assistant Division G-2.

He was a natty little Regular Army bastard in shiny boots, a nonregulation zipper jacket, and a scarf made from camouflage parachute silk around his neck. He carried both a .45 in a tanker's shoulder holster and a .45 ACP Grease Gun. If he had earned a Combat Infantry Badge, he hadn't sewn it to his fancy jacket.

He had come, he said, to place Charley Company on the alert for "a reconnaissance patrol possibly operating south of these coordinates."

Allen thought there wasn't much useful information in that . . .

What does "possibly" mean? Is there a patrol or not?

Whose patrol? How big a patrol?

What am I supposed to do if the patrol shows up?

What if the patrol gets in trouble and asks for help?

. . . but when Allen asked those questions of Major Masters, the answers had been something less than completely helpful.

Major Masters said he couldn't get into that, "for security reasons." All Allen had the need to know was that if the patrol showed up, he was to notify him by the most expeditious means. He clarified that somewhat by saying Allen should transmit the code words "Trojan Horse," on receipt of which further orders would be issued.

Major Masters had then gotten back in his jeep and driven off.

There were three possible communications links between the Charley Company roadblock and Division Headquarters, none of them direct. There was a radio in Allen's sandbagged command post — the CP — which sometimes could communicate with Battalion and/or Regiment. The Signal Corps equipment available was about as old and unreliable as everything else. Each of the tanks had radios that in theory permitted them to communicate with one another and with the CPs of the Regimental Tank Company and Regiment. Only two of the three tanks were on that "net," and communications with Tank Company and Regiment were the opposite of reliable.

Finally, there was a field telephone system, called a "landline," which connected the roadblock CP with the 1st Battalion Command Post by wire. That usually worked during the day, but only after the Signal Corps wire men had laid fresh wire to replace the wire Korean farmers had stolen during the previous hours of darkness.

With these problems in mind, Captain Allen had ordered that one of his three jeeps and a driver always be parked next to the CP, so that if either the enemy or the mysterious patrol showed up, and neither the radios nor the landline was functioning, he could shag ass — Paul Revere–like — down the road to Battalion, crying, "The gooks are coming! The gooks are coming!"

When word of a jeep flying an American flag on its antenna had appeared at the crest of a hill five hundred yards south of his roadblock, it came from George Patton, as Second Lieutenant George Parsons, USMA '49, of Regimental Tank Company had inevitably been dubbed. Captain Allen and Foster Four were in the CP discussing over a mug of coffee whether it would be safe or not to conduct yet another midnight requisition on the regimental ration dump.

The SOP was that one officer (First Sergeant Grass was included) would always be on the line in case something happened. When Allen and Foster Four got to the line, they saw George Patton in the turret of one of the Shermans and Grass in the left .50-caliber machine-gun emplacement, both studying the hill and the jeep through binoculars.

The jeep with the outsized flag hanging from its antenna was an odd sight, and Captain Allen was pleased that his order "No one fires at anything until the word is passed" had been obeyed. He hadn't been at all sure that it would be. When soldiers — even experienced soldiers, and his men were anything but that — are told there is nothing in front of them but the enemy, the natural inclination is to shoot at anything that comes into sight before it has a chance to shoot first.

The driver of the jeep was standing beside the vehicle, waving his arms over his head.

"First Sergeant, you want to take a chance and go out there and wave back?"

First Sergeant Grass handed his binoculars to Allen and walked in front of the sandbags. Allen then steadied himself on the sandbags and put the binoculars to his eyes.

The driver, leaving the jeep on the hill, walked back over the crest and disappeared.

A minute or so later, another soldier appeared . . . *That's not the same guy . . .*

waving his arms over his head, got in the jeep, and started easing it down the hill.

Sometimes you can't see diddly-shit through binoculars, and sometimes there is extraordinary clarity and detail. This time — even though it was rapidly getting dark — it luckily was the latter. Allen could even read the front bumper markings on the jeep: HH7DIV on the right, 36 on the left. The jeep was Vehicle #36 of those assigned to Headquarters and Headquarters Company, 7th Infantry Division.

The somewhat less than deep and confidence-inspiring voice of George Patton called from the turret of the Sherman to his right.

"Vehicle on the road, Captain!"

"I wonder who the hell that is?" Allen asked aloud, and then called back, "Americans?"

"An officer and somebody else in a jeep," the voice called back.

Allen pushed himself off the sandbags and climbed up on the tank to see for himself.

In a moment, he was able to identify the officer in the jeep. It was the assistant Division G-2, Major Masters.

Well, he probably had word that this mysterious patrol of his was coming in.

Allen climbed off the tank, and a minute or so later the jeep slid to a halt beside the tank and Major Masters jumped out.

Allen saluted. Masters returned it crisply.

"You were told to be on the alert for a patrol. . . ."

"Yes, sir," Allen said. "I think that's what's coming in now."

He pointed down the road.

"Did I or did I not, Captain, tell you to notify me by the most expeditious means when that happened?"

"Yes, sir, you did," Allen said. "This just happened, sir. Just a couple of minutes ago. I don't know if it's your patrol or not."

Major Masters peered carefully around the skirts over the tank's tracks.

"That's one man in a jeep," he declared, "not a patrol."

"The jeep came over the hill a couple of minutes ago, sir. The driver waved, we waved back, and now somebody else is driving the jeep."

Major Masters either grunted or snorted.

There was the sound of a carbine firing. One round.

The jeep skidded to a stop, and the driver got out and held both arms over his head.

"I think that was an accidental discharge, sir," Captain Allen said.

And if Sergeant Grass saw who fired it, he'll kick his ass all the way back to Japan.

"Unfortunate," Major Masters said.

"Only a few of my men have ever been in a situation like this, sir."

"Tell me about it," Major Masters said, then added: "Well, he's coming in. Let's see what he has to say."

They walked to the .50-caliber air-cooled Browning position on the left, arranged themselves behind its sandbags, and watched as the tall soldier, his arms still over his head, walked toward them.

The soldier was no boy, but there were no chevrons visible on the sleeves of his fatigue shirt.

When he was twenty yards away, Captain Allen stood up.

"Over here, soldier," he called.

The soldier trotted to the machine-gun emplacement, dropped his arms, and saluted.

"Who are you?" Major Masters demanded.

"Technical Sergeant Jennings, sir."

"Are you in charge of this . . . patrol?"

"No, sir. Sir, with respect, may I go wave the others in?"

"Go ahead, Sergeant," Allen said.

Masters gave him a dirty look, and when Jennings was just possibly out of hearing range, said, "I was talking to that man, Allen. You should not have interfered."

"Sorry, sir."

Fuck you! Until someone relieves me, I'm in command here, and you're just a goddamn visiting brass hat. A minor-league brass hat.

Jennings trotted halfway toward where he had stopped the jeep and gestured toward the hill that it was all right to come in. Then he trotted back to the machine-gun emplacement.

"Just who is in charge of your patrol, Sergeant?" Major Masters asked.

"Sir, with respect, if I don't find a slit trench in the next sixty seconds, I am going to have a personal catastrophe."

"Over there, Sergeant," Captain Allen said, chuckling as he pointed.

"Thank you, sir."

Masters gave him another dirty look.

"Vehicles coming down the hill, Captain!" the sergeant in the turret of one of the Shermans called.

Allen and Masters looked.

"What the hell is that?" Masters asked.

"Jesus, I don't know," Captain Allen said.

The vehicle leading the weapons carrier toward them was jeeplike but not a jeep. After a moment Allen remembered seeing pictures of a Russian vehicle like it in a magazine. *Or was it during one of those endless goddamn Know Your Enemy! briefings?*

"It looks like a Russian jeep," Allen said.

Major Masters snorted or grunted again;

Captain Allen wasn't sure.

The Russian, if that's what it was, jeep stopped behind the jeep the sergeant had left out there, and a man . . .

How do I know that guy is an old-time noncom? Allen thought.

. . . climbed out of it, got in the jeep, and led the Russian jeep and a weapons carrier into the roadblock.

When the jeep got close and he could see its stocky, barrel-chested driver, Captain Allen was even more sure he was a long-time noncom. He said so, calling out, "Sergeant, park your jeep behind the Sherman on the left."

The driver nodded his understanding.

The Russian vehicle — *That's what it is, I'm sure* — immediately followed.

With its headlights on, for Christ's sake! Doesn't this guy know that turns him into a bull's-eye?

"Turn those headlights off!" Captain Allen ordered firmly, even a little angrily, then impatiently signaled the Russian vehicle to move past him and get behind the closest of the three tanks.

As the weapons carrier rolled up to him, Allen ordered, "Put that behind that tank," and pointed to the third Sherman.

As the truck passed him, Allen saw that the truck bed was just about full of people. It was now dark, so he couldn't be sure, but he thought he saw at least two, maybe three, Orientals.

Major Masters marched purposefully toward the Russian vehicle, with Allen following.

The driver . . .

Who's not wearing a helmet . . .

Goddamn it, none of these people are!!!

. . . who looked a little old to be a private — there was no rank insignia in sight — was already out of the Russian vehicle, leaning against it, lighting a cigar with a wooden match.

"Are you in charge of this . . . *operation?*" Major Masters demanded.

"Yes, I am," the driver said, taking a deep, satisfied puff on his cigar, then examining the coal.

"And don't you salute officers, soldier?" Major Masters demanded icily.

"Sorry," the driver said, straightened, and saluted. Masters returned it impatiently. After a moment, Allen did so too.

"What's your name, soldier? Your outfit?" Major Masters demanded.

"My name is McCoy, Major," the driver said. "And I'm a Marine. Actually, I'm a Marine major."

Captain Allen accepted this immediately. There was something about this guy's voice, the smile on his face, that made the announcement credible. Major Masters

75

had trouble with it.

"Is there some reason you're not wearing the insignia of your rank, *Major?*"

"Who are you?" McCoy asked.

"My name is Masters. I'm the assistant G-2 of the 7th Division."

"You work for Colonel Lemuleson?" McCoy asked.

"As a matter of fact, I do," Masters admitted. The question had surprised him.

Zimmerman walked up to them. He saluted.

"Thanks for not shooting first and then asking questions," Zimmerman said.

"This is Master Gunner Zimmerman," McCoy said.

"Master Gunner?" Captain Allen asked as he offered his hand. "The Marine equivalent of our master sergeant?"

"Mr. Zimmerman is what the Army would call a chief warrant officer," McCoy corrected him.

"Neither of you is wearing any insignia —" Major Masters began.

"I know," McCoy interrupted, smiling.

Masters glowered at him.

"If you work for Colonel Lemuleson, you're just the man I want to see," McCoy went on.

"Is that so?"

"I need two things, Major," McCoy said. "I need to get a message to Colonel

Lemuleson, and —"

"Before we go any further, *Major*," Masters interrupted, "I'd like to see some identification and your orders. Who the hell are you?"

"If you work for Colonel Lemuleson, and he didn't tell you, then I guess he decided you don't have the need to know," McCoy said.

He turned to Allen.

"Have you got a landline I can use to call 7th Division, Captain?" McCoy asked.

"It was working fifteen minutes ago, sir," Allen said. He pointed toward his command post.

"I demand to see your identification, Major!" Masters said loudly.

His face was red. McCoy seemed amused rather than cowed.

"Colonel Lemuleson's holding all that for us, sorry. Why don't we see if we can get him on the horn?"

He started to walk toward the CP. Masters, red-faced, stood with his hands on his hips, watching McCoy walk away.

Allen started to follow him, saw Foster Four with a *May I go too?* look on his face, and nodded permission.

Allen caught up with McCoy.

"Somehow, sir, I get the feeling Major Masters is annoyed with you," he said.

McCoy chuckled.

"I . . . uh . . . didn't know what to think when I saw your jeep," Captain Allen said. "The first one, I mean. Or this thing . . ."

He stopped when he became aware that Major Masters was trotting after them.

"We've been doing a reconnaissance," McCoy said. "No big deal, but it's none of that guy's business."

"I thought the Marines were operating in Seoul, north of it," Allen said.

"They are," McCoy said.

"Where'd you get the Russian jeep?"

Major Masters was now walking beside them. He announced: "We'll see what Colonel Lemuleson has to say about all this."

McCoy acted as if he hadn't heard him. He turned to Allen. "We bagged some Inmun Gun. They were driving this thing. I figured, what the hell, why not take it with us?"

Major Masters picked up on that.

"Can I take that to mean you have engaged the enemy?"

"It wasn't much of an 'engagement.' They were coming up the road, Mr. Zimmerman shot the tires out on the first vehicle, and we bagged them."

"You have prisoners?" Masters demanded.

"Uh-huh," McCoy said. "That's the second thing I need from you, Major. Somebody to take four of the five off our hands.

One of them is a lieutenant colonel. He's a keeper."

"By which you mean?"

"That I'm going to take him to Seoul with me."

"I'll want to interrogate him, of course."

"You speak Korean?" McCoy asked.

"No, of course I don't speak Korean. There's Korean-speaking interrogators at Division. We'll take him — all of the prisoners — there."

They were down at the doorway to the CP.

McCoy stopped and looked at Major Masters.

"Sorry, the colonel goes with me," he said. "And if I can get Colonel Lemuleson on the phone, I'm not going anywhere near your headquarters."

"Let's clear the air here, Major," Major Masters said. "I'm the assistant G-2 —"

"So you said," McCoy interrupted.

Major Masters glowered at him, then picked up:

"— of the 7th Division. Interrogation of prisoners is my responsibility. You do understand that?"

"None of these people will tell any of your interrogators anything," McCoy said. "I think maybe, once he sees we're back in Seoul, the colonel may be more cooperative."

"We won't know what any of the prisoners will say, will we, Major, until we sit them down before an interrogator who speaks Korean?"

"Mr. Zimmerman and I both speak Korean, Major, and we've already talked to these people. And to clear the air, these are our prisoners, not yours."

"That brings us back to Question One, doesn't it?" Major Masters asked icily. "Just who the hell are you, Major? And what are you doing in the 7th Division's area?"

McCoy looked at him for a moment, then ducked through the narrow sandbagged opening into the CP without replying.

A slight, very young corporal was sitting on a folding metal chair by the radio and an EE-8 field telephone.

"Corporal," McCoy said, "see if you get through to G-2 at Division on the land-line."

The corporal looked to Captain Allen for guidance. Allen nodded. The corporal cranked the generator handle on the side of the leather-cased EE-8.

"Patch me through to Regiment," he ordered after a moment, and then, a moment after that, he ordered, "Patch me through to Division."

McCoy walked to him and took the handset from him.

"Wolf Two, please," he said.

Twenty miles away, in a small village called Anyang, seven miles or so south of Seoul, in what had been built to be the waiting room of the railway station, Technical Sergeant Richard Ward picked up the handset of one of three EE-8 field telephones on the shelf of his small, folding wooden field desk.

"Wolf Two, Sergeant Ward, sir."

"Trojan Horse Six for the colonel, Sergeant," McCoy said.

"Hold one," Ward said, and extended the handset to Lieutenant Colonel Charles Lemuleson, a short, thin forty-year-old in too large fatigues, who was the intelligence officer of the 7th Division.

"For you, Colonel," Ward said, and added, "Trojan Horse Six."

Colonel Lemuleson turned from the map board leaning against the wall.

"Good!" he said. "I was getting worried."

He took the handset, pressed the butterfly switch, and said, "Wolf Two."

"Trojan Horse Six, sir. Good evening, sir."

Captain Allen handed Major McCoy a china mug of steaming coffee. McCoy smiled his thanks.

"Welcome home," Colonel Lemuleson's voice came somewhat metallically over the landline. "You're all right? Where are you?"

"At a roadblock south of Suwon, sir. We just came through."

"And apparently nobody shot at you. I was concerned about that."

"Yes, sir, that was a concern."

"I've got a message for you. Ready?"

"Yes, sir."

" 'Kimpo oh nine hundred twenty-nine September. Acknowledge. Confirm. Signature Hart, Capt., USMCR, for Admiral Dewey.' Got it?"

"Yes, sir. Thank you."

"Got that just after you left," Colonel Lemuleson said. "It was in the clear. Couldn't get you on the radio."

"It was in the clear" meant that the message had not been encrypted, which meant further that someone had decided there wasn't time to go through the encryption process. And that it wasn't encrypted explained "Admiral Dewey." Captain George S. Hart, USMCR, aide-de-camp (and bodyguard) to Brigadier General Fleming Pickering, USMCR, Assistant Director for Asia of the Central Intelligence Agency, did not want to use Pickering's name in a non-encrypted message.

"The radio in the jeep went out before we were out of Seoul, sir," McCoy said. "Can you take a reply, sir?"

"Shoot."

"Acknowledge and confirm Kimpo oh nine hundred twenty-nine September. All well. Fresh eggs but no ham. Signature, McCoy."

Lieutenant Colonel Lemuleson said, "Got it," read it back for confirmation, and then asked, "Are you going to explain the ham and eggs business, McCoy? And who the hell is Admiral Dewey?"

"I better not, sir. But if memory serves, Admiral Dewey won the battle of Manila Bay in the Spanish-American War."

Lemuleson chuckled. "I knew I'd heard the name someplace. Anything else I can do for you, McCoy?"

"Yes, sir, there is. Sir, if I'm to be at Kimpo at 0900, I'd like to go there to-night —"

"That may be risky, McCoy," Lemuleson said. "I don't want to get a report in the morning that somebody shot first before asking any questions."

"Yes, sir. But I don't think I have much choice. Making things more difficult is that we picked up some prisoners. What I'd like to do is send four of them to you with one of my sergeants. You could give him that envelope —"

"It's under a thermite grenade in my safe," Lemuleson interrupted.

"— and he could bring it to us in Seoul at first light."

"And if you need some identification to-night?"

"I'll have to take that chance, sir."

"Your call, McCoy," Lemuleson said. "Done."

"May I have that phone, please, Major?" Major Masters asked. It was more of an order.

McCoy considered the request for a moment, then said, "Hold one, sir, please. Major Masters wants to talk to you."

"What the hell is he doing there?" Lemuleson said.

McCoy handed the handset to Masters.

"Masters, sir. These people have five prisoners, one of them a lieutenant colonel, and Major McCoy refuses to turn him over to me."

He looked triumphantly at McCoy.

McCoy and the others could hear only one side of the ensuing conversation.

"Trying to stay on the top of the situation, sir," Major Masters said, and then, "Yes, sir."

And then, "Yes, sir."

And then, "Yes, sir."

And then, "Yes, sir, I'll do that, sir."

Then he handed the handset back to McCoy.

"The colonel wants to speak to you, Major," he said.

"Yes, sir?" McCoy said.

"Sorry about that, McCoy. He doesn't know what's going on, and for obvious reasons — God save us all from well-meaning idiots — I didn't want to tell him."

"I understand, sir. No problem."

"I told him to do whatever you tell him to do, and to ask no questions."

"Thank you, sir."

"If you need anything else, give a call."

"Thank you very much, sir," McCoy said, and handed the handset to the corporal.

"Major, would you be willing to lead my Marines — the jeep and the weapons carrier — to Division?" McCoy asked.

"Certainly," Major Masters said. "Anything I can do to be of service. . . ."

[Two]
Seoul, South Korea
1935 28 September 1950

Staff Sergeant John J. Doheny, USMC, thought it highly unlikely that "fleeing remnants" of the North Korean Army would drive boldly up Korean National Route 1 with their headlights blazing, but it never hurt to be careful.

"Heads up!" Doheny ordered when the headlights first illuminated, then stopped at the wrecked and burned General Motors

6 x 6 truck he had ordered dragged into the middle of the road as sort of a prebarrier to his roadblock fifty yards up the road.

"Halt, who goes there?" a voice in the darkness called to the lights.

That was Corporal Daniel Meredith, USMCR, whom Doheny had stationed with three other Marines, one of them armed with a BAR, in the ditches on either side of the burned truck barrier.

On one hand, Doheny thought, that sounded a little silly, as if they were at Parris Island or someplace, waiting for a drill instructor to inspect the guard post and demand a recitation of the Ten General Orders, instead of here, in the middle of a war.

On the other hand, he couldn't think of any other challenge that could be made that did the job as well. What else could Meredith shout? *"Hi, there! Mind stopping there a moment, and telling me who you are?"* or maybe, *"Pardon me, sir, are you a friendly or a fucking gook Communist?"*

"Marines!" a deep voice called back.

The beam of one flashlight and then another appeared, one from each side of the road. If his orders had been followed — and Sergeant Doheny had no reason to think they hadn't — PFC Miller, the big hillbilly with the BAR, now had it trained on the vehicle on the road from his position nowhere near the flashlights, waiting for orders to fire from Meredith.

Sergeant Doheny could now see enough to know there was something really strange down there. There were three men in a strange-looking jeep. The two in the front had their hands over their heads. The one in the back just sat there.

There was an American flag draped over the hood of the vehicle.

As Doheny got to his feet, he saw Meredith come onto the road from behind the vehicle, holding his carbine at the ready.

A moment later, Corporal Meredith bellowed, "Sergeant Doheny, I think you better come down here!"

Doheny ran quickly down the ditch, pushing the safety off on his M-1 Garand as he did. When he was beside the funny-looking vehicle, he came out of the ditch, holding the Garand like a hunter expecting to flush a bird.

A not-at-all-friendly voice called to him from the vehicle.

"Doheny, tell that moron to get that fucking light out of my eyes, or I'll stick it up his ass!"

"Who is that?" Doheny called back.

"Gunner Zimmerman! Are you blind as well as deaf?"

I knew I knew that fucking voice!

Staff Sergeant Doheny and Master Gunner Zimmerman had been professionally associated at one time or another at the USMC Recruit Training Facility, Parris Island; Camp Lejeune; and Camp Pendleton.

Doheny was more than a little in awe of Master Gunner Zimmerman. He was a Marine's Marine: tough, competent, and fair. And — although Zimmerman had never said anything about it himself — Doheny knew that during War Two Zimmerman had been a Marine Raider.

"Turn those fucking flashlights off," Sergeant Doheny ordered. They were out immediately.

"Jesus, Mr. Zimmerman, what the fuck are you doing out here?" Doheny inquired.

"Major McCoy," Gunner Zimmerman said, "this is Staff Sergeant Doheny. He's not too bad a Marine — when he's sober."

Sergeant Doheny saluted.

"Sorry, sir," he said. "I didn't see any insignia. . . ."

"How are you tonight, Sergeant?" McCoy replied, returning the salute.

"Can't complain, sir. Sir, with respect, what the fuck is this vehicle?"

"We took it away from the prisoner in the backseat, Sergeant," McCoy said. "As best as I can tell, it's a Chinese copy of a

88

Russian vehicle the Russians copied after a German jeep."

"I'll be damned," Doheny said, and then stepped close to the vehicle and looked in the backseat. There was enough reflected light from the headlights for him to be able to see a hatless North Korean officer tightly trussed up and then tied to the backseat.

"What happened to the truck?" Zimmerman asked.

"No fucking idea. I had it drug into the road so anyone coming down the road would have to stop."

"Good thinking, Sergeant," McCoy said. "How do we get around it?"

"Sir, if you're careful, you can get around it in a jeep," Doheny said. "I done that. I don't know about in this."

"Well, we'll try. What's between here and Seoul, Sergeant?"

"There's a checkpoint at the pontoon bridge over the Han River, sir. And that's about it. So far as action is concerned, we've got it pretty well cleaned out, but there's action north and east."

He pointed. There were flashes of dull light, and booming noises. It could have been a distant thunderstorm. It was, in fact, artillery.

"You got a landline to the checkpoint?" Zimmerman said. "I would really hate to get this close only to get blown away because somebody thought if it's riding around in a gook vehicle, it's probably a gook."

Sergeant Doheny sensed that the explanation was a shot at the major.

"No problem, sir," he said. "Anything else I can do for you?"

The major turned around and said something to the North Korean officer, who, after a moment, responded. Then the major turned to Sergeant Doheny.

"The colonel needs to relieve himself, and so do I. Can your people untie him, and watch him?"

"Yes, sir. We're about fifty yards the other side of the truck."

"Okay. We'll do that next. And then . . . have you got any sandbags?"

"Yes, sir."

"I'll need a couple of them, please."

"Yes, sir. *Sandbags?*"

"Empty ones."

"I got stacks of them, sir."

"I think two will be enough, thank you."

[Three]
The House
Seoul, South Korea
2045 28 September 1950

The sound of the cannon fire and the muzzle flashes lighting the sky had grown progressively louder and brighter as they approached the center of Seoul. There was obviously fighting, heavy fighting, on the outskirts of the city.

They were stopped three times inside the city, twice by Army military policemen and once by a Marine patrol, but the American flag on the hood and Zimmerman's gruff declaration that they were "transporting a prisoner" — and, of course, the prisoner himself, with two sandbags over his head — was enough to satisfy the MPs and a Marine sergeant. They were not asked for either orders or identification.

The city was in ruins. The North Koreans had defended it block by block, and there was smell of burned wood and rotting flesh. The streets were full of debris, and their progress was slow.

But finally McCoy turned the Russian jeep off a narrow street, stopped before a wrought-iron fence in a brick wall, and blew the horn.

Immediately — startling them — floodlights mounted on the brick wall glowed red for an instant, then bathed them in a harsh white light.

Master Gunner Zimmerman bellowed the Korean equivalent of "Turn those fucking lights off!"

The lights died and the gate swung open. As McCoy drove though it, he saw that an air-cooled .30-caliber Browning machine gun was trained on them.

The building inside the wall looked European rather than Asiatic. It was of brick-and-stone construction, three stories tall. It had been built in 1925 for Hamburg Shipping, G.m.b.H., which had used it to house their man in Seoul. It was purchased from them in 1946 by Korean Textile Services, Ltd., a wholly owned subsidiary of Far East Fur & Textiles, Ltd., of Hong Kong, which, it was alleged, was owned several steps distant by the United States Central Intelligence Agency. It was known as "The House."

A Korean in U.S. Army fatigues came out of the front door as McCoy pulled the Russian jeep up in front of the veranda beside three jeeps and a three-quarter-ton ambulance. The overpainted Red Cross markings on the sides of the ambulance body were still visible.

The Korean — he was at least six feet tall and weighed about 200 pounds, enormous for a Korean — came down the stairs, slinging his Thompson submachine gun over his shoulder as he did.

He said nothing.

In Korean, McCoy ordered, "Take the colonel in the house. Put him in one of the basement rooms. Once he's there, put a guard on him, untie him, take the sandbags off his head, and give him something to eat. I want him alive and unhurt."

The enormous Korean nodded his understanding. "The others?" he asked in English.

"They'll be here early tomorrow morning, all of them," McCoy said. Then he asked, "Is he here?"

"In the library," the Korean replied, again in English.

McCoy nodded, and he and Zimmerman got out of the Russian jeep and walked into the house.

The library was the first door on the right off the foyer. McCoy pushed open the door and walked in.

The first time McCoy had been in the room, the bookshelves lining three walls had been full. Now they were bare. The Inmun Gun had stripped the house of everything reasonably portable as soon as they had taken over the building.

"It's not amazing how little is left," Dunston had philosophized, "but how much."

Dunston, a plump, comfortable-appearing

thirty-year-old whose Army identification card said that William R. Dunston was a major of the Army's Transportation Corps, sat at a heavy carved wooden table. A Coleman gasoline lantern on the table glowed white, and Dunston was using it to read *Stars and Stripes*, the Army newspaper.

Dunston was not actually a major, or even in the Army, despite his uniform and identity card. He was in fact a civilian employed by the Central Intelligence Agency, and before having been run out of Seoul by the advancing North Korean Army had been the Seoul CIA station chief. After the landings at Inchon, Dunston had flown back into the city as soon as enough of the runway at Kimpo Airfield had been cleared to take an Army observation aircraft.

McCoy and Zimmerman pulled chairs — one heavy and of carved wood matching the table, the other a GI folding metal chair — to the table and sat down.

"What's with the Coleman lantern?" McCoy asked by way of greeting. "I heard the generator. . . . The perimeter floodlights are working."

"No lightbulbs," Dunston replied. "I'm working on it. Probably tomorrow." He paused, then went on: "I was getting a little worried about you, Ken."

"We're all right," McCoy said. "But I'm hungry and thirsty."

"Hard or soft? There is also a case of Asahi cooling in the fridge."

"I think one medicinal belt, and then beer," McCoy said. "Food?"

"There's steaks and potatoes, no vegetables."

"Hot water?" Zimmerman asked.

Dunston nodded. "And your laundry awaits," he said.

"I'm going to have a beer, a shower, a drink, and a steak, in that order," Zimmerman said.

A door opened, and a middle-aged Korean woman stood in it waiting for orders.

Dunston, in Korean, told her to bring beer and whiskey and to prepare steaks.

"I think if you had found him, you'd have said something," Dunston said.

"Close, goddamn close, but no brass ring," McCoy said. "I wouldn't be surprised if he saw us looking for him."

"But you think he's alive?"

"I'm pretty sure he was alive six, eight, maybe twelve hours before we found his arrow."

"Did you tell the general?"

McCoy nodded.

"I sent a message through the 7th Division G-2," he said, "and sometime tonight, I want to get a message out to the *Badoeng Strait*."

The USS *Badoeng Strait* (CVE 116) was the aircraft carrier — a small one, dubbed a "Jeep Carrier" — from which Major Malcolm Pickering had taken off on his last flight. His wing commander, Lieutenant Colonel William "Billy" Dunn, USMC, was doing all he could to locate and rescue Pickering; McCoy wanted him to know what had happened on this last ground search mission.

"No problem," Dunston said.

"What's going on here?" McCoy asked.

"It says in here," Dunston said, dryly, tapping *Stars and Stripes*, "that Seoul has been liberated. I guess nobody told the artillery."

"I wondered what all that noise is," McCoy said. "But that's not what I meant. I got a message from Hart saying to be at Kimpo at 0900. What's that all about?"

"El Supremo's flying in. He's going to turn Seoul over to Syngman Rhee. I guess the general's coming with him."

El Supremo was General of the Army Douglas MacArthur, Supreme Commander, Allied Powers, and, since shortly after the Korean War began, Commander, United Nations Forces in Korea.

"They sent you a message?"

Dunston shook his head no.

"I'm a spy, Ken. I thought I told you. I've got a guy at Haneda. The *Bataan*'s being readied as we speak."

McCoy chuckled. Haneda was the airbase outside Tokyo where the *Bataan*, MacArthur's personal Douglas C-54 transport, was kept.

"I wish I had better news for the boss."

"That he's alive is good news."

"Yeah, and six hours after I tell him that, we'll find his body."

"The bastard walks through raindrops, Killer," Zimmerman said. "You know that."

"Where's General Howe? And did you tell him that MacArthur and the boss are coming?" McCoy asked.

Major General Ralph Howe, a World War I crony of then-Captain Harry S Truman, was in the Far East as the personal representative of the President of the United States and Commander-in-Chief of its Armed Forces.

"I got a message from him about six o'clock, saying he's with Chesty Puller's Marine regiment," Dunston said. "And no, I didn't tell him. (a) I figured they'd get word to him, and (b) I didn't want him to ask how come I knew."

The Korean woman came into the room carrying a tray. It held quart bottles of Asahi beer, a quart bottle of Famous Grouse scotch, and ice and glasses.

"Where'd you get all the booze?" Zimmerman asked.

"I paid a courtesy call on General Almond," Dunston said. "That general knows how to go to war. With a trailerload of hootch and cocktail snacks, and clean white sheets. Almond told his aide — Haig? — to take care of me."

"Why did Almond tell El Supremo Seoul's been liberated?" McCoy asked, indicating the pounding rumble of the heavy artillery with a finger pointed at the ceiling.

He reached for the bottle of whiskey and poured two inches in one of the glasses. Zimmerman picked up one of the beer bottles. Dunston slid him a bottle opener.

"I think it was the other way around," Dunston said. "And Almond is too smart to disagree with El Supremo. MacArthur said he wanted Seoul liberated within two weeks of the landing at Inchon, and by God, it has been liberated."

"We bagged a North Korean lieutenant colonel —" McCoy began.

"And his Russian jeep," Zimmerman interjected.

"And his jeep?" Dunston asked, smiling. "What are you going to do with that?"

Zimmerman opened the bottle, and then left the room, drinking from the bottle as he walked.

"— who I turned over to Paik Su," McCoy went on, "with instructions to put him in the basement, feed him, and make him comfortable. I think he's important. Probably an intelligence officer, maybe a political commissar, but somebody important. I think he should be interrogated by somebody besides Zimmerman and me — or, for that matter, you. This guy is not impressed by a couple of clowns riding around the boondocks in a jeep. But I think he might respond to somebody he thinks is important."

"Paik is very good at getting people to tell him things," Dunston said.

"And there is always thiopental sodium, but that also requires that the interrogator know what questions to ask. What we may get from this guy will be something — and I have a gut feeling there will be something — that he lets slip, not something Paik, or a needle in his arm, 'persuades' him to tell us."

"I know just the guy, an ROK bird colonel," Dunston said. "I'll handle it. Go get a shower and something to eat, Ken. You look beat."

"After I get a message off to the *Badoeng Strait*."

"I can do that, too, if you'd like," Dunston said.

"Thanks, Bill, but I'd rather do it myself," McCoy said.

He stood up and held the whiskey glass out. "And before I have another of these and go to sleep. I'm beat."

"You've been up since four, and I don't think you got much sleep last night," Dunston said. "Ken, if all you've got to tell Colonel Dunn is where Pickering was — or wasn't — I can use that overlay and send the message."

"I'd rather do it myself," McCoy said. "But for the second time, thanks, Bill."

He walked out of the library and climbed the stairs to the radio room on the third floor. Coleman lanterns were on each landing. The radio operator on duty was a not-unattractive Korean woman in her thirties. She sat at a table on which was an aluminum teapot on an electric stove, an ashtray, a typewriter, and a fully automatic M-2 .30-caliber carbine. The radio room had a lightbulb dangling naked from the ceiling.

McCoy nodded his head and said, "Di-San."

Possibly to restrain the romantic tendencies of McCoy's Marines, Dunston had told them that Di and her husband had been prewar employees, and that after torturing the husband for several hours, the North Koreans had finally killed him, then, after subjecting the woman to multiple rape, had for some reason let her go.

Her head barely moved in a nod acknowledging McCoy.

"I'll have a short message for the *Badoeng Strait*," McCoy said.

Her head bobbed almost imperceptibly again, and she turned to one of the radio sets and began to make the necessary adjustments.

McCoy took a map of Korea and a translucent overlay from a table drawer, put the overlay on the map, and made a pencil note of the coordinates on the overlay. Lieutenant Colonel Billy Dunn, on the aircraft carrier, had an identical overlay. Without the overlay, the coordinate keys would be useless.

Then he sat down at an old Underwood typewriter, which already — in anticipation of incoming messages — had paper in it. He paused thoughtfully for a moment, and then began to type.

```
SECRET
2125 28SEP50
FOR MOTHERHEN
FROM TROJANHORSE

POSITIVE INDICATIONS HOTSHOT AT
COORDINATES CHARLEY SEVEN SEVEN
TWO, MIKE ZERO FOUR ZERO TWO TO
TWELVE HOURS PRIOR TO 0900 28SEP50.
NO CONTACT. TROJANHORSE AT MONACO
0900 29SEP50. END.
```

He unrolled the sheet of paper from the typewriter and handed it to the Korean woman. She read it, looked at him, then said, "I will encrypt it if you like."

He nodded.

"I'm going to get something to eat, and then go to bed," he said in Korean. "If I don't hear from you, I will presume *Badoeng Strait* acknowledges."

She nodded.

"Thank you, Di-San," he said.

She nodded again.

McCoy left the radio room and walked back down the stairs to the ground floor. There was the glaring white light and hissing of a Coleman lantern coming from the dining room, and he went in there.

"I didn't wait," Zimmerman said, unnecessarily, as he mopped the last meat juices from his plate with a piece of bread. "I was starved."

"I got a message off to Billy Dunn," McCoy said.

Zimmerman grunted, and then got up.

"Make sure they wake me for breakfast," he said, and walked out.

McCoy nodded and sat down at the table. The older Korean woman came in almost immediately with a steak and french fried potatoes on a plate. She left and returned in a moment with a bottle of red wine.

The steak was enormous, and he couldn't eat all of it. He drained the wineglass, stood up, and left. He climbed the stairs to the second floor and walked down a dark corridor to and through a heavy door into a large, sparsely furnished room. There was a double bed, neatly made up with sheets and Army blankets. Beside it was a chair. There was a large wooden desk with a Coleman lantern glowing white on it.

Neatly folded on the bed were freshly washed linen, a freshly washed and starched set of Marine utilities, two towels, a facecloth, and a bar of Pond's soap. McCoy wondered where Dunston had found that. Next to the bed was a pair of Army combat boots. *Shined* Army combat boots.

McCoy sat on the bed and took off the Marine boots he was wearing. Then he took off the fatigue jacket, held it for a moment, and dropped it onto the floor. He stood up, took a Model 1911A1 Colt .45 ACP pistol from the small of his back, and put it on the chair beside the bed. Then he stripped off the rest of his clothes, leaving everything in a pile on the floor.

He took the freshly pressed and starched uniform from the bed and laid it over the pistol on the chair. Then he picked up the clean linen and the towels from the bed and walked to the bathroom door, returning in a moment for the Coleman lantern.

It took a long time for the hot water to work its way up from the boiler in the basement, but finally there was a steady, heavy stream of hot water. He stood under it a long time after he was clean.

Then he put on the underwear, carried the Coleman lantern back into the bedroom, sat on the bed, turned the lantern off, and got between the sheets.

In thirty seconds, he was asleep.

III

[One]
Hangar 13
Kimpo Airfield (K-16)
Seoul, South Korea
2205 28 September 1950

As Major McCoy slipped between the clean white sheets of his bed, Captain Howard C. Dunwood, USMCR — who, three months before, had been named "Salesman of the Month" at Mike O'Brien's DeSoto-Plymouth Agency in East Orange, New Jersey — sat in his underwear on the edge of his cot in a shrapnel-riddled hangar forking cold ham chunks and baked beans from an olive-drab Army ration can by the light of a small candle.

And like Major McCoy, Dunwood was fresh from his personal toilette: He had just shaved, then washed his face and crotch and his armpits with water held in a steel helmet. He had then used the same water to wash his change of socks and underwear, using a tiny chunk of soap that had come with a package of Chesterfield cigarettes, a small pack of toilet paper, and some other "comforts" with the field rations.

He actually felt a little guilty about the cot, having been taught, and believing, that officers should enjoy no creature comforts not available to their men. There were only ten folding wooden cots available to the men of Baker Company, 5th Marines.

His supply sergeant — Staff Sergeant Al Preston, USMC, who three months before had been on recruiting duty in Montgomery, Alabama — had "borrowed" them that morning from an Army ration dump in Ascom City, near the port of Inchon, while collecting their daily rations and the mail. There had not been very many rations, and almost no mail.

Preston had passed seven of the ten cots out to the senior noncoms of the company, then carried the remaining three into the officers' quarters — what had apparently been small offices off the hangar floor — and started setting them up.

"Can you go back and get some more cots for the men?" Dunwood had asked.

"Ten's all they had, sir," Preston had replied, then had taken the meaning of the question and added: "R.H.I.P., Skipper."

Dunwood doubted that "Rank Hath Its Privileges" justified his other two officers and himself, and the seven noncoms, having cots when none of the other men of

Baker Company would, but he let it go.

The floor of the officers' quarters was concrete, and he wasn't as young as he had been when he had made the Tarawa and Okinawa landings in War Two.

He decided that there was nothing wrong with being as comfortable as he could for as long as he could. Their current status was bound to change, sooner or later and probably sooner than later, and when it changed, things would almost certainly be worse.

Right now, despite the spartan and miserable living conditions in the shrapnel-holed hangar and the lousy rations, things were pretty good, considering the alternative, which was doing what they were supposed to be doing, fighting as a Marine infantry company on the line.

The lines of ambulances and the sound of the firing had made it obvious that taking Seoul back from the North Koreans had been a nasty job. To judge by the sound of artillery, it still was a nasty job.

Baker Company hadn't been involved. They were officially in what some G-3 major had told him was "Division Special Reserve." Exactly what that meant Dunwood didn't know, but he knew the result.

Since Baker Company had landed at Inchon eleven days before, with the exception of some minor harassing and intermittent fire, they had not been involved in any combat at all, and that meant there had been zero KIA, zero WIA, and zero MIA.

It hadn't been that way in the Pusan Perimeter, where the Army general, Walker, admitted publicly that he had used the 5th Marines as his "Fire Brigade," rushing its men in all over to save the Army's ass when it looked as if the North Koreans were about to break through.

There had been a lot of Killed in Action and Wounded in Action in Baker Company in the Pusan Perimeter. When they were pulled off the line so they could board ships and make the Inchon Landing, Baker Company had been down to three officers and ninety-eight men. They were supposed to have five officers and two hundred four men. Dunwood had been able to report zero Missing in Action in the perimeter; he took a little quiet pride in knowing he hadn't left any of his Marines behind.

When they got to the piers in Pusan, expecting to board the USS *Clymer* or the USS *Pickaway*, or another of the attack transports that would carry them to Yokohama, where the 1st Marine Division was being assembled, Baker Company had been loaded instead aboard LST-450. And they were the only Marines loaded, although she was big enough to carry a hell of a lot more people.

Just about as soon as they were out of the harbor and the LST's skipper, Lieutenant John X. McNear, USNR, had time for a little chat, he told Dunwood three things.

First, that he was, like Dunwood, a reserve officer involuntarily called up for Korea (he had been the golf professional at Happy Hollow Country Club, Phoenix, Arizona). Second, that he had just now sailed LST-450 from Bremerton, Washington, where she had been mothballed. And third, that they were now headed for Sasebo, not Yokohama. He said he had learned that only when he opened a sealed envelope on which was typed "OPEN ONLY WHEN AT SEA," and he hadn't any idea what was going on.

Dunwood had searched his mind for a possible explanation and had come up with very little, except the possibility that Baker Company would be reequipped and brought up to authorized strength at Sasebo.

When they got to Sasebo, Dunwood quickly learned that was not to be the case. Baker Company, the lieutenant colonel in charge of a team from 1st Marine Division Headquarters told him, had been selected for a "special mission of crucial importance to the landing at Inchon."

The lieutenant colonel made it sound

like an honor. Dunwood's experience as a Marine made him suspect it was a euphemistic description of a mission that would get a lot of Marines — probably including him — killed.

Baker Company was shortly thereafter assembled in the gymnasium of the U.S. Naval Base, Sasebo, where, after the windows were covered and guards posted at the doors, the colonel described their mission to them.

It seemed that to reach the landing beaches at Inchon, the invasion fleet would have to traverse the thirty-odd-mile-long Flying Fish Channel. In the channel were a number of islands, two of which, Taemuui-do and Yonghung-do, had to be invested and neutralized twenty-four hours before the invasion fleet arrived, otherwise the enemy could blow large holes in the sides of the transports with ordinary field artillery.

Baker Company had been given the mission, the honor, of investing Taemuui-do and Yonghung-do. Before they landed on the islands from Higgins boats, the islands would of course be subject to an enormous barrage of naval gunfire, which would effectively reduce to minimal the enemy's ability to resist Baker Company's invasion.

Actually, from that perspective, the colonel said, the real mission of Baker Company would be to occupy the two islands and prevent the enemy from coming back and bringing more artillery with them.

Captain Dunwood had gone ashore at Tarawa and Iwo Jima, on each occasion having been assured that following the massive preinvasion barrages of naval artillery to be laid on those islands, resistance would be minimal. That assurance had turned out to be bullshit, and he had therefore concluded that it was logical to presume this one was, too, and that Baker Company had just been handed the short end of the stick.

But he was a Marine, and Marines go where they are ordered to go, and he was a Marine officer, and Marine officers do whatever is humanly possible to reduce Marine losses by the only means that has ever looked like it works — training and more training.

By the time Baker Company reboarded LST-450, Captain Dunwood was sure that ninety-five percent of his Marines hated him for the regimen of training they had gone through under his command. And he was also sure that he had trained them as well and as thoroughly as he knew how, and that would probably result in fewer KIA and WIA than otherwise would have occurred.

At 0415 14 September, as the schedule

called for, LST-450 was at the mouth of the Flying Fish Channel, preparing to load the men of Baker Company aboard the Higgins boats for their assault on Taemuui-do and Yonghung-do islands.

Every ear, of course, was listening for the thunder, and every eye the flash, of the massive naval gunfire bombardment that was going to reduce the potential of the North Koreans to repel their assault to minimal. That was scheduled to begin at 0415 and last for a half hour.

At 0445, when Baker Company's Higgins boats were scheduled to depart LST-450 for the beaches of the islands, they were still listening, in vain. There had been some kind of a fuckup, obviously, and there wasn't going to be any massive barrage of naval gunfire.

Or, possibly, Captain Dunwood had thought privately, *some candy-ass chairwarming swabbie clerk-typist had made a little mistake typing the order — hitting the "5" instead of the "4" — and there would be a massive barrage of naval gunfire landing on Taemuui-do and Yonghung-do starting at 0515, five minutes after the first Higgins boat touched the shore, and Baker Company would be up to its ass in angry North Koreans.*

Marines go where they are ordered to go, with or without massive barrages of naval gunfire to reduce opposition to the minimum.

At 0510, on schedule, the first Higgins boat transporting Baker Company to the Flying Fish Channel Islands touched ashore and dropped its ramp.

Marines ran down the ramp and turned right and left, spreading out, weapons at the ready. Captain Dunwood was in the center of what ultimately was a formation in the shape of a V, holding his carbine in one hand.

"Hold your fire! Hold your fire!" a voice shouted, an obviously American voice.

A figure appeared. He was in black cotton pajamas and had a band of the same material around his forehead. He held his hands over his head in a gesture of surrender.

It soon became apparent that the Marines Had Landed and the situation was well in hand. The first landing had occurred before — long before, *weeks* before — Baker Company of the 5th Marines had arrived.

The character in the black pajamas was a technical sergeant named Jennings. The second character to appear in black pajamas had identified himself as Captain K. R. McCoy, USMCR, and he said he was "in charge of the operation."

At about that moment — just as

Dunwood was trying to reconcile McCoy with some candy-ass Marine he'd clashed with on a plane — the skies lit up and the earth trembled as a massive barrage of naval gunfire began. It flew overhead to land on Wolmi-do Island, miles farther down the Flying Fish Channel.

Captain McCoy explained to Captain Dunwood that the *real* role of Baker Company in the Inchon Invasion was to retake Taemuui-do and Yonghung-do islands in case something happened to him and his men.

Captain McCoy and his handful of men — some of them Korean — had then gotten into Baker Company's Higgins boats and left. Dunwood never had time to ask Captain McCoy what he was supposed to do next, or even to which Marine unit he belonged, or what was the reason for the black pajamas.

Two days later, other Higgins boats appeared at the island, under a Navy chief bosun's mate who knew only that he had been ordered to the island to pick up Baker Company and transport them to Inchon.

At Inchon, which had just been taken, Baker Company was placed in Division Special Reserve and Dunwood was shown where to bivouac and told to be prepared to move out on twenty minutes' notice.

No such notice ever came, and it had

not been necessary for Baker Company to fire a shot. Or, for that matter, to dodge any.

After five days in Division Special Reserve, half a company of amphibious trucks had come to their bivouac area under an old gunnery sergeant who reported that all Captain Strauley had told him was that he was to haul Baker Company to Kimpo Airfield.

By the time they reached Kimpo, the war had moved past the airfield. It was already in use.

Sergeant Preston had come to him within an hour, saying that he'd reconnoitered the field and found a hangar at the far end that was neither in use nor too badly shot up, and why didn't they take it over?

"At least, sir, until the fucking crotch gets its head out of its ass and decides what the fuck to do with us."

Under the circumstances, Captain Dunwood had decided that pending orders, moving into the hangar was the prudent thing to do.

A captain from G-3, Headquarters, 1st Marine Division, had shown up the next day and announced that Baker Company was still in Division Special Reserve and further orders would be forthcoming. He didn't say when, but warned Dunwood to be prepared to move out on four hours' notice, maximum.

Captain Dunwood's plan of action remained the same. Have Baker Company prepared to move out on command, and in the meantime to make his men as comfortable as possible, at the same time making no waves that would call attention to his command.

With a little bit of luck, they might be forgotten again.

When he finished his ham chunks and baked beans, he took a bite of the chocolate bar that came with the rations, spit it out, and decided it had probably already been bad when packaged just before the Civil War.

He slipped his feet into his boondockers, then sort of slid across the concrete floor to the door and went outside the hangar. He put a cigarette in his mouth and reached for his Zippo. Then he went back inside the building and, with his back to the door, lit the cigarette.

He thought it was highly unlikely that a North Korean sniper was lying in the mud out there somewhere, waiting to take a shot at some Marine careless enough to light a cigarette in the open and make a target of himself, but it never hurt to be careful.

Besides, he had warned his men of

snipers lying in the mud waiting for a chance to shoot a careless Marine so often that he felt he should practice what he preached.

Holding the cigarette with the coal in his cupped hand, he went outside again, thinking that for the evening's amusement he would watch the red glow of the artillery bounce off the clouds to the northeast of Seoul.

What he saw was the headlights — not the blackout lights — of two jeeps coming down the runway at high speed, and he wondered if no one had ever told them about North Korean snipers lying in the mud, hoping for an opportunity to shoot people foolish enough to run around at night with their headlights blazing.

Surprising him, the jeeps turned off the runway and onto the service road leading to his hangar.

A hundred yards from the hangar, they were stopped by one of Dunwood's perimeter guards. In the headlights, he could see the sentry gesturing toward him. Or, he thought, more accurately, the hangar, as there probably was not enough light to make him visible.

And then the jeeps were on him. There were two. In the first were three officers. The second was an MP jeep with a pedestal-mounted .30-caliber air-cooled Browning machine gun.

The driver of the jeep got out of it quickly and walked up to Dunwood. Dunwood saw that he was an Army officer, a major, wearing a classy fur-collar zipper jacket with the blue-and-white X Corps patch sewn to it. He was armed with a .45 in a tanker's shoulder holster.

Dunwood saluted.

The major returned the salute and inquired, not unpleasantly, "Who are you?"

"Captain Dunwood, sir. Commanding Baker Company, 5th Marines."

"When we couldn't find you, we thought you'd moved out."

"Sir?"

"You're 1st Marine Division Special Reserve, right?"

"Yes, sir."

"Well, you've been assigned to us for this mission," the major said.

"What mission is that, sir?"

The major didn't reply directly.

"We looked for you back there," the major said, indicating the main area of the airfield. "And when we couldn't find you, we thought you'd moved out. And we didn't expect to find anyone in this hangar."

"Yes, sir," Dunwood said.

"But all's well that ends well, right?" the major said, and turned to one of the officers with him, a young lieutenant. "Better get on the horn, Dick, and tell the colonel we've found the Marines, are now at the hangar, and we'll get back to them when we know more."

"Yes, sir," the young lieutenant said. He got into the backseat of the jeep, picked up a microphone, and called, "Jade Bird, this is Jade Bird Three."

"I'm the assistant Army Aviation officer for X Corps," the major said. "My name is Alex Donald." He put out his hand.

"How do you do, sir?"

"What's your strength, Captain? Nobody seemed to know."

"Three officers and ninety-eight men, sir."

"That ought to be enough. We can always get more if needed."

"Yes, sir. May I ask, enough for what?"

"To protect the aircraft," Major Donald said.

"What aircraft, sir?"

"This is to go no further than here, you understand?"

"Yes, sir."

"At first light, Captain, two aircraft are going to land here, and immediately be placed inside this hangar. . . . The doors do function, don't they?"

"I'm afraid I have no idea, sir," Dunwood said. He saw that Staff Sergeant

Al Preston had come around the corner of the hangar.

"Why not?" Major Donald asked.

"Sir, I had no reason to open them."

"Jesus Christ, Captain!" Major Donald exclaimed. "What good is a hangar if you can't get the doors open?"

"Yes, sir," Dunwood said. "Sergeant Preston, do you know if the doors of the hangar work?"

"Don't have a clue, sir."

"Get a couple of men and try to open them," Dunwood ordered.

"Aye, aye, sir," Sergeant Preston said.

Major Donald gave Captain Dunwood a thumbs-up.

"That's the spirit!" Major Donald said, and then explained, "It's very important that the enemy . . . and I think it's reasonable to assume they left spies behind when we ran them out of Seoul, don't you?"

"Yes, sir."

"It's important that the enemy not see these aircraft before we're ready for them to see them, you understand?"

"I think so. What kind of aircraft are these, Major?"

"I'm afraid you don't have the need to know that, Captain," Major Donald said. "And the problem is compounded because we think a senior officer, a *very* senior officer, is probably going to want to have a look at these aircraft — you take my meaning, Captain?"

"I'm afraid not, sir."

"Well, then, I'd better not get into that, either. It will all become clear at first light when these aircraft arrive."

"Yes, sir."

"I can tell you this, Captain," Major Donald said. "You are going to be present to personally witness the beginning of a new era in battlefield mobility."

"I don't know what that means, I'm afraid, sir."

"You'll see in the morning, Captain. But right now, I suggest you establish a really secure perimeter around this hangar."

"Yes, sir," Captain Dunwood said, and thought, *This is fucking surreal.* "With your permission, sir, I'll get dressed and see about setting up a perimeter guard."

Major Donald gave Captain Dunwood another thumbs-up signal and said, "That's the spirit!" Then he raised his voice. "Dick!"

"Yes, sir?"

"Get on the horn again and tell the colonel that everything's set up. And then bring in the sandwiches and coffee."

"Yes, sir," the young lieutenant replied.

"It's going to be a long night, but it's always better to be early than late."

"Yes, sir."

[Two]
Hangar 13
Kimpo Airfield (K-16)
Seoul, South Korea
0510 29 September 1950

Major Alex Donald, USA, and Captain Howard Dunwood, USMCR, stood on the tarmac before the open doors of Hangar 13. It had grown light enough in the last few minutes for Dunwood to see the perimeter guard he had established in the dark around the hangar.

The Marines of Baker Company were set up in and around foxholes, culverts, wrecked vehicles, crashed aircraft fuselages, and in a really shot-up little building painted in a black-and-white checkerboard pattern, their weapons forming fields of fire that would keep the enemy away from the hangar that was to house the aircraft soon to arrive.

Dunwood wondered about the purpose of the checkerboard building. Every airport seemed to have one, but he had no idea of what they were for.

Probably because he didn't really give much of a damn about either the Air Force or the Army, neither did he have any idea what the relationship between the two was with respect to airplanes. Now he was wondering about that, too. When, during the night, Major Alex Donald had taken off his spiffy fur-collared zipper jacket — which Dunwood had belatedly recognized to be a pilot's jacket — there were silver pilot's wings pinned to his chest. There were also metallic representations of the old-time wigwag signal flags on his collar point. Dunwood recognized that as the insignia of the Army Signal Corps.

Putting that all together, Major Donald was an Army Signal Corps officer — in other words, an officer whose specialty was communications — who was also a pilot, presumably of these secret aircraft about to arrive to usher in a new era of battlefield mobility.

Where did the Air Force fit into this? Weren't airplanes the province of the Air Force? Until just now, Dunwood thought the only airplanes the Army had were little Piper Cub–like two-seaters used for artillery spotting, and a handful of helicopters, tiny little flying machines in which the pilot sat in a huge plastic bubble and whose only purpose Dunwood could see was to haul either the brass from point to point or to haul the wounded in a side-mounted stretcher rack.

Dunwood knew that his success as a DeSoto-Plymouth salesman had been in large part due to his ability to get people to tell him just about anything he wanted them to. Knowing your customer was the first, and most important, step in making a sale, and he had been damned good at finding out whatever he had wanted to know.

That skill had failed him in the long hours of the night. Major Alex Donald had told him no more than what he'd told him when he had first appeared at the hangar, and finally had made it very clear that Dunwood's persistent curiosity was very unwelcome.

There came the sound of multiple aircraft engines.

Dunwood looked into the sky toward Inchon. There were three Corsairs slowly approaching the airfield. They were flying one above the other, separated by two hundred feet or so. The lowest was maybe 1,500 feet above the ground.

"There they are," Major Donald cried, excitement in his voice.

"Major," Dunwood said, "those are Corsairs. *Marine* Corsairs."

"Not there, Captain," Major Donald said, as if speaking to a retarded child. *"There!"*

Dunwood looked at him. The major had his arm extended toward the horizon in the direction of Inchon.

Dunwood looked where Donald was pointing.

There were two objects in the air, perhaps two hundred feet off the deck, approaching the airfield from the direction of Inchon. They looked not unlike olive-drab dragonflies, a large body supported by a lot of flapping wings, or whatever.

In a moment, Dunwood realized they were helicopters, the largest he had ever seen.

"Well, Captain," Major Donald said. "What do you think about that?"

Dunwood, who didn't know what to think, said nothing.

It was maybe sixty seconds before the first of the helicopters reached the hangar, flared, and then settled to the ground. By then, Dunwood saw, perhaps half of his men had climbed out of their foxholes and other emplacements to get a better look. Two Marines were standing on top of the checkerboard-painted building.

As they had rehearsed during the night, eight Marines under Sergeant Al Preston trotted up to push the aircraft into the hangar.

As it was pushed past him, Dunwood saw a legend painted in yellow on the fuselage just behind the side door of the cockpit: US ARMY MODEL H-19A.

The second helicopter settled to the ground.

"Shake a leg, men!" Major Alex Donald

shouted. "We've got to get these aircraft out of sight before anyone sees them."

[Three]
The House
Seoul, Korea
0550 29 September 1950

Major Kenneth R. McCoy, USMCR, now wearing crisply starched Marine utilities, with the gold oak leaves of his rank pinned in the prescribed place on the collar points, and even wearing aftershave lotion, walked into the dining room.

Master Gunner Ernest W. Zimmerman, USMC, similarly attired and shipshape, was sitting at one side of the heavy carved wooden table, spreading butter on a piece of toast.

The two men nodded at each other. Zimmerman opened his mouth as if to say something, but stopped when the middle-aged Korean woman entered from the kitchen carrying a silver coffeepot.

She bowed to McCoy, he bowed back, and she poured a cup of coffee for him. She asked him what he wanted for breakfast, and he asked what was available, and she told him, and he ordered what Gunner Zimmerman had had — ham, eggs up, home-fried potatoes, and toast.

When she passed through the door to the kitchen, McCoy sat down across the table from Zimmerman.

"I wonder what the other Marines in Korea are having for breakfast this morning," he said, helping himself to a piece of Zimmerman's toast.

"My mother used to try to make me eat oatmeal by telling me about the starving kids in India," Zimmerman said. "Same answer. I don't give a damn what's on anyone else's plate." He pointed at his plate. "This is the only one that counts."

"I'm shocked at your cruel selfishness," McCoy said in mock indignation.

"Neither do you, Killer," Zimmerman said, chuckling. "Be honest."

McCoy smiled.

"You know what I was thinking, though?" Zimmerman asked.

"No."

"What did finding your next day's uniform sitting all pressed and shipshape on your bed last night remind you of?"

"Shanghai, 4th Marines, houseboys?" McCoy responded. "Sergeant Zimmerman and Corporal McCoy?"

"Yeah."

"Hard whiskey and wild, wild women, before we became respectable, married, officers and gentlemen?"

"What I was thinking was we haven't

come that far in ten years," Zimmerman said.

"Then, ten years ago, I would have been happy to think I could make staff sergeant in ten years," McCoy said.

"So now you're a field-grade officer, and I make as much money as a captain —"

"And own half of Beaufort, South Carolina. . . ."

"— and people are still shooting at us."

"Nobody shot at us yesterday, Ernie."

"With you and that goddamn Russian jeep, we almost got blown away by our own side," Zimmerman said.

The door from the foyer opened and two middle-aged men in mussed and soiled Army fatigues walked in. One of them had a Garand rifle slung over his shoulder; there were two eight-round clips of ammunition on the strap. The other carried a U.S. Submachine Gun, Caliber .45 ACP M-3, in his hand. The weapon, made of mostly stamped parts, was called a Grease Gun because it looked like a grease gun.

Zimmerman glanced up at them, and then in a Pavlovian reflex jumped to his feet and barked, " 'Ten'hut on deck!"

McCoy, in another Pavlovian reflex, stood to attention.

"As you were," one of the two newcomers said, then added, "Good morning."

"Good morning, sir," McCoy and

128

Zimmerman said, almost in unison.

Major General Ralph Howe, NGUS, walked to the table and hung his Grease Gun over the back of one of the heavy chairs and sat down. He looked at Zimmerman.

"Ernie," he said. "I thought I told you I'd rather you didn't do that every time I walk into a room."

"Force of habit, sir," Zimmerman said. "Sorry, sir."

The other man, whose sleeves carried the stencil-painted chevrons of a master sergeant, shook his head in resignation, then hung his rifle over the back of another chair and sat down.

General Howe gestured with his hand for McCoy and Zimmerman to sit down.

"To judge by your spiffy appearance, I guess you heard who's due at Kimpo at 0900?" he said.

"I got a message from Hart, sir, to be at Kimpo at 0900," McCoy said. "No names were mentioned."

"El Supremo is going to turn Liberated Seoul back over to Syngman Rhee at about eleven," Howe said. "Maybe it'll really be liberated by then. Some of the North Koreans apparently didn't get the word."

McCoy chuckled.

"And Charley said that if anyone could get us a bath, a shave, and clean uniforms, it would be you two," Howe said.

"And maybe something besides powdered eggs for breakfast?" Master Sergeant Charley Rogers said.

He, too, was a National Guardsman. He had been Captain Howe's first sergeant and had been with him ever since. That meant when President Harry S Truman had ordered — actually asked, "Ralph, I need you" — General Howe to active duty, the first thing General Howe had done was ask just about the same question of Charley Rogers.

Zimmerman got up and went through the door to the kitchen.

"Are you going to have good news for your boss, Ken?" General Howe asked. "I am presuming he will be with the imperial entourage."

"I sent General Pickering a message last night, sir. Pick . . . Major Pickering . . . is out there somewhere, within a fifty-mile radius of Suwon. I don't think we missed him by more than a couple of hours, and I don't have any reason to believe he's in trouble."

"He's in trouble — we're all in trouble — until we get him back, Ken."

"Yes, sir."

"What's the problem, Ken? And how do we get around it?"

"The scenario is this, sir. Whenever they

can, Colonel Dunn's pilots look for the messages he leaves, ones he stamps out in rice paddy mud. Sometimes they eyeball them, sometimes the photo interpreters pick them out from aerial photographs. So we've had a rough idea where he is ever since he was shot down. Locating him precisely is part of the problem. And then, even if we do that, picking him up will then be the problem. The ideal way to do that is with a helicopter. The problem there —"

"— is that there aren't very many helicopters," General Howe picked up. "And those that exist are being used to haul wounded —"

"— or brass," McCoy began, and corrected himself: "— *senior officers* — where they have to go. And General Pickering doesn't want to take a chopper away from hauling the wounded to look for Pick or pick him up."

Zimmerman came back into the dining room, followed by the Korean housekeeper, who carried a tray with a silver coffee service on it.

"You were right, Charley," General Howe said. "While we're drinking three-day-old coffee from canteen cups, these two —"

"I told her to make ham and eggs, sir," Zimmerman said. "Will that be all right?"

"If that's the best you can do, Mr. Zimmerman, I guess it will have to do," Master Sergeant Rogers said.

Howe chuckled, then said: "We can't afford to have Major Pickering captured, Ken. We may have to borrow a helicopter for a while, General Pickering's feelings aside."

It was an observation more in the nature of a decision, and thus an order. While legally Major General Howe had no authority to order anyone to do anything, he was in Korea bearing orders signed by Harry S Truman, as President and Commander-in-Chief, which ordered that "all U.S. military and governmental agencies provide General Howe with whatever assistance of whatever kind he deems necessary for the accomplishment of his mission."

Howe, who had been a captain with Captain Harry S Truman in France in World War I, and who had risen to Major General in World War II, was in Korea as Truman's eyes.

No one from MacArthur down was going to refuse him anything he asked for.

McCoy didn't reply.

The door opened again, and "Major" William R. Dunston walked in.

"I just heard you were here, sir —" he began.

"Mooching breakfast," Howe interrupted

him. "And, I hope, a shower, shave, and some clean fatigues."

"Not a problem, sir," Dunston said.

"If you didn't know that General MacArthur's due at Kimpo sometime around nine, Bill, I'd be very surprised."

"I heard, sir," Dunston said. "Good morning, Charley."

Master Sergeant Rogers nodded and smiled.

"Did your guy get anything out of my guy, Bill?" McCoy asked.

"I was going to ask you to sit in on that," Dunston said. "You and Ernie. They're still in the basement."

"I'm in the dark," General Howe said simply.

"We took some prisoners yesterday, sir," McCoy began. "We were on our way here, and they just came barreling up the highway. The senior one's a lieutenant colonel. Arrogant sonofabitch. I've got a gut feeling he's somebody important. Ernie and I couldn't get anything out of him. The other four I turned over to 7th Division."

Howe nodded.

"I thought he might react to a senior officer, and Bill has had an ROK colonel interrogating him," McCoy went on.

"I can't believe anyone could get more out of a prisoner than you two can," Howe said.

"I don't think he knows anything about troop dispositions, that sort of thing," McCoy replied. "And if he does, he won't tell us. But I thought he might let something slip when trying to impress a senior officer with his own importance."

"And has he, Bill?" Howe asked.

Dunston looked uncomfortable.

"What does your man say he got from this fellow, Bill?" Howe persisted.

"I'm afraid Colonel Lee thinks he got more out of the prisoner than is the case, General," Dunston said.

"What?" Howe asked. There was now a hint of impatience in his voice.

"Something I would much rather not pass on, especially to someone as senior as you, until I had a hell of a lot to back it up," Dunston said.

"Specifically, what?" Howe demanded.

"Colonel Lee thinks this guy has information that the Chinese are coming in," Dunston said. "He didn't say that, in so many words. It's more of a gut feeling on Lee's part."

"Interesting," Master Sergeant Rogers said.

"General," Dunston said, "the first thing I was going to do — did — was ask Major McCoy and Mr. Zimmerman to talk first with Colonel Lee, and then the prisoner, and see what they think. And even — no

134

offense — if they thought there was something to it, think long and hard before passing it on."

Howe grunted.

"Afraid of calling, 'Wolf, wolf'?" he asked.

"Yes, sir," Dunston said, and added, "General, you've got me on a spot, sir —"

He was interrupted in midsentence by the Korean housekeeper, who entered the room with Howe's and Rogers's breakfasts.

No one spoke until she had laid the plates before them, poured coffee, and left the room.

"I understand, Bill," Howe resumed.

"General, I think the Chinese will come in," Dunston said. "But I don't want to be — you said it, sir — crying wolf until I have a lot more than this to back it up."

"I understand," Howe repeated, and started to say something else when the door from the foyer opened and another man came in.

This one was wearing a USMC flight suit, to the breast of which was fixed a leather patch bearing stamped-in-gold-leaf Naval aviator's wings, and the legend *W. C. Dunn, LtCol USMC*.

Lieutenant Colonel William C. Dunn, who was five feet six inches tall and weighed not quite one hundred forty pounds, was visibly surprised and discomfited when he saw the two silver stars of each collar point of General Howe's soiled and rumpled Army fatigues.

"I beg the general's pardon, sir," he said, coming almost to attention. "I didn't know the general was in here."

"Colonel Dunn, right?" Howe asked.

"Yes, sir."

"Your reputation precedes you, Colonel," General Howe said. "Please sit down. Have you had your breakfast?"

General Howe thought: *With that pink skin and blond crew cut, he really does look like "an overage cheerleader," which is how Ernie Zimmerman described him.*

"That's very kind, sir, but I fear I'm intruding."

"Not at all," Howe said. "And I was hoping for a chance to talk to you in the next day or so. My name is Howe."

He put out his hand.

"Yes, sir. I thought that's who you probably were," Dunn said.

"The old man in need of a shave and a bath is Master Sergeant Charley Rogers," Howe said. "I guess you know everybody else."

"Yes, sir, I do," Dunn said, and then rose out of his chair to offer his hand to Rogers. Zimmerman got up and went into the kitchen.

"I didn't expect to see you here, Colonel," Howe said.

"I happened to be in Seoul, sir, and I wanted to talk to Major McCoy," Dunn said.

"You 'happened to be' in Seoul?" Howe asked, smiling.

"Yes, sir, I had an early-morning mission — flying cover for a pair of enormous Army helicopters they flew off a transport into Kimpo — and I thought I'd take advantage of the opportunity."

McCoy's curiosity got the best of him.

"*Enormous* helicopters?" he blurted.

Dunn nodded.

"Sikorskys, I think. I saw a photo of them a while back."

"Why were you flying cover for them?" Howe asked.

"I guess they didn't want them shot down before they even got here, sir."

"How's the Army going to use them?" Howe asked. "You have any idea?"

"Not a clue, sir."

"You get my message last night, Colonel?" McCoy asked.

"I got it. One of the things I wanted to tell you was that both of the Corsairs with me — there were three of us — are going to take a lot of aerials over those coordinates you gave me —"

"Which were the coordinates for?" Howe interrupted.

"The last place we know Pick was for

sure, General," McCoy said.

"— on the way back to the *Badoeng Strait*," Dunn finished his sentence.

Zimmerman came back into the room.

"Chow's on the way, Colonel," he announced.

"Colonel, what I wanted to talk to you about is Major Pickering," Howe said.

"Yes, sir."

"How do we get him back, Colonel?"

Lieutenant Colonel Dunn was respectful of, but not cowed by, Major General Howe.

"With respect, sir, I'm an airplane driver. The Killer and Zimmerman are the experts in that sort of thing."

Howe chuckled. "You must really be old and good friends. I understand that's the only way you can get away with calling him that."

"Yes, sir. We are. We go back a long way."

"Let me rephrase, Colonel: If you were, say, the commanding general of the 1st Marine Division, and you were ordered to return Major Pickering to U.S. control, how would you do that?"

Dunn thought his answer over a moment before speaking.

"General, just about what's happening now. Giving *Major McCoy* whatever —"

"Much better. Thank you, sir," McCoy said.

"Ken, I'm sorry, it just slips out," Dunn said.

"You were saying, Colonel?" Howe said.

"The best way I can think of to get Major Pickering back, sir, is just what's happening now. Giving Major McCoy whatever he thinks he needs to do it."

"Is that happening, Ken?" Howe asked. "You have everything you need?"

"Yes, sir. It is. And I can't think of anything else I need. I've even managed to borrow an infantry company — actually about two platoons — from 1st MarDiv, in case we need them."

"The backup people for the Flying Fish Channel operation?" Howe asked.

"Yes, sir. They're at Kimpo."

"Probably wondering what the hell is going on," Zimmerman offered.

"In case you need them how, Ken?" Howe asked.

"Nothing specific, sir. But if we have to go any farther from our lines to grab Pick than we have so far, I'd rather have more people along."

"When you say you have everything you need, you mean, 'except of course for the helicopters that we don't want to take from hauling the wounded,' right?" Howe went on, looked at McCoy for a moment, and then turned to Dunn.

"Okay, Colonel," Howe said. "You say

139

you're an airplane driver. So, for the sake of argument, let's assume you have a helicopter — hell, say four helicopters — at your disposal. How would you, as an airplane driver, use them to get Major Pickering back?"

Dunn, visibly in deep thought, did not immediately reply.

"Add this unpleasant reality to your equation, Colonel," General Howe went on. "Stop thinking of Major Pickering as a Marine pilot. Start thinking of him as someone we simply cannot afford to have fall into the enemy's hands."

Dunn met his eyes but still did not instantly reply.

Finally, he exhaled audibly.

"The one sure way to keep Major Pickering out of the enemy's hands is to locate him positively within a one-hundred-yard circle and then napalm the hell out of the circle," he said.

"Jesus Christ, Billy!" McCoy exploded.

"General, I want you to understand that I understand what's at play here," Dunn said. "Pick Pickering was my wingman at Guadalcanal. I love the bastard. But I also understand he's General Pickering's son."

"Let's hope it doesn't come to napalm," Howe said. "And let's get back to your having four helicopters at your disposal."

"Sir, with respect, I drive airplanes.

Other people — in this case, that would be Major McCoy — tell me what they would like me to do with them."

"Okay," Howe said. "Okay, Ken. You have four helicopters at your disposal. How are you going to use them?"

McCoy didn't immediately reply.

"Certainly, Ken," Howe said, not unkindly, "you've thought about it."

"If we can find him, precisely locate him — which, so far, we haven't been able to do — then the standard Marine Corps procedure would almost certainly work. We arrange for fighter cover, send in one helicopter, and pick him up. I've already got that set up."

"What do you mean, you've already got it set up?" Howe asked.

"I've talked to the helicopter pilots. If we locate him, they'll go after him."

"I thought the decision has been made that helicopters will not be diverted for that purpose."

"If we can locate him," McCoy repeated, "a helicopter will be available to pick him up."

"Against orders?"

"We'll have to worry about that later."

"You took it upon yourself to order the pilots to disobey their orders?"

"I asked a couple of them, 'What if I find Pickering? Could you help?' And the answer was very simple: 'Give us thirty minutes' notice, and precise coordinates, and we'll go snatch him.' "

"So you don't need more than one helicopter?"

"I'd like to have eight, ten of them," McCoy said. "But since that's out of the question — there aren't that many — all I can use is one."

"And if you had eight or ten of them, Ken?" Dunn asked.

"I'd take that many Marines to the last marker he left. They'd drop us off and leave us. Then we'd follow his tracks. I think we could find him. If so, then we could call the helicopters back and have everybody picked up. But that's wishful thinking. Six or eight helicopters aren't available."

Howe grunted thoughtfully.

"And even if they were, General, that probably wouldn't work."

"Why not?"

"There are North Korean soldiers all over this area. And North Korean spies. Six or eight helicopters landing someplace all at once would attract a lot of attention."

"One helo taking in six or eight people one at a time?" Dunn asked.

"I thought about that, too," McCoy said. "Same answer — it would attract too much attention. And then if the NKs saw how few people there were, and went after us . . ."

"You could not be evacuated," Howe said.

"No, sir," McCoy said. "Not with one helo."

"General," Master Sergeant Rogers said. Howe looked at him. Rogers tapped his wristwatch. Howe nodded, then stood up.

"Shower time," he said. "You said you have some clean fatigues for us, Bill?"

"Yes, sir, clean and starched, but I don't know what we'll do for chevrons for Charley."

"Well, then I guess he'll just have to look like the oldest private in the Army," General Howe said, then turned to McCoy. "Ken, I want to hear what you and Ernie think of what this North Korean colonel has to say about the prospects of Chinese intervention."

"I'll go down there right now, sir," McCoy said.

Everyone rose from the table as General Howe and Master Sergeant Rogers walked out of the room.

One hundred yards away from the *Bataan*, General of the Army Douglas MacArthur's personal Douglas C-54, a very large MP sergeant, whose impeccable uniform included a chrome-plated steel helmet, a glistening leather Sam Browne belt, and paratrooper boots with white nylon laces, held up his hand to stop the 1950 black Buick Roadmaster.

The Buick had an oblong red plate with a silver star mounted to the bumper, identifying it as a car occupied by a brigadier general of the United States Marine Corps.

The MP bent over to look into the rear seat as the window rolled down.

There were two men in the rear seat, both of them wearing fur-collared zippered leather jackets officially known as Jacket, Flyers, Intermediate Type G-1. The driver was a U.S. Army sergeant.

"General Pickering," the younger of the two men in the backseat said.

There was no insignia on the leather jacket, but the silver railroad tracks of a captain were visible on the collar points of his shirt. The captain, in his early thirties,

144

was built like a circus strong man.

"Good morning, sir," the MP said, courteously, then added, a little uneasily, "Sir, the general is not on my list."

"Then your list is wrong, Sergeant," the captain said reasonably.

"Yes, sir," the MP said, straightened, came to attention, raised his hand in a crisp salute, and said, "Pass."

Both men in the back of the Buick returned the salute.

The Buick drove up to the mobile stairway to the glistening C-54, around which were gathered half a dozen officers and men, including two impeccably and ornately uniformed military policemen, one standing at parade rest at each side the ladder.

The driver of the Buick got out and hurriedly opened the rear door.

Brigadier General Fleming Pickering, a silver-haired man of six feet one, 190 pounds, who thought of himself as being one year past The Big Five Zero, got out of the car. The captain followed a moment later.

Colonel Sidney Huff, a large, somewhat plump fifty-year-old wearing the insignia of an aide-de-camp to a General of the Army, walked up and saluted.

"Good morning, General," he said. "I wasn't aware you were coming along."

Pickering and the captain returned the colonel's salute.

"Good morning, Sid," Pickering said, and added, "Neither was the MP back there."

"May I suggest you board, sir?" Colonel Huff said. "The Supreme Commander's due any moment, and you know he doesn't like to wait to board the *Bataan*."

Pickering nodded.

"See you on board, Sid," Pickering said, and started for the ladder, trailed by the captain, who now had a web pistol belt with a holstered Colt Model 1911A1 pistol in his hand.

The MPs at the foot of the stairway saluted as the two Marines climbed the ladder.

There was an Air Force master sergeant standing inside the aircraft at the door.

"Captain Hart will be sitting with me," Pickering said.

The sergeant obviously didn't like to hear that, but sergeants do not argue with brigadier generals.

"Yes, sir," he said. "How about the fourth row back on the left of the aircraft, sir?"

Pickering found the row, slid in, and took the window seat. The captain opened the overhead bin, put the pistol belt in it, then sat down beside Pickering.

Pickering pointed out the window.

An olive-drab 1950 Chevrolet staff car had stopped at the foot of the stairway. One of the Army officers hurried to open the rear door, as Colonel Huff stood by.

A slight, elderly, gray-haired Oriental in a business suit somewhat awkwardly extricated himself from the car, then turned to offer his hand to the other passenger. This was a Caucasian woman in a black dress.

"Rhee?" Captain Hart asked softly.

Pickering nodded.

Colonel Huff saluted, then waved the couple to the stairway.

A moment later they appeared inside the aircraft. The Air Force master sergeant led them to one of the two VIP suites, the one on the right.

"So where does the Palace Guard get to sit?" Hart whispered.

Pickering smiled at him but held his finger in front of his lips, suggesting that further observations of that nature would be inappropriate. Then he pointed out the window again.

The Chevrolet staff car was gone, replaced by a black 1942 Cadillac limousine, which had a small American flag mounted on the right front fender and a small flag with five stars in a circle mounted on the left fender.

Colonel Huff personally opened the passenger door.

General of the Army Douglas MacArthur, Supreme Commander, Allied Powers and United Nations Forces, got out.

MacArthur was wearing well-washed khakis, his famous battered, gold-encrusted uniform cap, and an Air Force A-2 leather flight jacket, not unlike the fur-collared Naval aviator's jackets Pickering and Hart were wearing.

Pickering was reasonably sure that his Naval aviator's jacket was not an authorized item of uniform for Marine officers, but he was equally sure that no one was going to call him on it. So far as he was concerned, his — and El Supremo's — leather jackets were a comfortable, practical garment for senior officers, who were not likely to find themselves rolling around in the dirt. Furthermore, he had heard somewhere that as a privilege of rank, general officers were permitted to select their own uniforms. He thought that if this were true, it probably applied only to Army officers, but had decided on the jacket anyway.

And had extended the privilege to his aide-de-camp (and bodyguard), Captain George F. Hart, as well.

"General, would it be all right if I got one of those leather jackets?" Hart had asked. "It would make hiding these a lot easier."

Hart had shown what he meant by first pulling up his trousers' leg and revealing a Smith & Wesson snub-nosed .38 Special five-shot revolver — his "backup" gun — in an ankle holster, then showing General Pickering his back and the Colt Model 1911-A1 semiautomatic .45-ACP-caliber pistol he carried in a skeleton holster in the small thereof.

Captain Hart, who as a civilian commanded the Homicide Bureau of the Saint Louis, Missouri, Police Department, had brought the weapons with him when recalled to the Corps for the Korean Conflict. He was never either without the pistols or very far from Brigadier General Pickering.

It makes sense, and if the Palace Guard doesn't like it, sorry about that.

"Sure, George. Why not?" Pickering had replied.

Hart now carried the .45 in a shoulder holster and the snub-nose in the right side pocket of the leather jacket.

And, predictably, the Palace Guard hadn't liked the sight of Captain Hart in a Naval aviator's leather jacket identical to that of General Pickering's, and had used it to take a shot at what really bothered them — Marine General Pickering wearing a leather jacket much like the one worn by the Supreme Commander, Allied Powers and United Nations Forces.

"General," Colonel Sidney Huff had said, "I'm sure you won't take offense where none is intended, but do you think your aide's leather jacket is appropriate?"

The translation of that, of course, was: *"Do you think* your *leather jacket is appropriate when (a) General MacArthur's leather jacket has become his trademark and (b) General MacArthur has made it plain he would prefer that his staff officers do not wear leather jackets or battered gold-bedecked uniform caps?"*

General Pickering had smiled at Colonel Huff.

"Let me think about that, Sid. Thank you for bringing the subject up."

After that, George's leather jacket — and of course his — were set in concrete. Brigadier General Pickering, the Assistant Director of the CIA for the Far East, was not a lowly brigadier on the staff of the Supreme Commander, as much as the staff — and probably El Supremo himself — would like it so. He was, *de jure,* subordinate only to the Director of the CIA, Rear Admiral Roscoe Hillencoetter, USN, but, *de facto,* only to President Harry S Truman.

MacArthur's people had to be reminded of that every once in a while. If the petty nonsense about who could wear leather jackets and who couldn't served to accomplish this, so much the better.

General MacArthur somewhat impatiently returned the salutes being offered and hurried up the stairway into the aircraft, trailed by Colonel Huff and some of the others.

Air Force ground crewmen hurried to move the stairway away from the aircraft, and there immediately came the whine of an aircraft engine being started.

MacArthur entered the cabin, knocked politely at the door of the VIP suite on the right, entered, and a moment later reappeared in the aisle.

He looked around, spotted what he was looking for, and gestured for Brigadier General Pickering to join him.

"I guess you get to sit on the right hand of God," Captain Hart said.

"George, you're going to get us both in trouble," Pickering said, but he was smiling.

Hart got out of the way, and Pickering made his way to the VIP cabin on the right.

There were six leather-upholstered seats in the compartment, two double sets facing forward, and two against a bulkhead that faced to the rear. A table, on which sat a coffee thermos, cups and saucers, and a

151

map case, was between the forward- and rear-facing seats.

MacArthur was in the window seat of the first forward-facing row, in the process of fastening his seat belt. He waved Pickering into one of the seats opposite him.

Colonel Huff stepped into the compartment.

"That will be all, Huff. Thank you," MacArthur said, dismissing him.

There was the sound of a second engine starting, and the aircraft began to move.

"Good morning, General," Pickering said.

"Good morning, Fleming," MacArthur replied. "I'm pleased you could come with me."

There was a discreet knock at the door, and then, without waiting for permission, an Air Force colonel entered.

"Good morning, General," he said.

"Storms, turbulence, and a bad headwind all the way, right?" MacArthur greeted him.

"Quite the contrary, sir. Weather's fine en route and there."

He laid a sheet of paper on the table and went on: "I think we'll be wheels-up at six thirty-five, which should put us in Seoul a few minutes before ten."

"Splendid! Thank you, Colonel."

The colonel left, and a white-jacketed airman came in with a plate of pastry.

The *Bataan* taxied to the end of the runway, ran the engines up quickly, and then began to race down the runway.

When the rumble of the wheels stopped and the whining of the gear being retracted ended, MacArthur said: "I think dignity and simplicity should be the style for this business in Seoul, Fleming. Do you agree?"

"I would trust your judgment about that above anyone else's," Pickering said.

I meant that, even if it made me sound like a member of the Palace Guard.

"Let me make a note or two," MacArthur said. He reached for a lined tablet on the table, then changed his mind and instead picked up the coffeepot.

He held it over a cup, then asked with a raised eyebrow if Pickering wanted some, and when Pickering said, "Please," poured coffee for him.

He poured a second cup for himself, then picked up a pencil and slid the tablet to him.

Pickering pulled the sheet of paper the pilot had left on the table to him.

It was their routing. There was a simple but adequate map, and the data:

Direct Haneda-Kimpo.
Ground Miles: 739
Estimated Air Speed en route 227 mph

Estimated Flight Time 3 hours 16 min
Rendezvous with fighter escort over Fukui
(before reaching Sea of Japan)
No Adverse Weather Expected.
Presuming Haneda Take-Off 0635
ETA Kimpo 0951

Pickering thought: *The Constellations cruise at 323; that's almost 100 knots faster than this. No wonder El Supremo wants one.*

General Pickering knew more about aircraft than he ever thought he would. In another life, he was chairman of the board of the Pacific and Far East Shipping Corporation. Among the wholly owned subsidiaries of P&FE was Trans-Global Airways.

The first president of Trans-Global — Pickering's only child, Malcolm, then just out of Marine Corps service as a fighter pilot — had argued long, passionately, and in the end successfully that Trans-Global should start up with Lockheed L-049 aircraft, rather than with surplus (and thus incredibly cheap) military aircraft.

Pick's argument had been threefold:

First, the maiden flight of the DC-4 — Air Force designation C-54 — had been in 1938, and the first Constellation flight in 1943, five years later. It had, thus, five years' design experience on the Douglas, longer really if you considered the development money thrown at the aviation industry with war on the horizon.

Second, Pick argued, the Connie had a range of 5,400 miles, more than twice the 2,500-mile range of the Douglas, which would permit them to open routes in the Pacific that the Douglas simply couldn't handle.

And third, Pick had argued, if the fledgling Trans-Global acquired, as it could with the 323-knot Constellation, a reputation for providing the fastest transoceanic service, it would keep that reputation even after the other airlines smartened up and got Connies themselves.

"Nobody, Pop, has ever accused Howard Hughes of being stupid."

The legendary Howard Hughes was known to have had a heavy hand in the design of the Constellation, and Trans-World Airlines, in which he held a majority interest, was equipping itself with Constellations as quickly as they could come off the Lockheed production line.

Fleming Pickering had given in to his son's recommendations, in part because he thought Pick was right and in part because he was — P&FE was — cash heavy from the sale of all but two of P&FE's passenger liners to the Navy during World War II.

Shortly after Pearl Harbor, Flem Pickering had flown over the Boeing plant in Seattle and seen long lines of B-17 aircraft, each plane capable of flying across any ocean in the world. He had known that day that the era of the luxurious passenger ship was over. Time was money.

He had willingly sold seventeen of his passenger ships to the Navy, but flatly refused to sell them one P&FE merchantman. Airplanes were not about to haul heavy materials.

When MacArthur ordered/invited Pickering to ride in his private compartment, Pickering had assumed MacArthur wanted to chat, either about military matters or the Good Old Days in Manila or Australia, or to perhaps deliver one of his lectures on strategy.

But, surprising Pickering, he busied himself with his lined pad until, forty-five minutes later, Pickering said, "General," and pointed out the window.

A Chance Vought Corsair fighter plane, with MARINES lettered large on its fuselage behind the cockpit, was on their wingtip. Others were visible elsewhere in the sky.

"Our fighter escort," MacArthur said needlessly.

The cockpit of the Corsair was open, and they could clearly see the pilot, a young redhead with earphones cocked on one ear. He saluted crisply, held his position a moment, then shoved the throttle to the firewall. The Corsair then pulled very rapidly ahead and upward, then turned and began to assume a position above and just ahead of the *Bataan.*

Major Malcolm S. Pickering, USMCR, had flown such an airplane in the Pacific, becoming an ace in the process, and had been flying such an airplane when he was shot down.

Brigadier General Pickering vainly hoped that General of the Army MacArthur would not see the tears that came to his eyes.

"Has there been any further word, Fleming?" MacArthur asked gently.

Pickering waited until he was sure he had control of his voice before replying.

"There was a message last night from Major McCoy, sir. He seems to feel that Pick is all right, and that he missed making contact with him by just a matter of hours."

"I would suggest, my friend, that McCoy is just the man for that job."

"I agree, sir."

"My heart goes out to you, Fleming," MacArthur said.

"Thank you."

MacArthur decided to change the subject.

"I suppose you've read the dossier on Rhee?" he asked.

"Yes, sir. Amazing man, apparently."

"Who in his youth fell under the spell of a Viennese . . . lady of the evening . . . and married her."

"I saw that," Pickering said. "I wonder how often a prominent man has done something like that without it becoming a matter of official record?"

"I would hate to hazard a guess," MacArthur said.

There was a discreet knock at the door.

MacArthur frowned, then said, "Come."

Colonel Sidney Huff came into the compartment.

"General, we just had word that the helicopters have arrived safely at Kimpo."

"What helicopters would that be, Huff?"

"The large-capacity Sikorsky helicopters, sir. Two of them."

"Is there some reason, Huff," MacArthur asked, not pleasantly, "why you felt I had to know that right now?"

"General, I thought there might be a public relations value in photographs of you with these aircraft."

"I would think photographs of me turning his capital back to Rhee would overshadow any photograph of me standing by an airplane."

"Yes, sir, of course they would. But I really think it might be valuable in the future. It would take only five minutes or so.

May I set it up, sir?"

MacArthur looked thoughtful, shrugged, and then nodded.

"Yes, Sid," he said. "You may."

"Thank you, sir," Huff said, and backed out of the compartment, closing the door after him.

"Fleming, do you have any idea how much I envy your anonymity?"

"Douglas, that's the price of being a living legend," Pickering said.

MacArthur considered that, and nodded.

"Getting back to where we were before Huff," MacArthur said. "Youthful indiscretions. You know the old Cavalry dine-in toast, don't you?"

"No, I'm afraid I don't."

" 'Here's to our wives and the women we love,' " MacArthur quoted, hoisting an imaginary glass. "Pause. *Long* pause. 'May they never meet.' "

Pickering chuckled.

"Somehow, Douglas, I don't think my Patricia or your Jean would be amused."

"Then we will just have to keep that between us, won't we?"

IV

Major General Ralph Howe and Master Sergeant Charles A. Rogers walked into the garage behind the house looking considerably neater and cleaner than they had at breakfast. They were showered, shaved, and in starched and pressed U.S. Army fatigues.

Major Kenneth R. McCoy and Master Gunner Zimmerman were examining the hood of what now had become "McCoy's Russian jeep."

Zimmerman spotted Howe and Rogers, stood erect, and opened his mouth.

General Howe very quickly raised his hand, palm outward, to silence him. McCoy sensed something unusual and looked over his shoulder. General Howe turned his palm-outward hand toward him. He lowered it only when he was sure McCoy wasn't going to bellow an automatic "Attention on Deck!"

160

"So this is the famous Russian jeep?" Howe said.

"Yes, sir," McCoy said.

"What are you doing to it?"

McCoy answered by pointing. There was now a large white star on the hood, and on either side the stenciled-in-black legend U S M C.

"I'm impressed," Howe said. "Where did you get the stencils?"

"I cut them," Zimmerman answered. "I cut one for you, too, Charley."

"Excuse me?"

"For chevrons," Zimmerman said, pointing at Rogers's bare sleeve. "You'll look like a Marine, but I thought you'd like that better than what the general said about you looking like the oldest private in the army."

"He has a point, Charley," General Howe said.

"Will the paint dry?" Rogers asked doubtfully. "We're going to have to get out to the airport."

"It'll dry," Zimmerman said. "I'm a Marine. You can trust me."

Rogers snorted but started to unbutton his fatigue jacket.

"Ken," Howe said, gently but as a reprimand, "I thought you understood I wanted to hear what the North Korean colonel had to say."

"Sir, they were supposed to tell me when you came downstairs."

"There was a little confusion in there," Howe replied. "The rest of your men showed up, hungry and dirty."

He took from his pocket a manila envelope, folded over and heavily sealed with Scotch tape, and handed it to McCoy. "Your sergeant said this was for you."

"Thank you, sir," McCoy said, and began to remove the tape as he went on: "Well, sir, Ernie and I talked to both the prisoner and the South Korean colonel. Which puts me in the same spot Bill Dunston's in. We think we're onto something, but we don't want to holler 'Fire' just yet, with nothing to back it up."

"Neither you nor Ernie could get anything out of this fellow?" Howe sounded both surprised and disappointed.

"All I can give you, sir," McCoy said carefully, "is what I think is one possible scenario. I have nothing to back it up but my gut feeling."

Howe made a *let's have it* gesture.

"I think this colonel is important. I'm pretty much convinced he's an intelligence officer. He had his own vehicles, for one thing, and he was obviously trying very hard to not get captured."

McCoy realized that he was not going to be able to remove the Scotch tape from the manila envelope with his fingernails. He muttered, "Shit," slipped his right hand up the sleeve of his utility jacket, and came out with a blue steel dagger, then continued without missing a syllable: "I think he's one of the NK officers who've been trained by the Chinese Communists, or the Russians, or both. . . ." McCoy dug the point into the Scotch tape, gave a little shove, and then almost effortlessly sliced through the layers of tape. "I know he speaks Cantonese, and I think he probably speaks — or at least understands — Russian." He wiped the blade of the dagger on his utility jacket, then replaced it in whatever held it to his left wrist. "If that's true — and that's a big 'if' —"

General Pickering had told General Howe about the knife McCoy carried on his left wrist. It was a Fairbairn, designed by the legendary Captain Bruce Fairbairn of the pre–World War II British-officered Shanghai Police. Fairbairn had taken a liking to a cocky young corporal of the 4th Marines, whom he had met at high-stakes poker games, had run him through his police knife-fighting course, and then given him one of his carefully guarded knives. Howe had never seen it before, although Pickering had told him McCoy was never without it.

McCoy took two leather wallets from the

now-sliced-open envelope, put them in his hip pocket, then tossed the third wallet the envelope had held to Zimmerman.

"— then it's possible, I think likely —" McCoy went on.

"What's that, your wallets?" Howe interrupted.

His curiosity had gotten the best of him.

"Yes, sir. And the CIA credentials. We left them with the 7th Division G-2 when we went south," McCoy said.

Howe thought: *Which suggests, of course, that you thought there was a very good chance you would have been captured — or killed — yourselves. In either event, you didn't want them to find the CIA identification.*

"Go on, Ken," Howe said.

"If all three things are true, sir, then *possibly* he's had access to contingency plans which said the Chinese will intervene under such and such circumstances. . . ."

"For example?"

"Maybe something vague, like we get too close to the Yalu River, and they feel we're not going to stop on the south riverbank there. There's a big electric-generating plant, the Suiho, on the Yalu. If we interrupted service from there, it would cause the Chinese a lot of trouble. Or maybe, for example, something specific, like we look like we're about to take Pyongyang. I don't know, sir."

"But you think this fellow has seen this, knows the trigger?"

"I think he's cocky because he believes the Chinese will come in, sir. But this is another of those cases, sir, where I don't know what the hell I'm talking about. He may not know any more about Chinese intentions than I do."

"If you were a betting man, Ken, what would the odds of Chinese intervention be?" Howe asked.

"Seven–three," McCoy said, "that they will."

"Can you think of anything that would increase the odds that they won't?"

"If we destroy the NK Army, maybe by chasing it halfway to the Yalu, then stop, they may not — may not — feel threatened."

"Two days ago, the Joint Chiefs authorized MacArthur to conduct military operations leading to the destruction of the North Korean armed forces north of the 38th Parallel," Howe said. "Did you hear that?"

"No, sir."

"Two caveats. Only South Korean troops can approach the Yalu, and our aircraft cannot fly over China or Russia."

"The Chinese won't care if our troops on their border are South Korean or American," McCoy said.

"You think that would change the odds?" Howe asked. "How bad?"

McCoy didn't reply directly.

"ROK troops on the Yalu would make it even worse," he said. "The Chinese would believe us, probably, if we said we weren't going across the river. But they don't know how much control we have of the ROKs, and would act accordingly."

"Changing the odds to?"

"Eight–two," McCoy said. "Maybe nine–one."

Howe exhaled audibly.

He looked at Charley Rogers, who was very carefully putting his arms into the sleeves of his fatigue jacket, on which the chevrons of a master sergeant had been stenciled in black paint that still looked wet.

"Much better, Charley," Howe said. "I would have hated to see you hauled off to wash pots in a field mess somewhere."

Then he turned back to McCoy.

"Forewarned is forearmed, Ken. There's a very determined-looking second lieutenant from the 7th Division outside the gate who wants his vehicles back. You need some help with that?"

"No, sir. Thank you. I saw that coming. That's one of the reasons I liberated the Russian jeep."

He turned to Zimmerman.

166

"Ernie, let them have the jeep and the weapons carrier. We'll see what we can scrounge from Tenth Corps or the division."

Zimmerman nodded and walked out of the garage.

"You about ready to head for Kimpo, Ken?" General Howe asked.

"Yes, sir."

"I was thinking I could ride with you in this magnificent vehicle of yours, and Zimmerman could ride in my jeep with Charley."

"Whatever you want to do, sir," McCoy said.

[Two]
Kimpo Airfield
Seoul, South Korea
0835 29 September 1950

The terminal building at Kimpo had been in the line of fire of both sides since the war began, and was in pretty bad shape. Army engineer troops were already at work trying to make it functional, but at the moment base operations was two squad tents set up end to end and the tower was mounted on the back of an Air Force General Motors 6 x 6 truck.

Two platoons of military police from the

4th Military Police Company, whose usual mission was the protection of the X Corps Headquarters, had been sent to the airport to provide the necessary security for the arrival of General MacArthur.

They had quickly established three areas, informally known as (1) For The Brass; (2) For The Press; and (3) For Everybody Else.

The area for (1) The Brass was immediately adjacent to the squad tents serving as base operations. Cotton tape usually used to show safe lanes through minefields had been strung in two lines, ten yards apart, from iron stakes intended to support barbed-wire entanglements.

(2) The Press was thus ten yards from The Brass, and kept from joining them by large MPs stationed at three-yard intervals. Still farther away from base operations, behind The Press, was another double row of minefield tape strung through the loops on top of the barbed-wire rods. Behind this was sequestered (3) Everybody Else.

Everybody Else included everyone with some reason, however questionable, to be in the area. There were perhaps two hundred people in this category, officers and enlisted, Marines and soldiers.

The entire area was surrounded by still more tape on rods to keep the rest of the world away. This was guarded by MPs, and the outer of the two MP checkpoints was located here.

Under the supervision of a military police second lieutenant, who was sitting with his driver in a jeep equipped with a pedestal-mounted .30-caliber air-cooled machine gun, a sergeant and three other MPs stopped every approaching vehicle to determine in which area the passengers belonged, if any, and to show them where to park their vehicles.

Getting a glimpse of General of the Army Douglas MacArthur in the flesh was right up there with, say, getting a look at Marilyn Monroe or Bob Hope.

No one really knew how the word of his pending arrival had gotten out, but no one was surprised that it had.

"Lieutenant!" the MP sergeant called when he saw the funny-looking vehicle fourth in line, and thought, but could not be sure, that he saw silver stars gleaming on the collar points of the passenger.

The MP lieutenant got out of his jeep in time to be at the sergeant's side when the funny-looking vehicle rolled up. His attention on the vehicle, he did not at first see the stars on General Howe's fatigues.

Then he did, jerked to attention, and saluted.

"Sorry, sir," he said. "The General's star

is not mounted on the bumper, and I didn't —"

"It's not my vehicle," Howe said reasonably. "No problem."

"Sir, VIP parking is right beside the tent," the lieutenant said, pointing.

"Thank you," Howe said. "The two in the jeep behind us are with us."

The lieutenant had seen the people in the jeep were a Marine master sergeant — he could tell because his chevrons were painted — and a warrant officer, and thus falling into Category (3), Everybody Else, but the lieutenant had been in the service long enough to know that it is far wiser to go along with general officers than to argue with them.

"Yes, sir," the lieutenant said, and raised his hand to salute again.

When both vehicles were out of earshot, the sergeant asked the lieutenant, "Sir, what the hell was that?"

"Damned if I know," the lieutenant confessed. "What was that, a Russian jeep?"

A high-pitched voice from The Press caught their attention.

The voice had screamed, "McCoy, you sonofabitch!"

The lieutenant and the sergeant looked. One of the members of The Press had ducked under the minefield tape and was running toward the Russian jeep, which

170

slowed and then stopped.

Two MPs rushed toward the member of The Press to keep the Fourth Estate where it belonged. The lieutenant and the sergeant rushed to join them.

The journalist, who had two 35-mm cameras hanging from the neck, nimbly dodged the two MPs intent on maintaining the established order, by force if necessary, reached the Russian jeep, and quickly scrambled into the backseat.

The lieutenant now could identify the errant member of the Fourth Estate as Miss Jeanette Priestly of the *Chicago Tribune*, primarily because as she climbed into the Russian jeep she dislodged her brimmed fatigue cap and long blond hair cascaded to her shoulders.

The lieutenant reached the Russian jeep.

"Sorry about this, General," he said, and added, sternly, to Miss Priestly, "Miss Priestly, you know the rules. You'll have to get behind the tape."

Miss Priestly smiled, revealing an attractive mouthful of white teeth, and said, "Fuck you!"

"Please don't cause a scene, Miss Priestly," the lieutenant implored.

"It's all right, Lieutenant," General Howe said. "Miss Priestly is also with us."

"General, she's supposed to . . ."

"If anyone gives you any trouble about

this, Lieutenant," Howe said, motioning for McCoy to drive on, "refer them to me."

How the hell am I supposed to refer anybody to you if I don't know who the hell you are?

"Yes, sir," the lieutenant said.

If either General Howe or Major McCoy expected at least a word of gratitude from Miss Priestly for having rescued her from the military police, it was not forthcoming.

"Killer, goddamn you," she said. "You promised to let me know what you found, you sonofa—"

McCoy snapped, "Shut up, Jeanette," and then added, evenly: "One more word out of that sewer of a mouth of yours and I'll drive you to the end of the runway and throw you out."

"Oh, sh—" she began, and then fell silent.

Why do I suspect, General Howe thought, *that at some time in the past McCoy has threatened her, then made good on the threat?*

An MP was directing the parking of senior officers' vehicles to the left of the base operations tents.

He saluted and had just started to say something to General Howe when a four-car convoy of olive-drab 1950 Chevrolet staff cars, preceded by an MP jeep, rolled up. The first car in line had a two-starred major general's license plate on its bumper.

A tall, erect captain in starched fatigues jumped out and trotted around the car to open the rear passenger door.

Major General Edward M. Almond, commanding general of X U.S. Corps, got out. He was in fatigues, but wearing his general officer's dress pistol belt* around his waist.

The tall captain said something to him, and Almond looked over at Howe and McCoy, then walked over to the Russian jeep. Howe and McCoy got out of the jeep. McCoy saluted crisply. Generals Howe and Almond sort of waved their right hands at each other.

"I'm glad you're here, General Howe," Almond said. "I know that's important to the Supreme Commander."

"Good morning, General," Howe said.

Almond looked at the backseat of the jeep.

"Good morning, Miss Priestly."

"Good morning, sir," Jeanette said with a warm smile, and very politely.

"McCoy," Almond said.

"Good morning, sir."

"I've been informed General Pickering is on the *Bataan*," Almond said. "Have you got some good news for him?"

*A calfskin leather belt and holster, fastened with a gold-plated circular buckle.

"Not good news, but not bad news, either, sir."

Almond looked at his wristwatch.

"I've also been informed the Supreme Commander's ETA is 0950," he went on. "So we have some time. Have you got a few minutes for me, General?"

"Of course," Howe said. "McCoy, why don't you take Miss Priestly aside and tell her what you know about Major Pickering?"

"Yes, sir."

"Where did you get the Russian jeep, McCoy?" Almond asked.

Howe answered for him: "He took it away from a North Korean colonel."

Almond leaned over the vehicle and inspected the interior.

"Interesting," he said, then turned to the tall captain.

"Al, why don't you set up the convoy," he said, "while General Howe and I ride over to the other side of the field."

He gestured for Howe to go to his staff car.

"Yes, sir," the captain replied.

Howe turned to Jeanette Priestly.

"You are going to behave, right, Jeanette?"

"Yes, sir," she said docilely.

Howe walked to Almond's staff car.

They went through a little "After you, Alfonse." / "No, after you, Gaston" routine dance at the door, but eventually Almond got in first, Howe slid in behind him, the tall captain closed the door, and the car, preceded by an MP jeep, drove off across the airfield.

"Interesting woman," Almond said. "What's she doing with you?"

"She's . . . romantically involved . . . with young Pickering, and she knows Mc-Coy's been looking for him."

"Without success, apparently?" Almond said. It was a question.

"He thinks he missed him yesterday by no more than a couple of hours," Howe said.

"That's a really awkward situation, isn't it? Is there anything I can do to help?"

"I asked McCoy. He says he has every-thing he needs."

Almond grunted.

"Where are we going?" Howe asked. "May I ask?"

"As I understand it, General, you can ask anyone anything you want to," Almond said, chuckling. "We're going to look at something my Army Aviation officer enthu-siastically assures me will 'usher in a new era of battlefield mobility.' "

"The secret helicopters?" Howe asked.

"You do hear things, don't you, Gen-eral?" Almond said. "Yeah, the secret heli-copters."

175

"And are they going to 'usher in a new era of battlefield mobility'?" Howe asked.

"Not today or tomorrow, I don't think," Almond said. "Eventually, possibly, maybe even probably. Between us?"

"That puts me on a spot, General. I'm supposed to report everything I think will interest my boss."

"So you are. Well, what the hell, you've been around, you'll see this for yourself. What this is, is a dog and pony show, intended to inspire the Supreme Commander to lean on the Joint Chiefs to come up with the necessary funding to buy lots of these machines. Apparently, the Joint Chiefs are first not very impressed with these machines, and even if they do everything the Army Aviation people say, the Joint Chiefs will believe that if it flies, it should belong to the Air Force."

"So they're staging a dog and pony show for you? And you're supposed to work on General MacArthur?"

"No. They're working on the Supreme Commander directly," Almond said. "He gets the show. When I got his revised ETA, I was also informed that the *Bataan* will taxi here after it lands to afford General MacArthur the opportunity to see these vehicles, and to have his picture taken with them."

Howe shook his head in amazement.

"Yeah," General Almond said. "Following which General MacArthur will turn over the liberated city of Seoul to President Syngman Rhee."

"I spent last night with Colonel Chesty Puller's Marine regiment," Howe said. It was a question.

"Seoul is liberated *enough*, General," Almond responded, "to the point where I feel the ceremony can be conducted with little or no risk to the Supreme Commander or President Rhee. I would have called this off if I didn't think so."

"I understand," Howe said.

"With a little luck, the artillery will fall silent long enough so that we can all hear General MacArthur's remarks on this momentous occasion," Almond said evenly.

Howe smiled at him.

"Well, here we are," Almond said as the Chevrolet stopped before the bullet-riddled hangar.

Major Alex Donald, the X Corps' assistant Army Aviation officer, walked briskly up to it, opened the door, and saluted.

General Howe got out first, his presence clearly confusing Major Donald. Then General Almond slid across the seat and got out.

"Good morning, sir," Major Donald said. "Everything is laid on, sir."

"Good," Almond said. "General Howe,

this is Major Donald."

They shook hands.

Howe spotted Captain Howard C. Dunwood, USMCR, standing close to the closed hangar doors with eight other Marines.

"Good morning, Captain," Howe said.

"Good morning, sir."

"Baker Company, 5th Marines, right?" Howe asked.

"Yes, sir."

Both Captain Dunwood and General Almond were visibly surprised that General Howe was possessed of that information. Almond admitted as much.

"How did you know that?" he asked.

Howe winked at him.

"Well, Donald, let's have a look at these machines before the Supreme Commander gets here," Almond said.

[Three]

As the staff car carrying Generals Almond and Howe started down the road beside the runway, McCoy paused long enough to wonder where they were going, then turned and motioned to Jeanette Priestly to get out of the Russian jeep.

He had given a lot of thought to Jeanette and to her relationship with Pickering.

178

Pick Pickering — a really legendary swordsman, of whom it was more or less honestly said he had two girls and often more in every port — had taken one look at Jeanette Priestly just over two months before and fallen in love with her.

And vice versa. The second time Jeanette — known as the "Ice Princess" among her peers in the press corps because no one, and many had tried, had ever been in her bed or pants — had seen him she had taken him to bed.

Everyone knew that "Love at First Sight" was bullshit, pure and simple, that what it really meant was "Lust at First Sight" and had everything to do with fucking and absolutely nothing to do with love.

Everybody knew that but Major Kenneth R. McCoy, USMCR. He knew there was such a thing as love at first sight because it had happened to him.

The first time he had seen Ernestine Sage he had known he would love her forever even though the chances of having her in his bed, without or with the sanction of holy matrimony, had ranged from zero to zilch, and he damned well knew it.

Ernie was from Pick's world. Her mother and Pick's mother had been roommates at college. Her father was chairman of the board of — and majority stockholder in —

American Personal Pharmaceuticals. Everyone thought that Pick and Ernie would marry.

There was no room in Ernestine Sage's life for a poor Scotch-Irish kid from Norristown who had enlisted in the Marine Corps at seventeen, been a corporal with the 4th Marines in Shanghai, and was now a second lieutenant primarily because he had learned how to read and write two kinds of Chinese, Japanese, and even some Russian and the Marine Corps was short of people like that, and thus willing to commission them, *temporarily,* for wartime service.

A week after Ernie Sage had seen Second Lieutenant McCoy sitting on the penthouse railing of her parents' Fifth Avenue apartment overlooking Central Park, his feet dangling over the side, she had told her mother that she had met the man whose babies she wanted to bear and intended to marry him just as soon as she could get him to the altar, or some judge's chambers, whichever came first.

Pick, and Pick's father, thought that was a splendid idea. Everybody else, including Lieutenant McCoy, had thought it was insanity, that their marriage just wouldn't — couldn't — work.

But Ernie had known it was love, and could not be dissuaded, even though Ken

180

had firmly declined the offer of her hand in wedded bliss. She had followed him around, proudly calling herself a camp follower, whenever and wherever he was in the United States during World War II.

She had written him every day, and when, toward the end of the war, he'd come home from a clandestine operation in the Gobi Desert a major on Presidential orders to attend the Army's Command and General Staff college, he was denied his final argument against their marriage — the very good chance that he either would not come home at all, or come home in a basket — she'd finally got him to the altar.

With conditions. He was a Marine, and wanted to stay a Marine. He would not take an entry-level executive training position with American Personal Pharmaceuticals — or with the Pacific & Far East Shipping Corporation — and she would not press him to do so. And they would live on his Marine pay, period.

There had been good times and bad in their marriage, but it had worked. The good times had included their year with the Army at C&GSC at Fort Leavenworth and a year at Quantico, which was close to Washington, so Ernie had a chance to see a lot of her parents. The Quantico assignment had ended when he had been reduced to captain, not because he'd done anything wrong, but because the Corps had shrunk and didn't need as many officers.

The Corps had a — maybe unwritten — policy that if you were reduced in grade, you were transferred, and that had seen them sent to Japan, where he had been a junior intelligence officer on the staff of the Commander, Naval Element, Supreme Headquarters, Allied Powers.

There, after a year or so, things had really gone wrong. He had come across what he believed to be compelling evidence that the North Koreans were going to invade the south. He'd worked long and hard to put it down on paper, and then turned it in to the Commander, Naval Element, Supreme Headquarters.

First, he got a "well done."

Then the Commander, Naval Element, Supreme Headquarters, called him back in and said, in effect, (1) "McCoy, you have never written an intelligence analysis of any kind regarding North Korean intentions, and certainly not one that had concluded 'war is inevitable,'" and (2) "Start packing. The Marine Corps has no further need of your services as a commissioned officer, and you will be separated from the Naval Service 1 July 1950. It will be determined later at what enlisted grade you may reenlist in the service if you desire to do so."

So far as Supreme Headquarters, Allied Powers, was concerned, McCoy's "war is coming" analysis no longer existed. Worse, it never had. All copies, McCoy was informed, had been destroyed.

McCoy found out why:

Major General Charles A. Willoughby, the Supreme Commander's intelligence officer, had just informed General MacArthur that there was absolutely no indication that the North Koreans had hostile intentions, and in any event their armed forces were incapable of doing anything more than causing mischief along the 38th Parallel. He did not want his judgment questioned by a lowly Marine captain.

When he had told Ernie he was getting the boot, Ernie had told him she wouldn't mind being a sergeant's wife.

He had realized then that it was his turn to make a few sacrifices.

What the hell, I might even like selling toothpaste and deodorant for American Personal Pharmaceuticals.

Once he had made that decision, there was one more decision to make, a big one. The Commander, Naval Element, Supreme Headquarters, Allied Powers, was wrong. All of the copies of McCoy's analysis had not been destroyed. He had his own copy of his analysis, his last draft before he had typed the whole thing over again before turning it in. He could not bring himself to either forget it or burn it.

After thinking hard and long, and fully aware that doing so could — probably would — see him facing a court-martial, he had given his draft copy of his analysis to Fleming Pickering.

Pickering was no longer a brigadier general and had no security clearance, and the Office of Strategic Services in which they had served in World War II no longer even existed. But he figured that Pickering could probably get the document into the hands of somebody who should have his information.

Whistling in the wind, he had told himself that the Corps might have a hard time court-martialing a civilian for the unlawful disclosure of a Top Secret document that wasn't supposed to ever have existed.

On his final, delay-en-route leave before reporting to Camp Pendleton for separation, he had been offered a civilian job he thought he might even really like, helping to develop an island off the coast of South Carolina as a retirement area.

It was the idea of Colonel Ed Banning, USMC, who was about to retire himself. Zimmerman, then stationed at Parris Island, had been enlisted in the project. He, like McCoy, had worked for Banning throughout World War II. As he and Ernie drove across the country to California, the idea of working with Colonel Banning and Ernie sounded like a hell of a better way than spending his life selling toothpaste and deodorant.

Orders were waiting for him when he reported into Camp Pendleton the night of 1 July 1950, but not the *Thank you for your service, and don't let the doorknob hit you in the ass on your way out* ones he expected, which would have ordered him to his home of official record.

Eight hours after reporting into Camp Pendleton — early the next morning — he had found himself sitting in the backseat of an Air Force F-94 taking off from Naval Air Station Miramar. He was traveling on orders bearing the code of the highest priority in the Armed Forces: DP. It stood for "By Direction of the President."

In Washington, he found out what had happened to the analysis he couldn't bring himself to burn.

Pickering had taken it to Rear Admiral Roscoe Hillencoetter, the Director of the Central Intelligence Agency, which had taken the place of the OSS. Hillencoetter had told Fleming Pickering that he didn't believe the analysis, but — Pickering had come to his office accompanied by Senator Richardson K. Fowler, and Pickering had been the Assistant Director of the OSS for

Asia — he said he would look into it.

Before that could happen, the North Koreans invaded South Korea.

When President Harry S Truman had demanded of Admiral Hillencoetter, in effect, "You mean to tell me you had absolutely no idea the North Koreans were going to do this?" the admiral had replied that there *was* one thing, and told him that the World War II Director of the OSS for Asia, the shipping magnate Fleming Pickering, had come to his office with Senator Fowler carrying an analysis written by a Marine captain predicting the North Korean invasion was inevitable.

The President had had some trouble getting Pickering on the telephone in the penthouse of the Foster San Franciscan Hotel on Nob Hill.

When the operator said, "General Pickering, please, the President is calling," it had been difficult to convince Mrs. Patricia Pickering that it wasn't one of her husband's drinking buddies thinking he was clever.

But eventually the President got through, and shortly thereafter — after a cross-country flight in an F-94 — Pickering found himself facing the President of the United States in the Foster Lafayette hotel suite of his friend, and Truman's bitter political enemy, Senator Richardson K.

Fowler, Republican of California.

After first demanding of the President that he give his word that no harm would come to Captain McCoy for his having turned his analysis over to him, Pickering told the President as much as he knew.

When he had finished, the President said, in effect, "I gave you my word because I wanted to, not because I had to."

Then he picked up the telephone, asked to be connected with the Commandant of the Marine Corps, and when, in less than sixty seconds, that officer came on the line, said, "This is the President, General. I understand you're acquainted with Brigadier General Fleming Pickering, USMC Reserve?"

There was a very short pause while the Commandant said, "Yes, sir."

"Please cause the necessary orders to be issued calling the general to active service for an indefinite period, effective immediately, and further placing him on duty with the Central Intelligence Agency," Truman ordered. "It won't be necessary to notify him; he's with me now."

The President had hung up and then turned to General Pickering.

"So far as this Captain McCoy is concerned, I've ordered that he be brought here as soon as he can be located. I want to see him myself."

Within days, Brigadier General Pickering, Captain McCoy, and Master Gunner Zimmerman were on a plane for Tokyo. The President had told Admiral Hillencoetter it was pretty obvious to him that a very good way to find out what had gone wrong with CIA intelligence-gathering procedures in the Far East — and to make sure the situation was corrected — was to send the man who'd run Far Eastern Operations for the OSS during World War II back over there.

General Pickering was named Assistant Director of the CIA for Asia.

This time Ernie had not sat dutifully and docilely at home while her husband went to war. They had been in Tokyo only a few days when there was a message saying Mrs. Kenneth McCoy would arrive in Tokyo aboard Trans-Global Airways Flight 4344 at ten the next morning.

She was now residing at No. 7 Saku-Tun, in the Denenchofu section of Tokyo, Japan. And she had told her husband that she had not only deceived him when they had been stationed in Tokyo — she had told him that she had found a very nice house at a rent they could afford that would keep them out of the small quarters they would have been given by the Navy, when the facts were she had bought the house — but also that, since the Marine

Corps had already let him know what they really thought of him, she had no intention of pretending any longer that they had only his pay to live on.

"Don't give me any trouble about this, Ken," she'd said firmly. "You're not supposed to upset a pregnant woman."

Ernie was in the sixth month of her pregnancy. Twice before, she had failed to carry to full term.

Major Ken McCoy had thought, as Ernie had stood before him, hands on her hips, her stomach just starting to show, making her declaration, that he loved her even more now than when he had first seen her on the patio of the penthouse, when it had really been Love at First Sight.

McCoy walked away from the base operations tents, and Jeanette Priestly had to trot to catch up with him.

"Where are they going?" she asked, indicating the car with Generals Howe and Almond in it.

"I thought you wanted to hear about Pick," McCoy replied.

She didn't reply, but caught his arm and stopped him.

He looked back at the tent, decided they were out of earshot, and stopped and told her everything he knew.

"So you think he's alive?" she asked

when he had finished.

He nodded.

"He was yesterday, I'm sure of it."

"So when are you going to look again?"

"You mean instead of standing around here waiting for El Supremo?"

She nodded.

"Well, for one thing, I was ordered to be here," he said. "And for another, I have no idea where he is. There's no sense going back south until I do."

"And when will that be?"

"Whenever there's another sighting of his arrows," McCoy said. "Billy Dunn was here early this morning, and he said he's going to photograph the hell out of the area where we just missed him. He'll almost certainly come up with something, and when he does, we'll go out again."

"When you go, can I go with you?"

"No, of course not. And if you try something clever, I'll have you on the next plane to Tokyo."

"You'd do that, too, wouldn't you, you sonofabitch?"

"You know I would, and stop calling me a sonofabitch."

She met his eyes.

"It's a term of endearment," she said. "I love you almost as much as I love that stupid bastard who got himself shot down."

She stood on her toes and kissed his cheek.

For a moment — just a moment — McCoy put his arms around her and hugged her.

[Four]

The *Bataan* made its landing approach from the direction of Seoul, passed low over the people gathered around the base operations tents, and touched down.

The military police had permitted a dozen still and motion picture photographers to detach themselves from the press area so that they would be able to photograph the *Bataan* taxiing up to base operations and the Supreme Commander himself getting off the airplane.

When the *Bataan,* instead of taxiing toward them, turned off the runway and taxied to a hangar on the far side of the field, a chorus of questions and protests rose from the Fourth Estate.

The phrase "Now, what the fuck is going on?" was heard, and several variations thereof.

The X Corps information officer, a bird colonel, who really had no idea what the hell was going on, managed to placate them somewhat by stating that it was "a security precaution" and that the *Bataan*

191

and General MacArthur would shortly move to base operations.

The press could see the *Bataan* stop in front of the hangar, and a flight of mobile stairs being rolled up to it.

The first three people to debark from the *Bataan* were three Army photographers, two still and one motion picture. The photographers took up positions by the mobile stairway. Next off was Colonel Sidney Huff, the Supreme Commander's senior aide-de-camp.

He exchanged salutes with Major Alex Donald, USA, and Captain Howard C. Dunwood, USMCR, who were standing on the ground, looked around to see there were enough heavily armed Marines around so there wasn't much immediate danger to General MacArthur, and then raised his eyes to the open door of the *Bataan* and saluted.

The Supreme Commander somewhat regally descended the stairs and the cameras whirred and clicked. There was another exchange of salutes, then MacArthur was led to the just-open-wide-enough doors and went inside.

As soon as he had gone inside, preceded and trailed by the photographers, Brigadier General Fleming Pickering and Captain George F. Hart came down the stairs and went into the hangar.

★ ★ ★

Major Generals Ralph Howe and Edward C. Almond were standing inside the hangar. They saluted, then Almond stepped toward MacArthur for the benefit of the photographers. General Howe went to the door to avoid the photographers and also to see if Pickering had gotten off the airplane.

Pickering and Hart came into the hangar and stood with Howe as Major Alex Donald showed General MacArthur around the closest of the two helicopters. General MacArthur declined Major Donald's invitation to climb aboard the helicopter, but obligingly posed for several minutes while the photographers recorded the event for posterity.

Then he shook hands with Major Donald and walked back toward the door.

"General Howe," MacArthur declared, "I'm really glad to see you here."

"Good morning, sir."

"This business out of the way, I presume we can get on with returning President Rhee's capital to him," MacArthur said. "How are we going to do that, Sid?"

"Sir, I suggest that you reboard the *Bataan*," Colonel Huff replied, "which will then taxi to base operations, where the press is waiting."

"What about General Almond?" MacArthur asked.

"I would suggest that General Almond ride back over there in his car, sir. That would eliminate any possible questions about whether he has come to Korea with you."

"All right, Ned?" MacArthur asked.

"Yes, sir."

"I think it would be appropriate," Huff went on, "if General Almond were to greet the general when he descends from the *Bataan.*"

"Yes, so do I," MacArthur said. "He is, after all, the liberator of Seoul." Then he added, jovially, "Well, then, Ned, why don't you saddle up, and hie thee to the other side of the airport?"

"Yes, sir," General Almond said. "You ready, Howe?"

"General," Howe said to MacArthur, "I'd like a moment of your time. Would it be all right if I rode over there with you?"

"I'd be delighted to have your company, General. Of course."

"Fleming," Howe said, "would you mind riding with General Almond?"

"Of course," Pickering said.

He, MacArthur, Almond, and Huff instantly decided that Howe had something to say to MacArthur that he didn't want anyone else to hear.

As Pickering, Hart, and Almond got into Almond's Chevrolet, MacArthur and Howe climbed the stairway to the *Bataan*. Colonel Huff and then the photographers followed them.

Pickering was a little curious about why Howe wanted a moment of El Supremo's time in private, but not concerned. Their relationship was not only one of mutual respect; they also liked each other. It never entered Pickering's mind that Howe was in any way going behind his back. He never had, and Pickering had no reason to suspect he would suddenly start now.

General Pickering was dead wrong. In this instance, Howe had something to say to the Supreme Commander that he absolutely did not want Pickering to know about.

"That will be all, Huff, thank you," MacArthur said, waited until Huff had closed the door, and then looked expectantly at Howe.

"General," Howe began carefully, "I fully understand that my role here is solely that of observer, and that I have neither the authority — and certainly not the expertise — to offer any sort of suggestion. . . ."

The *Bataan* began to taxi away from the hangar.

"General," MacArthur said, "I decide who has the expertise to offer a suggestion to me, and I would welcome any suggestion you might be good enough to offer."

"That's very gracious of you, sir," Howe said. "It's about those helicopters."

"Those helicopters?" MacArthur asked, surprised. "Or helicopters in general?"

"Those two helicopters, sir."

"Okay. Let's have it."

"While we were waiting for you to arrive, sir, Major Donald — the Army pilot in charge of them?"

MacArthur nodded.

"— gave General Almond and myself a well-thought-out briefing about those specific helicopters, and the future role of what he calls 'rotary-wing aircraft' in providing battlefield mobility."

"And you were, or were not, impressed?"

"May I speak frankly, sir?" Howe asked, and when MacArthur nodded, he went on, "Are you familiar with the phrase 'dog and pony show,' General?"

"I wouldn't be surprised if they used it at Valley Forge," MacArthur said.

"There are only five of those machines in the Army, General, according to Major Donald. Two are at the Army Aviation School at Fort Riley being studied, and the Air Force has a third, which they are subjecting to destructive engineering tests. In other words, the two here are the only two which are operational. I can't think of a place where they can be used for a really practical purpose, except perhaps to carry senior officers around, and neither can General Almond."

"So this is a dog and pony show?"

"I would suggest that it is, sir."

"In France, I staged more than one dog and pony show myself, to convince my seniors that a new gadget called the tank had a place in ground warfare."

Howe didn't reply directly.

"During Major Donald's enthusiastic presentation," Howe said, "I had two questions about the actual usefulness of these machines. The first thing, I thought, when he was telling us how useful they would be to transport senior officers, was that it would really be pretty stupid to load half a dozen generals or colonels on one of them. They are not immune to ground fire, and I don't know how safe they are, period."

MacArthur grunted.

"Same thing for carrying half a dozen wounded," Howe went on. "You don't often find half a dozen wounded in one place except in some place where what got them would also likely get a large, and fragile, helicopter."

"I hadn't thought about that," MacArthur said softly.

"They're capable of carrying six or seven infantrymen each. Say seven. But I can't think of a situation where fourteen men being flown into it would have much real effect."

"I take your point," MacArthur said. "So what is your suggestion? That I order these machines out of Korea? We can't really use them, and we shouldn't be wasting time and effort on a dog and pony show?"

"We haven't rescued Major Pickering, sir. Major McCoy told me he thinks he missed him on his last attempt by less than a couple of hours. Of course, he was riding in a jeep and weapons carrier convoy, and couldn't make very good time getting where he had to go."

"And McCoy could have flown in these machines to wherever he went in time to establish contact with young Pickering?"

"Possibly, sir. In fact, probably. With a dozen of his men, in case there was resistance when he got there."

MacArthur looked at Howe intently for a moment, and then glanced out the window.

"If those tents are where we're going, we're almost there," he said.

"Yes, sir."

"You and I are both aware that General Pickering might regard this as special treatment for his son," MacArthur said, "and not like it at all."

"I also think you and I would agree, General, that keeping the son of the Deputy Director of the CIA out of enemy hands is the first consideration, even at the risk of offending General Pickering's sense of chivalry. Or, for that matter, offending the entire Marine Corps."

"Well, I'd hate to do that," MacArthur said. "I have reason to suspect that I'm not a hallowed figure in the Halls of Montezuma as it is."

Howe chuckled.

"What I'm going to do, General Howe . . ." MacArthur began, then stopped, smiled, and said, " 'Oh what a tangled web we weave when ere we try to deceive,' " and went on: ". . . is wait until we're just about to take off for Tokyo, and then direct that these machines be immediately placed under the control of the CIA here in Korea, and state that my decision is not open for discussion."

He paused again, then explained: "That way, Colonel Huff will not connect our little chat with that order. And further, with a little luck, General Pickering will not hear of this until it is a *fait accompli.*"

"Yes, sir," Howe said.

"And when that inevitably happens, and he comes to me, as I strongly suspect he will, I will resort to the last defense of the

Machiavellians. I will tell the truth. These machines were brought to my attention; I concluded that at the moment I could see no really practical operational use for them, but thought that the CIA might find some use for them."

[Five]
The Capitol Building
Seoul, South Korea
1205 29 September 1950

"Mr. President," General of the Army Douglas MacArthur sonorously intoned, "in God's name, I herewith return the city of Seoul to you as the chief of its lawful government."

There came the shock wave of what most experienced soldiers and Marines in the building recognized as coming from a massive 155-mm cannon "time on target" — that is, the firing of perhaps ten, fifteen, or more heavy cannon nearly simultaneously, so that their projectiles would all land on the target at the same instant.

The shock wave caused plaster and glass to fall from the ceiling and walls of the bullet-pocked building. Many people cringed.

MacArthur did not seem to notice.

"I invite you now to join me in recitation

of the Lord's Prayer," he went on. "Our Father which art in heaven . . .."

"Am I allowed to ask questions?" Captain George F. Hart, USMCR, asked of Brigadier General Pickering ten minutes later.

"Shoot," Pickering said.

"That *was* the DSC El Supremo gave Almond and the other guy, Walker, wasn't it? The *cross*, as opposed to the *medal*? As in DSM?"

"A little decorum would be in order, Captain Hart. Yes, *General MacArthur* has just decorated *General* Almond and *General* Walker with the Distinguished Service *Cross*."

"I thought that was like the Navy Cross, that you only got it for courage above and beyond in combat."

"The DSC is the Army version of the Navy Cross. And General MacArthur apparently feels that the service of both general officers was above and beyond the call of the duty in combat. Any further questions, Captain Hart?"

"No, sir."

"Good," Pickering said. "One day, George, your curiosity is going to get us both in trouble." He paused. "Where's McCoy going to meet us?"

"Outside," Hart said. "He sent Zimmerman back out to Kimpo to see if Colonel Dunn had sent any fresh aerials, and wasn't sure they'd let Zimmerman in here without a fuss."

"Let's go. El Supremo told me he wants to get out of here as soon as possible."

Miss Jeanette Priestly was sitting in Mc-Coy's Russian jeep and he and Zimmerman were leaning against it. The men stood erect when they saw Pickering coming.

"You should have come inside, Ken," Pickering greeted him. "That was an historic moment."

"I wanted to see what, if anything, Billy Dunn came up with," McCoy said matter-of-factly, then added: "Nothing, I'm afraid, sir."

"And what do you make of that, Ken?" Pickering asked.

"He's moving again, sir. Probably north. Zimmerman told Colonel Dunn where we think he might be headed. Either almost due east, toward Wonju, or northeast, toward Chunchon. There's not many paved roads in that area, mostly rice paddies. I think he wants to be somewhere where there won't be much movement on the roads. . . ."

"Like yours, for instance," Jeanette said.

The men looked at her but said nothing.

". . . and where he can easily find rice

paddies to stamp out his arrows," McCoy finished.

"Explain that, please," Pickering said. " 'Easily find rice paddies'?"

"We have to presume, sir, that the NKs have also come across one of Pick's stampings. And that they would be looking for others. The advantage we have is that we've got air superiority, which means they have to look at paddies from the ground. The more paddies there are, the more they have to look at. . . ."

Pickering nodded.

"I take your point. You think Pick has thought of this?"

"I'm sure he has," McCoy replied. "General, there's often been two- and three-day intervals between sightings. There may be another this afternoon; if not, then probably tomorrow. When there is —"

"You'll go out again," Pickering finished the sentence for him.

"Yes, sir. Of course."

"Pick is really putting a lot of lives at risk, isn't he?" Pickering said, and then he heard what he had said and added: "That sounded pretty stupid, didn't it?"

"General," McCoy said, "we're Marines. We go after people who find themselves in trouble."

"What I meant to say was that the lives

we're putting at risk are yours and Zimmerman's, and I can't afford to lose either of you. Isn't there someone else who could go out there and look for him?"

"As of right now, sir, 1st MarDiv hasn't said anything about wanting to get back the people — it's an understrength company — who were on the Flying Fish Channel Islands. If I knew I could keep at least twenty or so of them, Ernie and I could bring them up to speed in three or four days. That would at least allow Ernie to go with one recon patrol, and me with another."

"You're talking about the Marines that are now at that hangar with the helicopters?"

"Yes, sir," McCoy said. "The problems with that are taking rations-and-quarters care of them, getting enough vehicles to carry them, and then deciding what, if anything, we tell them about why it's so important we get Pick back — and, for that matter, who Ernie and I work for. They're going to wonder."

Pickering considered that for a moment.

"I'll tell General Smith — he'll be at the airport — that I'd like to keep those Marines for a while. And I'll tell General Almond you're going to need jeeps and so forth."

"Yes, sir."

"And if General Smith goes along, I'll decide later what they're to be told."

"Yes, sir."

He looked back at the Capitol Building. Officers and other dignitaries were getting into the staff cars to accompany MacArthur back to Kimpo Airfield.

"The Imperial procession is forming," he said. "I've got to go." He put his hand out to Jeanette Priestly. "It was good to see you, Jeanette. Is there anything I can send you from Tokyo?"

"Thank you, but no thank you. I'm going with you."

"On the *Bataan*?" Pickering asked, surprised.

"I've already asked El Supremo," she said. "I don't know about you guys, but when I smile at him, I get just about anything I want."

She jumped nimbly out of the backseat of the Russian jeep.

[Six]
Kimpo Airfield
Seoul, South Korea
1425 29 September 1950

The two senior commanders in Korea, Lieutenant General Walton Walker, the Eighth Army commander, and Major General Edward M. Almond, the X Corps commander, accompanied the Supreme Commander to the stairs of the *Bataan*.

Both were still wearing their newly awarded Distinguished Service Crosses pinned to their fatigue jackets.

Of the two, the shorter, almost rotund Walker presented the most military appearance. His fatigues had obviously been tailored to his body, and they were starched. He wore a varnished helmet with the three silver stars of his rank fastened to it, and polished "tanker" boots, as he had while serving under General George S. Patton in Europe.

Almond was wearing clean but rumpled fatigues and what the Army called "combat" boots. These looked like rough-side-out work shoes to which had been sewn a band of smooth leather fastened to the lower calf with a double buckle. The only things that distinguished him from any of the soldiers in his command were the stars pinned to his collar points and fatigue cap — which was crumpled and looked too large for him — and the general officer's leather pistol belt around his waist.

"You are both to be congratulated," MacArthur intoned. "And I shall expect equally great things from you in the future."

He first shook Walker's hand, then let go. Walker saluted. MacArthur returned it. Then he shook Almond's hand, let it go, and returned his salute.

He then took one step up the stairway and stopped and turned.

"By the way, Ned . . ." he began.

"Yes, sir?" Almond asked.

"This is addressed to you in your capacity as Chief of Staff, Supreme Headquarters."

"Yes, sir?"

"Those helicopters we saw?"

"Yes, sir."

"Dog and pony shows are sometimes necessary, but under the present circumstances, I can't see that the time and effort are justified. Have them transferred immediately to the CIA here in Seoul."

"Sir?" Almond asked, more than a little surprised by the order.

"Do that today, if you can," MacArthur said. "The helicopters, the pilots, the mechanics, everything, go to the CIA, and I don't want to see photographs of them in the press. Clear?"

"Yes, sir."

MacArthur nodded at Almond, then went up the stairs and, ducking his head and without looking back, passed through the door.

"What the hell was that all about?" General Walker inquired of General Almond.

General Almond shrugged.

"I have no idea," he confessed, "but the Supreme Commander didn't leave any doubt about what he wants done, did he?"

They stood in front of the base operations tents watching as the *Bataan* taxied away, reached the end of the runway, ran up its engines quickly, and then raced down the runway.

The two men then looked at each another. There was no love lost between them, but there was a certain mutual respect.

"Well, Ned," Walker said as he put out his hand, "we'll no doubt be in touch."

Almond shook the hand, then saluted.

"Yes, of course we will," Almond said.

Walker nodded at him, then turned and started to walk to the Air Force C-47 that would carry him to his Eighth Army headquarters in the south.

Almond did not wait for the C-47 to take off. Even before Walker got to it, he walked toward the end of the base operations tents.

The fleet of staff cars that had been used to carry the Supreme Commander and his entourage from the airport to the Capitol Building and back — it had been assembled with no little effort; some cars had come from as far away as Pusan on an

LST for the occasion — was no longer needed. Outside Seoul, with few exceptions, the roads were unpaved, in very bad shape, and not usable by passenger cars. The staff cars had been turned over to an X Corps Transportation Corps captain, who had arranged them in neat rows and was waiting for orders on what to do with them.

Where they had once been lined up before the base operations tents, there was now a line of jeeps, the vehicles in which the senior officers had come from their units to participate in the liberation ceremony.

As General Almond walked toward his jeep, his aide-de-camp got out of the front seat and called his name.

"General Almond! Over here, sir."

Almond headed for his jeep. The aide took the canvas cover from the two-starred license plate.

Just as he reached the jeep, he was intercepted by Major Alex Donald.

"General Almond, if I may —"

Almond looked at him curiously, then held up his hand in a gesture telling him to wait.

"Al," he ordered, "see if you find Colonel Scott, or, failing him, Colonel Raymond, and bring one or the other here."

Colonel Charles Scott was the X Corps

G-2, and Lieutenant Colonel James Raymond his assistant.

"Yes, sir," Haig said, and walked quickly down the line of jeeps.

Almond turned to Major Donald.

"Okay, Major," he said. "Donald, isn't it? What can I do for you?"

"Sir, I wondered what General MacArthur's reaction to the helicopters was," Major Donald said.

"I've been wondering about that myself," Almond said. "Is that why you . . . ?"

"No, sir. Sir, I was going to suggest that rather than returning to the X Corps CP by jeep, you fly there in one of the H-19s."

"I don't think that will be possible," Almond said. "But thank you, Major, for the thought."

Major Donald was surprised and disappointed by the general's refusal, but he was not yet ready to quit. If General MacArthur were to ask General Almond what he thought of the H-19s — as he almost certainly would — Donald wanted to make sure he had kind, even enthusiastic, things to say about them.

"Sir, I can have you there in fifteen minutes, and, sir, I really would like to demonstrate the capabilities of the H-19s to you."

Almond looked at him a moment, then gestured for Donald to follow him. Almond walked far enough away from the line of jeeps so that he was sure no one could overhear the conversation, then stopped and faced Donald.

"Major," he said, "you will consider the following to be classified."

"Yes, sir."

"Top Secret, and to be related to no one without my specific permission in advance."

"Yes, sir."

"As of" — Almond consulted his wristwatch — "1445 hours, the helicopters, their crews and maintenance personnel, everything and everyone connected with them, are transferred to the Central Intelligence Agency."

"Sir?"

"What didn't you understand?" Almond asked.

Major Donald was visibly shaken. It took him a moment to frame his reply.

"I understood that the helicopters and everyone and everything connected with them have been transferred to the Central Intelligence Agency, sir. Sir, does that include me?"

"You are connected with the helicopters, are you not?"

"Yes, sir, but —"

"Then you're included in the package," Almond said, cutting him off. "What you will do now, Major, is go back to the

211

hangar. Someone will shortly contact you with further orders. Any questions?"

"No, sir."

"That will be all, Major," Almond said. "Thank you."

Major Donald saluted and then, after a moment, started to walk to where he had parked his jeep.

Almond looked toward the line of jeeps and saw that Haig had located Lieutenant Colonel James Raymond, the assistant G-2. He gestured for him to come to him. Haig looked dubious, so Almond gestured again, meaning for him to come along.

Lieutenant Colonel Raymond saluted.

"Yes, sir?"

"Raymond, do you know how to find the CIA's — 'headquarters,' I suppose is the word — in Seoul?"

Raymond looked slightly uncomfortable.

"Not officially, sir."

"Explain that to me."

"They don't like people to know where they are, sir. But they told Colonel Scott, and he thought I might have a need for the information, and he told me."

"But you know?"

"Yes, sir."

"I want you to go there, right now, and deliver a message for me to the station chief or his deputy. No one else. If necessary, wait there for one or the other to show up."

"Yes, sir."

When Almond did not hand him a sheet of paper or an envelope, Lieutenant Colonel Raymond took a small notebook and a pencil from his pocket.

"Don't write this down," Almond said. "Memorize it."

"Yes, sir."

" 'Classification Top Secret,' " Almond began to dictate. " 'As of 1445 hours this date, by order of the Supreme Commander, Allied Powers, two H-19 helicopters, together with their crews, maintenance personnel, and all available supporting equipment, have been transferred to you. The officer-in-charge has been notified, and is awaiting your orders in the hangar across from base operations at Kimpo Airfield. Signature, Almond, Major General, Chief of Staff, Allied Powers.' Got that?"

"Sir, would you give it to me again?" Lieutenant Colonel Raymond asked.

Almond did so.

"Got it, sir."

"When you have delivered the message, report to me at the CP," Almond ordered. "Let's go, Al."

V

Major Malcolm S. Pickering, USMCR, was
three quarters of the way toward the top of
a hill that had been terraced into rice paddies. He had only a vague idea where he
was, except . . .

He *knew* he was somewhere to the east
of where he had seen the jeep with the
American flag flying from its antenna.

He *knew* that he had been moving, and
making pretty good time, since daylight —
that is, for fifteen hours.

He *knew* that he had crossed a dirt road
three hours before and an hour after that a
paved road, which in Korea meant a
highway, and he *suspected* that it was the
highway connecting Suwon, to his west,
with Wonju, to his east.

And he *knew* that he had waded and
swum across a river, which he was *pretty
well convinced* was the Han.

From where he was sitting, on a dirt
footpath, his back resting against the earth-

wall dam of a rice paddy, he could see in the valley below him the "highway" bridge of the paved road across the river. The bridge had been mostly blown into the water, but there were signs that vehicles had forded the river near the shattered bridge.

He had no idea whose vehicles, or when they had crossed.

There were the burned remnants of buildings and stone-walled, thatch-roofed huts on both sides of the river by the bridge. There had been no signs of people or of travel on the dirt road, the highway, or the river when he had crossed them, and there had been no signs of anything human and alive in the thirty minutes he had been watching now.

The only sign of human life he had seen all day had been very early that morning, shortly after he had started moving, when he had come across three rice farmers tending a paddy.

They had had with them their lunch — balls of rice flecked with bits of chicken or pork — and two bottles of water. He had taken half the rice and one of the bottles of water, even though he was *almost positive* the water wasn't safe to drink, and had vowed he wasn't going to take a sip unless he absolutely had to.

He had paid for the rice and water with

a U.S. twenty-dollar bill from a thick wad of currency held together by a gold money clip that had been either a birthday or a Christmas present from either his mother or his father. He couldn't quite remember which.

He wasn't at all sure if the rice farmers knew what the twenty-dollar bill was, and was just about convinced the farmer's pleasure in taking it was because they would have been just as happy to take any colored piece of paper if that meant the large bearded American with the large pistol wasn't going to shoot them to ensure they would not report him to the authorities.

Pick had noticed aerial activity all through the day, from contrails laid almost certainly by Air Force B-29 bombers, to formations of twin-engine aircraft, either Air Force A-20s or B-26s flying at what was probably eight or ten thousand feet, to low-flying Air Force P-51s and even some Marine and Navy Corsairs flying to his west, right down on the deck, probably on interdiction missions.

None had been close enough for them to see him, and certainly not close enough for him to try to signal them with the mirror, even if he knew how to work that goddamn thing, and anyway, the flash of light from the goddamn mirror would almost certainly have been lost in the far brighter flashes of light coming from the sun bouncing off the water in the rice paddies.

He had filled both canteens and the bottle he'd bought from the rice farmers with water from what was probably the Han River, and felt *marginally* safer in drinking some of that now.

The decision he had before him now was when to have supper, before or after going to work.

He had not found a conveniently drained rice paddy, which meant that he was going to have to drain one himself. In two months, he had become rather expert in draining rice paddies, so that he would have a muddy surface into which he could stamp out his arrow and the letters *PP*.

It wasn't as simple a task as one might assume, not simply a matter of kicking a hole in the dirt dams and letting the water flow out.

There was a hell of a lot of water in each rice paddy, he had learned, and if you kicked too large an opening, the water would run out too quickly, taking with it more dirt, so that what had begun as a small trickle of water turned with astonishing speed into a raging torrent.

The torrent would soon overwhelm the capacity of the dirt path between adjacent paddies to carry it away, and flow into the rice paddy below it on the hill, where it would overwhelm that paddy's earth dam, and produce something like a chain reaction.

A line of drained paddies running down a hill was visible for miles, and would attract the kind of attention that would see him captured. He had caused one major chain-reaction draining and two not quite so spectacular — all three of which had seen excited farmers rushing to see what had happened — before he'd given the subject of paddy drainage a great deal of thought and come up with a technique that worked.

The trick was to go to one end of the paddy and scrape a *very* shallow trench at the top of the dam. The water would flow until it had fallen to the level of the trench and then stop. Then you moved five feet away and dug another *very* shallow trench, and repeated the process until the paddy was dry.

Major Pickering decided he would work *and* eat. He would dig the first *very* shallow trench with his boot, eat one of his nine rice balls as the water drained, then, when it had stopped flowing, dig another very shallow trench, eat a second ball of rice, and so on.

He pushed himself off the earth dam, walked to the end of the paddy, and scraped the first trench.

It was long after dark before the paddy was drained.

He looked down at the valley and saw some lights, but they were dim and not moving along the highway.

He moved uphill from the drained trench, sat down on the dirt path, popped dessert — the last of the nine rice balls — into his mouth, and then lay down.

He had a busy day tomorrow. He had to find food again, and move, and then find another suitable rice paddy.

[Two]
The House
Seoul, South Korea
1715 29 September 1950

When Colonel Scott, the X Corps G-2, had quietly passed on the location of the CIA station to Lieutenant Colonel Raymond, he of course had not simply given him the address. Neither officer spoke, much less read and wrote, Korean. Instead, he had prepared a rather detailed map, and provided a verbal description of how to get there, and of the building itself.

Still, what street signs remained were in Korean, and it took Raymond about two hours to make it to the house from Kimpo. And even when he blew his jeep's horn in front of the massive steel gates, he wasn't sure he was in the right place.

A moment later, an enormous Korean in U.S. Army fatigues came through a door in the gate, holding the butt of a Thompson submachine gun against his hip.

"Do you speak English?" Raymond asked.

There was no sign, verbal or otherwise, that the Korean had understood him.

"I'm here to see the station chief," Raymond said.

Again there was no response that Raymond could detect.

"I have orders from General Almond," Raymond said.

That triggered a response. The Korean gestured, and the right half of the gate swung inward. The Korean motioned Raymond to drive through it.

Inside, he saw a large stone European-looking house. There was a jeep and a Russian jeep parked to the left of the porte cochere in the center of the building. He remembered seeing a Russian jeep earlier at both the Capitol Building and Kimpo, and wondered if it was the same one. On the roof of the porte cochere an air-cooled .30-caliber machine gun had been set up behind sandbags. It was manned, and trained on the gate and the road from the gate. Raymond wondered if it was manned all the time, or whether his horn-blowing had been the trigger.

He stopped in front of the porte cochere and looked over his shoulder for the enormous Korean. The Korean, who was right behind him, pulled his finger across his throat, a signal to cut the engine, then pointed at the door of the house.

Then the Korean, the Thompson still resting on his hip, beat him to the door and motioned him through it.

Inside was a large marble-floored foyer. Another Korean, much smaller than the one who had been at the gate, sat at the foot of a wide staircase with an automatic carbine on his lap. The large Korean led Raymond to a door off the foyer, rapped on it with his knuckles, and then pushed it open.

Lieutenant Colonel Raymond was interested — perhaps even excited — to see what was in the room behind the door. The only previous contact he had had with the CIA was on paper. He had seen a number of their intelligence assessments, and he had met a number of CIA bureaucrats, some of whom had lectured at the Command & General Staff College when he had been a student there. But he had never before been in a CIA station and met actual CIA field officers.

He walked into the room.

There was a large dining table. On it sat two silver champagne coolers, each holding a liter bottle of Japanese Asahi beer. Two men in clean white T-shirts were sitting at the table, drinking beer, munching on Planters peanuts, and reading *Stars and Stripes*.

They hurriedly rose to their feet.

Those are enlisted men!

"Can I help you, Colonel?" the taller of them asked courteously.

"My name is Raymond," he said. "I have a message for the station chief from General Almond."

The taller of them jerked his thumb at the other one, which was apparently a signal for him to get the station chief.

"It'll be a minute, Colonel," the taller one said. "Can I offer you a beer?"

"I'd kill for a cold beer, thank you," Colonel Raymond blurted.

It was not, he instantly realized, what he would have said if he had considered his reply carefully — or, for that matter, at all. He was on duty as the personal messenger of the Corps commander, for one thing, and for another, field-grade officers do not drink with enlisted men.

But it had been a long day, and the beer looked so good.

The tall man found a glass —

That's a highball glass, a crystal highball glass!

Where are they getting all these creature comforts?

— filled it carefully with beer, and handed it to Lieutenant Colonel Raymond.

"There you go, sir."

"Thank you."

Raymond was on his second sip when three other men came into the room. They were also wearing crisp, clean white T-shirts. One was lithe and trim, the second barrel-chested and muscular — Raymond decided he, too, was an enlisted man, probably a senior sergeant — and the third was sort of pudgy and rumpled.

"What can we do for you, Colonel?" the pudgy one asked. He walked to the champagne cooler, poured beer, and handed glasses to the others.

"I have a message for the station chief from General Almond," Raymond said. "Is that you, sir?"

"Who are you, Colonel?" the pudgy one asked.

"Lieutenant Colonel Raymond, sir. I'm the assistant X Corps G-2."

"You work for Colonel Schneider, right?" the pudgy one said.

"No, sir, for Colonel Scott."

The pudgy one nodded at the trim one and confirmed, "That's the name of the X Corps G-2."

"Are you the station chief, sir?" Raymond asked the pudgy one.

The pudgy one pointed at the lithe one, and the lithe one pointed at the pudgy one.

Station Chief William R. Dunston had pointed at Major Kenneth R. McCoy for two reasons. First, he was always reluctant to identify himself to anyone — even an Army G-2 light bird — as the station chief, and second, he considered Ken McCoy to be *de facto* the senior CIA officer in South Korea.

There was no question in Dunston's mind that if there was an argument between him and McCoy, and General Pickering had to choose between them, McCoy would prevail. He had served under Pickering in the OSS in the Second World War, and they were personal friends as well.

Major McCoy had pointed at Dunston because Dunston *was* the station chief, even though both of them knew McCoy was calling the shots.

The chunky, muscular enlisted man chuckled when he saw the exchange.

"Mr. Zimmerman, it is not nice to mock your superiors," the lithe one said, which caused the other two enlisted men to laugh.

"May I presume that one of you is the station chief?" Lieutenant Colonel Raymond said. He realized he was smiling.

What did I expect to find in here? A Humphrey Bogart type in a trench coat?

"You may," the lithe one said, and put out his hand. "My name is McCoy. That's Major Dunston," he added, pointing, "and Master Gunner Zimmerman, Technical Sergeant Jennings, and Sergeant Cole."

"What's your message, Colonel?" Dunston asked.

Raymond ran it through his brain first before reciting, " 'Classification Top Secret. As of 1445 hours this date, by order of the Supreme Commander, Allied Powers, two H-19 helicopters, together with their crews, maintenance personnel, and all available supporting equipment, have been transferred to you. The officer-in-charge has been notified and is awaiting your orders in the hangar across from base operations at Kimpo Airfield. Signature, Almond, Major General, Chief of Staff, Allied Powers.' "

"Jesus!" Zimmerman said. "Helos? Two helos?"

"Could you do that again, please, Colonel?" McCoy asked.

Raymond did so.

"Did General Almond say what we're supposed to do with these helicopters?" Dunston asked.

"If these are the two big Sikorskys that flew into Kimpo this morning, I know what we can do with them," McCoy said.

"Yeah," Zimmerman said.

"That's General Almond's entire message, sir," Raymond said.

"Colonel, have you had your supper?" McCoy asked.

"Excuse me?"

"For two reasons, I hope you can have it with us," McCoy said. "The first is to thank you for the helos, and the second is that I think you're just the actor we need for a little amateur theatrical we're staging."

"Yeah," Zimmerman said. "And, Killer, if we can find Howe's stars — and I'll bet there's a spare set in his luggage — we can pin them on him."

"Even better," McCoy said.

"I have no idea what you're talking about," Lieutenant Colonel Raymond confessed.

"Colonel, we have a prisoner in the basement. A North Korean colonel," McCoy explained. "We're just about convinced (a) he's a high-level intelligence officer and (b) that he knows something about either a planned Chinese Communist intervention or the situation which will trigger such an intervention. We've been working on him without much success. The one thing we do know for sure is that he has an ego. He wants us to know how important he is.

What we've got set up for tonight is a dinner —"

"A dinner?" Raymond asked in disbelief.

"Roast beef, potatoes, rice, wine — lots of wine — and all served with as much class as we can muster."

Raymond had been eating his meals — prepared from Ten-In-One rations — off of a steel tray. There had been an infrequent beer, but it had been warm and in a can.

"Can I ask where you're getting all . . . of this?" he asked.

McCoy looked at him thoughtfully for a moment, then smiled. He said: "Dunston's people managed to hide a lot of the crystal and silver and even some of the wine before the North Koreans took Seoul, and the day before yesterday Sergeants Jennings and Cole toured Inchon Harbor, swapping North Korean souvenirs — flags, weapons, et cetera — with the crews of the cargo ships. You'd be surprised what a good Marine noncom can get for a Sudarev PPS-43 submachine gun."

Raymond chuckled.

"Jennings and Cole," McCoy went on, "came back with a weapons carrier — and its trailer — full of frozen food and beer. The freezers and the reefers here still work, so we're in pretty good shape for a while."

"So the idea is, you're going to feed this NK colonel and try to get him drunk?"

"I don't think he'll let us get him drunk, but he might take a little more wine than he should," McCoy said. "Enough to let something slip. Particularly if he thought he was impressing someone important. You're a distinguished-looking man, Colonel. Asiatics — who don't have much facial hair — are impressed with large mustaches. If we pin General Howe's stars on you, I think he'll buy you as a general officer."

"He speaks English?"

"I think he does, but won't admit it. Dunston, Zimmerman, and I speak Korean. I suppose it's too much to hope —"

"Nothing but German — I was there for four years — and not very good German."

In German, McCoy asked, "But if I said 'Look doubtful,' you'd understand?"

"Yes."

"And you could say, in German, 'What did he say?' when I give you the nod?"

"Yes, I guess I could."

"Colonel, I really hope you can stay for supper," McCoy said.

Why not? Raymond thought. *As long as I get back to the CP by twenty-four hundred, so I can relieve the colonel. . . .*

"If you think it would be useful, I will," Lieutenant Colonel Raymond said.

"You're really going into the general's

luggage and borrow his insignia?" Dunston said.

"Unless you've got a better idea where we can get a set of general's stars," McCoy said.

Lieutenant Colonel Raymond decided that the lithe one, McCoy, was the station chief. He was the one giving the orders.

[Three]
Haneda Airfield
Tokyo, Japan
1805 29 September 1950

Fleming Pickering glanced out the window as the *Bataan* taxied toward the hangar that served as the departure and arrival point for the Supreme Commander and his entourage.

He saw the line of staff cars lined up awaiting the *Bataan*'s passengers. MacArthur's black Cadillac limousine was first, and the cars of the other brass were behind it, strictly according to the rank of their intended passengers. Pickering saw his black Buick Roadmaster sitting alone in front of the hangar, facing in the opposite direction from the others.

Pickering knew this would annoy the Palace Guard, who would have greatly preferred to have his car with the others. His single star would have seen his car five or six cars behind MacArthur's limousine, reminding him that he was actually just a minor planet revolving around MacArthur.

MacArthur's staff — and, for that matter, El Supremo himself — really didn't like having anyone in their midst who did not have a precisely defined place in the hierarchy of the Supreme Commander, Allied Powers.

There were two such burrs under the saddles of the Supreme Commander and the Palace Guard, Major General Ralph Howe, NGUS, and Brigadier General Fleming Pickering, USMCR. Neither was subordinate to MacArthur, and both reported directly to the President of the United States.

Pickering had not been at all surprised when he came to Tokyo that the Palace Guard had immediately begun to attempt to get some degree of control over him — the more the better, obviously, from their point of view — and had been prepared to fight that battle, confident that he could win it again, as he had in the Second War.

The Buick — and his and George Hart's fur-collared Naval aviators' leather jackets — were more or less subtle statements that he was not subordinate to Supreme Headquarters, Allied Powers.

The Buick was his. He owned it.

When he had first come to Japan, he had been provided with an olive-drab Chevrolet staff car and a sergeant to drive it, and asked when it would be convenient for him to have the housing officer show him what government quarters were available for an officer of his rank, so that he could make a choice between them.

There was no question in Pickering's mind that the staff car drivers — three of them, on a rotating basis — were agents of the Counter-Intelligence Corps, and thus reporting to Major General Charles A. Willoughby, MacArthur's chief intelligence officer.

He had politely thanked the Headquarters Commandant for the offer of government quarters, but said that would prefer to stay where he was, in a suite in the Imperial Hotel. And he had sent an urgent radio message to Colonel Ed Banning, who was at Camp Pendleton, ordering him to immediately buy a small Buick or Oldsmobile and have it placed aboard the very next P&FE freighter bound for Japan, even if he had to drive to San Francisco to get it on the next ship.

Colonel Banning had, with the word "immediately" in his mind, looked at the small Buicks and Oldsmobiles available in San Diego, decided "The General" would really not like any of them — he could not imagine "The General" riding around Tokyo in a bright yellow little Olds, or a two-tone, mostly lavender little Buick — and instead, eight hours after getting his orders, had stood on a wharf watching the black Buick Roadmaster being lifted aboard the *Pacific Clipper*, which he had been assured was among the fastest vessels in the P&FE fleet.

As soon as the car arrived, Pickering had told the Headquarters Commandant he would no longer need the staff car; he would drive his own car. The Headquarters Commandant told him he'd really be more comfortable if he continued to provide drivers, just in case Pickering might find them useful.

Pickering could not think of a reason to decline the "courteous, innocent" offer, so the "drivers" remained assigned to him. They usually spent their entire tour of duty reading newspapers and magazines while sitting on a couch in the corridor outside his suite. But sometimes he did use them. One of them had driven the Buick to Haneda in the morning, and had brought the car back to carry him to the hotel now.

That had solved the problem of the CIC agent drivers reporting his every move to Willoughby, and McCoy had solved what Pickering knew was a major problem — how to keep the messages he and Howe were sending to Truman really secret.

Despite the TOP SECRET EYES ONLY THE PRESIDENT classification, eyes other than Truman's would see the messages both in Tokyo, where they would be encrypted and transmitted, and at Camp Pendleton, California, where they would be decrypted, typed, and dispatched by Marine officer courier to the White House.

Pickering was confident that there would be no leaks at Pendleton, where a Marine cryptographer working only for Colonel Ed Banning would handle the decryption, and just about as sure their messages would be read in the Dai Ichi Building communications center by people other than the cryptographers. An army sergeant was unlikely to chase away a colonel with all the security clearances — or, for that matter, Major General Charles Willoughby himself — when he was reading over his shoulder.

In Pusan, McCoy had run across a just-rushed-from-Germany-to-Korea Army Security Agency cryptographer, Master Sergeant Paul T. Keller, who didn't even know any of the Dai Ichi Building cryptographers. A message from General Howe to the Army Chief of Staff in Washington had seen Keller the next day transferred to the CIA, with a further assignment to the staff of the Assistant Director of the CIA for Asia.

Keller was told — more than likely unnecessarily — that if there were any leaks of EYES ONLY THE PRESIDENT messages they would know who had done the leaking.

Pickering also suspected that Willoughby was entirely capable of both tapping the telephones in his hotel suite and bugging the suite itself. Master Sergeant Keller had "swept" the hotel suite and found several microphones, which might, or might not, have been left over from the days of the Kempai-Tai, the Japanese Imperial Secret Police.

There was no way of finding out for sure without tearing walls down to trace the wires, so they had left them in place. When Pickering had something to say he didn't want Willoughby to hear, he held the conversation in the bathroom, with the shower running, the toilet flushing, and a roll of toilet tissue around the microphone in the left of the two lights on either side of the mirror.

Most of the time, however, when there was a meeting they didn't want overheard, they held the meeting in McCoy's house in Denenchofu. Keller swept the house on a regular basis.

The *Bataan* stopped, and the engines died.

General MacArthur looked at his watch,

then stood up and stretched.

"Jean and I would be pleased if you could come for dinner, Fleming. No one else will be there. Would eight be convenient for you?"

"Thank you," Pickering said. "I'd be delighted."

There was a discreet knock at the compartment door, and Huff's voice calling, "We're ready for you anytime, General."

MacArthur nodded at Pickering, pushed the door open, and went through it.

Pickering looked out the window again. Master Sergeant Keller was leaning on the Buick's fender.

That means he either has a message for me, or that he got a little bored in the hotel and decided to drive the Buick out here himself.

Pickering waited until all the brass had deplaned and gotten into their cars, then stood up and went into the aisle. Captain George F. Hart and Miss Jeanette Priestly were waiting for him.

"Keller's driving the car," Hart said.

"I saw," Pickering said.

"George said you were going to see Ernie," Jeanette said. "Can I bum a ride?"

"Your wish is my command, Fair Lady," Pickering said.

"Despite what people say about you, I think you'll be a fine father-in-law," she said.

If we get him back, Pickering thought, but said, "Was there ever any doubt about that in your mind?"

Hart chuckled.

They went down the staircase and walked to the Buick. Hart got in the front beside Keller. Keller started the engine, then turned and handed Pickering a sheet of paper, folded in thirds.

"Came in an hour ago, General," Keller said.

Pickering shifted in the seat so that Jeanette could not see what it was when he unfolded it.

TOP SECRET PRESIDENTIAL

SPECIAL CHANNEL

ONE COPY ONLY

EYES ONLY BRIG GEN FLEMING PICKERING USMCR

BLAIR HOUSE 0235 28 SEPTEMBER 1950

IN THE ABSENCE OF A REALLY COMPELLING REASON PRECLUDING YOUR TRAVEL, I WOULD LIKE TO SEE YOU HERE AS SOON AS POSSIBLE. BEST PERSONAL REGARDS HARRY S TRUMAN

TOP SECRET PRESIDENTIAL

Pickering refolded the message and

handed it to Hart.

"Read that, don't comment," he ordered, "and then do the magic trick for Jeanette."

"Magic trick?" Jeanette asked. "What was that? Am I allowed to ask?"

"No, you're not. Show her, George."

Hart turned to the backseat. He waved the sheet of paper in his hand.

"Now you see it, Jeanette . . ." he said.

He produced a Zippo lighter, flicked it open and touched the flame to the sheet of paper. There was a sudden white flash and a small cloud of smoke.

The sheet of paper disappeared.

". . . and now you don't," Hart finished unnecessarily.

"Jesus Christ, what was that?" Jeanette asked.

"That would be telling, Jeanette," Pickering said. "When we get to McCoy's house, set that up, please, George, including the appropriate reply."

"Yes, sir. When do we go?"

"I thought it said, 'as soon as possible,' " Pickering said.

"Yes, sir."

[Four]
No. 7 Saku-Tun
Denenchofu, Tokyo, Japan
1915 29 September 1950

A middle-aged Japanese woman in a black kimono came through the steel gate in the wall around McCoy's house, bowed to the black Buick, then went back inside the wall. A moment later, the double gates farther down the wall opened, and Keller drove the car inside.

Mrs. Ernestine Sage McCoy, who was standing outside the door of the sprawling, one-floor Japanese house, was also wearing a black kimono.

Pickering decided she was wearing it as a maternity dress rather than a cultural statement of some kind. He also thought that it was true that being in the family way did indeed give women sort of a glow. Ernie looked radiant.

She came down the shallow flight of stairs as Fleming, Jeanette, Hart, and Keller got out of the Buick.

As Ernie hugged Fleming, he could feel the swelling of her belly against him.

"How are you, sweetheart?" he asked.

"I'm fine," she said. "The question seems to be, How are the men in our extended little family?"

"Ken's fine," Jeanette answered for him.

"He looked like a recruiting poster when I saw him. Pick is still among the missing."

"Ken told me they had missed him by no more than a couple of hours yesterday," Pickering said. "They'll find him, I'm sure."

"Well, come on in the house, all of you, and have a drink. I didn't know how many of you were coming, or when, so dinner will have to be started from scratch."

"Then I'll have time to take a shower?" Jeanette asked. "Shower, hell, a long hot bath?"

"Come on with me," Ernie said. "Uncle Flem, you know where the bar is."

She put her arm around Jeanette and started to lead her into the interior of the house.

"Wow," Ernie said, first sniffing and then wrinkling her nose. "You really do need a bath, don't you?"

"You can go to hell," Jeanette said.

The middle-aged Japanese woman and a younger Japanese woman were already in the living room when Pickering led the others in. There were four bottles on the bar: bourbon, scotch, vodka, and beer.

The men indicated their choices — two scotches and a bourbon — by pointing. The young woman made the drinks, and the older woman put them on a tray and served them. The younger woman left the room, returning in a moment with a tray of bacon-wrapped smoked oysters.

Ernie came in as the oysters were being served.

"I would really like a very stiff one of those," she said. "But I am being the perfect pregnant woman."

"Good for you, sweetheart," Pickering said. "How about an oyster and a glass of soda?"

"Take what you can, when you can get it," Ernie said, and said something in Japanese to the younger woman, who started to fill a glass with soda water.

She turned to Pickering.

"Was Ken telling Jeanette the truth about Pick? Or whistling in the wind to make her feel good?"

"The truth, I'm sure," Pickering said.

"I really feel sorry for her," Ernie said.

"Ernie, two things. Thank you for dinner, but no thank you. MacArthur has invited me for dinner, and George and Paul have got things to do."

"Things that won't wait until they can eat?"

"That's the second thing. No, they can't wait. Don't tell Jeanette, but there's been a message from the President; he wants me in Washington as soon as I can get there."

"What's that all about?"

"I really don't know. But he's the President, Ernie. I do what he tells me to do."

"Don't tell Jeanette?"

"She's a reporter."

"She's Pick's . . . I was about to say girlfriend, but she's much more than that."

"I know," he said. "But I still don't want you to tell her."

"About you going to Washington, or about anything?"

"This will sound cruel, perhaps, but the less Jeanette knows about anything, the better. Let me, or Ken, decide what she can know."

"You're going to Washington, and Ken's in Korea," Ernie replied.

"Come to Washington with me," Pickering said.

"No."

"You could see your parents for at least a couple of days."

"No."

"And then come back here, if you'd like."

"No, Uncle Flem. Thank you, but no."

"You want to tell me why?"

"Ken's here. This is our home."

"A couple of days with your parents would be good for all concerned," Pickering argued.

"They would spend all their time arguing that I should stay with them, and then be really hurt when I wouldn't. It's better the way it is."

"You don't want your mother here when the time comes?"

"Not unless Ken's here, too. Then, sure."

"If she decides to come, you can't stop her, Ernie."

"She knows how I feel. Can we get off this subject?"

"Got your Minox, George?" Pickering asked.

"Yes, sir."

"Then take a couple of pictures of me and the hardheaded pregnant lady in the kimono."

"Okay," Ernie said, and smiled.

"And then we have to get out of here, sweetheart," Pickering said. "If you need anything, tell Paul. And if he can't get what you need, he knows how to contact General Howe, and Howe will get it for you."

"Thanks, Paul."

"Anything you need, Ernie," Paul Keller said. "Anything."

Pickering stood up and put his arm around Ernie's shoulders, and George Hart took three shots of them with the tiny Minox.

Captain Howard C. Dunwood, USMCR, was having breakfast — ham chunks with raisin sauce, out of a can — with Major Alex Donald, U.S. Army, when the small door in the left hangar door opened and a Marine corporal, a very large fair-skinned man in his early twenties, his field cap perched precariously on his head, came through, followed by four other men.

"Heads up!" Major Donald whispered. "That must be the people I was told to expect."

Captain Dunwood said nothing.

After a moment, he recognized two of the men. He had seen them before, the last time when Baker Company had landed on Tokchok-Kundo Island in the Flying Fish Channel leading to Pusan. At that time, both had been wearing black cotton pajamas, with bands of the same material wrapped around their foreheads. The tall and lanky one was now dressed in crisply starched utilities, with the chevrons of a technical sergeant painted on the sleeves. The other character who had been wearing black pajamas on the island was now in crisp utilities, with the gold leaves of a major pinned to his collar points.

Dunwood had seen that one once before Tokchok-Kundo.

At Haneda. On 15 August, the day I arrived in Japan from the States. Six weeks ago. It seems like a hell of a lot longer.

At Haneda the major had been wearing a tropical worsted uniform and the insignia of a captain. A Marine brigadier general and a strikingly beautiful woman had put him and a Navy lieutenant on a C-54 bound for Sasebo.

And I was half in the bag, and pegged him as a candy-ass chair warmer and made an ass of myself on the airplane, for which I paid with a dislocated thumb that still hurts sometimes. I suppose it's too much to hope he doesn't remember that incident.

Dunwood had no idea who the other two were — a Marine master gunner and an Army Transportation Corps major in a rumpled uniform — and absolutely no idea what was going on.

Major Donald — subtly making it clear that he was privy to highly classified information that he could, of course, not share with a lowly Marine captain — had told him only that "there had been a change of plans" and that "sometime in the immediate future, I will be contacted with further orders reflecting that change."

Major Donald put down his can of ham chunks in raisin sauce and marched to meet the newcomers. The crews of the two helicopters, who were also having their breakfast, sitting on the floor of their aircraft, watched with interest.

Dunwood shrugged, put his can of ham chunks in raisin sauce down, and walked after Major Donald. When Donald became aware he was being trailed, he turned to look at Dunwood.

And here's where the sonofabitch tells me to butt out.

"Hello, Dunwood. How are you?" McCoy said.

Dunwood saluted.

"Good morning, sir."

"You know Sergeant Jennings," McCoy said. "That's Gunner Zimmerman and that's Major Dunston."

"My name is Donald, Major."

"You're in charge of these aircraft?" McCoy asked.

"Yes, I am."

"And I understand you were told you'd be contacted about them?"

"Yes, I have."

"Well, here we are," McCoy said. "My name is McCoy."

"I wonder if I might see some identification?" Donald said.

"Ernie," McCoy said.

Zimmerman took a small leather wallet from his breast pocket, opened it, and held it so Donald could see it.

"Thank you," Donald said, then looked at McCoy. "I'm at your orders, sir."

"How much have you told anybody about any of this?" McCoy asked.

"Not a word to anyone, Major."

"I'd like to speak to the aircraft people right now," McCoy said. "Dunwood, you listen, and you decide which of your Marines you can tell, and what."

"Aye, aye, sir."

Donald walked to the closest of the H-19s and gestured for the men gathered around the second helicopter to come over.

When they were finally assembled, McCoy saw there were four pilots, two enlisted men also wearing flight suits, and half a dozen maintenance personnel, all noncoms but one, who was a warrant officer.

Donald barked "Atten-hut" and, when everybody was at attention, said, "This is Major McCoy."

"Stand at ease," McCoy ordered. "I'm sure you're all wondering what's going on. I'll tell you what I know, which frankly isn't much. What follows is classified Top Secret, and I don't know how many of you have that security clearance. For the time being, it should be enough to tell you that nothing about this operation is to be told to anyone. As I'm sure you all know, divulging Top Secret information will see you standing before a General Court-Martial. I'm dead serious about that. You don't tell your pals about this, and you don't write home telling your mother, your wife, or anyone else. If you do, we'll find out about it and you'll find yourself in front of a General Court. No second chances. We cannot afford to have loose mouths. Pay attention. The lives you'll save by keeping your mouths shut will be your own." He paused. "Any questions?"

He took the time to make eye contact with everyone, including Major Donald, and then went on.

"These aircraft, and all of you, have been assigned to the Central Intelligence Agency. You will continue to receive your orders from Major Donald, who will get his from the CIA station chief. Any questions?"

One of the pilots raised his hand.

"Okay," McCoy said.

"Sir, I always thought you had to volunteer for something like this."

"If you always thought that, Captain, you were always wrong," McCoy said.

There were chuckles from most of them.

Another hand went up.

"Sir, can I ask what we'll be doing?"

"Aside from flying those helicopters, no."

More chuckles.

A voice from somewhere called, jokingly, "How do we get out of this chickenshit outfit?"

"In handcuffs, a coffin, or when you retire," McCoy said, smiling. Now there was laughter. "I'll tell you what I can when I can. But for the time being, that's it."

"I'd like to see you alone, please, Major," McCoy said to Donald, and started walking toward the rear of the hangar. Dunston, Zimmerman, and Jennings followed him, and in a moment, so did Donald and Dunwood.

"Major," Donald said when they were out of earshot of the others, "if I'm . . . You can't tell me what we'll be doing, either?"

"Because that hasn't been decided," McCoy said. "We didn't know we were getting you and these aircraft until seventeen thirty yesterday. I don't think you should share that information."

"I understand."

"We have some ideas, but we won't know if they're any good until we know what these machines can and can't do. I never saw one of them until I walked into the hangar. Can we start with that?"

"Yes, sir. What would you like to know?"

"Everything," McCoy said.

Donald looked at him thoughtfully for a moment, then began what McCoy quickly decided was a recitation he had given before.

"These are Sikorsky H-19A helicopters," Donald recited. "They are powered by a Wright R 1340-57 550-horsepower engine, which gives them a maximum speed of 98 mph, a cruising speed of 80 mph, and a range of about 410 miles. The helicopter itself is 42 feet long and has a wingspan of 53 feet. The empty weight is 5,250 pounds and the maximum takeoff weight 7,500 pounds. There is a three-man crew, pilot, copilot, and crew chief. It can carry ten men, in addition to the crew."

McCoy smiled.

"I think you and Mr. Zimmerman will get along, Major. He, too, is a walking encyclopedia of technical information." He paused and then went on. "On the other hand, I have to have things explained to me."

"Ask away."

"You said the empty weight was . . ."

"Fifty-two hundred and fifty pounds," Donald furnished.

"And the maximum takeoff weight 7,500 pounds. Does that mean these things will carry — what is that? — 2,250 pounds?"

"You have to deduct the weight of the

fuel," Donald explained. "AvGas weighs about seven pounds a gallon."

"Okay. You said it will carry ten men. Riflemen? With their weapons? Ammo? Rations?"

"That figure is based on an average weight, man and equipment, of 180 pounds."

"But these things will carry 1,800 pounds of whatever 180 miles someplace, and then be able to return?"

"That would be pushing the envelope a little," Donald said.

"The what?" Zimmerman asked.

"They call the capabilities of aircraft 'the envelope,'" Donald explained. "Just about everything affects everything else. The more you exceed the cruising speed, for example, the more fuel you burn and the less range you get."

"What about carrying 1,500 pounds 150 miles and back?" McCoy asked.

"That could usually be done," Donald said.

"Do you need the crew chief?" McCoy asked. "If he weighs 180, that's twenty-five gallons of gas."

"Crew chiefs are handy if the bird breaks," Donald said. "And they have other in-flight duties."

"Essential, yes or no?" McCoy pressed.

"Desirable, not absolutely essential."

"And the second pilot? That's another

twenty-five gallons of gas."

"Same answer. There is also the possibility that pilots take hits, and a spare pilot is a nice thing to have."

"Desirable, but not absolutely essential?" McCoy pressed again.

"Right."

"You can fly one of these?" McCoy asked.

"Yes. I was the assistant project officer on this aircraft."

"Can you fly it without help?"

"If necessary. Why do you ask? If I can ask that."

"I'd like to see what you can see from the pilot's seat. I don't think anybody can see very much looking out the side door."

Donald nodded but didn't say anything.

"Do you have another pilot who can fly one of these things by himself?"

"They all can."

"Are these things fueled up and ready to go?"

"I had them topped off yesterday afternoon."

"When you flew them here, did you fly over Inchon?"

"I really don't know what route they took. I'll have to ask one of the pilots who did fly in here."

"What's going on, Kil— Major?" Zimmerman asked.

"I just had one of my famous inspirations," McCoy said. "Major, would you ask one of the pilots who flew over Inchon if he would join us?"

"Sure," Donald said, walked to the nearest H-19, and returned with a young-looking captain.

"This is Captain Schneider, Major," Donald said.

McCoy shook his hand, then asked, "When you flew here yesterday, Captain, did you fly over Inchon?"

"Yes, sir."

"There's supposed to be an Army vehicle depot there. Did you see it?"

"I saw a motor park of all kinds of vehicles, sir."

"Was there someplace in this motor park where you could land one of these aircraft?"

"I'd have to make a couple of passes over it to make sure there's no telephone or power lines, but yes, sir, there was plenty of room to land the H-19s."

"Okay. This is what I'm thinking. We need vehicles. *We* need them," he said, pointing to Dunston, Zimmerman, Jennings, and then himself. "And you need them. And the Marines need them. The original plan was to go there and dazzle whoever's in charge with our CIA identification and orders. We're authorized vehicles, but we get hung up in the bureaucracy. It just occurred to me that if we flew in there in these helos, showed them our orders, and said we needed the vehicles right now, they'd be double dazzled and we'd be out the gate before they had time to think things over — and try to get permission from somebody who would need three days to make a decision."

Major Donald and Captain Schneider smiled.

"How many vehicles are you going to need to support the helicopters and your men?" McCoy said. "Make a list right now. You, too, Dunwood."

"Aye, aye, sir," Dunwood said.

"If you had a tank truck, or tank trailers, could you get AvGas somewhere?" McCoy asked.

"From the Air Force," Donald said. "I don't know if there's a tank park at Inchon or not."

"Make sure you have tank trucks, or plenty of trailers, on your list," McCoy said.

"Yes, sir," Major Donald said.

"On the helos, I want enough men to drive what vehicles we're going to take, plus enough to manhandle the food and whatever else we're going to draw from the Quartermaster Depot," McCoy said.

[Six]

After the H-19s were pushed outside the hangar, Major McCoy managed with some difficulty to climb into the cockpit of one, and then — with some assistance from Major Donald — to strap himself into the copilot's seat.

Donald then handed him a headset and a microphone, and showed him how to press the microphone button to talk, and the switch that allowed selection of TRANSMIT and INTERCOM.

"Got it?" Donald's voice came through the earphones.

McCoy checked to make sure the switch was set on INTERCOM and then pressed the microphone button.

"Got it," he said.

Donald put his face to the open cockpit window.

"Wind it up, Schneider," he called to the other H-19.

A moment later, there came the whine of the engine cranking, a cloud of blue smoke, and a lot of vibration.

For the first time, McCoy realized that he and Donald were practically sitting on the engine.

The rotor blades began to turn very slowly, and then ever faster, over them. And produced more vibration.

He looked around Donald at the other helicopter and saw Zimmerman, who looked as uncomfortable as he felt, sitting beside Captain Schneider.

Donald checked a baffling array of instruments on the control panel and exercised the controls. McCoy had no idea what Donald was doing.

After about a minute, Donald's voice came over the earphones.

"You about ready, Schneider?"

"Anytime, sir," Schneider's metallic voice replied.

"K-16, Army 4003," Donald's voice said.

"Go ahead, Army 4003," a new voice responded.

"Army 4003, a flight of two H-19 helicopters, on the tarmac in front of the hangar across from base ops. Request takeoff permission for a low-level flight on a departure heading of 250 degrees."

"4003, where are you going?"

"K-16, Inchon. We will not exceed 1,000 feet en route."

"4003, understand departure heading 250 degrees, destination Inchon, flight level under 1,000. Be advised that there are multiengine aircraft in the pattern making an approach to runway 27. The altimeter is two niner niner. The winds are negligible. K-16 clears 4003 for immediate takeoff on a departure heading of 250 degrees. Advise when clear of the field."

"Roger, K-16. Army 4003 lifting off at this time."

Donald did something to the controls. The sound of the engine changed. There was more vibration. The tail of the helicopter seemed to rise, and then they were moving very slowly across the tarmac, just a few feet off the ground. The helicopter turned at the edge of the hangar, seemed to both accelerate and rise a few more feet off the ground.

Then, when it had passed over the airport boundary, it turned and climbed to about 500 feet.

Jesus Christ, Major Kenneth R. McCoy thought, *you can see just about everything from up here! This noisy goddamn machine is really going to be useful!*

[Seven]
Haneda Airfield
Tokyo, Japan
0905 30 September 1950

Captain Paul R. Jernigan, who would command Trans-Global Airways Flight 908 — *City of Los Angeles* — Lockheed Constellation Service from Tokyo to San Francisco with fuel stops at Wake Island and Honolulu, had no idea at all that he would be carrying Fleming Pickering until he looked out the window and saw him approaching the aircraft.

He pushed himself out of the seat, told his copilot and the flight engineer that "Jesus Christ, Pickering himself is getting on!" and then left the cockpit so that he could personally welcome aboard the man who owned the airline.

"Welcome aboard, sir," he said. "My name is Jernigan."

"Thank you, Captain," Pickering said, offering his hand. "This is another kind of captain, George Hart. My name is Pickering."

"Yes, sir. I know. It's a pleasure to have you aboard, gentlemen."

The senior stewardess who had been counting heads in the rear of the airplane saw the captain standing by the door and came quickly forward and saw who it was.

"We heard you were coming with us, Commodore," she said. "Welcome aboard. We have you in 1A, the window seat, and 1B."

Never thought to tell me, huh, you airhead! Captain Jernigan thought rather unkindly. He had been known to comment that if he had his choice between flying B-17s over Berlin, which he had done, or flying Connies with six stewardesses aboard, as he was doing now, he would take Berlin anytime.

"Thank you," Pickering said, and found his seat.

"You want the window, George?" he asked.

"Up to you, Boss. I don't care either way."

Pickering slid into the window seat.

"Once we're in the air, please feel free to come to the cockpit, Commodore," Captain Jernigan said. He had picked up on the title, and heard it was what they called the senior of a group of ship captains.

"Thank you," Pickering said.

"Commodore," the senior stewardess asked, "can I get you anything? Coffee? Something stronger? While we're waiting for our clearance?"

"No. Thank you very much," Pickering said, and then, a moment later: "Hold on. Bring me a Bloody Mary, please. Better make it a double."

George Hart looked at him in surprise. Pickering rarely drank at this time of day. Then he saw the silvered cast-aluminum plaque attached to the bulkhead before them, where they would see it all the way across the Pacific.

THIS TRANS-GLOBAL
LOCKHEED CONSTELLATION

"THE CITY OF LOS ANGELES"

ON JUNE 1, 1950

SET THE CURRENT SPEED RECORD FOR

COMMERCIAL AIR TRAVEL BETWEEN

SAN FRANCISCO AND TOKYO

CAPTAIN MALCOLM S. PICKERING

CHIEF PILOT OF TRANS-GLOBAL AIRWAYS

WAS IN COMMAND

Pickering saw Hart looking at him.
Hart turned to the stewardess.
"Make it two of those, please," he said.

VI

**[One]
8023 Transportation Company
  (Depot, Forward)
Inchon, South Korea
0935 30 September 1950**

Captain Francis P. MacNamara, Transportation Corps, his attention caught by the *fluckata-fluckata-fluckata* sound of rotor blades, stepped outside his office — a canvas fly — and looked skyward.

MacNamara, a stocky, redheaded thirty-five-year-old Irishman from South Boston, had earned a commission in World War II, risen to captain, decided he liked the Army, and elected to remain in service when the war was over. In 1946, while assigned to the Army of Occupation in Germany, he had been told that he was about to be RIF'd.

RIF'd was an unofficial but universally understood and used acronym. The Army didn't need as many Transportation Corps officers as it had during the war, and there was consequently a Reduction In Force program involuntarily releasing from active duty those officers it no longer needed. Those selected to be released were said to be RIF'd.

He had also been told that he could enlist as a master sergeant. He had been a PFC when he had gone to OCS. There was a lot to be said for being a master sergeant, and he had also learned that he could retire from the service after twenty years of service at fifty percent of his basic pay, and further that he could retire at the highest grade held in wartime — in other words, as a captain. He reenlisted.

First Sergeant Francis P. MacNamara, Headquarters and Headquarters Company, the Transportation Corps School, Fort Eustis, Virginia (Captain, TC, Reserve), had been recalled to active duty five days after the North Koreans crossed the 38th Parallel.

His first assignment had been at the Anniston, Alabama, Ordnance Depot, where he had been responsible for the acceptance by the Transportation Corps of wheeled vehicles stored by the Ordnance Corps, and then seeing them moved to the port of Mobile, Alabama, for shipment to the Far East. During this period, the 9th Transportation Company (Provisional) was activated, and he was given command.

The five officers and 145 enlisted men of the 9th Transportation Company, and 608 wheeled vehicles ranging from jeeps to tank transporters, sailed from Mobile to Yokohama, Japan, aboard the *Captain J.C. Buffett*, a Waterman Steamship Line freighter pressed into service. On arrival in Yokohama, the 9th Transportation Company (Provisional) was redesignated the 8023d Transportation Company (Depot, Forward) and Captain MacNamara was told that it would shortly sail aboard the *Captain J.C. Buffett* for Pusan for service with the Eighth U.S. Army.

That didn't happen. The *Captain J. C. Buffett* lay anchored in Yokohama Harbor until 10 September, when it weighed anchor and joined the fleet of vessels bound for the Inchon Invasion.

On 14 September, the *Captain J.C. Buffett* dropped anchor just outside the Flying Fish Channel leading to Inchon, from which position the next morning they could see the warships and attack transports sail into the channel for the invasion.

Commencing 20 September — once Inchon was secure — the 8023d and its 608 vehicles began to debark. This took some time, because of the tides at Inchon, which saw the *Captain J.C. Buffett* forced to hoist anchor, sail into Inchon, and offload as many vehicles as possible before the receding tides made it necessary for her to go back down the Flying Fish Channel, drop anchor again, and wait for the next high tide. The off-loading procedure was further hampered by the shortage of equipment in Inchon capable of lifting the tank transporters, heavy wreckers, and other outsized wheeled vehicles.

But finally everything and everybody was off-loaded, and Captain MacNamara set about setting up the company. Its purpose was to exchange new vehicles for vehicles that had either been damaged in combat or had otherwise failed, and then to make an effort to repair the damaged vehicles that had been turned in, so they could be reissued.

MacNamara had done much the same sort of thing in France during World War II, and most of his men were skilled in performing "third-echelon maintenance" on wheeled vehicles. All he had had to do was get everything running. He felt that he was ahead of schedule. He had found a building in which, once the Engineers got him some decent electrical power, he could perform the duty assigned to the 8023d.

The first thing to do was get what he thought of as "the pool" — the vehicles he had shepherded all the way from Anniston, Alabama — up and running. Actually, that was the second thing he had to do. The first was to lay barbed wire around the pool and set up guard shacks.

There were two things Captain Mac-Namara had learned in France. One was that an unguarded pool of vehicles would disappear overnight, and the other was that if you listened to some bullshit pull-at-your-heartstrings story of why some guy really needed a vehicle, and why he didn't have a vehicle to exchange for one from the pool, the pool would disappear almost as quickly.

MacNamara believed — after some painful experiences in France — that the Army knew what it was doing when it set the policy, the very simple policy, of "something happens to the vehicle you've been issued, take it to an Ordnance or Transportation Depot, turn it in, and they'll issue you a serviceable one."

Unspoken was: "No vehicle to turn in, no new vehicle."

The reason for that was pretty obvious. If you didn't have to turn a vehicle in, every sonofabitch and his brother would show up and take a vehicle. And the problem with that was that some colonel would show up with a half-dozen wrecked or shot-up jeeps and expect to get half a dozen replacements, and when you didn't have half a dozen jeeps to give him — you'd given every vehicle to every sonofabitch who'd shown up with a hard-luck story — he would ask, "What the hell happened to your pool?"

That had happened to MacNamara in France. They'd as much as accused him of selling vehicles on the black market, and he'd had the MPs' Criminal Investigation Division following him around for months, and he'd gotten a letter of reprimand.

He often thought that letter of reprimand was the reason he had been RIF'd. Now that he was a captain again, because they needed him, he was determined not to fuck up again. Being a captain was better than being a master sergeant, and maybe, if he didn't fuck up again by passing out the Army's vehicles to people who weren't supposed to have them, they'd let him stay on as a captain when this war was over. He might even make major if he didn't fuck up.

Captain MacNamara had spent a good deal of time on the way from the States writing a Standing Operating Procedure for the company that would make it absolutely impossible for anyone who didn't have a busted-up vehicle to turn in to get one from his pool.

He was looking over the SOP when he heard the *fluckata-fluckata-fluckata* of rotor blades.

He had heard the *fluckata-fluckata-fluckata* the day before, and had gone outside and seen two enormous helicopters — he didn't know they made them that big —

flying over Inchon headed for Seoul.

He had wondered what the hell they were yesterday, and he wondered what the hell they were now.

And then he was more than a little surprised to see first that they seemed to be heading for the 8023d, and then even more surprised when the first of them, and the second, stopped fifty feet over the open area where he was going to store the turned-in vehicles, and then fluttered to the ground.

The sound of their engines died, and the rotors seemed to be slowing.

Captain MacNamara marched toward the machines, his experience telling him that the passengers on something like this were almost certainly going to be heavy brass.

He got, instead, a somewhat rumpled-looking major of the Transportation Corps.

"Good morning, sir," MacNamara said as he saluted.

"Good morning, Captain."

Then he got two more majors, who climbed down from the cockpit — one of them an Army major and the other a Marine. MacNamara saluted again.

"Captain MacNamara," he reported. "Commanding 8023d TC Company."

"You're the senior officer?" the Marine asked him.

"Yes, sir."

The major took a leather wallet from his pocket, unfolded it, and extended it for MacNamara to read. It identified the major as a field officer of the Central Intelligence Agency. It was Captain MacNamara's first contact with the CIA.

"Yes, sir?" he asked.

"Read this, please, Captain," Major McCoy said, extending a business-size envelope to him.

"Yes, sir," MacNamara said, opened the envelope, and took out a single sheet of paper. He read it.

THE WHITE HOUSE

WASHINGTON, D.C.

JULY 8TH, 1950

TO WHOM IT MAY CONCERN:

BRIGADIER GENERAL FLEMING PICKERING, USMCR, IN CONNECTION WITH HIS MISSION FOR ME, WILL TRAVEL TO SUCH PLACES AT SUCH TIMES AS HE FEELS APPROPRIATE, ACCOMPANIED BY SUCH STAFF AS HE DESIRES.

GENERAL PICKERING IS GRANTED HEREWITH A TOP-SECRET/WHITE HOUSE CLEARANCE, AND MAY, AT HIS OPTION,

---

GRANT SUCH CLEARANCE TO HIS STAFF.

U.S. MILITARY AND GOVERNMENTAL AGENCIES ARE DIRECTED TO PROVIDE GENERAL PICKERING AND HIS STAFF WITH WHATEVER SUPPORT THEY MAY REQUIRE.

Harry S Truman
HARRY S TRUMAN
PRESIDENT OF THE UNITED STATES

1ST INDORSEMENT
1 SEPTEMBER 1950

THE UNDERSIGNED DESIGNATES THE FOLLOWING MEMBERS OF MY STAFF AS FOLLOWS, WITH THE ATTENDANT SECURITY CLEARANCES AND AUTHORITY TO ACT IN MY BEHALF.

KENNETH R. MCCOY: EXECUTIVE OFFICER
ERNEST W. ZIMMERMAN: DEPUTY
  EXECUTIVE OFFICER
GEORGE F. HART, CAPT, USMCR:
  ADMINISTRATIVE OFFICER

FLEMING PICKERING
FLEMING PICKERING
BRIGADIER GENERAL, USMCR

"Jesus H. Christ!" Captain MacNamara said.

"We're going to need some vehicles," McCoy said. "And right now. Is that going to cause any problems?"

Captain MacNamara looked at the lines of vehicles in his pool, then at the signature of the President of the United States, then back at the lines of vehicles in his pool, and then at Major McCoy.

He came to attention, licked his lips, and said, "Not with orders like those. No, sir."

"Good. May I have the orders back, please? And I won't have to tell you, will I, that you are not to reveal anything connected with this?"

"No, sir," MacNamara said, and then had a second thought. "But, sir, somebody will have to sign for the vehicles."

"That's what I'm here for, Captain," Dunston said.

"Sir, could I ask you for some identification?"

"Sure," Dunston said, and handed him an Army Adjutant General's Office photo identifying him as a major, Transportation Corps.

"Thank you, sir."

[Two]
Detachment A
8119 Quartermaster Company (Forward)
Inchon, South Korea
1020 30 September 1950

Major Kenneth R. McCoy, USMCR, who was sitting beside Major Alex Donald, USA, and Major William Dunston, USA, on the floor of the cargo compartment of one of the H-19s watching Master Gunner Zimmerman supervise the loading of rations, and other items, into a GMC 6 x 6, turned to Major Dunston and asked, "Do you think we'd be pushing our luck to try to get something from over there?"

He pointed across the Quartermaster Supply Point to an eight-man squad tent, before which was a corporal with a rifle sitting on a folding chair and a small wooden sign reading, "Class VI."

Class VI supplies are supposed to have — but usually don't have — the lowest priority for shipment to a combat area. The highest priority goes to medical supplies, followed by ammunition, rations, and so on, based on the military's best judgment of what is most essential.

Class VI supplies are bottled intoxicants, such as whiskey, gin, and rum. They are not issued, but purchased with "nonappropriated funds" intended for resale to officer and noncommissioned officer clubs. They are not subject to alcohol taxes of any kind. Their sale is rigidly controlled and only to "authorized entities."

"Why not?" Major Dunston replied. "We seem to be on a roll."

Captain MacNamara had given them every vehicle they had asked for, including a tanker truck and five tank trailers, as well as enough trucks, weapons carriers, and jeeps to make both Baker Company, 5th Marines, "the aviation detachment," and the station fully mobile on the ground.

The officer in charge of the Quartermaster Supply Point had been even more dazzled than Captain MacNamara when three field-grade officers bearing orders personally signed by the President of the United States descended upon his unit in machines he had never heard of.

The men — the Marines and the Army Aviation people — in the bullet- and shrapnel-riddled hangar would that night have a hot meal prepared on field stoves, and everyone would sleep that night on a cot in a sleeping bag. The only thing they would not have was cold beer — a means of refrigeration was not available — but as Mr. Zimmerman pointed out, warm beer was far better than no beer at all.

"Mr. Zimmerman!" McCoy called out, and Zimmerman marched over to them.

"Yes, sir?"

"I'm going to need some of our discretionary funds," McCoy said.

"I saw the sign," Zimmerman said, taking an oilcloth wallet from his rear pocket. "How much do you want?"

"We don't want to be greedy," McCoy said. "Give Major Dunston two — better make it three — hundred dollars."

Zimmerman opened the wallet, took from it a packet of money labeled "$500 — Twenty-Dollar Notes," and counted off two hundred dollars.

He handed what was left to Dunston.

"That should be three hundred," he said.

"I guess I'm going to try to buy the booze?" Dunston said.

"Uh-huh," McCoy said. "And into your capable hands, Major Dunston, I entrust the entire wagon train."

"Where are you going?"

"Major Donald is going to take Mr. Zimmerman and me on a reconnaissance mission."

"I'd like to go along," Dunston said.

"I don't think all three of us should go at the same time," McCoy said. "If this flying egg beater should crash and burn with all of us on it, the entire war could well be lost."

"Indeed it could," Dunston said.

"Where are we going?" Major Donald asked.

"Not far from Suwon," McCoy said. "How well do you know the area?"

"I've flown over it. Not a hell of a lot."

"One of the things we hope to do with your aircraft, Major, is locate and pick up a shot-down Marine pilot who's down there somewhere."

"I thought the Marines did that sort of thing themselves," Donald said.

"Yes, they do," McCoy said. "But this is sort of a special case. I'll tell you about it at The House."

"The House?"

"Where we stay in Seoul," McCoy explained.

"Do you have any idea where this pilot is?" Donald asked.

"We know where he was thirty-six hours ago."

He took a map from his pocket, opened it, and pointed out the rice paddy where Pickering had last stamped out his arrow and his initials.

"Can you find that?"

Donald glanced at the map and nodded. "No problem." Then he looked at McCoy. "You think he's there?"

"He was there. He's not now."

"How do you know?"

"Because we were there," McCoy said.

"That area's not secure," Donald blurted. "The whole NK army is trying to escape through there."

"So Zimmerman told me," McCoy said.

Donald digested that a moment, then asked, "Where do you think this pilot is now?"

"I have no idea. Maybe he's heading east. Maybe we'll get lucky."

"Whatever you say," Donald said.

"Send the other helo back to Kimpo and have it put in the hangar," McCoy ordered.

"Right."

"We'll see you at the hangar, Bill," McCoy said. "And I think I should tell you this: I don't know how it is in the Army, but in the Marine Corps, officers who fail to adequately protect their Class VI supplies are castrated."

"I'll keep that in mind," Dunston said.

[Three]
Two Miles NNE of Hoengsong,
South Korea
1115 30 September 1950

Major Malcolm S. Pickering's efforts to drain the rice paddy near Yoju the previous evening so that he could stamp out his initials and the arrow had failed.

It would have been a waste of effort to try to stamp the *Here I am, for Christ's sake, come and get me* message in the dark, so he had waited until morning, hoping that the ground would still be wet and soft enough for the stamping.

The reverse proved to be true. When it grew light enough for him for see, he saw that the rice paddy was covered with water, only an inch or two deep, but covered with water.

He thought at first that he hadn't kicked away enough of the earthen dam to completely drain the water. But a quick investigation of the site showed that the paddy was a natural depression in the hillside, and the only way it could possibly be drained would be to dig a trench and empty it across the dirt path into the next-lower rice paddy.

To dig a trench like that, he quickly saw, would require a pick and shovel, and he had neither tool.

This was not the first time he'd had trouble draining a paddy. Very much the same thing had happened to him three times before. This knowledge of itself was not very comforting.

He had put the A-Frame over his shoulders and climbed up and over the crest of that hill, then worked his way eastward.

He had risen at first light, and left the

undrained paddy forty minutes later. By eleven-fifteen, he had moved, in his best guess, about ten or eleven miles. As the crow flies, about four.

He was at the crest of another hill — he hadn't counted, but he thought it was probably the fourth crest — when he heard the *fluckata-fluckata-fluckata* of a helicopter.

His first reaction was fear. It was not the *fluckata-fluckata-fluckata* of any of the three helicopters he knew — the Bell, Hiller, and Sikorsky aircraft — all small two-man machines. This *fluckata-fluckata-fluckata* was louder, heavier, and *different*.

Since so far as he knew the only U.S. helicopters in Korea were those assigned to the 1st Marine Air Wing, and they were Bells, logic dictated that the aircraft making this *fluckata-fluckata-fluckata* were not American. It was entirely possible, he thought after a minute, that in the nine thousand years since he had been shot down, the Army or the Air Force had finally gotten its act in gear and gotten some of their own helicopters to Korea, and this was what he was hearing.

But then he thought that the only place the Army could get helicopters was from Bell or Hiller . . .

He recalled then that the Navy had some helos to pick aviators from the drink if they missed a carrier landing or takeoff — he'd actually seen them while practicing carrier takeoffs and recovery off San Diego — but when he thought about that, he remembered the *fluckata-fluckata-fluckata* they'd made, and it wasn't the *fluckata-fluckata-fluckata* he was hearing now.

. . . and he knew the *fluckata-fluckata-fluckata* he was hearing now wasn't coming from a Bell or a Hiller, so it had to be made by something else. Like a *Russian* helicopter. The Russians had helicopters. Hell, the Russians had invented helicopters. Both Sikorsky and Piasecki were Russians before they came to the States.

What he needed was a cave to hide in.

There being no convenient caves, he did the next best thing. He put his back against the earthen wall of a rice paddy, then held the A-Frame over him. It would, he believed, break his human figure outline, shade his face from the sun, and make him difficult to see from the air.

The *fluckata-fluckata-fluckata* grew louder. Pickering pushed the A-Frame away from his head and glanced skyward, trying to get a look at it.

Where the hell is it? Jesus Christ, it sounds like it's right here!

He leaned his neck back as far as it would go, just in time to see the shiny olive-drab fuselage of an enormous helicopter — the largest he had ever seen — hanging beneath an enormous rotor cone flash — *fluckata-fluckata-fluckata-fluckata-fluckata-fluckata* — not more than 100 feet over him. It headed down the hill, then turned to the left.

Pickering could see U.S. ARMY painted in large letters on the fuselage.

The helicopter turned right, rose above the crest of the next hill, and then dropped out of sight below it.

He waited for a long time to see — *Please, God!* — if it would reappear again, and maybe turn around and come back.

It didn't.

[Four]
Headquarters, First Marine Division
Seoul, South Korea
1225 30 September 1950

Master Gunnery Sergeant Allan J. Macey, USMC, who looked very much like Master Gunner Ernest W. Zimmerman, backed through the canvas flap that served as the door to the office of Major General Oliver P. Smith, Commanding 1st MarDiv. He held a stainless-steel food tray and a mess kit set of spoon, knife, and fork in each hand.

"Chow, sir," he announced. "Salisbury

steak, for a real treat."

He laid the trays on a simple wooden picnic-type table.

"I'll get the coffee, sir," Gunny Macey said, and looked at General Smith's luncheon guest. "Canned cow and sugar, General?"

"No, thanks," Major General Ralph Howe, NGUS, said. "Black's fine. You'll take care of Sergeant Rogers, right?"

"We old men have to stick together, General," Macey said.

"I apologize for the scarcity of the fare, General," Smith said.

"I'm an old infantryman General," Howe said. "If it's warm and served inside, that's all I ask, and I'm grateful to get it."

Smith smiled and grunted. He waved Howe to a seat at the table.

"So what can I do for you today, General?" Smith asked.

"General Almond told me an hour ago about MacArthur's plan to move the division by sea to Wonsan as soon as Eighth Army cleans up the peninsula as far as Seoul," Howe said.

Smith grunted again and said nothing.

"That was in the nature of a question, General," Howe pursued.

Gunny Lacey came back through the flap with a white china mug of coffee in one hand and a canteen cup of coffee in the other. He set the mug before Howe and the canteen cup before Smith and then left.

"Why do I think he gave me your mug?" Howe asked, and reached for the canteen cup.

"That's his mug," Smith said. "I broke mine. I guess he likes you."

"I've got a couple of spares in the jeep," Howe said. "You can have them."

"Thanks, but no thanks. I would be very surprised if Macey didn't have me one by supper. Probably before."

"You're welcome to them," Howe said, shrugging.

"What you're asking, General, is what do I think of the idea."

"That's what I'm here for."

"I'm a Marine. Marines go where they're ordered, and fight whomever they're ordered to fight," Smith said.

"In other words, you think it's a dumb idea," Howe said.

"Your words, General, not mine."

"Whatever you tell me will go to no one but the President," Howe said. "No. The President and General Pickering. We have an arrangement to share information."

"Did they find his boy?"

"They think he's still alive, somewhere around Suwon," Howe said.

"That has to be tough for him."

"It is."

"Is there anything I can do to help?"

"If there were, I'd ask. You know Major McCoy?"

"Killer McCoy? I've met him a couple of times. Is he in charge of finding Pickering's son?"

Howe nodded. "And I think if anybody can get young Pickering back, McCoy can," he said.

Smith grunted.

"In terrain like that of northeast Korea, General," Smith said, "cohesion of your forces is critical. You can't string them out, and, worse, you can't outrun your logistics."

"I know. I had a division in Italy. It's hard to get ammunition — not to mention hot rations — up the side of a mountain in a snowstorm."

"So, I understand General Almond had a division in Italy," Smith said. "And in the presumption that General Almond learned what you did there, and will not issue orders requiring me to separate elements of the division, or order me to move so far or so fast that my ration and ammo trains will be strained, I have no objection to the Marines going ashore at Wonsan. Or anywhere else they think we can do the job."

"Thank you," Howe said. "That will not go further than Pickering and the President."

"God, I hate canned peaches," Smith said, holding a peach half aloft on his fork.

"I hate to admit this, but I'm getting to like the Salisbury steak," Howe said.

"You've been here too long, General," Smith said, chuckling.

"You ever see McCoy?" Smith asked.

"Frequently."

"When you see him, ask him, please — tell him I told you to ask — what, if anything, I can do to help him."

"I will, of course, but he will say, 'Thank you, sir, I have everything I need.' "

Smith looked at him for a moment. "Why do I think something went unsaid, General?" he asked.

"General, does Baker Company, 5th Marines, ring a bell?" Howe asked.

"Yes. They're the people who were the reserve for the clandestine operation on the Flying Fish Channel Islands."

"They're now at K-16, guarding a couple of secret Army helicopters."

"Secret Army helicopters?" Smith parroted incredulously. "Almond asked me if he could have them for a couple of days. I said, 'Yes, sir.' I didn't know what they would be doing."

"McCoy doesn't have enough people," Howe said.

"Is that what he's doing now, guarding secret Army helicopters?"

"I meant for his intelligence activities, and looking for Major Pickering."

"He tell you that?"

"That's my opinion."

"And he asked for these people?"

"No."

Smith grunted, then raised his voice. "Gunny!"

Master Gunnery Sergeant Macey came through the canvas flap.

"Sir?"

"Baker Company, 5th Marines," Smith said.

"They're in Division Special Reserve, sir. They're the people who were detached when we left the Perimeter —"

"I know," Smith cut him off. "Tell the G-3 they are to remain in Special Reserve until released by me, personally."

"Aye, aye, sir."

"And send a messenger to the company commander . . . Where did you say they were, General Howe?"

"In a hangar across from base operations at K-16," Howe furnished.

". . . that, until further orders from me to the contrary, he will take his orders from Major McCoy. He knows who he is."

"Aye, aye, sir."

[Five]
The House
Seoul, South Korea
1625 30 September 1950

Major Alex Donald, who was in the act of extending his hand to take a crystal whiskey glass full of beer from a tray extended to him by a middle-aged Korean woman, was surprised when Majors McCoy and Dunston, Master Gunner Zimmerman, and Technical Sergeant Jennings suddenly rose to their feet and stood to attention as military men do when a senior officer suddenly appears.

This — "mansion" was the only word that fit — did not seem to be a bastion of the fine points of military courtesy and the customs of the service. And neither did its inhabitants. Technical sergeants do not normally sit around drinking with officers.

He took the glass of beer, then glanced at the door. A graying master sergeant in fatigues was coming through it. Then another man in fatigues came through, and there were two silver stars on each of his collar points.

Donald popped somewhat awkwardly to attention, the glass of beer in his hand.

"Stand at ease, gentlemen," General Ralph Howe said. He smiled and added:

"We'd hoped to arrive at the cocktail hour."

"Or at least before you drank everything," Master Sergeant Charley Rogers said.

He smiled at the Korean woman and held up two fingers. She bowed and left the room.

Howe looked curiously at Major Donald.

"General, this is Major Donald," McCoy said.

"I think we've met, haven't we, Major?" Howe asked.

"Yes, sir," Donald said. "Yesterday, at Kimpo."

"Right," Howe said, as if remembering. "You're the man with the new helicopters."

"Yes, sir."

Howe looked at McCoy for an explanation.

"General," McCoy said, "those helicopters — and Major Donald and his people — have been assigned to us."

Howe pursed his lips thoughtfully.

"Interesting," he said. He looked at Donald. "How did that happen?"

Donald looked at McCoy, remembering what McCoy had said about telling anyone anything.

"You can tell General Howe, Donald. You can — and you'd better — answer anything and everything he asks.'"

"Sir, at Kimpo, General Almond told me that, at the direction of General MacArthur, the helicopters and everyone associated with them were transferred to Major McCoy."

"He said, 'Transferred to Major McCoy'?"

"No, sir," Donald said. "He said the CIA. And that someone would contact me with further orders. And then Major McCoy, and these other officers, came to Kimpo."

"But he didn't say 'to Major McCoy'?"

"No, sir. I misspoke. General Almond said 'to the CIA.' "

"Interesting," Howe said. "I wonder what General MacArthur had in mind. You know anything about this, Ken? Dunston?"

Dunston said, "No, sir."

McCoy said, "Not a hint, sir."

"I presume by now, Major," Howe said to Donald, "that you have received from Major McCoy, or Major Dunston, the speech about what happens to people who talk too much?"

"Yes, sir, I have."

The Korean woman came back into the room with two crystal whiskey glasses of beer. Howe took one and raised it to Donald.

"Well, in that case, Major, welcome to the CIA and McCoy's private army."

"Yes, sir. Thank you, sir."

Howe and Master Sergeant Charley Rogers exchanged glances, and both thought just about the same thing: *Good. McCoy has no idea that it was arranged by Major General Ralph Howe, NGUS.*

"Can you use these aircraft, Ken?" Howe asked. "Have you given that any thought?"

"We already have, General," Zimmerman said happily. "We made a very successful raid on supply depots at Inchon in them."

McCoy flashed him a dirty look.

"And then we went looking for Pickering," McCoy said.

"Oh? How did that go?"

"We didn't find him, or any sign of him, but if we had had these helos just a week ago, I think we'd have him back. They're going to be very useful. I've already got some other ideas. Actually, sir, that's what we were about to get into when you came in. We just got back."

"I'd like to sit in on that," Howe said. "But before you get started, two important things. I've got to get a message off. General Almond told me MacArthur ordered him to reembark X Corps 'as soon as possible after Eighth Army makes it up the peninsula to Seoul.' He wants to land them on the East Coast, probably at Wonsan, and cut off the North Korean retreat northward." He paused. "I want to make sure the President knows about that."

"Sir, wouldn't General Pickering have heard about that, and sent that intel?"

"I don't know if he knows, Ken, and it's better not to assume that he does. I presume you know he's on his way to Washington?"

"No, sir, I didn't," McCoy said, and looked at Dunston, who shook his head no.

"Give Charley time to get that message off, and for the both of us to have a shower, and then we can talk about how you're planning to use the helicopters."

"Yes, sir," McCoy said.

Everyone was sitting around the table waiting for Master Sergeant Rogers to finish his shower when the Korean woman who was in charge of the radio room came in and handed McCoy a sheet of typewriter paper.

He read it, then slid it across the table to General Howe.

"From Billy Dunn," he explained to the others. "No sign, either visual or from aerial photographs, of our wanderer."

"Which does not mean he's not out there, right?" Howe said.

"No, sir, it doesn't."

"And, from what you've seen, these helicopters MacArthur gave you are going to be useful in getting him back?"

"Absolutely, sir."

Master Sergeant Rogers came into the room.

"Sorry to keep you waiting, but I thought that was important enough to wait for an acknowledgment."

"And you got one?" Howe asked.

"Keller must have been sitting on his radio," Rogers said. "He acknowledged, told us to Hold One, and then sent, 'I have acknowledgment from Camp Pendleton.' "

"Good man, Charley," Howe said. "And I'm sure Colonel Banning will make sure General Pickering sees it before he leaves the coast for Washington."

He turned to McCoy.

"Okay, Ken, tell us how you're going to use General MacArthur's helicopters."

"Aside from looking for Pickering, the first thing that comes to mind is using them to insert and extract people behind the NK lines. Maybe even other places, too. . . ."

When he sensed Howe was about to say something, McCoy stopped. Howe paused, his mouth open, and then said nothing.

". . . But before I can start seriously thinking about any of this, there's a lot I have to know."

"For example?" Howe asked.

McCoy looked at Donald.

"What should I call you? Donald or Alex?"

"Either's fine."

"My name is Ken," McCoy said. "Dunston's is Bill."

"Okay," Donald said.

"Let me give you the problem, and then you give me the solution."

"Okay."

"When the helos first came to K-16, I presume they went through the same kind of radio chatter — 'Kimpo, this is Army six six six or whatever, request landing instructions,' et cetera — that you went through when you brought us back?"

"Yes, they did."

"We have to presume NK agents saw the helos flying over Inchon to come here. And it's a given that somewhere within range of the Kimpo tower is an NK agent with a radio. So they heard that radio chatter. So they now know there are two H-19s in Korea. And didn't you give them a number?"

"What they call the 'tail number,' " Donald said. "You use that to identify yourself when you call the tower."

"And when the other chopper went back to Kimpo, alone, he used his tail number?"

Donald nodded.

"So now they know we have two helos, and even know their tail numbers." He paused, smiled, and went on: "What all the secrecy, all the Marines guarding the hangar, has done is keep the H-19s a secret from everybody but the enemy."

"That's a problem, Ken?" Howe asked. "What's the difference? The enemy will see them eventually."

"Yes, sir. But if we're going to use the helos to insert and extract agents across the line, I don't want to telegraph our intentions. They now know we have helos. They'll figure out in a hurry that we're using them to do the insertions and extractions. That's not a problem. The problem is if we have to go on the radio every time we take off, that's when they'll start looking for helicopters."

"I get it."

"Another thing I don't know is when General Pickering is coming back here," McCoy said. "Can you tell me, sir?"

"All I know is that he was sent for," Howe said. "What do you need from him?"

"I was going to ask him to ask General Smith if we could keep at least some of the Flying Fish Marines," McCoy said. "They're at the hangar with the helos. General Almond had them guarding them."

"I saw them," General Howe said.

He exchanged glances with Master Sergeant Rogers, who knew about his luncheon conversation with General Smith.

"Would you like me to ask General Smith for those men, Ken? To at least loan them to you for a while?"

"I hate to ask you to do that, sir. And for all I know, the 1st MarDiv may need them."

"All he can say is no," Howe said. "I'll ask him when I see him in the morning."

"If you think it would be all right, sir."

"I have a feeling it will be," Howe said. "Okay, Ken. Presuming you can keep the Flying Fish Channel Marines for a while, what are you going to do with them?"

"These helos are supposed to be able to carry ten men. That would be twelve, if we got rid of the copilot and the crew chief. I figure that's about the same weight as a pretty heavily armed eight-man fire team. I'd like to train maybe six or eight teams to get carried somewhere — for example, if we find Pick, or to pick up an agent the NKs have discovered on their side of the line."

"You think that can be done?"

"We won't know until we try it, sir."

"It sounds like a pretty good idea to me."

"That still leaves us with the problem of how to get the helos into the air without going on the radio and announcing, 'Here we come.' "

"Is there any way, Major," Howe asked Donald, "not to use the radios?"

"Not on an airfield, sir. It's a question of being clear to land or take off — I mean, so there's no midair collisions."

"You'd need, in other words, your own airfield?" Howe asked.

"Where would we get our own airfield?" McCoy asked.

"Killer," Zimmerman said. "You don't need an airfield for these things. You saw where we landed at Inchon. All we need is a good-sized parking lot, far enough away from an airfield so airplanes don't run into them."

"He's right, McCoy," Donald said.

"Okay. Shoot this down, please," McCoy said. "We find a large enough parking lot someplace, preferably with a building we can hide the helos in in the daytime —"

"You get me some canvas and some camouflage netting, and I'll hide them," Zimmerman said.

"— Okay. And we paint them black, so they can't be seen at night."

"Black or not, they make a hell of a racket," Zimmerman said.

"But they would be harder to see," McCoy said.

It was not an argument, Major Donald

understood. The almost new, very expensive, glossy olive-drab paint scheme on the H-19s was about to be covered with flat black paint.

"What do we do now?" Zimmerman asked. "Start looking for a parking lot?"

"That would seem logical, Mr. Zimmerman," McCoy said, lightly sarcastic.

"It would be easier if we knew where to look for a parking lot."

"Ken, do you know Socho-Ri?" Dunston asked.

McCoy shook his head no.

"It's on the east coast, close to the 38th Parallel," Dunston went on.

"And?" McCoy asked.

Dunston looked at Donald. It was obvious that he was deciding whether to go on in the presence of someone who was not in the CIA.

McCoy picked up on this.

"He has to know, Bill," he said.

"Before the war, I used it as a base for the *Wind of Good Fortune*," Dunston said. "There is — *was* — a dozen or so thatch-roofed hootches and sort of a wharf, and a —"

"I don't understand," Donald said, and parroted, "Wind of good fortune?"

"You don't know what's there now?" McCoy asked, ignoring Donald's question, and then, before Dunston could reply, asked, "Is there room for the helos?"

"I had them clear a landing strip for an L-19," Dunston said, "to take the wounded out if necessary. I never had to use it. And when the war started, the NKs were there before I could get an L-19 or anything else over there to try to evacuate them. I lost some good men there."

"And you don't know what's there now?"

"I'm not even sure the ROKs have gone that far north yet," Dunston said.

"But there was a landing strip?" Zimmerman said, and went on without waiting for a response. "If there was a landing strip, there's room to operate helos."

"I think we should have a look at this place as soon as we can," McCoy said. He turned to Donald. "Two questions. I don't want to use helos if I don't really have to. So, Question One: What's the chances — without calling a lot of attention to it — of getting an L-19 from the X Corps Air Section long enough for us to fly over there? Question Two: If you had an L-19, could you find Socho-Ri if Dunston marked it on a map?"

"I think we could get an L-19 without any trouble, particularly if you showed Colonel Jamison, the X Corps Army Aviation officer, your credentials," Donald said. "And sure, I could find it using a map."

"I noticed, Major," General Howe said, "that you said, 'We could get an L-19.' That's the attitude Major McCoy needs from you. Whether you like it or not, you're part of this now."

"Yes, sir," Donald said.

"Maybe, with a little bit of luck, we could do that at first light," McCoy said. "And maybe we can get around flashing credentials at this colonel."

"Maybe we can," Donald said.

"Where's the X Corps airstrip?" McCoy asked.

"At what used to be the Seoul race-track," Donald said.

"Jennings, how are we fixed for black paint?" McCoy said.

"There must be fifty gallons of it, sir, over the garage. There's also some white, and some red. I guess the NKs missed it when they were here."

"Or booby-trapped it," McCoy said. "After supper, I want you to load twenty gallons of paint, a generator, and the spray gun in a weapons carrier. Take it to the hangar. What I'm going to do is drive Major Donald over there so that he can tell them the helos will be painted, and then bring him back here so that we can get an early start in the morning. Any problem with that, Donald?"

"None," Donald said.

"I wonder, Bill," McCoy said, "how much the X Corps G-2 and/or G-3 would know about how far the South Koreans have moved up the east coast?"

"Probably very little," Dunston said. "The impression I get is that Eighth Army doesn't talk to X Corps unless absolutely necessary, and vice versa."

"Well, give it a shot anyway, will you? Maybe we'll get lucky. We really need to know where they are."

"I'll go to the X Corps CP after supper," Dunston said.

[Six]
The House
Seoul, South Korea
2105 30 September 1950

"Dunston's back from the X Corps CP," Major Kenneth R. McCoy announced unnecessarily to Major Alex Donald as they pulled up to the front of the house in the Russian jeep.

They found him and Zimmerman sitting at the dining room table. Dunston was bent over a stereoptical viewing device looking at an aerial photograph. Zimmerman was flipping through a three-inch-high stack of ten-by-ten-inch aerials on the table.

Dunston raised his eyes from the device as McCoy and Donald came into the room.

"These are yesterday's Air Force aerials," he said. "I got them just before the X Corps G-2 was going to burn them."

"They wouldn't give you today's?" McCoy asked.

"No. And they have no idea what, if any, South Korean troops are in this area. The last word — yesterday — was that 'lead elements' of I ROK* Corps — probably the Capital ROK Division — were about ten miles south. They may have moved that far today, but even if they have, I don't think they went into Socho-Ri."

"Why not?" McCoy asked.

Dunston got out of his chair and waved McCoy into it.

McCoy sat down and bent over the device, which functioned on the same principle as the disposable glasses given to 3-D motion picture patrons. There were two lenses mounted on a wire frame. They provided a three-dimensional view of a photograph placed under it.

McCoy saw what looked like eighteen or twenty burned-out stone Korean houses, their thatch roofs gone.

*Republic of (South) Korea — ROK — Corps were numbered, like U.S. Army Corps, with Roman numerals.

"What am I looking at?" he asked, raising his head.

"That's Socho-Ri," Dunston said. "It's obviously been torched. We don't know when or by whom. My people could have torched it right after the invasion. Or the NKs may have torched it then, or two days ago."

McCoy got out of the chair and motioned Donald into it.

"Okay," McCoy said. "Tell me about this place."

"In the first part of 1949, I realized I needed a base for the *Wind of Good Fortune . . .*" Dunston began.

Without raising his eyes from the viewing device, Donald asked, "Can I ask what that is?"

"It's our navy, Major," Zimmerman said.

McCoy chuckled, then explained: "It looks like your typical, ordinary junk. You know. High prow and stern, one mast, with a square sail that's raised and lowered like a venetian blind."

"Okay," Donald said. "What do you use it for? Can I ask?"

"To insert and extract agents in North Korea," Dunston said.

"You did that with a *junk?*" Donald asked incredulously.

"I said the *Wind of Good Fortune* looks like a typical junk," McCoy said. "But she was prepared for the smuggling trade by some very good shipwrights in Macao. You know, near Hong Kong?"

Donald nodded.

"How prepared?" he asked.

"*Wind of Good Fortune* has a two-hundred-horse Caterpillar diesel, and fuel tanks therefore in her holds," McCoy said. "And some basic, but pretty reliable, radio direction finder equipment. She'll make thirteen, fourteen knots, even with her sail acting as a windbreak."

"Sound like something out of *Terry and the Pirates*," Donald said, referring to Milton Caniff's popular comic strip.

"Why Socho-Ri?" McCoy asked. "Why there?"

Dunston went to the stack of aerials, searched through them, and slipped one under the viewing device.

"For several reasons," he said. "For one thing, it's tiny. For another, it's about fifteen miles south of the 38th Parallel. Highway Five runs up to the border, but — since it had nowhere to go beyond the border — the closer it got to the border it was less traveled and not maintained. And even better, between the highway and the shoreline" — he took a pencil and used it as a pointer on the aerial — "there's this line of hills. You can't tell from the aerial, but they're (a) too steep-sided to build rice paddies on them and (b) from 100 to 200 feet high, so that you can't see the village from Highway 5."

McCoy touched Donald's shoulder. Donald moved his head out of the way, and McCoy studied the aerial.

"I'm surprised I don't see much of a road," he said.

"We didn't use the road — actually just a path — unless we had to. We supplied the place using the *Wind of Good Fortune*."

"Okay," McCoy said.

"When I found Socho-Ri," Dunston went on, "there were about a dozen fishermen and their families in the village. They (a) not only hated the North Koreans but (b) were delighted to find someone willing to buy their dried fish from them, and at a better price than they had been able to get after having to take it by oxcart south to Kangnung, the closest 'city,' thirty miles to the south.

"So I hired the fishermen to build four more stone, thatch-roofed houses, and to repair the existing, fallen-into-repair-because-their-small-boats-didn't-need-it wharf so the *Wind of Good Fortune* could tie up to it," Dunston went on. "And then went to work."

"How did it work?" McCoy asked.

"The *Wind of Good Fortune* called on Socho-Ri on an irregular basis. Sometimes once a week, sometimes twice, sometimes not for two weeks. She sailed into Socho-Ri late in the afternoon, unloaded rice, live chickens, the occasional porker, and started taking aboard dried fish. And, at first light the next morning, sailed away."

"And during the night . . ." McCoy began admiringly.

Dunston smiled.

"We fired up her diesels and did our business up north. Always being careful to be back at Socho-Ri before dawn."

"And you never got caught?" Zimmerman asked.

"Honestly, Zimmerman, I don't think they suspected a thing," Dunston said. "Not even when we built the new buildings. They were visible from the sea."

"And used for what?" Donald asked.

"They housed a diesel generator, radios, weapons, and a detachment of from four to six agents."

"And what do you see when you look at these aerials?" McCoy asked.

"Twenty burned-out hootches, and no people," Dunston said.

"Alex," McCoy asked. "Are these aerials going to help you find this place?"

"Oh, sure."

"Well, then, I guess we'll find out what happened at Socho-Ri in the morning, won't we?" McCoy said.

[Seven]
Near Socho-Ri, South Korea
0805 1 October 1950

The view afforded the observer — Major Kenneth R. McCoy, USMCR — in the backseat of the high-winged, two-place, single-engine L-19 was all that could be asked for. But despite looking very carefully, and twice making the pilot — Major Alex Donald, USA — turn around for a better, lower-level look, McCoy didn't see any sign of Major Malcolm S. Pickering, USMCR, in the one hour and twenty minutes it took them to fly from the Municipal Race Track in Seoul to the east coast just above Kangnung.

There, north of the city on Highway 5, they could look down on what were apparently elements of the South Korean army, but attempts to make radio contact with what they saw failed, and there didn't seem to be a place where Donald could safely land the airplane.

They flew north.

"There it is," Donald said, pointing.

"Can you land there?" McCoy asked.

"I'll make a couple of passes and see," Donald said. "But I have to tell you, when we leave, we're going to have to fly straight back to Seoul. We have less than half fuel."

"Okay."

Alex made two low-level passes over the tiny village, then turned a final time and touched down smoothly on a narrow, half-sand, half-grassed field.

McCoy raised the side window of the L-19, then opened the door, got out, and reached back inside and came out with a Thompson submachine gun. Then he waited for Donald to get out.

Donald nodded at the Thompson.

"If we're going to be doing more of this sort of thing, I'd be more comfortable if I had one of those."

"Can you shoot one?"

"I had, you know, familiarization."

"I'll have Jennings get you an automatic carbine," McCoy said. "Thompsons are a lot harder to shoot than it seems in the movies."

He started walking toward the burned-out hootches.

Before they reached it, there was the smell of putrefying flesh, and then they came across the first, near-skeletal body.

"Jesus Christ!" Donald exclaimed, fighting back nausea.

McCoy didn't reply.

He walked into the village, where there were more bodies, including three with their hands tied behind them.

"Jesus, what happened here?" Donald asked.

"If I had to guess, I would guess that a

North Korean patrol, covering the flanks, or maybe just coming down the coastline, came here, found something — the generator, the radios, anything — that suggested these people had some government connection."

"You mean, they knew what this place was used for?"

"No. I mean they thought it was a government outpost of some sort. So, to make everybody understand the rules of the liberation, they shot everybody they could find, then burned the place down."

"And didn't bury the bodies."

"They may not have had the time," McCoy said, "or there may have been a political officer who decided that rotting bodies would really send the message he wanted to send."

Donald blurted what he was thinking. "You don't seem overly upset about this."

"Alex, you have no idea how close I am to tossing my cookies," McCoy said. "Let's get the fuck out of here!"

They trotted back to the L-19.

[Eight]
Near Seoul, South Korea
0935 1 October 1950

McCoy pressed the black button on his microphone and asked Donald, "Is there some reason we can't land at Kimpo, K-16?"

"No. You want to go to the hangar?"

"I've just decided I'm going to use some of the Marines there before they take them away from me," McCoy said.

"I thought the general said he was going to speak to the CG of the Marine Division about them."

"He did. And the 1st MarDiv CG may say, 'Not only no, but hell no.' Take us to the hangar."

"Captain," Major McCoy said to Captain Howard C. Dunwood, USMCR, as they stood outside the hangar, "I don't know what, if any, authority I have over you and your Marines, but —"

"Sir, I can answer that question."

"Okay, Captain, answer it."

"There was a captain from 1st MarDiv G-3 here yesterday, sir. He said my orders, until I hear to the contrary, are to take my orders from you."

"Yesterday, you said? Not today?"

"Late yesterday afternoon, sir."

"Never look a gift horse in the mouth, Captain. Write that down."

Dunwood smiled.

"Aye, aye, sir."

"There's a tiny fishing village on the east coast called Socho-Ri. I want you to leave enough men here to keep the curious away from the helos, and make for this village with the rest. Take everything with you we got from the dumps. Don't take any chances. If you run into North Koreans, turn around and run. Getting to this village is the priority. By the time you're loaded up, Master Gunner Zimmerman will be here. He'll have maps, radios, et cetera."

"Yes, sir."

"When you get to the village, clean it up — there's bodies all over it. Find someplace to bury them, and do what you can to collect identification, et cetera."

"Aye, aye, sir."

"Then set up a perimeter guard, and stay there. I'll be in touch."

"Can I ask what this is all about, Major?"

"Not yet. I'll tell you when I can."

"Aye, aye, sir."

VII

San Francisco International Airport
San Francisco, California
1145 3 October 1950

Two cars, a black Chevrolet with the insignia of the U.S. Immigration and Naturalization Service painted on its doors and a black Lincoln limousine bearing the California license plate US SEN 1, followed a Ford truck with stairs mounted in back toward the *City of Los Angeles* as the aircraft shut down its engines.

An INS officer and an officer from the Bureau of Customs got out of the Chevrolet, and a Marine colonel got out of the limousine. As soon as the stairs had been put in place against the Constellation and the rear door had been opened, they all went up the stairs.

They found Brigadier General Fleming Pickering in seat 1-A.

"That's all the hell I need," Pickering said to the Marine colonel as he put out his hand, "a full bull colonel of the Regular Marine Corps to look askance at my appearance."

308

Two hours into the final Honolulu–San Francisco leg of his flight, as he was having his breakfast, there was unexpected turbulence, and the front of his uniform jacket still showed — despite the frenzied, even valiant efforts of two stewardi — the remnants of most of a cup of coffee, a half-glass of tomato juice, and two poached eggs.

"You look shipshape to me, General," Colonel Edward J. Banning, an erect, stocky, six-foot-tall, 200-pound forty-five-year-old, said with a straight face.

Pickering snorted, then asked, "What's going on here, Ed? Isn't that Senator Fowler's car?"

"Yes, sir, it is."

"Fowler's car? Or Fowler himself?" Pickering asked.

"Senator Fowler himself, General."

"What the hell does he want?" Pickering asked rhetorically.

"General," the customs officer said, extending a printed form to him. "If you'll just sign this, sir, it will complete the Customs and Immigration procedure."

Pickering scrawled his signature on the form and handed it and the pen back to the customs officer.

"What about our luggage?" Pickering asked, looking at Banning.

"It'll be off-loaded first, sir. While you're still on the tarmac."

"Well, at least that will limit the number of people who'll get a look at this," Pickering said, gesturing with both hands toward the mess on his tunic. "Let's go, George."

"Had a little accident, did you, sir?" the INS officer asked sympathetically.

" 'Little' isn't the word," Pickering said sharply, and then added: "But it certainly wasn't your fault. I didn't mean to snap at you."

The INS officer raised both hands, palms outward, indicating the apology wasn't necessary, then stepped out of the way so Hart and Pickering could precede him off the airplane.

Fred Delmore, a tall, gray-haired black man who had been Senator Fowler's chauffeur for twenty years, had the rear door of the limousine open before Pickering reached it. Pickering motioned for Banning to get in first, then followed him. Hart ran around and got in the front passenger seat.

Senator Richardson K. Fowler, a tall, silver-haired, regal-looking sixty-seven-year-old, was sitting on the right side. He and Pickering looked at each other but didn't speak for a moment.

"I was just wondering, Flem," the senator said finally, "if you'd had your breakfast. I suppose I have the answer before me."

"Fuck you, Dick," General Pickering said.

"My, we are back in the Marines, aren't we?" Fowler said. "Such language!"

"Fuck you twice, Dick," Pickering said.

"Is he always this way, George?" Fowler asked innocently. "Or has he been at the booze?"

"Not yet," Pickering replied. "To what do I owe this dubious honor, Dick?"

Fowler shook his head in resignation and smiled.

"As a courtesy, one of Truman's people called to tell me you were on your way, and when, but that they doubted there would be time to meet, as you were to be immediately transferred to Travis Air Force Base for your trip to Washington. An Air Force plane —"

"Not that again," Pickering interrupted.

"Not what again?"

"The last time he sent for me, I flew across the country in the backseat of an Air Force jet."

"Oh, yes, I remember. Today, I understand, we will travel in a backup airplane — one of the big Douglases — to the *Independence*."

"*We* will travel?"

"*We*. I invited myself to go with you. I thought you might need some moral support. As I was saying, your aircraft awaits at Travis."

"Sir," Colonel Banning said, "if I may interrupt, I think you'd better take a look at this."

He handed Pickering a sealed, business-size envelope.

Pickering opened the envelope, read the message it contained, and then handed it to Hart.

"That's already in Washington, sir," Banning said.

Hart put the message back in the envelope and handed it back to Banning, who put it carefully into his hip pocket.

"I suppose what that is is none of my business," Senator Fowler said.

"Dick, you're putting me on a spot," Pickering said.

"And what the hell, I'm only a United States Senator, right?"

"Let him see it, Ed," Pickering ordered.

Banning handed Fowler the envelope.

"That's from General Howe to Truman," Pickering said. "MacArthur plans to reembark X Corps and reland it far up the east coast."

"I know you won't believe this, Fleming, but I do know how to read," Fowler said as he took the message from the envelope.

He read it, put in back in the envelope, and handed it to Banning.

"Thank you, Colonel," Fowler said, then

turned to Pickering. "What's the significance of that?"

"I think Howe wants the President to know MacArthur may take his time 'advising' the Joint Chiefs of his intentions," Pickering said. "They have a tendency to want to take time to consider things carefully, and MacArthur (a) likes to strike when the iron is hot and (b) does not like the idea of having to ask permission to do something in 'his' war."

"And whose side are you on?"

"The Joint Chiefs were the opposite of enthusiastic about the landing at Inchon. MacArthur is difficult, but he's one hell of a general."

There was the sound of the trunk slamming.

"That's the luggage, sir," Hart said.

"Okay, Fred," Senator Fowler said. "Travis Air Force Base."

"No, Fred," Pickering said. "Take us to the San Franciscan."

He turned to Fowler. "That'll just have to wait. I need a bath, George needs a bath, and, as you were so kind to point out, I need a clean uniform."

"You don't think it behooves you to instantly comply with an order from your Commander-in-Chief?"

"Fuck you yet again, Dick," Pickering said. "A whole cup of coffee went down

313

my front. . . ."

"And some tomato juice," Hart offered helpfully from the front seat.

Pickering pointed a threatening finger at Hart.

"The San Franciscan, please, Fred," Pickering ordered.

Fowler nodded. The limousine started to move.

"What's the President want from me, anyway, Dick?" Pickering asked. "What's this all about?"

"I think he's going to offer you the CIA," Fowler said. "Actually, I'm pretty positive he will."

"Well, we can handle that with a telephone call," Pickering said. "I don't want the CIA."

"I don't think 'No, thank you' is one of your options," Fowler said. "What I can probably help you to do is get some concessions vis-à-vis what you'll do with it, what your authority will be, when you get it."

Pickering looked at him thoughtfully for a moment, then said, "That's another reason I'm not going to jump on another airplane right now. We're going to have to talk about this, Dick."

Fowler nodded.

"Thank you," Pickering said.

Fowler nodded again.

[Two]
The Penthouse
The Foster San Franciscan Hotel
Nob Hill, San Francisco, California
1250 3 October 1950

The husband of the chairwoman of the board of the Foster Hotel Corporation entered the Foster San Franciscan Hotel through the rear basement door normally used to remove garbage from the kitchen, and rode to what for tax purposes was known as "The Foster Hotel Corporation Executive Conference Center" in the service elevator.

There was a large conference room in what everyone called "The Penthouse," and two or three times a year it was actually used for that purpose. With that exception, however, The Penthouse was *de facto* the Pickering's San Francisco apartment.

Pickering started to get out of his soiled uniform the moment he stepped off the service elevator into the kitchen. He was trailed by Hart — carrying their two ValvPaks — and Fowler and Banning.

Pickering laid his tunic on the kitchen table and started to untie his necktie.

"George," he said, turning to Hart, "in this order. Get on the horn and call Travis Air Force Base and tell them we'll be delayed, probably overnight."

"Aye, aye, sir."

"Then get on the house phone and tell the manager we have urgent need of the valet, coffee, and some lunch. . . ."

"Aye, aye, sir."

"And then get on the horn to P&FE, ask for Mr. Kensington — he handles transportation — and tell him I said to get you on the next plane to Saint Louis. Call me at the Lafayette in Washington tomorrow night, and I'll let you know how long you can stay."

"No, sir," Hart said. "Thank you, sir, but no thank you."

"Excuse me?"

"I don't want to go home, sir. I can't."

"Why the hell not?"

"I wouldn't be able to look any of the families of my Marines in the face," Hart said.

"What the hell is he talking about, Ed?" Pickering demanded of Colonel Banning.

"I think I know, sir. This has to do with disestablishment of your company, right, George?"

"Yes, sir," Hart said.

"What the hell are *you* talking about?" Pickering demanded. "What company?"

"George had a company, an infantry company, in the Marine Corps reserve," Banning explained. "It was activated, and ordered to Camp Pendleton. As soon as they got there, it was disestablished — broken up — and the men sent as fillers to the 1st Provisional Marine Brigade."

"I trained those Marines, General," Hart said. "And I told their families I'd take care of them."

"Why did they do that?" Pickering asked. "Break up his company?"

"I have no goddamn idea," Hart said bitterly. "They just did it. The fucking Marine Corps!"

"Hey!" Banning said warningly, holding up his hand.

Captain Hart was silent, but he did not seem repentant.

"It was a cold-blooded, necessary decision," Banning explained. "The priority was finding bodies to fill up the Provisional Brigade, find them anywhere, and George showed up with two hundred bodies. It was as simple as that."

"I should have been with them in the Pusan Perimeter, and I should have been with them at Inchon," Hart said. "They were my Marines!"

"George," Senator Fowler said, "in the big picture, you're making a greater contribution, meeting a greater responsibility, in taking care of General Pickering than you would have been able to do —"

"Sir," Banning turned on him. "With respect —"

"Dick," Pickering interrupted, "you don't understand. George is a Marine officer. There is no greater responsibility, no greater privilege, than leading Marines in combat. I know exactly how George feels."

Fowler shrugged as if to say, *I was only trying to help.*

Pickering turned to Hart.

"You didn't mention any of this to me, George."

"You said it, General, I'm a Marine officer. Marine officers go where they're sent and do what they're told to do. But I am not going to go home to Saint Louis so long as my Marines are in Korea."

Pickering looked at him for a long moment.

"Okay, Captain," he said finally, "change of orders. After you call Travis and tell them we'll be delayed —"

"I'll take care of that, Fleming," Senator Fowler interrupted.

"Okay. Then — and this is an order, Captain — you will get on the horn and tell your wife to pack her bags because in the next hour or two a man named Kensington is going to call her and tell her on which flight she and your kids are booked for Washington."

"General —" Hart said, almost visibly trying to frame his objections.

"Captain Hart," Pickering interrupted

318

him, "the proper response from a Marine officer who has been given an order is 'Aye, aye, sir,' which translates to mean 'I understand the order and will comply.' "

"Aye, aye, sir," Hart said.

"Good," Pickering said. "And just for the record, George, Fowler's right. What you do for me is important. I don't know what the hell I would do without you."

Hart nodded.

"General," Banning said, "have you got anything for General Howe? Or McCoy? I've got to get back to Pendleton."

Pickering thought it over.

"Message them Hart and I made it this far and will be in Washington tomorrow," he said. "But that's about it."

"Aye, aye, sir."

[Three]

Fleming Pickering marched into the kitchen of The Penthouse, freshly bathed, shaven, and attired in a fresh white T-shirt, boxer shorts, and stockings held up with garters.

"I still don't have a uniform?" he demanded of Captain Hart. "For Christ's sake, all they had to do was press the spare in the suitcase."

"And I'm sure they're working on doing just that," Senator Fowler said. "Have a cup of coffee and calm down."

He pointed to a coffee service on the kitchen table.

"You've got a clean uniform," Pickering said accusingly, to Hart.

"I didn't have mine pressed," Hart said. "You said you wanted yours pressed."

"And he didn't spill his breakfast on his," Fowler offered helpfully.

Pickering glared at him.

"I've got to call Patricia," he said.

"I did that for you. She'll be at the Lafayette when you get there," Fowler said. And then he giggled as much as a dignified U.S. Senator can giggle. "I told her about . . . your uniform difficulties, and that you were in the shower."

That earned Senator Fowler another dirty look.

"Jesus, I've got to call Ernie Sage. I promised Ernie I would as soon as I got here."

He went to the wall-mounted telephone and connected with the long-distance operator, who said she was required to ask, because of the increased telephone traffic caused by the war, if the call was necessary.

"Trust me, Operator, I know there's a war, and this call is necessary."

He then informed her that he wished to be connected, person-to-person, with Mr.

Ernest Sage at the corporate headquarters of American Personal Pharmaceuticals in New York City.

The call to Mr. Sage's office went through quickly enough, but Mr. Sage's secretary, he was told, "was away from her desk" and her telephone was being answered by someone else, who, to the scarcely concealed amusement of Senator Fowler and Captain Hart, had never heard of Fleming Pickering, and more or less politely demanded to know what it was that he wished to speak to Mr. Sage about.

"I brushed my teeth with your lousy toothpaste and my teeth fell out," General Pickering replied. "Now, get him on the phone!"

The someone else answering the telephone decided that she had best at least relay the information that some furiously angry man was on the phone to Mr. Sage's secretary, who had accompanied her boss to an important staff meeting, and did so.

That lady came next on the line, and asked Pickering if he could possibly call back later, as Mr. Sage was conducting a very important meeting and she hated to disturb him.

"I don't give a damn if he's conducting the New York Philharmonic," Pickering replied. "Get him on the phone now!"

Mr. Sage then came on the line.

"Is something wrong, Fleming?"

"Not at all. I just thought you would be interested in a report about your daughter."

"Flem, could I ask you to call Elaine?"

"And report to her, you mean?"

"Yeah. I'm really up to my ears in this meeting, Flem."

"Ernie, I will not call Elaine and tell her myself," Pickering said, "because I can tell you what I have to say in two seconds, and it would take twenty minutes to tell Elaine, and I don't have any more time to waste."

"Well, Jesus, Flem, don't take my head off."

"That's not what I would like to cut off, Ernie," Pickering said. "Now, listen carefully. Write this down. Ernie is fine. She sends her love. Got it?"

"You did try, right, Flem, to get her to come home?"

"Yes, I did. And she said no. I have to go, Ernie. Go back to your meeting."

Pickering hung up the telephone.

"You were a little rough on Sage, Flem," Fowler said.

"If I had a six-months-pregnant daughter halfway around the world and someone called me to report on her, any goddamned meeting I was having would have to wait."

Fowler shrugged.

322

The service elevator door opened and two bellmen carrying freshly pressed uniforms came in.

"Finally," Pickering said.

He took the uniforms from them and walked out of the kitchen.

Senator Fowler waited until Pickering was out of earshot, then asked, "Is he all right, George?"

"He's fine, sir."

"How the hell can he be fine when no one knows where Pick is? Or even if he's alive."

"McCoy and Zimmerman think he's alive," Hart said. "On the run, but alive."

"So Banning told me," Fowler said. "What do you think his chances are?"

"If he's made it this far, pretty good. That war's just about over."

"I devoutly pray you're right, George."

The telephone on a side table in the living room rang several minutes later as two bellmen were laying out their lunch.

Fowler was closest to it, so he answered it.

"Just a moment, please," he said, and then, to Hart: "Go tell him he's got a phone call."

Pickering, now wearing trousers and a shirt, came into the living room.

"That goddamn well better not be Elaine

Sage," he said, taking the telephone from Fowler.

"It's not," Fowler said.

"Pickering," he snarled into the telephone, then: "Yes, Brigadier General Pickering."

Then he said quietly in an aside to Hart and Fowler, "Jesus Christ, it's Truman."

Then he said into the phone, "Good afternoon, Mr. President. I'm very sorry, sir, about the delay in getting to the airport. I was just about to reschedule. We can be in the air in no more than two . . ."

There was a short pause as Fleming listened to the President.

"It's not?"

A pause.

"The last sighting of the signs he's leaving was several days ago, Mr. President, so we know he was alive then. Major McCoy seems to feel there's a good chance of getting him back."

A very long pause, followed by a barely audible sigh from Fleming.

"That's very kind of you, Mr. President. I'm convinced that everything that can be done is being done. I'm deeply touched by your interest."

Brief pause.

"Yes, sir, Mr. President, I look forward to seeing you soon, too. Good afternoon, Mr. President."

He put the telephone in its cradle.

"I was rough on Ernie Sage, was I? That sonofabitch didn't even ask about Pick. The President of the United States just did."

Fowler looked at Pickering, then turned to Hart.

"George, unless I'm mistaken, there's a two-year supply of Famous Grouse in the last cabinet on the left of the sink. Why don't you make us all a little nip?"

"Aye, aye, sir," Hart said.

[Four]
Base Operations
Kimpo Airfield (K-16)
Seoul, South Korea
0405 4 October 1950

Lieutenant Colonel Allan C. Lowman, USAF, a tall, good-looking thirty-five-year-old, who would have much preferred to be flying Sabrejets but who the powers that be had decided could make a greater contribution to the Air Force and the war as Commander, K-16 USAF Base, had elected to set up his cot in an unused-at-the moment radio van mounted on a GMC 6 x 6 truck.

There were several advantages to this. The van had its own electrical generator, driven by a gasoline engine. The generator was primarily intended to power the radio equipment, but it also provided electric lights and the current necessary to operate his electric razor, an electric hot plate, and his Zenith Transoceanic portable radio, on which it was possible to listen — usually — to the Armed Forces Network Radio Station in Tokyo, and even — sometimes — civilian radio stations as far away as Hawaii and the West Coast.

When someone knocked at the rear door of the van, waking him, the luminescent hands of his Rolex — a gift from his wife — told him it was a little after 0400.

He had left orders with the duty NCO to wake him at 0500, so this was obviously a problem of some sort. The question was what kind of a problem.

Feeling a little foolish — it was probably the duty NCO bearing an early-morning teletype message that required his attention — he felt around on the floor until he found his .45, took it from the holster, pulled the slide back, chambered a cartridge, and only then got off the cot and walked barefoot in his underwear to the door.

"Who is it?"

"Sergeant Alvarez, Colonel."

Colonel Lowman put his right arm — and the .45 — behind his back and then opened the door.

It was Sergeant Alvarez, all right, but with him were three officers, all majors. Two of them were Army — a plump, rumpled Army major and an Army aviator. The third was a Marine who had a Thompson submachine gun slung from his shoulder.

"These officers insisted on seeing you, Colonel," Sergeant Alvarez said.

"What can I do for you?" Colonel Lowman asked, aware that he felt a little foolish standing there in his underwear with his pistol hidden behind his back.

"May we come in, please, sir?" the Marine asked.

Colonel Lowman could not think of an excuse not to let them into the van. He backed up and gestured for them to climb up the short flight of stairs.

"Thank you, Sergeant," the Marine said.

"If you'll pull that door closed, we can turn the lights on," Lowman said.

The Marine pulled the door closed and latched it. Lowman switched the lights on.

The rumpled, stout major held out a small leather wallet to Lowman.

Lowman saw the credentials of a Special Agent of the United States Central Intelligence Agency. It was his first contact of any kind with the CIA.

"How can I help the CIA?" Lowman asked.

"In that hangar across the field, Colonel, as I'm sure you know, are two Sikorsky helicopters," the Marine said.

"Yeah, I know. This has to do with them?"

"What we want to do, in the next few minutes, is get them out of here with as few people as possible knowing about it," the Marine said.

"I'm not sure I understand," Lowman confessed.

"We don't want to talk to the tower, sir," the Army aviator said.

"Why not?"

"We have to presume the NKs have people monitoring your tower traffic," the rumpled major said.

"What we hope to do, sir," the Marine said, "by taking off in the dark, and not talking to the tower, is get those machines out of here without letting the NKs know."

"You really think they're listening to the tower traffic?" Lowman asked.

That possibility had never occurred to him.

"I'm sure they are," the Marine said. "And since they were listening when the helos first arrived, and when the helos made their only flight out of here and back, they know about the helos. What we hope to do now is get the helos out of here without them knowing — with a little luck,

328

thinking they're still in that hangar."

"How do you propose to do that?" Lowman asked.

"Sir, we'll fire them up, warm them up, inside the hangar," the Army aviator said. "Then shut them down and roll them out of the hangar. Then we'll call the tower — 'K-16, this is Air Force two oh seven, radio check.' If there's no reason we can't take off, the tower will give the radio check. We'll then reply, 'K-16, thank you,' fire them up again, and take off immediately. If you have incoming or departing traffic, just ignore our call, and we'll wait five minutes and call again."

Colonel Lowman considered that a moment.

"That should work. You want me to be in the tower, right?"

"If you would, please, sir," the Marine said. "And if you would, sir, make the point to your tower people that they didn't hear or see anything at all."

"Got it," Colonel Lowman said. "At this hour, there's only one — well, maybe two — guys in there anyway. Give me a minute to get my clothes on."

There were two NCOs, a staff sergeant and a buck sergeant, in the control tower — which was also mounted on a GMC 6 x 6 truck — when Colonel

Lowman climbed up on the truck and went into the small, green, glass-walled, boxlike structure. Both, visibly surprised to see The Colonel, came to attention.

"Good morning," Lowman said. "What's going on?"

"Quiet as a tomb, sir," the staff sergeant said. "It won't be light for another thirty minutes or so."

"We heard some engines starting, sir," the buck sergeant said. "Over there."

He pointed across the field.

"You're sure?" Colonel Lowman said doubtfully.

"Well, sir, it *sounded* as if it was coming from over there."

"As far as I know, there's nothing over there but a shot-up hangar," Colonel Lowman said.

The ground-to-air radio came to life.

"K-16, Air Force two oh seven, radio check."

"We don't have anything coming in or going out right now, do we?" Colonel Lowman asked.

"No, sir," the staff sergeant said.

Colonel Lowman took the microphone the buck sergeant held in his hand.

Into it he said, "Air Force two oh seven, read you five by five. Niner, eight, seven, six, fiver, four, three, two, one."

"K-16, thank you," the radio said.

Colonel Lowman handed the microphone back to the staff sergeant.

Across the field, there were suddenly two spots of orange light, as if coming from the exhaust of an engine. And a moment later, there was the rumble of an engine and a *fluckata-fluckata-fluckata*.

"There it is again," the buck sergeant said. "I knew damned well I heard something."

"I don't hear anything," Colonel Lowman said.

"From over *there*, Colonel!" the buck sergeant insisted.

"Sounds like a helicopter to me, sir. Helicopter*s*," the staff sergeant said.

The *fluckata-fluckata-fluckata fluckata-fluckata-fluckata fluckata-fluckata-fluckata* sound grew louder.

Lowman thought he could just faintly see one of the H-19s moving rapidly across the field, then taking off into the darkness.

"Goddammit," the staff sergeant said. "That was two helicopters, and not a goddamn navigation light on either of them. What the fuck?"

"I want you two to listen to me carefully," Colonel Lowman said. "I have been here all the time with you. I neither heard or saw anything that sounded remotely like a helicopter."

"But, sir —" the staff sergeant said.

"And neither did you," Colonel Lowman said. "Do we understand each other?"

"Yes, sir," they said, almost in unison.

"And I don't want it to get back to me that whatever you thought you saw or heard, but didn't, is the subject of any conversation anywhere. Clear?"

"Yes, sir," they said.

"Keep up the good work, men," Colonel Lowman said, smiled at them, and left the control tower.

Outside, he could hear the *fluckata-fluckata-fluckata* of rotor blades diminishing to the southeast.

Colonel Lowman wondered where the hell they were going with the H-19s and what they were going to do with them.

But there had been something in the eyes of the Marine major that had told him that his curiosity would have been not only highly unwelcome but maybe even a little dangerous, and he hadn't asked.

[Five]
Socho-Ri, South Korea
0545 4 October 1950

Major Donald had told McCoy there were three ways to get to Socho-Ri, one flying at an altitude that would permit them to look for an arrow stamped out in a rice paddy.

332

The trouble with that option was, Donald said, that if they could see a sign like that, people on the ground could see them.

The second option was to fly what he called "nap of the earth," which meant flying just a few feet off the ground. That would expose them to eyes on the ground for only a fleeting moment, but flying at ninety knots, that wouldn't be much different from driving over the ground at that speed; the chances of spotting a stamped-out arrow would be slim, unless they just happened to fly right over it and were paying close enough attention not to miss it.

The third option — which Donald recommended — would be to ascend quickly to, say, 9,000 feet, which would for all practical purposes make them invisible to eyes on the ground, and incidentally keep them safely above any rock-filled clouds they might encounter en route. There was a line of mountains running down the peninsula, Donald said, and he did not have a deep and abiding faith in the navigation charts he had been given.

McCoy opted for the high altitude. The priority was to get the helos to Socho-Ri intact and undetected. Even if they were spotted by only friendly forces — I ROK Corps — the sudden appearance of two black helicopters would very likely cause some South Korean commander to make a report of "unidentified, black, type previously not seen, rotary-wing aircraft" flying over his position.

There was also a chance that the two helos would be spotted by Air Force, Navy, or Marine fighters making an early-morning reconnaissance. Their pilots would more than likely — out of curiosity, if nothing else — make a pass at them before shooting them down. In that case, Donald said, he would get on the emergency radio frequency and try to contact them.

"You could enthusiastically sing 'The Marines' Hymn,' " Donald said.

Pick would just have to wait. There had been no word from the *Badoeng Strait* that any signs of Pick had been found, anyway.

But as it had grown light, turned into day, as they had flown eastward across the peninsula, McCoy rarely took his eyes from the ground far below them.

When the coastline appeared and Donald flew over it and above the Sea of Japan, McCoy wondered what was happening and looked at Donald, who read his mind.

"I'm going to fly a couple of miles out to sea before I make the descent," Donald explained. "And then approach Socho-Ri with our wheels just far enough above the water to keep them from getting wet."

McCoy gave him a thumbs-up.

"You're pretty good at this, Alex. A quick learner."

"I had another thought," Alex said. "Just now. How are you and Dunston going to get back to Seoul?"

"I thought we'd get in a jeep. Maybe we could talk somebody in I ROK Corps into giving us a ride. Dunston and I talked about it. He said they have a few L-4s and L-19s."

"And if they won't, it's a long ride back to Seoul," Donald said. "We need our own fixed-wing airplane," Donald said. "What we really need is an L-20, a Beaver, but I think we'd have a better chance of getting an L-19."

"What's a Beaver?"

"Single-engine, six-place DeHavilland. Canadian. Designed for use in the Alaskan bush. The Army bought a dozen — and ordered a hell of a lot more — off the shelf when this started. There were six of them on the baby aircraft carrier with the H-19s. The brass will be fighting over them like a nymphomaniac at a high school dance."

"I think you had better get in the jeep with me, and see about getting us one or the other," McCoy said.

His stomach then rose in his chest as Donald put the H-19 into a steep descending turn.

★ ★ ★

As they approached the coastline, not fifty feet off the water, they came across a junk plodding slowly southward, maybe a mile and a half offshore and half a mile away from them.

"That has to be the *Wind of Good Fortune*," McCoy said.

"You want me to take a closer look?"

"God, no! There's an air-cooled .50 on the prow, and another on the stern. By now — they've seen us — they've taken the covers off and fed ammo belts into both."

"Why is it leaving Socho-Ri?"

"She dropped off a generator, a good base station radio, and some other supplies," McCoy replied. "Chow, a couple of rubber boats, sandbags, stuff — I guess you call it 'thatch' — to put the roofs back on the hootches. And some of Dunston's Koreans. And then she got out of there before anyone could draw the right conclusion."

Donald took his hand off the cyclic control long enough to point. They were approaching Socho-Ri. As McCoy followed Donald's pointing, Donald put the H-19 into a steep turn to the left, then to the right, and then as suddenly straightened up. They were now lined up with the dirt strip.

McCoy could see enough of the activity

on the ground to know that Zimmerman — and Dunwood's Marines — had done a lot of work even before the *Wind of Good Fortune* had brought them the supplies they needed.

He saw what had to be Marines in two emplacements overlooking the path from Route 5, and another emplacement facing out to the Sea of Japan.

And a patch of recently turned earth twenty-five feet by eight. Burying the bodies had obviously been a priority.

Jesus, that's a hell of a big hole to have to dig by hand!

The H-19 stopped forward movement, and a moment later its wheels touched the ground.

McCoy saw the second helo flutter to the ground to their right, and then Dunwood and Zimmerman walking out to them.

Donald began to shut the machine down. McCoy unfastened his seat and shoulder belts but made no move to get out until the rotor blades stopped turning.

He had just jumped to the ground from the wheel when the smell of putrefying flesh hit him.

Dunston and the pilot of the other helicopter started to walk over to them. The pilot didn't make it. He suddenly bent over and threw up.

Dunston ignored him and joined the others in time to hear McCoy snap at Zimmerman: "Jesus! When did you finally get around to burying the bodies?"

"We waited until this morning, of course, Killer, knowing you were coming," Zimmerman answered, not daunted by McCoy's anger. "Jesus! It was the first thing we did. We could smell this place a mile off."

"How do we get rid of the smell?" McCoy asked.

"Sir," Dunwood said, "we don't think it's coming from the bodies, from the grave, but from the ground where they were lying. I was thinking maybe if we soaked the ground with gas, and then —"

"Do it," McCoy said.

"Aye, aye, sir."

"Some of the bodies were in the hootches, Killer. And they stink too."

"Well, use gas on them before we put the roofs back on," McCoy said. "That smell's got to go."

Zimmerman nodded.

He looked at Major Donald.

"I don't suppose we could just drape fishnet over those propellers, could we, Major?"

He made a swirling motion with his index finger, pointing at the helicopter.

"Rotors," Donald corrected him. "No. I

don't think that would be smart."

"I was afraid of that," Zimmerman said, and pointed toward the side of the landward hill, one hundred yards from where they stood. "That's what I came up with."

Against two very steep parts of the slope, two enormous flies of fishnet had been erected. Their outer edges were supported by flimsy "poles" made of short, nailed, and tied-together pieces of wood. Vegetation of all sorts had been laced into the net.

McCoy thought: *Boy, that's really a jury-rig!*

"And they won't stay up long," Zimmerman said, reading McCoy's mind, "if you get close to them with the *rotors* turning."

"Collect some men and push them over and get them out of sight," McCoy ordered.

Zimmerman nodded.

Dunston walked away from them, toward the mass grave.

"You want some breakfast, Killer?" Zimmerman asked innocently. "Couple of fresh eggs, maybe? The *Wind of Good Fortune* brought some. And a couple of fresh suckling pigs, too, come to thing of it."

McCoy glowered at him.

"You want me to throw up, too, right?" he said, pointing toward the helicopter pilot, who was now sitting, pale-faced, on the ground, trying to regain control of himself.

Zimmerman smiled at him.

McCoy, Dunston, Zimmerman, Dunwood, and Donald were sitting on the stone wharf, where the smell didn't seem as bad. There was a breeze from the sea, and the smoke of the fires built over where the dead had been left to rot had sort of diluted the smell of the bodies.

"Then we're agreed?" Dunston asked.

McCoy looked at him and made a little *come on* gesture with his hand.

Dunston began to lay out the plan of action. "The priority is to get some agents up north as quickly as possible, the more the better, but for right now, three teams is all that seems feasible.

"We call the *Wind of Good Fortune* back, to dock here an hour after dark. She picks up the agents and goes north. Using just one of the rubber boats — keeping the other in reserve; the *Wind of Good Fortune* can bring more boats on her next trip — she puts them ashore and then heads for Pusan. She has enough fuel aboard to run the diesel, balls to the wall, all night.

"Unless they come across something really interesting, the agents will not get on the radio for twenty-four hours, or forty-eight. If they get in trouble, they will yell for help. If they do — Donald makes the decision whether or not the risk is manageable — we'll send one of the helicopters after them and see what happens.

"Presuming they don't get in trouble: Donald, Dunwood, and Zimmerman will start preparing to use the choppers as flying trucks to take a squad of men wherever they have to go. As I understand you, Alex, most of that training will be pretty basic.

"First, Zimmerman decides how they'll be armed and equipped. Then we'll find out how many men we can load on a chopper. Then we practice their getting out of the chopper in a hurry. None of this will require flying the choppers. When they get pretty good at that, we'll start making dry runs, first just taking off and landing here, and finally, flying inland a little to practice insertion and withdrawal on the kind of terrain they'll find up north.

"By the time we do all this, maybe the war will be over. If not, the *Wind of Good Fortune* will be back here, and we'll decide what to do next." He paused. "That's about it."

"Ernie?" McCoy asked.

"Sounds fine to me," Zimmerman said.

"Donald?"

"What about me going back with you,

McCoy? We talked about that. To see about getting a fixed-wing airplane? I'd rather stay here, but . . ."

"Let's see what Dunston and I can do, begging on our knees," McCoy said.

Donald nodded.

"Dunwood?" McCoy asked.

"I don't have any problems with any of this," Dunwood said.

"Okay. That's it," McCoy said, and then added: "I don't think Bill Dunston and I should go back to Seoul together. I think we should go separately — say, an hour apart, in two jeeps. Dunwood, can you let each of us have, say, six Marines? With a couple of BARs?"

"No problem," Dunwood said.

"You go first, McCoy," Dunston said. "I'll want to explain all this to the Koreans, and I'd like to see what I can do about identifying my people the NKs found here."

"The sooner I get out of here, the better," McCoy said, scrambling to his feet. "Ernie, I don't care if you have to keep those fires burning all week."

"That thought ran through my mind, Major, sir," Zimmerman said.

rack of radios in the back.

He drove up to it, the second jeep following.

The guards raised their rifles.

"Stand at ease," McCoy barked in Korean. The guards assumed a position not unlike Parade Rest, and saluted by crossing their right hands to the muzzles of the Garands.

McCoy got out of the jeep and walked into the tent.

It was full of officers and soldiers, radios, telephone switchboards, and desks.

A Korean colonel wearing impeccably fitting and perfectly starched and pressed fatigues, polished boots, with a .45 in a tanker's shoulder holster turned from the map board when McCoy pushed the flap aside and light entered the tent.

McCoy saluted.

"Good morning, Colonel," he said in Korean. "May I have a moment of your time?"

Everybody in the tent was now looking at him.

The colonel returned McCoy's salute crisply.

"Good morning," he said in faultless English. "I'm Colonel Pak. I'm surprised, Major, to see a Marine officer this far east."

"May I have a moment of the colonel's

time?" McCoy said, continuing in Korean.

"And, if you don't mind my saying so, one who speaks Korean so well," the colonel replied in English. "How may I be of service to the Marines?"

McCoy decided the colonel was an officer who had most likely learned his English while an officer in the Japanese Army, and had then been one of the rare ex-Japanese officers selected to start up the South Korean Army, and as a result of that had been sent to one or more U.S. Army schools in the States. His English was American accented.

"May I come to the map board, sir?"

Colonel Pak gestured that he could.

McCoy went to the map, found Socho-Ri, and pointed to it.

"Sir, I have established a small camp here," he said.

"That far north?" Pak asked rhetorically. "How long have you been there?"

"The first element arrived two days ago, sir."

"Why do I suspect you are not the lead elements of the First Marine Division?"

"We are not, sir," McCoy said.

Colonel Pak grunted.

"What can I do for you, Major?"

"Two things, sir. I hoped you could get word to your people before they move in that direction that my people are there."

Pak nodded, then picked up a grease pencil and made a check mark on the acetate covering the map.

"And the second?"

"Colonel, it is important that I get to Seoul as quickly as possible," McCoy said.

"And you would like a ride in one of our L-4s?"

"If they are not required for a more important mission, yes, sir."

"At the moment, the CG is at I ROK Corps seeking permission to move north," the general said. "Until we get that permission, they are not very busy. Observation has not revealed any enemy forces within thirty miles of here. Have you seen any indications of the enemy?"

"No, sir. I suspect — but do not know for sure — that they are no closer than twenty miles north of Socho-Ri."

Colonel Pak grunted.

"As I said, our aircraft are not being utilized at the moment, Major. But the problem I have is that I cannot afford to lose either of them — either to enemy action or, bluntly, to one of my fellow senior ROK officers who might commandeer it at the Race Track in Seoul. Having one's own aircraft, I'm afraid, has become the ROK equivalent of the German field marshal's baton. My general is known for his temper; I don't want to have to tell him, when he flies back in here in the third of our air-craft, that I loaned one of the others to a Marine who didn't give it back."

McCoy smiled.

"Colonel, if you would have me dropped at the Race Track, your pilot would not even have to shut the engine down, and anyone trying to commandeer your air-plane would have to go through me."

Colonel Pak grunted, then replied: "At Quantico, Major, one of the lessons I learned — in addition to how to drink martinis — was that a Marine officer's word is his bond."

"We try to keep it that way, sir," McCoy said, and then curiosity got the better of him. "May I ask what you were doing at Quantico, sir?"

"The idea was that South Korea was to have Marines," the general said. "But that, obviously, is going to have to be put off for the moment." He smiled at McCoy. "May I offer you a cup of tea before you take off, Major?"

"That's kind, but unnecessary, sir."

"It would be my pleasure, I insist," Col-onel Pak said. "And, if you don't mind, I'd like to have your — unofficial, of course — thoughts on the possibility that the Chinese will enter this conflict."

"Frankly, sir, I was wondering if I could ask you the same thing," McCoy said.

Twenty minutes later, one of the Capital ROK Division's two aircraft bounced down National Route 5 and lifted off, very slowly, into the air.

It took an hour and forty minutes against a headwind to reach the Race Track in Seoul.

McCoy spent the entire time looking down at the ground for a stamped-out arrow or any other sign of Pick Pickering. He found none.

But there was time to think, of course, and he thought that perhaps if he couldn't get anybody to let him have an L-19 — not to mention the other airplane Donald had said would be really useful, the Beaver — he might be able to get his hands on an L-4.

And he wondered what Dunston's agents were going to find up north. Both he and Colonel Pak — whom he now thought of as "the Quantico ROK colonel" — were uncomfortable with the idea that the war was just about over, and that the Chinese and the Russians were just going to stand idly by and watch while their surrogate army was annihilated by the Americans and their surrogate forces.

And the Quantico ROK colonel was right about the hunger of senior ROK officers for their own airplanes, too. No sooner had the L-4 landed at the Race

Track and taxied to a fuel truck than an ROK colonel appeared and told the L-4 pilot that he had an important mission and would require the use of the L-4.

"You'll have to look elsewhere, Colonel, I'm afraid," McCoy said. "This aircraft has been assigned to me."

McCoy showed him his CIA credentials. He thought the colonel backed off more because of McCoy's fluent Korean than because of the credentials. Since the Korean didn't try to argue with him in English, there was a good chance he had no idea what the CIA credentials were, or what they said.

He stayed with the L-4 until it taxied off to the strip for takeoff.

And then, when he tried — and failed — to get a jeep from the officer in charge of the airstrip to take him to the house, he had to make his own irregular requisition.

He walked to a street not far from the Race Track, waited until the first Marine vehicle — a weapons carrier — came down it, flagged it down, and told the corporal driving that he needed a ride.

"Sir, I can't —"

"All I want to hear from you, Corporal, is 'Aye, aye, sir.' "

"Aye, aye, sir."

[Seven]
The House
Seoul, South Korea
1145 4 October 1950

Technical Sergeant J. M. Jennings came through the door in the metal gate to the house as the weapons carrier carrying McCoy stopped in front of it.

"That was a quick trip, sir," he said as he saluted.

"I got lucky," McCoy said. "Get a phone number from the corporal, and then get on the horn and tell his officer I had to borrow the truck."

"Aye, aye, sir," Jennings said. "Major, there's an Army light colonel inside. . . ."

"How did he get inside?" McCoy asked.

"Sir, I'm a tech sergeant, and he showed me orders signed by some general at UNC."

"Did he say what he wants?"

"He wants to see Major Dunston," Jennings said.

"Where's General Howe?"

"He went south to see General Walker," Jennings said. "He said to tell you he'll try to get back tonight, if not first thing in the morning."

"I'll deal with it," McCoy said. "When you talk to the corporal's officer, say something nice about the corporal."

"Aye, aye, sir."

★ ★ ★

A stocky, neat, but not natty Army lieutenant colonel was sitting at the dining room table with a tall, thin, natty Army first lieutenant. Both were drinking coffee.

"Can I help you, Colonel?"

"I'm looking for Major William Dunston," the colonel said.

"He's not here right now," McCoy said.

"Where is he?"

"May I ask who you are, Colonel?"

"And you are?"

"My name is McCoy, sir."

"My name is Vandenburg," the colonel said, then took a sheet of paper folded twice from the breast pocket of his fatigues and laid it on the table. "Those are my orders."

McCoy went to the table, picked up the orders, and unfolded them.

TOP SECRET

**Supreme Headquarters
Commander-in-Chief
United Nations Command
Tokyo, Japan**

2 October 1950

SUBJECT: Letter Orders

TO: LtCol D.J. Vandenburg, Inf
　　　Headquarters CINCUNC

---

1. You will proceed at the earliest possible date to Korea, and such other places as you may deem necessary to carry out a mission of great importance, taking with you such personnel as you may deem necessary. Travel priority AAAAA-1 is assigned.

2. In order to facilitate the execution of your mission, authority is granted for you to requisition whatever support you may require from any source, and all UNC commands are directed to provide such support.

3. Any questions regarding your mission are to be directed to the undersigned.

FOR THE SUPREME COMMANDER:

Charles Willoughby
CHARLES WILLOUGHBY
Major General
Assistant Chief of Staff, J-2

TOP SECRET

McCoy refolded the orders and handed them back to Lieutenant Colonel Vandenburg.

"Thank you, sir."

"With regard to paragraph two of those orders," Vandenburg said, "what I require of you is your helicopters. And these premises, which I will use as my headquarters."

McCoy didn't reply.

"Where are those helicopters, Major?"

"With respect, sir, I don't think you have the need to know that."

"You can read, Major, can't you?"

"Yes, sir. I can read."

"You did notice those orders were issued in the name of the Supreme Commander, General MacArthur, and signed by the Supreme Commander's intelligence officer, Major General Willoughby?"

"With respect, sir, we are not a subordinate unit of the United Nations Command. And I'm sure, sir, if you would ask General Willoughby, he would confirm that."

Lieutenant Colonel Vandenburg tried to stare McCoy down, and failed.

"Harry," he said. "Take a walk."

The slim, natty lieutenant, surprise on his face, got to his feet and walked out of the room.

When the door had closed, Vandenburg smiled at McCoy and said: "You're not what I expected, Killer. I sort of expected a gorilla in a Marine Corps uniform."

McCoy didn't reply.

"You're not going to deny that you're

the legendary Killer McCoy, are you, Major?"

"I've been called that, sir," McCoy said. "I don't like it."

"Relax, Killer," Vandenburg said. "I'm one of the good guys. We even have a mutual friend."

McCoy said nothing.

"You're not curious, Killer, who that might be?"

"Yes, sir, I'm curious."

"Back in War Two, when Charley Willoughby and his boss finally got off the dime and sent an officer in a submarine onto Mindanao to establish contact with Wendell Fertig, what General Fertig told that officer — me — was that Killer McCoy and some other Marines had beat me there by two weeks."

Vandenburg let that sink in, then smiled.

"That shook you up a little, didn't it, Killer?" he asked.

McCoy didn't reply.

"Come on, fess up," Vandenburg said.

"I heard an Army officer went in later," McCoy said. "I wasn't there long."

"Let me tell you why I'm here, Killer," Vandenburg said. "You know what happened to General Dean of the 24th Division?"

"He was captured, early on, in Taejon."

"Well, the Army — the Chief of Staff of

the U.S. Army — wants him back. I work for him, despite what those orders say, not Willoughby. My primary mission here is to spring Dean from durance vile. The first thing I have to do is find out where he is, and then I want to mount a mission to spring him. To find out where he is, I have to put agents into North Korea. And to spring him, I need some method of grabbing him by surprise. It occurred to me on the way over here that using those Sikorskys is the best way to do both. When I got to where they were supposed to be, in a hangar at K-16, the base commander — very reluctantly — told me that CIA had them and had flown them out. He didn't know where to. So I came here to see Major Dunston. You with me so far?"

"Yes, sir."

"There's two ways we can handle this, Killer," Vandenburg said. "We can wage a turf war, which will neither help me get Dean back nor you do whatever it is you're doing. Or we can cooperate. Most of the Army doesn't like people like me any more than most of the Marine Corps likes people like you. We're social pariahs. But between us, I think we could probably do one hell of a job, even if there would be damned little appreciation down the road."

McCoy didn't reply.

"I went looking for your boss, General

Pickering. He's not at the Imperial Hotel. You want to tell me where he is?"

McCoy hesitated before replying.

"He's in the States. The President sent for him."

"And left you minding the store?"

"Yes, sir."

"Then the decision to cooperate, or not, is really yours to make, isn't it?"

"I don't know how you're defining 'cooperate,' Colonel. I don't want — General Pickering absolutely does not want — anyone around here who's going to report what he sees to General Willoughby."

"I don't like the sonofabitch any more than you do," Vandenburg said.

"You could be expected to say something like that."

"No I wouldn't," Vandenburg said indignantly, then chuckled. "Yeah, of course I would. But that happens to be the truth."

"I wish I could believe that," McCoy said.

"I wish you could, too. What about it — do we cooperate?"

"I still don't have your definition of the word."

"Very basic. You scratch my back, and I'll scratch yours."

"We have plans for the helos," McCoy said. "We're going to use them to insert

357

and extract agents up north. There's a few of us who aren't so sure this war will be over in two weeks. We have to know what's going on."

"I don't think it will be, either," Vandenburg said. "You already have people up north?"

"We're going to make the first insertions tonight, by boat, if we get lucky," McCoy said. "We're also in the first stages of training some fire teams to use the helos. But I can't see any reason — with the understanding I don't lose control of them — why you couldn't have the helos, and for that matter, the fire teams, to make a raid to spring General Dean. Presuming you can find him. We haven't heard anything, and I wouldn't be surprised to finally learn he's in Peking."

"Either would I," Lieutenant Colonel Vandenburg said. "Okay. It looks like we have a deal. I was wondering where I could get the men for the snatch operation and get them trained. Right now, my entire command is me and Harry. Aside from West Point and having had a Chinese nanny who taught him Cantonese, he doesn't have many qualifications for the sort of thing you and I do."

McCoy nodded.

"Your turn, Killer. What can I do for you?"

"You can stop calling me 'Killer,' " McCoy said.

Vandenburg laughed.

"I wondered when you were going to get around to that. Fertig told me you hate it. That's all?"

"You know what a Beaver is?"

"The airplane?"

McCoy nodded. "I need one. I would also like to have an L-19."

"There's a couple in Pusan. You have somebody who knows how to fly one?"

"I think so. Half a dozen pilots came with the helicopters. One of them should be able to fly a Beaver."

"I'll see what I can do," Vandenburg said. "I only promise what I know I can deliver. Chances are I *can* get you a Beaver and an L-19. I'll give it my best shot. Okay?"

"Thank you," McCoy said.

"Does this also mean Harry and I can stay in this palace of yours?"

"Like you said, Colonel. We're social pariahs. We have to stick together."

VIII

**The Marquis de Lafayette Suite
The Foster Lafayette Hotel
Washington, D.C.
0905 5 October 1950**

Mrs. Patricia Foster Fleming, a tall, shapely, aristocratic-looking woman whose silver hair was simply but elegantly coiffured, was in the living room of the suite when Pickering, Hart, two bellmen, and the on-duty manager entered.

She was at a Louis XV escritoire, talking on the telephone.

She held up a finger as an order to wait.

She talked another thirty seconds on the telephone, then abruptly announced that she would have to call back later, hung the phone up, and walked across the room to her husband and Hart.

"Hello, George," she said to Hart, "it's good to see you."

She kissed him on the cheek, then turned to her husband and kissed him on the cheek.

Pickering thought that he had been

360

kissed by his wife with all the enthusiasm with which she had kissed George Hart.

Honey, that's not fair. I didn't want Pick to get shot down.

"Okay," Pickering said to the manager and Hart. "We have an understanding, right? All calls to me except from the President, Senator Fowler, and Colonel Banning go through Captain Hart, who'll be operating out of the Monroe Suite. All calls to Mrs. Pickering go on line three, which I will not answer. Right?"

"That's already set up, General," the manager said.

"Captain Hart will need the car to go to the airport to pick up his family at two-fifteen. Which means he will have to leave here at one-thirty."

"The car will be available."

"Okay, George. Take whatever time you need to get settled, then hop in a cab and go over to the CIA. Give my compliments to Admiral Hillencoetter and tell him I'm at his disposal, and that I've sent you there to get the latest briefing."

"Aye, aye, sir. Sir, Louise is perfectly capable of getting a cab at the airport. . . ."

"Do what you're told, George," Pickering said, not unkindly. "How are you fixed for cash?"

Hart hesitated, then said, "Just fine, sir."

Pickering pointed at the manager.

"Give Captain Hart five hundred dollars. Charge it to me."

"Certainly, Mr. Pickering."

"That's *General* Pickering, Richard," Mrs. Pickering said to the manager. "You can tell by the uniform and the stars all over it and by the way he gives orders with such underwhelming tact."

"Sorry, General," the manager said. "I really do know better."

"Forget it," Pickering said.

General and Mrs. Pickering looked at each other, but neither spoke or touched until they were alone in the suite.

Then Pickering's eyebrow went up as he waited.

"God, I really despise you in that uniform," Patricia said finally. "I think I hate all uniforms."

"They make it easy to tell who's doing a job that has to be done, and who's getting a free ride," Pickering said.

"You did your job when you were a kid in France, and you did your job in World War Two. When does it stop? When does somebody else take over and start doing your job?"

He looked at her for a long moment, then said: "Ken McCoy says he has every reason to believe Pick is alive and in good shape, and that we'll have him back in short order."

"And you believe him?"

"Yes, honey, I do."

"I wish I shared your faith," she said bitterly.

He didn't reply.

"For the last four days," Patricia said, "ever since Dick Fowler called and told me you were on your way to Washington, I have had fantasies of having your arms around me. And I promised myself I would remember it isn't your fault . . . what's happened to Pick . . . and that I wouldn't be a bitch. . . ."

He looked at her a moment, then nodded.

"If you promise not to bite my jugular, Patricia," he said softly, "I'll put my arms around you."

She didn't reply.

He took a step toward her, then held his arms open. Very slowly, she walked into them, and he held her against him.

"Oh, my God, Flem," she said softly, and then she began to sob. "Oh, God, I've missed you!"

"Me, too, honey." His voice was not quite under control.

He held her a long time, until her sobs subsided.

Then she said, "I wish you'd take off that goddamn uniform."

"I'll still be a Marine, honey," he said.

"My fantasy was to feel your bare arms around me," she said softly.

"Well," he said. "I guess it is like riding a bicycle. You never forget how."

He was lying on his back in their bed. She was lying half on him.

She pinched him, painfully, on the soft flesh of his inner thigh.

He yelped.

"I'd forgotten you do that, too," he said.

She didn't reply.

"Pick's got a girl," he said.

"Pick has always had a girl," she said. "He wasn't even five years old when he talked Ernie Sage into playing doctor, and it went downhill from there."

"This is serious, I think," Pickering said.

"I have heard that before, and find it very hard to believe."

"In many ways, she's very much like you."

"You know her? That *is* unusual."

"Yeah. I know her. And Ernie knows her and likes her too; they've become quite close."

She propped herself up on her elbows and looked down at him. "Tell me about her. What do you mean, she's like me?"

"Tough, smart, competent, and, I think, very much surprised to find herself in love with Pick. She's a reporter, a war correspondent. Jeanette Priestly, of the *Chicago Tribune*."

"I've seen her stories," she said. "No pictures."

"Tall, graceful . . . like you. Long blond hair. Not peroxide. Blue eyes. Good-looking young woman."

"I had a mental picture of a middle-aged frump with a short haircut," Patricia said.

"No. Very nice."

"And they're in love?"

"Yeah. And I mean love, rather than lust."

"If you think that, then it is serious."

"It had to happen eventually," Pickering said. "It's the natural order of things."

"How's . . . what's her name? Jeanette? . . . taking what's happened to Pick?"

"About like you, me, and Ernie," Pickering said. "Stiff upper lip. She doesn't say much. But there's really not much that can be said, is there?"

"Do you know what happened — I mean, in detail — to Pick? How was he shot down?"

"He was flying what they call 'low-altitude tactical interdiction sorties, seeking targets of opportunity,' " Pickering said. "What he was doing was shooting up locomotives."

"Railroad locomotives?" she asked, surprised.

"If you can take out, for example, an enemy supply train, that denies the enemy supplies and ammunition, and so on. Pick was apparently pretty good at it. He had three locomotives painted on the nose of his airplane."

"I thought he was shot down by another airplane."

"We pretty much have what is known as air superiority," Pickering said. "A lot — most — of aviation activity is in close support of the troops on the ground."

"So it was antiaircraft fire?"

"What Billy Dunn . . . You remember Colonel Dunn?"

"The tiny little man with an Alabama accent you can cut with a knife?"

"That's him," Pickering said. "Billy thinks that a locomotive blew up just as Pick was passing over it, and there was damage to the aircraft, most likely to the engine, from parts of the locomotive. Pick had to make an emergency landing; he couldn't get back to the *Badoeng Strait*, the aircraft carrier."

"Was he hurt?" she asked softly.

"Billy didn't think so, and the proof seems to be that he's covered a lot of distance. If he was injured, he couldn't move as fast and as far as he has."

"That sounds as if you know where he is," she said.

"We have an idea where he is," Pickering said. "He finds a rice paddy somewhere, and stamps out an arrow and his initials."

"If you know where he is, then why can't you go get him?"

"Because he has to keep moving. By the time a pilot who spots one of the arrows gets back to his aircraft carrier to report it, or by the time they can spot one of his arrows on an aerial photo — which is what happens most — and we can get people to that spot, he's three, four, five miles away. McCoy said the last time he doesn't think they missed him by more than a couple of hours."

"But you really believe he's . . . going to come back?"

"Yeah, I do."

"Don't lie to me, Flem."

The cold truth is that I don't know whether my faith that he's coming back is based on my professional assessment of the situation, or whether I'm just pissing in the wind.

"I'm not, honey."

The telephone on the bedside table rang.

"Don't answer it," Patricia said. "God, we're entitled to at least a few minutes."

"I have to, honey," he said, and stretched his arm out for the telephone.

Patricia didn't move off him.

"Pickering," he said.

"The President wants to see you," Senator Fowler said without any preliminaries.

"When?"

"Right now."

"Where?"

"Here."

"He's with you?"

"That's right."

"It'll take me a few minutes to get dressed."

[Two]

There were two neatly dressed muscular men — obviously Secret Service agents — in the corridor when Pickering left his suite and walked down it toward Senator Fowler's suite.

"The President is expecting you, General," one of them said to Pickering, then knocked at Fowler's door and opened it without waiting for a reply.

Harry S Truman, President of the United States and Commander-in-Chief of its Armed Forces, was sitting on a couch in Fowler's sitting room drinking a cup of coffee. His hat was on the table, and he was wearing one of his trademark bow ties. He stood up and smiled as Pickering entered the room.

"I'm sorry to interrupt your homecoming . . ." he said, extending his hand.

"Good morning, Mr. President," Pickering said.

". . . but as I was taking my walk, it occurred to me this would be a good time to speak with you," Truman finished. "I wanted to do that before having to make some decisions."

"I'm at your disposal, Mr. President."

"Will you excuse me, Mr. President?" Senator Fowler asked.

Truman considered that.

"Okay, Dick, if you'd rather not hear this," he said. "But you're welcome to stay."

Fowler considered the reply, then sat down.

"When I was in the Senate, General, I learned that there were a few members of the loyal opposition who could be trusted to place the country's interest above partisan politics, and Dick headed that list."

"Thank you, Mr. President," Fowler said.

"They were most often wrong about things," Truman said with a smile, "but they could be trusted."

Fowler smiled at him.

"Will you have some coffee, General?" Truman asked. "And please sit down."

Truman pointed to the couch on which he was sitting, poured Pickering a cup of coffee, then slid to the far end of the couch and turned so that he was facing Pickering. He waited until Pickering had picked up his cup before continuing.

"Ralph Howe has told me of MacArthur's intention to move the X Corps around the Korean Peninsula and land it somewhere around Wonsan," he said.

Pickering understood it was a question.

"Yes, sir. I know. General Howe sent me a copy of his message to you. I got it in California."

"And?" Truman asked.

"Mr. President, I'm not qualified to question General MacArthur's strategy," Pickering said.

"I'll be the judge of that," Truman said. "What do you think?"

"Mr. President, there were a lot of people who thought that the Inchon Landing was a very bad idea. And from what I've learned, putting X Corps ashore at Wonsan will be a good deal easier than the Inchon operation."

"No Flying Fish Islands to deal with?" Truman asked.

How the hell did he hear about that?

"No, sir."

"You're aware that General Marshall has become Secretary of Defense?"

"Yes, sir."

"General Marshall tells me that MacArthur staged a clandestine operation under

General Willoughby to take those islands just before the invasion."

Pickering didn't reply.

"Apparently, General Willoughby sent an officer to brief General Marshall on how the Inchon Landing was planned and carried out," Truman said.

"Yes, sir."

"And General Marshall told me," Truman said.

Pickering didn't reply.

"I was a little surprised to hear the story," Truman said. "I hadn't heard it from the CIA — Admiral Hillencoetter — at all, and the story I got from Ralph Howe was that it was your clandestine operation, and that not even General MacArthur knew about it until it was a done deed."

Pickering didn't reply.

"I'd like an explanation, if you don't mind, General," Truman said.

"Mr. President, I accept responsibility for what happened," Pickering said.

"Why did you feel it was necessary to keep the Supreme Commander in the dark?" Truman said.

"Sir, I was at the Dai Ichi Building meetings at which the landing was discussed. Very senior members of the planning staff raised the question of the Flying Fish Channel Islands, and when was the best time to neutralize them. It was General MacArthur's decision that they be neutralized as the invasion fleet steamed down the channel. I thought —"

" 'MacArthur is wrong. Those islands have to be neutralized earlier, and I can do it'?" Truman asked.

"I didn't think I would have much chance of getting General MacArthur to reverse his position, as doing so would fly in the face of the recommendations of his staff officers."

"So you took it upon yourself to stage this clandestine operation, without telling either General MacArthur or seeking permission from Admiral Hillencoetter to take an action known to be contrary to the wishes of General MacArthur?"

"Sir, if my operation failed, the original plan to neutralize the islands would have taken place."

"So you took it upon yourself to stage this clandestine operation, without telling either General MacArthur or seeking permission from Admiral Hillencoetter to take an action known to be contrary to the wishes of General MacArthur?" Truman asked verbatim again.

"Yes, sir. That's what I did."

"I think some people would describe that behavior as . . . the phrase 'loose cannon' comes to mind."

Pickering didn't respond.

Senator Fowler shook his head in disbelief, or perhaps resignation, at what Truman had revealed.

"I'm not one of those people," Truman said. "Sometimes you have to do what you know is right, regardless of the consequences."

He let that sink in.

"And what did the Supreme Commander have to say to you when he found out what you had done?"

Pickering, without realizing what he was doing, smiled at the memory.

"Why are you smiling, General?"

"Sir . . . When I told General MacArthur, he announced to his staff that it was his clandestine operation."

Truman smiled back.

" 'Victory has a thousand fathers'? Something like that? He wasn't angry with you?"

"If he was, it didn't show, Mr. President."

"Ralph tells me that, too," Truman said. "That MacArthur seems genuinely fond of you."

Pickering didn't reply.

"That was really a question, General," Truman said.

"I'm not sure if 'fond' is the right word, Mr. President," Pickering replied. "I admire him —"

"Warts and all?" Truman interrupted.

"The latter overwhelm the former, Mr. President. I think his biggest wart . . . he's something like the architect Frank Lloyd Wright, who said, 'It's difficult to be humble when you know you're great.' "

Truman chuckled.

"I'll have to remember that one," he said.

"When they made me a sergeant in France, Mr. President, a wise old gunnery sergeant took me aside and told me the worst mistake I could make as a sergeant was to think I could be friends with my men."

Truman nodded.

"I think MacArthur knows that, practices that. What I suppose I'm saying is that he and Jean are lonely in the residence. Then I show up. Three things: I knew him — slightly — socially in Manila before the war. And I was with him through most of the Second War. And I'm not subordinate to him. And he knows that I like him. For those reasons, they include me in . . . how do I say this? . . . their personal family."

"In other words, he's not trying to either pick your brain or influence me through you?"

"That, too, sir, frankly."

"Tell me how you think he's going to act with regard to the new Secretary of Defense, General Ma[...]

"I don't think h[...]
Secretary Johnson, [...]

"That wasn't the [...]

"I think he will be [...]
dier as Secretary of [...]
dent."

"Even one he once [...]
ciency report, as 'not [...]
mental command'?" Tru[...]

"Yes, sir. I know tha[...]
question was 'How will [...]
General Marshall?' I don'[...]
be any problems in that re[...]

"Did you ever hear tha[...]
General Eisenhower as 'th[...]
ever had'?" Truman asked.

"Yes, sir. I've heard that st[...]

"The United Nations ha[...]
permit the UN Command —[...]
course General MacArthur —[...]
North Korea and destroy th[...]
rean Army," Truman sa[...]
of that, right?"

"Yes, sir."

"I'm co[...]
might [...]
b[...]

375

icular, en-
rshall." parent
e had much re de-
Mr. President.
question."
pleased to have ch
Defense, Mr. te
th
s
escribed, in an
being fit for you
man challenged Mac-
story, sir. Y t they
e get along wi missed,
think there wi
gard." er a per-
t he described much the
e best clerk I — saying
ory." him here,"
s voted was that he
which is at this time' to
to ent of course, if he
North K have been won-
re awa t what he said, or
ething go wrong —
war, for example —
would be my fault,
to leave the Far

"Sir, I thi ndably reluc-
tant to giv d, for any
length of tin

"I'm the President, General. I'm the Commander-in-Chief. When I send for somebody, they should come."

"Sir, you asked my opinion," Pickering said.

"Yes, I did, and you gave it," Truman said, and suddenly got to his feet. "Thank you for your candor, General."

He started for the door and then turned.

"I'm meeting General MacArthur halfway," Truman said. "That is, the Commander-in-Chief of this country is going to get on an airplane and fly to Wake Island and meet one of his generals, who is too busy to come here."

"Yes, sir," Pickering said.

"I may decide I want you to go with me. Or would that interfere with your schedule?"

"Mr. President, I'm completely at your disposal."

"Thank you," Truman said, and walked out the door.

"Jesus H. Christ!" Pickering said when the door had closed.

"Indeed," Senator Fowler chuckled. "I would hazard the guess that Ol' Harry's just a little piqued with MacArthur."

"And I'm probably at least partially responsible," Pickering said.

"I wouldn't flatter myself and think that, Flem," Fowler said.

"Well, finding the silver lining in that black cloud," Pickering said. "I guess that settles the question of his offering me the CIA, doesn't it?"

"In my professional opinion, Fleming, you are absolutely wrong about that."

"You're kidding!"

"Uh-uh," Senator Fowler said, shaking his head. "I'll give you seven-to-three for a hundred bucks that I'm looking at the next Director of the Central Intelligence Agency."

[Three]
The House
Seoul, South Korea
0725 6 October 1950

"That's the fifth time you've looked at your watch in the last five minutes," Lieutenant Colonel D. J. Vandenburg said to Major Kenneth R. McCoy. "Expecting somebody?"

They were at the dining room table. The dishes and silverware had been cleaned away, and the table was covered with large maps of Korea, and with stacks of reports — many of them written in Korean — that reported sightings of Prisoners of War held by the North Koreans.

"Dunston," McCoy said. "I guess he couldn't catch a ride in an airplane. And

General Howe. I'm getting a little worried about both of them."

"General Howe is fine, thank you for your concern," Major General Ralph Howe said, walking into the dining room trailed by Master Sergeant Charley Rogers.

Howe draped the web strap of his M-2 Grease Gun on the back of a chair and sat down. Then he gestured impatiently for McCoy and Vandenburg, who had come to attention, to relax. Rogers, after glancing at the map, sat down on the other side of the table.

"Sir," McCoy said, "this is Lieutenant Colonel Vandenburg. Colonel, General Howe."

Howe extended his hand.

"How do you do, Colonel?" he said. "This is Master Sergeant Charley Rogers." He paused. "That out of the way, have we missed breakfast?"

"Of course not, sir," McCoy said. "Ham and eggs?"

"That would be very nice," Howe said.

McCoy walked to the kitchen, spoke to the housekeeper, and then came back into the room.

"We tried to make it back here last night, it got dark, so we sat down on a First Cav airstrip and spent the night," Rogers said. "We passed on the cold rations that were offered, the horses kept us up all night, and we passed on a cold breakfast. So we are hungry."

Howe chuckled.

"Not really horses," he said. "But apparently in the Cav their sentinels are taught to shoot first, and then challenge, 'Halt, who goes there?' Charley's a little too long in the tooth to keep jumping up all night the way he did."

"The 7th Cav CP sounded like the O.K. Corral," Rogers said. "And I kept remembering what happened to them at the Little Big Horn."

Vandenburg laughed.

"Well, we're here," Howe said. "I guess Dunston is not? Where is he?"

"We took the helos to Socho-Ri yesterday, sir. I came back as soon as I could. Dunston stayed on to start the agent insertions. I caught a ride back in a Capital ROK Division L-4. I guess he couldn't get an airplane and had to drive."

Howe nodded, then turned to Vandenburg.

"Colonel, since Major McCoy is talking about inserting agents from Socho-Ri, I presume you have the need to know about such things."

"Sir," Vandenburg said, smiling, "since Major McCoy has told me who you are, I presume it's all right to tell you I'm here to see about getting General Dean back."

380

"Okay," Howe said. "I think I know about that. You came from the States for that purpose, right?"

"Yes, sir. My orders are from DCSOPS,* but I have been led to believe the orders came from the Chief of Staff."

"You were led wrong, then," Howe said. "They came from the top. One of the first questions the President put to the new Chief of Staff, General Bradley, was 'What can we do about getting General Dean back?' I have a message from the President — it arrived here just after General Pickering left for the States — saying that somebody was being sent here, and ordering me to do what I could to help."

"I didn't know that, sir," Vandenburg said.

"If you had come to me, I would have referred you to Major McCoy, so you've come to the right place. You weren't told to contact me?"

"I was told to contact General Pickering, sir. But not you, sir. Maybe there wasn't time. An hour after I got my orders, I was on a plane for the West Coast."

"Or maybe," Howe said, thinking out loud, "what happened was that I got a copy of the President's message to General

*The acronym for the Deputy Chief of Staff for Operations, Headquarters, U.S. Army.

Pickering, in case that didn't reach him before he left."

"Yes, sir," Vandenburg said.

"I was a little surprised with the message. I'm not supposed to get involved in operations here; I'm strictly an observer. Now it makes sense. Anyway, we know what the orders are. Let's see what we can do about getting General Dean back. Is that what this is all about?"

He waved a hand toward the map and reports.

"Yes, sir," McCoy said. "But we don't have anything of value."

He patted one of the stacks of reports.

"These are mostly pre-Inchon," he said. "They locate POW holding points we know are no longer there . . ."

"Spit it out, Ken," Howe said.

"My gut feeling is that General Dean may already be in Peking," he said. "The ChiComs know what a valuable propaganda tool he could be — hell, *is* — and they know we'll probably stage an operation to get him back. If he's in China — even just a couple of miles across the border . . ."

"I take your point," Howe said. "McCoy, this is in the nature of an order. Even 'a couple of miles across the border' is not the Flying Fish Channel Islands. I don't want you staging any kind of an operation across the border unless the President gives the okay. You understand me?"

"Aye, aye, sir," McCoy said.

"So tell me what you two have decided," Howe ordered.

"Aside from dividing the peninsula between us, sir, with Colonel Vandenburg looking on the west and me on the east, not much. And I thought we'd better wait and talk to Dunston before we decide even that."

"And he's not here," Howe said. "You said he had to drive?"

"Probably, sir."

"Why couldn't he have used one of the helicopters?"

"We're going to keep them as quiet as possible, as long as possible, sir," McCoy said.

"What we need is a couple of regular airplanes, General," Vandenburg said.

"A couple?"

"An L-19," McCoy said. "I'll settle for an L-4. And a Beaver."

"What's a Beaver?"

"Six-place, single-engine high-wing, General," Vandenburg said. "Designed for Alaska, Canada. Rugged, and they can land on a dime."

"I think I've seen one," Howe said. "Okay. I'll see what I can do."

"General, I'm pretty sure I can get both,

but hanging on to them — especially the Beaver — is going to be a real problem. They're in short supply, and every general in Korea thinks he should have one. And probably should."

"But you need one more than they do, eh?"

"Yes, sir. I think it's a question of deciding priorities. I think getting General Dean back qualifies."

"Yeah, so do I. Not to mention getting young Pickering back," Howe said. "Has McCoy told you about him?"

"No, sir."

"Okay. Major Pickering, General Pickering's son, was shot down about two months ago, and has been evading capture ever since. . . ."

"You know that, sir? That he's alive and hasn't been captured?"

"McCoy thinks he's alive," Howe said.

"Where is he?" Vandenburg said, turning to McCoy.

"The last sighting was east of Wonju," McCoy said.

"You sighted him?"

"We sighted where he had stamped out a signal . . . his initials and an arrow on the ground, not him. I figure we missed him by no more than a couple of hours."

"You couldn't pick him up with a chopper?"

"We didn't have the choppers then, and we couldn't take one away from the 1st MarDiv — they're using them to transport wounded."

" 'Couldn't take one' from the Marines — or anyone else who has one — is past tense, Ken," Howe said. "The rules have changed."

"Sir?"

"This is absolutely not for dissemination," Howe said. "I think the reason the President called General Pickering to Washington is to give him the CIA. He asked me what kind of a director I thought he'd make, and I told him I couldn't think of anyone better qualified to take it over and straighten it out. So what we have is a changed priority with regard to Major Pickering. We can't afford to have the son of the Director on the CIA in enemy hands." He paused. "That, too, Ken, is in the nature of an order."

"Aye, aye, sir."

"Okay, Colonel," Howe went on. "You lay your hands on these airplanes you need, and I will do my damnedest to see that no one takes them away from you."

"Sir, may I offer a suggestion about how that might be done?" Vandenburg asked.

"Shoot."

"I notice the general doesn't have an aide-de-camp."

"I don't need one," Howe said simply, then chuckled and added: "I shine my own shoes."

"Sir, I respectfully suggest that you do need an aide-de-camp," Vandenburg said. "A fairly senior one. And I volunteer for the duty."

"Where are you going with that idea?"

"I don't think any general here, from MacArthur on down, would try to take an airplane away from the aide-de-camp of — What's your official title, sir?"

"We're the Presidential Mission to the Supreme Command, United Nations Command," Master Sergeant Rogers said. "His official title is Chief of Mission. Boss, I think the colonel's had a fine idea."

Howe thought it over for ten seconds.

"Okay," he said. "Do it. Type up something appropriate, Charley, naming the colonel my deputy. Somehow, he doesn't look like an aide-de-camp."

"Even better, sir," Vandenburg said.

"Yes, sir," Rogers said. "And we get to use the airplanes, too, right?"

"Of course," Vandenburg said.

"You're a . . . I was about to say 'devious man,' Colonel," Howe said admiringly. "But I think the word I'm looking for is 'ruthless.' I can see where you and The Killer are going to get along just fine."

[Four]
USAF Airfield K-1
Pusan, South Korea
0945 8 October 1950

The breakout — and advance northward — from the Pusan Perimeter of the Eighth Army had done little or nothing to reduce the pressure on what had once been the only operational airfield in South Korea.

It had become, however, more of a passenger and freight terminal than a base for the fighters and light bombers it had been when the Pusan Perimeter needed fighting aircraft to keep from being pushed into the sea.

When the USAF C-47 from Seoul arrived at the port city, it had to take its place at the end of a long line of aircraft making their approaches to the field. Many of the aircraft ahead of them were four-engine C-54 transports bearing the insignia of the Military Air Transport Command, and there were four essentially identical aircraft wearing the insignia of the civilian airlines from which they had been chartered.

The warplanes were not entirely gone. The stack also held a dozen or more warplanes, USAF P-51 Mustang fighters, A-20 and A-26 attack bombers, and several Corsairs from the Marine Corps and Navy.

And when, after more than a half hour in

the stack, the Gooney Bird from Seoul finally touched down and taxied to the tarmac in front of base operations, there was even a Lockheed Constellation of Trans-Global Airways sitting there taking on enough fuel to get it to Japan, where it would be topped off. The glistening, sleek, triple-tailed aircraft looked out of place among the others.

When the Gooney Bird shut down its engines and the door opened, sixteen people, ranging in rank from PFC to full colonel, got off and most of them walked into base operations to see about getting themselves some ground transportation.

Four of the passengers — a lieutenant colonel, a major, a captain, and a lieutenant, the latter three wearing the wings of Army aviators — did not go into base operations but started walking across the field to a hangar before which sat a small fleet of Army aircraft.

When they got close to the hangar, they saw a small group of officers and men standing around an L-20 DeHavilland Beaver, watching as a corporal put the final touches to the insignia of the Eighth United States Army he had painted on the door. The aircraft looked as if it was not only just about brand new but also freshly polished.

The senior of the officers was a major,

also an Army aviator. He saluted the lieutenant colonel and smiled at his brother aviators.

"Good morning, sir," he said. "This came off the ship at 2100 last night," he went on, indicating the Beaver. "And as soon as that paint dries, it's going to Eighth Army Forward. How's that for efficiency?"

"Commendable," the lieutenant colonel said, then spoke to the soldier with the paintbrush: "Son, have you got some paint thinner in your kit?"

"Yes, sir," the corporal said, visibly confused.

"Then how about taking that off the door?" the lieutenant colonel said. "I don't want that insignia on there."

"Sir?" the major asked incredulously.

"I said I don't want that insignia on the door," the lieutenant colonel explained, reasonably, "and asked the corporal to start taking it off."

"Sir, this aircraft is assigned to Eighth Army Forward," the major said.

"It *was* assigned to Eighth Army Forward," the lieutenant colonel said. "Now I'm taking it."

"Sir, you . . . you can't do that," the major said.

"Yes I can. And I will also require two L-19s."

"Sir, I can't just give you this airplane," the major said, "or any aircraft, for that matter, without authority from United Nations Command."

"You *are* the officer in charge?" the lieutenant colonel asked.

"No, sir. I'm the deputy."

"Well, then, son, if you have problems with this, why don't you ask the officer in charge to come talk to me?"

"Yes, sir. I'll do that, sir."

"And in the meantime, Corporal, you start getting that insignia off the doors," the lieutenant colonel said.

The major walked quickly — almost trotted — to a Quonset hut set up beside a hangar and returned in less than two minutes, followed by a portly lieutenant colonel wearing pilot's wings and the insignia of an aide-de-camp to a three-star general, and another lieutenant colonel, also a pilot, whose collar carried the insignia of the Transportation Corps.

"Colonel," the portly lieutenant colonel said, "this is some sort of joke, right?"

"What's a joke?"

"About you taking this airplane."

"I wasn't joking about that."

"This airplane belongs to General Walker," the portly lieutenant colonel said. "Do you understand that?"

"Colonel, this airplane belongs to the

U.S. Army," Vandenburg said. "And I have what I'm sure is the highest priority to put it to use."

"I'd like to see that authority!"

"Certainly," Vandenburg said, and handed him an envelope.

The eyes of both lieutenant colonels grew wide as they read it.

THE WHITE HOUSE

WASHINGTON, D.C.

JULY 8TH, 1950

TO WHOM IT MAY CONCERN:

MAJOR GENERAL RALPH HOWE, USAR, IN CONNECTION WITH HIS MISSION FOR ME, WILL TRAVEL TO SUCH PLACES AT SUCH TIMES AS HE FEELS APPROPRIATE, ACCOMPANIED BY SUCH STAFF AS HE DESIRES.

GENERAL HOWE IS GRANTED HEREWITH A TOP-SECRET/WHITE HOUSE CLEARANCE, AND MAY, AT HIS OPTION, GRANT SUCH CLEARANCE TO HIS STAFF.

U.S. MILITARY AND GOVERNMENTAL AGENCIES ARE DIRECTED TO PROVIDE

GENERAL HOWE AND HIS STAFF WITH
WHATEVER SUPPORT THEY MAY REQUIRE.

Harry S Truman
HARRY S TRUMAN
PRESIDENT OF THE UNITED STATES

1st Indorsement
Headquarters, Presidential Mission
In the Field (Korea) 7 October 1950

Lieutenant Colonel D. J. Vandenburg, USA,
of my staff is designated Deputy Chief of
Mission.

Major Kenneth R. McCoy, USMCR, of my
staff is designated Vice Chief of Mission.

Ralph Howe
Ralph Howe
Major General
Chief of Mission

"Are there any questions, gentlemen?"

"General Walker's not going to like this!" the lieutenant colonel with the aide-de-camp insignia said as he handed the orders back.

"Colonel," Vandenburg said, man-to-man, "I understand how you feel. In your place, I'd feel the same way. Hell hath no fury like a general who doesn't get what he wants, right? But what can I do? We all live under the Chain of Command. General Howe, who reports directly to the President, doesn't need any more authority than what I've shown you he has. And he sent me here to get a Beaver and two L-19s. I don't have any more choice in this matter than you do."

Neither lieutenant colonel replied.

"Now, while the corporal is taking that paint off the door, can we look at what L-19s are available?" Vandenburg asked reasonably.

"There's only one here at the moment," the Transportation Corps lieutenant colonel said. "There should be some more coming in in the next three or four days."

"I can only hope General Howe will understand," Vandenburg said, his voice suggesting he didn't believe that at all. "He sent me to get two."

[Five]
Hangar 13
Kimpo Airfield (K-16)
Seoul, South Korea
1245 8 October 1950

Major Kenneth R. McCoy was driving the Russian jeep and Major William Dunston was sitting behind him. The Marines on perimeter guard around the hangar recognized them and passed them without question, but the moment they reached the hangar, Staff Sergeant Sam Klegger, who had been left in charge when the others went to Socho-Ri, came through the door.

He saluted, and McCoy and Dunston returned it.

"From the look on your face, Sergeant," McCoy said, "you have a question on your mind."

"Good afternoon, sir," Staff Sergeant Klegger said. "Yes, sir. Actually, some of the men have been a little curious why we're guarding a hangar with nothing in it."

"There is about to be something in it," McCoy said. "About an hour ago, we got a message from Taejon saying that two airplanes will arrive here right about now. A Beaver and an L-19. When they get close to the hangar, I want the doors opened, quickly, and as quickly closed once we get the airplanes inside."

"Aye, aye, sir. Is that what they call those helos, 'Beavers'?"

"No. A Beaver is a regular airplane," McCoy said.

"Sir, can I ask what's going on? What are we going to do with these airplanes?"

"We 'borrowed' them from the Army,"

McCoy said. "We're going to use them to look for a Marine aviator who's down somewhere between Suwon and the east coast."

"You 'borrowed' them from the Army?"

"You could put it that way, Sergeant, yes," McCoy said.

Staff Sergeant Klegger smiled approvingly.

Dunston touched McCoy's arm, and, when he had his attention, pointed skyward.

A Beaver was making its final approach.

"Right on time," McCoy said.

"If that's ours," Dunston said.

"Odds are it is," McCoy said. "There aren't that many of them."

They lost sight of the Beaver as it landed, but it quickly appeared on a taxiway headed for them.

"Open the doors, Sergeant," McCoy ordered.

Five Marines grunted as they slid open the hangar doors.

The Beaver stopped before the open doors and shut down the engine. Lieutenant Colonel D. J. Vandenburg and Major Alex Donald climbed down from the cockpit. The Marines and all the officers pushed it into the hangar. Before they were finished, an L-19 taxied up, shut down its engine, and was pushed into the hangar by the two officers in it. The doors were closed with a loud screeching noise.

"The good news," Lieutenant Colonel Vandenburg said to Majors McCoy and Dunston, "is that — obviously — I was able to make good on my promise to try to get us a Beaver and an L-19. The bad news is that that particular Beaver was supposed to go to the Eighth Army commander, and I think we have to count on General Walker making a serious — one might even say furious — effort to get it back."

"Ouch," McCoy said.

"If we can keep General Walker, or his people, from getting their hands on it — or us — for three, four days, a week, I think they'll probably be able to get him another one, and the furor will die down. But until then . . ."

"You have any ideas how we can do that?" McCoy asked.

"As a matter of fact, Major Donald and I did discuss the problem on the way up here," Vandenburg said, smiling.

"All suggestions gratefully received, Colonel," Dunston said, smiling.

"Since we can't hide the Beaver, I suggest we camouflage it," Vandenburg said, a little smugly.

"I don't follow you, sir."

"We change the tail number,"

Vandenburg said. "They will be looking for . . ." He looked up at the Beaver. ". . . 507179. We change that to, say, 507167. General Walker's Beaver is now invisible."

"Very clever," McCoy said.

"We landed here as Army five zero mumble mumble mumble," Donald said. "When they asked me to 'say again,' I blew into the microphone. I figured that might buy us a little time."

"Only a little," Vandenburg said. "I think General Walker's pilot was on the horn to him before we took off from Pusan. It won't take them long to figure out we're the airplane Walker is looking for."

"And there are problems with painting new tail numbers," Donald said. "It can't be done in fifteen minutes, even if we had somebody to do it, and the paint to do it with. There's paint in the mechanics' tool kits, but they're at Socho-Ri."

"Then we'll have to change them at Socho-Ri," McCoy said. "Why can't we just take off now and tell the tower we're headed for the Race Track?"

"And never land there, you mean?" Donald asked.

McCoy nodded.

"If the Race Track tower asks questions, I'll think of something to mumble," Donald said. "But we don't have enough fuel to make it to Socho-Ri. We're going to have to refuel the airplanes."

"Sergeant," McCoy said to Staff Sergeant Klegger, "isn't there a trailer of AvGas here?"

"Yes, sir. Two, each with five hundred gallons."

"Drag one of them in here, and get started refueling these airplanes," McCoy ordered.

"Aye, aye, sir."

"And then get ready to move out," McCoy went on. "Mr. Zimmerman left you maps so that you can drive to Socho-Ri, right?"

"Yes, sir."

"As soon after the airplanes take off as you can, you get going."

"Aye, aye, sir."

"Bill, can you stay with them until they're out of Seoul?" McCoy asked Dunston. "Get them through roadblocks?"

"Sure. You're going with them?"

"Yeah. I want to show Colonel Vandenburg what we have at Socho-Ri, and the sooner we can put the L-19 to work conducting our own search for Pickering, the better."

The hangar door screeched open wide enough to admit a tanker trailer.

[Six]
8023d Transportation Company
(Depot, Forward)
Inchon, South Korea
1425 8 October 1950

Captain Francis P. MacNamara, Transportation Corps, was not at all surprised when he got a "heads-up" call that the X Corps Transportation Officer, Colonel T. Howard Kennedy, would be in the Inchon area and would pay the Eighty-Twenty-Three a visit.

MacNamara had been expecting such a "visit." He would not have been surprised if he had gotten an official call announcing a formal inspection of the unit. Certainly, the status of readiness of the Eighty-Twenty-Three would be of interest to the staff officers of X Corps, and so far there had been no contact of any sort.

He was, of course, a little nervous. He knew that the purpose of an inspection — by whatever name — was to find fault with whatever was being inspected.

But he was ready. There had been very little "business" for the Eighty-Twenty-Three since he'd started to set up shop. There had been that interesting business of issuing vehicles to the CIA a week before, and he had exchanged twenty-seven of his vehicles for damaged vehicles. But that had not at all taxed the capabilities of the

Eighty-Twenty-Three. He felt sure he could conduct one hundred vehicle exchanges a day easily, and more if pressed.

But the lack of business had permitted getting the Eighty-Twenty-Three into very good shape. Not only had his shops repaired all but seven of the exchanged vehicles and returned them to the Ready for Exchange lines, but there had been time to establish creature comforts for his men.

The squad tents in which they were housed now had wooden floors, doors, and electric lights. A section of the garage building had been converted to a mess hall, with picnic-table-type seating for the lower ranks, and chairs and tables for First Three Graders and officers.

He was serving three hot meals a day, and had set up two shower points, one for the men and a second for the noncoms and officers, which they shared on a simple schedule. Similarly, he had set up three latrines, one outside under canvas, and two — by repairing existing facilities — in the main building, one for the officers and another for the noncoms.

He had even established a unit laundry. He'd had to bend regulations a little to do this. Koreans were performing this service, in exchange for the garbage from the mess and five jerry cans of gasoline daily. Inasmuch as this service was provided outside the depot area, he didn't think it would come to the attention of anyone visiting the Eighty-Twenty-Three. If it did, he was prepared to argue that it was a question of troop morale. Men whose uniforms quickly became grease- and oil-stained, and who took a great deal of comfort in knowing that after their shower they could put on fresh clothing, were obviously going to be happier than those who had to either wash their clothing themselves or go to one of the X Corps shower points outside the depot and exchange them.

Not to mention, of course, that his laundry service returned uniforms that were even pressed. In the case of the officers, starched and pressed. The uniforms available for exchange were those that had simply been washed and dried in the enormous machines of the shower point.

Immediately after the "heads-up" call, Captain MacNamara had sent his runner to announce an officer's call, and when his four lieutenants came to the CP, he told them what was going to happen.

He said that when he walked through the shop and around the depot perimeter, as he planned to do in thirty minutes, he didn't want to see anyone unshaved or in a dirty uniform. He said, as they knew, he didn't insist that steel helmets and web gear be worn while the men were working, but he expected to see both near those working. Those on perimeter guard he expected to see looking alert and with their weapons as clean as possible, and they better be wearing their helmets and web gear.

And thirty minutes later he took a quick tour of the Eighty-Twenty-Three, and found only a few things — he insisted that a large poster of a nearly naked redhead be removed from the wall of one of the work bays, for example — that needed correction. Then he started a second tour of the Eighty-Twenty-Three, this time a slow one.

He thought it would look better if Colonel T. Howard Kennedy found him keeping a personal supervisory eye on things, rather than sitting in the CP, drinking coffee, and reading *Stars and Stripes*.

From what MacNamara had heard — and, for that matter, seen — the war was just about over. The linkup with Eighth Army advancing from the south had been made, and he'd heard that the UN had given permission to MacArthur to chase the North Koreans back across the 38th Parallel and destroy what was left of their army.

There were a lot of implications to be drawn from that, and MacNamara had been around the Army long enough to make them.

Many of the troops here would be withdrawn, either — at first, at least — to Japan or all the way back to the States. That didn't mean they would take all their wheeled vehicles with them. For one thing, that would take a lot of shipping, and for another, it didn't make a lot of sense to haul vehicles that had been used hard in the war and needed Third and Fourth Echelon maintenance all the way back to the States when that maintenance could be performed a lot cheaper in Japan.

And MacNamara believed that it was unlikely the Army was going to allow itself to be caught again with its pants down, logistically speaking. From what he'd seen and heard, there had been almost nothing in the depots in Japan when the war started, and that had hurt bad.

It seemed very likely to MacNamara that what would happen, once the war was over in a couple of weeks, was that the Army would restock the depots in Japan with the vehicles that had come from the States. There would be ordnance depots in Japan like the Anniston Depot in Alabama, with stocks of rebuilt-to-specification vehicles ready for immediate issue.

And there was certainly a role to play in that for units like the Eighty-Twenty-Three generally, and, if he played his cards right, for Captain Francis P. MacNamara specifically.

He didn't want to get too enthusiastic about it, only to be later kicked in the balls, but it seemed possible, even likely, that he could stay on active duty long enough to get his promotion to major. He was eligible.

If that happened, that meant he would be retired as a major when he had his twenty years in, even if he got RIF'd again back to master sergeant.

But it was also possible, if less likely, that he could stay on active duty, particularly if he was right about the Army setting up an Anniston-type depot in Japan when the war was over, and go all the way to twenty years and retirement as a major.

Hell, maybe even make lieutenant colonel before he retired.

All it would take for this to happen would be for the brass to notice that he had done a hell of a good job with the Eighty-Twenty-Three and was just the man they needed for what was going to happen after the war.

Colonel Kennedy arrived fifteen minutes into Captain MacNamara's second tour of the depot.

MacNamara saw him arrive — in a three-jeep convoy — but pretended not to see him until the "visiting party" had parked their jeeps and walked down to him between two rows of Ready for Exchange vehicles.

Then he hurriedly walked to them, saluted, and announced, "Good morning, sir. Captain MacNamara, Francis P., commanding."

Colonel Kennedy returned the salute.

"Quite an operation you have here, Captain," he said. "Very impressive."

"Thank you, sir."

"Can you give me some quick stats? What's ready for issue?"

"Everything you see, sir, except for those beyond-my-capacity-to-repair vehicles" — he pointed — "over there. There are seven in that category, sir. There are five hundred seventy-nine wheeled vehicles of all types ready for issue, sir."

"Five hundred seventy-nine, eh?"

"Yes, sir. Would the colonel like a specific breakdown?"

"That won't be necessary," Colonel Kennedy said. "I didn't really realize there were that many."

"Yes, sir. And all ready for immediate exchange."

"I understand there was some difficulty in getting them off-loaded at Inchon when you came."

"The heavier stuff — the tank trans-

porters, some of the larger wreckers —
gave us a little trouble, sir. But we managed to get everything off-loaded without
trouble."

"And the tides, too, I'm sure, posed a
problem?"

"Yes, sir. We really had to push when
the ship was at the dock to get as much off
before the ship had to go back down the
channel again."

"Somebody said, you know, that Inchon
was the worst possible place, because of
those tides, to stage a landing."

"Well, we did it, sir."

"And you think you learned from the experience?"

"Yes, sir. I'm sure we did."

"Well, perhaps that will make things a
little easier for you now," Colonel Kennedy
said.

"Sir?"

"As soon as you can, Captain, start
moving your vehicles back to Inchon.
Check with the port captain, and see where
he wants you to operate for the onloading."

"Yes, sir. I'll get right on it. I'm a little
surprised that we're going back to Japan so
soon."

"I didn't say anything about Japan,
Captain," Colonel Kennedy said. "X
Corps has been ordered to reembark to

make another landing elsewhere."

"Yes, sir. Where would that be?"

"You'll be informed in good time," Colonel Kennedy said. He put out his hand. "You've done a good job here, Captain. Keep it up."

"Yes, sir," MacNamara said.

IX

[One]
Blair House
Pennsylvania Avenue
Washington, D.C.
1005 11 October 1950

There was a knock at the closed door of Harry S Truman's study, but the President, who was reading what he thought of as one more windy damned report, didn't pay much attention to it.

There were knocks at his study door all day and all night, followed a moment later by whoever was there — his secretary, usually — opening it and standing there waiting until she had his attention.

When, a full sixty seconds later, Truman raised his eyes to see who it was, the door was still closed. He watched the door, waiting for it to open. It didn't. He had just about decided that he hadn't heard a knock after all when there was another.

"Come in," the President called, not entirely cordially.

The door immediately opened and a Marine sergeant in dress blue uniform marched

408

in, stopped precisely eighteen inches from the President's desk, saluted crisply, and barked, "An eyes-only message for the Commander-in-Chief, sir!" and extended a business-size white envelope toward the President.

"Thank you, son," Truman said, and returned the salute.

Harry S Truman knew very well that salutes were supposed to be only for members of the armed forces in uniform, but had rationalized that by reminding himself that not only was he Commander-in-Chief, but every month the Treasurer of the United States mailed a pension check to Colonel Harry S Truman, NG, Retired. He'd worn the uniform, and if he wanted to return this boy's salute, he damned well was going to.

The sergeant snapped to a Parade Rest position.

"Stand at ease," Truman said.

The sergeant snapped to a slightly — only slightly — less rigid position and stared eight inches over the President's head.

There was little question in the President's mind that he was about to read a message from Ralph Howe. All other messages were delivered by either his secretary or, in the case of Eyes-Only, by one of the Signal Corps officers or warrant officers in the message center.

Except for Eyes-Only messages from Ralph Howe and Fleming Pickering. These were invariably delivered by a Marine. Truman had finally figured out that the Marines had stationed two of their own in the message center, round-the-clock, a Marine cryptographer who got all the messages from Camp Pendleton addressed to the President, and decoded it, and another Marine in dress blues to personally deliver it.

It was just like the Marines, the President thought, to do something like that.

He realized and admitted that the thought was much less sarcastic than it had been before this damned Korean business started. He had not then been much of a fan of the United States Marine Corps, and had been quoted as saying he didn't see why the Navy needed its own army, and perhaps — to save the taxpayer's dollar — it was time to do away with it.

Korea had changed that. The Army had really dropped the ball over there, and the Marine Corps had saved their ass. That wasn't Marine Corps public relations talking. Ralph Howe had reported that from over there, and even General Walker had come right out and said that if it hadn't been for the Marines, he didn't think he would have been able to hold at the Pusan Perimeter.

Truman slit the envelope open with a small penknife, took out the contents — four sheets of neatly single-spaced type-writer copy — and read them twice. First, a quick glance, and then again, slowly.

Then he folded the sheets of paper and put them back in the envelope. He looked at the Marine sergeant.

"Sergeant . . ." The Marine snapped to attention like a spring. "That'll be all, son. Would you ask one of the Secret Service agents to come in, please? Thank you."

"Aye, aye, sir," the Marine barked, and snapped his rigid hand to his eyebrow.

Truman returned the salute again.

The Marine did a snappy About-Face movement and marched out of the office.

Truman picked up one of his telephones.

"See if you can get General Pickering for me, will you, please?" he said, and hung up.

There was another knock at the door, and the door opened and two Secret Service agents stepped into the room without waiting for permission.

"Yes, Mr. President?" one of them asked.

"I want one of you to take this," Truman said, holding out the envelope, "across the street to General Pickering in the Foster Lafayette. When he's finished reading it, bring it back."

411

The telephone buzzed. Truman reached to pick it up before the Secret Service agent could take the envelope from his hand.

"I have General Pickering, Mr. President," the White House Operator said.

"Pickering?" the President said.

"Yes, Mr. President?"

The President of the United States changed his mind.

That wasn't good news about his son. The least I can do is deliver it myself.

And I need to get him off the hook about the CIA anyway.

This is as good a time to do that as any.

"Have you got a few minutes for me? Right now?"

"I'll be there immediately, Mr. President."

"Hold your position, General," Truman said. "You're in your apartment, right?"

"Yes, Mr. President."

"Order up some coffee, General, if you'd be so kind. I'll be right there. I need the walk."

"It'll be waiting, Mr. President."

The President hung up and looked at the Secret Service agents.

"Organize the parade," he ordered. "I'm going across the street to the Foster Lafayette."

The parade, as Truman referred to his

Secret Service bodyguard escort, was waiting when Truman came down the steps of Blair House, turned right, and walked briskly down Pennsylvania Avenue toward the Foster Lafayette Hotel.

Truman looked across Pennsylvania Avenue at the White House. There were all sorts of signs of work on the "repairs" under way. It was more than repairs, Truman thought. The building, which had been literally at the point of collapse, had been gutted and was being rebuilt.

He waved and smiled at tourists, but completely ignored the questions called out to him by a dozen members of the press who had joined the parade the moment it was formed.

They were waiting for him at the Foster Lafayette. The doorman held the door open for him, and, inside, four Secret Service agents made sort of a path to an elevator waiting for him.

Brigadier General Fleming Pickering, USMCR, was standing in the corridor outside the door to his suite.

"Morning," the President said.

One of the Secret Service agents walked quickly through the door.

"Good morning, Mr. President," Pickering said as the President walked past him into the sitting room of the Marquis de Lafayette Suite.

Two waiters were making final adjustments to an array of food on a table covered with a white tablecloth.

"That's very nice, General," Truman said, "but all I asked for was a cup of coffee."

"Mr. President, if you'd given them another couple of minutes, there would be a steamboat round of beef and pheasant under glass on that table," Pickering said.

"It's a little early for something like that, but that pastry is tempting," Truman said. He walked to the table and spoke to the waiters. "That's very nice, thank you very much."

He picked up a white sugarcoated breakfast roll and looked at the Secret Service agents.

"Would you leave us, please?" he ordered.

He took a bite of the roll, then laid it down and poured a cup of coffee from a silver pitcher. He looked at Pickering, asking with raised eyebrows if Pickering wanted coffee.

"Yes, please, thank you, sir," Pickering said.

Truman poured the coffee and handed the cup and saucer to Pickering. Then he took his own cup and saucer and the breakfast roll and sat down on a couch.

"Please sit down, General," he said.

"Thank you, sir."

"I just got a message from Ralph Howe," the President said. "I thought you would like to see it."

He took the white envelope from his suit jacket pocket and handed it to Pickering.

"Thank you, sir," Pickering said, and opened the envelope and read it.

TOP SECRET/PRESIDENTIAL

OPERATIONAL IMMEDIATE
DUPLICATION FORBIDDEN

0845 TOKYO TIME 10OCTOBER1950

FROM: CHIEF PRESIDENTIAL MISSION TO
      FAR EAST

VIA: USMC SPECIAL COMMUNICATIONS
     CENTER CAMP PENDLETON CAL

TO: WHITE HOUSE COMMUNICATIONS
    CENTER WASHINGTON DC
    EYES ONLY THE PRESIDENT OF THE
    UNITED STATES

BEGIN PERSONAL MESSAGE FROM MAJOR
GENERAL HOWE

DEAR HARRY

IN RESPONSE TO YOUR REQUEST THAT I
SEND WHATEVER I THINK YOU WOULD
FIND USEFUL AT WAKE ISLAND

IN RE THE RELANDING OF X CORPS ON
EAST COAST OF KOREAN PENINSULA

MACARTHUR GAVE ME A PERSONAL
BRIEFING ON HIS PLANS AND INTENTIONS
IN WHICH HE CONVINCINGLY SAID THE
OPERATION WILL PERMIT HIM TO QUICKLY
REACH THE YALU RIVER AND THUS KEEP
THE FLEEING NORTH KOREAN ARMY FROM
ESCAPING INTO CHINA AND THUS PERMIT
ITS COMPLETE DESTRUCTION

HE CONVINCINGLY SAID THERE IS
ABSOLUTELY NO MILITARY REASON FOR
HIM TO CROSS THE BORDER

I RAISED THE CONCERNS OF MAJOR
GENERAL OLIVER SMITH OF FIRST MARDIV
AS PREVIOUSLY REPORTED TO YOU THAT
THE TERRAIN OF NORTH KOREA AND THE
EXTENDED SUPPLY LINES POSE
PROBLEMS

MACARTHUR SAID BOTH HE AND GENERAL
ALMOND ARE VERY MUCH AWARE OF THE

PROBLEMS AND WILL DEAL WITH THEM
ACCORDINGLY

I DON'T KNOW HOW MUCH MACARTHUR
KNOWS ABOUT FIGHTING IN THE
MOUNTAINS BUT ALMOND FOUGHT HIS
DIVISION IN THE MOUNTAINS OF ITALY IN
THE WINTER AND CERTAINLY LEARNED
FROM THAT EXPERIENCE

I HAVE THE FEELING THAT MACARTHUR
DIDN'T SEEK GUIDANCE AND APPROVAL
FOR THE OPERATION FROM THE JOINT
CHIEFS BECAUSE HE THINKS HE HAS A
MANDATE TO OPERATE WITHOUT IT AND
ALSO BECAUSE HE REGARDS AS DO
ALMOND AND SMITH THIS OPERATION AS
CONSIDERABLY SIMPLER THAN THE
INCHON LANDING

THE NAVY HAS NO PROBLEMS WITH THE
OPERATION EXCEPT FOR THE ANTICIPATED
LACK OF PORT FACILITIES WHICH WILL
PROBABLY DELAY THE OFF LOADING OF
HEAVY EQUIPMENT SUCH AS TANKS
ETCETERA

I HAD A LONG TALK WITH GENERAL
WALKER WHO HAS MOVED HIS FORWARD
HEADQUARTERS TO KOREA FROM JAPAN
AND PLANS TO OPEN IT IN SEOUL AS

SOON AS HE CAN TO CONTROL
OPERATIONS IN NORTH WESTERN KOREA

HE SEEMS TO HAVE NO SERIOUS
OBJECTIONS TO THE X CORPS OPERATION
EXCEPT THAT HE REMAINS INDIGNANT
THAT X CORPS HAS NOT BEEN PLACED
UNDER HIS COMMAND

WALKER MAKES THE POINT THAT ALL
KOREAN OPERATIONS SHOULD BE
COORDINATED AND THIS REQUIRES THAT
THE X CORPS COMMANDER TAKE HIS
ORDERS FROM THE EIGHTH ARMY
COMMANDER

WALKER WAS ALSO HIGHLY INDIGNANT
THAT AN L-20 BEAVER SIX PLACE LIAISON
AIRCRAFT WHICH HE CONSIDERS
NECESSARY TO MOVE HIMSELF AND
MEMBERS OF HIS STAFF AROUND KOREA
WAS STOLEN BY A SO FAR UNLOCATABLE
ARMY OFFICER WHILE EN ROUTE TO HIM

IN RE CHICOM INTERVENTION

MACARTHUR, WALKER FEEL THE POSSIBILITY
IS VERY SLIGHT

ALMOND AND SMITH FEAR THAT ANY
CROSSING OF THE BORDER FOR WHATEVER

REASON MIGHT TRIGGER INTERVENTION
BUT THAT THE CHINESE DO NOT POSSESS
EITHER SUFFICIENT FORCES OR LOGISTICS
TO CAUSE A MAJOR OR LASTING PROBLEM
FOR EITHER EIGHTH ARMY OR X CORPS

IN OTHER WORDS THE MOST THEY COULD
DO WAS FORCE US BACK SEVERAL MILES
FROM THE BORDER

SEE ADDITIONAL COMMENTS BELOW

IN RE RESCUE OF GENERAL DEAN AND
MAJOR PICKERING

LT COL D J VANDENBURG SENT BY
DCSOPS TO DEAL WITH DEAN ARRIVED
HERE A WEEK AGO AND IMMEDIATELY
MADE CONTACT WITH MAJOR MCCOY AND
KOREA CIA STATION CHIEF DUNSTON

VANDENBURG IS AN IMPRESSIVE
OPERATOR AND BOTH HE AND MCCOY
FEEL IT HIGHLY PROBABLE THAT GENERAL
DEAN HAS BEEN TAKEN TO CHINA AND
THAT THEREFORE HIS RESCUE IS HIGHLY
DOUBTFUL

THEY HAVE HOWEVER POOLED
RESOURCES AND DIVIDED RESPONSIBILITY
AND BEGUN TO ATTACK THE PROBLEM
VIGOROUSLY

VANDENBURG WILL OPERATE ON WEST OF

PENINSULA AND MCCOY ON EAST

MCCOY AND DUNSTON WHO HAVE THE
EXPERIENCE HAVE ALREADY BEGUN THE
INSERTION OF AGENTS INTO NORTH
KOREA WHO WILL BOTH ATTEMPT TO
LOCATE DEAN AND POSSIBLY PICKERING
AND ATTEMPT TO DETERMINE STRENGTH
OF BOTH REMAINING NORTH KOREAN
FORCES AND CHINESE FORCES ACROSS
THE BORDER

BOTH UNDERSTAND THEY ARE NOT TO
STAGE ANY SORT OF A CROSS BORDER
OPERATION WITHOUT YOUR SPECIFIC
APPROVAL

MCCOY IS OPERATING OUT OF A SMALL
FISHING VILLAGE ON EAST COAST
PREVIOUSLY USED BY DUNSTON BEFORE
THE WAR

VANDENBURG SOMEHOW ACQUIRED AN
L-20 BEAVER SIX PLACE LIAISON AIRCRAFT
AND HAS MADE IT AVAILABLE TO
DUNSTON AND MCCOY FOR TRAVEL
BETWEEN PUSAN SEOUL AND SOCHO RI
FISHING VILLAGE

ADDITIONALLY MACARTHUR ORDERED
THAT TWO SIKORSKY HELICOPTERS SENT

TO KOREA BE TRANSFERRED TO THE CIA
AND THEY WILL BE USED FOR INSERTION
AND EXTRACTION OF AGENTS AND ALSO
TO RESCUE GENERAL DEAN AND OR
MAJOR PICKERING IF THEY CAN BE
LOCATED

THERE HAVE BEEN NO SIGHTINGS OF THE
SIGNALS PICKERING HAS BEEN LEAVING IN
THE PAST SEVEN DAYS WHICH MCCOY
SAYS MAY BE BECAUSE HE IS MOVING
EASTWARD AND THERE ARE FEWER PLACES
WHERE HE CAN MAKE THEM

BOTH MCCOY AND DUNSTON HAVE TOLD
ME WITH THE CAVEAT THEY HAVE NO
PROOF TO SUPPORT THEIR POSITION THAT
CHINESE INTERVENTION IS VERY POSSIBLE
MAYBE EVEN PROBABLE

AT THE RISK OF REPEATING MYSELF I
GROW MORE AND MORE CONVINCED
THAT THE PROBLEMS OF THE CIA ARE ITS
BUREAUCRACY

PEOPLE LIKE MCCOY AND DUNSTON AND
I THINK VANDENBURG TOO DO THEIR
JOBS ONLY TO HAVE THEIR LABOR GO
FOR NAUGHT BECAUSE IT DOESN'T FIT
THE PRECONCEIVED NOTIONS OF
SOMEBODY SITTING BEHIND A DESK FAR

FROM WHAT IS HAPPENING

I DON'T KNOW HOW EFFECTIVE FLEMING
PICKERING WOULD BE IN SHAPING UP
THE CIA BUT I CAN'T THINK OF ANYBODY
WHO COULD DO BETTER

THANK YOU FOR UNDERSTANDING THAT I
WOULD JUST BE EXCESS BAGGAGE AT
WAKE ISLAND AND THAT I AM RELUCTANT
TO LEAVE HERE WITH PICKERING GONE

RESPECTFULLY, AND WITH BEST REGARDS
TO BESS

RALPH

END PERSONAL MESSAGE FROM GENERAL
HOWE

TOP SECRET/PRESIDENTIAL

Pickering put the message back in the
envelope and handed it back to Truman.

"Thank you, sir," he said.

"I'd hoped there would be better news
about your boy," Truman said.

"Thank you, sir," Pickering said.

Truman smiled.

"Did you get the feeling that General
Walker's missing airplane and the airplane

Colonel Vandenburg 'somehow acquired' are in any way connected?"

Pickering chuckled. He said, "General Howe didn't seem to share General Walker's indignation, did he?"

"Well, maybe the airplane'll be useful in trying to locate your son," the President said.

"I hope so, sir," Pickering said. "I just hope that the airplane, and those helicopters — that was the first I'd heard about that — aren't needed somewhere else more than —"

"I would think that right now the insertion of agents is very important. We need to know what the Chinese may be up to, and we have to make every effort to get both General Dean and your son back."

"Yes, sir."

"I'm sure you're aware, General, that I've given a good deal of thought to replacing Admiral Hillencoetter at the CIA. And I'm sure you're aware you were high on my list of potential directors."

"I was afraid of that, sir. I really don't think I'm qualified to take it over."

"I do, and so does Ralph Howe, in whose judgment I place a lot of trust, but it's not going to be you, and I suppose the real reason I came over here was to tell you that face-to-face."

"Sir, you could have sent me a postcard,

as long as that was the message."

Truman chuckled. "You really didn't want it, did you?"

"No, sir, I did not."

"But you would have taken it, had I asked?"

"Yes, sir."

"Do you know General Walter Bedell Smith?"

"I know who he is, sir, but I've never met him."

"He didn't want the job, either," Truman said. "I had to work hard to convince him it was important to the country."

"From what I know of him, sir, he's far better qualified than I am for the job."

"That's what he said about you," Truman said, smiling. "He said that he had virtually no experience with the nuts and bolts of the intelligence business, and you had an enormous amount of practical on-the-job experience." He paused, then added: "He knew a great deal about you, General."

"Maybe he said that because he really didn't want the job, either," Pickering said. "I've never regarded myself as anything but an amateur who found himself in water far over his head."

"General Donovan used very much the same words to describe his own feelings," Truman said.

"You're talking about Wild Bill Donovan of the OSS, Mr. President?" Pickering asked, as if confused.

Truman nodded.

"I understand you were great friends," the President said, his smile making it clear he knew exactly the opposite to be true.

Pickering smiled back at the President and chuckled.

"I made a mistake when I disestablished the OSS," Truman said. "When I realized the country needed an organization like the OSS, I asked Donovan to come see me, to ask what he thought we needed, and how we should go about getting it."

"Despite our differences, Mr. President, I don't think anyone can fault General Donovan's leadership of the OSS in the Second War."

"What he said, in essence, was that he could have done a far better job if he had been perceived as a member of the military establishment, rather than as 'an amateur with friends in high places in water over his head.' "

"The OSS was not very popular with the military establishment, Mr. President. I don't think the CIA is, either." He paused as understanding dawned, and then said, "Oh."

"Uh-huh," Truman said. "I can't think of anyone who is as much a respected, liked, admired, proven member of the military establishment than General Eisenhower's World War Two Chief of Staff, General Walter Bedell Smith."

Pickering nodded, and said, "I completely agree, sir."

"Admiral Hillencoetter was gracious enough to offer his resignation right after this war started. When I asked him who he thought should replace him, he said I might think about bringing General Donovan back, or, failing that, to offer the job to you. General Donovan had already made it plain he wasn't interested, so your name was on my list from the beginning."

"I'm really surprised to hear that, Mr. President. I only met Admiral Hillencoetter that one time."

"At which meeting you handed him intelligence that the North Koreans were preparing for war, something which had not filtered up to him from his people in the field," Truman said. "The admiral is a good man, General. He had egg on his face, but he was man enough to admit it, and it never entered his mind to shoot the messenger."

Pickering considered that and nodded.

"So General Smith will be my new boss?"

Truman nodded.

"How does he feel about me? Mr. President, I would be happy to give up my position in the CIA. I would like to stay on active duty, if possible, until we see what's going to happen with my son."

"I didn't come here to ask for your resignation," the President said. "I came to tell you why I thought it best to name General Smith CIA Director. Which I will do as soon as I get back to my office. He's at the Army-Navy Club hoping to hear I've changed my mind. I want you to get together with him as soon as possible . . . maybe even this afternoon. The more you can tell him before we go to Wake Island, the better."

"He's going with you to Wake Island? That's a good idea, Mr. President. I think he'll mesh well with General MacArthur."

"He's not going to Wake Island, General, you are," the President said. "And after that meeting, you're going on to Tokyo, where you will implement the changes General Smith has ordered."

"Do you know what he has in mind, sir?"

"No. And neither will he until you and he get together and decide what they'll be." He paused long enough for that to sink in, then added: "But when those orders are issued, I'm sure General Smith will let it be known throughout the military establishment that they came from him, and not some 'amateur who finds himself in water over his head.' I'm also sure that he will make it known that he was quite pleased that you agreed to stay on."

"Because you told him that?"

"No. The ironic thing here is that he feels he is the amateur in deep water. He was really worried that you would want to leave."

The President stood up and, when Pickering got to his feet, put out his hand. Truman looked as if was going to say something but changed his mind.

He nodded at Pickering, shook his hand, and walked to the door.

[Two]
The Army-Navy Club
Washington, D.C.
1215 11 October 1950

General Walter Bedell Smith's entire suite on the fourth floor of the Army-Navy Club would have fit, with room to spare, into Brigadier General Fleming Pickering's sitting room in the Foster Lafayette.

Smith, who was wearing a dark gray suit, a crisp white shirt, and a rep-striped necktie, opened the door to Pickering's knock himself and put out his hand.

"Thank you for coming on such short notice, General," Smith said.

How the hell do I reply to that? "You're welcome"? "My pleasure"? This chap is a four-star general who is about to become the Director of the CIA. People like that don't have to thank underlings for coming quickly when summoned.

Smith looked at his watch.

"Fifteen minutes," he said, smiling. "That's quick."

"General, this is Captain Hart," Pickering said. "If you have no objection, I'd like him to sit in on this. He has an uncanny ability to later recall who said what and to whom."

"None whatever," Smith said, and offered Hart his hand. "I suppose that 'uncanny ability' was useful to you as a policeman. Or is that an acquired skill?"

Jesus, he knows all about George.

"I think I got it from my father, sir," Hart said. "He was a cop, too."

"Have you had lunch?" Smith asked.

"No, sir," Pickering said.

"Well, we could go downstairs, but if we ordered a sandwich here — they do a very nice open-faced roast beef, and a chicken club — we could talk while we eat. Your call."

"An open-faced roast beef sandwich sounds fine to me, General," Pickering said.

"Captain?"

"Roast beef's fine with me, sir."

Smith went to the telephone and ordered the sandwiches and "a very large pot of coffee." Then he turned to Pickering. "To get to the starting line, the President will have a press conference at five o'clock, at which he will announce my appointment as Director of the CIA. I will have to be there, so we have until, say, half past four. That should be enough time, don't you think?"

"Yes, sir," Pickering said.

Smith took an envelope from his jacket pocket and extended it to Pickering.

"The President sent this over," Smith said. "I understand you've seen it."

Pickering opened the envelope. It held the message from General Howe that Truman had shown him earlier.

"Yes, sir, I have," Pickering said.

"Have you?" Smith asked of Hart.

"No, sir."

"I told George what I thought he should know, sir," Pickering said.

"I think it would be useful if you saw the whole thing," Smith said.

Pickering handed Hart the envelope.

"Before the waiter gets here, General," Smith said, "I'd like your opinion of why this war came as a complete surprise not only to General MacArthur but to the CIA as well."

Christ, he goes right for the jugular!

Screw it. When you don't know what to say, try telling the truth.

"When the intelligence gathered by some of MacArthur's intelligence people went against the intelligence conclusions of MacArthur's G-2, it was buried," Pickering said.

"Okay. That explains MacArthur's surprise. But why did the CIA fail so completely?"

"The CIA Tokyo station chief regarded himself as a member of MacArthur's staff," Pickering said. "And was not about to disagree with the conclusions of General Willoughby, as endorsed by General MacArthur."

"And you think he should have disagreed?"

"I think he should have drawn his own conclusions from his own sources and sent them directly to Admiral Hillencoetter without discussing them with — and certainly not allowing them to be censored by — anyone in the Dai Ichi Building."

"What you're saying, General, is that the Tokyo station chief was derelict in the performance of his duties?"

"Yes, sir, I guess I am."

"Then why didn't you relieve him when you went over there and came to this conclusion?"

"There were several reasons, sir," Pickering said. "For one thing, McCoy told me he had developed his own sources —"

"I'm really looking forward to meeting Major 'Killer' McCoy," Smith interrupted. "The President seems very taken with him. Where is he now?"

"Probably in North Korea — or China — looking for General Dean," Pickering replied, and added, "and my son."

Smith met Pickering's eyes for a long moment but did not respond directly.

"You were saying McCoy said he had his own sources?"

"Which had proven to be more reliable than those of General Willoughby," Pickering went on, "so I didn't need the station chief's intel . . . which, presumably, he was already furnishing to Willoughby and Hillencoetter anyway. I didn't know if I had the authority to relieve him, or whether that had to be cleared with the CIA, and the moment I started to relieve him, Willoughby would learn of it, possibly cause trouble here, and certainly make him keep a closer eye on me than he already was."

"The President's right," Smith said. "You do have a loose-cannon tendency, don't you?"

"Is that what he said?" Pickering said.

This is not going well. If I were this man, I would not want me working for me.

So what do I do now?

Ask the Marine Corps to keep me on at least until we find out what happened to Pick?

Ask for immediate release from active duty and just stay in Tokyo? If I do that, I probably wouldn't be able to get permission to go to Korea.

"That's what he said," Smith replied, evenly, with a little smile, then asked: "What do you want to do about the Tokyo Station Chief?" Smith asked.

"If I were to become your deputy for Asia . . ."

"Please don't tell me you're having second thoughts about that," Smith said. "I need you over there."

Jesus, I didn't expect that!

"We don't know how well we would work together," Pickering said.

"I think I'll be considerably easier for you to work with than General Donovan was," Smith said. "I understand that your personal relationship with him . . ."

"Was about as bad as a relationship can be," Pickering said.

"You are taking the job, right?"

"I'm surprised it's still being offered," Pickering said.

"What are you doing, General, fishing for a compliment? Yes, it's still being offered, because both the President and I think you're the best man to do what has to be done."

They locked eyes for a moment.

"Yes, sir, I'll take the job," Pickering said. "Thank you."

"Okay. Now, what do you want to do about the Tokyo station chief?"

"One of the reasons I didn't relieve him when I first got to Tokyo was that I was afraid he'd go to Washington and spend all his time throwing monkey wrenches into my gears."

"He's gone," Smith said. "Or will be as soon as I can order him home. And he will not be sniping at you from the rear. What about his replacement?"

"Off the top of my head, I have no idea," Pickering admitted.

"I thought I was going to hear two names," Smith said. "Major K. R. McCoy and Colonel Edward Banning. I don't think McCoy has the experience, but what's wrong with Banning?"

"Absolutely nothing is wrong with Colonel Banning," Pickering said quickly and firmly.

"Why have you got him sitting around Camp Pendleton doing a job that could be done by a lot of far more junior people who don't have a tenth of his experience as an intelligence officer?" When Pickering didn't immediately reply, Smith added: "I know that he worked for you in the Second War, and what he did."

"I guess the truth, General," Pickering said, "is that while I often thought how much I need Ed Banning in Tokyo, I didn't have the balls to make waves. Either about getting rid of the Tokyo station chief or about asking Admiral Hillencoetter to name Banning in his place."

"It usually helps, if you're going to make waves, to be sure of your authority," Smith said. "Now that that question has been resolved, I take it if I named Colonel Banning as Tokyo station chief, I would have your concurrence?"

"Yes, sir."

"I'll issue the necessary orders tomorrow, as my first order of business. Or maybe even tonight. I thought I would drop by there tonight, unannounced, just to see what I could see. How soon do you want Banning in Tokyo?"

"As soon as possible, sir."

[Three]
Office of the Chief of Staff
Headquarters X U.S. Corps
Seoul, South Korea
0825 11 October 1950

There were three full colonels sitting on folding chairs facing the folding desk of the chief of staff, who was also a full colonel.

A somewhat irreverent thought occurred to Colonel T. Howard Kennedy, the X Corps Transportation Officer: *It's like Orwell said. Some pigs are more equal than other pigs.*

"The general does not want any delays when we go aboard the ships," the chief of staff — the most equal of all the pigs — said. "Comments, please."

T. Howard Kennedy had another irreverent thought: *That's a nice thought, but it's like hoping for a white Christmas. Nice if you can get it, but unlikely.*

There were going to be delays in loading X Corps aboard the ships that would constitute the invasion fleet for the Wonsan landing. That was a given. There were always delays.

This maneuver was probably going to have more delays than the general was going to like, which was going to be a problem for everybody in the chief of staff's office. Major General Edward M. Almond expected his orders to be obeyed as he wanted them to be obeyed, which was sometimes impossible to accomplish, and when that happened, Almond's temper was legendary.

The chief of staff was looking at Colonel Kennedy, which told Kennedy that the chief of staff considered this meeting a conference, which was different from just being summoned by the chief of staff to receive orders. In a conference, comments were solicited before orders were issued. And conferees presented their comments in reverse order of rank, most junior first. This ensured that whatever the junior officer had to say was not influenced by the comments of the officers senior to him.

The pecking order here placed Kennedy at the bottom. The Transportation Office wasn't even a G-Section, but rather a subsection of the Office of the Assistant Chief of Staff for Plans and Operations, G-3. The G-3 and the G-4 (Supply) were supposed to be more or less equal, but the G-3 called the shots.

"There are six truck companies available," Kennedy said. "Four — two with the Marines and two with the 7th Division — are operational, and will of course be available to move people and gear to Inchon when the orders are issued. Two are in reserve, and I have given operational control of one of them to the G-4 so that he can start moving whatever he wants to move to Inchon whenever he wants to move it. Similarly, I have given operational control of half of the remaining truck company to the Headquarters Commandant here for the same purpose. The other half remains in reserve.

"The only unit over which I exercise staff control is the vehicle exchange company, the 8023d. Five days ago, I started to move it to the wharfs in Inchon for on-loading."

"Howard," the G-4 said, "I hope you're not going to tell me they're already on-loaded?"

"No. They are probably in the process by now, but, no, they're not on-loaded. I was going to go down there this morning and see how things are going."

"I'm a little confused," the G-3 said. "You said you told them to move five days ago. And they're only 'probably' in the process of on-loading? How long does it take them to move from one side of Inchon to the other?"

The chief of staff snorted.

"Bob, there are almost six hundred vehicles in the 8023d —" Kennedy started to reply.

"Almost?" the G-4 interrupted.

"Five hundred seventy-nine, Gerry," Kennedy finished.

"And their condition?"

"I sent you a report, Gerry," Kennedy said. "There are five hundred seventy-nine ready for issue, plus seven beyond the company's ability to repair. They have exchanged far fewer vehicles than was anticipated, somewhere around twenty, mostly jeeps and six-by-sixes."

"I must not have gotten your report,"

438

the G-4 said, and wrote in a wire-bound notebook.

"Okay," the G-3 said. "Six hundred, give or take, vehicles. And it's taken this long to move from one side of Inchon to the other?"

"They were set up for exchange, Bob," Kennedy explained patiently. "The CO did a very good job. But we're talking here about (a) on-loading all the vehicles, and (b) doing so according to that loading sequence schedule you sent me. That takes time."

"Time spent here will save time when we get on Wonsan," the G-3 said. "Last on/ first off makes sense. A lot of thought has gone into that loading sequence schedule."

"All I'm saying, Bob, is that it takes some time to accomplish. This is not like driving these vehicles to the Battery and right onto the Staten Island Ferry. They have to be sorted at the wharf according to what goes on first."

"I can do without the sarcasm, thank you very much, Howard," the G-3 said coldly.

"I didn't think Howard was being sarcastic, Bob," the chief of staff said.

Colonel Kennedy thought: *That either got me off the hook or sunk me deeper in the deep shit.*

"We're going to need those vehicles at

Inchon," the G-4 said. "It seems pretty obvious to me that a replacement of only twenty vehicles means that a good deal more are on the edge of needing replacement, and even more will be needing replacement after we get them ashore at Wonsan. I'd really like to see these vehicles moved up — as far up as possible — on the off-loading schedule."

"Gerry's got a point, Bob," the chief of staff said.

"I'll see what I can do."

"The general would be very unhappy if our dash for the Chinese border was delayed by broken-down trucks," the chief of staff said. "I don't want that to happen."

"I'll review the off-loading schedule and get you my suggested changes," the G-3 said.

"Great! And, just to satisfy my general curiosity, Howard, how is this vehicle exchange company fixed for tank retrievers and wreckers?"

"I believe there are twenty wreckers and fifteen tank retrievers," Kennedy said.

"Bob, make sure that when you review your on-/off-loading schedule that some wreckers — a half a dozen, anyway — and, say, five tank retrievers are near the head of the line," the chief of staff ordered.

"Even if that means off-loading them if

they've already been on-loaded?" Kennedy asked.

The chief of staff thought that over for ten seconds.

"Yeah, Howard, even if it comes down to that. And come see me, please, after you've had a chance to see how things are going down there."

"Right," Colonel Kennedy said.

**[Four]
Wharf 3
Inchon, South Korea
1130 11 October 1950**

The Waterman Steamship Line freighter *Captain J.C. Buffett* was tied up to Wharf 3 when Colonel Kennedy drove up to the wharf. In bumper-to-bumper lines parallel to the ship were the vehicles of the 8023d Transportation Company (Depot, Forward) waiting to be loaded.

Halfway down the lines, Kennedy touched the arm of his jeep driver and ordered, "Stop here, Tom."

He got out of the jeep and walked down the line of vehicles, looking carefully at each one. He was pleased with what he saw and the few truck tires he kicked. All the vehicles seemed ready for duty.

But when he got close to the end of the

line, and the ship itself, he saw something that pleased him not at all.

A squat, ruddy-faced, middle-aged sailor was standing on the wharf. He held both hands extended before him, palms up.

Kennedy knew what he was doing, signaling the operators of the crane and winch operators on the ship as they prepared to load a vehicle aboard. Two things annoyed Colonel Kennedy: first, that an ordinary seaman, rather than an officer, was supervising the operation, and second, that the vehicle about to be loaded aboard the *Captain J.C. Buffett* was a heavy-duty wrecker.

He didn't have the revised on-/off-loading schedule yet, but the chief of staff had made it very clear that the first vehicles he wanted unloaded at Wonsan were heavy-duty wreckers and tank retriever vehicles. That meant they would have to be loaded last, so they could be unloaded first.

He walked up to the seaman on the wharf who was directing the boom and winch operators.

"Excuse me," he said.

"Not now, buddy. Can't you see I'm working?"

With slow and gentle, even graceful, movements the seaman signaled the winch operators on the deck of the *Captain J.C. Buffett* to begin to *very slowly* haul aboard what the White Manufacturing Company called a Wrecker, Special, Heavy Duty and the U.S. Army called a Vehicle, Heavy Vehicle Recovery 6 x 6 Mark III A2.

The Army and the White Manufacturing Company were agreed that the truck was heavy. It had been heavy when built for civilian use, designed to be able to pick up a broken-down tractor for eighteen-wheeler rigs. The Army had demanded a number of modifications to the basic design. The front (steering) wheels of the basic model had not been powered. The Army demanded that their version have all-wheel drive. The frame and body had been reinforced to take both the weight of the more powerful lifting arm and the additional weight it was intended to lift. And there were lifting hooks welded to the frame in places determined to be the best places to put them so the weight would be evenly distributed when it had to be loaded aboard a ship.

There was the whining hum of an electric motor and the limp cables attached to the lifting hooks on the front of the wrecker grew taut, and then the hum of another electric motor and the cables attached three quarters of the way down the frame began to draw taut.

Well, screw you, Colonel Kennedy thought, *just as soon as you get that wrecker*

443

loaded aboard, at least just as soon as I can have a word with the captain, you'll just have to take it back off.

Kennedy saw Captain Francis P. MacNamara, commanding officer of the 8023d Transportation Company (Depot, Forward), standing by his jeep on the other side of the seaman supervising the loading and walked over to him.

MacNamara saluted.

"Good afternoon, sir," he said.

"How are you, MacNamara?" Kennedy replied.

"We've just started to load, sir," MacNamara said. "I thought it best to arrange the vehicles so they could be loaded according to the last on/first off schedule before we actually started the procedure."

"Good thinking, MacNamara," Kennedy said. "There's been some changes to that schedule. I'll want to talk to you about them, but I think we might as well wait until we can talk to the captain at the same time."

"Yes, sir."

There was a screeching sound of unknown origin, which lasted about fifteen seconds, then the sound of the seaman's voice.

"Jesus H. Fucking Christ!"

He sounded disgusted, or frustrated, or both.

The Vehicle, Heavy Vehicle Recovery 6 x 6 Mark III A2 was now suspended five feet in the air, swinging slowly back and forth.

"I said slowly, you dumb sonofabitch!" the seaman called to someone on deck. His voice did not need amplification.

The seaman then made very small, very gentle upward movements of his hands. There was another electric motor hum, and, just perceptibly, the Vehicle, Heavy Vehicle Recovery 6 x 6 Mark III A2 began to inch upward again.

Then there was another screeching noise, this time lasting no more than ten seconds.

The wrecker continued to rise very slowly until it was about level with the deck.

The seaman made a cutting motion across his throat.

The wrecker stopped rising and swung back and forth on the cables.

Very slowly the seaman, the palms of his hands now vertical, made a pushing motion with his left hand. There was the sound of an electric motor, and very slowly the boom holding the rear of the wrecker moved inward. When the wrecker was perpendicular to the wharf, the seaman made a cutting motion with his left hand and then a pushing motion with his right. The boom holding the cables attached to the front of the wrecker began to swing inward. After thirty seconds — which seemed longer — the truck was completely inboard and again aligned with the keel of the *Captain J.C. Buffett.*

"Okay!" the seaman shouted. "For the love of Christ, don't let that heavy sonofabitch get away from you! Slowly, *fucking slowly!*"

Very slowly, the wrecker began to descend into a hold of the *Captain J.C. Buffett.* In thirty seconds or so it was out of sight, but the seaman continued to stand on the wharf, his hands on his hips, looking upward until the hum of the electric motors died.

A moment after that there was another electrical hum, a lesser sound this time. And then one of the booms swung outward.

Colonel Kennedy and Captain Mac-Namara were both surprised to see another seaman standing on the hook at the end of the cable being lowered to the wharf. The seaman stepped casually off the hook, then engaged in a short conversation with the seaman in charge of the operation.

Both shook their heads, and then the seaman who had ridden down on the hook shrugged, as the seaman who'd been on the wharf threw up his hands in a gesture of resignation, or frustration, or both.

The seaman who had been on the hook

stepped back onto it, made a *take me up* gesture with his hand, and immediately began to rise into the air.

It reminded Colonel Kennedy of how a circus high-wire performer rises to the high wire.

The seaman walked over to Colonel Kennedy and Captain MacNamara. He addressed Captain MacNamara.

"That's it, pal," he announced. "That's the last of the big fuckers I'm going to try to take aboard."

"I beg your pardon?" Colonel Kennedy said.

"I said that's the last of those heavy fucking trucks that goes aboard the *Captain J.C. Buffett*."

"That's simply not acceptable," Colonel Kennedy said.

" 'Acceptable'?" the seaman parroted. "Who the fuck are you to tell me what goes aboard the *Captain J.C. Buffett*?"

"I think I had better discuss this with one of the ship's officers," Kennedy said. "Preferably with her captain. Presumably I can find him aboard?"

"You are discussing this with her captain," the seaman said. "Who the fuck did you think you were talking to?"

"You're the captain?"

"Captain John F. X. Moran at your service, Colonel."

"Captain, obviously I owe you an apology —"

"Not yet," Captain Moran interrupted.

"Thank you," Kennedy said. "Captain, the vehicles we're trying to load aboard your ship are essential to an operation. . . ."

"Putting the X Corps ashore at Wonsan," Moran offered helpfully.

Colonel Kennedy found that helpfulness disturbing. For one thing, that the invasion force was headed for Wonsan was classified Top Secret. Colonel Kennedy wasn't at all sure that Captain Moran had that kind of a security clearance, much less the Need to Know, at this point, the destination. He was sure that he was not supposed to casually introduce it into conversation the way he had.

"Wonsan?" Kennedy asked. "Who said anything about Wonsan?"

"Jesus Christ!" Moran said disgustedly. "If you really don't know about Wonsan, Colonel, what's going on here is the reloading of X Corps, which will then be transported around to the other side of the Korean Peninsula and landed at Wonsan."

Colonel Kennedy decided not to respond directly.

"The X Corps Operations Officer sent me here to see that the heavy vehicles, such as the wrecker you just loaded aboard, were loaded aboard last, so they may be unloaded first when you reach your destination."

"Colonel, let me try to explain this to you. When I off-loaded those vehicles when we came here, I just about completely fucked up the motors, booms, winches, and other equipment aboard. I knew it would. My gear is not designed to handle such heavy loads. But I figured, what the hell, the important thing is to get these vehicles ashore — I can get the gear repaired when I'm back in San Diego. But now I'm told I'm going to Wonsan, not 'Diego, and I have to load all this stuff back aboard, and then unload it again at Wonsan — where I understand there will be no functioning shoreside equipment to unload me." He paused, then went on: "Still with me, Colonel?"

Colonel Kennedy nodded and said, "Go on, please."

"What I can do, Colonel," Moran went on, "is use the ship's gear to load the lighter stuff — the jeeps, three-quarter-ton ammo carriers, and the six-by-sixes. I can also probably unload them in Wonsan, presuming I don't fuck up my gear any more than it's already fucked up by loading the heavy stuff." He paused, and went on: "Am I getting through to you, Colonel?"

"Yes, you are," Colonel Kennedy said.

"There's absolutely no chance —"

"Not a fucking chance. Now, do I start to see how much of the light stuff I can get aboard before the fucking tide starts going down and leaves me stranded in the fucking mud? Or what?"

"Under the circumstances, I think it would be best to start loading the lighter vehicles," Colonel Kennedy said.

"Believe it or not, I'm sorry as hell about this," Captain Moran said, and then walked back to where he had originally been standing.

He looked up at the ship.

"Okay, get those fucking lines down here," he called. "We're now going to start loading the light stuff."

Colonel Kennedy turned to Captain MacNamara.

"It looks as if we have a problem, Captain," he said. "What I suppose I'm going to have to do is see the Port Master, and see if these heavy vehicles can be loaded aboard another vessel."

"Yes, sir," MacNamara said. "Colonel, can I make a suggestion?"

"Absolutely."

"Let me take them overland, across the peninsula," MacNamara said.

"I don't think I follow you," Kennedy admitted.

"Colonel, maybe I jumped the gun a

little, but when Captain Moran told me that X Corps was going to be relanded at Wonsan, I looked at the maps."

"And?"

"Excuse me, sir, I have to get the line moving," MacNamara said, and trotted toward the lines of vehicles ready to be loaded. He jumped up on the running board of a GMC 6 x 6, and a moment later Kennedy saw a soldier appear behind the wheel. He started the 6 x 6's engine and drove down the wharf toward where Captain Moran was impatiently waiting for the truck with MacNamara still on the running board.

MacNamara dropped nimbly off the truck as it passed Kennedy.

"Sorry, sir. That man was asleep," MacNamara said, as if he considered that a personal insult.

"You were saying something, Captain, about moving the heavy vehicles overland?" Kennedy asked.

"Yes, sir. Colonel, I've got a map in my jeep. Can I show you what I think?"

"Why not?" Kennedy said.

[Five]
Office of the Chief of Staff
Headquarters X U.S. Corps
Seoul, South Korea
1720 11 October 1950

"Kennedy," the chief of staff said, "this was not what I expected to hear from you when I told you to report on your progress."

"I know," Colonel Kennedy said. "I wish it were otherwise."

"Well, what do you want to do about it?"

"If we could get an LST . . ."

"Fine. See the Port Captain, and tell him I want these heavy vehicles available as soon as possible at Wonsan."

"Sir, I did that. He says there is no space on the available LSTs. They can't carry all the tanks we want to move as it is."

"Jesus Christ! Kennedy, we've got to do something!"

"Captain MacNamara has an off-the-wall idea —"

"Who's he?"

"He commands the vehicle exchange unit."

"Let's hear it."

"He suggests moving the wreckers and the tank retrieval vehicles by road."

Kennedy was surprised when the chief of staff did not frown, snort derisively, or say

"Jesus Christ!" disgustedly, as he was wont to do when presented with a wild and/or stupid idea. In fact, the chief of staff was apparently giving the idea some thought.

The chief of staff snorted, but thoughtfully, not derisively.

"Think of it as a chess game, Kennedy," he said. "As we move pieces around the board — in this case the landing beaches at Wonsan."

"Okay," Kennedy said agreeably.

"First the landing craft go in."

"Right."

"And right on the heels of the landing craft — sometimes right with them — come the LSTs."

"Right."

"And what happens to the LSTs after they land the tanks? They get out of the way, right?"

"That's true."

"They wait for the freighters to come in close and drop anchor, right, and then take on supplies and ferry them to the beach, right?"

"Uh-huh."

The chief of staff raised his voice: "Sergeant Miller! Bring me a map of the east coast."

"Coming up, sir!" Sergeant Miller replied, and a moment later entered the chief of staff's office, removing a map from its tube as he walked. He laid it on the chief of staff's desk, anchoring its corners with two cans of Planters peanuts, a coffee cup, and a large stapler.

The chief of staff stood up and leaned over the map. Colonel Kennedy walked around the desk and stood beside him.

"We own Suwon," the chief of staff said, pointing. "And we own Wonju and Kangnung. And Highway Four runs all the way from Suwon to Kangnung. And we're only talking about" — he made a compass with his fingers — "about 120, maybe 140 miles, tops. All of it on a paved highway."

"That's about right," Colonel Kennedy agreed.

The chief of staff used his fingers as a compass again.

"And about that far, 120 miles or so, from Kangnung to Wonsan."

"Uh-huh, that's about right."

"The last I heard, the Capital ROK Division has moved at least this far" — he pointed — "close to Kansong, which is only seventy-five miles, give or take, from Wonsan, and on another paved highway."

After a moment's hesitation, Colonel Kennedy said, "According to the map, the highway ends fifteen miles north of Kansong."

Now Colonel Kennedy received one of

the chief of staff's derisive snorts.

"The *highway* does, Howard. But there are villages all along the coast here" — he pointed — "from Kuum-ni to Tokchong. I'll bet there are roads of some sort to all of them."

"There probably are," Colonel Kennedy agreed.

"Tokchong is only thirty-five miles south of Wonsan," the chief of staff said. "I think there is a good chance that by the time the invasion fleet arrives off Wonsan, we'll own that real estate."

"That would seem a reasonable assumption," Kennedy agreed.

"Worst case," the chief of staff said, "for some reason, the vehicles cannot make it over the highway to Kangnung. That seems unlikely."

"Uh-huh."

"Presuming they can make it Kangnung, they can't make it much farther north along Highway Five. That also seems unlikely, but let's take that for the purpose of argument. The LSTs dump their tanks at Wonsan and immediately head for Kangnung. They make about fifteen miles an hour, which would get them there in eight hours. An hour there to load the trucks and another eight hours back to Wonsan, where — since the vehicles would not have to be unloaded by cranes, et cetera — they could simply be driven off the LSTs and be available."

"Interesting," Colonel Kennedy said.

"That's a lot better — getting them there seventeen hours after the landing — than not getting them there at all, right?"

"Absolutely."

"And the farther north they could go along Highway Five, the less travel time for the LSTs. And if the Capital ROK Division has by that time taken Wonsan, which I think is likely, we won't have to use the LSTs at all. Just drive these vehicles all the way to Wonsan, and set up shop, maybe even before X Corps lands there."

"That's certainly a possibility," Colonel Kennedy agreed.

"Okay. So the thing to do, I think, is see if the vehicles can make it to Kangnung. I suggest the best way to do that is make a trial run. Send a couple of wreckers and a couple of tank retrievers and see what happens. It would probably be best — the NKs may have some left-behinds in the area — to send a couple of tanks with them."

"I agree."

"If the test run is successful, we can start moving all the heavy vehicles. Obviously, it would be better to have them on the east coast, however close to Wonsan, than sitting on the wharf in Inchon, on the other side of the peninsula."

"Obviously," Colonel Kennedy agreed.

"Go see Bob and tell him I said to give you a couple of tanks, and then get your show on the road, Howard."

"Right," Colonel Kennedy said.

[Six]
Andrews Air Force Base
Washington, D.C.
1105 13 October 1950

There was already a line of limousines parked not far from the *Independence*, the President's Douglas C-54 transport, when Senator Richardson K. Fowler's Packard limousine was passed by the Secret Service agents and allowed to drive onto the tarmac.

The dignitaries the other limousines had carried to the airport, and some of their aides, were gathered around the movable stairway leading up to the aircraft. Two USAF master sergeants stood at Parade Rest on either side of the stairs.

When Fowler's Packard stopped, Captain George F. Hart, USMCR, got out of the front passenger seat and immediately went to the trunk, opened it, and took out two Valv-Paks and handed them over to another Air Force master sergeant, who was in charge of the luggage.

Fred Delmore, Fowler's chauffeur, got from behind the wheel and opened the rear passenger door. Mrs. Patricia Fleming, in a thigh-length Persian lamb coat, got out first, followed by Senator Fowler and finally Brigadier General Fleming Pickering, USMCR.

Fowler stood by the car, making no effort to join, or even greet, the dignitaries gathered at the stairway. After a moment, one of the dignitaries, a bald Army officer, broke away from the group and walked to the Fowler limousine.

He was wearing an ordinary woolen olive-drab "Ike" jacket-and-trousers uniform, identical to those worn by enlisted men. The only differences were the solid gold piping on his overseas cap and a small circle of five stars pinned to each epaulet. General of the Army Omar Bradley had recently been promoted to the highest rank in the Army by Truman, the first — and, as it turned out, only — such promotion since World War II.

After a moment, several of the others started after him.

"Good morning, Senator," Bradley said, smiling and putting out his hand.

"General Bradley, how are you, sir?" Fowler replied. "I don't think you know General and Mrs. Pickering, do you?"

"I'm afraid I don't," Bradley said. He offered his hand to Patricia Fleming. "An honor, ma'am," he said.

Pickering saluted, and Bradley returned it. They shook hands.

"How do you do, sir?" Pickering said.

"I've been looking forward to meeting you, General," Bradley said. "General Smith has been saying all sorts of nice things about you, and I wanted you to know that I'm really pleased that the two of you will be running the CIA."

"General Smith will be running it, General," Pickering said. "I'm just a temporary hired hand."

Three other men had now walked up to them.

"I don't think you know any of these people, do you, Flem?" Fowler said, then proceeded to introduce him to Secretary of the Army Frank Pace — whose youth surprised Pickering — and two State Department officers, Dean Rusk and Philip Jessup.

There wasn't time to do more than shake hands as the Presidential caravan rolled up.

Harry S Truman got out the black Cadillac first, and a moment later a tall, thin man in what Pickering thought of as a "banker's black" suit joined him. He was Averill Harriman, who was Truman's National Security Adviser. He held the personal rank of Ambassador-at-Large.

Truman headed for the stairway, but then saw Fowler and the Pickerings and turned and walked toward them. After a moment, Harriman followed him.

"Senator," Truman said, smiling. "How nice of you to come to see us off."

"Your Majesty's loyal opposition could do no less," Fowler replied.

Pickering saluted. Truman nodded and smiled at him.

"I'm sorry he didn't have more time at home, Mrs. Pickering," Truman said.

"A little time is better than none, Mr. President," Patricia Fleming replied.

"How nice to see you, Patricia!" Harriman exclaimed, putting out his hand.

Her face was stony, and she ignored the greeting and the hand.

The smile vanished from Harriman's face, and he turned and walked directly toward the stairway.

"Jesus, Pat," Pickering said.

"Mr. President," Patricia Fleming said, "I'm not among Averill Harriman's legion of female admirers. . . ."

"I somehow sensed that," the President said.

"I'm one of those old-fashioned women who think husbands should not sleep with other people's wives, and if they can't manage that level of decency, they should

460

at least not flaunt their infidelity in their wife's face."

"I'm married, oddly enough," Truman said, "to a woman who shares that philosophy. I'm going to have to get you and Bess together, Mrs. Pickering." He paused, and added: "It was nice to see you again."

He started toward the *Independence*.

Pickering looked at his wife.

"Was that necessary?"

"I thought so," his wife replied.

They looked at each other a moment.

"Bring Pick home, Flem," she said softly.

"I'll damned sure try, honey," he said.

She nodded, then wrapped her arms around him.

She stayed that way a moment, then raised her face to his and kissed him.

Then he walked quickly to the steps to the *Independence*, where George Hart was waiting for him.

As soon as they had gone through the door, the steps were pulled away and there came the sound of an engine starting.

[Seven]

There were no layovers. The *Independence* stopped at San Francisco, but just long enough to take on fuel and food, and to give the President and his aides time to deal with the messages that had come in for him while they were flying across the country. No one got off the airplane.

There was a Presidential compartment — and two others, one occupied by General Bradley and the other by Ambassador Harriman — on the *Independence* and there was a steady stream of visitors to both. Pickering did not expect to be summoned to any of the meetings, and he wasn't. He wasn't at all sure why Truman had ordered him to make the trip, and he suspected that Harriman would probably do his best to have the President ignore him.

At San Francisco — not surprisingly, it was Trans-Global's headquarters — there were four Trans-Global Lockheed Constellations, one of which sat, its engines idling, at the end of the runway when the *Independence* took off for Hawaii.

Pickering thought that not only was it a far more graceful-looking aircraft than the Presidential Douglas, but also a hundred miles an hour faster. He wondered why the President wasn't furnished with the fastest aircraft available, and then he thought, again, how wise Pick had been in insisting that Trans-Global buy the Lockheeds, rather than take advantage of the surplus

Air Force Douglas transports available so cheaply.

He then thought that the war was making a good deal of money for Trans-Global. The Air Force had not only contracted for as many contract flights as Trans-Global could make aircraft available for but also was filling every seat made available on the regularly scheduled flights, and there were now far more of those than there had been when the war started.

That was the good news, Pickering thought. The bad news was that Chief Pilot Pickering wasn't around to see how well his airline was doing. Worse than that, Pickering was growing less and less confident that Pick would be found. He refused to allow himself to dwell on the details of why that was likely, even probable, as all of them were unpleasant to contemplate.

He had no idea how he was going to deal with Patricia if his growing fears turned out to be justified.

From San Francisco, the *Independence* flew across the Pacific to the Barber's Point Naval Air Station, which is about fifteen miles from Honolulu.

As they were making their approach to the airfield, Pickering idly wondered if they would wake the President — there were beds in all three compartments — for the landing. The question was answered immediately after the airplane stopped moving when Truman, obviously freshly shaved, appeared in the rear compartment and went around making small talk with everyone there from Army Secretary Pace through Brigadier General Pickering to a young man in civilian clothes whom Hart had identified to Pickering as an Army Warrant Officer Cryptographer.

Truman went down the stairway to both greet Admiral Arthur W. Radford, Commander-in-Chief, Pacific, and to stretch his legs a little while the aircraft was being fueled and fresh food brought aboard. His walk was cut short when another batch of messages requiring his immediate attention was brought to the aircraft.

They were on the ground less than an hour.

Pickering had just about made himself as comfortable as possible in his seat for the Hawaii–Wake Island leg of the flight when one of the Air Force stewards touched his shoulder.

"The President would like to see you, General," he said.

Truman, now in his shirtsleeves, was alone in his compartment when Pickering entered it. The Presidential bed had been returned to its couch function, and Truman was sitting on it before a table covered with documents.

"You wanted to see me, Mr. President?"

Truman held out two sheets of message paper.

"Have a look at this, please, and tell me what you think, please," the President said.

```
TOP SECRET/PRESIDENTIAL

OPERATIONAL IMMEDIATE
DUPLICATION FORBIDDEN

FROM SECRETARY OF DEFENSE
VIA WHITE HOUSE COMMUNICATIONS
  CENTER
0905 WASHINGTON TIME 14OCTOBER1950

TO COMMANDER IN CHIEF PACIFIC
EYES ONLY ADMIRAL RADFORD

PLEASE INSURE FOLLOWING MESSAGE
FROM CHIEF PRESIDENTIAL MISSION TO
FAR EAST TO THE COMMANDER IN CHIEF
CLASSIFIED TOP SECRET/PRESIDENTIAL IS
DELIVERED TO THE PRESIDENT ONLY
REPEAT TO THE PRESIDENT ONLY ON
ARRIVAL AT BARBERS POINT

BEST PERSONAL REGARDS

GEORGE C MARSHALL
```

BEGIN PERSONAL MESSAGE FROM MAJOR GENERAL HOWE

1235 TOKYO TIME 13OCTOBER1950

DEAR HARRY

WONSAN ON EAST COAST OF KOREA FELL TO CAPITAL ROK DIVISION SEVERAL HOURS AGO

MACARTHUR NEVERTHELESS INTENDS TO CONTINUE WITH PLAN TO MOVE X CORPS BY SEA TO WONSAN AND TOLD ME THAT DESPITE QUOTE BRILLIANT PERFORMANCE ENDQUOTE OF ROKS THEY DO NOT HAVE THE NECESSARY TRANSPORT AND HEAVY ARTILLERY HE FEELS IS NECESSARY TO SUPPORT RAPID MOVEMENT TOWARD CHINESE BORDER AT YALU RIVER

IN MY OPINION HE IS CORRECT AS ROK FORCES ARE STILL EQUIPPED MOSTLY WITH HAND-ME-DOWNS

I ALSO HAVE THE FEELING THAT HE WANTS A STRONG AMERICAN PRESENCE THERE TO INSURE (A) THE CAPTURE OF PYONGYANG AS SOON AS POSSIBLE (B) THE ROKS DO NOT GO ANY FARTHER

THAN THE YALU AND (C) THE ROKS PAY
MORE ATTENTION TO THE GENEVA
CONVENTION THAN THEY PROBABLY
WOULD IF AMERICANS WERE NOT AROUND

WHAT THE NORTH KOREANS DID TO THE
SOUTH KOREANS DEFIES DESCRIPTION
AND THEY WILL CERTAINLY SEEK
VENGEANCE UNLESS HE SITS ON THEM

MACARTHUR ALSO SAID HE IS QUOTE
THINKING ABOUT ENDQUOTE TRYING TO
FORM AN ARMORED COLUMN TO TAKE
PYONGYANG EVEN SOONER THAN
X CORPS COULD GET THERE

HE SAYS HE IS REASONABLY CONFIDENT
ORGANIZED RESISTANCE WILL END BY
THANKSGIVING AND THAT HE HAS QUOTE
REASONABLE HOPES ENDQUOTE OF BEING
ABLE TO WITHDRAW EIGHTH ARMY TO
KOREA BY CHRISTMAS

THE REPORTS OF AGENTS INSERTED BY
CIA (MAJOR MCCOY) IN THE EAST AND
LTCOL VANDENBURG IN THE WEST IN
WHICH I PLACE MORE FAITH THAN INTEL
MACARTHUR IS GETTING FROM HIS
SOURCES ALL REPORT (A) BREAKDOWN
OF NORTH KOREAN EFFECTIVENESS

(B) THAT NORTH KOREANS MADE STRONG EFFORT TO TAKE OUR POWS WITH THEM

VANDENBURG TELLS ME HE THINKS RESCUE OF GENERAL DEAN BECOMES MORE UNLIKELY BY THE DAY ALTHOUGH HE AND MCCOY ARE PREPARED TO STAGE RAID USING HELICOPTERS IF HE CAN BE LOCATED

MCCOY INSISTS NO NEWS IS GOOD NEWS ABOUT PICKERING'S SON

I CAN ONLY HOPE HE'S RIGHT

MCCOY SAYS HE IS GETTING QUOTE UNCONFIRMED AND THUS UNRELIABLE ENDQUOTE REPORTS OF EXTENSIVE MOVEMENT OF CHINESE TROOPS TOWARD YALU

REMEMBERING HOW RIGHT MCCOY WAS THE LAST TIME I CAN ONLY HOPE HE WILL BE WRONG NOW

GENERAL WILLOUGHBY AND MACARTHUR FEEL INTERVENTION IS NOT EVEN A REMOTE POSSIBILITY

I STILL THINK PICKERING WOULD HAVE

BEEN BEST CHOICE TO STRAIGHTEN OUT
THE CIA BUT I UNDERSTAND YOUR
CHOICE OF BEDELL SMITH WHO VERY
MUCH IMPRESSED ME THE FEW TIMES
I MET HIM

RESPECTFULLY

RALPH

END PERSONAL MESSAGE FROM GENERAL
HOWE

TOP SECRET/PRESIDENTIAL

Pickering read it and handed it back to the President.

"Anything in there you don't agree with?" the President asked.

"I don't think General Howe is right about me and the CIA, Mr. President."

Truman smiled.

"Anything else?"

"No, sir."

"I'm sorry there's no better news about your son, General," the President said. "But I'm one of those people who believe that the opera isn't over until the fat lady sings."

"I've heard that, Mr. President," Pickering said.

"That'll be all, General," the President said. "Would you ask one of the sergeants to ask General Bradley to come up here?"

"Yes, sir."

X

Clad only in underpants and brassiere, Miss Jeanette Priestly, of the *Chicago Tribune*, bent over a bed while stuffing an Army-issue rucksack. She looked up as Mrs. Ernestine Sage McCoy — whose exquisitely embroidered kimono almost but not quite concealed the evidence of her advanced pregnancy — came into the bedroom.

Jeanette smiled as Ernie carefully lowered herself onto the foot of the mattress.

"I used to have one of those," Ernie said.

"A rucksack?" Jeanette replied, surprised. "You were a Girl Scout?"

"I meant a flat belly, with a cute little navel that used to drive the boys wild when I wore a bikini," Ernie said. "Now look at me!" She patted her stomach. "I look like a boa constrictor that just swallowed a whole pig."

471

Jeanette laughed. "Not quite that bad," she said.

"Bad enough," Ernie said.

Jeanette's tone turned serious. "Can I offer a word of advice?"

"No," Ernie replied sharply, then softened the edge. "Thank you, but no. I know what you're going to say: Go home and have the baby."

"I feel like a shit leaving you alone in your condition," Jeanette said.

"I'm not due until the middle of December," Ernie said. "You'll be back before then, right?"

"I'll be back in a week," Jeanette said. "But I don't want to walk in here a week from now and . . . hear something unpleasant."

"You want to be here when something unpleasant happens, right?"

"That's not what I meant, and you know it," Jeanette said. "But yeah, if something does go wrong — and so far you have a lousy record of going all the way through the childbearing process — I'd like to be here."

"What'll happen will happen," Ernie said. "I'm doing everything the doctor told me to do, which really means not doing anything on a long list of things I'm not supposed to do. I'll be all right."

"If I say, reassuringly, 'Certainly, you'll

be all right,' you'll use that as an excuse not to go home. If I say —"

"Jeanette, this *is* home. This is the first house Ken and I have ever owned."

"A fact — you told me — you carefully concealed from him until very recently."

"I thought of it as my house, our house," Ernie said. "You know why I couldn't tell him. He was trying to be a good Marine officer."

"And for being a very good Marine officer, they started to kick him out of the Marine Corps. There's a moral in there somewhere."

Ernie exhaled audibly.

"So what happens to him when this war is over?" Jeanette asked. "Which it may be by the time I get to Korea, from what they're saying at the Dai Ichi Building."

"I wish I knew," Ernie said. "He doesn't say anything — good Marine officers don't criticize the sacred Marine Corps — but he has to be bitter about what they did to him."

"What would you like to happen?"

"What almost did," Ernie said. "When we thought he was being 'involuntarily released,' which is the euphemism for getting kicked out, we went to see Colonel Ed Banning and his wife, and the Zimmermans, in Charleston. . . ."

"Who's Banning?"

"He and Ken and Ernie go all the way back to the 4th Marines in Shanghai. He's the one who sent Ken to Officer Candidate School. They were together all through World War Two. Anyway, before this goddamn war came along, Banning — who was about to retire — and Zimmerman were going to develop an island. . . ."

"Develop an island?" Jeanette parroted.

"You know, build houses on it and sell them. Their idea was to sell them to retired Marines. But I saw the island, and I think they could sell them to just about anybody. The island is just off the coast, and it's just beautiful. Anyway —"

"Where are they going to get the money to do something like that?" Jeanette interrupted.

"Banning owns the island; he has money," Ernie replied. "A lot of money. He was Ken's role model for living on Marine pay, but he doesn't have to play poor when he retires. And Ernie's wife has the King Midas touch. They own a half-dozen businesses outside Parris Island. Anyway, they asked Ken to go in with them. He seemed to think it was a good idea. But that was when his choices were going back to being a sergeant or the island. Now . . . now they gave him his golden major's oak leaf back. I don't know what he'll do."

"It'll be your choice," Ernie said. "Like I say, I know him. He's really a great guy. But he's not a saint. What he is is a man, and all of them are selfish. They want what they want, and all we can do is learn to live with it. If we can't do that, we lose the man."

"Jesus Christ! And here I was feeling sorry for you."

"Don't feel sorry for me. I like my life — I love my life — with Ken."

"Yeah, that shows," Jeanette said. "Jesus Christ, Jeanette Priestly, wife, mother, and diaper changer!"

"Jeanette Pickering," Ernie corrected her.

"That does have a nice ring to it, doesn't it?" Jeanette asked.

She closed the rucksack and pulled the straps tight.

"You noticed, I'm sure, that amongst my delicate feminine apparel were two sets of GI long johns?"

"I noticed."

"They itch," Jeanette said. "But Korea is cold at night. It is better to itch and scratch than to freeze your ass. Write that down."

Ernie laughed.

"You don't have to go with me to Haneda," Jeanette said.

"Yeah, I do," Ernie said.

Jeanette reached down to the bed and picked up and put on an olive-drab undershirt and a pair of olive-drab men's shorts. Over this, she put on a set of fatigues, then slipped her feet first into Army-issue woolen cushion sole socks and then into combat boots.

She looked at Ernie.

"How do I look?" she asked.

"Oddly enough," Ernie said, "very feminine."

"Bullshit, but thanks anyway."

She picked up the rucksack and walked out of the bedroom.

[Two]
Near Jaeun-Ri, South Korea
1145 14 October 1950

Major Malcolm S. Pickering, USMCR, who had at first known to the minute how many days and hours and minutes it had been since he had had to set his Corsair down — how long he had been on the run — now didn't have any idea at all.

He wasn't even sure if he had eaten his last rice ball yesterday or the day before yesterday.

All he was sure about was that deciding to move northeastward was probably the worst fucking mistake he had made in his life. And might well be the last major mistake of his life.

There was nothing in this part of Korea but steep hills and more steep hills. No rice paddies. Damned few roads, and from what he'd seen of the traffic on them, it was mostly long lines of retreating North Korean soldiers, most of them on foot.

North American P-51 fighters, carrying the insignia of the South Korean Air Force, regularly flew over the roads, strafing anything they saw moving. They flew so low that there was no question in Pickering's mind that if he just stood in the middle of one of the roads he would be seen by one of the P-51 pilots, who would then stand the airplane on its wing, do a quick one-eighty, and then come back and let him have a burst from the eight .50-caliber Brownings in its wings.

The P-51 pilot would logically presume that anyone on these roads was a North Korean. The South Koreans were holed up someplace out of sight. He'd also come across, making his way over the mountains, a dozen or more rock formations that by stretching the term could be called caves. They didn't go deep into the mountains, but far enough so that a family of five or six could go into one of them and not be visible from either the ground or the air.

When one of the South Korean P-51s, or

a section of them, caught a platoon, or a company, of North Koreans in the open and strafed them, the dead and wounded were left where they had been hit. There were very few North Korean vehicles of any kind, and the few trucks he had seen — some of them captured 6 x 6s and weapons carriers — were jammed with the walking wounded. They had kept their arms and used them to guarantee their positions on the trucks.

There was therefore the smell of rotting bodies that seemed to be getting worse, not better, even though it was getting chilly all the time, and freezing cold at night.

There was no question that the tide of war had changed. The North Koreans were not only retreating but bore little resemblance to an organized military force.

So obviously all he had to do was . . .

Make himself invisible to the P-51 pilots, so they wouldn't blow him away. To that end, he had plastered his face and hands with mud, so they would not be a bright spot on the ground to be investigated and strafed. Or maybe just strafed, skipping the investigation, and . . .

Make himself invisible to the retreating North Koreans, who would almost certainly shoot him if they could, not for a military reason but to see if he had anything to eat, and . . .

Wait for friendly troops to come up one of the roads. There were several problems with that. Friendly troops would, like the P-51 pilots, conclude that anybody here in the middle of nowhere was a North Korean. American troops might take such people prisoner. From what he had seen, the South Koreans would not.

The major problem was that he had been on short rations since he'd been shot down, and over the last four or five days the short rations had diminished to zero. And since he had stopped eating, he could feel his strength diminishing with each step — each labored breath — he took.

He didn't think, in other words, that he was going to make it.

He was not going to give up, but on the other hand there wasn't much difference between what he was able to do and giving up. Unless, of course, he gave up by taking a dive off the nearby cliff or putting the .45 to his temple, and even being hungry, dirty, tired, and sick seemed better than those options. With his luck, he thought, he wouldn't get killed taking a dive off the cliff, he would break both legs and arms and lie in agony for Christ only knew how long.

There was another option to checking out, if that's what was going to happen, and that was to lie on one of the boulders and let the sun warm him while he thought of Jeanette.

At first, when he thought of Jeanette, the thoughts were erotic. Now when he thought of her, there was little lust in the fantasy. He remembered how she smelled and the soft touch of her fingers on his face.

It would be very nice, he thought, if he wasn't going to make it, if he went to sleep in the sun thinking of Jeanette and then just never woke up.

He thought about asking God to give him at least that, but decided against it. He asked God to make it as easy on Jeanette and his mother and father, and Ernie, and even Killer McCoy. It wasn't right, he thought, to ask God for special treatment, but his parents and Jeanette and the others shouldn't have pain on his account. Maybe God would see it that way, too.

He had just turned onto his stomach when he heard the sound of tearing metal. That caught his attention, and then he heard the sound of clashing gears and an engine racing.

He got up, and walked as quickly as he could manage around an outcropping of rock to the cliff he decided he would not take a dive from, and looked down at the road.

It was a convoy of U.S. Army vehicles. A

very strange one. In the lead was a jeep. Behind it were two M-26 tanks, a tank recovery vehicle, a heavy-duty wrecker, another tank recovery vehicle, and then another heavy-duty wrecker.

Pickering closed his eyes and shook his head to make sure he wasn't delusionary. When he opened his eyes again, the convoy was still there. It wasn't moving, and he saw why. The first heavy-duty wrecker had collided with the trailer of the tank recovery vehicle and knocked its rear wheels off the road.

Pickering went down the hill as fast as he could.

He made it to the road.

He put his hands over his head and started walking down it.

"American!" he shouted. "Don't shoot!"

And then he began to sing and shout, as loud as he could manage:

"From the Halls of Montezuma,

"American! Don't shoot!

"To the Shores of Tripoli

"American! Don't shoot!

"We will fight our nation's battles!

"American! Don't shoot!

"On the Land and on the Sea!

"American! Don't shoot!"

Captain Francis P. MacNamara, commanding officer of the 8023d Transportation Company (Depot, Forward), who had elected to lead the test over-the-road run to the east coast, who was examining the considerable damage the wrecker had done to the retrieval trailer, heard the noise.

He drew his .45, worked the action, shouted "Heads up!" and stepped into the center of the road.

A tall, thin human being, too large for a Korean, was walking down the center of the road with his hands in the air. He was wearing what looked like the remnants of some kind of coveralls. His face was streaked with mud.

And he was making strange sounds.

I'll be a sonofabitch if he isn't singing! And it's "The Marines' Hymn"! I'll be a sonofabitch!

"Who the hell are you?" Captain MacNamara demanded.

"Major Malcolm S. Pickering, United States Marine Corps," Pick croaked . . . and then fell first to his knees, and then flat on his face.

MacNamara hurriedly holstered his .45 and ran to him.

He first felt for signs of life, then turned him over and wrapped his arms around him and held him like a baby.

"Get some water up here!" he shouted. "And there's a bottle of bourbon in the glove compartment in my jeep. Bring that. And some blankets."

"And if you happen to have some food," the walking skeleton in his arms said, very faintly.

"You got it, Major," Captain MacNamara said.

Five minutes later, Major Malcolm Pickering, USMCR, was laid out on several blankets on the trailer of the tank recovery vehicle. He had been given a stiff drink of Captain MacNamara's Old Forester — which he had promptly thrown up — and half a dozen spoonfuls of ham chunks in pineapple sauce, three of which he had managed to keep down.

The blankets had been provided by Technical Sergeant Alvin H. Donn, U.S. Army, who was the NCO in charge of the M-26 tanks. He had also held Major Pickering up in a sitting position while Captain MacNamara had, with all the tenderness of a mother, spoon-fed him the ham chunks in pineapple sauce, and while he had thrown up.

There were now a dozen men standing at the side of the tank recovery trailer looking down with mingled amazement, curiosity, and pity at the human skeleton on the blankets.

Sergeant Donn pointed to Staff Sergeant

James D. Buckley, the commander of the second tank.

"Stay with the major," he ordered. "Try to get some food in him. No more booze."

When Buckley had taken his place, Donn slid off the trailer and nodded his head at Captain MacNamara, a signal he wanted a word with him. MacNamara followed him to the recovery vehicle tractor.

He had made a snap judgment when he had first met Sergeant Donn. A goddamn good NCO, as he himself had been. He had then thereafter treated him accordingly.

"That guy's in really bad shape," Sergeant Donn said. "We've got to get him to a hospital."

"We'll have to get this out of the way," MacNamara agreed, slamming the tank retriever trailer with his fist. "Fuck it, we'll just push it the rest of the way off the road. Maybe we could lay him on the hood of the jeep. But where the hell do we take him?"

"I've got a radio in the tank that sometimes lets me talk to light aircraft," Donn said. "We could give that a shot."

MacNamara nodded his head.

They walked past the second tank to the first, and crawled onto it. Donn lowered himself into the turret and came up a minute later with a microphone and a headset.

"What do they call this circus?"

"Task Force Road Service," MacNamara said. That had been Colonel Kennedy's whimsical suggestion/order.

Donn pushed the round black TRANSMIT button on the microphone.

"Road Service to any U.S. aircraft hearing my call," he said. "Road Service to any U.S. aircraft hearing my call."

There was no reply.

He made the call twice again. This time there was a reply.

"Go ahead, Road Service."

"Who are you?" Donn asked.

"I'm an Air Force P-51, call sign Air Force three oh seven."

"Air Force three oh seven, we just picked up a shot-down pilot. We have to get him to a hospital, and right now."

"Who and where are you, Road Service?"

"We're a small convoy, two M-26s and wreckers and tank recovery vehicles. We are approximately six miles northeast of Jaeun-Ri."

"Say again location?"

"We are approximately six miles northeast of Jaeun-Ri."

"Hold one, I'll see if I can find it on the chart."

There was a long silence before Air Force three oh seven came back on the air.

"Road Service, I think I have you. I think I'm about twenty miles south. Let me get a positive location, and then I'll try to get a helicopter from the Navy. I should be there in a couple of minutes."

Another voice came over the air.

"Road Service, say again your location."

"Approximately six miles northeast of Jaeun-Ri. Who are you?"

There was a long silence.

"I'm about five miles from your position. Have you got any flares?"

"Affirmative. Who are you?"

"Wait sixty seconds, and then start shooting flares at sixty-second intervals."

"Okay. Who are you?"

There was no reply.

It took Sergeant Donn about sixty seconds to get flares from inside the tank. As soon as he had one loaded, he shot it off.

He had just fired the third flare when there was a strange noise.

Fluckata-fluckata-fluckata fluckata-fluckata-fluckata.

"What the hell is that?" Sergeant Donn asked.

"It's a helicopter," Captain MacNamara said. He had heard the sound before.

"Jesus, the Navy sent one that quick?"

"I don't think that's a Navy helicopter," MacNamara said.

"Okay," the radio said. "Enough flares. I

have you in sight. Are there any telephone wires, cables, anything like that down there?"

Donn and MacNamara looked.

"Negative. No wires or cables."

"Okay. Here we come."

A Sikorsky H-19A helicopter, painted black, came down the valley, flew over the convoy, slowed, stopped forward movement, turned around, and fluttered to the ground.

A half-dozen heavily armed men, dressed in what looked like black pajamas, erupted from the passenger compartment. Another one started climbing down from the cockpit.

"What the hell is this?" Sergeant Donn asked.

The man who had climbed down from the cockpit trotted up to them. When he saw Captain MacNamara, he said, "Oh, Jesus, look who it is!" And then, "Where's the pilot?"

MacNamara pointed to the tank recovery vehicle trailer.

The man made a *follow me* signal with his hand to the other men in black pajamas as he started to trot to the trailer. They began to trot after him.

So did Sergeant Donn, who was more than a little curious about the guys in the black pajamas, and the black helicopter with no markings in which they had arrived.

He got there about the time the first guy in the black pajamas did.

The first guy looked down at the human skeleton.

"Hello, you ugly bastard," he said. "Where the hell have you been hiding?"

The human skeleton raised one hand and grasped the hand of the guy in the black pajamas. Sergeant Donn saw tears form and roll down the human skeleton's cheeks, and when he glanced at the guy from the chopper, he saw tears on his cheeks, too.

After a moment, the guy from the chopper turned his head.

"Okay, let's get him on the bird," he ordered. He turned again to the human skeleton. "You hurt, Pick?"

"I'm fine," the human skeleton said.

"Three guys on each side of the blankets," the guy in the pajamas ordered. "And be careful with him."

"Aye, aye, sir," one of the men in pajamas said.

An Army major wearing pilot's wings walked quickly — almost trotted — up to them.

"Can you raise the *Badoeng Strait*?" the man in pajamas, Major Ken McCoy, said.

"Jesus, I don't think so, Ken," the pilot,

490

Major Alex Donald, said.

"Hell!"

"Maybe the P-51 can," Donald said.

"And you can talk to him?" McCoy asked.

"No problem."

"How are we fixed for fuel?"

"Not well. No matter where we go, we'll have to refuel first."

"Okay. Let's go."

Donald started for the helicopter.

McCoy turned to MacNamara. "MacNamara, right?"

"Yes, sir."

"What the hell are you doing out here in the middle of nowhere?"

"Trying to get to Wonsan."

"You're not going to get there on this road," McCoy said. "It ends at a lake — no ferry — about three miles from here. I'll leave one of my men with you, and he'll get you onto a road around the lake."

"Thank you," MacNamara said. "I appreciate that."

"I owe you," McCoy said. He put out his hand and then trotted to the helicopter.

Before he got there, an Air Force P-51 flew over them, very slowly.

When McCoy climbed into the cockpit, the voice of the P-51 pilot was already coming over the headset.

"Road Service, Air Force three oh seven. I have you in sight. How do you read?"

McCoy grabbed the microphone.

"Air Force three oh seven, this is Army four zero zero three."

"Zero zero three, are you the black helicopter on the ground?"

"Air Force three oh seven, can you contact the aircraft carrier *Badoeng Strait*? They're operating in the Sea of Japan."

"I don't know. Who is this?"

"Please call the *Badoeng Strait*. Let me know if you get through."

"Who is this?"

"A friendly word of advice, Air Force three oh seven — do what I ask, and do it now."

"Stand by."

There was a sixty-second wait, and then: "Negative on contact with the *Badoeng Strait*."

Major Donald was now sitting beside McCoy. He put his hand out for the microphone, and McCoy gave it up.

"Three oh seven," Donald ordered, "climb to ten thousand and try it again on the emergency frequency."

"Stand by."

This time the delay was on the order of four minutes, which gave Donald time to fire up the H-19A.

"Army four zero zero three, Air Force

three oh seven is in contact with the *Badoeng Strait.*"

Donald handed McCoy the microphone.

"Air Force three oh seven, stand by to relay message to *Badoeng Strait.* Message follows: 'For Colonel William Dunn. Bingo. Killer. Heads up. En route.' Got that?"

"Got it. Stand by."

This time the wait was less than sixty seconds.

"Army four zero zero three, *Badoeng Strait* acknowledges."

"How are you fixed for fuel?"

"What do you have in mind?"

"Could you fly cover for us for a while?"

"Affirmative. I have one hour fuel aboard. Who are you?"

"Thank you, Air Force three oh seven. We're taking off now."

McCoy turned to Donald and made a lifting motion — take it up — with his hands.

Then he said, "Oh, shit!"

Donald took his hands off the controls and looked at McCoy.

"I told MacNamara I'd leave him somebody to get him on the right road," McCoy said.

He leaned between the seats of the cockpit so that he could shout into the passenger compartment.

"The Army's lost," he called. "Leave two men and a map behind to get them on the road around the lake."

Sixty seconds after that, two men in black pajamas got out of the H-19A and ran just far enough away so that Donald could see them. When he did, the H-19A lifted off.

[Three]
USS *Badoeng Strait* (CVE 116)
37.9 Degrees North Latitude
129.59 Degrees East Longitude
The Sea of Japan
1305 14 October 1950

Lieutenant Colonel William Dunn, USMC, still in his flight suit, had been on the bridge ever since the captain had sent for him after getting the cryptic message from Air Force three oh seven on the emergency frequency.

"Bridge, Radar," the squawk box announced.

"Bridge," the talker replied.

"We have a slow-moving aircraft at a thousand feet at fifteen miles heading three hundred degrees."

"Acknowledged," the captain responded personally. "Keep me advised."

The captain turned to Colonel Dunn.

"That's probably your helo," he said.

"Who else would it be?"

"Sir," Dunn said, "it just occurred to me that an Army pilot probably has never made a carrier landing."

"Why the hell is he coming here?" the captain asked, and then without waiting for a reply, ordered: "Turn into the wind. Prepare to recover U.S. Army helicopter." Then he had another thought, and issued other orders. "Engine room, full astern. Flight deck, make all preparations for a crash landing."

"Turn into the wind, aye, aye, sir," the talker parroted into his microphone. "Prepare to recover U.S. Army helicopter, aye, aye, sir. Engine room, full astern, aye, aye, sir. Flight deck, make all preparations for a crash landing, aye, aye, sir."

There was immediately the sound of a Klaxon, and another voice on the squawk box: "Make all preparations for a crash landing. Firemen and Corpsmen, man your stations. Make all preparations for a crash landing. Firemen and Corpsmen, man your stations."

Then another voice on the squawk box.

"Bridge, Radio."

"Bridge," the talker replied.

"We are in radio contact with Army four zero zero three on Emergency Frequency One."

"Acknowledge," the captain said.

"Acknowledged," the talker parroted.

The captain turned to a small control panel near his seat, moved several switches, and picked up a microphone.

"This is the captain of the *Badoeng Strait*," he said.

"Good afternoon, sir," the speaker replied metallically.

"Have you ever made a carrier landing?"

"No, sir, I have not."

"Jesus Christ!" the captain softly said to Dunn, and then pressed the microphone button again. "I'm going to turn you over to Colonel Dunn, who is a highly experienced carrier aviator. I'm sure he'll be able to help you."

He handed the microphone to Dunn.

"Army zero three," Dunn called, "what we're doing now is losing headway — losing speed — so that the deck, which will be your runway, will be moving as slow as possible. You with me so far?"

"How slow is 'as slow as possible'?" Major Alex Donald inquired.

"Just fast enough to maintain what we call steerageway," Dunn said. "You'll hardly notice that it's moving at all. But we can't stop a ship this large right away. Have you enough fuel to circle around for a couple of minutes?"

"Affirmative," Donald replied.

"And you won't have to worry about the

wind, either. The ship will be heading into it."

"Okay."

The captain issued another order.

"Engine room, make turns to maintain steerageway."

The talker repeated the order.

"*Badoeng Strait*, can I fly over the deck? Approaching from the back end, into the wind?"

The captain raised his eyebrows in exasperation, then nodded.

"Permission granted," Dunn said.

The H-19A approached the *Badoeng Strait* head-on.

"I thought he said he was coming in over the 'back end'?" the captain said.

When the H-19A was several hundred feet from the ship, it veered to its right and flew down the length of the carrier at about the height of the flight deck. Dunn and the captain could see the pilot looking at the ship.

When the H-19A was several hundred feet aft of the ship, Donald turned it around and then flew toward the stern, carefully adjusting his speed to that of the carrier, so that he was moving very slowly toward the deck.

"Jesus Christ, look at that!" Donald's voice came over the radio. "The whole fucking fire department's waiting for us."

It was clear to both Colonel Dunn and the captain that the pilot of the helicopter believed his microphone switch was in INTER-COM rather than where it was, in TRANSMIT.

Neither officer felt this was the appropriate time to bring the pilot's error to his attention.

"Don't fuck this up, Alex," another voice said, one Colonel Dunn recognized as that of Major Kenneth R. "The Killer" McCoy, USMCR.

"I have no intention of fucking this up," Donald said.

The exchange caused snickers, chuckles, and several laughs from officers and sailors on the bridge and elsewhere on the ship.

The amusement on the bridge was instantly stilled when the captain said, "Knock that off!"

The H-19A was now over the aft edge of the deck, thirty feet above it. It inched down its length.

When it reached the bridge, on the superstructure called "the island," both the captain and Colonel Dunn could see the men in the cockpit. And vice versa. Major McCoy recognized Colonel Dunn and waved and smiled at him.

"Jesus H. Christ!" the captain said.

Colonel Dunn nevertheless waved back.

The H-19A continued its slow passage over the flight deck.

"I think I have this fucking oversized ferry figured out, Ken," Donald's voice said. "What's happening is that the deck is moving faster than we are."

"So?"

"Not much faster," Donald said, thought-fully. "So if I went right up to the front . . . and sat down very carefully, what would happen? All we would do is maybe roll back a little. Shall I give it a shot?"

"Why not?"

The captain grabbed his microphone and opened his mouth. And then closed it.

The captain, an experienced aviator himself, realized that the pilot of the helicopter had condensed the essentials of carrier landing to one sentence: *Sit down very carefully.* In the time available, the captain realized he had nothing to add to that.

The H-19A was now at the forward end of the landing deck, where, very slowly, it inched downward toward the deck. One wheel touched down, and then, very quickly, the other three.

"I'll be a sonofabitch," the captain said softly. "He's down!" Then he raised his voice. "Mr. Clanton, you have the conn!"

To which Lieutenant Commander Clanton, a stern-faced thirty-five-year-old, replied, "I have the conn, sir. Captain is leaving the bridge!"

The captain, with Colonel Dunn on his

heels, headed for the ladder to the flight deck.

On the flight deck, fifty men — a dozen of them in aluminum-faced firefighting suits and another dozen in Corpsmen's whites, six of these pushing two gurneys — raced toward the helicopter. Through them moved tractors and firefighting vehicles loaded with other sailors.

They all reached the helicopter even before Donald had shut down the engine, and long before he could apply the brake to the rotor.

By the time the captain and Colonel Dunn reached the helicopter, a very thin, very dirty, heavily bearded human skeleton in what was just barely recognizable as a flight suit was very gently removed from the passenger compartment and onto a gurney.

The human skeleton recognized both Colonel Dunn and the captain. His hand, fingers stiff, came up his temple.

"Hey, Billy!" he said, then: "Permission to come aboard, sir?"

"Permission granted, you sonofabitch!" Colonel Dunn replied as he returned the salute. Despite his best efforts, his voice broke halfway through the sentence.

"Make way!" one of the doctors ordered, and the gurney started to roll toward the island.

McCoy climbed down from the cockpit.

The sight of a man in black pajamas in itself attracted some attention, as did the black helicopter with no markings. Eyes grew even wider when the man in black pajamas saluted the captain crisply, barked, "Permission to come aboard, sir?" and then crisply saluted the national colors.

The captain returned the salute.

"Good to see you again, Major," the captain said.

"Where'd you find him, Killer?" Dunn asked.

"The Army found him — actually, he found an Army convoy that got lost trying to get to Wonsan — in the middle of the Taebaek Mountains. We must have flown right over him fifty times in the last ten days."

"Me, too," Dunn said. "That's rough territory. Hard to spot anything from the air."

Major Alex Donald walked around the tail assembly of the H-19A. Not being at all familiar with the customs of the Naval service, he did not ask permission to come aboard, but instead simply saluted the captain and Lieutenant Colonel Dunn.

"Well done, Major," the captain said.

"He needed some help, as soon as we could get it for him," Donald replied.

"I presume, Major," the captain said to

McCoy, "that's why you felt the risks in bringing him here were justified?"

"Yes, sir. That and because I knew you have the communications facilities I need."

"Well, Colonel Dunn will see that you have what you need," the captain said. "And when you're finished, perhaps you would be good enough to come to the bridge and tell me what you can to satisfy my curiosity."

"Yes, sir. Thank you, sir," McCoy said.

[Four]
Communications Center
USS *Badoeng Strait* (CVE 116)
37.9 Degrees North Latitude
129.56 Degrees East Longitude
The Sea of Japan
1315 14 October 1950

The communications officer on duty answered the buzz to unlock the port himself. When he saw Lieutenant Colonel Dunn and a man wearing what appeared to be black pajamas, he opened his mouth to say something, but Dunn cut him off.

"This officer has a message to dispatch," Dunn said.

"Yes, sir?"

"You want to let us in, please?" Dunn asked.

"Yes, sir," the commo officer said, and stepped out of the way.

"May I have the message, sir?" the commo officer said.

"I'll have to type it out," McCoy said.

"One of my men will be happy —"

"I'll type it myself, thank you," McCoy said. "Lieutenant, this is one of those messages that the fewer people see, the better. There will be no copies. Can you handle a Top Secret encryption yourself?"

The commo officer looked between McCoy and Dunn, then said, "That's unusual, but yes, sir."

"Can I have that typewriter a moment?" McCoy asked a white hat seated at a work table.

The commo officer nodded his approval and the white hat stood up.

McCoy sat down, rolled the carriage to eject a standard message form made up of an original and three carbons, then rolled a single sheet of paper into the machine.

He typed very rapidly, then took the message from the typewriter and handed it to Dunn, who read it.

"Two things, Ken," he said, somewhat hesitantly. "Considering the addressees, isn't that 'dirty, unshaven, and very hungry' business a little informal?"

"If I just said, 'in pretty good shape' or something like that, everyone would wonder what I wasn't saying," McCoy said.

"And can you do that? Ask somebody 'not to disseminate' Top Secret information, and then give it to them?"

"I guess we'll find out soon enough, won't we?" McCoy said, and smiled, took the sheet of paper from Dunn, and handed it to the commo officer.

"Will you encrypt this and send it Operational Immediate, please?"

The commo officer took it, read it, looked at McCoy, and then sat down at the cryptographic machine and began to enter McCoy's message.

TOP SECRET

OPERATIONAL IMMEDIATE
1320 14OCT1950
DUPLICATION FORBIDDEN

FROM OFFICER IN CHARGE CIA SEOUL
ABOARD USS BADOENG STRAIT

EYES ONLY MASTER SERGEANT PAUL T
KELLER USA COMMUNICATIONS CENTER
SUPREME HEADQUARTERS UNITED
NATIONS COMMAND TOKYO

ENCRYPT USING SPECIAL CODE AND
TRANSMIT AS OPERATIONAL IMMEDIATE
THE FOLLOWING

MESSAGE BEGINS

EYES ONLY
DIRECTOR CIA WASHINGTON DC
DEPUTY DIRECTOR CIA FOR ASIA
CHIEF PRESIDENTIAL MISSION TO KOREA
SEOUL
CIA STATION CHIEF SEOUL
COMMANDANT USMC WASHINGTON DC

MAJOR MALCOLM S. PICKERING USMCR
RETURNED TO US CONTROL 1200
14OCT1950. TRANSPORTED USS BADOENG
STRAIT AS OF 1300 14OCT1950.

SUBJECT OFFICER IS DIRTY, UNSHAVEN,
AND VERY HUNGRY, BUT IS UNWOUNDED,
UNINJURED, AND IN SOUND
PSYCHOLOGICAL CONDITION.

FOLLOWING CIVILIAN PERSONNEL SHOULD
BE CONTACTED BY MOST EXPEDITIOUS
MEANS, ASKED NOT TO DISSEMINATE
INFORMATION ABOVE TO OTHERS AND ON
AGREEMENT BE NOTIFIED OF SUBJECT
OFFICER'S RETURN AND CONDITION.

MRS FLEMING PICKERING C/O FOSTER
HOTELS SAN FRANCISCO CAL
MRS K.R. MCCOY, TOKYO, JAPAN

[Five]

The captain, who was sitting in his chair facing aft, as if expecting them, waved Lieutenant Colonel Dunn and Major McCoy onto the bridge.

"Colonel Dunn get you everything you needed, Major?" the captain asked.

"Yes, sir, thank you," McCoy said.

"The ship's surgeon was just here," the captain said. "There's nothing life-threatening wrong with Major Pickering. But that's because he's here. The doc said he wouldn't like to hazard a guess how much longer he would have lasted if you hadn't found him when you did." He paused, and shook his head. "And what a way to die that would have been."

"Sir?"

"I suppose I'm violating the major's privacy, but I think you have a right to know, if I do. What was really threatening his life was dehydration. He has dysentery. That's unpleasant anytime, but it usually won't kill you, according to the doc, if you have enough liquids. Pickering heard somewhere that you get dysentery from bad water — and he'd had some bad water and had dysentery — so what he decided to do was not drink water he hadn't boiled. That might not cure the dysentery, but it might. Drinking more bad water would not cure it."

"My God!" Dunn said.

"Major Pickering told the doc," the captain went on, "that he'd run out of boiled water four, five days ago, and hadn't had a chance to boil any more. So he didn't drink anything. Meanwhile, the dysentery continued to drain what liquids were left in his body. They're dripping glucose into both arms now, and the doc says he should have the dysentery under control shortly. The doc also says he belongs on a hospital ship, not here."

"Sir, I knew you had the communications I needed," McCoy said.

"I won't ask you questions, McCoy, that I know you won't answer. But those pajamas of yours do make me curious."

"When I put them on this morning, sir, I

had no intention of going aboard a man-of-war."

"Meaning you're not going to explain them, right?" the captain said, smiling.

"They're sort of a disguise, sir. I can't pass for an Asiatic in the daylight, but at night, in clothes like this, if they can't get a good look at me, I can."

"Until you open your mouth, you mean?"

"I speak Korean, sir."

"Who don't you want to spot you as an American? Can I ask that?"

"At first light this morning, sir, we inserted agents north of Wonsan," McCoy said.

"Using that black Sikorsky?"

"Yes, sir."

"You were on the ground, behind enemy lines, this morning?"

"Yes, sir."

"How often do you do that sort of thing?"

"It's what we do, sir. We do it just about daily."

"You're a braver man than I am, Gunga Din," the captain said.

"It's not what you think, sir. If you know what you're doing, it's not all that dangerous."

The captain snorted.

"I'm not being modest, sir. What scared me was just now."

"Excuse me?"

"When we came out to the *Badoeng Strait*, sir, and Major Donald told me had no idea how we were going to land on a carrier. That was high-pucker-factor time for me, sir."

The captain smiled. "I took the liberty of seeing what I could do about that," he said. "Take a look."

He pointed down to the flight deck. McCoy followed his finger and saw Major Alex Donald and two other men in flight suits standing near the H-19A. They were making gestures with their hands. Donald was nodding his head.

"Those are helo pilots," the captain said. "I asked them to give your pilot a quick course in carrier takeoff in a helicopter."

"Sir, I am profoundly grateful," McCoy said.

"Major, I would be pleased if you and Colonel Dunn and your pilot would take lunch with me in my cabin," the captain said.

"That's very kind, sir."

Major McCoy suspected — correctly — that even the captain of a vessel like the USS *Badoeng Strait* did not routinely luncheon on what was served by a white-jacketed steward to the four of them in the captain's cabin.

It began with cream of mushroom soup,

went through roast beef with Yorkshire pudding, baked potatoes, and green beans, and ended with strawberry shortcake.

Over their coffee, the captain asked another question.

"If you're uncomfortable answering this, McCoy, just don't answer it. But do your agents get information for you? Anything you can tell me?"

McCoy hesitated, then said: "May I have your word that it will go no further than this cabin, sir?"

"You've got it."

"In the last several days, we've been getting reports that elements of the Fourth Chinese Field Army — which has been at the Korean border since June — have begun to send at least elements of the 38th, 39th, 40th, and 42d armies across the border."

"My God!" Dunn blurted.

"I suppose my ignorance is showing," the captain said. "Fourth Field Army? What did you say, 38th, 39th, 40th, and 41st armies? Five *armies?*"

"Fortieth and *42d,*" McCoy said. "The Chinese *field* army is something like one of ours. Like the Eighth Army. What we would call a 'corps' they call an 'army.' A field army is made up of two or more armies, like our armies usually have two or more corps. The last reliable word I had was that the strength of the Fourth Field Army was about six hundred thousand men."

"My God, and you say they're crossing the border, Ken?" Dunn asked.

"What I said, and why I don't want any of this to go further than this cabin, is that I have been getting *reports,* which I so far can't confirm, that *elements* of the Fourth Field Army — *elements* of those numbered armies — have begun to slip across the Yalu."

"We've been flying — and so has the Air Force — reconnaissance missions all over that area," the captain protested.

"Bill Dunston, the Korea station chief, saw the last intelligence from Supreme Headquarters, the stuff they furnished Eighth Army and X Corps. According to that, aerial reconnaissance — even the covert stuff, across the border — has not detected the Fourth Field Army as being there, and I know it's there."

"It's the first I've heard of it," the captain said, more than a little doubtfully. "How the hell can you hide — what did you say, six hundred thousand men?"

"In caves, in valleys, in buildings, you put them down by first light, and nobody moves, *absolutely nobody moves,* during daylight. They've had a lot of experience doing that," McCoy said.

"I'm having trouble — no offense, McCoy — accepting this," the captain said.

"None taken, sir."

"You think the Chinese are going to come in, don't you, Ken?" Dunn asked.

"I think it's a strong possibility."

"What — can I ask this? — do you do with your intelligence, these reports, who do you send them to?" the captain asked. "Can I presume they go through Supreme Headquarters?"

"I'm right on the line of what I can't say, sir," McCoy said. "We share some of our intelligence with Supreme Headquarters, General Willoughby. My boss, the Assistant Director of the CIA for Asia, gets my reports, and the decision as to what to do with them is his."

"You share 'some' of your intelligence with Supreme Headquarters?" the captain asked. "Why not all of it?"

"That's politics, sir," McCoy said.

"What's politics got to do with it?"

"If there is a difference of opinion, sir, about the reliability of some intel . . . What General Willoughby puts out, he puts out in the name of General MacArthur. If Willoughby says the moon is made of blue Roquefort cheese, that means MacArthur agrees. Once that announcement is made, we can't say the moon is made of Gorgonzola, even if we are sure it is, because that would be telling General MacArthur that he's wrong." He paused. "I suspect I'm having diarrhea of the mouth, sir."

"I don't know about that, Major," the captain said, "but frankly, it seems to me that, for a relatively junior officer, you seem to know a hell of a lot about how things work at the highest levels."

"Sir," Dunn said. "I have something to say that (a) will almost certainly annoy Major McCoy and (b) should not leave this cabin."

"Let's hear it," the captain said, "whether or not the major is annoyed."

"Christ, Billy!" McCoy protested.

"Let's have it, Colonel," the captain ordered.

"When Major McCoy was attached to Naval Element, Supreme Headquarters," Dunn said, "he turned in to Supreme Headquarters an analysis which indicated the North Koreans were planning to invade South Korea in June. His conclusions went against those formed by General Willoughby. Not only was McCoy's analysis ordered destroyed, but they tried to kick him out of the Marine Corps, and almost succeeded."

"I find that, too, hard to believe," the captain said. "Where did you get that?"

Dunn replied, "From General Pickering,

sir, the Deputy Director of the CIA for Asia."

"Jesus H. Christ!" the captain said.

"In what I personally regard an act of courage," Dunn went on, "McCoy got his draft copy of his analysis to General Pickering, for whom he had worked when they were both in the OSS during World War Two. General Pickering took McCoy's analysis to Admiral Hillencoetter, the Director of the CIA. The Admiral didn't believe it, either, apparently, until the North Koreans came across the border. But when that happened, the admiral gave McCoy's analysis to the President, who thereupon called General Pickering to active duty, named him Deputy Director of the CIA for Asia, and ordered the Commandant of the Marine Corps that McCoy not only not be involuntarily separated but that he be assigned to General Pickering."

"I really don't know what to say," the captain said.

"Sir," McCoy said, "with all possible respect, I ask you to forget this conversation ever took place."

"Forget this conversation? How could I ever do that? But you have my word that what was said in this cabin will never get out of this cabin. And if I owe you an apology, Major, consider it humbly offered."

"No apology is necessary, sir. None of this conversation would have happened if I hadn't run off at the mouth."

"What I think happened there, Killer," Dunn said, "is that even you, the legendary Killer McCoy, was understandably emotionally upset with relief when you snatched your best friend literally from death's door. Under those circumstances, a moment's indiscretion is understandable."

"I didn't do anything, Billy," McCoy said. "I told you, Pick found a lost army convoy."

Thirty minutes later, the black H-19A lifted off the flight deck of the USS *Badoeng Strait* without incident and headed for the eastern shore of the Korean Peninsula.

[Six]
USAF Airfield K-1
Pusan, South Korea
1405 14 October 1950

After Ernie McCoy dropped her at Haneda Airfield, outside Tokyo, Miss Jeanette Priestly of the *Chicago Tribune* had been told that there were no direct flights from Japan to the airstrip at Wonsan. Just returned to service, the airstrip would take nothing larger than twin-engined C-47 aircraft. But inasmuch as there were very limited refueling capabilities at Wonsan, and the C-47 could not make it to Wonsan from Tokyo with enough fuel remaining to make it back to K-1 at Pusan, Tokyo–Wonsan service was out of the question.

What she would have to do is fly first to K-1, then see what she could do there about further transportation to Wonsan.

With some difficulty, she managed to get a seat on the next Pusan-bound C-54.

The dispatcher at Pusan base operations was polite but firm.

To board a Wonsan-bound aircraft, it would be necessary for her to have an authorization from the Eighth Army Rear Press Officer. There could be no exceptions. And no, he could not provide her with transportation to the Eighth Army Rear Press Office. Perhaps if she called them, they might be willing to send a jeep for her.

Jeanette went to the highway, took off her cap, unbraided her long blond hair, and let it fall around her shoulders.

The drivers of the first two jeeps to pass her stared openmouthed at the sight of a fatigues-clad lady with long blond hair hitchhiking. The driver of the third jeep slammed on his brakes, backed up, and told her he would carry her anywhere in the Orient she wanted to go.

He dropped her at the Eighth Army Rear Press Office, a collection of Quonset huts near the railroad station in downtown Pusan.

There, first a corporal, then a technical sergeant, then a captain, and finally a major with a very neatly trimmed pencil-line mustache told her essentially the same thing, that there was a lot of demand for air passage to Wonsan — *"Every reporter in Korea wants to be able to say they were waiting on the beach when X Corps landed"* — and there was only a limited amount of space available for nonessential travelers, like reporters.

There was a list, to which her name would be appended. With a little luck, she might be able to get on a plane to Wonsan tomorrow, but it would most likely not be until the day after.

Jeanette hitchhiked back to K-1, and wandered around the field until she saw a C-47 standing in front of a hangar from the doors of which hung a huge red cross.

A little investigation revealed that this was the point at which medical supplies, which have the highest priority, were loaded aboard transport aircraft.

She dazzled the pilot with a smile, asked him where he was going, and was told that he was going round robin Pusan–Seoul–Wonsan–Pusan, which meant, he explained, that he would first fly to Seoul, where he would discharge cargo and take on enough fuel to fly across the peninsula to Wonsan, where he would discharge the rest of his cargo and take aboard wounded requiring evacuation via Pusan, and fly to Pusan.

Jeanette told him that was really fascinating, the sort of a human-interest story her editors were always interested in, the sort of a story that would be reprinted in a lot of newspapers.

"Where did you say you were from, Lieutenant?" Jeanette asked, taking the lens cap off her Leica.

"Louisville, Kentucky."

"*The Louisville Courier* usually prints everything I write," Jeanette said. "Why don't you just stand there by the boxes with the big red crosses on them."

"That's human blood, ma'am," he said, "fresh human blood, straight from the States."

"Fascinating," Jeanette said. "Let me make sure I have your name spelled right."

Lieutenant Jefferson C. Whaleburton, of Louisville, Kentucky, did not question Miss Priestly's statement that he didn't have to get permission to take her on the round robin, that journalists such as herself could go anywhere the story took them. She showed him her "invitational orders" from Supreme Headquarters, which authorized her to travel anywhere with the Far East Command.

As they flew up the Korean Peninsula — Jeanette sat on a fold-down seat between the pilot's and copilot's seats — Lieutenant Whaleburton pointed out the windshield and told her the dark clouds on the horizon were a front moving down from Manchuria.

"Weather said it's not moving very fast and shouldn't give us any trouble, either to Seoul or across to Wonsan," he said.

[Seven]
No. 7 Saku-Tun
Denenchofu, Tokyo, Japan
1505 14 October 1950

Jai-Hu-san, the housekeeper for Major and Mrs. Kenneth R. McCoy, did not speak English. Master Sergeant Paul T. Keller, U.S. Army, did not speak Japanese. Jai-Hu-san, moreover, was very fond of Mrs. Ernestine McCoy, aware of the problems of her pregnancy, and absolutely unwilling to disturb her rest by waking her simply because some Yankee soldier said he had to speak to her.

It was only when the barbarian sergeant began to shout Ernie-san's name that Jai-Hu-san relented and went to the McCoy bedroom.

"The sergeant with the red face is here," Jai-Hu-san announced after gently waking her employer. "He is very rude, and he will not go away."

"I'll deal with it," Ernie said, "thank you."

She hurriedly put on and buttoned a kimono over her sleeping gown and swollen belly. Then she saw herself in the mirror. Not only was her hair mussed, but she had smeared her makeup tossing around on the bed, trying to get to sleep.

The baby was now kicking with some regularity, very often when she was trying to take her mind off Ken, Pick, and her condition and get some sleep.

"I can't go out there like this!" she said, aloud, and went into her bathroom.

She began to remove her lipstick with a tissue.

Who am I kidding? I don't give a damn what I look like. I'm afraid to go to the door. Paul wouldn't be here in the middle of the afternoon unless he had something to tell me that won't wait. And I'm afraid to hear what it is that won't wait.

She reapplied her lipstick and ran a brush through her hair, then looked at herself in the mirror again, exhaled audibly, and then walked through the house to the front door. Jai-Hu-san walked behind her.

"Hi, Paul," she called cheerfully. "What's up?"

"What did I do, get you out of bed? The Dragon Lady wouldn't let me in until I raised hell."

"I was taking a nap," Ernie said. "What's going on?"

"Major Pickering is aboard the *Badoeng Strait*," Keller said. " 'Dirty, unshaven, very hungry, but not wounded or injured, and in sound psychological condition.' "

"Major Pickering has never been in sound psychological condition," Ernie said. "Are you sure, Paul? How do you know?"

"There was an Operational Immediate from the *Badoeng Strait*," Keller said. "Signed by the major."

"What major?"

"Your husband, my boss," Keller said. "I guess the Killer carried him there after he found him. I just finished encrypting it and sending it to the States."

"Don't call him Killer," Ernie said.

And then she felt herself starting to fall, and the lights went out.

The next thing she knew, she was looking up at Keller, who was gently wiping her face with a cool wet cloth.

Ernie pushed his hand away and sat up.

She saw she was on cushions on the tatami.

"Jesus, you went down like a polled ox, whatever the hell that means," Paul said.

"Are you all right, Ernie?"

"I'm fine."

"You're sure?"

Ernie saw the look on Jai-Hu-san's face. It was clear that she thought Keller had told her something so awful that it had caused her to pass out.

"The red-faced barbarian brought very good news, Jai-Hu-san," Ernie said. "He is a very good man."

"You went unconscious," Jai-Hu-san said. "You could have hurt yourself and the baby."

"I think I better call for an ambulance," Paul Keller said, getting to his feet.

"No," Ernie said flatly. "I don't need an ambulance."

"I think I should call an ambulance," Paul said.

Ernie looked at him.

He's trembling; his face is as white as a sheet.

Christ, is he going to faint?

"What you should do, Paul," Ernie said, "is first sit down. Before you fall down. Jai-Hu-san will get you a stiff drink. I will watch you drink it, because I don't get any in my condition. That out of the way, we will then try to put a call in to Pick's mother."

"At least let me call a doctor."

"If I thought I needed a doctor, I'd tell you," Ernie said.

Then she had another thought.

"Where's the general?" she said.

"He's with the President, on the way to Wake Island. MacArthur left here for Wake at seven this morning."

"How will he hear about this?"

"The President is never out of touch," Keller said. "They will forward my — Major McCoy's — message to him wherever he is, and there's always a cryptographer with the President. He'll get it, Ernie."

"And we're going to have to get word to Jeanette, too," Ernie said. "She's on her way to Wonsan."

"I wish you'd let me call a doctor."

"Do you think you can find her?"

"That shouldn't be hard," Keller said. "As soon as I leave here, I'll start calling around. She's probably at the Press Center in Pusan."

"First things first, Paul," Ernie said. "Go sit on the couch before you fall down, and Jai-Hu-san will bring you a drink."

"First things first I'm going to get you a doctor!"

Ernie, laboriously, assisted by Jai-Hu-san, got to her feet.

She walked to Keller, who was just over six feet one and weighed just over two hundred pounds, put her hands on her hips, and looked up at him.

"For Christ's sake, Paul, go sit on the goddamn couch!"

Master Sergeant Paul T. Keller, USA, walked over to the couch and sat down.

[Eight]

The weather was getting nasty by the time Lieutenant Whaleburton put the C-47 down at K-16, and by the time they took off the weather was, in Whaleburton's phraseology, "marginal."

"Not a problem, Miss Priestly," he said. "If it gets any worse, we'll just head for Pusan."

The weather got worse.

Thirty minutes out of Seoul, Lieutenant Whaleburton said, "If I get up in that soup, I'll never find Wonsan, so what I'm going to do is drop down below it. And if it gets any worse than this, I'm going to head for Pusan. But I really would like to get that blood to Wonsan."

It quickly got worse, much worse, with lots of turbulence.

When Lieutenant Whaleburton saw the ridge in the Taebaek mountain range ahead of him, he of course pulled back on the yoke to get over it.

He almost made it.

The right wingtip made contact with the

granite of the peak, spinning the aircraft around and down. Before it stopped moving down the mountainside, it came apart and the aviation gasoline exploded.

Lieutenant Whaleburton didn't even have time to make a radio report.

XI

[One]
Wake Island
0625 15 October 1950

As the *Independence* landed, Brigadier General Fleming Pickering saw, with a sense of relief, that the *Bataan* was already on the ground. He'd overheard some of President Truman's staff wondering if that was going to happen, whether, in other words, MacArthur would time his landing so that the President would arrive first and have to wait for the Supreme Commander to arrive from Tokyo.

At first, Pickering had dismissed the conjecture as utter nonsense, but then he thought about it and had to admit that MacArthur was indeed capable of doing something like that. It was, he thought, like two children playing King of the Hill, except that Truman and MacArthur were not children, and Truman was, if not a king, than certainly the most powerful man on the planet. A king worried that one of his faithful subjects had his eyes on the throne.

Pickering had realized — maybe especially after he'd met with General Walter Bedell Smith — that Truman was anything but the flaming liberal incompetent the Republican party had painted him to be.

He had then realized — the late-dawning realization making him feel like a fool — that Senator Richardson K. Fowler, who was as much entitled to be called "Mr. Republican" as any politician, was fully aware of this.

That had led him to recall Truman's visit to tell him he was naming General Walter Bedell Smith to replace Admiral Hillencoetter. When he had told Truman he had always felt he was in water over his head, Truman had told him that not only had "Beetle" Smith said the same thing, but Wild Bill Donovan as well. Pickering had been so surprised — in the case of Donovan, astonished — to hear that that it was only later that he recalled what Truman had said when he'd assumed the presidency on Roosevelt's death, that was going to need all the help he could get."

That certainly suggested that Truman thought he had been given responsibility he wasn't at all sure he was qualified to handle.

And the truth was that Truman had proven himself wrong. Almost all the decisions he had made — right from the beginning, when he'd ordered the atomic bombs to be dropped on Japan — had been the right ones.

He of course had been mistaken to give in to the brass and disestablish the Office of Strategic Services. And Fleming Pickering found Truman's suggestion that it was about time to disband the U.S. Marine Corps to be stupid and outrageous. But Truman had realized he'd made a mistake about the OSS, and quickly formed the CIA, and after the performance of the Marines in the Pusan Perimeter and at Inchon, Truman had changed his mind about the Marines and said so.

Truman's selection of General Smith to head the CIA had been the right one, even though his old friend Ralph Howe, the one general officer he really trusted, had relentlessly pushed Pickering for the job, and appointing Pickering would have pleased Senator Fowler personally and silenced a lot of Republican criticism.

As the *Independence* stopped, Pickering saw from his window the Supreme Commander, United Nations Command, standing on the tarmac waiting for the Commander-in-Chief.

MacArthur was wearing his trademark washed-out khakis and battered, gold-encrusted cap.

Jesus, Truman is the Commander-in-Chief! At least El Supremo could have put on a tunic and neck scarf!

Then he saw the others in the MacArthur party. Brigadier General Courtney Whitney was among them; Major General Charles Willoughby was not. That was surprising.

He wondered if Willoughby, who was almost invariably at the Supreme Commander's side, might somehow have fallen into displeasure.

Is El Supremo punishing Willoughby for something by bringing Whitney here and leaving Willoughby in Japan? I know damned well Willoughby would want to be here.

The two were, in Pickering's judgment, the most shameless of the Bataan Gang in sucking up to MacArthur, in constant competition for his approval, or even for an invitation to cocktails and dinner.

Both disliked Pickering. He had long before decided this was because of his personal relationship with MacArthur, which was far closer than their own. Pickering declined more invitations to cocktails, or bridge, or dinner with the MacArthurs than both of them received. And MacArthur often addressed Pickering by his first name, an "honor" he rarely accorded Willoughby or Whitney or, for that matter, anyone else.

There was more than that, of course. Pickering had never been subordinate to

MacArthur. Worse than that, they knew —
and there was no denying this — that he
was, in effect, a spy in their midst, making
frequent reports on MacArthur's activities
that they never got to see.

In the case of Whitney, Pickering had
made a social gaucherie the day he had
met MacArthur when he arrived in Australia from the Philippines with members of
his staff — soon to be dubbed the "Bataan
Gang." He had not recognized Major
Whitney as a Manila lawyer he had known
before the war.

The truth was that he simply hadn't remembered the man. Whitney had decided
he had been intentionally snubbed, and
had never gotten over it.

Pickering had written his wife from Australia, in early 1942, that his relations with
MacArthur's staff ranged from frigid to
frozen, and that had been when he had
been a temporarily commissioned Navy
captain sent to the Pacific by Navy Secretary Frank Knox. The temperature had
dropped even lower when he had been sent
to the Pacific as a Marine brigadier general
and with the title of Deputy Director of the
OSS for Asia.

MacArthur — with the encouragement of
Willoughby and Whitney, Pickering had
come to understand — had not wanted the
OSS in his theater of operations. Wil-

loughby, MacArthur's intelligence officer, and Whitney, who had been commissioned a major in the Philippines just before the war, and was serving as sort of an adviser, were agreed that intelligence activities should be under MacArthur's intelligence officer. Whitney, moreover, had decided he had the background to become spymaster under Willoughby.

MacArthur had not *refused* to accept the OSS in his theater, he had simply been *not able to find time in his busy schedule* to receive the OSS officer sent to his headquarters by Wild Bill Donovan, the head of the OSS.

Donovan, who was a close personal friend of Roosevelt, had complained to him about MacArthur's behavior, and Roosevelt had solved the problem by commissioning Pickering into the Marine Corps, assigning him to the OSS, and sending him to deal with MacArthur.

Pickering had a dozen clashes with the Bataan Gang during World War II, the most galling to Willoughby and Whitney his making contact with an officer fighting as a guerrilla on Mindanao after MacArthur — acting on Willoughby's advice — had informed the President there "was absolutely no possibility of U.S. guerrilla activity in the Philippines at this time."

Pickering had sent a team commanded

by a young Marine intelligence officer —
Lieutenant K. R. McCoy — to Japanese-
occupied Mindanao on a Navy submarine.
McCoy had established contact with a reserve lieutenant colonel named Wendell
Fertig, who had refused to surrender, promoted himself to brigadier general, announced he was "Commanding General of
United States Forces in the Philippines,"
and begun guerrilla warfare against the Japanese occupiers.

When, late in the war, MacArthur's
troops landed on Mindanao, they found
Brigadier General Fertig waiting for them
with 30,000 armed and uniformed troops,
including a band. Pickering had had
Fertig's forces supplied by Navy subma-
rines all through the war.

Every report of Fertig's successes — even
of a successful completion of a submarine
supply mission to him — during the war
had been a galling reminder to the Bataan
Gang that Pickering had done what Mac-
Arthur had said — on their advice — was
impossible to do.

Pickering had learned that MacArthur
had a petty side to his character. The one
manifestation of this that annoyed Pickering the most — even more than Mac-
Arthur's refusal to award the 4th Marines
on Corregidor the Presidential Unit Citation because "the Marines already have

enough medals" — was MacArthur's refusal to promote Fertig above his actual rank of lieutenant colonel even though Fertig had successfully commanded 30,000 troops in combat. An Army corps has that many troops and is commanded by a three-star general.

Whitney had risen steadily upward in rank — he ended World War II as a colonel and was now a brigadier general — and this added to Pickering's annoyance and even contempt.

Aware that he was being a little childish himself, Pickering took pleasure in knowing that Brigadier General Whitney's pleasure with himself for being at El Supremo's elbow when he met with the President would be pretty well soured when he saw Pickering get off the Presidential aircraft.

There turned out to be less of an arrival ceremony for the President than there had been at K-16 when MacArthur had landed there to turn the seat of the South Korean government back to Syngman Rhee.

The door of the *Independence* opened, and two Secret Service men and a still cameraman and a motion picture cameraman went down the stairs. Then Truman came out of his compartment and went down the stairs.

MacArthur saluted. Truman smiled and put out his hand, then started shaking hands with the others of MacArthur's party.

The first man off the *Independence* after Truman was a stocky Army chief warrant officer in his mid-thirties. He carried a leather briefcase in one hand and a heavy canvas equipment bag in the other. He wore a web pistol belt with a holstered .45 around his waist. A jeep was waiting for him. He got in it and drove off before General of the Army Omar Bradley came down the stairs.

George Hart knew — and had told Pickering — what the equipment bag contained, and what Chief Warrant Officer Delbert LeMoine, of the Army Security Agency, was doing with it. LeMoine was the Presidential cryptographer. Messages intended for the President that had come in since they left Hawaii had been forwarded to Wake Island. Wake Island, however, did not have the codes. The President would have to wait for his mail until LeMoine decrypted it.

The dignitaries aboard the *Independence* came down the stairs one by one and shook hands with MacArthur and the members of his staff he had brought with him from Tokyo. Pickering decided he was not an official member of the Truman party, and waited until the handshaking was over before he got off the *Independence*.

He gave Brigadier General Courtney

Whitney a friendly wave. Whitney returned it with a nod and a strained smile.

Truman and MacArthur got in the backseat of a something less than Presidential — or MacArthurian — 1949 Chevrolet staff car and drove off for a private meeting.

Then everyone else was loaded, without ceremony, into a convoy of cars and jeeps and driven to one of the single-story frame buildings lining the tarmac. Inside, a simple buffet of coffee and doughnuts had been laid out for them.

Pickering had just taken a bite of his second doughnut when another Army warrant officer touched his arm.

"Would you come with me, please, General?" he asked.

"Sure," Pickering said. "What's up?"

The warrant officer didn't reply, but when Hart started to follow them, he said, "Just the general, Captain."

The warrant officer led Pickering to a frame building — identical to the one where coffee and doughnuts were being served — a hundred yards away and held open the door for him.

There was an interior office, guarded by a sergeant armed with a Thompson submachine gun. He stepped out of the way as Pickering and the warrant officer approached, and then the warrant officer knocked at the door. A moment later LeMoine unlocked the door, opened it, and motioned Pickering inside.

Then he closed and locked the door and turned to Pickering with a smile.

"We have a mutual friend, General," he said.

"Who's that?"

"Master Sergeant Paul Keller," LeMoine said. "He worked for me when we were in Moscow."

"Good man," Pickering said.

"He says much the same about you, General," LeMoine said. "And he has the same kind of problems I do, wondering who gets to see what and when."

"I'm not sure I follow you," Pickering said.

"Why don't you have a chair, General?" LeMoine said. "I've got to take a leak, and I'll see if I can't get us some coffee."

He pulled a chair on wheels away from a table, waited until Pickering sat down, then walked to the door, unlocked it, walked through it, and then closed and locked it.

There was one sheet of paper on the table.

Pickering wondered why LeMoine had left it on display.

A man like that does not make mistakes. Christ, whatever it is, he wants me to see it!

Pickering picked it up and read it.

TOP SECRET — PRESIDENTIAL

WASHINGTON 2215 14OCT1950

FROM DIRECTOR CIA
TO (EYES ONLY) THE PRESIDENT OF THE
UNITED STATES

FOLLOWING RECEIVED 2207 14OCT1950
FROM MAJOR K R MCCOY USMCR

MESSAGE BEGINS

MAJOR MALCOLM S. PICKERING USMCR
RETURNED TO US CONTROL 1200
14OCT1950. TRANSPORTED USS BADOENG
STRAIT AS OF 1300 14OCT1950.

SUBJECT OFFICER IS DIRTY, UNSHAVEN,
AND VERY HUNGRY, BUT IS UNWOUNDED,
UNINJURED, AND IN SOUND
PSYCHOLOGICAL CONDITION.

FOLLOWING CIVILIAN PERSONNEL
SHOULD BE CONTACTED BY MOST
EXPEDITIOUS MEANS, ASKED NOT TO
DISSEMINATE INFORMATION ABOVE TO
OTHERS AND ON AGREEMENT BE
NOTIFIED OF SUBJECT OFFICER'S RETURN
AND CONDITION.

```
MRS FLEMING PICKERING C/O FOSTER
HOTELS SAN FRANCISCO CAL
MRS K. R. MCCOY, TOKYO, JAPAN

MISS JEANETTE PRIESTLY C/O PRESS
RELATIONS OFFICER, SUPREME
HEADQUARTERS UNITED NATIONS
COMMAND, TOKYO

MCCOY MAJ USMCR

MESSAGE ENDS

IN PRESUMPTION YOU WILL INFORM
GENERAL PICKERING I WILL NOT DO SO

W. B. SMITH

DIRECTOR
```

There was the sound of the door being unlocked.

Fleming Pickering swallowed hard and stood up, but did not turn around for a moment, until he felt he had his voice and himself under control.

"Ready for some coffee, General?" LeMoine asked.

"Thank you," Pickering said.

LeMoine set a coffee mug on the table.

"A little sugar for your coffee, General?" LeMoine asked. He held a silver pocket flask over the cup.

"Can I do that myself?" Pickering asked.

LeMoine handed him the flask.

Pickering put it to his lips and took a healthy swig.

"Thank you," he said after a moment.

"Have another. There's more where that came from," LeMoine said.

Pickering took another pull, then handed the flask to LeMoine.

"Thank you," he said again.

"Oh, look what I did!" LeMoine said. He picked up the decrypted message. "I really should have put this in the envelope for the President."

"I didn't see it," Pickering said.

LeMoine met his eyes and nodded.

"I don't think anyone's going to question the Assistant Director of the CIA for Asia coming in here to ask if I had anything for him," LeMoine said. "But, after I told you I didn't, they might wonder why you hung around. Will you excuse me, please, General?"

"Thank you for the coffee," Pickering said.

"When you see Sergeant Keller," LeMoine said, "tell him I asked about him."

"I'll do that," Pickering said as he walked to the door.

As he walked back to the coffee-and-doughnuts building, Pickering saw that the people who had been on the *Independence* and the *Bataan* were now — in separate knots — gathered around a Quonset hut. As he walked toward it, the door of the Quonset opened and first Truman and then MacArthur came out.

General Bradley walked up to them, then led them toward another of the identical frame buildings.

Pickering decided that since he had not been invited to attend the official conference, he would just stay in the background. He was glad for the opportunity: That Pick was coming home didn't seem quite real yet. He realized that he had really given up hope, and was ashamed that he had. He knew he needed a couple of minutes to set himself in order.

He walked between two of the frame buildings and leaned against the wall of one of them. He became aware that his forehead was sweaty, and took a handkerchief from his pocket to mop it.

Jesus Christ, he's really alive! And unhurt. Thank you, God!

"General, the President would like to see you, sir," an Army colonel said. Pickering hadn't seen him come between the buildings.

"Right away, of course," Pickering said, and pushed himself off the building.

"General, are you all right? Sir, you look —"

"Colonel, I couldn't possibly be any better," Pickering replied.

When he turned the corner of the building, he saw the President standing with General Bradley and MacArthur in front of the conference building. When Truman saw Pickering, he motioned him over.

Pickering wasn't sure what the protocol was, whether he was supposed to salute or not. He decided if he was going to err, it would be on the side of caution. He saluted, which seemed to surprise both Bradley and MacArthur, who nevertheless returned it.

"Delbert," the President began, ". . . the cryptographer? . . . has had time to decode only a couple of messages. One of them is this one. I thought you'd be interested."

The President handed him the message.

"General, I can't tell you how happy that message made me," Truman said as Pickering read the message again.

"Thank you, sir," Pickering said.

"May I show it to General Bradley and General MacArthur?" the President asked.

"Yes, sir. Of course."

Bradley read it first.

"That's very good news, indeed," he said as he handed the message to MacArthur.

MacArthur's left eyebrow rose in curiosity as he read the message. Then he wrapped an arm around Pickering's shoulder.

"My dear Fleming!" he exclaimed emotionally. "Almighty God has answered our prayers! A valiant airman will be returned to the bosom of his family! Jean will be so happy!"

Bradley could not keep a look of amazement off his face.

"I'd like a word with General Bradley before we go in here," Truman said. "I think if you two went in, the others would follow suit."

"Of course, Mr. President," MacArthur said.

"I'm to be at the meeting?" Pickering blurted.

"Of course," Truman said. "You're really the middleman, General. You're the only one who knows everybody."

MacArthur entered the building with Pickering on his heels. Truman waited until they were out of earshot, then until the others who would participate in the conference had entered the building, and then turned to Bradley.

"General, I want that young officer returned to the United States as soon as he's fit to travel. And I want to make sure the people Major McCoy named are notified

542

as soon as possible, by an appropriate person. Have you got someone who can handle that for me?"

"Yes, sir," Bradley said. He raised his voice, just slightly. "General Mason!"

An Army major general walked quickly to them.

"General," Bradley said. "I want you to read this."

General Mason read the message and raised his eyes curiously to Bradley.

"General," Bradley began, "the President desires —"

"What the President desires," Truman interrupted, "is that Major Pickering — as soon as he is physically up to it — be flown to the United States to whichever Naval hospital is most convenient for his mother. And I want the people listed in that message to be notified personally — without anything said to them about keeping this a secret — by a suitable person just as soon as that can be arranged. You understand?"

"Yes, sir."

"Thank you," the President said.

"May I keep this message, sir?"

"Why not?" Truman said, then gestured for Bradley to precede him into the conference building.

Truman slipped into an ordinary wooden

office chair at the head of a table around which the participants had arranged themselves, those who had come with the President on one side, and MacArthur and those who had come from Tokyo with him on the other.

Everyone was standing, in deference to the President.

"Take your seats, please," Truman said. "General Bradley will take notes, and each of you will later get a copy, but it is for your personal use only, and not to be shared with anyone else. Clear?"

There was a chorus of "Yessir."

"But before we get started, I want to tell you that General Pickering has just been informed that his son, a Marine pilot, who was shot down early in the war . . . How long ago, General?"

"Seventy-seven days ago, Mr. President," Pickering said softly.

". . . who was shot down seventy-seven days ago," the President went on, "and has gone through God only knows what evading capture, was rescued behind the lines yesterday and is as we speak aboard the carrier USS *Badoeng Strait.*"

There was a round of applause.

"Mr. President," MacArthur said. "If I may?"

Truman gestured for him to go on.

"Perhaps only I know nearly as much as

General Pickering does about what Major Pickering was facing and has come through. One of the unpleasant things I have had to do recently is compose the phrasing of the citation for the decoration it was my intention to award — posthumously, I was forced to think — to this heroic young officer. I would like your permission, Mr. President, to —"

"Give him the medal anyway?" Truman interrupted. "What did you have in mind?"

"Mr. President, it is self-evident that Major Pickering's valor on the battlefield was distinguished."

"The Distinguished Service Cross?" Truman asked.

"The major is a Marine, Mr. President," General Bradley said. "It would be the Navy Cross."

"Yes, of course," the President said. "I agree. I don't know how that's done, but I'm sure that General Bradley and General MacArthur can handle that between them."

"Yes, sir," Bradley said.

The President wasn't finished: "I also think whoever rescued him from behind enemy lines needs recognition," he went on. "That would be Major McCoy, wouldn't it, General Pickering?"

"Either McCoy or one of his men, sir," Pickering said.

"I would suggest, Mr. President," Mac-Arthur said, "the Silver Star for the officer who risked his life to snatch Major Pickering from the midst of the enemy, and Bronze Stars for the others."

Truman looked at Omar Bradley.

"I agree, Mr. President," Bradley said.

"You'll take care of all this?"

"Yes, sir."

"Okay," the President said. "Let's get started with this. The first thing . . ."

[Two]
Aboard the *Bataan*
30.59 Degrees North Latitude
172.44 Degrees East Longitude
The Pacific Ocean
1615 15 October 1950

Captain George F. Hart, USMCR, gently nudged Brigadier General Fleming Pickering, USMCR, with his elbow, and, when he had his attention, directed it with a just-perceptible nod of his head down the aisle of the *Bataan*.

There were few passengers on the Douglas C-54 four-engine transport. Pickering and Hart were seated toward the rear, in what Hart called "the cheap seats." In them were seated the junior officers — including the aides-de-camp of the senior officers — and the warrant officers and noncoms brought from Tokyo to do whatever was necessary for the senior officers.

Pickering saw Brigadier General Courtney Whitney coming down the aisle to the rear of the airplane. In doing so he passed a number of rows of empty seats. There was little question in Pickering's mind that Whitney was headed for him. He was the only senior officer sitting in the cheap seats.

Whitney stopped at Pickering's seat.

"General Pickering," he said, "the Supreme Commander would like to see you at your convenience."

"Thank you, General Whitney," Pickering said.

Whitney turned and started back toward the front of the aircraft.

Pickering looked at Hart with a raised eyebrow. Hart smiled, hunched his shoulders, and feigned a shiver. Pickering smiled back. It had indeed been an icy encounter. Another one.

Brigadier General Whitney and Brigadier General Pickering had not exchanged a word on Wake Island, and Pickering hadn't thought — until Whitney came down the aisle — that they would exchange one on the way to Japan.

Pickering waited until Whitney had taken his seat before unfastening his seat belt and standing up. Whitney took the seat nearest to the door of MacArthur's compartment. It was the seat traditionally reserved for the most senior of MacArthur's staff aboard.

Pickering knocked at the door to MacArthur's compartment and was told to come in.

"Ah, Fleming!" MacArthur said, coming half out of his chair to offer Pickering his hand. "I was afraid you might have been asleep. I told Whitney not to disturb you."

"I was awake, sir," Pickering said.

MacArthur waved him into the seat facing his.

"First, of course, I had to go through the messages from Tokyo." He indicated several manila folders that were imprinted with TOP SECRET in red. "And then I had to let poor Whitney down gently."

"Sir?"

"Entre nous," MacArthur said. "I have been trying for some time to get him a second star. I thought perhaps a private word between myself and General Bradley might help —"

My God! Pickering thought. *He actually tried to use a meeting between him and the President of the United States to get one of the Bataan Gang promoted!*

He wanted to make a man who never commanded a company, much less a regiment, a major general!

Who are you to talk, General *Pickering? The only unit you've ever commanded was a squad.*

MacArthur had left the rest of the sentence unspoken, but when he saw the surprise on Pickering's face, he went on.

"I was surprised, too," he said. "I thought Bradley would arrange it as a personal courtesy to me, but all he said was that he would 'look into it,' which, of course, is a polite way of saying no."

Pickering couldn't think of a reply.

"I thought I would tell you this," MacArthur went on, "because you've just learned you're not going to get the promotion you so richly deserved."

"Are you talking about General Smith being named Director of the CIA, sir?"

"Of course."

"You heard that I was being considered?"

"I have a few friends in the Pentagon," MacArthur said. "Not many, but a few. You were the logical choice for the job. But you were obviously tarnished with the brush of being someone held in very high regard by the Viceroy of Japan."

Pickering's surprise was again evident on his face.

"Oh, I know they call me that," MacArthur said. "They also call me 'Dugout Doug,' which I don't really think is fair. And 'El Supremo.' "

549

"I'm guilty of the latter, General," Pickering said. "I don't think anyone uses that as a pejorative. It's sort of like calling a company commander 'the Old Man.' "

MacArthur smiled but said, "That too. 'The Old Man in the Dai Ichi Building.' "

"General, before President Truman named General Smith, I told him I didn't think I was qualified to be Director of the CIA."

"It got as far — before you took a Pentagon knife in the back — as the President actually offering you the job, did it?"

"The President told me, when he told me that he had named General Smith, that he had considered me but decided General Smith was the best man for the job. I told him I completely agreed."

"You know Smith?"

"I met him for the first time after I spoke with the President."

"From everything I hear, he was the brains behind Eisenhower," MacArthur said. "Well, for the record, I think you would have been the best man for the job."

"I respectfully disagree," Pickering said with a smile.

"Well, it's water over the dam," MacArthur said.

"Yes, sir, it is."

"As soon as we get within radio range of Tokyo, I'll set the wheels in motion about your son," MacArthur said. "The first step, obviously, is to get a more precise indication of his physical condition than . . . What did the message say, 'very dirty and very hungry'?"

Pickering chuckled.

"It also said, 'uninjured, unwounded, and in sound psychological condition,' " he said.

MacArthur acted as if Pickering hadn't spoken.

"And once we have that information," he went on, "which shouldn't take long to acquire, we can decide whether it would be best for you to fly out to the *Badoeng Strait,* and arrange for that, or to wait until your boy is to be flown from the carrier to Tokyo."

"That's very kind of you, General," Pickering said.

"Not at all," MacArthur said. "I'm delighted that everything has turned out so well for you."

MacArthur stood up. After a moment, Pickering realized that he was being dismissed and got hurriedly to his feet.

MacArthur put his hand on Pickering's arm in an affectionate gesture.

"I hate to turn you into a runner, but would you mind sending Colonel Thebideaux in here as you pass through the cabin? He's the plump little chap with the shiny cranium."

"Yes, sir, of course. And thank you again, General."

MacArthur didn't reply. He smiled faintly and sat back down.

Pickering left the compartment, closing the door after him. Halfway down the aisle, he spotted a plump little lieutenant colonel with a shiny cranium. When he got closer, he saw that he was wearing a nameplate with THEBIDEAUX etched on it. When he got to the seat, Pickering squatted.

"Colonel Thebideaux," he said, "General MacArthur would like to see you."

"Yes, sir. Thank you, sir."

Pickering went to the cheap seats and slipped in beside George Hart.

"What's up?"

"As soon as we're in radio contact with Tokyo," Pickering replied, "El Supremo will 'set the wheels in motion' to get me together with Pick. Either fly me out to the carrier or have Pick flown to Tokyo."

"That was nice of him," Hart said.

"I thought so."

"That's all he wanted?"

"That's all he wanted."

Hart pursed his lips and shrugged.

[Three]
Haneda Airfield
Tokyo, Japan
2105 15 October 1950

As the *Bataan* taxied up to what he thought of as "El Supremo's Hangar," Brigadier General Fleming Pickering saw Master Sergeant Paul Keller leaning on the front fender of his Buick.

So much for the secrecy about El Supremo's movements, he thought. *Willoughby and Company almost certainly didn't call Keller and give him our ETA. Paul knows how to find out "top secret" things like that.*

As usual, he waited until the important members of MacArthur's staff deplaned before unfastening his seat belt and standing up.

When he came down the stairs, he was surprised to see MacArthur standing impatiently by the open door of his black Cadillac limousine. Willoughby was with him.

When MacArthur saw him, he motioned him over.

"Fleming, why don't you get a good night's sleep and then come by the office first thing in the morning?" MacArthur said. "Willoughby is still collecting information about your boy, and by, say, eight, we should know just about everything."

"Yes, sir. Thank you."

MacArthur nodded and ducked inside the Cadillac. Willoughby trotted around the rear of the limousine and got in beside him. The limousine, preceded by the usual escort of chrome-helmeted MPs in highly polished jeeps, rolled off.

Pickering walked to his Buick. Keller straightened and saluted. Pickering returned it.

"You got the good news, General?" Keller asked.

"The President told me at Wake Island," Pickering said, and got in the front seat. Keller got behind the wheel and turned to him.

"Okay, while George is getting the luggage, this is what I know," Keller said.

Master sergeants are not supposed to refer to commissioned officers by their Christian names, but rather than being disrespectful, Pickering thought, it was an indication that Keller both liked Hart and considered everybody part of a special team.

"As soon as I got The Killer's message off," Keller began, "I went to Denenchofu and told Ernie."

"Good for you," Pickering said.

"Whereupon, she passed out," Keller said. "Scaring the bejesus out of me."

"My God! Is she all right?"

"She says she is. I tried to make her go

to the hospital, or at least let me call a doctor, but she wouldn't let me."

"Before we go to the hotel, Paul, we'll swing by Denenchofu," Pickering ordered.

"Yes, sir."

"Did she hurt herself when she fell?"

"She says no, but I still think she ought to see a doctor."

"So do I."

"Anyway, right after that happened, we put in a call to Mrs. Pickering. We found her in Washington."

"So she knows?"

"Yes, sir. She said that she'd just gotten off the line with Colonel Banning and he'd already told her."

"He probably called her immediately after reading the decrypt of McCoy's message."

"Yes, sir, that's what I thought. I haven't been able to get in touch with the blond war correspondent. Ernie said I missed her at the house by a couple of hours, that she's on her way to Wonsan. I tried to call her at Wonsan. They said she wasn't there, so I called the Press Center at Eighth Army Rear in Pusan. They didn't know where she was, but she's on a list of press people trying to get to Wonsan. She'll turn up."

"And what do we hear about my son?"

"All I know is what's in Killer's message.

I think that's probably what it is. He isn't hurt, he's okay psychologically, he's hungry, and he needs a shower and a shave."

"Thank you, Paul," Pickering said. "I suppose we'll have more news in the morning."

"I'm sure we will, sir."

[Four]
The Imperial Hotel
Tokyo, Japan
0210 15 October 1950

Master Sergeant Paul Keller answered the telephone before it had a chance to ring twice.

"General Pickering's quarters, Sergeant Keller," he said. Then he listened briefly, covered the microphone with his hand, and turned to Pickering, who was sitting sprawled beside Captain George Hart on the couch. Both were holding drinks in their hands.

"I've got Mrs. Pickering on the horn, General."

"Thank you," Pickering said. "You two can now go to bed."

Hart stood up, drained his drink, and nodded at Keller as a signal for him to precede him out of the room. When Keller had gone through the door, Hart looked at

Pickering, who was looking at him curiously, his raised eyebrow asking, "Jesus, right now, George?"

"General," Hart said, "would it be too much to ask Mrs. Pickering to call my wife and tell her we got Pick back? She's been holding her breath. Actually, she's been praying."

"Of course not," Pickering said, reaching out his hand for the telephone.

"Good night, sir," Hart said, and walked out of the room.

"Patricia?" Pickering said to the telephone.

"Flem?"

She sounds sleepy.

Jesus Christ, I have no idea what time it is in the States. Did I wake her up?

"How many other calls do you get from men at this time of day?"

"Quite a few, actually," she said. "And two minutes ago I got a telegram from the Secretary of the Navy . . ." She paused, and he had a mental image of her picking it up and reading from it. ". . . who is 'pleased to inform you that your son Major Malcolm Pickering has been returned to U.S. control' and that 'further information will be furnished when available.' "

"I guess the system kicked in," he said.

"Have you seen him? Where are you?"

"In the Imperial. We got back here a

couple of hours ago."

"Thank you for calling me immediately," she said sarcastically.

"I was with Ernie," he said, trying to explain and apologize. "Trying to get her to see a doctor."

"What's wrong with her?" she asked, concern replacing her anger.

"I don't think anything is. But when Keller told her about Pick, she fainted."

"What did the doctor say?"

"She wouldn't see a doctor," he said.

"Tell her that her mother and I are on the way," Patricia said.

"Here?"

"No, to Acapulco."

"I don't think that's such a good idea, sweetheart."

"My son has just been rescued after more than two months and my pregnant goddaughter has just passed out, and it's not a good idea that her mother and I come over there? What the hell is wrong with you?"

"As soon as he's up to it, they're going to fly him to the States. You're going to be asked to which hospital he should be sent."

"How do you know that?"

"Harry Truman told me."

"Spare me your sarcasm, Flem."

"Just before he took off from Wake Island, the President told me that he has ordered that Pick be sent to the States as soon as his physical condition permits."

" 'As soon as his physical condition permits'? What do you know that I don't? When Ernie called, she said he was in great shape."

"He's in the sick bay on the *Badoeng Strait*. Patricia, he spent seventy-seven days running around Korea avoiding capture; they haven't found anything wrong with him, according to McCoy, but they . . . they want to make sure nothing is wrong with him."

"So something is wrong with him."

"I expect a full report on his condition in the morning. As soon as I get it, I'll call."

"Elaine and I will be traveling by tomorrow morning," Patricia declared. "She's on her way here from New Jersey."

Elaine Sage was Ernie's mother.

"Ernie doesn't want her mother over here, she told me."

"She's pregnant — she doesn't know what she wants."

"Obviously, I can't stop either of you, but if you come over here, it will be one goddamned big mistake. What's probably going to happen is that when you get here, you'll learn that you passed Pick flying in the other direction in the middle of the Pacific," Pickering said.

There was a long pause.

"So what are you telling me you think we should do, Flem?" she asked finally.

"Go to San Francisco. To the apartment. By the time you get there, I'll have more information. I'll call and give it to you."

"Elaine's determined to go over there."

"Talk her out of it, sweetheart."

"You'll call me at the apartment the minute you hear anything?"

"Of course I will."

"You sound tired, Flem."

"I am tired."

"Get some rest."

"I will," he said, then added: "Patricia, would you please call George Hart's wife in Saint Louis and tell her."

"I will, but —"

"George said she's been praying for him. Call her, please, Pat."

"I said I would."

"I don't know what the hell you're mad at me for."

"I'm not mad at you, Flem."

"That's not what it sounds like."

"I love you, Flem. I often wonder why."

"I love you, too, and I know why."

"I'll talk to you tomorrow," Patricia said, and hung up.

[Five]
The Dai Ichi Building
Tokyo, Japan
0805 16 October 1950

A chrome-helmeted MP stepped into the street and held up his hand somewhat imperiously to stop Pickering's Buick.

"El Supremo's coming," Master Sergeant Paul Keller, who was in the front seat beside the driver, said. "Everybody look busy."

Pickering and Hart, in the backseat, laughed. The sergeant driver — no one knew his name; they changed frequently, and were, not in their hearing, universally referred to as "the CIC guy" — looked at Hart, visibly surprised that a sergeant would dare mock the Supreme Commander, and even more so that a brigadier general and his aide-de-camp would laugh with him.

And it was indeed the Supreme Commander, United Nations Command & U.S. Forces, Far East, arriving at his headquarters.

Preceded by a jeep loaded with chrome-helmeted MPs, his black Cadillac limousine rolled regally past Pickering's Buick, and other cars behind it, and up before the steps leading to the door of the Dai Ichi Building.

A crowd of people, mostly Japanese but including some Americans and others in uniform, waited on the sidewalk behind a line of MPs.

Two more chrome-helmeted MPs stood on the sidewalk at the spot where the rear door of the limousine would open. As it approached them, they raised their hands in salute and held it. The instant the Cadillac stopped, one of them opened the door while the other held his salute.

MacArthur came out of the limousine and, looking straight ahead, walked quickly up the stairs to the building. He acknowledged the salutes given him three times.

Colonel Sidney Huff, MacArthur's senior aide-de-camp, got out of the limousine and followed MacArthur into the building.

The limousine drove off. The crowd — the show over — began to disperse. The MP who had stopped them now motioned just as regally for them to start moving.

When the car stopped before the building, Pickering was out of the backseat before either the CIC guy or Keller could get out of his seat to open it for him.

Trailed by Hart and Keller, Pickering walked across the lobby to the bank of elevators.

"If there's anything of interest, bring it upstairs," Pickering said to Keller.

"Yes, sir."

Keller got on one elevator, which would carry him to the Communications/Cryptographic Center in the basement, and Pickering and Hart got on another, which carried them to the lobby outside the door of the Office of the Supreme Commander.

Hart walked quickly to the door, pushed it inward, and held it open for Pickering.

There were two outer offices, one manned by one of MacArthur's junior aides, a receptionist, and other clerical types. Pickering strode purposefully through the first outer office into the second, which was occupied by Colonel Sidney Huff and some clerical types.

Shortly after arriving in Tokyo, he had decided that stopping in the outer office and asking to see Colonel Huff was not the thing to do. It gave him a place in the pecking order. He was not only a brigadier general but the Deputy Director of the CIA. He did not need to ask a major if he could see a colonel on MacArthur's staff, even if that colonel was MacArthur's aide-de-camp and a founding member of the Bataan Gang.

"Good morning, Sid," Pickering said. "General MacArthur expects me. Would you tell him I'm here?"

"Good morning, sir," Huff said. "Before you see the Supreme Commander, may I have a minute of your time?"

"Sure, Sid. What can I do for you?"

"I thought you would be interested in this, General," Huff said. "And I don't think I have to tell you we were all delighted to hear that Major Pickering came through his ordeal."

"Thank you, Sid," Pickering said, and reached out for the first of several documents Huff was obviously prepared to hand him.

```
SECRET
URGENT
FROM BADOENG STRAIT
0300 16 OCTOBER 1950

TO CHAIRMAN JOINT CHIEFS OF STAFF
ATTN MAJGEN MASON

INFO CHIEF OF NAVAL OPERATIONS
SUPREME COMMANDER UNC
COMMANDER-IN-CHIEF PACIFIC
COMMANDANT USMC

1. REFERENCE YOUR URGENT DIRECTION
OF THE PRESIDENT SUBJ: PICKERING, MAJ
MALCOLM USMCR 15OCT50

2. SUBJECT OFFICER SUFFERED NO
WOUNDS OR INJURIES DURING THE
CRASH LANDING OF HIS AIRCRAFT OR IN
```

THE PERIOD FOLLOWING UNTIL HIS RESCUE.

3. ON ARRIVAL BADOENG STRAIT SUBJECT OFFICER SUFFERED FROM EFFECTS OF MALNUTRITION AND DYSENTERY AND WAS INFESTED WITH INTESTINAL PARASITES. AS A RESULT OF THE FOREGOING, HE HAS LOST BOTH FAT AND MUSCLE TISSUE AND WEIGHS 58 (FIFTY-EIGHT) POUNDS LESS THAN HE DID AT THE TIME OF HIS LAST FLIGHT PHYSICAL EXAMINATION. IT IS NOT BELIEVED THAT HE WILL LOSE ANY TEETH, ALTHOUGH THE CONDITION OF HIS GUMS REFLECTS THE AFOREMENTIONED MALNUTRITION AND DYSENTERY.

4. SUBJECT OFFICER'S DYSENTERY HAS REACTED TO ANTI-BIOTIC TREATMENT, AND THE INTERNAL PARASITES HAVE REACTED TO ATABRINE AND OTHER TREATMENT. HE HAS BEEN PLACED ON A HIGH PROTEIN DIET.

5. THERE IS NO REASON SUBJECT OFFICER CANNOT BE AIR-LIFTED TO THE ZONE OF THE INTERIOR AT ANY TIME. HE CAN BE TRANSPORTED FROM BADOENG STRAIT EITHER BY TBM-3G AVENGER AIRCRAFT OR BY UNDER-WAY TRANSFER TO A DESTROYER OR DESTROYER ESCORT.

6. IN THE OPINION OF THE UNDERSIGNED, PRESENT AND PROJECTED WEATHER CONDITIONS MAKE AT-SEA TRANSFER THE LESS HAZARDOUS MEANS OF TRANSPORT. REQUEST DIRECTION.

7. BADOENG STRAIT PROCEEDING.

NORTON, CAPT USN
COMMANDING

Pickering read the message and handed it back to Huff.

"Fifty-eight pounds," he said. "Jesus, he must look like a skeleton."

Huff handed him another message.

SECRET
URGENT
FROM COMMANDER-IN-CHIEF PACIFIC
0405 16 OCTOBER 1950

TO BADOENG STRAIT

INFO SUPREME COMMANDER UNC TOKYO
CHIEF OF NAVAL OPERATIONS WASHINGTON
COMMANDANT USMC WASHINGTON
COMMANDER USNAVY BASE SASEBO
JAPAN

1. REFERENCE IS MADE TO

A. MESSAGE DIRECTION OF THE PRESIDENT SUBJ: PICKERING, MAJ MALCOLM USMCR 15OCT50
B. YOUR SECRET URGENT SUBJECT AS ABOVE 0300 16 OCTOBER 1950

2. CINCPAC DIRECTS
A. DETACHMENT OF DESTROYER OR DESTROYER ESCORT FROM COVERING FORCE FOR PURPOSE OF TRANSPORTING SUBJECT OFFICER TO NEAREST PORT OFFERING SUITABLE AIR TRANSPORT OF SUBJECT OFFICER TO USNAVY HOSPITAL USNAVY BASE SASEBO JAPAN.
B. SUBJECT OFFICER BE ACCOMPANIED BY NAVY PHYSICIAN DURING MOVEMENT FROM BADOENG STRAIT TO SASEBO. TRANSFER TO TRANSPORTING VESSEL TO TAKE PLACE WHENEVER AND WHEREVER BADOENG STRAIT DEEMS ADVISABLE.
C. BADOENG STRAIT WILL ADVISE CINCPAC AND ADDRESSEES HEREON BY URGENT MESSAGE OF SUCCESSFUL TRANSFER OF SUBJECT OFFICER TO TRANSPORTING VESSEL, PORT OF DESTINATION, AND ETA THEREAT.

3. BADOENG STRAIT WILL PASS FOLLOWING PERSONAL MESSAGE FROM CINCPAC TO

SUBJECT OFFICER AT EARLIEST
OPPORTUNITY. QUOTE WELL DONE. YOUR
RECENT ACTIONS IN HIGHEST TRADITIONS
OF USMC AND NAVAL SERVICE. WELCOME
BACK. END QUOTE

FOR THE COMMANDER-IN-CHIEF, PACIFIC

STEVENS, VICE ADMIRAL, CHIEF OF STAFF

Pickering read the message and handed it back to Huff. Huff held the other messages up.

"You can read these, of course, if you like," he said. "But they are simply administrative messages to implement what's going to happen. The thumbnail of the situation is that a Navy R4-D hospital plane will be waiting at Pusan — that's the nearest port — to fly your son to Sasebo. The Supreme Commander has arranged for you to be flown to either Pusan or Sasebo, whichever you prefer —"

"Sasebo," Pickering interrupted. "I don't see much point in going to Korea just to come back. And I would just be in the way."

And it smacks of special treatment — not for Pick, for me.

"Yes, sir. There are two remaining problems."

"Which are?"

"The President has directed that Major Pickering be flown to the naval hospital in the United States most convenient for Mrs. Pickering. They have apparently been unable to contact her."

"San Diego," Pickering said. "Send him to the Navy Hospital in San Diego."

"Yes, sir."

"And the second problem?"

"Miss Priestly. We haven't been able to locate her. We know she's in Korea, and probably in Pusan, but we haven't been able to find her so far."

"I understand she was headed for Wonsan."

"We've checked Wonsan. They don't know where she is, and her name does not appear on any flight manifest of flights from Pusan to Wonsan." He paused, then added: "We'll find her, General."

"I'm sure you will," Pickering said. "Thank you, Sid."

"I know the Supreme Commander is expecting you, sir," Huff said. "I'll tell him you're here."

[Six]

When Colonel Huff opened the door to MacArthur's office and announced, "General Pickering, sir," MacArthur and Major

General Charles Willoughby, his intelligence officer, were standing at a table to one side of the room, looking down at a map.

"Ah, come on in, Fleming!" MacArthur called heartily. "I've been waiting for you."

"Good morning, sir," Pickering said, and saluted.

Marines and sailors do not salute indoors — unless under arms or "covered" (wearing a hat or cap) — soldiers do. Pickering had decided nine years before, in Australia, that it was wiser to follow the Army custom. His relationships with the officers around MacArthur were bad enough as it was without adding "the arrogant SOB doesn't even salute" to the listings of what was wrong with him.

"The Supreme Commander has just told me about your son, Pickering," General Willoughby said. "What good news!"

"Thank you, General," Pickering said.

"And Huff has you up to speed, right, on what's happened about that this morning?" MacArthur asked.

"Yes, sir, he has."

"Are you going out to the carrier, or to Korea?"

"No, sir. I think I'd just be in the way. I'll go to Sasebo and wait there."

"Probably the wisest thing to do. Huff will arrange whatever is necessary."

"Thank you."

"Willoughby has been bringing me up to speed on what's happening. Would you like to listen, or are you anxious to leave for Sasebo?"

"I'd prefer to hear General Willoughby's briefing, sir, if I may."

"Start from the beginning, Willoughby," MacArthur ordered.

"Yes, sir," Willoughby said. "On the west coast," he began, using his swagger stick as a pointer, "I Corps is poised to take Pyongyang. . . ."

The briefing took only ten minutes. It was upbeat and confident. The implication was that the Korea Peace Action was just about over.

MacArthur had asked only two questions of Willoughby.

"And the Wonsan mines, Willoughby?"

"Admiral Struble's Joint Task Force Seven, as of this morning, sir, has nineteen mine-sweeping vessels working on the problem."

"And?"

"X Corps will sail today from Inchon, General," Willoughby said. "I have every confidence that by the time the invasion fleet arrives off Wonsan, the mines will no longer pose any problem at all."

"And the Chinese?"

"There has been no reliable intelligence of any movement of Chinese troops toward the border, sir," Willoughby said. "I've personally taken a look at a good deal of the Air Force photography. There's simply nothing there."

Pickering had another unkind thought about Major General Charles Willoughby:

He obviously believes what he's saying, but that is not the same thing as saying that what he believes is true.

What I should do, I suppose, is stand up and say, "General, please remember that Willoughby is the guy who told you guerrilla operations in the Philippines were absolutely impossible, and that there was no indication of hostile intentions on the part of North Korea, and his confident statements about no mines and no Chinese should be judged accordingly."

Why don't I? Because I don't know *if the mines are gone from the approaches to Wonsan or not, and I don't* know *if the Chinese are going to come in the war, and absent proof of either, MacArthur's going to go with Willoughby.*

And, furthermore, Bedell Smith made the point that the intelligence-gathering function of the CIA ends with passing it on to those charged with making decisions. Making decisions is not our responsibility.

MacArthur interrupted his thoughts. "Have you any questions for Willoughby, Fleming?"

"No, sir."

"In that case, Willoughby, would you give General Pickering and me a moment?"

"Yes, sir, of course."

Willoughby went through the door into Huff's office.

"Willoughby tells me that you have sent the CIA Tokyo station chief home," MacArthur said, making it a question.

I can answer that tactfully, which means lie, and say Bedell Smith ordered it.

Or I can tell the blunt truth, and probably antagonize him.

It's probably time for the blunt truth.

"In my judgment, General, he needed to be replaced. For one thing, he failed to gain intelligence of North Korea's intentions when this war started, and for another — and no disrespect is intended — he was entirely too close to members of your staff, especially General Willoughby."

MacArthur considered that a full fifteen seconds.

"Have you decided on a replacement?"

"Colonel Ed Banning, sir. Do you remember him?"

"Of course. He was your deputy in the Second War."

"Yes, sir, he was."

"It's always nice, Fleming, to have old comrades-in-arms in one's inner command circle. You know they can be trusted,"

MacArthur said, then smiled. "Well, I suppose you're anxious to head for Sasebo, aren't you?"

He meant Willoughby in that philosophical observation, not Ed Banning.

Is he asking me to understand his relationship with Willoughby?

"Yes, sir, I am."

Pickering saluted again, then walked out of MacArthur's office into Huff's office, where Captain Hart and Master Sergeant Keller were waiting for him. Willoughby nodded at Pickering, then went back into MacArthur's office.

"This is the most interesting one, General," Keller said, handing him a sheet of paper. "And it was delivered by a Jap on a bicycle."

FROM TRANSGLOBAL HONOLULU

TO TRANSGLOBAL TOKYO

PLEASE PASS TO GENERAL PICKERING
THAT COLONEL EDWARD BANNING, USMC,
IS ABOARD TGF 1022 DUE TO ARRIVE IN
TOKYO 1230 TOKYO TIME OCTOBER 16.

WILLIAMSON TG HONOLULU

"Well, I guess we'd better be at Haneda to meet him, hadn't we, Paul?" Pickering said.

XII

Captain George Hart knocked lightly on the door to Brigadier General Pickering's bedroom, and then, as was his custom, without waiting for a reply, opened the door wide enough to look inside.

Pickering's bedroom was actually a suite within a suite. There was a bedroom, a private bath, and a small room holding a desk and chair and a leather-upholstered chair with a footstool.

Pickering was sitting in the chair, holding a cup of coffee. He was not on the telephone, which meant that his conversation with Mrs. Pickering was over.

Hart signaled with a wave of his hand for Master Sergeant Paul Keller to follow him into the small room.

Pickering didn't seem to notice their presence.

"It's about that time, boss," Hart said. "We better get out to Haneda. Trans-Global

575

may surprise us all by arriving on time."

Hart got neither the laugh nor the dirty look he expected from Pickering. Instead, Pickering looked at them thoughtfully.

"Sir?" Hart asked.

"I want a straight answer from you two," Pickering said. "You listening, Paul?"

"Yes, sir?"

"A lot has gone on in Korea that I don't — we don't, and especially Colonel Banning doesn't — know much about. The helicopters, for one thing, and this Army lieutenant colonel who apparently has not only stolen a Beaver from the Eighth Army Commander but seems to have taken over our villa in Seoul," Pickering said. "Right?"

"That's right, sir," Hart said. "Are you worried about Colonel Vandenberg?"

Pickering didn't respond.

"George," he went on, "you and I have never been inside the Seoul villa, and all we know about it is what Bill Dunston has told us about it."

"The Killer seems impressed with this Vandenburg guy," Hart said.

Again, Pickering didn't respond.

"Neither have we been to Socho-Ri," Pickering said.

"No, we haven't," Hart agreed.

"And obviously, Banning should meet Dunston and Vandenburg, and have them and McCoy and Zimmerman bring him up to speed on what's going on. All of these things would seem to indicate that we get Banning and ourselves to Seoul as quickly as possible, even if Ed Banning's ass is dragging after having flown halfway around the world."

"Makes sense to me, boss," Hart said.

"Okay, here's the question, and kindness should not color your answer: Who made that decision, your steel-backed, cold-blooded commander thinking of nothing but the mission, or a father who desperately wants to see his son?"

There was silence.

"You first, Paul," Pickering said.

"Jesus, General," Keller said. "If it was me, and if my son, if I had one, was just coming back from wherever the hell he's been, I'd be on the next plane to Korea, and I wouldn't even think of Dunston and Socho-Ri and the rest of it."

Pickering met his eyes for a moment, then looked around for Hart. Hart was across the room, on the telephone.

"Whoever that it is, George, it'll have to wait," Pickering said. "I want an answer."

Hart covered the telephone microphone with his hand.

"Where are we going? Pusan or Seoul?" he asked.

"Meaning what?"

"Meaning if we can get on the 1500 courier plane to Seoul, you'll have time to meet Colonel Vandenburg this afternoon and tonight, then fly to Socho-Ri in the morning and see the Killer and Zimmerman, and then be in Pusan probably four, five hours before the tin can can get Pick off the carrier and deliver him there. Which means, your choice, you can have Dunston fly to Seoul from Pusan this afternoon — my suggestion — or have him wait for you in Pusan."

"That's not an answer to my question," Pickering said.

"Yes it is, boss," Hart said softly but firmly. "I kept my mouth shut when you and the Killer were going through that 'we can't use a helicopter that's needed to transport the wounded to look for him' noble Marine Corps bullshit, but enough's enough. You have valid reasons to go to Korea. Be glad you do. You and Pick are entitled to get together. Now, where are we going, Pusan or Seoul?"

After a long pause, Pickering said, "Seoul."

Hart nodded and returned to the telephone.

"Brigadier General F. Pickering, USMC, will require three seats on the 1500 courier to Seoul," he said.

Whoever he was talking to said something.

"Hey, Captain!" Hart barked into the phone, interrupting the person on the other end. "Whoa! Save your breath! I don't give a good goddamn if you have seats available or not. We have a priority that'll bump anybody but Douglas MacArthur, and we intend to use it. Am I getting through to you?"

Hart turned to Pickering, intending to smile at him. He saw that Pickering had stood up and was looking out the window. As Hart watched, Pickering blew his nose loudly.

"We're on the 1500, boss," Hart said.

General Pickering nodded his understanding, but he didn't trust his voice to speak.

[Two]
USS *Mansfield* (DD 728)
37.54 Degrees North Latitude
130.05 Degrees East Longitude
The Sea of Japan
1505 16 October 1950

Lieutenant Commander C. Lewis Matthews III, USN, a very large, open-faced thirty-nine-year-old, took a final look out the spray-soaked window of his bridge, then walked to the rear of the bridge and pressed the ANNOUNCE lever on the public-address system control panel mounted on the bulkhead.

"Attention all hands. This is the captain speaking," he announced. He knew that within seconds he would have the attention of every man aboard.

On being given command of the *Mansfield*, he had received advice from both his father and grandfather. In addition to a good deal else, they had both told him to stay the hell off the PA system unless he had something important to say.

"Don't fall in love with the sound of your own voice," Vice Admiral Charles L. Matthews, USN, Ret., his grandfather, had told him. "Remember the little kid who kept crying 'wolf.' "

Rear Admiral C. L. Matthews, Jr., his father, had put much the same thought this way: "Stay off the squawk box, Lew, unless you have something really important to say. When you say 'This is the captain speaking,' you want everybody to pay attention, not groan and say, 'Jesus Christ, again?' "

Lew Matthews had taken that advice, and right now was glad he had.

"We're about to pull alongside the *Badoeng Strait*," Captain Lew Matthews announced. "We are going to make an underway transfer of two officers from *Badoeng Strait*. One of them is a physician.

The other is a Marine pilot who was shot down right after this war started, and has been behind the enemy's lines until his rescue yesterday. Once we have them aboard, we will make for Pusan at best speed, where a hospital plane will be waiting to fly the Marine to the hospital at Sasebo. Do this right. The one thing this Marine doesn't need after all he's gone through is to take a bath in the Sea of Japan."

He let go of the ANNOUNCE lever and walked to the spray-soaked window of the bridge, took a look at the seas and the gray bulk of the *Badoeng Strait* dead ahead, and shook his head.

He turned and caught the attention of the officer of the deck, then pointed to himself.

"The captain has the conn!" the officer of the deck announced.

"Bring us alongside the *Badoeng Strait*," Matthews ordered the helmsman, describing with his finger how he wanted the *Mansfield* to move and where.

He turned to the officer of the deck and nodded.

The officer of the deck went to the control panel, depressed the ANNOUNCE lever, and said, "Attention all hands. Make all preparations for underway personnel transfer."

[Three]
USS *Badoeng Strait* (CVE 116)
37.54 Degrees North Latitude
130.05 Degrees East Longitude
The Sea of Japan
1515 16 October 1950

Lieutenant Bruce D. Patterson, MC, USNR, wearing foul-weather gear and an inflated life jacket, was sitting in a bosun's chair. The chair — an item of Navy gear evolved from a sort of canvas seat that hauled sailors aloft to work on masts and sails, and thus was probably as old as the anchor — was suspended under a cable that had been rigged between one of the higher decks of the USS *Mansfield* and an interior strong point in the USS *Badoeng Strait* that was accessible through a square port in her side.

"All things considered, Major Pickering," Lieutenant Patterson said, "I very much regret ever having met you."

Major Malcolm S. Pickering, USMCR, who was also wearing foul-weather gear and an inflated life jacket, and was strapped into a second bosun's chair, smiled, shrugged, held out both hands in front of him, and said, "Jeez, Doc, I thought you liked me."

There was laughter from the dozen Marine aviators who were on hand to watch

Good Ol' Pick get transferred to the destroyer.

Another Marine aviator in a flight suit walked up to them.

"I don't suppose it occurred to any of you guys that you might be in the way down here," Lieutenant Colonel William C. Dunn, USMC, said.

Lieutenant Colonel Dunn was not in a very good mood. He had just finished what he considered the most unpleasant duty laid upon a commanding officer.

And it was still painfully fresh in his mind:

USS BADOENG STRAIT (CVE-116)

MARINE AIR GROUP 33

AT SEA

16 OCTOBER 1950

MRS. BARBARA C. MITCHELL
APARTMENT 12-D, "OCEANVIEW"
1005 OCEAN DRIVE
SAN DIEGO, CALIFORNIA

DEAR BABS:

 BY NOW, I'M SURE THAT YOU HAVE BEEN OFFICIALLY NOTIFIED OF DICK'S DEATH.

I THOUGHT THAT YOU WOULD BE INTERESTED IN WHAT I CAN TELL YOU OF WHAT HAPPENED.

WE WERE IN A SIX-CORSAIR FLIGHT OVER NORTH KOREA, NEAR HUNGNAM, ON THE EAST COAST OF THE KOREAN PENINSULA. OUR MISSION WAS IN SUPPORT OF THE I REPUBLIC OF KOREA CORPS, WHICH IS IN PURSUIT OF RETREATING NORTH KOREAN ARMY FORCES.

WHAT WE WERE CHARGED WITH DOING WAS INTERDICTING NORTH KOREA TROOPS TO BOTH SLOW THEIR RETREAT AND HIT THEM AS HARD AS WE CAN. WHEN THE SOUTH KOREANS DID NOT HAVE A TARGET FOR US, WE MADE SWEEPS OVER THE AREA, LOOKING FOR SUITABLE TARGETS OURSELVES.

ON THE AFTERNOON OF 14 OCTOBER, I DIVIDED THE FLIGHT INTO THREE TWO-CORSAIR ELEMENTS, WITH MYSELF AND MY WINGMAN, LIEUTENANT STAN SUPROWSKI, IN THE LEAD AND FIVE HUNDRED FEET ABOVE THE SECOND ELEMENT, WHICH WAS CAPTAIN JACK DERWINSKI, WHOM I KNOW YOU KNOW, AND WHO WAS A CLOSE FRIEND OF DICK'S. LIEUTENANT SAM WILLIAMS

WAS FLYING AS JACK'S WINGMAN. THEY WERE FIVE HUNDRED FEET ABOVE THE THIRD ELEMENT, WHICH WAS DICK, WITH CAPTAIN LESTER STEPPES FLYING ON HIS WING.

A LITTLE AFTER TWO-THIRTY, FROM MY GREATER ALTITUDE, I WAS ABLE TO SEE A COLUMN OF TROOPS MIXED WITH SOME TRUCKS AND OTHER VEHICLES. TO MAKE SURE THEY WERE NOT FRIENDLY FORCES, I PASSED THE WORD THAT I WOULD MAKE A PASS OVER THEM, AND THAT IF THEY WERE INDEED THE ENEMY, THE OTHERS WERE TO ATTACK, STARTING WITH SUPROWSKI, WHO WAS NOW A THOUSAND FEET BEHIND ME, AND THEN THE OTHER TWO ELEMENTS.

I MADE THE PASS, AND RECEIVED SOME SMALL-CALIBER FIRE, WHEREUPON I GAVE THE ORDER FOR THE OTHERS TO ATTACK.

I THEN PULLED UP, MADE A 180-DEGREE TURN, AND SHORTLY THEREAFTER WAS FLYING A THOUSAND FEET OR SO BEHIND DICK AND CAPTAIN STEPPES AT NO MORE THAN TWO HUNDRED FEET OFF THE DECK. I COULD SEE DICK AND LESTER'S TRACER AMMUNITION STRIKING THE ENEMY COLUMN.

AND THEN, TO MY HORROR, I SAW DICK GO IN. ACTUALLY, IT HAPPENED SO QUICKLY THAT THE FIRST SIGN OF TROUBLE I SAW WAS THE FIREBALL OF DICK'S AIRCRAFT.

THERE IS NO QUESTION WHATEVER IN MY MIND THAT HE DIED INSTANTLY, AND IT IS ENTIRELY LIKELY THAT DICK WAS STRUCK AND KILLED BY ANTIAIRCRAFT MACHINE-GUN FIRE BEFORE HIS CORSAIR CRASHED.

ON MY FIRST PASS OVER THE CRASH SITE — SECONDS LATER — THERE WAS NOTHING TO BE SEEN BUT THE FIREBALL. ON SUBSEQUENT PASSES, AFTER THE FIRE HAD BURNED ITSELF OUT, I WAS FORCED TO CONCLUDE THAT NO ONE COULD HAVE SURVIVED THE CRASH.

ON RETURNING TO THE BADOENG STRAIT, I WAS ABLE TO MAKE CONTACT WITH A MARINE UNIT ON SHORE WHICH HAS ACCESS TO AN H-19 HELICOPTER, AND THEY ARE AS THIS IS WRITTEN IN THE PROCESS OF GETTING DICK'S REMAINS. I KNOW THEY WILL DO THEIR VERY BEST, NOT ONLY AS FELLOW MARINES, BUT BECAUSE AMONG THEM IS A MASTER GUNNER WHO KNEW DICK IN NORTH

CAROLINA, AND HELD HIM IN BOTH HIGH
ESTEEM AND AFFECTION.

AS SOON AS I LEARN ANYTHING ABOUT
THIS, I WILL IMMEDIATELY LET YOU KNOW.

I DON'T THINK I HAVE TO TELL YOU HOW
ALL THE MARINES IN MAG33 FELT ABOUT
DICK. HE WAS A SUPERB PILOT, AND A
FINE MARINE OFFICER, AND WE SHALL ALL
MISS HIM VERY MUCH.

THIS WILL PROBABLY OFFER LITTLE IN THE
WAY OF CONSOLATION, BUT I HAVE JUST
BEEN NOTIFIED THAT MY
RECOMMENDATION FOR THE AWARD OF
THE DISTINGUISHED FLYING CROSS HAS
BEEN APPROVED. THAT WILL BE HIS THIRD
AWARD OF THE DFC.

IF THERE IS ANYTHING I CAN DO TO BE
OF SERVICE AT ANY TIME, PLEASE LET ME
KNOW.

Sincerely,

William C. Dunn

William C. Dunn
Lieutenant Colonel, USMC
Commanding

Dunn walked up to Pickering.

"Jesus, Billy," Pickering said. "How about cutting a little slack? The guys just came to see me off."

Dunn didn't respond directly. He thrust a large oilskin envelope at Pickering. "Can I rely on you to get this in the mail as soon as you get to Japan?" he asked.

"Depends on what's in it," Pick said.

"My condolence letter to Babs Mitchell."

Pick's smile faded. "Sure," he said, and took the envelope and stuffed it inside the foul-weather gear.

Dunn walked to the open door and peered out.

He saw that while weather conditions could not — yet — be accurately described as a storm, there were strong winds, five- to eight-foot swells, and it was raining, sometimes in gusts.

He saw that as the *Mansfield* and *Badoeng Strait* moved through the sea, with an intended space of fifty feet between them, they did not move up and down in unison. Only when the *Mansfield*, moving upward, for example, was exactly on a level with the *Badoeng Strait*, moving downward, was the cable stretched between them fairly level.

At all other times, it formed a loop, with one of the vessels at the top of the loop and the other at the bottom.

In addition, if the seas caused one vessel

to lean to port and the other to starboard, the cable would be subject to a stress capable of snapping it as they moved apart unless additional cable was released from the winch. Conversely, if the vessels leaned toward each other, the lower part of the loop tended to go into the water, unless the cable was quickly winched in.

Dunn pulled his head in and looked at Chief Petty Officer Felix J. Orlovski, who had been in the Navy longer than many of his sailors were old.

"How are we doing with this, Chief?"

"We're about to make a test run, sir," the chief said, and pointed upward to the cable. A third bosun's chair was hooked to it.

"What's that strapped inside?" Dunn asked.

"The doc's medical bag, sir, and some weights to bring it to two hundred pounds. You want me to go ahead, sir?"

Dunn nodded, and Chief Orlovski bellowed, "CHAIR AWAY!"

The chair began to move between the ships. When it was almost exactly in the middle between them, the two vessels leaned toward each other. The loop in the cable dropped the bosun's chair to the surface of the sea, where it sank briefly beneath it.

When the two ships leaned away from each other, the loop straightened and the bosun's chair rose out of the water. As it continued to move toward the *Mansfield*, everyone watching the "transfer" could see that Lieutenant Patterson's medical bag and the weights that had been in the seat were no longer there.

Major Pickering said, "I am offering three-to-five the doc never makes it" — there was appreciative laughter from the pilots — "in which case, the colonel's going to have to think of some better way to get me off this vessel."

More laughter.

Dunn looked coldly at Pickering but said nothing.

He had been giving Pickering a lot of thought ever since the Air Force pilot had relayed McCoy's "Bingo, heads up" message.

His first reaction had been personal: joy and relief that Pickering had not perished in some desolate rice paddy or at the end of some North Korean's bayonet. That was understandable. They had been close friends since Guadalcanal, when, flying VMF-229 Grumman Wildcats off of Fighter One, Second Lieutenant Pickering had been First Lieutenant Dunn's wingman.

His second reaction, he'd originally thought, was sort of cold-blooded professional. Pickering's return to the *Badoeng Strait* after everyone — including himself — had decided he wouldn't come back at all was going to do a great deal to restore the sagging morale Dick Mitchell's death had caused among his pilots.

The first unkind or unpleasant thought had come when the Army pilot had flown the black H-19A out to the *Badoeng Strait*. For one thing, he had heard and believed that helicopters — particularly new ones, and the H-19A was as new as they came — were notoriously unreliable. Somebody who knew what he was talking about had told him that if it were not for the helicopter's ability to land practically anywhere — or, for that matter, to flutter without power to the ground in what they called an "autorotation" — they would be banned as a general hazard to mankind.

It was well over one hundred miles from Socho-Ri to where the *Badoeng Strait* cruised in the Sea of Japan. Finding the ship itself was risky. And if the H-19A had engine trouble, the "can land anywhere" and "autorotation" safety features would be useless at sea. It could flutter to the sea intact, of course, but then it would immediately begin to sink.

Dunn hadn't thought the H-19A would have life jackets — much less a rubber lifeboat — aboard, and he checked, and it didn't. Everybody on board would have died if they hadn't been able to make it to the *Badoeng Strait*.

And that was only the beginning of the problem. The Army aviator who had flown the machine had never landed on an aircraft carrier before. Dunn had admired his courage, and later his flying skill, but he had thought that if it hadn't been for Pick trying to become the first Marine locomotive ace, he wouldn't have been shot down, and no one would have had to risk their lives to save his ass.

That Pick had not been brought up short by a direct order to stop flying all over the Korean landscape looking for a locomotive to shoot up instead of what he was supposed to do, was what was known at the Command and General Staff College as a failure of command supervision. Major Pickering's asshole behavior had been tolerated, not stopped, by his commander, whose name was Dunn, William C.

Phrased another way, what that meant was that Colonel Billy Dunn was really responsible for all the lives risked, and all the effort spent, to save Pick Pickering's ass, because if he had done his job, Pick would not have been shot down trying to become the first locomotive ace in the Marine Corps.

"You ready, Doc?" Chief Orlovski asked.

"As ready as I'll ever be," Patterson replied.

"CHAIR AWAY!" Orlovski bellowed.

Dr. Patterson, in disturbingly quick order, felt himself being hauled up vertically, then moving horizontally off the *Badoeng Strait*, then sinking suddenly toward the Sea of Japan, then felt his feet being knocked out from under him as they actually encountered the Sea of Japan, then rising vertically and sideways at once, and then having strong male arms wrapped around him, and then dropping with a thump to the deck as someone released the bosun's chair from the cable.

Major Pickering turned to Lieutenant Colonel Dunn.

"I really don't want to do that, Billy," he said.

"Shut up, Pick," Dunn said, not very pleasantly.

Two sailors, supervised by a chief petty officer, began to attach Major Pickering's chair to the cable.

"As a matter of fact," Major Pickering said, "I'll be goddamned if I'll do that." He looked over his shoulder, saw Chief Orlovski, and ordered: "Get me out of this thing, Chief."

Pick started to unfasten the straps, and was startled to find Colonel Dunn's hand roughly knocking his fingers away from the buckle.

"Hook him up, Chief," Dunn ordered. "He's going."

"I am like hell!" Pick protested.

"You're going, Pick," Colonel Dunn said. "Goddamn you!"

"In my delicate condition, I really think it's ill-advised," Pick said lightly, and added, "I really would prefer to wait for weather that will permit me to fly off this vessel, as befitting a Marine officer, aviator, and gentleman, if that's all right with you, Colonel, sir."

"No, it's not all right with me, you self-important sonofabitch," Dunn said furiously. "Your delicate condition is your own goddamn fault. And we both know it." Dunn turned to Orlovski: "Snap it up, Chief!"

"What the hell is wrong with you, Billy?" Pick demanded.

"There's not a damn thing wrong with me. Your problem is that you have never, not fucking ever, really understood you're a Marine officer who does what he's ordered to do."

"What brought this on?" Pick asked, genuinely surprised at Dunn's tone.

"You really don't care how much trouble your childish behavior has caused, do you? Or how many good people have put their necks out to save you from the consequences of your sophomoric showboating, do you?"

"Jesus Christ!" Pick said softly.

"Haul him away, Chief!" Dunn ordered coldly.

Chief Petty Officer Felix J. Orlovski bellowed, "CHAIR AWAY!"

Ninety seconds later, after a brief but thoroughly soaking dip in the Sea of Japan, Major Pickering was sitting on the deck of the USS *Mansfield.*

A ruddy-faced chief bent over Pickering to help him out of the bosun's chair.

"I'm really sorry you got dunked, Major," he said, obviously meaning it. "It was the last goddamn thing I wanted to have happen to you."

"Chief, the skipper says the major is to go to his cabin," a voice said.

Pickering moved his head and saw a full lieutenant standing beside the chief.

"You all right, sir?" the lieutenant asked.

"I'm fine," Pick said.

The chief and the lieutenant hauled him to his feet and gently led him through a port into the *Mansfield*'s superstructure.

Pick felt the *Mansfield* lean as she turned away from the *Badoeng Strait.*

[Four]
USAF Airfield K-16
Seoul, South Korea
1750 16 October 1950

Major William R. Dunston, TC, USA, was waiting in the passenger section of base operations at K-16 when the 1500 courier flight from Haneda arrived.

He saluted somewhat sloppily when Pickering walked into the building, trailed by Banning and Hart.

Pickering restrained a smile when he saw that Dunston, who was not what could be described as a fine figure of a man, and additionally was wearing mussed, somewhat soiled fatigues and could have used a haircut, had failed the First Impressions Test of Colonel Edward J. Banning, USMC.

"Bill, this is Colonel Ed Banning," Pickering said.

"Welcome to the Land of the Morning Calm," Dunston said. "Your reputation precedes you."

"Does it really?" Banning said a little stiffly.

Pickering thought: *What's ruffling Banning's feathers? Dunston's appearance? Or that he hasn't used the word "sir"?*

"Yeah," Dunston continued, "when the Killer heard you were coming, he told me all about you."

Pickering saw that Hart was also amused by the exchange.

"Where is Major McCoy?" Pickering asked.

"I don't really know," Dunston said. "When I got the heads-up from Keller, I got on the horn to Socho-Ri, and Zimmerman said they got the three clicks a little after three this morning."

" 'The three clicks'?" Banning asked.

"Meaning they got ashore okay. . . . Should we be talking about this in here?"

"Good point. Let's go outside," Pickering said.

Dunston led them to the end of a line of parked vehicles.

"What the hell is this thing?" Pickering asked.

"This is the Killer's Russian jeep," Dunston said. "He took it away from an NK colonel. He had it over in Socho-Ri, but when he sent Jennings here, he sent the Russian Rolls with him and said to keep it here."

"Is that what you call it, the Russian Rolls?" Pickering asked, chuckling.

"Who's Jennings?" Banning asked. It was almost an interruption.

"Tech Sergeant," Dunston said. "He and Zimmerman and the Killer were in the Marine Raiders. Good man. He's been with us since Pusan."

"You know McCoy hates to be called Killer, don't you, Major?" Banning asked.

"Yeah, well, I guess I'm one of the privileged few who can," Dunston said. "We're pretty close, Colonel."

Pickering saw that Banning found that hard to accept.

Dunston got behind the wheel, and Pickering got in beside him.

"Nobody can hear us here," Pickering said when Banning and Hart had climbed over the back into the rear seat. "What about McCoy? Where is he?"

"Well, they — the Killer and two of my Koreans — went ashore a few miles north of Chongjin," Dunston said. "The *Wind of Good Fortune* got the three clicks a little after three this morning."

"*Your* Koreans?" Banning asked.

"The *Wind of Good Fortune* is the flagship of our fleet, Colonel," George Hart offered quickly. "It's a diesel-powered junk."

He did that, Pickering thought, *because he sensed that Dunston has had enough of Banning's attitude and was about to snap back at Banning. What the hell is wrong with Ed Banning?*

Banning's glance at Hart did not suggest anything close to gratitude.

"*My* Koreans, Colonel," Dunston said coldly, "are what few agents I have left of the agents I had before the war. McCoy's Koreans are the ones he's borrowed from Colonel Pak at I ROK Corps. We tell them apart that way."

"Three clicks?" Pickering asked, more to forestall another question from Banning than for information. He had made a guess — as it turned out, the right one — about what three clicks meant.

"You push the mike button three times, General, but don't say anything," Dunston said. "It means you're safely ashore."

"Ashore a few miles north of where?" Banning asked.

"Chongjin," Dunston said. "It's a town —"

"On the Sea of Japan, about sixty miles from the Chinese and Russian borders," Banning said impatiently. "I know where it is. What's he doing there?"

"Vandenburg got him some radios from the Army Security Agency," Dunston said. "He's going to listen to what he calls low-level Russian radio traffic."

"I was under the impression the ASA was responsible for intercepting enemy communications," Banning said.

"That's their job," Dunston agreed a little sarcastically.

"Then what —"

Pickering, who was sitting sidewards on the front seat of the vehicle, dropped his hand to Banning's knee and silenced him.

Pickering thought: *I don't know what's wrong with Banning — maybe fatigue from the long flight; or maybe he doesn't think Dunston is showing him the proper respect — but he's acting like an inspector general, and Dunston doesn't like it. I don't want — can't have — the two of them scrapping.*

Dunston started the engine and backed out of the parking slot.

[Five]
The House
Seoul, South Korea
1910 16 October 1950

Major General Ralph Howe, NGUS, Lieutenant Colonel D. J. Vandenburg, USA, Master Sergeant Charley Rogers, NGUS, Technical Sergeant J. M. Jennings, USMC, and an Army captain wearing a fur-collared aviator's jacket were sitting at the dining room table when Pickering, Banning, Hart, and Dunston walked in.

Everyone but Howe made some movement to stand. Pickering signaled for them to stay where they were.

"I will claim the privilege of rank, Flem," Howe said, "and be the first to tell you how delighted I am your son's safe."

"Thank you," Pickering said.

600

"I suppose I'd better do the introductions," Howe said. "General, this is Colonel D. J. Vandenburg . . ."

Pickering offered him his hand.

"How are you, Colonel?"

"Sir, we're all happy Major Pickering is back with us."

"Thank you," Pickering said.

". . . and this is Captain Lew Miller," Howe went on, "who flies the Beaver."

"I've heard about the Beaver," Pickering said, smiling at Vandenburg. "How are you, Captain?"

"How do you do, sir?" Miller said.

"And J. M. Jennings," Howe said, "who has the dubious distinction of having been a Marine Raider with McCoy and Zimmerman."

" 'Dubious distinction'?" Jennings said, and then: "How do you do, sir?"

"The phrase, General Howe," Pickering said, "is *great distinction.*"

"Thank you, sir," Jennings said.

"I'm sorry, Sergeant," Pickering said, "that you've had to be alone with all these dogfaces, but that's changed. Ed Banning and I have landed, and the situation is well in hand."

"Oh, God!" Howe said, shaking his head. He put out his hand to Banning. "I've heard a lot about you, Colonel, all good. And this is Charley Rogers, who the jarheads around here refer to — behind our backs, of course — as the 'Retread Doggie General's Retread Dog Robber.' "

"How do you do, General?" Banning said to Howe, and shook his hand. He shook Rogers's hand but said nothing to him.

Howe said, "I don't know if Marines drink champagne — for that matter, if they even know what it is — but when Bill Dunston heard about your son and you coming, he put a couple of bottles in the refrigerator in case a celebration was in order, and I suggest one is."

"My God!" Pickering said. "A house like this, with champagne in a refrigerator, in what my favorite journalist refers to as 'the battered capital of this war-torn nation'? Pay attention, Ed, these doggies really know how to live. See if you can find out how they do it!"

There was laughter from everyone but Banning, who came up with a somewhat restrained smile.

Dunston went through the door to the kitchen, and a moment later Lai-Min, the housekeeper, came through it carrying a tray with two bottles of champagne in coolers and champagne glasses on it. She set it on the table, went back into the kitchen, and came back with another tray. This one held hors d'oeuvres.

"I will be damned!" Pickering said.

"More than likely," Howe said, mock serious.

Dunston came back into the room, and he and Hart opened the champagne and poured.

Howe raised his glass. "Major Malcolm S. Pickering," he toasted. "Who has proved he's as good a Marine as his father, and probably a lot smarter."

Pickering took a swallow and then raised his glass again.

"How about to Major Ken McCoy and whoever was with him when he found Pick?" he said.

"Well, I'll drink to the Killer anytime," Howe said. "But that's not exactly what happened, Flem."

"Excuse me?"

Howe gestured to Jennings, whose face showed he would much rather not have to tell the story.

"Sir, what happened was that we were coming back to Socho-Ri in a Big Black Bird after having picked up a recon patrol —"

"You're talking about a helicopter?" Banning interrupted.

"Yes, sir," Jennings said. "And we heard somebody — 'Road Service' — calling for any U.S. aircraft —"

"Road Service?" Banning parroted.

Pickering looked at him sharply.

"Yes, sir," Jennings went on. "We found out later it was an Army convoy, a couple of tanks and some heavy vehicles, trying to find a land route to Wonsan. We even knew them. Anyway, we didn't reply, of course —"

"Why not?" Banning interrupted.

"Ed, for Christ's sake, let Sergeant Jennings finish," Pickering snapped, and immediately regretted it.

The remark earned him a look of gratitude from Jennings and a look of astonishment, even hurt, from Banning.

"But an Air Force P-51 did," Jennings went on. "And Road Service told him they'd just picked up a shot-down pilot and needed to get him to a hospital. The Air Force guy asked for a location, and it was about five miles from where we were, so the Kil . . . Major McCoy told Major Donald to go there, and see if we could land, and so we did. What we found was that the Army was lost, and Major Pickering had seen them and come out from where he was hiding."

Pickering saw Jennings smile.

"What's funny, Sergeant?" he asked.

"Well, sir, what Major Pickering did was come down the road to the doggie convoy with his hands over his head, singing 'The Marines' Hymn' as loud as he could and

604

shouting 'Don't shoot' between lines."

"Jesus Christ!" Pickering said, smiling at the image.

"Anyway, sir, we could get in where they were, so we loaded Major Pickering on the Big Black Bird — they left me behind to show the Army the road to Wonsan — and flew on to Socho-Ri, took on fuel, and then flew him out to the aircraft carrier. But we didn't find him, sir, although God knows we sure looked hard for him — the major found the Army."

Pickering smiled and shook his head.

"What difference does it make, Flem?" Howe asked. "He's back. That's all that counts."

"There's a small problem," Pickering said, smiling. "It has been decided at the highest level — by that I mean agreement between El Supremo, General of the Army Omar Bradley, and the President himself — that McCoy gets the Silver Star for his valor in finding Pick —"

"Goddamn!" Jennings said, chuckling.

"And everybody with him gets the Bronze Star," Pickering went on. He stopped himself as he was about to add "and the President agreed with MacArthur that Pick gets the Navy Cross."

Why did I stop? So Proud Papa won't be boasting?

No, it's something else.

605

Because I don't see where what he did deserves the Navy Cross?

I didn't think I deserved mine, either. I was just doing what a Marine is supposed to do.

Isn't that what Pick did? What a Marine is supposed to do?

How the hell did I get on this line of thought?

"General," Jennings said, "I didn't do anything that should get me the Bronze Star."

"I'll straighten it out," Pickering said. He raised his champagne glass to Jennings and smiled.

"I'm about to send a message I think you ought to see," Howe said. "Can we go upstairs for a minute?"

"Sure," Pickering said. "What's upstairs?"

"The communications," Howe said. He smiled. "I keep forgetting the laird of this manor has never been here before. I'll have to show you around."

"It's not what I expected," Pickering said.

"Very few things ever are," Howe said with a smile as he waved Pickering out of the room ahead of him.

They went through the foyer and up the stairs. Pickering was not surprised to find Koreans armed with Thompson submachine guns blocking entrance to the corridors on both the second and third floors, but he was surprised when Howe knocked on a door on the third floor and it was answered by a Korean woman holding a .45-ACP-caliber Grease Gun.

"Di-san," Howe said, "this is General Pickering."

She smiled. In perfect English, she said, "General, we were happy to hear your son has been rescued."

"Thank you," Pickering said.

"I want to show General Pickering my message," Howe said.

She nodded, motioned them into the room, and took several sheets of typewriter paper from a table.

```
TOP SECRET/PRESIDENTIAL

OPERATIONAL IMMEDIATE
DUPLICATION FORBIDDEN

<<<<<INSERT TIME BEFORE
TRANSMISSION>>>>> TOKYO TIME
16 OCTOBER 1950

FROM: CHIEF PRESIDENTIAL MISSION TO
      FAR EAST

VIA: USMC SPECIAL COMMUNICATIONS
     CENTER CAMP PENDLETON CAL
```

TO: WHITE HOUSE COMMUNICATIONS
    CENTER WASHINGTON DC
    EYES ONLY THE PRESIDENT OF THE
    UNITED STATES

BEGIN PERSONAL MESSAGE FROM MAJOR

GENERAL HOWE

DEAR HARRY

I JUST GOT WORD THAT GENERAL
PICKERING IS ON HIS WAY HERE TO
SEOUL. HIS SON IS TO BE TAKEN FROM
THE CARRIER BADOENG STRAIT TO PUSAN
ON A DESTROYER AND FLOWN FROM
THERE TO SASEBO AND FROM THERE TO
THE STATES. PICKERING UNDERSTANDABLY
WANTS TO SEE HIM BEFORE HE GOES
HOME.

BUT TYPICAL OF PICKERING, DUTY FIRST.
BEFORE HE GOES TO PUSAN HE'S COMING
HERE AND TO SOCHO-RI, THE BASE FROM
WHICH MCCOY OPERATES ON THE EAST
COAST. HE HAS WITH HIM COLONEL
BANNING, WHO HAS BEEN HANDLING
THESE COMMUNICATIONS AT CAMP
PENDLETON, AND WHO WILL NOW, I
PRESUME, SERVE AS HIS DEPUTY HERE.

THE FIRST BAD NEWS IS THAT I DON'T THINK WE ARE GOING TO GET GENERAL DEAN BACK. THIS I'M PRETTY SURE OF AS IT COMES FROM LT COL VANDENBURG, THE OFFICER SENT WITH THE MISSION OF GETTING HIM BACK, MCCOY, AND BILL DUNSTON, THE CIA SEOUL STATION CHIEF. THEIR AGENTS, OR THEY PERSONALLY, HAVE SPENT A GOOD DEAL OF TIME BEHIND THE ENEMY'S LINES AND THEY ALL TELL ME, AND I BELIEVE, THAT DEAN HAS BEEN TAKEN TO CHINA.

SECOND, UNLESS SOMETHING HAS HAPPENED THAT I DON'T KNOW ABOUT, MACARTHUR PROBABLY TOLD YOU ON WAKE ISLAND WHAT HE TOLD ME BEFORE HE LEFT, THAT THE CHINESE AND/OR THE RUSSIANS ARE NOT GOING TO COME INTO THE WAR AND THAT IT'S REALLY A MOOT QUESTION, BECAUSE EVEN IF THEY DID IT WOULD NOT POSE A PROBLEM AND WOULD GIVE US A CHANCE TO BLOODY THEIR NOSE.

MCCOY AS I WRITE THIS IS SOMEWHERE BEHIND THE ENEMY'S LINES IN THE FAR NORTH TRYING TO EAVESDROP ON SOVIET ARMY RADIO COMMUNICATIONS TO SEE IF HE CAN LEARN SOMETHING OF THEIR DISPERSAL, SIZE, AND INTENTIONS.

HE IS NOT DOING THE SAME FOR THE CHINESE COMMUNISTS BECAUSE HE BELIEVES THAT THERE ARE SOME SIX HUNDRED THOUSAND CHINESE — THAT'S RIGHT, SIX HUNDRED THOUSAND — IN THE FOURTH FIELD ARMY EITHER ON THE BORDER OR ALREADY SLIPPING INTO NORTH KOREA AND THEY ARE NOT USING THEIR RADIOS.

THERE IS NO QUESTION IN EITHER MCCOY'S OR DUNSTON'S MIND THAT THE CHINESE ARE COMING INTO THE WAR. THEY ACKNOWLEDGE THEY DON'T HAVE ENOUGH HARD INTELLIGENCE TO MAKE THAT JUDGMENT VIS-A-VIS THE RUSSIANS.

WHEN I, WITHOUT MENTIONING MCCOY OR DUNSTON, ASKED MAJ GEN CHARLES WILLOUGHBY, MACARTHUR'S INTELLIGENCE OFFICER, WHETHER HE HAS ANY INFORMATION ABOUT CHINESE BEING ON THE BORDER, HE FLATLY STATED THERE WERE NOT, AND IF THERE HAD BEEN ANY UNUSUAL MOVEMENT OF CHINESE TROOPS HE WOULD KNOW ABOUT IT, AND ASSURED ME THAT IT WOULD BE IMPOSSIBLE TO HIDE THE MOVEMENT, OR THE PRESENCE, OF "SUBSTANTIAL TROOP FORMATIONS."

THIS AFTERNOON X CORPS WILL SAIL
FROM INCHON AROUND THE TIP OF THE
PENINSULA TO WONSAN. THE ORIGINAL
IDEA WAS THEY WOULD MAKE AN
AMPHIBIOUS LANDING AT WONSAN, AND
THEN STRIKE BACK ACROSS THE
PENINSULA, TOWARD PYONGYANG,
CUTTING OFF THE RETREATING NORTH
KOREANS.

THERE ARE SEVERAL PROBLEMS WITH
THIS. FOR ONE THING THE I ROK CORPS
IS ALREADY IN WONSAN, AND THE SEA
APPROACHES TO WONSAN AND
HUNGNAM HAVE BEEN MINED. MCCOY'S
PEOPLE HAVE INTERCEPTED
COMMUNICATION BETWEEN THE
MINELAYING VESSELS IN RUSSIAN, WHICH
SUGGESTS TO HIM THAT THE RUSSIANS
ARE LAYING THE MINES.

I SAW DUNSTON'S MESSAGE A WEEK AGO
TO THE TOKYO CIA STATION CHIEF IN
WHICH HE REPORTED THIS. PRESUMABLY
THIS INTELLIGENCE WAS PASSED ON TO
WILLOUGHBY. SO FAR AS I CAN FIND OUT,
IT WAS NEVER PASSED ON TO X CORPS,
EIGHTH ARMY, OR THE NAVY. THE FIRST
THE NAVY LEARNED OF THE MINES WAS
WHEN A HELICOPTER FROM ONE OF THE
BABY CARRIERS ON A DOWNED PILOT

RESCUE MISSION FLEW LOW OVER THE APPROACHES TO HAMHUNG AND SAW THE MINES IN THE WATER. THE NAVY SENT A MINESWEEPER TO CHECK AND IT HIT A MINE AND SANK.

THIS MEANS THAT WHEN X CORPS ARRIVES OFF WONSAN OR HAMHUNG SOMETIME TOMORROW OR THE DAY AFTER, THEY WILL HAVE TO SAIL BACK AND FORTH UNTIL THE MINES ARE SWEPT, AND THAT WILL TAKE THREE TO FIVE DAYS.

MEANWHILE, ON THE WEST COAST, GENERAL WALKER'S EIGHTH ARMY IS IN PURSUIT OF THE RETREATING NORTH KOREANS. ONE OF THE WAYS THEY ARE DOING THIS IS WITH A DROP OF THE 173RD PARACHUTE INFANTRY REGIMENT. THE ONLY JUSTIFICATION I HAVE HEARD FOR THIS IS THAT THERE ARE A NUMBER OF PARACHUTE OFFICERS ON THE EIGHTH ARMY STAFF WHO DIDN'T WANT THE PARATROOPS LEFT OUT OF THE WAR.

One of the radio teletype machines in the room began to clatter, and Pickering stopped reading the message.

Di-san went quickly to it, then turned to Howe and Pickering.

"It's a back-channel from Sergeant Keller," she announced. "Depending on how long it is, it will take me a couple of minutes to type it into the decryption machine."

A back-channel message is one sent between operators at two communications facilities, in this case the Dai Ichi Building (UNC) communications center and the communications room in the house. Intended primarily to announce schedules, down equipment, and other technical matters, they are not logged and officially do not exist.

Pickering smiled and nodded his understanding, then turned to Howe.

"Why don't you tell the President what you really think, Ralph, without being so polite?"

Howe chuckled.

"Read on, Flem," he said. "It gets better."

Pickering dropped his eyes to the yet-to-be-transmitted message.

> ANYWAY, WITHIN A COUPLE OF DAYS, EIGHTH ARMY WILL ALMOST CERTAINLY TAKE PYONGYANG.
>
> MCCOY AND DUNSTON (SEPARATELY) HAVE TOLD ME THE CAPTURE OF THE NORTH KOREA CAPITAL MAY BE THE

TRIGGER FOR THE CHINESE TO ENTER THE WAR. OPERATIVE WORDS MAY BE THE TRIGGER.

BY THE TIME EIGHTH ARMY TAKES PYONGYANG, THE MINES ON THE EAST COAST WILL PROBABLY BE CLEARED, AND X CORPS CAN LAND. THE QUESTION THEN BECOMES WHAT WILL X CORPS HAVE TO DO? SINCE PYONGYANG WILL HAVE FALLEN, THERE IS NO POINT IN HAVING X CORPS RECROSS THE PENINSULA TO TAKE IT. THE ONLY THING LEFT FOR THEM TO DO IS MOVE NORTHWARD ALONG THE EAST COAST TOWARD THE CHINESE BORDER.

THE SOUTH KOREANS ARE ALREADY MOVING TOWARD THE BORDER.

MCCOY AND DUNSTON (AGAIN SEPARATELY) HAVE BOTH TOLD ME THAT WHILE THE CHINESE MIGHT NOT REGARD THE SOUTH KOREANS AS A REAL THREAT — THEY HAVE TO RELY ON U.S. LOGISTICS — ONCE THE CHINESE LEARN THAT THE X CORPS IS COMING THAT WAY THEY VERY LIKELY WILL CONSIDER THAT MACARTHUR IS PLANNING TO STRIKE ACROSS THE BORDER. MACARTHUR HAS TOLD ME, AND I BELIEVE, HE HAS NO PLANS TO GO

ACROSS THE CHINESE BORDER, BUT THAT ISN'T THE POINT. WHAT THE CHINESE THINK IS WHAT'S IMPORTANT. MCCOY AND DUNSTON THINK THAT ONCE THE CHINESE LEARN THAT X CORPS IS APPROACHING THE BORDER, THEY WILL COME INTO THE WAR. I CANNOT FAULT THEIR LOGIC.

IT CAN BE ARGUED — AND GENERAL WALKER DOES SO EFFECTIVELY — THAT IF HE HAD COMMAND OF X CORPS, THERE WOULD BE OVERALL CONTROL AND COORDINATION. HE SPENT ALMOST AS MUCH TIME EXPLAINING THIS TO ME AS HE DID COMPLAINING ABOUT HIS MISSING AIRPLANE. I HAVE THE FEELING THAT IF HE WERE GIVEN COMMAND, THE FIRST THING HE WOULD DO WOULD BE TO RELIEVE GENERAL ALMOND, WHOM HE CORDIALLY DETESTS, AND VICE VERSA.

THERE IS NOT MUCH LOVE LOST BETWEEN MACARTHUR AND WALKER EITHER, WHICH IS ONE OF THE REASONS HE IS NOT ABOUT TO PLACE X CORPS UNDER EIGHTH ARMY. THERE ARE OTHERS, WHICH INCLUDE ALMOND — WHO IS A GOOD MAN — AGREEING WITH MACARTHUR'S CONCEPT OF FIGHTING THIS WAR. ANOTHER, OF COURSE, IS THAT IF X CORPS IS UNDER

EIGHTH ARMY, ALMOND COULD NOT
CONTINUE TO WEAR BOTH HATS, THAT OF
X CORPS COMMANDER AND CHIEF OF
STAFF TO MACARTHUR. IF ALMOND WERE
RELIEVED AS X CORPS COMMANDER, "ONE
OF WALKER'S MEN" WOULD GET IT. IF HE
WERE RELIEVED AS CHIEF OF STAFF, THAT
WOULD PERMIT THE PENTAGON TO SEND
A REPLACEMENT OF THEIR CHOOSING.
NEITHER ALTERNATIVE IS ACCEPTABLE TO
MACARTHUR.

I HAVE NO IDEA HOW EVEN YOU CAN
STOP THIS INTERNECINE WARFARE
BETWEEN YOUR SENIOR OFFICERS, BUT I
HAVE BEEN BOTH WORKING WITH
PICKERING AND FILLING IN FOR HIM LONG
ENOUGH SO THAT I FEEL COMFORTABLE
OFFERING SOME ADVICE ABOUT
INTELLIGENCE GENERALLY AND THE CIA IN
PARTICULAR.

YOU WERE WRONG — AS YOU TOLD ME —
WHEN YOU DISESTABLISHED THE OSS,
AND YOUR APPOINTMENT OF ADMIRAL
HILLENCOETTER TO HEAD THE CIA
OBVIOUSLY HASN'T WORKED. IF MCCOY
HADN'T GONE TO PICKERING AND
PICKERING'S FRIENDSHIP WITH SENATOR
FOWLER HADN'T GOTTEN HIM IN TO SEE
HILLENCOETTER WE WOULD NEVER HAVE

KNOWN THAT THERE WAS INTELLIGENCE SAYING THE NORTH KOREANS WERE GOING TO ATTACK. AND THAT WOULD HAVE MEANT THE MILITARY ESTABLISHMENT COULD CLAIM, AND WOULD HAVE CLAIMED, THAT THIS PROVED THE CIA WAS ESSENTIALLY USELESS AND USING UP APPROPRIATIONS THAT THEY COULD PUT TO BETTER USE.

ROOSEVELT'S AND DONOVAN'S IDEA THAT THERE SHOULD BE A CENTRAL AGENCY FOR INTELLIGENCE NOT SUBORDINATE TO ANYONE IN THE MILITARY WAS A GOOD ONE, EVEN IF THE MILITARY ESTABLISHMENT IMMEDIATELY PUT THEIR WAGONS IN A CIRCLE TO FIGHT THE OSS, AND HAVE ALREADY STARTED TO DO SO WITH THE CIA.

THE FIRST THING TO DO THEN IS MAKE SURE WALTER BEDELL SMITH UNDERSTANDS THAT HIS TITLE IS "MR. DIRECTOR" AND NOT "GENERAL" AND THAT HE ANSWERS TO NO ONE BUT YOU. IF HE'S TO DO A GOOD JOB, HE HAS TO BE FREE OF THE MILITARY ESTABLISHMENT AND ITS OLD BOY NETWORK.

THE SECOND THING TO DO IS MAKE SURE THAT INTELLIGENCE GATHERED ANYWHERE

IN THE WORLD, BUT RIGHT NOW
ESPECIALLY HERE, GOES DIRECTLY TO
WASHINGTON, WHERE IT SHOULD BE
EVALUATED BY SMITH AND THEN SENT TO
WHOEVER MIGHT HAVE USE FOR IT. IF
THAT IS DONE, THE VARIOUS COMMANDS
WILL NOT BE ABLE TO IGNORE
INTELLIGENCE THAT DOESN'T FIT THEIR
AGENDA.

FOR ALL I KNOW, YOU MAY HAVE
ALREADY STARTED SOMETHING LIKE THIS.
PICKERING, YOU TOLD ME, WAS GOING TO
MEET WITH SMITH. I'M SURE PICKERING
TOLD HIM HOW HE THINKS IT SHOULD BE
DONE, AND HE APPARENTLY DID THAT
WELL ENOUGH TO HAVE COME BACK
OVER HERE WITH AT LEAST SOME OF THE
AUTHORITY HE NEEDS. I HAVE LEARNED
THAT HE HAS RELIEVED THE CIA TOKYO
STATION CHIEF, WHO WAS BOTH
INCOMPETENT AND THOUGHT OF HIMSELF
AS A MEMBER OF MACARTHUR'S STAFF. I
DON'T KNOW THIS, BUT I SUSPECT
PICKERING WILL REPLACE HIM WITH
COLONEL BANNING, WHO WORKED FOR
HIM IN WAR TWO AND IS HELD IN HIGH
REGARD BY MCCOY AND OTHERS. AND
WHO WILL WORK FOR PICKERING, THAT IS
THE CIA, NOT MACARTHUR.

IN THIS LATTER CONNECTION, I AM VERY
IMPRESSED WITH VANDENBURG AND VERY
WORRIED THAT WILLOUGHBY WILL TRY —
AND PROBABLY SUCCEED — TO GET
CONTROL OF HIM. I RECOMMEND THAT
YOU ORDER — AS OPPOSED TO SUGGEST
— THAT HE BE PLACED ON TDY TO THE
CIA AND PLACED UNDER PICKERING.

BY NOW, HARRY, YOU MUST SENSE THAT
MY POSITION IS "A POX ON BOTH THEIR
HOUSES." IT IS. YOU MUST ALSO SENSE
THAT I HAVE TAKEN SIDES. I HAVE. I
REALLY THINK MY USEFULNESS TO YOU
HERE IS OVER, AND I RESPECTFULLY
REQUEST RELIEF.

PICKERING CAN DO FOR YOU WHAT I
HAVE BEEN DOING, AND IF YOU THINK
ABOUT IT THAT'S THE WAY IT SHOULD
HAVE BEEN DONE ALL ALONG. AS
COMMANDER-IN-CHIEF YOU ARE ENTITLED
TO GET THE FACTS, AND IT SEEMS TO ME
THAT THE CIA IS WHERE YOU SHOULD
GET THEM.

I'M GOING TO SHOW PICKERING THIS
BEFORE I SEND IT, LARGELY BECAUSE I
WANT HIM TO KNOW WHAT I'M TELLING
YOU.

RESPECTFULLY, AND WITH BEST REGARDS TO BESS

RALPH

END PERSONAL MESSAGE FROM GENERAL HOWE

TOP SECRET/PRESIDENTIAL

Pickering raised his eyes to Howe.

"Jesus, Ralph," he said.

"Is there anything in there you disagree with?" Howe asked.

"No," Pickering said simply. "Except you wanting to leave me here to face the lions all by myself."

"I've outlived my usefulness," Howe said. "And I really think you can do anything for the President that I can."

He put out his hand for the message, and when Pickering handed it to him, he turned to Di-san. She was sitting at the keyboard of the decryption machine, her fingers flying over the keys.

As they watched, the electric typewriter section of the machine began to clatter as it typed the now decrypted message.

She waited until it had finished, then ripped the yellow paper from the machine and handed it to Howe.

"Thank you," he said, and handed her

his message. "Put the correct date time block on this, please, and send it."

Di-san nodded and turned back to the keyboard.

Howe read the back-channel, then handed it to Pickering.

FROM KELLER
TO ROGERS OR JENNINGS

PASS TO GEN PICKERING ON ARRIVAL:
COL HUFF CAME TO IMPERIAL LOOKING
FOR HIM. HE FINALLY TOLD ME WHY.
MACARTHUR HAD SENT HIM TO TELL THE
GENERAL THAT MAJ PICKERING WAS
TRANSFERRED FROM THE CARRIER TO THE
DESTROYER MANSFIELD AT 1500.
MANSFIELD IS EN ROUTE PUSAN, ETA
EARLY TOMORROW. MAJ PICKERING WILL
BE FLOWN IN HOSPITAL PLANE TO
SASEBO, AND THEN ON TO THE NAVY
HOSPITAL IN SAN DIEGO. TELL THE
GENERAL I THOUGHT ERNIE AND MRS
PICKERING WOULD WANT TO KNOW, AND
SO I HAVE PASSED THE WORD.

"Well," Howe said, "I guess you'll want to be in Pusan when he gets there."

"I'll have Hart get us seats on the Round Robin in the morning," Pickering said.

"The Beaver's at your disposal, Flem," Howe said. "If you want, you can use that."

"I hadn't thought about that," Pickering replied. "I guess what I could do is leave early, and go to Pusan by way of Socho-Ri. Would that be possible?"

"You could also wait to go to Socho-Ri after you see your boy," Howe said. "Your call, Flem."

"Let's go see what the pilot says," Pickering said, and then had another thought. "Keller didn't mention Jeanette Priestly. I'm sure Pick's lady friend'll want to see him. She's in Wonsan, right? Maybe we could pick her up at the same time."

"I don't know if she's in Wonsan or not," Howe said. "Or, for that matter, where she is."

"Really?" His surprise showed in his voice.

"I know Dunston and McCoy were looking for her, but I never heard where they found her."

"Well, let's go find out," Pickering said. "I think Pick will be far more interested in seeing her than me."

"General," Bill Dunston said a little uncomfortably. "The first thing I did when I got the Killer's Operational Immediate was call the Press Center at Eighth Army Rear in Pusan. They told me they expected her but she hadn't arrived yet. I left word for her to call me the minute she got in."

"And she didn't call?" Pickering said.

"No, she didn't. So — maybe around suppertime — I went there myself. She had been there — they told me they had given her my message, and that she had signed on to the roster for a Gooney Bird flight to Wonsan. They said it was a long roster and she almost certainly wouldn't get out the next day, more likely the day after that. They didn't know where she was. So I called around town, and couldn't find her."

"And you left it there?" Colonel Ed Banning inquired, not pleasantly.

Dunston replied, "You don't know this lady, Banning . . ."

Pickering picked up on that — "Banning," not "Colonel" — and thought, *Dunston's resentment is starting to show.*

". . . she's a free spirit," Dunston went on. "There's no telling where she would be. I figured maybe she arranged her own ride to Wonsan — she doesn't like waiting — and that that had happened in such a way that she didn't have time to call me. Or didn't want to."

"So you stopped looking?" Banning asked.

"What I did, Banning, was get on the horn to Wonsan, specifically to the Capital ROK Division — we have a friend there, a colonel named Pak — and asked him to look for her, to have her call me, and then

I called Zimmerman at Socho-Ri. Ernie knew about the major having been picked up, and he had already started checking around for the Priestly woman. I told him to keep looking, and to give me a yell if he found her."

"And he never called, Bill?" Pickering asked.

"He never called."

"Gunner Zimmerman looked all over for her, sir," Jennings said, "and when I came here, he told me to call him and let him know where she was. I guess he figured if she wasn't in Wonsan, or anywhere on the east coast, she had to be either here or in Pusan."

"So the bottom line," Banning began unpleasantly, "is that you were ordered to find Miss Priestly, and not only haven't done so, but didn't inform anyone that you failed —"

"That will enough, Colonel," Pickering interrupted him, coldly.

Banning was visibly surprised by both the order and the tone of Pickering's voice.

"He's right, General," Dunston said. "I guess I dropped the ball."

"I don't look at it that way," Pickering said. "You did what you thought had to be done. But I'm open for suggestions."

"I'll go out to K-16 and check with the Air Force," Dunston said. "The base commander is a pretty good guy. And while I'm doing that, Jennings is first going to get on the horn to Zimmerman, and then start calling all the division public information officers. She has to be here somewhere."

"When are you going to do this?" Pickering asked.

"That whoosh you hear, General, is me going out the door," Dunston said. He put his champagne glass on the table. "I'll finish this," he said, "when I have put my hands on the lady."

He walked out of the dining room. Zimmerman followed him.

Pickering looked at Banning.

"Come with me, please, Colonel," he said.

He walked out of the dining room with Banning on his heels, and led him out of the building into the courtyard. He stopped in the middle.

"Okay, Ed," he said. "You've got a hair up your ass. Tell me what it's all about."

"Sir, I don't know what you —"

"You've been pissing everybody off with your attitude since you got here, and I want to know why."

"With respect, sir, I don't —"

"You can either tell me what's bothering you, Ed, or I'm going to tell George to get you a seat on the first flight out of here tomorrow, and that will be the first leg of your flight to the States. I like you, we're — I have always thought — old and good friends, but I cannot afford to have you come in here with an attitude that's pissing off good people. You understand me?"

They locked eyes.

"That was a question, Colonel," Pickering said.

Banning exhaled audibly.

"Milla's in the hospital," he said softly.

"Milla's in the hospital? When did this happen?"

"She went in yesterday, or the day before — I don't even know what day it is in the States, much less what time — to have a lump removed from her breast. Or maybe the whole breast, depending on what they find."

"Then what the hell are you doing here?" Pickering said.

"You sent for me," Banning said simply.

"Jesus H. Christ! If I had known about your wife . . ."

"I'm a Marine officer," Banning said.

"And a good one. But as a human being, you're a goddamn fool," Pickering said.

"I'm sorry you feel that way, sir," Banning said.

"Where is she? What hospital?"

"Charleston," Banning said.

"These are your orders, Colonel. You are to go up to the third floor of this building. There you will find a Korean woman named Di-san. You will order her to send an Urgent Message to the Commanding Officer, Marine Barracks, Charleston. Quote — Urgently require report status Mrs. Milla Banning, presently in Whateverthehell Hospital Charleston. Update hourly or more frequently, as necessary, until notified otherwise. Signature, Pickering, Brig. Gen. CIA Deputy Director for Asia — Unquote."

"General, with respect, that's . . ."

"What? Not authorized?"

"No, sir."

"Well, maybe not, Colonel. But the only person who can challenge me is a retired Army general named Smith, and I don't think he will. You have your orders, Colonel."

After a long moment, Ed Banning said, "Aye, aye, sir."

He started back toward the entrance and then turned.

"Sir, I'd really be grateful if you could keep this between us."

"You'd rather appear to be a horse's ass than admit you have human emotions? Like hell I will."

Banning didn't reply, but neither did he continue toward the house.

"Get moving, Ed," Pickering said. After a moment, Banning nodded and then walked quickly toward the house.

XIII

[One]
USS *Badoeng Strait* (CVE-116)
39.58 Degrees North Latitude
128.33 Degrees East Longitude
The Sea of Japan
1125 17 October 1950

The *Badoeng Strait* was at sea about fifty miles east of a midpoint between Hungnam and Wonsan.

There had not been much call for air strikes from any of the units of I ROK Corps, which was pursuing the retreating North Korean army up the rugged east coast of the Korean Peninsula.

With about two-thirds of his fuel remaining, Lieutenant Colonel William C. Dunn, USMC, had decided to take his three-Corsair flight north of Chongjin, which would place them close to the borders between North Korea and China, and North Korea and Manchuria.

He could then take a look around, then fly down the east coast of the peninsula, looking for targets of opportunity on the way back to the *Badoeng Strait*.

For a number of reasons, starting with the fact that he was a good Marine officer who obeyed his orders, he was very careful not only not to cross the border but to keep far enough south of it so that it could not be credibly charged that he had violated either Chinese or Russian territory, even by mistake.

But he did take the flight inland far enough and high enough so that over extreme Northern Korea, he could look down and across the borders into both China and Manchuria.

He saw nothing that suggested the presence of troops massed on either side of the border prepared to enter the conflict. He had in mind, of course, what McCoy had told him and the skipper in the captain's cabin on the *Badoeng Strait* about 600,000 Chinese either on their side of the border, or already starting to cross into North Korea.

It was possible, of course, that McCoy was dead wrong. It was also possible that McCoy was right. Again.

On the way back down the coast, they found the targets of opportunity they knew would be there, and made strafing passes at North Korean troops either on the roads or hiding on either side of them. They stopped this only when the fuel available became sort of questionable and most of their ammunition had been expended. It made no sense to either run out of fuel or to return to the *Badoeng Strait* with a lot of ammunition unfired.

Colonel Dunn brought the flight down pretty close to the deck and flew over Socho-Ri. The H-19As were not in sight, which meant either that their camouflage was very good or that they were off someplace. He decided it was the camouflage, because Major Donald, the Army pilot, had told him they preferred to make their flights in the very early hours or just before nightfall, so as to provide as small a "window of possible observation" as possible.

He dipped his wings as Marines on the ground, recognizing the gull-winged fighters, came out of the thatch-roofed, stone-walled houses and waved at them.

Then he climbed to 5,000 feet and headed for the *Badoeng Strait.*

He landed last, as was his custom, caught the second wire, and was jerked to a halt.

As he hauled himself out of the cockpit, he saw one of the ship's officers on the deck, obviously waiting for him.

The officer, a blond-headed lieutenant j.g., saluted as Dunn jumped from the wing root to the deck.

"Shooting back, were they, Colonel?"

"Excuse me?" Dunn asked as he returned the salute.

The j.g. pointed to the rear of the Corsair's fuselage and its vertical stabilizer.

"I'll be damned!" Dunn said. There were seven holes in the Corsair — five in the fuselage and two in the vertical stabilizer. They looked like .50-caliber holes.

"I didn't see any tracers coming close," Dunn said, as much to himself as to the j.g.

"The captain's compliments, Colonel. The captain would be pleased if you would take lunch with him."

"Would the captain be pleased to see me immediately, or more pleased after I've had a shower?"

"I think the captain would prefer the latter, sir," the j.g. said, smiling.

"My compliments to the captain, Lieutenant."

"Aye, aye, sir."

Dunn went to the pilot's ready room and listened as Captain Jack Derwinski and Lieutenant Sam Williams, the two pilots who had flown the sortie with him, were debriefed by an air intelligence officer.

Finally, the AIO turned to him.

"Colonel?"

"I have nothing to add," Dunn said. That was true. They had flown an observation/interdiction mission, seen nothing of

interest, and engaged targets of opportunity — small units of North Korean
ground troops — and then come home.
Then he remembered, and added: "There
was some antiaircraft fire from the ground,
probably .50-caliber machine gun."

"How do you know that, Colonel? For
the record."

"Because there are seven half-inch holes
in my fuselage and vertical stabilizer,"
Dunn said, "that I know weren't there
when I took off."

"No shit, Colonel?" Jack Derwinski said,
obviously surprised. "I didn't see any
tracers."

"Either did I, Captain Derwinski," Dunn
said with a smile, "which, as a devout be-
liever in the adage that the one that gets
you is the one you don't see, I find just a
wee bit disconcerting."

"You didn't feel anything?" Derwinski
pursued.

Dunn shook his head no.

"They must have just gone through the
skin without hitting anything else," Dunn
said, then turned to the AIO. "You better
make that fourteen holes in my airplane.
Seven in and seven, thank the good Lord,
out."

"Yes, sir," the AIO said, smiling. "*Fourteen* holes."

Dunn filled a china mug with coffee

from the machine and carried it with him to his cabin.

He showered, shaved, put on fresh khakis, and made his way to the bridge.

The captain waved him onto the bridge.

"I understand the bad guys have been shooting back at you, Colonel," he said.

"Worse than that, sir," Dunn said. "Somebody has apparently been teaching them how to shoot."

"Ready for a little lunch?"

"Yes, sir. Thank you, sir."

The captain pushed himself out of his chair and led Dunn off the bridge to his cabin, where a white-jacketed steward and a table set for two were waiting for them.

"We can serve ourselves, Danny. Thank you," the captain said to the steward as he waved Dunn into a chair.

He waited for the steward to leave them, then said, "You went pretty far north today, did you?"

"Yes, sir."

"See anything interesting? Of the sort your friend in the black pajamas was talking about?"

"No, sir."

"He scared me with that talk of six hundred thousand Chinese," the captain said. "You think he was right?"

"Killer McCoy, over the years, has been right most of the time," Dunn said.

The captain lifted a dome off one serving plate and then another, and lowered the domes to the table. Lunch was pork chops, mashed potatoes, and green beans.

"Help yourself," the captain said as he forked a pork chop to his plate.

Dunn, filling his plate, said: "I was thinking — today, as a matter of fact, on our way back to the ship, when I didn't see a sign of a Chinese platoon, much less a field army — that if I had to bet, I'd bet on McCoy. He doesn't say something unless he believes it."

"I hope he's wrong now," the captain said. "This part of the world is a lousy place to have to fight a war in the winter."

"The troops seem to think they'll be home for Christmas," Dunn said.

"Let's hope they're right," the captain said, then: "Changing the subject, you have a message straight from CNO."

"I have a message from CNO?"

"Yeah," the captain said, then took it from his pocket and handed it to him.

"I thought you were pulling my chain, sir," Dunn said as he unfolded the single sheet of teletypewriter paper.

WASHINGTON DC 0945 16 OCTOBER 1950

FROM: CHIEF OF NAVAL OPERATIONS

SUBJECT: CITATION FOR DECORATION FOR MAJOR M.S. PICKERING, USMCR

TO: COMMANDING OFFICER MAG 33 ABOARD BADOENG STRAIT

INFO: CHAIRMAN JOINT CHIEFS OF STAFF NAVAL LIAISON OFFICER TO THE PRESIDENT SUPREME COMMANDER UNITED NATIONS COMMAND TOKYO COMMANDANT USMC COMMANDER-IN-CHIEF PACIFIC

1. IT IS THE DESIRE OF THE PRESIDENT THAT MAJOR MALCOLM S. PICKERING, USMCR, BE AWARDED THE NAVY CROSS FOR HIS HEROISM AND VALOR ABOVE AND BEYOND THE CALL OF DUTY DURING THE PERIOD HE SPENT BEHIND ENEMY LINES BETWEEN HIS BEING SHOT DOWN AND HIS RESCUE.

2. IT IS DIRECTED THAT YOU

A. ACKNOWLEDGE RECEIPT OF THIS MESSAGE BY URGENT MESSAGE.

B. IMMEDIATELY PREPARE A SUITABLE CITATION FOR THIS AWARD AND FORWARD IT BY THE MOST EXPEDITIOUS MEANS THROUGH APPROPRIATE CHANNELS TO CHIEF OF NAVAL OPERATIONS, ATTN: CHIEF, AWARDS BRANCH.

C. FURNISH CNO A COPY OF THE PROPOSED CITATION BY URGENT MESSAGE AT THE TIME YOU BEGIN TO FORWARD IT THROUGH APPROPRIATE CHANNELS. (SEE 2.A. ABOVE)

FOR THE CHIEF OF NAVAL OPERATIONS

WALLACE T. GERARD
VICE ADMIRAL
DEPUTY CNO

SECRET

"No," Dunn blurted. "I won't do it."

"Excuse me?"

"I won't do it," Dunn repeated.

"What are you talking about, Billy?" the captain asked.

"Pickering did nothing that merits the award of the Navy Cross," Dunn said.

"The President seems to think he does," the captain said.

"Pickering did what he was expected to do," Dunn said. "He evaded capture until he was able to get back. That's all."

"Colonel," the captain said formally, then reached over and took the message from Dunn's hand and read from it: " 'It is the desire of the President that Major Malcolm S. Pickering, USMCR, be awarded the Navy Cross.' That seems to settle the question, wouldn't you agree?"

"Let the President write the citation. I won't."

The captain dropped his eyes to the message and read from it again: " 'You will immediately prepare a suitable citation for this award. . . .' That sounds pretty clear to me."

"Not only was Pickering not doing anything more than any shot-down pilot is expected to do, but it was his fault — and mine — that he got shot down in the first place."

"You want to explain that to me, Colonel?" the captain asked somewhat coldly.

"What he was doing when he was shot down was trying to become the first locomotive ace in the Marine Corps," Dunn said. "I knew what he was doing, and I didn't stop him."

"What do you mean, 'locomotive ace'?"

"He wanted credit for shooting up five locomotives; in his mind that would make

638

him a locomotive ace. He'd already checked with the Air Force to see if any Air Force pilot was credited with more locomotives in World War Two."

The captain looked at him, shook his head, but said nothing.

"It was a joke to him," Dunn said. "The whole war is a joke to him. And I knew what he was doing and didn't stop him."

"I thought you were old pals."

"He was my wingman at Guadalcanal," Dunn said. "I love the sonofabitch, but I am not going to go through with this nonsense of giving him the Navy Cross. What he did was cause a lot of good people to put their dicks on the chopping block to save his sorry ass, and I am not going to help him get a medal like that for being a three-star horse's ass and, for that matter, a lousy Marine officer."

"Calm down, Colonel," the captain said.

"I beg your pardon for my language, sir," Dunn said. "But I am not going to go along with this bullshit."

The captain raised his hand in a gesture that meant *take it easy*.

"Jesus!" Dunn said disgustedly.

The captain said nothing.

"There was a standing order at Fighter One on the 'Canal," Dunn said. "No buzzing the field, period. We couldn't risk the airplanes. Pick used to do full-emergency-power *barrel rolls* over the field every time he shot down an airplane," Dunn said. "And sometimes just whenever the hell he felt like it. That's when I should have pulled the wiseass bastard up short."

"When you have your emotions under control, Colonel, let me know," the captain said coldly.

Dunn looked at him for a long moment.

"My apologies, sir," he said finally.

"What are you going to do?" the captain asked. "You have been ordered by the Chief of Naval Operations to immediately prepare 'a suitable citation.' "

"I'm unable to comply with that order, sir."

The captain said nothing.

"A lot of good men have *earned* the Navy Cross —" Dunn began.

"Including you, Colonel," the captain interrupted. "Is that what this is about?"

"— and giving Major Pickering the decoration for having done nothing beyond what he was expected to do," Dunn went on, "would be an insult to every one of them."

"Be that as it may, the Commander-in-Chief 'desires' that Pickering be awarded the Navy Cross. You can't fight that, Colonel. You have an order. You have no choice but to obey it."

"I am unable to do that, sir," Dunn said.

* * *

Thirty minutes later, a message went out from the *Badoeng Strait*.

SECRET

URGENT

BADOENG STRAIT 1405 17 OCTOBER 1950

FROM: COMMANDING OFFICER MAG 33

TO: CHIEF OF NAVAL OPERATIONS
ATTN: CHIEF, AWARDS BRANCH

1. REFERENCE PARA 2. MSG CNO SUBJ:
CITATION FOR DECORATION FOR MAJOR
M.S. PICKERING, USMCR DATED 16 OCT 1950

2. THE UNDERSIGNED IS UNABLE TO
COMPLY.

WILLIAM C. DUNN
LIEUTENANT COLONEL, USMC
COMMANDING

SECRET

[Two]
U.S. Naval Hospital
U.S. Navy Base, Sasebo
Sasebo, Japan
1625 18 October 1950

Lieutenant (j.g.) Rosemary Hills, Nurse Corps, USNR — a five-three, one-hundred-fifteen-pound twenty-three-year-old from Chicago — had the duty, which placed her at a desk in the nurses' station of Ward 4-G between 1600 and 2400 hours.

There were six Corpsmen always on duty in Ward 4-G, and usually two or three of them could be found at the nurses' station. They dealt with the routine operations of Ward 4-G, and turned to Lieutenant Hills only when something required the attention of the ward nurse on duty, a registered nurse, or a commissioned officer, or any combination thereof.

She was a little uncomfortable when she glanced up from her desk and saw a Marine standing on the other side of the counter, obviously wanting something, and saw there was no Corpsman behind the counter — or anywhere in sight — to deal with him.

Lieutenant Hills had not been in the Navy very long, and was not completely familiar with all the subtleties of Navy rank and protocol, and was even less familiar with those of the Marine Corps.

She knew from the rank insignia on his collar points and shoulders that the man standing before her was a master gunner, which was the equivalent of a Navy warrant officer, which meant that he ranked between the senior enlisted Marine and the junior Marine officer.

She remembered, too, from orientation at the Great Lakes Naval Training Center, that Marine master gunners were special, as lieutenants — Marine and Navy — were ordinary. There were very few master gunners, and they were all ex–senior enlisted Marines with all sorts of experience that qualified them to be master gunners.

The ribbons and other decorations on this one's tunic — she recognized only a few of them — seemed to attest to that. Judging by just the number of them, this master gunner had been in every war since the American Revolution, and wounded in all of them.

One of the medals on his chest she did recognize was the Purple Heart, awarded for having been wounded in action. She had seen enough of them pinned on hospital gowns here in the ward to know what that was. The master gunner's Purple Heart medal was just about covered with little things — Lieutenant Hills had forgotten what they called the little things —

pinned to it. But she knew that each one of the little things meant a different award of the Purple Heart for getting wounded in action.

Lieutenant Hills saw that he was carrying a small canvas bag in his left hand, as a woman carries a bag. She wondered what was in it.

Then she realized that she had no idea how master gunners were addressed.

Do you call them "Master Gunner," as you would call a major "Major"? If not, then what?

"May I help you, sir?" Lieutenant Hills finally asked, even though she knew that as a lieutenant j.g. she outranked the master gunner and therefore he was not entitled to be called "sir."

"Major Pickering," the master gunner said.

"What about Major Pickering?" she asked. "Where is he?"

I think he was supposed to say, "Where is he, ma'am?"

"He's in 404," Lieutenant Hill said. "But he's on Restricted Visitors. If you want to visit him, you'll have to go to . . ."

The master gunner nodded at her, then turned and marched down the corridor toward room 404.

"Just a minute, please," Lieutenant Hills called after him as firmly as she could manage. "Didn't you hear me? Major

Pickering is on Restricted Visitors. You have to have permission of the medical officer of the day —"

When she realized she was being totally ignored, she stopped in midsentence.

She came from behind the nurses' station counter and looked down the corridor in time to see the gunner enter room 404.

Master Gunner Ernest Zimmerman, USMC, marched to the foot of the cranked-up hospital bed in which Major Malcolm S. Pickering was sitting and looked at him without speaking.

"Look what the goddamn tide washed up!" Pick cried happily. "I'll be goddamned, Ernie, it's good to see you!"

"You won't think so in a minute, Pick," Zimmerman said. "Can you handle some really shitty news?"

There was a just-perceptible pause, long enough for his bright smile to vanish before Pickering asked, "Jesus Christ, not the Killer?"

"Not the Killer," Zimmerman said.

"Dad? Has something happened to my father?"

Zimmerman opened the straps on his canvas bag and extended it to Pickering.

"What's this?" Pick asked, but looked, and then reached inside without waiting for an answer.

He came out with a fire-blackened object that only after a moment he recognized as a camera.

"Jeanette's camera," Zimmerman said, and then when Pick looked at him curiously, went on: "I picked it up yesterday near where the plane went in."

"Jeanette's?" Pick asked. "What plane?"

"An Air Force Gooney Bird headed for Wonsan," Zimmerman said. "It clipped a mountain and blew up. Nobody got out."

"Jeanette was on the Gooney Bird?"

"Yeah."

"You're sure?" Pick asked softly.

"Yeah."

"How can you be sure? How did you get involved?"

"From the top?"

"From the fucking top, Ernie," Pickering said, struggling to keep his voice from breaking as a tear slipped down his cheek. "Every fucking tiny little fucking detail."

Lieutenant Hills went back behind the nurses' station aware that she had two choices. She could ignore what had happened, or she could report it. She had just decided to ignore the breach of orders —

What harm was really being done? It wasn't, after all, as if Major Pickering was at death's door. What they were trying to do for him was fatten him up, and making sure the dysentery wouldn't recur. And having a visitor might make him feel better. He looked so unhappy, which was sort of funny because he was just back from escaping from the enemy, and you'd think that would make someone happy.

— when she was forced to reverse it. The hospital commander, Captain F. Howard Schermer, MC, USN, was now standing at her nurses' station.

With him was a very pretty, very pregnant young woman.

"Good afternoon, sir," Lieutenant Hills said.

"This is Mrs. McCoy, Lieutenant," Captain Schermer said. "She is to be the exception to the Restricted Visitors on Major Pickering. They're old friends, and she just came from Tokyo to see him."

Schermer had received a telephone call that morning from Major Pickering's father, who was a Marine brigadier, saying that Mrs. McCoy, "the wife of one of my officers," was on the way to Sasebo to see his son.

"They're very close, they grew up together. They're like brother and sister."

"We'll be happy to take care of her, General."

"You may have to. She's very pregnant and traveling against medical advice."

"Yes, sir," Lieutenant Hills said.

"Four oh four, right?" Captain Schermer asked.

"Yes, sir," Lieutenant Hills said. "Captain, Major Pickering already has a visitor."

"Who would that be?" Captain Schermer asked, not very pleasantly. "You were aware, were you not, of the Restricted Visitors?"

"Sir, I tried to tell him, but he just ignored me."

"A journalist? Was the person who ignored you a journalist? Is that why he thought he could ignore you? Because he was a journalist?"

"No, sir. Sir, it's a Marine, a master gunner Marine. . . ."

"About this tall?" Mrs. McCoy said, holding up her hand. "Built like a tank?"

Lieutenant Hills smiled and nodded.

"That has to be Ernie Zimmerman," Mrs. McCoy said. She turned to Captain Schermer and added, "He works for General Pickering."

"I see," Captain Schermer said with a somewhat strained smile. "Well, why don't we . . . ?" He waved Mrs. McCoy down the corridor toward 404.

Master Gunner Zimmerman stopped in midsentence as the door swung open.

Major Malcolm S. Pickering looked angrily at Captain F. Howard Schermer, USN, and was about to say something when Mrs. K. R. McCoy brushed past the captain.

"I've seen you looking better," she said, and went to the bed and bent over him and kissed him. "But I'm glad to see you anyway."

"I guess you haven't heard, huh?" Pick said.

"Heard what?" Ernie replied, and turned to Zimmerman. "What's going on, Ernie?"

"Obviously, you haven't," Pick said. "Carry on, Mr. Zimmerman. Maybe you better start from the top again." Then he looked at Ernie McCoy and added: "I think maybe you better sit down, mother-to-be. I don't think you're going to like this." He gestured toward a folding chair, then made a *go on* gesture to Zimmerman.

"Well," Zimmerman began, "we don't know how she got from Pusan to Seoul —"

"She being Jeanette?" Ernie McCoy asked. "You mean Jeanette doesn't know we've got Pick back yet? Jesus Christ, why not?"

"Let him finish, Ernie," Pick said. "And I meant it, sit down."

"I think I will," Ernie said, and lowered herself into the folding chair.

"— whether on the Air Corps medical Gooney Bird or some other way,"

Zimmerman went on. "She wasn't on any manifest that we could find."

"Okay," Pick said. "But clever fucking OSS agent that you are, you have deduced that she was on the fucking medical Gooney Bird when it took off from Seoul for Wonsan, right? Because she was on it when it crashed?"

"Oh, my God!" Ernie said. "Is she all right?"

Zimmerman looked at her.

"Sorry, Ernie," Zimmerman said.

"You were saying, Mr. Zimmerman?" Pick said.

"What Dunston did was, when the general found out we hadn't told her about you and sent him to find her, was go out to K-16 and ask the Air Corps guy what possibilities there were," Zimmerman said. "The only thing he could think of was that maybe she'd hitched a ride aboard the Gooney Bird that had gone missing. Then he — the Air Force guy — found out they'd located the crash site."

"What made him think Jeanette was on this plane?" Ernie McCoy asked.

Zimmerman ignored the question.

"They'd gone looking for it after it had gone missing," he went on. "There were no Maydays or anything. Anyway, they found the crash site near the top of a goddamn mountain, but (a) they hadn't been able to get anybody to it, because it was in middle of nowhere, and (b) it had exploded and burned, and there were no signs of survivors, and it was . . . Getting to the site could wait until they'd been to other crash sites where there could be survivors."

"So?" Pick asked.

"So Dunston called me —"

"Where's the Killer been all this time?" Pick interrupted.

Zimmerman took a look at Captain Schermer, then shrugged.

"He's in North Korea, listening to the Russians," Zimmerman said. "We're going to pick him up tomorrow morning at first light."

"You had to tell her that, right?" Pick snapped. "Sometimes you have the sensitivity of an alligator."

"I'm a big girl, Pick," Ernie said. "I know what Ken does."

"Captain," Zimmerman said to Schermer. "With respect, do I have to tell you that whatever is said in here has to stay here?"

"I understand," Schermer said.

"So Dunston called me, gave me the coordinates, and at first light this morning, we went to the site."

"We is who?" Ernie McCoy asked. "And I thought you said getting to the site was difficult?"

"We is me, a doggie major — real good guy — named Alex Donald, who flew the Big Black Bird, and four Marines in case they were needed."

"By which, Ernie, he means a great big Sikorsky helicopter painted black," Pick said. "Your husband has a couple of them."

"And?" Ernie replied, impatience in her voice.

"Well, we found the crash site. The Gooney Bird clipped the top of a mountain, went in, exploded, and then slid down the mountain. Nobody walked away from the crash. And it was quick. No question about that."

"Well, that's comforting," Pick said sarcastically. "To know it was quick. And you found — what's the euphemism? — the *remains* of those on board?"

"We found four bodies," Zimmerman said. "There was a three-man crew on the Gooney Bird. We figured, even before I found the camera, that the fourth had to be Jeanette."

"You couldn't tell?" Ernie asked.

"There was a lot of fuel on the Gooney Bird," Zimmerman said. "They topped off their tanks at K-16. They were planning to go on to Pusan, and maybe all the way to Japan, after Wonsan. There wasn't much left of the bodies."

"So where are the remains?" Pick asked.

"We took them to Seoul, to Eighth Army Graves Registration. It'll take them at least a couple of days to identify them."

"Well, that's no problem, really, is it?" Pick said. "There's no rush, right? As a matter of fact, who the hell cares?"

"Pick," Ernie McCoy said. "Oh, Pick, I'm so sorry."

"Yeah, so am I," Pick said unpleasantly. "But I should have known better. Something that good was never really going to happen to me."

"Pick," she said, and started to push herself out of the chair.

Her face suddenly showed pain and went pale.

"Oh, for Christ's sake!" she said faintly but angrily.

"Mrs. McCoy, are you all right?" Captain Schermer said as he walked across the room to her.

"No, I don't think I am," Ernie said. "Goddamn it all to hell!"

Captain Schermer took a close, if brief, look at her.

"Young woman, you stay right where you are," he ordered, and then went to the door.

"Nurse!" he called loudly. "Get a gurney in here!"

He went back to Ernie.

"Doctor, I don't want to lose this baby," she said softly.

"Of course you don't," Captain Schermer said. "And we're going to do everything we can to see that you don't."

"Jesus H. Christ!" Pick said.

"Hang in there, Ernie!" Pick called as the gurney rolled out the door.

"Oh, shit," Ernie Zimmerman said when the gurney was gone and the door had swung closed. "Why the hell did I tell her about Jeanette?"

"She would have found out," Pick said. "If you are looking for the culprit in this little tragedy, you have to look no further than me."

"What the hell are you talking about?" Zimmerman asked.

"Think about it, old buddy," Pick said. "If I hadn't been engaged in trying to become the first locomotive ace in Marine Corps history, I wouldn't have been shot down, would I?"

"I don't know what the fuck you're talking about, Pick," Zimmerman said.

"And if I hadn't been shot down, then Ernie wouldn't have been worried about me for all that time, would she?"

"We were all worried about you," Zimmerman said.

"Yeah, but I don't think you love me,

old buddy, and, more to the point, you are not with child," Pick said. "This is the fourth time she's tried to make the Killer a daddy. Did you know that?"

"He told me."

"And having been shot down, and not having the balls to do the decent thing, I hung around for all that time, until God, in his infinite wisdom, made that Army convoy make a wrong turn, so I could find them and thus save my miserable ass."

"Jesus!"

"And if I had not been flown here, then Ernie would not have felt obliged to take a daylong train ride in her delicate condition to come all the way down here to welcome the hero home, would she?"

"Coming here was dumb," Zimmerman agreed.

"Where, upon arrival, you told her that the hero's girlfriend, her friend because of me, was now a corpse burned beyond recognition. . . ."

"Jesus, I told you I feel sorry as hell about that. I should have known better."

"And I told you she would have found out," Pick said. "This isn't your fault, old buddy, it's mine."

The door opened and Lieutenant (j.g.) Rosemary Hills entered the room.

"Mrs. McCoy has been taken to the women's ward," she announced. "There are several very skilled gynecologists on staff —"

"Whoopee!" Pickering said sharply.

"Captain Schermer says that you are to wait here for him," Lieutenant Hills said to Zimmerman. "He wants to talk to you."

"Okay," Zimmerman said.

"And he wants the telephone number of her sponsor."

"What the hell is a sponsor?" Pick asked.

"Her husband, for example."

"Her husband doesn't have a telephone right now," Zimmerman said.

"He's in Korea?" Lieutenant Hills asked. Zimmerman nodded. "Then we'll want to send a message to his unit," she said.

"That's not possible," Zimmerman said.

"Why not?" she asked.

"I can't get into that," Zimmerman said.

"You're going to have to explain that," she said.

"I don't have to explain anything to you," Zimmerman said flatly.

"What would you say, Florence Nightingale," Pick asked, "if I were to tell you that the lady's husband, as we speak, is in enemy territory, behind the lines, so to speak, eavesdropping on the Russians?"

She looked at him almost in horror.

"And if it's all the same to you," Pick went on, "I would rather not have him learn right now that the man the poor

656

bastard thinks of as his best friend has caused his wife to have another miscarriage."

"Pick, shut the fuck up," Zimmerman said.

Lieutenant Hills looked between them, then fled the room.

[Three]
The USS *DeHaven* (DD 727)
39 Degrees 36 Minutes North Latitude
128 Degrees 43 Minutes East Longitude
The Sea of Japan
0725 19 October 1950

The vessels transporting the X United States Army Corps from Inchon to Wonsan — attack transports, cargo ships, tankers, and the "screening force" to protect them against any potential danger — were spread out over miles of the Sea of Japan.

At the head of the screening force as it steamed north was the destroyer *DeHaven*. Her commander, Commander J. Brewer Welsh, USN, a lithe thirty-seven-year-old with closely cropped brown hair, was on the bridge.

"Captain," the officer of the deck said. "I have a radar target five miles dead ahead."

Captain Welsh was interested but not

alarmed. There was no reason to believe the target in any way posed a danger to the invasion fleet. Carrier aircraft were patrolling the area. They would have reported the presence of any naval force long before the *DeHaven*'s radar picked it up.

Captain Walsh looked at the radar screen.

"Probably a fishing boat of some kind," he opined. "He's about to get a surprise, isn't he?"

He nevertheless reached for the ship-to-ship microphone.

"*McKinley, DeHaven,*" he said.

The USS *Mount McKinley* was the command vessel of the convoy. It carried aboard both the senior Naval officer of the convoy and the senior officer of the Army and Marine Corps troops who were to be landed.

"Go, *DeHaven,*" an officer on the bridge of the *McKinley* replied.

"I have a radar target at about five miles, probably a fishing vessel."

"And?"

"I'm waiting until I have him in sight until I do anything."

"There's some Corsairs overhead. I'll have them take a look, and advise."

"Roger, thank you. *DeHaven* out."

0728 19 October 1950

Two Navy Corsairs approached the *DeHaven* from dead ahead at less than a thousand feet, dipped their wings, and then began to climb.

0729 19 October 1950

"*DeHaven, McKinley*, the Corsairs report it's a junk. I think that they probably woke them up, and they'll get out of the way."

"Thank you, *McKinley*."

0731 19 October 1950

"*McKinley, DeHaven*, I have the junk in sight. Unless they're blind, they have to see us, but they are not changing course. And it looks to me as if she's under power."

"Junks don't have power, *DeHaven*. They are propelled by what are called 'sails.'"

"Thank you so much."

"They'll probably get out of the way when they see more than one vessel headed their way. Advise."

"Will do."

0735 19 October 1950

"*McKinley, DeHaven*, my junk is not changing course."

"Well, we don't want to run over him,

do we? The admiral says to get him to change course."

"Understand. I'll make a run across his bow."

0741 19 October 1950

"*McKinley*, you're not going to believe this, but my junk just hoisted a large American flag. And she is not changing course."

"The admiral does not want the junk to approach the convoy."

"What am I supposed to do, fire a shot across her bow?"

A new voice came over the ship-to-ship.

"*DeHaven*, this is Admiral Feeney. If putting a shot across her bow is necessary, then that's what you should do."

"Aye, aye, sir. Sir, it is my intention to come alongside the vessel and signal an order to her to change course."

"Proceed," the admiral said.

0746 19 October 1950

"*McKinley*, *DeHaven* is alongside the junk. She is under power. A man in what looks like black pajamas has hailed *DeHaven* with a loudspeaker and says he is a Marine major named McCoy and desires to approach *McKinley*. Request guidance."

"*DeHaven*, Admiral Feeney. The junk is

not, repeat not, to approach the *McKinley*. Take whatever action is appropriate."

"Aye, aye, sir."

[Four]
The Bridge, USS *Mount McKinley* (LCC-20)
39 Degrees 34 Minutes North Latitude
128 Degrees 43 Minutes East Longitude
The Sea of Japan
0747 19 October 1950

"I think I know who that is," Major General Edward M. Almond, USA, said to Rear Admiral Ignatius Feeney, USN.

"You what?"

"I suggest you give him approval to approach your ship," Almond went on. "It might prove very interesting."

"You're serious, Ned, aren't you?" Admiral Feeney asked, surprised.

Almond nodded. "Remember the islands in the Flying Fish Channel that were cleared before we got there?" he asked. "Unless I'm mistaken, that's the man who cleared them. OSS."

"OSS? Really?" Rear Admiral Feeney said. He reached for the ship-to-ship microphone. "*DeHaven*, permit the junk to approach the *McKinley*."

Both Navy reconnaissance aircraft and

minesweepers on the scene had reported that there were still enough mines in the approaches to the harbors of both Wonsan and Hamhung to preclude the movement of oceangoing vessels into the harbors.

The invasion fleet, both to conserve fuel and because there was no point in making speed when the anticipated course for the next thirty-six hours was one large circle after another, was moving at ten knots.

Ten knots was still considerably faster than what Admiral Feeney — who, with General Almond, was now on the *McKinley*'s flying bridge — understood the maximum speed of a junk under sail to be, and he was thus more than a little surprised when the junk approached the *McKinley* head-on, made a quick 180-degree turn, and then pulled alongside.

"I'll be damned," Admiral Feeney said. "That junk *is* motorized."

A man wearing black pajamas stood on the forecastle of the junk, holding an electric megaphone in his hand.

"Ahoy, *McKinley*. Can you hear me?"

"Loud and clear," Admiral Feeney said into the microphone of his electric megaphone.

"I have three wounded aboard," the man in the black pajamas called.

"Including Major McCoy, apparently," General Almond said. "Look at his leg."

The left leg of the pajamas was torn off above the knee. A bloody compress was on the upper thigh.

"Is that your OSS man?" Admiral Feeney asked.

Almond nodded. "Admiral, you are looking at the legendary Killer McCoy, U.S. Marine Corps," he said.

"I don't want that junk crashing into the hull," Admiral Feeney said almost to himself, then took the few short steps onto the bridge.

"The admiral is on the bridge!" a talker called out.

Admiral Feeney approached Captain Joseph L. Farmer, USN, the captain of the *McKinley*, and asked, "Have you a minute for me, sir?"

"You have the conn," Captain Farmer said to his executive officer, then followed Feeney out onto the flying bridge.

Admiral Feeney began, "The master of that vessel —"

"Jesus, he's been wounded!" Captain Farmer blurted.

"— reports that he has three wounded aboard. I was wondering what you think of lowering a lifeboat to the junk — not into the water — and transferring the wounded to the lifeboat from the junk as a means of getting them aboard."

"I think we can do that, sir," Captain Farmer said.

He went back onto the bridge.

A piercing whistle and then Captain Farmer's voice came over the ship's loudspeakers a moment later. "Attention all hands. All, repeat all, nonessential personnel will immediately leave the port-side boat deck immediately. Port-side Lifeboat One Crew report to your station immediately. Medical Emergency Team report to port-side Lifeboat One immediately."

The captain came back on the flying bridge.

A much younger voice — that of the talker — repeated the orders he had just broadcast.

The admiral, the general, and the captain watched silently from the flying bridge as the port-side Number One lifeboat's davits swung the lifeboat away from the ship, and then — after an ensign and three white hats got aboard — lowered it slowly toward the sea.

When the lifeboat was even with the forecastle of the junk, the man with the bandage on his upper left thigh threw a line to a white hat in the lifeboat, who hauled on it and pulled the junk slowly sidewards to the lifeboat.

Five men in black pajamas, all Orientals, appeared on the deck of the junk, then

664

began to move three wounded men up onto the forecastle. Two of them had to be carried. The third was able, with help, to make it up the ladder on his feet.

Balancing precariously on the forecastle, they managed to manhandle the two more seriously wounded men into the lifeboat. Then the man who could walk and finally the American jumped into the lifeboat.

The line holding the junk to the lifeboat was cut, and the junk's helmsman turned her away from the *Mount McKinley*.

Electric motors whirred and the lifeboat began to rise against the McKinley's hull, and then was swung inboard.

The American with the bloody compress on his thigh jumped to the deck first.

He winced in pain, then saluted an officer on the deck.

"Permission to board, sir?" he asked.

"Granted," the officer said, visibly surprised.

The man saluted the colors aft.

A Navy doctor and half a dozen Corpsmen began to take the wounded from the lifeboat and to place them on aluminum stretchers.

"How are you, Major McCoy?" General Edward M. Almond asked. "That is not pro forma. What's with your leg?"

McCoy saluted him.

"I took a piece of shrapnel, sir," he said.

"I don't think it's serious."

"Take Major McCoy to sick bay," Almond ordered.

"Sir, with respect, I need to get a message off as soon as I can. Sick bay will have to wait."

"What sort of a message?"

"We lost our radios, sir," McCoy said. "I don't want them mounting a rescue mission when they don't hear from us."

Almond turned to Admiral Feeney.

"The Navy can accommodate the major, can it not?" he asked. "Admiral, this is Major McCoy."

"Welcome aboard, son," Admiral Feeney said. "If you're able to walk, I know the way to the radio room."

"I can walk, sir. Thank you."

McCoy gave the chief radioman the frequency, then eased himself into a plastic upholstered metal chair before a rack of communications equipment. The chief handed him a microphone and headset.

"Fishbase, this is Flying Fish," McCoy said into the microphone. "Fishbase, Flying Fish."

The reply came immediately: "Go, Flying Fish."

"Flying Fish is three clicks as of 0530."

"Understand three clicks as of 0530. What are your coordinates?"

"Aboard a Navy vessel at sea. If Bail Out is under way, cancel. If Bail Out is under way, cancel. Acknowledge."

"Acknowledge cancel Bail Out. Bail Out was just about to launch."

"Who is this?"

"Car Salesman."

"Killer here. Where Fat Kraut?"

"Sasebo."

"Say again?"

"Fat Kraut Sasebo. Big Daddy en route Sasebo."

"What's up?"

"From Big Daddy. Killer will proceed Sasebo ASAP. Acknowledge."

"Acknowledge proceed Sasebo ASAP. What's up?"

"Little Daddy is in Sasebo. Lady Friend bought farm. Fat Kraut carrying bad news."

"Say again?"

"Fat Kraut carrying bad news, Lady Friend bought farm, to Little Daddy in Sasebo."

"Understand Lady Friend bought farm. Where's Beaver?"

"Beaver here."

"Send Beaver Korean Marine. Wait for me. Acknowledge."

"Acknowledge Beaver to wait for you at Korean Marine."

"Contact Wild Bill Junior. Arrange transportation for me Seoul Sasebo. ETA Korean Marine 1200. Acknowledge."

"Acknowledge Killer ETA Korean Marine 1200. Wild Bill Junior to arrange transportation Seoul Sasebo."

"What happened to Lady Friend?"

"Gooney Bird went in on way to Wonsan."

"Advise Big Daddy I'm en route Sasebo. Acknowledge."

"Acknowledge advise Big Daddy Killer en route Sasebo."

"Send replacement crew for Wind on Beaver. We took two KIA, three WIA. Acknowledge."

"Acknowledge replacement crew on Beaver. How Killer?"

"Killer fine. Mind the store, Car Salesman. Flying Fish out."

"Fishbase clear."

McCoy laid the microphone on the desk and took off the headset.

"About the only thing I understood about all that, Major McCoy," General Almond said, "was 'Killer fine.' And that's just not so. You're bleeding all over the linoleum."

He pointed. There was a small puddle of blood on the linoleum under McCoy's chair.

"Can you make it to sick bay under your

own power? Or shall we get you onto a stretcher?" Almond asked.

"I've got to get to Wonsan, sir. I'm all right."

"You're not going anywhere until they have a look at your leg. Clear?"

"Yes, sir."

"Well, there's nothing in there," Lieutenant Warren Warbasse, MC, USNR, said to Major McCoy, who was lying prone on a medical table in sick bay. "And no serious muscle damage that I can see."

"They got lucky," McCoy said. "Hitting something with a mortar from a small boat under way isn't easy. I think I actually saw the round coming in."

"A half inch the other way, and what sliced your thigh would not have bounced off," Dr. Warbasse said.

"Four inches the other way, and I'd be a soprano," McCoy said.

"The sutures I'm going to put in will disappear," Dr. Warbasse said. "There is a danger of infection, of course. The penicillin I'll give you will probably take care of that. You need a day on your back, and when you get up, it will hurt like hell every time you put weight on it."

"I don't have time to spend a day on my back. Can you give me something for the pain that won't turn me into a zombie?"

"I can give you something — reluctantly — that will handle the pain," Dr. Warbasse said as he started the first stitch. "The more you take of it, the more you'll become a zombie."

"Fair enough," McCoy said evenly, then: "Jesus, that hurt!"

"If I don't put these in right, they won't stay in. Understand?"

"May I come in?" Major General Almond asked from the doorway.

Dr. Warbasse looked up from McCoy's thigh.

"Yes, sir," he said.

"How is he?"

"He was very lucky," Dr. Warbasse said. "And what he should do is spend at least a day on his back."

"Unfortunately, Major McCoy is not subject to my orders," Almond said.

Almond held an olive-drab shirt, and trousers and a field jacket, in his hands.

"A present from Al Haig, McCoy," he said. "You're pretty much the same size."

"Thank you, sir. Tell him thank you, please."

As Almond watched, Dr. Warbasse finished the installation of the last of half a dozen sutures, painted the area with a purple antiseptic, covered the sutured area with an adhesive bandage, and then wrapped the leg with gauze.

"If you get off that table, Major," Dr. Warbasse said, "you are doing so against medical advice."

"Thank you, Doctor," McCoy said, and sat up.

Dr. Warbasse prepared a hypodermic and stabbed McCoy three times, twice in the thigh and once in the arm.

"With that much of this stuff in you, if you were so inclined, Major, you could carouse all night with little chance of acquiring a social disease," Dr. Warbasse said. "I will now go get you a bottle of zombie pills."

"Thanks," McCoy said.

When he left the treatment room, Dr. Warbasse left the door open. Almond went to it and closed it.

"You want to tell me what's happened, McCoy?" Almond said. "Officially, or otherwise?"

McCoy did not immediately respond.

"Where were you when this happened?" Almond asked.

"A couple of miles offshore of Chongjin," McCoy said.

"You had been ashore?" Almond asked.

McCoy nodded.

"Doing?"

"Listening to Red Army low-echelon radio chatter," McCoy said.

"And?"

"I don't think the Russians are going to come in, at least now," McCoy said.

"And the Chinese?"

McCoy didn't answer.

"Why do I suspect your analysis of the situation is again not in agreement with that of General Willoughby?"

"The Chinese are going to come in, General," McCoy said. "I think there's probably as many as fifty thousand of them already in North Korea, and I now know there's five, maybe six times that many just across the border waiting to come in."

"Waiting for what?"

"Waiting for the Americans to get close to the Yalu," McCoy said.

"You have anything to substantiate that belief? Something hard?"

"No, sir."

"Nothing that would get General Willoughby to reconsider his analysis?"

"No, sir."

"Inasmuch as General Walker is about to, or already has, taken Pyongyang, the initial purpose of X Corps landing at Wonsan and striking across the peninsula is no longer valid. Under those circumstances, I suspect that I will get orders to strike with all possible speed toward the border. You think there will be Chinese intervention when we get close?"

"Yes, sir. That's what I think they'll do."

"Who have you told of your analysis?"

"I will tell General Pickering when I see him at Sasebo, sir."

"What's he doing at Sasebo?"

"I don't know, sir. Captain Dunwood just told me he's on his way there. It probably has to do with Major Pickering, sir. I think they moved him to the Navy hospital there."

"Who's Captain Dunwood?"

"He commands the Marines we borrowed from First MarDiv, sir. He's at a little base we have at Socho-Ri, on the coast."

"What was that business about a lady?"

"I didn't pick up much more than Major Pickering's girlfriend, the war correspondent, Jeanette Priestly? . . ."

"I know her."

". . . was killed in a plane crash on her way to Wonsan. One of my officers — Master Gunner Zimmerman, 'Fat Kraut' — was somehow involved in finding that out, and went to Sasebo to tell Major Pickering."

"That's tragic," Almond said. "The poor fellow. All that time . . . and when he's finally out of it, they have to tell him . . ."

"Yes, sir. It's a bitch." He paused, then added: "I suspect — I don't know — that's why General Pickering is headed for Sasebo."

"And why does he want you there?"

"I don't know, sir. But he wouldn't have sent for me unless he thought it was important." He reached for Al Haig's trousers and shirt. "Which means, sir, I have to get back aboard the *Wind of Good Fortune*."

"That's that powered junk?"

"Yes, sir. And head for Wonsan. We have a Beaver that will pick me up at the Capital ROK Division airstrip and take me to Seoul. I'll catch a plane there. Maybe a direct flight to Sasebo, if not through Tokyo."

McCoy pushed himself off the surgical table. There was pain, and he winced. He turned his back to Almond and slid the black pajama trousers down, and then, with effort, put his leg into the Army trousers.

"What happened this morning, McCoy? How did you take the hit?"

"Bad luck, sir. We had just gotten aboard the *Wind of Good Fortune* when all of a sudden there was a floodlight on us, and a North Korean — or maybe a Russian — patrol boat out there. We had .50 Brownings fore and aft, and we shot it up pretty quickly. But not until after they got their machine gun — and the damned mortar that got me — into action."

McCoy put on Captain Haig's shirt, then tucked it into the trousers.

"Tell Al thanks, please, sir," he said. "I really didn't want to have to go find a uniform somewhere."

"He will be pleased he could help," Almond said. "You're sure you're all right to get back on the junk?"

"Once I get aboard, I'll be all right, General. I was thinking maybe they could rig a bosun's chair and lower me into her."

"I'm sure they can," Almond said. "Thank you, McCoy."

"No thanks necessary, sir," McCoy said. "I'm just glad they don't shoot the messenger with the bad news anymore."

Ten minutes later, McCoy was lowered without incident in a bosun's chair onto the forecastle of the *Wind of Good Fortune*. As soon as he was aboard and out of the chair, she turned away from the *Mount McKinley* and headed westward toward Wonsan.

"Admiral, how much trouble is it going to be to get a message to the commanding officer of the hospital at Sasebo?" General Almond asked of Rear Admiral Feeney.

"No problem at all. What's the message?"

Almond handed him a sheet of paper fresh from Captain Al Haig's portable typewriter.

URGENT
UNCLASSIFIED

COMMANDING OFFICER, NAVY HOSPITAL, SASEBO

TO BE DELIVERED TO BRIGADIER GENERAL FLEMING PICKERING, USMC, AS SOON AS POSSIBLE

PERSONAL MESSAGE FROM MAJOR GENERAL ALMOND, X CORPS

PERSONAL MESSAGE BEGINS

DEAR FLEMING,

YOU KNOW WHERE I AM. I HAVE JUST MET WITH MAJOR MCCOY, WHO IS EN ROUTE TO SASEBO PER YOUR ORDERS.

HE GAVE ME SOME DISTRESSING INFORMATION WHICH I AM SURE HE WILL SHARE WITH YOU. IT IS A GREAT PITY THAT HE HAS NOTHING SOLID ENOUGH TO BACK IT UP TO FORCE A CHANGE OF ANALYSIS BY THOSE WHO HAVE TO BE CONVINCED. I AM CONVINCED HE IS RIGHT, BUT THAT DOESN'T MATTER, DOES IT?

MAJOR MCCOY IS TRAVELING AGAINST MEDICAL ADVICE, HAVING SUFFERED WOUNDS IN AN EARLY MORNING ENGAGEMENT TODAY. HE DID THE NEXT THING TO REFUSING MEDICAL TREATMENT IN ORDER TO COMPLETE HIS MISSION AND COMPLY WITH YOUR ORDER THAT HE GO TO SASEBO.

INASMUCH AS I STRONGLY SUSPECT THAT HE WILL NOT MENTION THIS TO YOU, AND THUS IT WILL NOT BECOME A MATTER OF OFFICIAL RECORD, I TELL YOU SO THAT HE MAY AT LEAST BE AWARDED THE PURPLE HEART.

IT SHOULD GO WITHOUT SAYING THAT I AM DELIGHTED THAT YOUR SON IS BACK FROM HIS UNIMAGINABLE ORDEAL.

WHERE DO THESE FINE YOUNG MEN COME FROM?

I LOOK FORWARD TO SEEING YOU SOON. BEST PERSONAL REGARDS.

NED

END PERSONAL MESSAGE FROM GEN ALMOND TO GEN PICKERING

XIV

**Fishbase Communications Hootch
Socho-Ri, South Korea
0747 19 October 1950**

"Cancel Bail Out, sir?" Staff Sergeant Al Preston, USMC, asked just as soon as Captain Dunwood had taken off his headset and turned from the radio.

Staff Sergeant Preston was wearing black pajamas and a black headband, and his face was smeared with black and dark brown grease. He had a Thompson .45-ACP-caliber submachine gun slung from his right shoulder. A canvas bag bulging with spare Thompson magazines and hand grenades hung from his left shoulder.

"Bail Out will not be necessary. Major McCoy is aboard 'a Navy vessel at sea,'" Dunwood said. "He couldn't say which one in the clear, but more than likely one of the ships carrying First MarDiv to Wonsan."

"What did they do, lose their radio?" Preston asked.

I really can't tell, Dunwood thought, *if Preston is relieved that Bail Out has been*

678

canceled, or disappointed.

"That, too, I'm sure. Something went wrong," Dunwood said. "Major McCoy didn't say what, but he said there are two KIA and three WIA. We're to send a replacement crew for the *Wind of Good Fortune* to Wonsan. On the Beaver."

"Sir, is there any reason I couldn't get in on that?"

"You surprise me, Preston," Dunwood said. "Here you are, a Marine with over six years' combat experience, and a staff sergeant. You're supposed to be bright enough to know that volunteering is something smart Marines just don't do."

"Sir, this is different," Preston said a little uncomfortably.

"How so?" Dunwood asked.

"This isn't like the regular Corps, sir. You know?"

Preston gestured around the communications hootch.

"You mean because of the refrigerator?" Dunwood asked innocently.

The hootch — because of the generator powering the radios, and because there was always an officer or senior noncom on duty — also housed a bright white Kenmore refrigerator that they had flown in on the Beaver from The House in Seoul.

"The refrigerator?" Preston asked, confused.

"You're right," Dunwood said. "I don't think even the commanding general of First MarDiv has a refrigerator full of Asahi beer."

"I wasn't talking about the refrigerator, sir," Preston said. "Jesus!"

"I'm a little confused, Preston. What are you talking about?"

"Sir, this isn't the Pusan Perimeter, is it?"

"No, it's not. I can't ever remember getting a cold beer when we were in the perimeter. Or, for that matter, a warm one."

Preston looked at him in bafflement for a long moment. Finally, he asked, "Sir, is there any particular reason the captain is pulling the sergeant's chain?"

"Oddly enough, Preston, there is."

"What's that, sir?"

"It can't go any further than this hootch," Dunwood said.

"Yes, sir."

"I've been thinking of volunteering myself," Dunwood said.

"For what, sir?"

"What I have been thinking is that sooner or later, they're going to send us back to the 5th Marines, and I don't really want to go back."

"I've been wondering how long this detail will last," Preston said.

"And I really don't want to go back to

the 5th Marines," Dunwood went on. "Where one of two things would happen. They'd bring the company back up to strength, run us through some kind of training cycle, and put us back on the line. It would be the perimeter all over again. Or the war will be over, and they'll bring the company back up to strength, run us through a longer training cycle, and it would be Camp Pendleton all over again."

"Yeah," Preston said. "I've been thinking about that, too. So what are you thinking of volunteering for?"

"The CIA," Dunwood said.

"How would you do that?"

"I don't really know. What I do know is that Major McCoy and Gunner Zimmerman are Marines — good ones, they were both Marine Raiders — and they're in the CIA. And we work for General Pickering, who's a Marine. I don't know how it works, but I'm really thinking seriously about asking Major McCoy what he thinks."

Sergeant Preston looked at him for a long time, expressionless, before he finally asked, "Sir, is there any way I could get in on that?"

"I'm not pulling your chain now, Preston. I'm serious about this."

"I sort of like this operation," Preston said.

"Major McCoy — I just told you — said he took two KIA and three WIA. To which his reaction was, send a replacement crew. You like that?"

"I'm not saying this is fun, sir. Don't get me wrong. But I know what we're doing here is important. I suppose when we were running around the perimeter saving the Army's ass, that was important, too. But if I'm going to get blown away, I'd rather it was because I fucked up, not because I was trying to un-fuck-up what some stranger's fucked up. You know what I mean?"

"Yes, I do," Dunwood said.

"What I really like about this operation is that the major and Gunner Zimmerman get things done. And they tell you what to do and don't stand over your shoulder making sure you do it. Shit, when the gunner left here after we found that lady's crispy corpse, all he said was, 'Take over, Captain Dunwood.' "

" 'Crispy corpse'? Jesus Christ, Preston! Show a little respect!"

"I wasn't being disrespectful, sir. That's what it was. When we put them bodies in the shelter halves, they was crisp. Like a barbecued pig."

"You know what I thought when the gunner left me in charge?" Dunwood asked, as much of himself as Preston. "I was happy, proud, like a second lieutenant getting his first platoon. And then I thought I must be crazy. I'm not a real Marine. I'm a weekend warrior, a goddamned car salesman — where do you think Major McCoy got Car Salesman as my call sign? Gunner Zimmerman is fat and German, and he's Fat Kraut, and I'm Car Salesman, because that's all I really am, a car salesman that got called up —"

"You're a Marine, sir, a goddamned good one," Preston interrupted. "Don't tell me different. I was in the perimeter with you from day fucking one until they pulled us out."

"What I was about to say," Dunwood went on after a moment, "was that the proof of that was that here I was, a captain, taking orders from a master gunner, and it didn't bother me at all. And then I realized I liked being here, doing what we're doing, a hell of a lot more than I ever liked selling cars."

"How the hell do you think I feel?" Preston asked. "Christ, sir, I was on *recruiting duty*. One minute telling some pimply-faced high school kid that once he gets to put on dress blues, he won't be able to handle all the pussy that'll be coming his way, and the next minute telling his mother that Sonny Boy not only will have a chance to further his education in the crotch, but will receive, just about every day, moral counseling from a clergyman of his choice of faith."

Dunwood laughed out loud.

"Are you suggesting, Sergeant Preston, that when I raise the question of CIA service to Major McCoy, I should mention your name?"

Preston considered that for a long moment.

"No, sir," he said finally. "I don't want you to do that."

"Change your mind, all of a sudden?"

"If the rest of the guys heard I did that, they'd all be pissed. I can't think of a one of them that really wants to go back to the 5th Marines. What I'll do, if you tell me what Major McCoy tells you, and it looks at least possible, is go see him myself."

Dunwood didn't reply.

"Or . . ." Preston had a second thought. "How much time do we have before the major gets back and you talk to him?"

"I have no idea when he'll be back. Or Gunner Zimmerman."

"I can ask the guys, who wants to go back to the crotch, and who wants to stay here . . . and get in the CIA official. And then everybody who wants the CIA can go see the major together."

"All right," Dunwood said. "I'll let you know what Major McCoy says."

"What about me going as replacement crew on the boat?"

"Take someone with you — another Marine. The rest Koreans. If Major McCoy or Gunner Zimmerman says you can go on the *Wind of Good Fortune*, it's okay with me. But get that grease off your face and get out of the pajamas before you go. You better take a replacement radio, too."

"Aye, aye, sir," Staff Sergeant Preston said.

[Two]
Office of the Chief, Awards Branch
Office of the Chief of Naval Operations
Washington, D.C.
1640 19 October 1950

The duty day at CNO/CAB ended at 1600, but when Commander John T. Davis, USN, went to the office door of Captain Archie M. Young, USN, the chief, and found him still hard at work at his desk, he was not at all surprised.

There were gold aviator's wings on Captain Young's breast, and submariner's gold dolphins on Commander Davis's breast. They pinned them on each day — as they had every right to do — even though Commander Davis had left the silent service four years before, and Captain Young had last sat in a cockpit eight years before.

Both had "busted the physical" and been

disqualified for further service in the air/beneath the sea. Captain Young had told his career counselor in the Bureau of Personnel that he would really rather find anything else useful to do around the Navy than be a grounded aviator at a Naval air station or aboard a carrier, and Commander Davis had told his career counselor that he would rather do anything but stand on a wharf somewhere and watch a boat head out on patrol.

Neither wanted a berth in the surface Navy, either. That didn't leave much — unless they wanted to go back to school and get a law degree, or something along that line — but supply and personnel. They had each given personnel a shot, and to their surprise learned that it was really not as boring as they thought it would be — actually, sometimes it was a hell of a challenge — and that they were very good at their new specialty.

Today, Commander Davis thought, was one of those times when it appeared there was going to be a hell of a challenge.

Captain Young raised his eyes from his desk and took off his glasses.

"What have you got, Jack, that has kept you from rushing home to a cold martini?"

"I thought I would seek your wise guidance on this one, sir," Davis said. "Commander MAG-33 has been heard from."

He walked into the office and laid the message from Lieutenant Colonel William C. Dunn on Captain Young's desk.

"I'll be damned," Young said when he'd read the message, then read from it: " 'The undersigned is unable to comply.' "

"What the hell does that mean?"

"Start out, Commander, by having faith in your fellow man," Young said. "It may mean just what he says. He is unable to comply. That is different, wouldn't you agree, from 'unwilling to comply'?"

"Yes, sir."

"And then, Commander, we must consider the circumstances. Actually, these circumstances should be considered first. The President has spoken. He thinks this officer should be awarded the Navy Cross. He *desires* that this officer be awarded the Navy Cross. What the President of the United States *desires* has the force and effect of a lawful order."

"Yes, sir," Commander Davis said, smiling.

"Furthermore, this jarhead obviously deserves a medal. Jesus Christ, he was shot down, and then evaded capture . . . three months?"

"About that, sir."

"Furthermore, when the Commander-in-Chief desires something, he desires it right then. He is not interested — and indeed, should not be — with administrative problems that get in the way of his desires. Agreed?"

"Yes, sir."

"Given (a) and (b) above, we cannot let a little thing like a *misplaced* citation get in the way of our carrying out what is clearly our duty, can we?" Captain Young asked reasonably.

"No, sir, we cannot."

"Why don't we ask Harrison to step in here for a minute, Commander?"

"Excellent idea, sir," Commander Davis said, and walked out of the office.

He returned a moment later with Chief Personnelman Robert C. Harrison, a slight thirty-five-year-old with eighteen years' naval service and a perfectly manicured pencil-line mustache.

"Yes, sir?" Harrison asked.

"Chief, we have a small problem that requires your literary skills," Captain Young said.

"Commander Davis showed me the TWX, Captain," Harrison said.

"Since the citation has been *misplaced,* Chief," Captain Young said, "we're going to have to duplicate what it must have said here so we don't keep the CNO — and indeed, the President — waiting. You take my meaning?"

"Yes, sir."

"Have you got your pad?"

"Yes, sir."

"Let's go over this together," Captain Young said. "What do we know, Commander Davis?"

"We know the major was shot down, sir."

"Okay. Let's go with that. To get shot down, he had to go up, right?"

"Yes, sir."

"Despite severe weather conditions that in other circumstances would not have permitted flight operations, Major . . . What's his name?"

"Pickering, sir, Major Malcolm S., USMCR," Harrison furnished.

"Hereafter Pickering," Captain Young went on, ". . . took off from the USS *Badoeng Strait* to render air support' — make that 'desperately needed air support' — 'to U.S. Marine forces then engaged in combat' — make that 'outnumbered U.S. Marine forces' and 'fierce combat' . . ."

"Sir, I get the idea," Chief Harrison said. "Why don't you give me the basics and let me fill in the blanks?"

"Okay. He was shot down while doing this."

"Wounded?"

"I don't think so, but he almost certainly suffered painful injuries making the crash landing. . . ."

"Because he crash-landed the airplane away from civilian houses?" Chief Harrison asked.

"Good thought, Harrison!" Captain Young agreed. "And if he got shot down, the plane had to be on fire, right?"

"Got it," Harrison said. "Then what?"

"While he was supporting the troops on the ground, he encountered fierce antiaircraft fire. . . ."

"Which, at great risk, he ignored?"

"Right."

"Then what?"

"He spent the next . . . what?"

"Find out when he was shot down and when he was rescued. That many days. 'Avoiding the determined efforts of the enemy to capture him,' et cetera. . . ."

"Got it, sir."

"We need that now, Harrison."

"Aye, aye, sir."

"Length is a criterion here, too. Make sure that the citation fills a sheet of paper, and that the signature block goes on the next page," Captain Young said.

"Signature blocks sometimes get lost, sir, right?"

"I guess they do," Captain Young said.

"Take me thirty or forty minutes, sir."

"Good man, Harrison!"

[Three]
U.S. Naval Hospital
U.S. Navy Base, Sasebo
Sasebo, Japan
2205 19 October 1950

Security for U.S. Naval Hospital, Sasebo — the guards at the gate and around the perimeter — was provided by a five-man detachment of U.S. Marines who set up and supervised the system, using sailors from the hospital staff — Corpsmen, others — assigned to "Shore Patrol" duty on a roster basis to man the various posts.

Sergeant Victor C. Wandowski, USMC, very rarely spent any time at all at Post Number One, which was the guard shack at the main gate, but tonight was an exception. He had been given a heads-up that a Marine major, named McCoy, was going to arrive at the hospital either sometime tonight or — probably — early tomorrow morning. The major was to be sent immediately to see the medical officer of the day, and the hospital commander, Captain Schermer himself, was to be notified of Major McCoy's arrival, no matter what the hour.

Under these circumstances, Sergeant Wandowski had decided, it behooved him to be at the main gate around 2200. He knew there was a courier flight arriving at the airfield around 2130, and it seemed likely this Major McCoy would be on it.

When he saw an Air Force jeep approaching just after 2200, Sergeant Wandowski congratulated himself on his foresight. If one of the swabbie pecker-checkers fucked up meeting this major — which was very likely — it would have been his ass in the crack, not theirs.

"I'll handle this one," he said to the swabbie on duty, and stepped out of the guard shack, crisply raising his hand to stop the jeep.

An Air Force buck sergeant was driving the jeep. If his passenger was a Marine major, he goddamned sure didn't look like it.

He was coverless, insignia-less, and wearing an Army field jacket.

Whatever it was, it did not rate a salute, and Sergeant Wandowski did not offer one.

"What can I do for you?" he demanded.

"You can tell me where I can find Brigadier General Pickering," McCoy said.

"Never heard of him," Sergeant Wandowski said, both truthfully and as sort of a challenge.

"Trust me, Sergeant," McCoy said. "He's somewhere around here. How about getting on the horn and calling the officer of the guard and asking?"

"I'm the officer of the guard," Wandowski said.

"Then call the officer of the day," McCoy said patiently.

"Can I ask who you are?"

"My name is McCoy," McCoy said.

"You're *Major* McCoy?"

McCoy nodded.

Sergeant Wandowski was unable to accept that.

"Sir, have you got any identification?"

"Get on the horn — and right now, Sergeant," McCoy said icily. "Call the OD and tell him to get word to General Pickering that Major McCoy is at the gate."

There was something about Major McCoy's tone of voice that made Sergeant Wandowski decide that he really didn't have to check the major's ID card.

He picked up the telephone, and had the operator connect him with the commanding officer's quarters.

"Hold the major there, Sergeant," Captain Schermer ordered. "Someone will be there shortly."

Captain Schermer's Navy-gray 1950 Ford station wagon rolled up to the main gate several minutes later. A Marine captain, who looked like a circus strong man, jumped out of the front passenger seat and walked quickly to where Sergeant Wandowski was standing by the Air Force jeep. Sergeant Wandowski saluted.

The Marine captain returned the salute.

"Good evening, sir," he said.

Major McCoy, shaking his head, returned the salute.

"The general's compliments, sir," the Marine captain went on. "The general hopes that you had a pleasant flight, sir, and asks that you join him in his car."

Sergeant Wandowski took a closer look at the Ford station wagon. There was a man in the backseat from whose collar points and epaulets gleamed the silver stars of a brigadier general. Sergeant Wandowski popped to attention and saluted. The general returned the salute.

"Thank you, Captain," McCoy said. "I would be delighted to do so." He got out of the Air Force jeep, said, "Thanks for the ride, Sergeant," to the driver, and walked toward the Ford. The captain ran ahead of him, pulled the rear door of the station wagon open, and stood to attention as Major McCoy got in the back beside the brigadier general. Then he ran around the front and got in beside the driver.

As the station wagon drove away, Sergeant Wandowski saluted again. The captain returned his salute.

"What the hell was that all about?" Brigadier General Pickering asked.

"Considering the circumstances," Captain George F. Hart said, "I thought a little levity was in order."

"What circumstances, George?" McCoy asked.

"Where should I start?" Hart said. "For openers, Banning showed up with a hair up his ass, and the boss had to pull it out of him that Milla's in the hospital in Charleston with breast cancer."

"Jesus Christ!"

"You could have phrased that with a bit more tact, and substantially more respect for a senior officer," Pickering said. "But let's start with you, Ken. How are you?"

"Fine, sir."

"Then you weren't wounded very early this morning?"

"How'd you hear about that?" McCoy asked, genuinely surprised. "I took a little shrapnel hit, nothing serious."

"We shall shortly find out how accurate a statement that is," Pickering said.

"Sir?"

Pickering pointed out the windshield. McCoy looked and saw they were approaching a three-story building. An illuminated arrow pointed to the emergency entrance.

"General, I just had this thing bandaged. . . ."

"And now the hospital commander himself is going to have a look at it," Pickering said.

Two hospital Corpsmen, a nurse, and a gurney were waiting outside the emergency room door.

"I don't need that," McCoy protested.

"I had to talk him out of sending an ambulance to the airport," Hart said.

One hospital Corpsman and the nurse came quickly to the station wagon. The second Corpsman pushed the gurney up to it.

McCoy winced when he got out of the station wagon. Pickering saw it.

"I don't need that," McCoy said. "Thanks anyway."

"Get on the gurney, Ken," Pickering said. "That's not a friendly suggestion. The response I expect is 'Aye, aye, sir.' "

"Aye, aye, sir," McCoy said.

He winced again as the Corpsmen helped him onto the stretcher.

"Where'd you get it, Ken?" Hart asked.

"Left leg, four inches from the family jewels," McCoy said, and then remembered the nurse, and added, "Sorry."

The nurse ignored the apology.

"Where were you first treated, Major?" she asked. "Forward aid station?"

"In the sick bay of the *Mount McKinley*," McCoy answered, then made the connection. "Oh. What did General Almond do? Send a message?"

"He suspected — correctly, obviously —

that you might not mention what had happened to you," Pickering said.

Captain F. Howard Schermer, MC, USN, looked up from his examination of McCoy's now-unbandaged upper thigh.

"Couldn't have done it better myself," he said, then stepped away from the table and made a gesture to the nurse to apply fresh bandages.

"I presume you've been given some penicillin, Major?"

McCoy reached into the pocket of Al Haig's Army OD shirt, took out a folded sheet of paper, and handed it to the doctor.

"The doctor gave me this as I was walking out of sick bay, sir," he said.

"Walking or limping, Major?" Captain Schermer asked. He read the note. "Well, you're full of penicillin. Did he give you anything for the pain?"

McCoy went back in the shirt pocket, came out with a small vial of pills, and handed it to Captain Schermer.

"How many of these have you taken? And when?"

"None, sir."

"You're a real tough Marine, are you? Or maybe a masochist? That has to hurt like hell every time you move."

McCoy didn't reply.

Dr. Schermer walked to a sink and came back with a paper water cup.

"Take two of these now," he said, and turned to the nurse. "See that he gets one every four hours. Make sure his chart says 'do not wake to administer.' And start penicillin again in the morning."

"Yes, sir," the nurse said.

Schermer turned to Pickering.

"Well, General, the major gets at least ninety-six hours in bed," he said. "At least forty-eight of which he should spend offering prayers of gratitude that whatever hit him didn't go an inch deeper. Or four inches higher." He looked at McCoy. "I said take two of those, Major."

"Sir, could I hold off until I can call my wife? She's in Tokyo. I don't want to sound like a zombie."

"Which brings us to Mrs. McCoy," Dr. Schermer said. "Had you planned to tell your wife about your leg, Major?"

"Nothing to tell," McCoy said.

"I think she'll be just a little curious when she sees that bandaged leg," Dr. Schermer said.

"She's not going to see it, sir."

"Ernie's here, Ken," Pickering said.

"She's here?"

"She came to see Pick," Pickering said.

Schermer added, "And a combination of the train ride down here, seeing Major

Pickering, and learning of Miss Priestly's death almost — I say almost — caused her to lose the baby."

"Oh, shit!"

"At the moment, her condition ranges from stable to improving slightly," Dr. Schermer said.

"I want to see her," McCoy said.

"I am wondering what her reaction will be to learning she almost lost her husband," Dr. Schermer said.

"She's a pretty tough girl," Pickering said.

"I noticed," Schermer said.

"Ken," Pickering said, "Pick took Jeanette's death pretty badly."

"I suppose," McCoy said.

"Dr. Schermer thought, and I agree, that in addition to her own worries, Ernie didn't need to be any more upset by him. So he's on his way to the States."

"He was that bad?" McCoy asked.

"He needs a lot of rest, Major. Physically and emotionally. He wasn't going to get much emotional rest here — sending him to the States, we hope, will sort of close a door on what happened to him here — and the hospital at San Diego has the facilities to take better care of him than we can here."

"I guess that answers my question, doesn't it?"

"What he did, Ken," Pickering said, "when he finally broke down, was start to cry. And he couldn't stop. And since he didn't want Ernie, or George, or Zimmerman, or me, to see him crying, that made it worse."

"A vicious emotional circle, Major," Captain Schermer said. "We got it under control here, temporarily, with medicine, but what Major Pickering needs is a lot of time with a good psychiatrist, and they've got better ones in San Diego."

"And we haven't told Ernie about this yet, either," Pickering said.

"Jesus H. Christ!"

"Your call, Major," Dr. Schermer said. "How do we deal with your wife? If you think a telephone call would be better, if you think learning that you've been wounded would upset her even more . . . ."

"I'm not going to be wheeled into her room on a gurney," McCoy said.

"Can you walk?"

"And I want to go in alone," McCoy said. "And not in Al Haig's Army pants and shirt."

"Is that where that came from?" Pickering asked, chuckling. "Doctor, Captain Haig is General Almond's aide-de-camp."

"There's an officers' sales store in the hospital," Dr. Schermer said. "If you will agree to be rolled there in a wheelchair — and from there to your wife's room?"

"Deal," McCoy said. "That is, if General Pickering will loan me enough money to buy a uniform."

"I think that can be worked out," Pickering said.

[Four]

Major Kenneth R. McCoy sat with a white hospital blanket over his knees in a wheelchair in a small dressing cubicle in the officers' sales store. He was waiting for his new uniform trousers to be taken in an inch at the waist, and for them to be provided with precisely the correct crotch-to-cuff length. While he was waiting, he was giving serious, just about completely futile, thought about what bright and witty comment, or comments, he would make to his wife when he walked into her room.

He had just about decided that he was not going to be able to come up with something useful when his reverie was interrupted by Captain George F. Hart coming into the cubicle with a dozen roses.

"Where the hell did you get those?" McCoy asked.

"It wasn't easy," Hart said. "A lesser dog robber than myself probably would have had to settle for one of those miniature trees —"

"Bonsai," McCoy furnished.

"— of which the Japanese seem so fond."

"Thanks, George."

"On the other hand, maybe a bonsai tree would have been better," Hart said. "The roses are going to wilt. The bonsai would last for the next century, as a souvenir of this unexpected encounter."

A Japanese seamstress pushed the curtain aside, handed McCoy the trousers, and then folded her arms over her breast, obviously intending to see how well she had done her job.

"Would you please wait outside for a minute?" McCoy said to her.

Her eyes widened when she heard the faultless Japanese. She bowed and backed out of the dressing cubicle.

"That always bugs me," Hart said. "They're always surprised as hell when one of us speaks Japanese, but a hell of a lot of them speak English."

"That's because we're barbarians, George," McCoy said. He handed Hart the hospital blanket, then started to put his left leg in the trousers. He winced.

"You need some help with that?" Hart asked.

"They are surprised when we use indoor

plumbing, take showers, and don't eat with our fingers," McCoy went on as if he hadn't heard the offer of help.

He got the right leg mostly inside the trousers, and then, awkwardly, got out of the wheelchair and pulled them up. He tucked his shirttail in, then pulled up the zipper and closed the belt.

"Hand me the field scarf, please," he asked, pointing to the necktie hanging from a hook.

Hart handed it to him, and McCoy turned around to face the mirror and worked the field scarf under his shirt collar.

"That hurt. I was better off before I let the doc talk me into the wheelchair."

"What did you do on the plane?" Hart asked.

"Planes," McCoy corrected him. "The Beaver from Wonsan to Seoul, and it hurt to move when I got out of that. Then a C-54 to Pusan. I walked up and down the aisle in that — it was the courier plane, full of chair warmers giving me dirty looks because I was wearing Al Haig's shirt and pants — and it didn't hurt — or hurt less — when I got off it. And I walked — not far — around Pusan to keep it from getting stiff until I got on a Navy Gooney Bird that brought me here. Hospital plane, full of wounded Marines. I walked up and down the aisle of that one, too. And I was doing pretty good until I got here. Now it hurts like hell."

"Moving pulls on the sutures," Hart said.

"Thank you, Dr. Hart. I had no idea what was making me hurt."

He pulled on a tunic, examined himself in the mirror, then turned away from it.

"I think I'll pass on the wheelchair," he said.

"Not only did you give your word as an officer and gentleman, but Ernie's room is way to hell and gone across the hospital."

"Well, maybe I can ride part of the way," McCoy said, and carefully lowered himself into the wheelchair.

Outside the room with the sign "McCoy, Mrs. Ernestine NO VISITORS," Hart took the roses from McCoy's lap and held them while McCoy got out of the wheelchair and painfully moved his leg around. Then, when McCoy nodded, Hart handed him the roses and pushed open the heavy door.

"That will be all, Captain Hart, thank you," McCoy said, and walked into the room.

Ernie was in bed, with the back raised, reading a book. She looked up when she saw him.

"You apparently can't read, Major," she said after a long moment. "The sign says no visitors."

"What are you reading?"

"A novel. *The Egyptian.*"

"Is it any good?"

"It is not about Korea or childbearing," Ernie said. "What's with the roses?"

He walked to the bed and handed them to her.

If I limped, she didn't seem to notice.

"Knowing you as I do, these were somebody else's idea," Ernie said.

"Hart's," McCoy admitted. "You almost got a bonsai tree."

"Are you going to put your arms around me, or I am that repulsive in my bloated condition?"

He leaned over the bed and put his arms around her.

"Oh, Ken, I've missed you!" she said into his neck.

"Me, too, baby," he said.

"How much do you know?" Ernie asked, still speaking into his neck.

"I know it was a damned fool thing to do, taking a train down here," he said.

"I almost lost it," she said. "But I had to see Pick."

"I know."

She let him go, and sort of pushed him away.

"Okay. Now what's wrong with you?" she asked.

"Nothing's wrong with me," he said.

"You're as pale as a sheet, and there's something wrong with your leg," she said.

"I took a little piece of shrapnel," he said.

"Is that why you're walking that way?"

"What way?"

"Ken, is that why you're walking that way?"

"I suppose."

"You want to lie down with me?"

"I want to, but is it smart?"

She shifted herself to the far side of the narrow bed, then patted the near side.

He very carefully got into the bed beside her, but was unable to do so without wincing several times.

"I don't think this is going to work," he said.

"You want to feel him or her? Him or her just kicked me again."

"Is that good or bad?"

She took his hand and guided it to her stomach.

"Jesus!" he said. "Does it do that all the time?"

"Him or her does that frequently," Ernie said. "Do not call him or her 'it.'"

"Yes, ma'am."

Their eyes met again. He moved his hand from her stomach to her face.

"My God, I love you so much," he said.

"It took you long enough to say it," she said.

The door swung open, and Captain F. Howard Schermer, MC, USN, marched in, followed by a middle-aged, gray-haired, short and stocky nurse whose badge identified her as Commander J. V. Stenten, NC, USN, Chief Nursing Services, and Brigadier General Fleming Pickering, USMCR.

"When I told you, Major McCoy," Captain Schermer said, "that you would have to spend at least the next four days in bed, I really had a bed of your own in mind."

McCoy, looking guilty, started to swing his legs out of bed.

"Belay that!" Captain Schermer ordered.

McCoy stopped moving.

"How bad is he, Doctor?" Ernie asked.

"He has been sewn up," Dr. Schermer said. "If he does what he's ordered to do, in three weeks or a month he should be as good as new."

"He very seldom does what he's ordered to do," Ernie said.

"So General Pickering has been telling me," Dr. Schermer said.

"Is there any reason another bed can't be brought in here for him?" Ernie said. "I'll see he does what he's told to do."

"It is against both regulation and policy," Dr. Schermer said.

"That wasn't her question, Captain

Schermer," Pickering said.

"Doctor, the sumo bed?" Commander Stenten asked.

"You're one step ahead of me again, Commander Stenten," Captain Schermer said. He turned to Pickering. "What I was thinking, General, was that if, in contravention of regulation and policy, we rolled another bed in here for Major McCoy" — he pointed across the room — "the first thing either or both of them would do the minute the door was closed would be to push the beds close to each other. Neither of them should be (a) on their feet and (b) pushing furniture around. This applies even more to Major McCoy, since he is about to take the medicine for pain prescribed, which is certain to make him more than a little groggy."

"Will you behave, Ken?" Pickering asked.

Captain Schermer ordered: "Get the bed, Commander."

"Aye, aye, sir," Chief of Nursing Services Stenten said, and went to the telephone on Ernie's bedside table. She dialed a number and then issued several orders of her own: "Chief, this is Commander Stenten. Get the sumo bed out of the attic. Bring it, now, to 308 in the Maternity Ward, together with two new mattresses and linen." She hung up, then turned to Captain Schermer. "On the way, sir."

"As a matter of historical interest," Captain Schermer said, "when we took over this hospital after the last war, we found that it was equipped to handle sumo wrestlers in need of medical attention. Some of them weigh well over two hundred kilograms — more than four hundred pounds — and they apparently didn't fit in standard Japanese hospital beds. I think these two should both fit comfortably into it."

"Thank you," Pickering said.

"But I think I should tell you, Major," Commander Stenten said, "that if you don't behave, you will almost instantly find yourself in a single bed in Ward F-7, where we care for those suffering from what is euphemistically called 'social disease.' "

"Commander Stenten, Major," Captain Schermer said, "is more or less affectionately called, behind her back, of course, 'The Dragon Lady.' Don't cross her."

[Five]
Supreme Headquarters, United Nations
  Command
The Dai Ichi Building
Tokyo, Japan
0900 21 October 1950

As they started down the corridor to the office of the Supreme Commander, Brigadier

709

General Fleming Pickering, USMCR, caught the arm of Colonel Edward Banning, USMC, who stopped and looked at him.

"When we march in there, Ed, we salute," Pickering said. "The Army salutes indoors."

"Yes, sir," Banning said. "I remember."

Pickering waved him down the corridor.

In the outer office, Colonel Sidney L. Huff, MacArthur's senior aide-de-camp, stood up when Pickering and Banning walked in.

"Good morning, General," he said.

"How are you, Sid?" Pickering said. "You remember Ed Banning, don't you?"

"It's been a long time, Colonel," Huff said, and put out his hand.

Neither Pickering nor Banning thought his smile looked very sincere.

"The Supreme Commander will see you now, General. He's been expecting you."

"Not for long, certainly, Sid," Pickering said. "You said nine o'clock, and Banning and I stood out in the corridor for fifteen minutes looking at his very expensive Rolex until it was oh eight fifty-nine fifty-five."

"Yes, sir," Huff said.

He opened the right of the double doors to MacArthur's office and announced, "General Pickering, sir."

Pickering saw that Major General Charles M. Willoughby was in the office, sitting in an armchair by a coffee table.

"Come on in, Fleming," MacArthur called.

The two Marines marched in, stopped eighteen inches from MacArthur's desk, and saluted.

"Good morning, sir," Pickering said. "Thank you for seeing me on such short notice."

"It's always a pleasure to see you, as I've told you time and again. Will you have some coffee?"

"Yes, thank you. General, you remember Colonel Banning, don't you?"

"Yes, of course," MacArthur said. "Good to see you again, Colonel. And you remember General Willoughby, of course?"

"Yes, sir, I do," Banning said.

Willoughby gave Banning his hand but didn't say anything.

"This is fortuitous, General," Pickering said to Willoughby. "I was hoping to get a couple of minutes of your time this morning."

"I'm at your disposal, General," Willoughby said.

"Thank you," Pickering said. "The reason I asked to see you, sir, was to introduce — reintroduce? — Colonel Banning to you as my deputy."

"What does that make him, General?" Willoughby asked. "His title, I mean?"

Pickering chuckled. "General, General Smith and I got a laugh out of that, too, in Washington, when he made the appointment. General Smith asked, 'If Colonel Banning is going to be Deputy to the Deputy Director of the CIA for Asia, what are we going to call his number two, when he inevitably appoints one? The Deputy to the Deputy to the Deputy Director?'"

MacArthur chuckled.

"Obviously, the nomenclature on your manning chart needs some work. But Banning is obviously a sound choice for the job, whatever the title, and I look forward to working with you again, Colonel, and I'm sure General Willoughby is similarly pleased."

"Thank you, sir," Banning said.

"Speaking of intelligence, Fleming," MacArthur said, "I got several interesting bits of intelligence just now by officer courier from Ned Almond — on an Interoffice Memorandum form, which also seems a bit incongruous, with Ned's office right now being on the *Mount McKinley* and mine here — which I really wanted to talk to you about."

"Yes, sir?"

"Ned said that he'd run into your man McCoy — more about that in a moment — and that McCoy had told him it is his belief that the Russians will not enter this war, but that the Chinese certainly will."

It was a question as well as a statement.

"If Major McCoy said anything like that — and I don't doubt that he did — it was unofficial, out of channels, and if the rank difference were not so great, I'd say between friends. That was not the CIA speaking."

"General Almond took pains to make sure I understood that," MacArthur said. "McCoy, he said, admitted that he had absolutely nothing concrete on which to base this conclusion. But your man McCoy obviously impressed Ned to the point where Ned thought he should pass it on to me. And I would be grateful to learn what you think."

"General," Pickering said, "unofficially, out of channels, and between friends — if I may so presume — and absolutely not as a statement, or even an opinion, of the CIA, I'd bet on McCoy."

"My sources, General Pickering," Willoughby said coldly, "have turned up nothing that suggests that either the Chinese or the Soviets are coming in."

"Which I find disappointing," MacArthur said. He stopped when he saw the look on Willoughby's face. "Because, Willoughby," he went on, "if they crossed the border into northern Korea, I would have the opportunity to bloody the Chinese nose, something which could be rather easily accomplished with our available airpower, and without the political ramifications incident to our crossing the border into China."

MacArthur paused, then went on: "I was disappointed in the conclusions you have drawn from your intelligence, Willoughby, not with the intelligence."

"Yes, sir. Thank you, sir."

"Do you follow my reasoning, Fleming?" MacArthur asked.

"I'm not sure, sir."

"We're talking about face," MacArthur explained. "The importance of which never seems to be understood in Washington. Let me try to explain: My basic reasoning in not wanting to cross the Chinese border for any purpose, in any strength, for any distance — and, Fleming, I am fully aware there are many Washingtonians who sincerely believe I am frothing at the mouth for any excuse to cross the border — is face.

"A *platoon* of American soldiers in Manchuria would cause the Chinese to lose face. They would be forced to regain face, not only by expelling the American force, but by retaliating. They would feel wholly justified to send a company — or even a battalion — across the border to regain face. What would happen next I can only conjecture, but I know as certainly as I do that the sun will rise in the morning that the only circumstances under which a war with China should be fought is when the objective is total victory, the total destruction of the Chinese Communist infrastructure of government. I doubt if that could be accomplished without the use of nuclear weapons. And I certainly am not advocating such a move or, indeed, *any* military action which, even by accident, sees even the aforementioned platoon of infantry cross the border."

Pickering thought: *He wants to give me — and probably Banning, and maybe even Charley Willoughby — this little lecture, of course, but I think he hopes — maybe expects — that I will immediately report it to Truman. Which, of course, I will. Am I thereby being manipulated? Or just doing my job?*

"However," MacArthur went on, "the reverse is not true. If the Chinese were to be so misguided as to send a military force — even a substantial one, say a hundred thousand men, even two hundred thousand — across the border, and we annihilated most of it — as we are completely prepared to do — and sent the rest fleeing in chaotic retreat back across the border, while they would lose some face, they wouldn't lose much. The

Chinese capacity for self-delusion is limitless. They would immediately say the force they sent was inconsequential, and that they withdrew of their own choosing. And, since face does not govern my military actions, we would not retaliate — for the reasons I have just given — and the incident would end there. To our advantage. We would have reduced a substantial military force to ineffectiveness, and bloodied their nose, imparting the lesson that the United States of America cannot be pushed around with impunity."

Pickering thought: *He believes that, and he's just about got me convinced, too. I wonder what Beetle Smith would think, if he were here?*

"For those reasons, Fleming," MacArthur went on, "unofficially, out of channels, and between friends — if I may so presume — and absolutely not as a statement, or even an opinion, of the UNC Supreme Commander . . ."

He paused, waiting for appreciation of his wit, got it in the form of smiles and chuckles, and then went on: ". . . I really hope that General Willoughby is wrong, and your man McCoy right."

There were more appreciative responses.

"Which brings us to him," MacArthur went on again. "Your man McCoy."

"Yes, sir?"

"Ned also told me that he had been wounded in action."

"Yes, sir. That's true."

"While behind the enemy's lines on some mission?"

"He was wounded while being exfiltrated from North Korea, where he had gone to eavesdrop on what he called 'low-level Russian radio traffic,' " Pickering said.

"Isn't that the job of the Army Security Agency?" General Willoughby asked.

"I can only suppose that Major McCoy didn't get what he wanted to hear from the ASA, General," Pickering said coldly.

"You'd agree, General, wouldn't you, that coordination would have ensured that your man McCoy didn't have to waste his effort — and indeed get shot in the process — if he had let the ASA do their job while he did his?"

"The trouble with that, Charley —" Pickering snapped, and was immediately aware that his mouth was about to run away with him. He stopped.

Charm and courtesy is what is called for here.

Dutch Willoughby is El Supremo's fair-haired boy.

Fuck it.

"— is that you don't mean 'coordination.' You mean control by Charley Willoughby," Pickering went on. "I fired my

Tokyo station chief primarily because he 'coordinated' entirely too much with you. That's not our function — one of the things I wanted to make sure you understood clearly when I met with you later on to discuss your relationship with Ed Banning."

Willoughby's face showed anger and surprise. He looked at MacArthur to get his reaction.

"According to Ned Almond," MacArthur said, as if he had not heard a word of the exchange, "while it could easily have been worse, the wound — while quite painful — is not serious."

"He's in the Navy Hospital in Sasebo, sir," Pickering said.

"With your son? That's — I hate to say fortunate — but if they have to be in hospital, it's fortunate that they can be together," MacArthur said.

"My son is on his way to San Diego, sir," Pickering said. "They felt 'Diego could give him more of what he needs than they could." He paused and smiled. "But Major McCoy is not alone. Mrs. McCoy went to Sasebo to see my son, and they — concerned for her advanced pregnancy — ordered her to bed."

"She's all right?"

"She was as of when we left last night, sir. Dr. Schermer says having McCoy there is very good for her."

"Almond also said that he was afraid that McCoy would not mention his wounds to you, and if he did, you would not mention them to me. Ned wants him to have the Purple Heart."

"General Almond sent me a message to that effect, sir. One of the first things that the Deputy to the Deputy here is charged with doing is finding out how I can get a Purple Heart for him."

"That won't be a problem, Colonel," MacArthur said. "Major McCoy will receive his Purple Heart from my hands."

"Sir?" Banning and Pickering asked, surprised, in chorus.

"Whenever I can," MacArthur said, "I like to visit my wounded in hospital, and personally pin the Purple Heart medal on them. I had already planned to fly to Sasebo tomorrow to do so there. And I will take great pleasure in seeing that your man McCoy is properly decorated."

"That's very kind of you, sir," Pickering said.

"There is, of course, as always, room for you on the *Bataan*."

"I appreciate that, sir, but I have a lot to do here."

"It'll be a quick trip. Depart Sasebo at 0600, go to the hospital, and then come right back."

Pickering didn't reply immediately, and MacArthur went on: "A photo of your man McCoy getting his medals from me, with you and his wife looking on — even if not for publication — would be something I daresay they would treasure for the rest of their lives."

Pickering thought: *Goddamn it, he's right.*

"You're right, sir. I'll be at Haneda at 0600."

"Willoughby," MacArthur asked. "When can you make time in your schedule for General Pickering and Colonel Banning?"

"At any time, sir."

"Now, for example?"

"Yes, sir."

"Well, that's it, then. Welcome back to the Far East, Colonel. Good luck on your new assignment. And I'll see you, Fleming, first thing in the morning."

[Six]
Room 308, Maternity Ward
U.S. Naval Hospital
U.S. Navy Base, Sasebo
Sasebo, Japan
0915 23 October 1950

Captain George F. Hart, USMCR, came through the door trailed by an Army captain — who had a Leica 35-mm camera

720

hanging around his neck, and a brassard reading 'PIO' around his right sleeve — and Lieutenant (j.g.) Rosemary Hills, NC, USNR.

"Well, how are things in Honeymoon Heaven today?" he inquired cheerfully.

"What the hell are you doing here, George?" Major Kenneth R. McCoy — who was sitting propped up in the over-sized Sumo Wrestler's Special Bed sharing *Stars and Stripes* with his wife — inquired.

"Captain, the ugly one, with the inhospitable attitude," Hart said, "is Major McCoy. The good-looking one is Mrs. McCoy."

"Good morning," the captain said.

"What the hell is going on, George?" McCoy asked.

"You are about to be decorated with the Purple Heart medal by El Supremo himself," Hart said.

"Oh, bullshit!" McCoy said.

"And the Silver Star," the captain said.

"But not in that bed," Hart said. "When Colonel Huff heard about the two of you cozily together in the wrestler's bed, he made the point that it lacks the proper military flavor for this momentous occasion."

"Screw him!"

"Ken!" Mrs. McCoy said.

"And General Pickering agreed with him. You will get your Purple Heart in a wheelchair, as Mrs. McCoy, in her wheelchair, looks adoringly on."

"And the Silver Star," the captain repeated. "The Purple Heart and the Silver Star."

"What the hell is he talking about, Silver Star?" McCoy asked.

"Sir, you are about to be awarded the Silver Star and the Purple Heart," the captain said.

"We don't have much time," Lieutenant (j.g.) Hills said, and rolled a wheelchair up to Ernie's side of the bed. "Can you make it all right, Mrs. McCoy?"

"I'll be all right. But would you hand me my cosmetics kit and the hand mirror from the bathroom?"

"Just as soon as we get you into the chair," Nurse Hills said.

"You need some help, Ken?" Hart asked.

"What I want to know is, what the hell he's talking about," McCoy said. "What about the Silver Star?"

"Sir, you are about to receive, third award, the Silver Star medal," the captain said.

"For what?" McCoy asked, genuinely confused.

The captain reached into his tunic pocket and came out with a thin stack of folded paper. He searched through it, peeled one sheet away from the others, and started to hand it to McCoy.

"Here's the citation, sir," he said.

"Wait until he's in the wheelchair," Hart said. "El Supremo and entourage are hot on our heels. You can read it after you're decorated."

Hart rolled a second wheelchair to the bed. McCoy, wincing, threw the light hospital blanket and sheet off his legs, swung them out of bed, and gingerly lowered himself first to the floor and then into the wheelchair.

Hart snatched the blanket from the bed and began to arrange it around his legs.

"Jesus Christ, George!" McCoy said.

"Why don't we put the chairs against the window?" the captain said. "If we close the drapes, we have our background."

"Let me see that citation, Captain," McCoy ordered as Hart rolled him toward the window.

The captain handed it to him, and McCoy started to read it.

"This is absolute bullshit!" McCoy announced angrily.

"Ken!" Ernie cautioned again.

"I don't know what the hell is going on here," McCoy said. "But I'm not going to have a goddamn thing to do with it. This is pure, unadulterated bullshit!"

The door was swung open by Captain F. Howard Schermer, MC, USN, who commanded, "Attention on deck!"

General of the Army Douglas MacArthur

marched into the room, trailed by Mrs. Jean MacArthur; Brigadier General Fleming Pickering, USMCR; Colonel Sidney G. Huff; two other aides-de-camp, a major and a captain; one Army photographer — the master sergeant who was usually at MacArthur's side; one Navy photographer; and half a dozen members of the medical staff of the U.S. Naval Hospital, Sasebo, including Commander J. V. Stenten, NC, USN, who was in Navy blues, and wearing all of her medals — not the ribbon representations thereof — and which occupied a substantial portion of the left side of her tunic.

"As you were," the Supreme Commander ordered as he followed Mrs. MacArthur to Mrs. McCoy in her wheelchair.

"I'm glad to see you looking so well, my dear," Jean MacArthur said, and leaned over and kissed her. Then she handed her a box of Whitman chocolates.

"Thank you," Ernie said softly.

"Good to see you again, Major McCoy," MacArthur said. "How's the leg?"

"Getting better, sir," McCoy said.

"Good," MacArthur said. "Unfortunately, we are really pressed for time. Get on with it, Sid."

"Attention to orders," Colonel Huff barked. "Supreme Headquarters, United Nations Command, Tokyo, 21 October

1950. Subject: Award of the Silver Star Medal. By direction of the President, the Silver Star Medal, Third Award, is presented to Major Kenneth R. McCoy —"

"Excuse me, sir," Major McCoy said.

Huff looked at McCoy, frowned, and went on: "— United States Marine Corps Reserve —"

"Excuse me, sir," Major McCoy said, louder.

"Yes, what is it, Major?" Colonel Huff asked icily.

"With all possible respect, sir, I have read that citation, and it's . . . it's not true, sir."

"— for conspicuous gallantry in action above and beyond the call of duty —"

"Sir, I cannot accept that medal."

"Major, be silent!" Colonel Huff ordered.

"Just a minute, Sid," MacArthur said. He gestured with a regal wave of his hand for everybody to leave the room. Mrs. MacArthur, General Pickering, Colonel Huff, and Captain Schermer remained behind.

"Let me see the citation," Pickering said.

McCoy handed it to him. Pickering read it and extended it to MacArthur.

"I didn't know about the Silver Star, sir," Pickering said. "If I had, this . . . situation could have been avoided."

MacArthur read it, then raised his eyes to McCoy.

"There is something faulty, in your opinion, about the citation? Is that it, Major?"

"Yes, sir. It's completely faulty. I didn't rescue Major Pickering. He found a lost Army convoy. . . ."

"So General Pickering has told me," MacArthur said. "But I put it to you, Major McCoy, that in my judgment, and I'm sure in General Pickering's as well, the citation is not entirely faulty. There is the phrase 'for conspicuous gallantry in action above and beyond the call of duty.' I find that completely justified, even if the details in the citation attached may be something less than entirely accurate."

"Sir —"

"Let me finish, Major, please," MacArthur said.

"Sorry, sir."

"What we have here is a situation in which the Commander-in-Chief, having been made aware of your conspicuous gallantry above and beyond the call of duty, decided, and announced before witnesses, including General Pickering and myself, that it was his desire your valor be recognized by the award of the Silver Star."

"Sir, I didn't do anything that citation says I did."

"That I think can be remedied," MacArthur said. "Sid, see that the citation attached is changed to read, 'for services of a covert and classified nature behind the enemy's lines' with no further specificity."

"Yes, sir."

"Does that satisfy you, Major McCoy?" MacArthur asked.

"Sir, I don't deserve the Silver Star."

"I think you do, Ken," Pickering said.

"And so do I. More important, so does the President," MacArthur said. "Now, Major, may I presume that when we get the others back in here, Colonel Huff can proceed without any further interruptions from you?"

After a moment, Major McCoy said, "Yes, sir."

"Get them back in here, Sid," the Supreme Commander ordered.

[Seven]
Aboard Naval Air Transport Service
** Flight 203 (Medical Evacuation)**
32.42 Degrees North Latitude
120.296 Degrees West Longitude
The Pacific Ocean
1630 25 October 1950

Lieutenant Commander Dwayne G. Fisher, USNR, a slightly plump, pleasant-appearing thirty-nine-year-old, came out of the door to the flight deck of the four-engined Douglas C-54 and made his way slowly down the aisle to the rear of the passenger compartment.

The aircraft was configured to carry litters. There were two lines of them, stacked three high. Almost all of the litters were occupied, and almost all of the injured were Marines. They were all strapped securely to the litters, which had thin inflatable mattresses, olive drab in color, but not unlike the air mattresses used in swimming pools. About one-third of the injured were connected to rubber tubing feeding them saline solutions, pain-deadening narcotics, or fresh human blood, or various combinations thereof.

Commander Fisher stopped at just about every row of litters. Sometimes he just smiled, and sometimes he said things like "How you doing, pal?" or "We're almost there. About another hour and we'll be in San Diego."

Sometimes the injured men replied, if only with a single word or two or a faint smile. Some stared at him without response. Four of the men in the litters were covered with sheets. They had not survived the flight.

At the rear of the fuselage, where they had been loaded last so they could be off-loaded first, were the NPs. The stress of war had been too much for them, and they were headed for the Neuro-Psychiatric Wards of the San Diego Naval Hospital. They had all been sedated, and strapped to their litters more securely.

Commander Fisher stopped at each row of NPs, but they were out of it, and he didn't speak to them, only gave them a little smile.

At the extreme rear of the passenger compartment was a patient whom Dwayne Fisher wanted to talk to. He was an NP, but the flight physician had told him that was probably just a technical classification to get him to the States. The poor bastard was a Marine fighter pilot who'd just been rescued after three months behind the enemy's lines.

"He's nothing but skin and bones, but he's not over the edge," the flight physician had told him.

"Hi!" Commander Fisher said.

What does this asshole want?

"I understand you're also an airplane driver."

What are you doing, writing a book?

"Guilty."

"Fighters?"

And also Lockheed 1049s. You are conversing, sir, with the current holder of the Trans-Pacific scheduled passenger service speed record.

"Corsairs."

"I flew P-38s in War Two," Fisher said. "Which twin-engine time I parlayed into a job with Eastern. Where I flew these. Which kept me out of fighters when they called me up."

"Reservist?"

Dumb fucking question. If he was called up, he was in the reserve.

"Yeah. You?"

"Me, too. I was flying for Trans-Global."

"Ten-forty-nines?"

"That's all Trans-Global has."

"Nice airplane."

"Very nice."

"You were shot down?"

Back to your fucking book, are we?

"Uh-huh."

"I'm surprised they didn't grab you for NATS," Commander Fisher said. "Most of our guys are called-up airline pilots."

"They didn't."

"I just called our ETA — one hour — to San Diego," Fisher said. "It's been a long haul."

It's been a fucking nightmare.

"It's been a nightmare."

"Walking down that aisle is tough," Fisher said. "The amazing thing is, you don't get complaints."

Not from the drugged or the dead, I guess you don't.

"A couple of hours out of Honolulu, I

went to the head. I saw . . . the sheets. How many didn't make it?"

"I counted four."

"I guess the rest of us are lucky, huh?"

"From what I hear, you're luckier than most. You were behind the enemy's lines for three months, right?"

"Yeah."

"And you're walking around. You look like you're in pretty good condition?"

"Yeah. I'm in good condition."

The way my commanding officer put it, with devastating honesty, Commander, is that I am a self-important sonofabitch whose delicate condition is my own goddamn fault. He went on to say that my childish behavior caused a lot of good people to put their necks out to save me from the consequences of my sophomoric showboating.

That should be me under one of those white sheets.

Commander Fisher put out his hand.

"I better get back up and drive the bus," he said. "Nice to meet you, Major. Good luck."

"Thanks."

Eight

Naval Air Station, San Diego
San Diego, California
1740 25 October 1950

As the C-54 taxied through the rain, Pick could see a line of ambulances and buses, and beside them a small army of medical personnel and a long line of poncho-covered gurneys.

The C-54 stopped on the tarmac before the passenger terminal, and when the cargo door opened, Pick saw that a forklift had been driven up to the aircraft. It held a platform, on which were four gurneys and eight Corpsmen in raincoats with Red Cross brassards.

The dead were off-loaded first. Four Corpsmen came onto the aircraft, went to one of the bodies, unfastened the litter, and carried it down the aisle to the door and the waiting gurneys. The body was gently moved from the litter to the gurney and covered with a poncho, but not before enough rain had fallen on the sheet to make it translucent.

Then the litter was carried back onto the aircraft, and a second body on its litter carried out to the gurneys waiting in the rain.

When all four gurneys had bodies, the forklift lowered the platform.

When it came back up, there were four

Corpsmen, different ones, on it. The flight physician was now waiting for them. They exchanged a few words, then the flight physician turned to Pick.

"Okay, Major, you're next," he said. "Do you need help to go out there and get on a gurney?"

"I don't need a gurney."

"It's policy."

"Fuck your policy."

"You made it all the way here without giving anybody any trouble. Please don't start now."

"I'm not going to get on a fucking gurney."

"You're going to get on it, Major. The only question is whether you do it now or after I sedate you."

"Major," one of the Corpsmen said, "with respect. It's raining out here. Please."

Pick stood up, walked through the door, and climbed onto one of the gurneys. One of the Corpsmen laid a poncho over him.

Three more NPs were brought off the aircraft. They were not transferred to the gurneys. Rather, their litters were laid on top of the gurneys and then they were strapped to it.

A Corpsman appeared with two lengths of canvas webbing.

"Let me get this around you, and we're

on our way," he said.

"You're going to strap me to this fucking thing?"

"That's the SOP," the Corpsman said. "Take it easy. The sooner we get to the hospital, the sooner we can take it off."

Fuck it.

What do I care?

What do I care about anything?

When the straps were in place, Pick could not move his arms and wipe the rain from his exposed face.

So what the fuck?

The forklift lowered the platform, and the gurneys were rolled off it — Pick's first — with a double bump, and then to one of the buses. The buses had enormous rear doors that permitted the gurneys to be wheeled aboard them.

The way he was strapped in, he could raise his head. But all he could see out the bus's windshield was the open door of the bus ahead of his.

He laid his head back down.

Several minutes later, he heard the door being closed, and when he looked up, he saw a white hat come down the aisle, get behind the wheel, and start the engine.

The bus turned out of the line.

The next thing Pick saw was a sign: WELCOME TO THE U.S. NAVAL HOSPITAL, SAN DIEGO!

XV

One

Room 308, Maternity Ward
U.S. Naval Hospital
U.S. Navy Base, Sasebo
Sasebo, Japan
0815 25 October 1950

Captain F. Howard Schermer, MC, USN, as Hospital Commander, was not required to make routine morning or afternoon rounds with members of his medical staff — after all, he had a lot else to occupy his time — but of course he had the unquestioned right to do so.

When he had the time, in other words, he often would join one of the teams making rounds to keep his fingers, so to speak, on the pulse of the hospital. And he would usually ask Commander J. V. Stenten, NC, USN, his Chief of Nursing Services, to accompany him. Between the two of them, very little that needed correction escaped notice.

Since *McCoy, Mrs. Ernestine* and later *McCoy, Major K. R.* had been admitted, Captain Schermer had found the time to make morning and afternoon rounds of the maternity ward every day, and Commander Stenten had been free to accompany him.

There were several reasons for this, and chief among them was that both Captain Schermer and Commander Stenten genuinely liked the young couple sharing the sumo wrestler's bed. But Schermer was also aware that he had a delicate situation in his care of Major and Mrs. McCoy.

It hadn't been, for example, the first time General of the Army and Mrs. MacArthur had come to Sasebo to visit the wounded and ill. Since the war had started, they had made ten, maybe twelve such visits. But never had Mrs. MacArthur brought a box of candy to a maternity ward patient.

And never, to his knowledge, had the hospital had in its care a CIA agent who had suffered wounds behind enemy lines. And whose commanding officer, a brigadier general, the assistant director of the CIA for Asia, obviously had an interest in both of them that went beyond official to *in loco parentis.*

Captain Schermer, followed by Commander Stenten and then by the Rounds Staff, marched into room 308, where the patients were lying beside one another reading *Stars and Stripes* and *So, You're Going to Be a Mother!*

"Good morning," Captain Schermer said. "And how are we this morning?"

"I don't know how *we* are, Doctor," Mrs. McCoy replied. "But speaking for my husband and myself, I'm pregnant and uncomfortable, ready to go home, and he's pawing the ground to get out of here."

Commander Stenten chuckled.

Captain Schermer picked up their medical record clipboards from the foot of the bed and studied both.

"Well," he said. "Why don't we get Major McCoy into a wheelchair, and have Dr. Haverty have a look at you?"

One of the nurses rolled a wheelchair to his side of the bed, and another started to pull the drapes around the bed.

"I won't need that, thank you," McCoy said, and got out of the bed and slid his feet into slippers.

Dr. Schermer thought: *He seems to be able to do so without pain.*

Or without much pain.

Or he's very good at concealing pain.

As the privacy drapes were drawn around the bed and Lieutenant Commander Robert Haverty, MC, USNR, Chief of Gynecological Services, and a nurse went behind it, McCoy walked to the window and rested his rear end on the sill.

Dr. Schermer walked over to him.

"She means that, sir," McCoy said. "She

737

wants to go home. Is there any reason she can't?"

"To the States? I'm afraid she doesn't meet the criteria for medical evacuation, and I don't think a flight that long would be the thing for her to do."

"She means Tokyo, sir," McCoy said. "We have a house there."

"You know what happened when she came here from Tokyo," Schermer said.

"She couldn't get a sleeper — for that matter, even a first-class seat — on the train, so she sat up all the way, all night, on a wooden seat in third class," McCoy said.

"I didn't know that," Schermer said as Commander Stenten stepped up beside him.

"Neither did I, until I tried to talk her out of going back to Tokyo," McCoy said. "You're going to have to convince her there is good reason — that she would lose the baby — if she went back to Tokyo in a sleeper on the train."

"Why does she want to go to Tokyo?" Commander Stenten asked.

"She says she'd rather be in her own bed, at home, than here."

"Especially since you won't be here?" Commander Stenten asked.

"Yes, ma'am," McCoy said.

"Let me think — long and hard — about

this. After I speak with Dr. Haverty," Dr. Schermer said.

"Yes, sir. Thank you."

"And how's your leg?"

"I don't think I'd want to do any squat jumps, sir," McCoy said. "But I can maneuver, and I really have to get out of here and back to work."

"Back to what you were doing when you were hit?" Commander Stenten asked.

"No, ma'am," McCoy said, chuckling. "I don't think I'm quite up to that yet. But I'm okay for limited duty."

"Let me talk this over with Dr. Haverty," Dr. Schermer said.

[Two]
Office of the Hospital Commander
U.S. Naval Hospital
U.S. Navy Base, Sasebo
Sasebo, Japan
0855 25 October 1950

"I didn't know about her sitting up all night on a train," Dr. Haverty said. "That explains a good deal."

"How is she?" Dr. Schermer asked.

"At the moment, she's fine," Haverty replied. "But the idea of her taking another train ride . . ."

"Even flat on her back in a sleeper?"

Commander Stenten asked.

The question seemed argumentative. Nurses are not permitted to question the opinions of physicians, much less argue with them. But this was not an ordinary nurse, this was the Dragon Lady.

"Well, what if she had trouble on the way?" Dr. Haverty asked.

"Yeah," Dr. Schermer agreed. "The husband wouldn't be much help. If something happened . . . anything could start her off again."

"She would need medical attention right then," Dr. Haverty said.

"But nothing a nurse couldn't handle, right?" the Dragon Lady asked. "Worst case, she starts —"

"You're not suggesting we send a nurse with her, are you?" Dr. Schermer asked. "I couldn't authorize anything like that."

"In addition to the train ride," the Dragon Lady said, "she got a hell of an emotional shock when she heard her friend had been killed. And when she got a good look at Major Pickering. You don't think that had anything to do with the trouble she had?"

"Of course it did," Dr. Haverty said.

"Then you would suggest her mental peace would be a factor in whether she can carry to term or not?"

"Obviously," Dr. Haverty said.

"She's a nice young woman, a very nice

young woman," the Dragon Lady said. "Tough, but not as tough as she thinks she is. Who is far from home and alone."

"That's true."

"The prospect of being here alone terrifies her. She wants to be in her own home," the Dragon Lady said. "I can understand that."

"So can I," Captain Schermer agreed. "But what if something happens at home? She'd be alone there, too."

"They have three live-in servants. She speaks Japanese."

"Three live-in servants?" Captain Schermer said. "In a major's quarters?"

"How do you know that?" Dr. Haverty asked.

"I've talked to her. Yeah, three live-in servants. Maybe the CIA pays better than the Marine Corps. But she's got three servants, and she doesn't live in government quarters. They own a house in Denen-chofu."

"Which brings us back to the question of the trip to Tokyo. As much as I'd like to, I can't authorize sending a nurse with her."

"I'm up to my ears in use-it-or-lose-it leave," the Dragon Lady said. "I herewith apply for up to thirty days' ordinary leave."

They both looked at her in surprise.

"I've got some friends at Tokyo General," the Dragon Lady said. "I can explain the situation to them and make sure they lay on whatever might be needed if it's needed."

Dr. Schermer looked at Dr. Haverty, and said, "Bob, if she's not in immediate danger of losing the baby . . ."

"She really would be better off in her own bedroom. If she had quarters here, I'd recommend her release and tell her to get in bed and stay there, and to call for help the moment . . . But she doesn't have quarters here."

"So the question, then, is how to get her to her quarters?"

Haverty nodded.

"Commander Stenten," Captain Schermer said, "in connection with your Temporary Duty to confer with the nursing staff of the U.S. Army General Hospital, Tokyo, you are authorized up to thirty days' ordinary leave."

"Thank you, sir," the Dragon Lady said.

[Three]
Room 16, Neuro-Psychiatric Ward
U.S. Naval Hospital
San Diego, California
0830 26 October 1950

"Come on in, Major," Lieutenant Patrick McGrory, MC, USN, said to Major Mal-

742

colm S. Pickering, USMCR.

Pickering was in pajamas, a blue bathrobe, and felt slippers. After a moment's hesitation, he walked into the office.

"Have a seat," McGrory said. "I'm Pat McGrory."

He leaned across his desk and put his hand out.

Pick made no move to take the hand.

"Funny about the seat," Pick said. "I seem to remember that officers are supposed to get out of *their* seats when a more senior officer enters a room."

McGrory stood up. "Sorry," he said.

"As you were," Pick said.

McGrory smiled.

"Does that mean I can sit down now?" he asked.

"Be my guest, Mr. McGrory," Pick said.

"Actually, that's Dr. McGrory, sir."

"Be my guest, Dr. McGrory."

"I'm a psychiatrist," McGrory said as he sat and motioned for Pick to do the same. "And you are in the psychiatric ward of the U.S. Naval Hospital, San Diego. This is our initial — sometimes called 'the welcoming' — interview."

"I never would have guessed, with the locked doors and the steel screens on the windows."

McGrory smiled at him.

"Funny, nobody told me I was nuts in

Japan," Pick said. "They told me — rather unnecessarily — that I was a little underweight and that my teeth are loose in my gums, but the word 'nuts' never came up. At least until yesterday when the guy on the airplane threatened to stick a needle in my arm unless I got on his gurney and allowed myself to be strapped in."

"I heard about that," McGrory said. "And I understand you said rude things to the nurse when she wouldn't let you use the telephone."

"I wanted to call my mother," Pick said. "And I am unable to understand why I couldn't."

"Well, for one thing, you had just got in, and you hadn't had your initial interview, in which the rules are explained. You can call your mother as soon as we're finished here."

"And when will that be?"

"Shortly."

"Tell me about the rules," Pick said.

"They vary from patient to patient —"

"Tell me about the ones that apply to me."

"— depending on that patient's problems."

"My problems are my teeth are a little loose in my gums and I'm a little underweight."

"You have gone through what I understand is one hell of an ordeal. Do you

744

want to tell me about that?"

"No."

"Any reason why not?"

"I'd prefer to forget about it."

"That's understandable," McGrory said. "But from my viewpoint, the Navy's viewpoint, we have to wonder what damage your ordeal caused."

"We're back to the loose teeth and lost weight," Pick said.

"The lost weight we can deal with by giving you a lot to eat. The food here's pretty good. And, I'm told, as you get your weight back, the loose teeth problem will gradually go away."

"Then why am I locked up in the booby hatch? That's all that's wrong with me."

"And I hope to be able to soon certify, after we've talked some, that there are fifty-two cards in your deck."

"Plus a couple of jokers. Take my word for it."

"There are three categories of patients here. You — because you just got here and have not been evaluated — are in Category One, which means that you are restricted to the ward. If you need anything from the Ship's Store, for example, you give a list to the nurse, and she'll see that you'll get it. You're not allowed to have money in your possession. When you move up to Category Two . . ."

"Let me guess. I can have money in my possession?"

"With which you can settle your Ship's Store bill. Which brings that up. When was the last time you were paid?"

"I guess four months ago, something like that."

McGrory made a note on a lined pad.

"When you move up to Category Two, they'll give you a partial pay," he went on. "It will take some time before your records catch up with you."

"What other great privileges go with Category Two?"

"You have freedom of the building, which means that you can go to the Ship's Store, and the movies —"

"Whoopee!"

"— and the Officers' Club for your meals, if you so desire, and where, I understand, intoxicants of various types are on sale."

"You trust the loonies with booze, do you?"

"Until they demonstrate they can't be trusted with it," McGrory said. "The uniform for Category Two patients is the bathrobe and pajamas. That's so we can easily recognize them if they give in to temptation and walk out the door. Then they're brought back and it's Category One all over again."

"Fascinating! And Category Three?"

"When you work your way up to Category Three, you are permitted passes. That means you can go, in uniform, on little tours of the local area we organize. Free bus service, of course. And, sometimes, when accompanied by a responsible family member or friend — have you got a girlfriend?"

"Not anymore."

"Pity. What happened?"

"None of your goddamn business, Doctor."

"Well, in Category Three, if you had — or get — a girlfriend, and we thought she was responsible, you could get a six-hour, sometimes an all-day, pass with her."

"No girlfriend."

"As I said, a pity."

"Is there a Category Four?"

"No. If we don't think you're going to hurt yourself or someone else, there's no sense in keeping you here."

"Why don't we just start with that? I'm not going to hurt myself or anyone else. I'm probably at least as sane as you are. So why do we have to play this game?"

"It's policy."

"Fuck your policy."

"You're fond of that phrase, aren't you? That's what you told the doctor on the med-evacuation flight."

"It's a useful phrase."

"Any questions, Major?"

"How do I get out of this chickenshit outfit?"

McGrory laughed.

"By working your way up through Category Three. That means we're going to have to talk."

"About . . . what was it you said, my 'ordeal'?"

"Uh-huh."

"Don't hold your breath, Doctor."

"I hadn't intended to," McGrory said. "Well, that's it. You can go back to your room and fill out your Ship's Store list. And call your mother. If she wants to come see you, that can be arranged. The nurse'll explain the rules, visiting hours, et cetera. I'll see you later."

"I don't have any choice there, do I?"

"No. Afraid not. For what it's worth, Major: You can make this as easy or hard as you want. Your choice."

Pick stood up, looked at Dr. McGrory for a moment, and then started out of the office.

His right foot came out of the slipper. He looked down, then kicked off the left slipper and walked down the corridor barefoot.

[Four]
The Race Track
Seoul, South Korea
1230 28 October 1950

Brigadier General Fleming Pickering, USMCR, jumped nimbly to the ground from the rear door of the Beaver, exchanged salutes with Lieutenant Colonel D. J. Vandenburg, USA, and then looked back at the airplane. Major Kenneth R. McCoy, USMCR, was climbing down from the copilot's seat.

McCoy could not conceal that stretching his leg to get his foot onto the step mounted on the landing gear strut was painful, or that it hurt like hell when he jumped the rest of the way to the ground.

Pickering glanced at Vandenburg and saw on his face that he had seen the same thing he had.

McCoy saluted Vandenburg crisply and smiled.

"I see the colonel has appropriated my vehicle," he said, gesturing toward the Russian jeep.

"I didn't expect to see you back so soon," Vandenburg said.

"He says he's fine," Pickering said. "I have very serious doubts about that."

"I'm all right, sir," McCoy said.

"In a pig's ass, you are," Vandenburg said. Major Alex Donald, who had flown to

Pusan to pick up Pickering and McCoy, finished shutting down the airplane and climbed down from the cockpit.

He saluted Vandenburg and said, "Every time I come in here in the Beaver, I devoutly hope there is truth in that crack that the best place to hide something is in plain sight."

"I'm told General Walker remains convinced his missing airplane is somewhere in Korea," Vandenburg said. "The last I heard, he was looking around Pusan." He paused and then looked at Pickering. "We're going to have to talk about that, sir. The Beaver is assigned to the Presidential Mission, and General Howe —"

"Let's talk about it at lunch," Pickering said. "Is there going to be any trouble about the airplane while it's here?"

Vandenburg pointed toward the base operations shack. Coming toward them from it were Technical Sergeant J. M. Jennings, USMC, and two other Marines, all armed with Thompson submachine guns.

"I thought a perimeter guard might be in order," Vandenburg said matter-of-factly.

Jennings saluted.

"You all right, Major?" he asked. "We heard you got —"

"I'm fine, Jennings, thank you," McCoy said.

"You may have to carry him to the Russian jeep, Sergeant," Pickering said. "But aside from that —"

McCoy trotted to the Russian jeep, jumped nimbly into the backseat, and called, "Anytime the general is ready, sir!"

Pickering turned his back to him and said to Vandenburg and Jennings, "That obviously hurt him. Let's act as if we don't think so. But one of the things I intended to tell you, Colonel, is that under no circumstances is he to go forward of our lines."

"I understand, sir."

"And if you or any of your men hear that he's planning to do something like that, Sergeant, you are to tell Colonel Vandenburg."

Jennings nodded. "Aye, aye, sir."

"Let's go get some lunch," Pickering said, and started toward the jeep.

Major General Ralph Howe, NGUS, was sitting at the dining room table in The House, drinking coffee with Master Sergeant Charley Rogers. The table was set for lunch.

"I'm surprised to see you, McCoy," Howe said. "General Almond told me you took a pretty good hit."

"A little piece of shrapnel, sir," McCoy replied. "I'm all right."

"That is not exactly the truth, the whole

truth, and nothing but," Pickering said as he shook hands with Howe. "Major McCoy is on limited duty. You do understand that, don't you, Major McCoy? Limited?"

"Yes, sir."

"Okay. Then let's have some lunch and decide where we go from here."

Master Sergeant Charley Rogers stood up and went through the swinging door into the kitchen. A moment later, two Korean women came through it carrying china tureens. Rogers followed them into the room.

"Fish chowder and chicken and dumplings," he said. "If it tastes as good as it smells, we're in luck."

"So far as I'm concerned in your where-we-go-from-here scenario, Fleming," General Howe said, "Charley and I are on the 1700 courier flight to Tokyo, where I will make my manners to General MacArthur, and then get on a plane — a Trans-Global flight, you should be pleased to learn — for the States."

"You're really determined to leave me all alone here, are you?"

"There are a lot of things I have to say to the President that I don't want to put on paper," Howe said. "After I tell him what I think he should hear, and he wants me to come back over here, I will."

Pickering nodded.

"I think the first thing on this agenda," Howe said as he smiled thanks for the fish chowder being ladled into his bowl, "should be Colonel Van's new status, with which he's not entirely delighted. I wanted to make sure he understands that while I'm sure you're delighted to have him, his transfer to the CIA — you — was my idea, not yours."

"I have to tell you, Colonel," Pickering said, "that it makes sense to me, and I feel a little foolish for not having thought of it myself."

Vandenburg didn't say anything, but it was clear that he had made the decision not to say what he was thinking.

"Let's get it out in the open, Colonel," Pickering said. "What's on your mind?"

Vandenburg met Pickering's eyes, then shrugged.

"General, in War Two, when I was asked to join the OSS, I decided I could be of more use where I was, in counter-intelligence. I never regretted that decision to stay in the Army. Especially after the war, when the OSS was disbanded and my friends who had gone into the OSS — I'm talking about career officers — went back to the Army. They were treated like lepers, sir."

McCoy snorted. "Lepers with a social

disease?" he asked. " 'Where were you when we were fighting the war?' "

"Exactly." Vandenburg looked at Pickering and then went on: "Ken told me just about the same thing happened to him when he went back to the Marine Corps."

"I didn't realize until right now that it was that bad, Ken," Pickering said, and then remembered: "Weren't you offered a chance to go into the CIA?"

McCoy nodded.

"Why didn't you?"

"I was a Marine," McCoy said. "I know what the colonel's talking about. He's a soldier."

"The same thing happened to me, in 1948, in Greece," Vandenburg went on. "They really wanted me in the CIA there, and I really didn't want to go. And I didn't. And now, all of a sudden, I'm told I'm now in the CIA. This time nobody asked me."

"Okay, I'm the villain," Howe said. "But don't mistake that for an apology, Colonel. It was my judgment that unless we got you out of the Army, you were about to be co-opted by General Willoughby, and I decided you were too valuable an asset for General Pickering to lose."

"General, I wasn't looking for an apology," Vandenburg said. "I'm a soldier — I go where I'm sent. But General

Pickering asked what was on my mind."

"And I'm glad you told me," Howe said. "The President's going to hear about this."

"General, I wish you wouldn't do that. I'm not whining," Vandenburg said.

"I didn't think you were, Colonel," Howe said. "But my job is to tell the President what I think he would be interested in hearing. And that's what I'm going to do."

"Ken," Pickering asked, "did the same sort of thing happen to Ed Banning when the OSS was disestablished?"

"Sir, Colonel Banning was a regular before the war. He's a Citadel graduate. You know what a fine Marine he is. He was never given command of a battalion, much less a regiment, and he was never promoted above colonel. For that matter, they never used him as an intelligence officer."

"Then why did he stay in the Marine Corps?" Pickering blurted. "God knows, he doesn't need the money."

"He's a Marine, General," McCoy said. "He knows it, even if there are a lot of bastards in the Corps who don't want to acknowledge it."

"That's the end of my contribution to this," General Howe said. "But I'm going to stick around so that I'll be able to tell the President what the new broom is sweeping, and where."

"I'd like to know what you two,"

Pickering said, pointing at Vandenburg and McCoy, "think the priorities are. You first, McCoy."

"Finding out when the Chinese are coming in," McCoy said. "The 1st MarDiv landed at Wonsan yesterday —"

"Only part of them, McCoy," Howe interrupted. "The 1st Marine Air Wing is ashore and operating out of Wonsan — and Bob Hope and a USO troupe have entertained them there. Even I was there. But there are still elements of the division sailing around in circles waiting for the mines at Wonsan to be cleared. When I saw General Almond — when he told me what had happened to you — he had just had himself flown off the *Mount McKinley* on a helicopter. I guess by tonight — certainly by tomorrow — everybody should be ashore. The Marines, I mean. They're not going to even try to land the 7th Infantry Division at Wonsan; they're going to land at Iwon."

"That's a hundred sixty, seventy miles north of Wonsan," McCoy said. "When's that supposed to happen?"

"Tomorrow," Howe said.

"Pyongyang has fallen," McCoy said. "Which means there is no need for X Corps to start back across the peninsula. Which means that pretty soon they'll be ordered to move north instead —"

"They already have been," Howe interrupted again. He looked at Pickering. "I was in Wonsan last night and this morning. I used the L-19." Pickering nodded. "Almond already has his orders. The Capital ROK Division will continue advancing up the coastline toward the Russian border. The ROK 3rd Division is going to go north from Hamhung to the Chosin Reservoir, and then up to the Manchurian border. When the 1st MarDiv gets organized ashore, they will follow the 3rd ROK, and — I don't think the 3rd ROK has been told this — pass through their lines, probably near the reservoir, and beat them to the Manchurian border to make sure our Koreans don't cross it. The 7th Division, once it's ashore at Iwon, will attack north straight for the Manchurian border."

"I didn't hear any of this in Tokyo," Pickering said, more than a little bitterly.

"Did you talk to MacArthur?" Howe asked.

Pickering shook his head no.

"Almond told me he got his orders via officer courier," Howe went on. "They're probably known only to the Bataan Gang in the Dai Ichi Building, and they wouldn't tell you unless MacArthur specifically ordered them to. . . ."

"And I didn't ask," Pickering said.

"They wouldn't have lied to me if I asked, but I didn't ask."

"Okay. Well, that's it," Howe said. "That's all I know."

"Sir, in these circumstances," McCoy said, "our obvious priority is to get as early a warning of the Chinese intervention as possible, especially since no one else thinks it will happen."

"I think General Almond does," Howe said. "He didn't come right out and say so, but I had the feeling he won't be terribly surprised to encounter the Chinese Red Army."

"How do you propose to get 'as early a warning as possible'?" Pickering asked.

"Well, that opens a new can of worms," McCoy said.

"Let's have it," Pickering said.

"Well, while Colonel Van and I were looking for General Dean and Pick —"

"One final question about that," Howe interrupted. "What about General Dean? I know the President will ask."

"I'm afraid all indications are that he's in China, sir," Vandenburg said.

"Okay. You did your best, and I'll make sure the President knows that," Howe said. "Go on, McCoy. Sorry for the interruption."

"When we were looking for the General and Pick, we also trained the men — the

Marines we have on loan — as overnight stay-behinds. By that I mean, we dropped them off and went back the next day and got them."

"Using the Sikorsky helicopters, you mean?" Pickering asked.

"Yes, sir."

"And using — what was the term you used — 'overnight stay-behinds'?"

"That's my term, sir. It's not in any book."

"Very little of anything you've ever done since I've known you has been in any book," Pickering said.

"What they do, General," Vandenburg said, "is find someplace where they won't be seen — where nobody would expect them to be — and then they just listen. The last thing they want to do is get in a firefight. There's no way they could win."

"How do you know where to put them?" Pickering said.

"We fly over in the daytime in one of the L-19s," McCoy said. "Zimmerman or I go along in the backseat. We point out to the pilot where we would like to leave them — usually on some hilltop — and the pilot — who will fly the Big Black Bird — decides if he can go in there or not."

"You're landing helicopters on mountaintops?" Pickering demanded of Major Alex Donald.

"Most of the time we just hover, sir," Donald said. "A couple of feet off the ground. There's no place to touch the wheels down."

"You've been making these flights?" Pickering asked.

"Most of them," McCoy answered for him.

"And this works?"

"Not all the time. But it's all we've got," McCoy said.

"Did you know about this?" Pickering asked Howe.

Howe shook his head no. "This is not my area of expertise," he said.

"What did you mean, Ken, when you said 'a new can of worms'?" Pickering asked.

"Well, sir, when we did it north of the line, Zimmerman and I and some of the original Marines from the Flying Fish Channel operation, plus, of course, our Koreans, did it. We never did it with the Marines we borrowed from the 5th Marines."

"Why not?"

"Our Marines are volunteers, sir. The guys we borrowed from the 5th Marines didn't volunteer for anything. I don't think we should send people to do something like this if they're not volunteers."

"Why not?" Howe said. "I don't remember anybody saying 'volunteers take one step forward' when the 5th Marines were ordered to land at Inchon."

"If our guys are discovered, sir, that's just about it for them. That's not like Inchon. We can't go get them."

"And you don't think they'd volunteer if they were asked?"

"I think they probably would, sir, but . . ."

"But what?"

"We borrowed them, sir. The 5th Marines expect them back. What do we say if we can't return them? That they're missing on a mission we can't talk about?"

"Why not?" Howe asked.

"The Marines don't leave people behind, sir. There would be a lot of questions asked we couldn't answer. But people would keep asking them. Pretty soon, a lot of eyes — angry eyes — would be looking at us, looking damned close at us, and we just can't afford that."

"There wouldn't be that problem, would there, if the men from the 5th Marines were no longer assigned to the 5th Marines?" Howe asked.

"What are you thinking, Ralph?" Pickering asked.

"I think McCoy should go to Socho-Ri, explain what he wants these guys to do, explain why they can only do it if they're in the CIA, ask if anyone wants to be in the CIA, and send the names of those that do to Tokyo. Between you and me, Fleming, with an Operational Immediate message or two, they can be in the CIA by this time tomorrow."

Pickering happened to glance at Colonel Vandenburg.

"You've been pretty quiet through all this, Colonel," Pickering said.

"Sir, no one's said anything I disagree with," Vandenburg said.

"And you have no suggestion or comment to make?"

"Yes, sir. I suggest you get on the 1700 courier with General Howe, so you can run this transfer to the CIA business through from Tokyo. McCoy's right — we have to get off the dime. Either do this, if these men volunteer, or think of something else. And right now, I can't think of anything else."

"That'll teach you to ask questions, Fleming," General Howe said.

[Five]
Emergency Room
U.S. Naval Hospital
San Diego, California
2305 27 October 1950
(1505 28 October 1950 Socho-Ri Local Time)

"What the hell is this?" Lieutenant Marjorie Wallace, NC, USN, asked of Lieutenant (j.g.) James C. Levell, MC, USNR, pointing out the door.

Lieutenant (j.g.) Levell was the medical officer on duty in the emergency room, and Lieutenant Wallace the nurse in charge. They were in a small glass-walled cubicle savoring a rare moment of respite from their late-evening emergency room duties.

A Packard limousine had stopped outside the emergency room. A civilian couple — a tall, slim, silver-haired woman in her fifties, and a portly, dignified, somewhat jowly man who looked about ten years older — were marching purposefully into the emergency room entrance lobby.

"I've seen him before, somewhere," Lieutenant (j.g.) Levell said, adding, "Let the Corpsman handle it."

The Corpsman with the responsibility of dealing with whatever came through the emergency room door proved unable to handle it. Ninety seconds later, he came into the glass-walled cubicle where Dr. Levell and Nurse Wallace were.

"Sir," the Corpsman said, "there's a civilian — two civilians . . ."

"I saw them. What's up?"

"They want to see whoever's in charge, sir," the Corpsman said.

"Now what?" Dr. Levell said, stubbed out his cigarette, pushed himself off the desk, and walked out of the glass-walled cubicle.

He walked up to the couple — *I know this guy from somewhere* — and smiled at them.

"May I help you, sir?"

"We're here to see one of your patients," the man said, and added an explanation that was more of an accusation. "There's no one answering the door at the main entrance."

"Well, sir, the main entrance closes after visiting hours, which are over at nine, I'm afraid."

"Lieutenant, I think the best way to get this over with quickly would be for you to get the hospital commander on the line."

"I'm not sure I follow you, sir," Dr. Levell said, "but I'd like to suggest that you come back at nine tomorrow morning, when visiting hours begin. There's just no way —"

"Get the hospital commander on the phone, Lieutenant," the man said. "Tell him Senator Fowler is in his emergency room."

Oh, Jesus. That's who it is! Richardson K. Fowler in the goddamn flesh! I knew I knew that face!

"Senator, will you come with me, please? We'll see if we can get the hospital commander on the phone for you."

"Thank you very much," Senator Fowler said.

"Senator," Captain W. Ainsley Unger, Jr., MC, USN, said five minutes later, "there's obviously been a communications foul-up somewhere. If I had known you were coming . . . ."

"Captain — or do I call you 'Doctor'?"

"Either's fine, Senator."

"This is Mrs. Patricia — Mrs. Fleming — Pickering. Her son, Major Malcolm S. Pickering, Marine Reserves, was flown in here last night from Japan. We want to see him."

"Well, Senator, visiting hours —"

"Are over. The young doctor made that clear. Let me put it this way: Mrs. Pickering is determined to see her son, who spent most of the last three months evading capture in Korea, and I am determined that she shall. Now, can you arrange this for us, or should I get on the tele-phone to the Secretary of the Navy?"

"I'm sure an exception can be made," Captain Unger said. "Do you happen to know where in the hospital your son is, Mrs. Pickering?"

"Room 16," Patricia Fleming said, "NP Ward."

The effect of that announcement was ev-ident on Dr. Unger's face.

"I suspect NP stands for Neuro-Psychiatric," Patricia Fleming said. "Does it?"

"Yes, ma'am, it does. And that may compli-cate things, as you can well understand."

"I want to see my son," Patricia Fleming said flatly.

"May I make a suggestion, Mrs. Picker-ing?" Dr. Unger said.

"Of course."

"I think it would be best if you had a word with his attending physician before you see him."

"That makes sense, Patty," Senator Fowler said.

"Okay," Patricia Fleming said, "as long as I have the word with him now, tonight."

"Yes, of course," Dr. Unger said.

Lieutenant Patrick McGrory, MC, USN, looked a little flushed when he came into Captain Unger's office. Senator Fowler wondered if he was flushed because he had run or trotted in response to the captain's call, or whether, perhaps, the young Navy doctor had had a belt or two.

Dr. McGrory immediately put the question to rest.

"I was in the Officers' Club, sir," he said to Captain Unger. "I didn't expect to be called upon to discuss Major Pickering tonight."

"You're not drunk, certainly."

"Well, I wouldn't want to drive, sir, but I'm not drunk."

"Doctor, you probably recognize Senator Fowler," Captain Unger said.

"Yes, sir, indeed I do," McGrory said with a smile, putting out his hand. "I even voted for you, Senator, thereby enraging my staunchly Democrat family."

Fowler beamed.

"How do you do, Doctor?" Fowler said. "I have myself been known to take a little nip at the end of a hard day."

"You've a connection with Major Pickering, Senator?"

"I'm his godfather," Fowler said. "And this is his mother, Mrs. Patricia Pickering, who has herself been known to take a little nip after duty hours." He paused and looked at Captain Unger. "I mention that, Captain, to make the point that neither Mrs. Pickering nor I are in any way offended because Dr. McGrory has had a drink or two."

"I'm glad you understand," Unger said. "And I know how hard Dr. McGrory works."

"Let's talk about my son," Patricia Pickering said.

"Okay," McGrory said. "He's a hard-nose. I'm pleased to see that it's probably genetic, rather than a symptom of his condition."

"I would suggest, Doctor, that the trait may be genetically inherited from both parents," Fowler offered. "Has he spoken of his father?"

"No. Right now, he's not talking to me at all."

"What, exactly, is wrong with him?" Patricia Fleming demanded.

"Physically, he's thirty, forty, maybe more pounds underweight. He apparently didn't get much to eat while he was evading capture. His teeth are a little loose in his gums, but a dental surgeon assures me that the situation will clear itself up as we fatten him up. He looks like a scarecrow; be prepared for that when you see him."

"He's in the Neuro-Psychiatric Ward," Patricia Fleming stated, making it a question. As McGrory framed his response, she impatiently demanded, "Why?"

"Well, despite what healthy, hearty, courageous young men like your son like to think, Mrs. Pickering, experience has shown that no one goes through what your son has gone through without some psychological effect."

"And in his case, what is that effect?" she snapped.

"Just so we understand one another, Mrs. Pickering," McGrory said, "I'm on your son's side. I'm going to help him. I'm one of the good guys."

"I'm sorry," she said.

"Okay. Right now he's acting like a perfectly normal young man. That doesn't mean he is perfectly normal. And I won't be able to judge what damage he's suffered, or begin to deal with it, until he tells me what he went through, and he's told me that's none of my business."

"There's something I think I should tell you, Doctor," Fowler said. "For the first time in his life, I think, he was in love. I mean, his father tells me that he was in love."

"You mentioned his father before," McGrory said. "Is there something you think I should know about him, about Major Pickering's relationship with his father? Have there been problems there?"

"They're two peas from the same pod," Patricia Fleming said. "They are so alike, it's frightening."

"His father is Brigadier General Pickering, US Marine Corps," Fowler said. "The Deputy Director of the CIA for Asia."

"He didn't get into that at all, and I certainly would have remembered that," McGrory said. "What about this love affair? Did that give him problems?"

"The day before Pick was rescued," Fowler said, "his girlfriend — she was more to him than 'girlfriend' implies — who was a war correspondent . . . Jeanette Priestly, of the *Chicago Tribune*? . . ."

McGrory nodded, indicating that he knew who she was.

". . . was on an Air Force medical supply airplane. Trying to get into Wonsan, North Korea, it crashed, exploded, and burned. There were no survivors."

"Oh, the poor bastard!" McGrory said, and sighed audibly. And then, having heard himself, he quickly added: "I beg your pardon, Mrs. Pickering."

"Doctor, the way you said that proved to me that you meant what you said about being on Pick's side. You are one of the good guys, and I apologize for my rudeness to you before."

"Okay," McGrory said after a moment. "We're friends. That will help a good deal."

"May I ask what happens now?" Patricia asked.

"Well — don't misunderstand this; I'm grateful to hear about anything that's given him a problem — we first have to get him to talk about what he went through, and then about the girl." He paused, visibly in thought, and then went on. "Just before I was summoned here from the club, with three, four drinks in me, I had just about decided that the standard technique for dealing with patients who won't talk probably won't work with Major Pickering."

"I don't understand," Patricia said.

"The carrot and the stick," McGrory said. "If they're cooperative, they get to go to the club, even on passes — short, four- or six-hour passes, with a responsible person — and if they don't, we keep them in the ward in their bathrobes and slippers."

"I see," she said. "He's not going to like that. But it's also likely to get his back up, and —"

"The thought occurred to me," McGrory interrupted her, "that if he could evade capture for as long as he did, escaping from the ward would be child's play for him. We'd catch him, eventually, of course, but that would only serve to increase his resentment. And what we're trying to do is help him, not make him obey the rules. Let me think about that some more. If he understands that he's not going back to duty until I say so, then maybe he will start talking to me. Maybe a couple of stiff belts every afternoon at seventeen hundred is medically indicated."

He looked between them.

"Okay. Do you want to see him now?"

"Can we?" Patricia Pickering said.

"He's outside. He doesn't know why. But I know him at least well enough to know that having you two see him in the NP Ward would not be good for him." He looked at Captain Unger. "May we use your office for about five minutes, Captain?"

"Of course," Unger said. "Would you like me to leave?"

"No, sir, I'd rather that you stayed," McGrory said. "Mrs. Pickering, you heard the five minutes?"

"I'm grateful for that, Doctor," Patricia Pickering said.

"You can come back tomorrow, of course, but I really wish you wouldn't come every day."

"Whatever you say, Doctor."

McGrory got to his feet and walked to the door.

"You may come in now, Major Pickering," he said, and stepped out of the way.

Pick marched somewhat warily into the room and saw his mother.

He stopped.

Fowler thought: *Jesus Christ, he looks like*

a cadaver. I hope Patty can keep a straight face.

"Boy, I thought we'd done this for the last time," Pick said. He raised his voice to a teenage falsetto: "Momma, Uncle Dick, I don't care what they told you I did, I didn't do it."

Fowler chuckled. "Dr. McGrory," he explained, "I have often found myself accompanying Mrs. Pickering to one of Pick's boarding schools when he had some difficulty with the rules."

"How are you, son?" Patricia Pickering asked.

"Well, now that they've stopped beating me, taken off the chains, and let me out of the straitjacket, not so bad, really. How about yourself?"

"Am I going to get a kiss and a hug?"

"Sure. You're still my best girl," Pick said, and went to his mother and put his arms around her. Then he hugged her very tight.

Fowler saw that tears were running down Pick's cheeks. He looked at Dr. McGrory, caught his eye, then quickly pointed to his own cheeks.

McGrory nodded, smiled, winked, and gave him a thumbs-up.

Pick let go of his mother. He put out his hand to Fowler.

"How are you, Uncle Dick?" he asked.

[Six]
Fishbase
Socho-Ri, South Korea
1535 28 October 1950

The message exchange had been in the clear and cryptic. Captain Howard C. Dunwood, USMCR, had taken it himself.

"Fishbase, this is House. How read?"

"House, Fishbase. Read you five by five," Dunwood had replied into the microphone in the commo hootch.

"Killer en route Fishbase. ETA fifteen-twenty. Acknowledge."

"Fishbase acknowledges Killer ETA fifteen-twenty."

"House, clear."

"Fishbase, clear."

That had been a little over an hour ago. Dunwood figured if it was going to take the Killer — Major McCoy — about an hour, and the message had come from the house, that made it pretty clear that McCoy was coming from Seoul, and in the Beaver.

Dunwood was a little surprised that McCoy was returning to Socho-Ri so soon. Both Master Gunner Zimmerman and Major Alex Donald had told him McCoy had taken a fairly serious hit while exfiltrating from up north on the *Wind of*

Good Fortune, and the last word Dunwood had had was that he was in the Naval Hospital in Sasebo.

He wondered if Master Gunner Zimmerman had heard McCoy was coming and hadn't, intentionally or otherwise, told him. Dunwood thought — and it was not a criticism — that Zimmerman was the High Priest of Need to Know. Since there was no reason why Dunwood needed to be told McCoy was coming back, if Zimmerman knew, he hadn't told Dunwood.

But when Dunwood left the commo hootch and went to Zimmerman — who was inspecting the two teams who would be practicing insertions at twilight — and told him, Zimmerman looked surprised.

He didn't say anything, he just looked surprised and nodded.

Zimmerman, it could be fairly said, was the opposite of loquacious.

For that reason, Dunwood had not discussed his thoughts about having himself — and as many of his Marines as wanted to — officially transferred to the CIA. He didn't think he would get any answer beyond "you better talk to the Killer" out of Zimmerman.

From the time he'd first told Staff Sergeant Al Preston, USMC, about his idea — the day McCoy had finally called in to say he was okay, just as Dunwood

was about to launch the Bailout Mission —
he'd given it a lot of thought.

There was a lot to think about.

He realized there was a real possibility
that when he finally said something — not
knowing when, or even if, McCoy was
coming back, he had Major Dunston in
mind as the man to talk to — he would be
told, politely or otherwise, "No, thanks,
Dunwood. We're about through with you
and your men, and you'll soon be back
with the 5th Marines."

With that possibility in mind, Dunwood had given a lot of thought to counter-
arguments.

For one thing, he had been running
Fishbase since Zimmerman had been ordered to Sasebo, even before they thought
McCoy had probably been detected and
gone missing up north. He had had the
Bailout Mission up and ready to go. That
was a hell of a lot different than running
a perimeter guard around the hangar at
K-16.

While Dunwood liked what for lack of a
better word was the "informality" of
Fishbase, he had to admit that the absolute
absence of an official chain of command
posed some problems.

There was an unofficial chain of command, of course. Master Gunner Zimmerman, USMC, gave the orders, and Captain

Dunwood, USMCR, and Major Alex Donald, USA, obeyed them. In the normal military scheme of things, majors give orders to captains who give them to warrant officers, not the other way around.

At least Alex Donald and the pilots and crews of the Big Black Birds — and now the "borrowed" Beaver, and the two L-19s — knew where they stood. By command of General MacArthur himself they had been transferred to the CIA. By stretching it a little, you could say that Donald was getting his orders from the Army lieutenant colonel, Vandenburg, at The House in Seoul.

But the facts there were that Zimmerman told Vandenburg only what he thought Vandenburg had the need to know, and so far as Dunwood knew, Vandenburg hadn't even offered a suggestion about what the people at Fishbase should be doing.

Officially, Charley Company, 5th Marines, Captain Howard C. Dunwood, USMCR, commanding, was, by verbal order of the Commanding General, 1st MarDiv, on temporary duty of an unspecified nature for an indefinite period. And there were problems with that.

For one thing, Dunwood very seriously doubted if anyone in the 5th Marines — for that matter, the entire 1st MarDiv — had any idea where they were. He knew the division had landed at Wonsan.

He knew no one in 1st MarDiv knew what they were doing. Which lately had been practicing insertions and extractions using the Big Black Birds, which nobody was supposed to know about. And practicing for what? The shot-down Marine pilot they had been looking for had been found. Or he had found the Army. Anyway, he didn't need to be found, so what were they doing with the practice insertions/extractions?

The latest wrinkle in that was the idea of one of his Marines. Instead of jumping out of the door of the H-19s as they hovered several feet off the ground, they made the insertion by half sliding, half climbing down a twenty-foot-long knotted rope from the door of the Big Black Birds.

What the hell were they practicing for, night after night?

When Captain Dunwood had posed, as tactfully as he knew how, that question to Master Gunner Zimmerman, the response had been succinct but not very illuminating: "Because that's what the Killer said to do."

There were administrative problems, too. Every other day or so, when the Beaver made a supply run, it carried with it a bag of mail from home, and took out the letters the Marines had written. No stamps were necessary; you wrote "Free" on the envelope where the stamp would normally go.

Among his other duties, Captain Dunwood had been appointed censor for Fishbase, not only for his Marines but for everybody else, including the Army Aviation people. Master Gunner Zimmerman had made the appointment, and his accompanying orders had been brief.

"You read anything about where we are, what we're doing, or the Big Black Birds, anything, burn the letter."

Presumably, everybody's service records were with the 5th Marines. That meant that no one was getting paid. No one had been paid since they went to Sasebo from Pusan, before the Inchon invasion.

It didn't matter, practically. There was nothing on which to spend money, or for that matter anywhere to spend it. And the Beaver — and trucks — brought in a steady stream of supplies, including creature comforts, cigarettes, cigars, shaving cream, and the like, and of course beer, all of which was free. There had even been a shipment of utilities, underwear, winter clothing, and boots.

In the just over an hour between the heads-up from The House and the arrival of the Beaver, Captain Dunwood made up his mind. The first thing he was going to do when Major McCoy got out of the airplane was ask for a minute of his time.

He didn't know exactly what he was going to say, but he would think of something.

He could always think of something to say. Being able to think on his feet, say the right thing, was what had made him "Salesman of the Month" at Mike O'Brien's DeSoto-Plymouth Agency in East Orange, New Jersey, month after month.

Major Kenneth R. McCoy, USMCR, climbed down somewhat awkwardly from the right side of the Beaver and surveyed his staff — Captain Dunwood and Master Gunner Zimmerman — who were on hand to greet him.

"You're back?" Zimmerman asked. "What's with the leg?"

"I'm all right," McCoy said. "We brought two pigs and three crates of chickens, which have made a real mess of the airplane. Get it cleaned up before that — 'shit' is the word — has a chance to dry."

"Okay," Zimmerman said.

"Use Koreans; I need to talk to the Marines. Your Marines, Dunwood."

"Yes, sir," Dunwood said. "Sir, may I have a minute or two?"

"Just as soon as I finish talking to your Marines," McCoy said. "Get them under the camouflage."

"Aye, aye, sir," Dunwood said. "I just need a couple of minutes, sir."

"When I'm finished talking to your Marines," McCoy said, not very pleasantly.

"Yes, sir."

Jesus Christ, is he going to tell us, "Thank you. And give my regards to the 5th Marines when you get back there"?

"Can everybody hear me?" Major McCoy asked five minutes later, as he stood on the landing-gear strut of one of the H-19s under the camouflage netting.

There were murmurs that he could be heard.

"I don't really know where to begin," McCoy said. "Okay. Say what's on my mind. One of the first things I learned when I came in the Corps was never to volunteer for anything. So what I'm looking for here is volunteers."

There was laughter.

"Major, we heard you was shot?" a voice called.

"I took a piece of shrapnel," McCoy said. "I was almost a soprano, but aside from that, I'm okay."

He looked around the Marines gathered in a half-circle around him.

"From here on, what I say is Top Secret," he said. "If the wrong people hear what I'm about to say, people will die. I

781

want that clearly understood."

There had been murmurs and whispered conversation. Now there was silence.

"X Corps has landed farther north," McCoy began. "Their orders are to strike northward, past the Chosin Reservoir, to the Manchurian border. There is a very good chance the Chinese are going to come into the war just as soon as we get close to the border.

"I think there are several hundred thousand of them. I don't think many people agree with me. I know they don't. But that's what I believe. So what I need to do is put people out ahead of our forces — both 1st MarDiv and the Army's 7th Infantry Division — to find out where the Chinese are, so that our people at least have some warning.

"The way to do that, I think, is to insert people, listening posts, in enemy territory. That's what you've been practicing to do. There are lots of problems with this, starting with the fact that if the Chinese detect you there, that'll be it. We can't risk losing one or both of the Big Black Birds trying to rescue people. The two we have is all there is.

"And I can't either send you on missions like these as Marines, even as volunteers. Marines don't abandon people to the enemy. We're going to have to do just that.

And since this whole thing is secret, we can't afford to have some well-meaning Marine wanting to live up to 'we're Marines, we don't leave people, dead or alive, behind,' and asking questions we can't answer."

"So what are you asking, Major?" a voice called.

"The rules don't apply to Marines serving in the CIA," McCoy said. "So I need people to volunteer for the CIA."

Now there were murmurs.

Captain Dunwood, who had been standing to one side of the half-circle, walked toward the center.

"Sir?"

McCoy silenced him with a hand raised, palm outward.

"There will be no pressure on anybody to volunteer. I'm not sure I would. But now that the cat's out of the bag — and this isn't a threat — what happens now is that we're all in the bag. Mail will come in, but none goes out, except for a final letter saying you'll be out of touch for a while. And when this is over, those who don't think going into the CIA makes sense will be sent to the States. If there's a leak, Naval Intelligence will find out, and there'll be court-martials. But if you keep your mouth shut, no one will even know you were asked to volunteer."

"Sir?" Dunwood said again.

McCoy glared at him.

"You have something to say, Captain?"

"Yes, sir. Sir, the thing is, some of us, the noncoms and me, and the noncoms and the Marines, having been trying to think of a way to ask you how we could transfer to the CIA."

"It's not all air-delivered live pigs and cold beer, Captain. You're aware of that?"

"Yes, sir, we know that."

"And when you finally get back to the Corps, if you get back to the Corps, some sonofabitch is going to ask where you were when he was fighting the war, and you won't be able to tell him. You understand that, too?"

"Yes, sir."

"Those of you who would like to go into the CIA, give your names to Captain Dunwood," McCoy said.

There was a sudden mass movement to get close to Captain Dunwood.

McCoy jumped off the landing strut and went into the passenger compartment of the H-19.

Zimmerman quickly moved — almost ran — from where he had been standing to the helicopter and climbed inside.

He found McCoy leaning against the fuselage wall. There were tears on McCoy's cheeks.

"When this fucking leg hurts, it fucking hurts," McCoy said. "I didn't want to let them see me."

"Your leg, my ass," Zimmerman said. "What did you expect, Killer? Those guys are Marines."

XVI

[One]
Room 39A, Neuro-Psychiatric Ward
U.S. Naval Hospital
San Diego, California
0830 30 October 1950

The room assigned to Major Malcolm S. Pickering, USMCR, was furnished with a hospital bed, a white cabinet to the left of the bed, a white table to the right, a plastic-upholstered chrome armchair, and a folding metal chair.

When the door swung open, Major Pickering was sitting in the armchair with his slippered bare feet resting on the folding chair. He was reading *Time* magazine.

He glanced up from the magazine and started to get to his feet.

"As you were," Brigadier General Clyde W. Dawkins, USMC, a tall, tanned, thin, sharp-featured forty-year-old, said, and reinforced the order by making a pushing motion with his right hand.

Major Pickering ignored both the order and the signal and stood up.

"Good morning, sir," Pick said.

Dawkins smiled, turned, and waved another officer, a captain, festooned with the regalia of an aide-de-camp, into the room.

"Captain McGowan," General Dawkins inquired, "looking at that ugly, skinny officer, would you believe he had half the Marines in Korea looking for him?"

"Sir, I understand there's a shortage of pilots," Captain Arthur McGowan, a tall, slim twenty-nine-year-old, who wore the ring of the United States Naval Academy, said with a smile.

Dawkins saw Pick's face.

"Not funny?"

"No, sir."

Dawkins nodded.

"How are you, Pick?" he asked, putting out his hand. "It's good to see you."

"It's good to see you, sir," Pick said, shaking it.

"That doesn't answer my question."

"Sir, as of today, I have been promoted to Loony Category Two, which means I no longer have to give the nurse a list of what I need from the Ship's Store. And they are going to give me a partial pay."

"You look like hell," Dawkins said. "But your legendary fast lip is obviously still functioning well."

"No disrespect was intended, sir."

"I wish you'd sit down," Dawkins said.

"Aye, aye, sir," Pick said, and sat down.

"Art," Dawkins said as he turned the folding chair around and sat backward in it. "Flash your smile at the nurse and see if you can't get us some coffee."

"Yes, sir," McGowan said. "How do you take yours, Major?"

"Black, please," Pick said.

McGowan left the room.

"Billy Dunn tell you I was here?" Pick asked.

"Actually, the news came from a little higher up in the chain of command. How is Billy?"

"He was fine, the last time I saw him. More than a little disgusted with me — and justifiably so — but fine."

"I have no idea what you're talking about, Pick," Dawkins said.

"Just before the bosun's chair moved me from the *Badoeng Strait* to the destroyer *Mansfield* —"

"You mean while you were under way?" Dawkins asked.

"Yes, sir."

"I've seen that, but I've never done it," Dawkins said. "I don't like the notion of being dangled over the ocean like that. How was it?"

"Not very pleasant, sir. Sir, may I go on?"

"Sorry, Pick. You were saying?"

"I was saying that Colonel Dunn told me what he thought of me," Pick said. "What he said was that I was a self-important showboating sonofabitch whose current troubles were my own fault, that I had put the necks of a lot of good people at risk because of my showboating, and that I have never really understood that I'm a Marine officer."

Dawkins looked at him for a moment in surprise.

"My first reaction is that Billy must have had a very bad day," Dawkins said.

"Just before I got in the bosun's chair, Billy handed me a letter to mail from Japan he'd written to the wife — correction, the widow — of one of his guys who had just plowed in," Pick said. "Dick Mitchell. Writing those letters is always tough for Billy. But that wasn't what was bothering him."

"What was?"

"Me. Everything he said about me was absolutely true."

"You want to explain that?"

"What I was doing when I went in was shooting up locomotives," Pick said.

"So what?"

"I was doing this because it amused me," Pick said. "I thought it would be amusing to become the first Marine Corps locomotive ace in history."

Dawkins looked at him without saying anything.

"I had three steam engines painted on the fuselage of my Corsair," Pick went on, "under the impressive row of Japanese meatballs from War Two. I even wrote the Air Force asking if they had a record of how many steam engines had been shot up in War Two, and if so, by who, to see who and what I was competing against."

"Jesus!" Dawkins said.

"Billy, of course, thought this was bullshit, dangerous bullshit, and told me to stop. And of course I ignored him, a senior officer. Proving his point that I have never understood that I am a Marine officer."

"What happened when you went in?"

"You mean, what put me on the ground?"

Dawkins nodded.

"I made a run at a train," Pick said. "Came in over the end of it, right on the deck, and worked my fire up the length of it. Sometimes, if there's gas on the train, you can set it off with tracer rounds; we were loading one tracer in five rounds. I don't remember any gasoline explosion, but I saw the locomotive go up just before I passed over it and began my pull up. Immediately, large and small parts of the locomotive punctured my beautiful Corsair in Lord knows how many places. I lost power, hydraulics, et cetera, et cetera. There was a rather large rice paddy convenient, so I set it down, got out, and got maybe one hundred yards away — maybe a little farther — before it caught on fire and blew up. The landing wasn't really all that bad. I dumped a Corsair on Tinian just before the war was over — couldn't get the right gear down — that was really a hell of a lot worse."

The door opened and Captain McGowan returned with three china cups of coffee.

"Be careful," he said. "It's hotter than hell."

"Thank you, Art," Dawkins said, then turned back to Pick. "Were you on fire?"

"No, sir."

"I thought maybe the antiaircraft, tracers, or exploding shells might have got you."

"No, sir. No ack-ack."

"And you're sure you weren't on fire?"

"Yes, sir."

"How badly were you hurt in the crash?"

"Not at all, sir."

"How close did you come to the village?"

"Sir?"

"Was there a village where you went in?"

"No, sir."

"Give me the citation, Art," Dawkins ordered. McGowan went into his tunic pocket and came out with an envelope. Dawkins took a sheet of paper from it and read it.

"Where were the Marines — the grunts — when all this happened?" Dawkins asked.

"I was nowhere near the lines, sir. I guess I was four, maybe five miles into enemy territory."

"And the weather? What was the weather like?"

"It was good weather, sir."

"Just about everything you have told me, Major Pickering," Dawkins said, "is inconsistent with this."

"What is that, sir?"

"It's the citation to accompany your Navy Cross," Dawkins said, meeting his eyes.

"What Navy Cross, sir?" Pick asked, visibly confused.

"The one the President is going to pin on you," Dawkins said. "Or if he can't fit you into his busy schedule, and the commandant is similarly occupied, and the commanding general of Camp Pendleton can't make it, I will pin on you."

"May I see that, sir?"

Dawkins handed it to him, and Pick read it.

As he did, he shook his head and several

times muttered an obscenity.

"This is somebody else's citation," he said, finally, as he handed the sheet of paper back to Dawkins. "It has to be. The weather — I told you — was good. Ceiling and visibility were unlimited. I was not flying close support for the grunts. There was no antiaircraft. I was not on fire, and if there was a village or a school, I didn't see either. Jesus, what a fuckup!"

"I don't think there's more than one Major Malcolm S. Pickering in the Corps, Pick, and that's the name on the citation," Dawkins said.

"General, that's not my citation. I did nothing to deserve any kind of a medal. I probably should have been court-martialed for what I was doing."

"I'll look into this," Dawkins said. "In the meantime — this is an order, Pick — I don't want you saying anything to anybody about this."

"Aye, aye, sir," Pick said. "If that got out, the Corps would look pretty goddamn stupid."

"The order to give you the Navy Cross, I am reliably informed, came from the President, personally," Dawkins said. "Anything to say about that?"

"Only that I really don't understand any of this, sir," Pick said.

"Okay. I'll look into it and get back to

you," Dawkins said. He smiled at Pick. "This Chinese fire drill aside, I'm really glad that you made it back, Pick. You were gone so long that we were all really getting worried."

"Thank you, sir."

"As soon as they'll let you, my wife wants you to come out to the base for dinner."

"I accept, thank you. I'm not entirely sure about you, sir, but I'm sure Mrs. Dawkins qualifies."

"Qualifies for what?"

"When they give me a pass out of this place, it has to be in the company of a responsible person."

Dawkins looked at him a moment, shaking his head as if in disbelief.

"Captain McGowan," he said. "We have just had proof that this officer belongs in the Neuro-Psychiatric Ward. No sane Marine major would say such a thing to a very senior officer such as myself. Even if he did on more than one occasion save my tail while we were off winning World War Two all by ourselves."

"Yes, sir," Captain McGowan said.

"You understood, Pick, that it was an order you are not to mention this Navy Cross business to anyone, right?"

"Yes, sir. Not a problem, sir. The only visitor I expect is my mother, and I wouldn't tell her something like that. And I don't expect any more visitors. The fewer people who know where I am, the better."

"Hey, you have absolutely nothing to be embarrassed about being in here. Despite what Billy Dunn said when his mouth ran away with him, I'm sure he is as proud of the way you evaded capture for so long as I am. And so are just about all of the pilots who know what you must have gone through. What you did — proving it can be done — is probably going to keep a lot of other shot-down pilots from giving up."

"The general's right, Major," Captain McGowan said.

"I'm always right, Art," Dawkins said. "I'm a general. Write that down."

Pick and McGowan chuckled.

Dawkins pushed himself out of the folding chair and extended his hand to Pick.

"Welcome home, Pick," he said. "We'll see you soon."

[Two]
Headquarters X U.S. Corps
Wonsan, North Korea
0620 30 October 1950

"Jade, Jade," Major Alex Donald said into his microphone. "How do you read?"

795

"Jade reads aircraft calling five by five," a metallic voice responded.

"Jade, this is Army four zero zero three."

"Go ahead, four zero zero three."

"Jade, four double zero three is approximately three miles from your field. Be advised four double zero three is a Sikorsky H-19 helicopter painted black in color. I say again, an H-19 painted black in color."

The control tower at Jade — the landing strip serving X Corps Headquarters — took a good thirty seconds to respond, and when it did there was a new voice on the radio.

"Four zero zero three, Jade reads a black H-19. Confirm."

"Four double zero three confirms. Please take necessary action to ensure strip defense does not engage. I say again, make sure no one shoots at us."

"Four zero zero three. Do not approach at this time. Action requested will take five or more minutes. Jade will advise when you may approach."

"Thank you, Jade," Donald said, looked at Major Kenneth R. McCoy in the copilot's seat, and released the microphone switch.

Major Donald was genuinely concerned about the strip defense. He had set it up himself. There had been virtually no enemy aerial attacks on American ground forces, or for that matter even enemy aerial observation of American positions. But that didn't mean there were never going to be any.

He had, therefore, when he had been the Assistant X Corps Army Aviation Officer, spent a good deal of time thinking, planning, and setting up airfield defense. The basic weapons of the defense he had planned and set up were .50-caliber Browning machine guns, four of them, in a mount permitting simultaneous fire by one man, on White half-tracked armored cars.

There were "multiple-fifties" located at each end of the strip. The other two were positioned, depending on where the strip was located, so that they could fire on attacking aircraft without firing into the rather extensive X Corps headquarters tents or buildings.

The multiple-fifties put out a lot of fire.

There were other machine guns positioned around the landing strip, but it was the multiple-fifties he was worried about. He had had a good deal of trouble getting them onto the Table of Authorized Equipment, and then talking the G-1 into providing their crews. Each weapon had a four-man crew: the vehicle driver, the assistant vehicle driver, the gunner, and the assistant gunner. The assistant vehicle driver also functioned as an assistant gunner, which meant he kept a steady supply of loaded cans of .50-caliber ammunition moving from the ammunition trailer that the White towed, and helped the assistant gunner in other ways, including using an entrenchment tool to shovel red-hot fired cartridge cases from the bed of the White.

A really astonishing number of them would accumulate whenever the four Brownings were fired.

One of the problems Major Donald had recognized and done what he could to get around was that the crews of the multiple-fifties were aware that the enemy had yet to stage aerial attacks on an Army airstrip. That translated to mean that their assignment was bullshit. They just sat there in the hot sun (or, now, the getting-colder-by-the-day icy winds) and nothing happened.

Major Donald had done what he could to motivate them. He told them that if the enemy attacked from the air, they would be the first, and really only, defense the airstrip and indeed the entire X Corps Headquarters complex was going to have. He told them they had a great responsibility.

And he also arranged for them to have quickly removable canvas sun shields to protect them in the summer, and, preparing for the winter, to have oil-fired stoves called Cannon heaters specially rigged so they could be mounted in the bed of each of the Whites and keep the crews warm in the cold.

Thus, Donald had spent a lot of time and thought and effort establishing airstrip protection, and thought he had done a good job, especially in motivating the men. He was convinced they were on the alert, ready to instantly fill the skies over the airstrip with a steady stream of .50-caliber projectiles the moment they thought the airstrip was being threatened.

Threatened, for example, by a rotary-wing aircraft of a type they had not seen before, and which was painted black and completely devoid of American markings.

Major Donald knew that the Killer wouldn't have ordered him to fly into the X Corps airstrip on the way back from dropping two stay-behind teams in the mountains unless there was a good reason, but wished that the Killer had elected to travel by some other means than in one of the Big Black Birds.

Major Donald thought there was a very good chance his careful planning and training for the defense of the X Corps airstrip was about to come around and bite him in the ass.

Major Donald had ten — not five — minutes to consider what the fire from a multiple-fifty would do to the delicate innards of an H-19A Sikorsky before the radio went off.

"Army four zero zero three, Jade."

"Go."

"You are cleared for an approach from the north and touchdown on the threshold of the active runway. You will hold, I say again, you will hold, on the threshold until further orders. Be advised there is light aircraft traffic in the area. Acknowledge."

"Four double zero three understand approach from the north and hold on the threshold after touchdown. Beginning approach at this time."

As he made the approach, Major Donald was able to clearly see — which surprised him not at all — the four large black barrels of the White-mounted multiple-fifty tracking his approach with care and what he thought might just be eagerness.

"Jade, I'm on the ground and holding on the threshold."

"Four zero zero three, I have you in sight. You will be met."

McCoy pointed out the cockpit window. Two jeeps, each with a pedestal-mounted .30-caliber air-cooled Browning, were racing down the runway toward them.

Both stopped twenty yards from the Big Black Bird. The .30s were now trained on the cockpit.

A lieutenant colonel got out of one of the jeeps, drew his pistol, and marched somewhat warily up to the helicopter.

Donald put his head and both of his arms out his window and waved.

"Sir, it's Donald," he called from the window.

The lieutenant colonel almost certainly couldn't hear over the roar of the engine, but he recognized the face.

Neither could Donald nor McCoy hear the lieutenant colonel mutter, in either disbelief or disgust, "Jesus H. Christ!"

But they saw him holster his pistol, make arm signals to both the machine-gunners in the jeeps and in the multiple-fifty half-track, telling them there was no hazard and to deflect their weapons. Then he made a *follow me* gesture to the Big Black Bird and got in his jeep and started back down the runway.

Donald waited until the jeeps were halfway down the runway, then taxied the H-19 down it after them.

They stopped before an obviously hastily built corrugated tin building on which was a sign: OPERATIONS.

McCoy very carefully climbed down from the cockpit and went inside the fuselage. Donald climbed down far more agilely and went to the lieutenant colonel, who shook his hand and gestured unbelievingly at the Big Black Bird.

When McCoy came out of the fuselage, everybody saw that not only was he wearing what looked like black pajamas but that he was carrying a wire hanger over his shoulder. Its white paper wrapping read NAVY EXCHANGE SERVICE SASEBO.

"Colonel, this is Major McCoy," Donald said.

"That's an interesting uniform you're wearing, Major," the lieutenant colonel said. "And what is that, somebody's laundry?"

"Yes, sir. That's just what it is," McCoy said. "It belongs to Captain Haig. And I'd really like to get him on the phone as soon as I can."

"You want to tell me what's going on here?"

"Respectfully, sir, no, I don't," McCoy said. "May I use the phone, please, sir?"

"Of course," the lieutenant colonel said. He waved McCoy ahead of him into the tin building and handed him a field telephone, then cranked it for him. "Haig's number is Jade Seven," he said.

"Jade Seven," McCoy told the operator, and a moment later Al Haig's voice came over the line.

"Haig, this is McCoy. I'd really like to talk to the general."

"That can very easily be arranged, sir,"

Captain Haig said. "My last orders in that area were 'If that's who I think it is, get him up here. The airstrip'll give you a jeep.' "

"Thank you," McCoy said. He handed the telephone back to the lieutenant colonel. "Sir, could we get a ride to the CP?"

"I'll take you myself," the lieutenant colonel said.

The X Corps Command Post was a dirt-floored Quonset hut. Captain Al Haig was standing in front of it waiting for McCoy.

"I thought you were in the hospital," Haig said in greeting.

"I was," McCoy said, and handed him the hanger. "Your uniform. Thanks for the loan."

"You actually had this stuff dry-cleaned?" Haig said.

"It seemed like the thing to do," McCoy said.

"Well, thank you very much," Haig said. "The general is waiting for you. In his mess."

The Jade Room, the General's Mess, was another dirt-floored Quonset hut a few yards from the Command Post. One end of it was partitioned off to provide privacy for the half-dozen general officers of Headquarters, X United States Corps.

Only one of them, the Corps Commander, was in the mess. He was sitting on a folding metal chair before a rough-appearing wooden table. There was a tablecloth, however, and white china.

"Hello, McCoy," Major General Edward M. Almond said. "Have you had breakfast?"

"Good morning, sir," McCoy replied. "No, sir, I have not."

"Sit down," Almond ordered, and then saw what Captain Haig had in his hand. "What's that, Al?"

"Major McCoy returned the uniform he borrowed, sir," Haig said.

Almond shook his head.

"There were some real eggs from the *Mount McKinley*," Almond said. "But they never got up here. I'm sure there's some left in the sergeant's mess, but what I can offer is powdered eggs with a lot of Tabasco."

"Anything is fine, sir," McCoy said.

"I watched your helicopter come in," Almond said. "Does that mean the secret is compromised?"

"We'll have to go on that premise, sir," McCoy said. "All we can do is hope they won't be able to figure out right away what we're doing with them."

"Which is?"

"We're leaving overnight observation teams where we hope they'll be able to learn something about the Chinese."

"Hence the black pajamas? I'm surprised you're up to doing something like that."

"I hadn't planned to stay overnight, sir. They're a precaution."

"How's the leg?"

"Getting better every day, thank you, sir."

"We've had an interesting development, McCoy," Almond said as he buttered a piece of toast.

"Yes, sir?"

"The 3d ROK Division, which had been advancing toward — and was close to — the Chosin Reservoir, has encountered unusually strong resistance. They have, in fact, been turned, and are in a retrograde movement."

"I'm sorry to hear that, sir."

"They have reported they came under attack by what they estimate to be three regiments of the enemy, supported by artillery and tanks."

"That's a good deal more North Korean strength than I would have thought they had in that area, sir," McCoy replied.

"I was a little surprised myself, McCoy," Almond said. "The 3d ROK is taking up — has taken up — a defensive position south of the reservoir. As soon as I finish my breakfast, I'm going to helicopter up there and have a personal look at the situation."

"Yes, sir."

"And one of the things I hope to do

when I'm there is be able to put to rest a rumor circulating that this division-sized enemy force is not North Korean but rather Chinese."

"There's a rumor like that, sir?"

"Now, you and I both know that's highly unlikely, if not outright impossible, don't we? General Willoughby has assured us there is virtually no chance of, and certainly no intelligence suggesting, Chinese intervention, hasn't he?"

"Yes, sir. He certainly has."

"I thought you might find that interesting, Major McCoy," General Almond said. "If I had a means to do so, I'd suggest you come along with me. But unfortunately, I have only two operational helicopters, H-13s, and so there is room only for me and one of my Korean interpreters, who speaks Chinese. I can't even take Al Haig with me."

"General, I wonder how you and your interpreter and Captain Haig would feel about going with me in my Big Black Bird? The problem there is that it doesn't have any markings on it. . . ."

"Major, I would think that would fall under what is known as 'an exigency of the military service.' It's regretful that you were unable to fully comply with the Rules of Land Warfare by applying the required identification markings to your helicopter, but I don't think that should keep us from using it, do you?"

"Sir, my concern was friendly fire from the 3d ROK. They've never seen a helicopter like this."

"Al," Almond ordered, "before we go, have someone get in touch with 3d ROK and tell them they are not, repeat not, to engage any aerial target until I personally give orders to the contrary. If necessary, send an L-19, and drop a written order."

"Yes, sir."

"On second thought, both communicate with and send an L-19," Almond ordered.

"I'll get right on it, sir," Captain Haig said.

"Al, could you call the airstrip and make sure Donald fuels the Big Black Bird?" McCoy asked.

"Done," Haig said.

Almond chuckled.

"You're speaking of Major Donald?" the general asked. "My former assistant Army Aviation officer? Now a member of your . . . organization?"

"Yes, sir."

"Have you got him wearing pajamas?"

"No, sir. He has more faith in his helo than I do."

" 'All things come to he who waits,' " Almond quoted. "I believe that."

"Sir?"

"The day General MacArthur ordered me to transfer those machines to you, and I told Major Donald, he was heartbroken that he would not be able to show me what a wonderful machine his new toy was. Now he can."

"Major Donald and the helicopters have been very useful, sir," McCoy replied.

"That's what he said, McCoy. He told me — and General MacArthur — that the helicopter was going to . . . What exactly did he say? Oh, yes: 'usher in a new era of battlefield mobility.' "

"I've heard the sales pitch, sir. Many times."

Almond chuckled, then looked at him thoughtfully.

"How are they going to function in the snow, McCoy? In twenty-, thirty-degrees-below-zero weather?"

"I guess we're about to find out, sir."

"On the subject of your organization, McCoy, I've got to warn you that the commanding general of 1st MarDiv is looking for your scalp."

"Do you know why, sir?"

"Something about that company of Marines I borrowed to guard Major Donald's hangar in Seoul. He has been informed they won't be returning; that they are now members of your organization."

"Yes, sir, they are."

"He asked me if I knew anything about the transfer. I told him no. Then he said . . . I don't think I'd better tell you what he said. But he did ask me to tell him if you ever showed up here."

"Their transfer was General Howe's idea, sir. His and General Pickering's."

"I have the feeling he suspects you were behind it," Almond said. "Or that I was and don't want to admit it."

"Why would he doubt your word, sir?"

"I have the feeling he's not in my legion of admirers," Almond said. "His primary purpose in coming to see me was to discuss . . . No. To be honest, it was to question, to request that I reconsider my orders to the 1st MarDiv. They've been ordered to proceed as quickly as possible past the Chosin Reservoir. . . ."

"General Howe told me, sir. And he told me those were General MacArthur's orders to you. That the quick dash to the border was not your idea."

Almond looked at McCoy for a minute.

"Let me explain something to you, Major," he said. "In case you ever find yourself far more senior and in a position like mine. The orders came from General MacArthur. When I got them — They came by officer courier, did General Howe tell you that?"

"Yes, sir."

"— I had the choice of saying 'Yes, sir' and carrying them out, or asking permission to discuss my questions, my doubts about them, with General MacArthur. I decided that General MacArthur had his reasons for the order, and that, my personal reservations about them aside, I had no grounds to ask him to reconsider them. When I made that decision, they became my orders. You can't tell a subordinate, 'Here's your orders. I don't like them much, but here they are. Don't blame me. They came from above.' I'm surprised you haven't learned that."

"I understand, sir."

"And since I gave *my* orders to General Smith regarding what *I* want the 1st MarDiv to do, I have had a chance to reflect on General MacArthur's orders to me. They were obviously based on General MacArthur's assessment of the situation. I remembered the doubts many people had about the Inchon Landing. The general was right then, and I must presume he made the correct decision in this instance."

"Yes, sir."

"His decision obviously was based on his consideration of the intelligence available to him. That intelligence concluded — General Willoughby concluded — there is only a very remote possibility that the Chinese will enter this conflict. When General

MacArthur accepted General Willoughby's conclusions, it became his conclusion. A Corps Commander is not permitted to question conclusions drawn by the Supreme Commander. You following me, Major?"

"Yes, sir."

"Only a superior headquarters can question the Supreme Commander's judgments. And a subordinate organization commander cannot go over the head of the Supreme Commander to make his doubts known to higher headquarters."

"Yes, sir."

Almond looked at him again for a long moment.

"I don't know what we're going to find when we get to the 3d ROK, Major McCoy. But I'm not going to comment on whatever we do. I want to be in a position — and I want you to be in a position — to be able to truthfully state that whatever you report to your superiors was in no way influenced by me."

"Yes, sir. I understand."

McCoy got one final long look.

"I really hope you do, McCoy," he said, finally. "Now, if you've finished your breakfast, why don't we see what's going on at the 3d ROK Division?"

[Three]
Headquarters, 3d ROK Division
Eleven Miles Southeast of East Shore,
Chosin Reservoir
0805 30 October 1950

McCoy had suggested — and General Almond had quickly agreed — that the Corps Commander should ride in the copilot's seat "because he could get a better look at the terrain from there."

McCoy rode in the passenger compartment with Captain Haig, an ROK major named Pak Sun, and two X Corps Military Policemen armed with Thompson submachine guns. With the exception of Haig, no one had ever ridden in a helicopter before, and it was obvious — at least at first — that they were more afraid of the helicopter than they were of the prospect of meeting the enemy.

Major Sun shouted in McCoy's ear, over the roar of the engine, announcing that he had attended the University of California, Los Angeles, on a swimming scholarship. McCoy just nodded and smiled.

The flight took about fifteen minutes, and as they made their approach, McCoy saw a Cessna L-19, with the X Corps' blue-and-white "X" shoulder patch painted on the engine nacelle. The small, high-wing observation aircraft was flying a circular pattern around the landing strip, which was a gravel "paved" road running parallel to the line of rocky hills on which the 3d ROK Division had set up its defensive positions.

He wondered if the airplane was there on orders, in case it was required to provide something, or whether the pilot was just curious about the black, unmarked H-19.

An ROK major general in a surprisingly natty fatigue uniform was waiting for them with a driver and two MPs in a highly polished jeep.

Major Sun began to translate the introductions, and presented Major General Lee Do, ROK, to Major General Edward M. Almond, USA. General Almond looked at McCoy with a question on his face. McCoy shook his head no, and Almond said, "Leave Major McCoy out of this, Sun."

Sun nodded his head in acknowledgment and McCoy was not introduced.

General Almond said he wanted to go up the hill, to the emplacements, to see for himself what was going on.

"Do you want to go, McCoy?"

Instead of replying directly, McCoy turned to the ROK general.

"General," he asked in faultless Korean, "where are you keeping your prisoners?"

Major Sun was as surprised that McCoy

spoke Korean as was the ROK general.

The ROK general pointed down the road. McCoy saw the prisoners, and the moment he saw them — both from the bones of their faces and their quilted cotton uniforms — he knew they were Chinese.

"They don't look Korean to me, sir," McCoy said to Almond. "With General Do's permission, I think I'll go talk to them."

"I think it's best you do that alone, Major McCoy," Almond said.

"Yes, sir."

"Do you want Haig to go with you?" Almond asked.

"No, sir. Thank you. Major Donald and I have a little good cop–bad cop routine we've practiced, in anticipation of something like this. Put on your nasty face, Major Donald, and lead me to the prisoners."

"Yes, sir," Donald said.

"I'm sorry I'm going to miss that," General Almond said as he got in the front seat of the shiny jeep. Haig and the two MPs got in the back. Since that left no room for him, the driver was left behind when General Do got behind the wheel and drove off.

McCoy went into the fuselage and came out with a Thompson. He handed it to the

ROK soldier, a young sergeant.

"You come with us, please, Sergeant," McCoy ordered. "What I want you to do is point the weapon at the prisoners, acting as if nothing would give you greater pleasure than if the major gave you permission to shoot them."

"Are we going to shoot them, sir?" the ROK sergeant asked.

"Unfortunately, Sergeant, they are more valuable alive than dead."

"Yes, sir," the sergeant said. He was visibly disappointed.

"Okay, Alex, lead on," McCoy said.

The prisoners — there were sixteen of them; McCoy counted as he and Donald walked down the line — were sitting lined up against the side of the road, their backs against a vertical section of rocky hill that had been excavated. Two ROK soldiers, one with a Garand and the other with a carbine, guarded them.

The prisoners' hands and feet were bound. The ropes on their feet were further tied to the prisoner on either side, to discourage somebody from running away.

There was a double purpose — triple if you counted simple curiosity — in the march past. McCoy wanted them all to see Alex Donald glowering at them. And he wanted to see if he could detect from boots or a wristwatch, or simply an attitude, whether one or more of them, despite the enlisted men's uniforms they were all wearing, was an officer.

Alex finished his march past and stood in the road, about halfway down the line of prisoners, and glowered at them. McCoy walked in front of him. The driver took the Thompson from his shoulder and chambered a round. The prisoners looked at him nervously.

Number Four is glaring, McCoy thought. *His uniform is pretty clean, too. I think I have found an officer.*

"Good morning," McCoy said in Cantonese. "The officer is from the headquarters of Generalissimo MacArthur."

Well, they speak Cantonese. There are three looks of noncomprehension. The rest are fascinated. Which almost certainly means the three "who don't understand" — including Number Four — are either officers or noncoms. Probably officers.

"He wishes to ask you all some questions," McCoy went on almost conversationally, in Cantonese. "Your answers will determine which of you will be taken to a prisoner-of-war compound and which will not."

He switched to English. "Shall we shoot one or two to put them in the right frame of mind?"

"Let's wait a bit," Donald replied.

Either none of them speaks English, or they're better at concealing fear than I think they are.

He turned and spoke softly to Major Donald.

"Start with Number Four," he said. "Let's take a chance. You say to me, 'I think this one is an officer.' We'll wing it from there."

Donald nodded, then made a curt *follow me* gesture and walked toward the fourth prisoner in the line.

[Four]

```
TOP SECRET

URGENT HQ X CORPS 1015 30 OCTOBER 1950

EYES ONLY SUPREME COMMANDER UNC

PERSONAL MESSAGE FROM MAJGEN
ALMOND TO GENARMY MACARTHUR
BEGINS

SIR

REFERENCE: OPERATIONAL MAP 403
```

1. AT APPROXIMATELY 2100 29OCT50 THE 26TH INFANTRY 3D ROK DIV THEN ADVANCING TOWARD THE CHOSIN RESERVOIR ALONG THE LINE COORDINATES 323.121 DASH 324.303 CAME UNDER MASSIVE ATTACK BY A LARGE, TANK REINFORCED ENEMY FORCE OF DIVISIONAL STRENGTH.

2. THE LINES OF THE 26TH WERE BREACHED, AND THE REGIMENT IN SOME DISARRAY WAS FORCED TO WITHDRAW SOUTHEASTWARDLY AND HAS ESTABLISHED DEFENSIVE POSITIONS ALONG THE LINE COORDINATES 313.405 DASH 312.555.

3. AT FIRST LIGHT THIS MORNING I WENT TO HQ 3D ROK DIV TO CONFER WITH MAJGEN LEE DO. IT IS HIS OPINION THAT THE ATTACKING FORCE WAS NOT NORTH KOREAN BUT CHINESE. AFTER INTERROGATION OF SIXTEEN (16) ENEMY PRISONERS IN MY PRESENCE BY ROK MAJ SUN OF MY HEADQUARTERS WHO IS FLUENT IN CHINESE I AM FORCED TO CONCLUDE THAT THE PRISONERS TAKEN ARE IN FACT CHINESE, SPECIFICALLY MEMBERS OF THE 124TH RED CHINESE INFANTRY DIVISION.

4. ALL OF THE PRISONERS WERE CAPTURED WHILE ON A RECONNAISSANCE MISSION. TWO ARE OFFICERS, A MAJOR AND A SENIOR LIEUTENANT. BOTH, DURING THE INTERROGATION I WITNESSED, ADMITTED THEY WERE CHINESE, AND ASSIGNED TO THE 124TH RED CHINESE DIVISION. BOTH STATED THAT THE 124TH IS NOT REPEAT NOT ATTACHED TO OR SUBORDINATE TO ANY NORTH KOREAN COMMAND OR HEADQUARTERS BUT IS OPERATING ON ITS OWN, UNDER THE COMMAND OF THE RED CHINESE 42D FIELD ARMY. THE CAPTAIN STATED THE 42D FIELD ARMY IS ENTIRELY INSIDE NORTH KOREA, AND HAS THE MISSION OF EXPELLING UNITED NATIONS FORCES QUOTE FROM ALL AREAS NOW OCCUPIED BY UNITED NATIONS FORCES ENDQUOTE.

5. HE FURTHER STATED THERE WERE OTHER RED CHINESE FORCES NOW PRESENT IN NORTH KOREA, CONSISTING OF AT LEAST ONE MORE FIELD ARMY, CHARGED WITH THE SAME MISSION, BUT WAS UNABLE OR UNWILLING TO MAKE FURTHER IDENTIFICATION OF SUCH FORCES.

RESPECTFULLY SUBMITTED

EDWARD M. ALMOND
MAJOR GENERAL
COMMANDING X US CORPS

END PERSONAL MESSAGE FROM MAJGEN
ALMOND TO GENARMY MACARTHUR

TOP SECRET

[Five]

TOP SECRET

OPERATIONAL IMMEDIATE

FISHBASE 1125 30 OCTOBER 1950

EYES ONLY BRIG GEN FLEMING PICKERING
TOKYO VIA STATION CHIEFS SEOUL AND
PUSAN

TO ENSURE DELIVERY BOTH INTERMEDIATE
ADDRESSEES WILL FORWARD FOLLOWING
MESSAGE TO GENERAL PICKERING
IMMEDIATELY ON RECEIPT

MESSAGE BEGINS

AT APPROXIMATELY 0900 THIS DATE
UNDERSIGNED COMPLETED INTERROGATION

OF TWO SIGNIFICANT PRISONERS HELD BY 3D ROK DIVISION IN VICINITY OF CHOSIN RESERVOIR. MAJOR SIN HOW LEE AND SENIOR LIEUTENANT WONG SU OF CHICOM 42D ARMY WERE CAPTURED BY ROKS WHILE ON A RECONNAISSANCE MISSION PRECEDING A SUCCESSFUL DIVISION SIZE ATTACK, WITH ARMOR, ON 26TH INFANTRY, 3D ROKDIV BY CHICOM 124TH INFANTRY DIVISION. THE ATTACK SUCCEEDED AND ENTIRE 3D ROK DIVISION WAS RENDERED SEVENTY-FIVE PERCENT INEFFECTIVE.

BOTH OFFICERS WERE UNUSUALLY COOPERATIVE DURING INTERROGATION BECAUSE OF THEIR BELIEF THAT AN OVERWHELMING STRENGTH OF CHINESE FORCES WAS ABOUT TO ENTER WAR, AND THEY WILL SHORTLY BE RELEASED FROM CAPTIVITY.

THE INFORMATION THEY PROVIDED CONFIRMS IN EVERY IMPORTANT DETAIL WHAT THE UNDERSIGNED HAS LEARNED FROM OTHER SOURCES. MOREOVER, BOTH OFFICERS, WHO SAID THEY SERVED IN INTELLIGENCE LIAISON CAPACITIES BETWEEN CHICOM 4TH FIELD ARMY AND 42D ARMY, HAD AN USUALLY DETAILED KNOWLEDGE OF US X CORPS INTENTIONS.

THEY STATED CHICOM ATTACKS ON ROK UNITS WILL CONTINUE BUT ATTACKS ON US FORCES WILL PROBABLY WAIT UNTIL US FORCES ARE STRETCHED OUT BETWEEN EAST COAST PORTS AND THE CHINESE BORDER, WHEN QUOTE THEY WILL BE EASIER TO COMPLETELY ANNIHILATE ENDQUOTE.

BASED ON INFORMATION PROVIDED, STAY-BEHINDS WILL BE INSERTED TONIGHT AT VARIOUS PLACES WHERE THEY WILL BE IN A POSITION TO LOCATE AND CONFIRM IDENTITY OF CHICOM FORCES AS DESCRIBED BY PRISONERS. THEIR CONFIRMATION WILL FOLLOW IMMEDIATELY IF AND WHEN AVAILABLE.

IN VIEW OF THE COOPERATIVE SPIRIT OF THE PRISONERS ONCE THEY BELIEVED THEY WERE BEING INTERVIEWED BY SENIOR US INTELLIGENCE OFFICERS BOTH WITH REGARD TO IDENTIFYING AND LOCATING CHICOM FORCES AND SPEAKING OF CHICOM INTENTIONS THE POSSIBILITY MUST BE CONSIDERED THAT THEY WERE ORDERED TO PERMIT THEMSELVES TO BE CAPTURED SO THAT AMERICAN COMMANDERS WOULD RECONSIDER OR CANCEL MOVEMENT TO THE CHINESE BORDER. THIS POSSIBILITY

WOULD SEEM MORE LIKELY IF STAY-
BEHINDS INDEPENDENTLY VERIFY CHICOM
UNIT IDENTITY, LOCATION, AND STRENGTH.

THIS INTEL HAS NOT REPEAT NOT BEEN
FURNISHED TO X CORPS OR 1ST MARDIV.
IN LATTER CASE, THIS IS BECAUSE
UNDERSIGNED HAS LEARNED GEN SMITH
IS VERY DISPLEASED WITH TRANSFER OF
PERSONNEL TO CIA.

MCCOY, MAJ, USMCR

TOP SECRET

[Six]
Room 39A, Neuro-Psychiatric Ward
U.S. Naval Hospital
San Diego, California
0945 31 October 1950

When Lieutenant Patrick McGrory, MC,
USN, pushed open the door he found
Major Malcolm S. Pickering in pajamas and
robe sitting in his plastic-upholstered chrome
armchair attempting, without much success,
to spin playing cards into his wastebasket,
which he had placed on his metal folding
chair.

"A little bored, are we?" McGrory inquired.

"I'm looking forward with immense anticipation to the arrival, about now, of a Corpsman who will ask if I would like some canned grapefruit juice, if you find that of interest, Doctor."

"Well, cheer up, you're about to have a visitor."

"Well, then I guess I'd better clean up the mess" — he pointed to what looked like far more than one deck of playing cards on and beneath the folding chair. McGrory remembered the Ship's Store sold playing cards in packs of four decks — "before Mommy gets here, hadn't I?"

"It's not your mother," McGrory said. "It's somebody's wife. Can I leave here assured that you will behave as an officer and a gentleman?"

"Is her name Dawkins? Tiny little woman?"

"No. It's somebody else's wife. You are going to behave?"

"What does she want?"

"To bring a little cheer into your drab life, I suppose."

"I don't want to see anybody."

"Too late, I cleared her in. If there is misbehavior, there will not be martinis at the cocktail hour. Understood?"

Pick gave him the finger.

McGrory put his right hand on his hip, waved the left, and in a feminine lisp said,

"Oh, you Marines are so crude!"

Pick had to laugh.

"I'll see you in a while," McGrory said, and the door swung closed.

Three minutes later, just after Pick had finished picking up the cards, dumping them in the wastebasket, and putting the wastebasket back where it belonged, the door opened.

A good-looking young woman put her head into the room.

Wholesome, not striking, Major Pickering thought. *But, all in all, a very attractive package.*

"Major Pickering?" she asked.

"Guilty," he said.

"I'm Barbara Mitchell," she said.

"Yes, ma'am?"

"Dick's wife," she said, and then corrected herself: "Dick's widow."

Oh, shit! Jesus Christ, did that fucking McGrory know this? Is this his idea of therapy?

"I was sorry to hear about Dick," Pick said as he got to his feet. "He was a fine man."

"May I come in?"

"Of course," Pick said. And then his mouth ran away with him. "I'll even let you sit in the upholstered chair."

She gave him a strange look.

"I'm sorry," he said. "I guess you no-

825

ticed this is the lunatic ward. I'm afraid you'll have to take that into account."

"It's all right," she said. "And that doctor — McGrory? — said that you were in here only for evaluation, that you were . . ."

"Harmless? True. Ill-mannered, but harmless."

She walked past him and sat down in the armchair.

Nice tail.

What the fuck's the matter with you?

This is not a potential piece of tail; this is a lady whose husband just went in.

And what would you do with a piece of tail if one jumped at you?

Even one not the widow of a fellow Marine officer and Naval aviator fallen in honorable combat?

Being the prick you know you are, you'd probably nail it.

"I got a very nice letter about Dick from Colonel Dunn," Mrs. Mitchell said. "Actually, I got a letter about a week ago, and then yesterday there was another letter from Colonel Dunn, with a carbon copy of the first letter. He said that he wanted to make sure I had gotten the first. He said he'd given it to you to mail when you were taken off the *Badoeng Strait,* but that you were in pretty bad shape and it might have been . . . misplaced."

He didn't reply.

"Anyway, somewhere in his second letter he said that you were being sent here, so I had the impulse, and gave in to it, to come see if there was anything I could do for you. Bad idea, huh?"

"Not at all," Pick said. "I very much appreciate your coming."

"Really?"

"Really. Dr. McGrory is a fine fellow, but he's not much to look at."

She smiled uneasily.

Your fucking mouth is out of control. There was a clear implication there that you like looking at her.

What a fucking insensitive thing to say to a widow!

I hope she thinks I am nuts.

"Is there?" she asked.

"Is there what?"

"Anything I can do for you? Anything you need?"

Don't even start to think what you started to think. You sonofabitch!

"I'm really in pretty good shape. I really think I should be asking you that question. How are you doing?"

"Well, you tell yourself over and over that you married a Marine pilot, and that sometimes they go away and don't come back. But when it happens, you just don't believe it for a while. It's unreal."

Yeah, I know. When it happens, you just don't believe it for a while.

"I think I understand," Pick said.

She didn't challenge the statement, but he saw in her eyes that she simply thought he was being nice.

She doesn't want to hear your problems. She's got a load of her own.

"The same day I was rescued," he heard himself saying, "my girlfriend — we were talking about getting married — was in an Air Force medical supply Gooney Bird that went down in Korea."

"Oh, how terrible for you!" she said.

"You're right, you just don't believe it for a while," he said.

"She was a nurse?"

"A war correspondent," he said. "Jeanette Priestly. Of the *Chicago Tribune.*"

"Oh, I saw that in the paper," she said. "I'm so sorry."

"Thank you," he said.

"I didn't believe it when the notification team came," she said. "I guess I didn't believe it until yesterday, when they called up to ask 'what my wishes were with regard to funeral arrangements.' Then it really sank in."

"What were they talking about?" Pick asked.

"Well, they've recovered what they call Dick's 'remains.' Why can't they say 'body'?"

"I don't know," Pick confessed.

"And they wanted to know 'my wishes.' "

"What about? Where to . . . bury him?"

"Uh-huh. And when did I want to accept his Distinguished Flying Cross? At the funeral, or separately?"

"What did you decide?"

"Well, he's not going back to Arkansas. He hated Arkansas."

"That's where his family is?"

She nodded. "Mine, too."

"Are you going there? What are you going to do?"

"I don't know. The only thing I know is that I'm not going to go back to Arkansas. I'm going to bury Dick here. We were happy here."

"You mean in San Diego?"

"At the National Cemetery, on Point Loma?"

"I know it."

"It overlooks the ocean. Dick loved the ocean. I do, too. Maybe because there's no ocean in Arkansas."

"I grew up on the ocean," Pick said. "And I love it, too."

"Where?"

"San Francisco," Pick said. "My parents have a place on the ocean a little south of San Francisco."

"You're not a regular, are you?" she asked.

He shook his head no.

"Just a weekend warrior," he said.

"What did you do as a civilian?"

"I flew for an airline," he said. "Trans-Global."

"That's what I'd like to do," she said.

"Fly for an airline? I don't think they have lady pilots."

She giggled, and smiled at him.

Jesus Christ, I could fall into those eyes.

"No, silly. I meant see if I could get a job as a stewardess. Maybe I could get a recommendation from you at Trans-Global? Absolutely no experience, but willing to learn. Free to travel. No family ties."

"I thought you said your family was in Arkansas."

"They were annoyed — Dick's family and mine, both — when I wouldn't go 'home' when Dick shipped out. There were words then. And when I wouldn't go home . . . after Dick died, there were more words."

"I'm sorry to hear that," Pick said.

"And I'm sorry I told you," she said, and stood up. "I really am. I came here to see what I could do for you, and here I am, telling you all about my woes."

"Haven't you ever heard 'misery loves company'?"

"Yeah, but I don't think it means what you're suggesting."

"What do you think it means?"

"It means that people that complain, whine a lot, like to be around people who complain and whine a lot."

"I think people like you and me, Mrs. Mitchell, who have lost the most important person in our lives, have every right to feel a little sorry for ourselves. This miserable person, Mrs. Mitchell, hopes that your standing up doesn't mean you're going to leave."

She met his eyes again.

Jesus, she looks right through me!

"I was about to say 'I have to run,' " she said. "That would have implied I have somewhere to go. I don't, really. So if you'd like me to stay awhile, Major Pickering, I'd like to."

"Pick," he said. "My name is Malcolm, but nobody calls me that."

She put out her hand.

"Babs," she said. "How do you do?"

"You mean aside from being in the loony bin?"

She giggled and looked at him again and smiled, and Pick realized he was holding on to her hand longer than he should be. He quickly let go. He saw a faint blush on her face, and decided that proved she had picked up on the hand-holding.

You may relax, Mrs. Babs Mitchell. The one thing this miserable sonofabitch is not going to do is one fucking thing that will give you any reason to suspect that I'm even thinking of anything that could resemble a pass.

[Seven]
Room 39A, Neuro-Psychiatric Ward
U.S. Naval Hospital
San Diego, California
1305 31 October 1950

"I was wondering when you were going to show up," Major Malcolm S. Pickering said to Lieutenant Patrick McGrory, MC, USN, when McGrory came into the room.

"I'm flattered," McGrory said. "I didn't think you cared. Especially after I saw you and your visitor in the O Club."

"It was lunchtime, I offered to take her to lunch," Pick said. "That's all there was to that. No, that's not true. Tell me how much I have to tell you about my terrible ordeal to get a six-hour pass the day after tomorrow."

"What the hell was it, lust at first sight?"

"The lady is burying her husband. She asked me to attend the service and the funeral. Jesus Christ, McGrory!"

"She told me she was a Marine pilot's wife. She didn't say he was dead."

"He flew a Corsair off the *Badoeng Strait*

832

and then into the ground," Pick said. "He was a very nice guy. She doesn't have any family, and I intend to be there with her when she buries him. Don't fuck with me on this, Doc."

"I won't even demand that you describe your ordeal, Pick," McGrory said. "You probably wouldn't tell me the truth anyway. I want you to talk about it with me when you want to, not before."

"I get the pass?"

McGrory nodded.

"Thank you."

"I don't know if I'm saying this as your friend or your physician, Pick, but either way, I think it has to be said."

"What has to be said?"

"There's what I call the boomerang syndrome in the relations between men and women. Most commonly it's when a divorced guy, after lifting the skirts of every bimbo in town, finds and falls in love with a twin — physically or psychologically, and often both — of his detested ex-wife. When there is a death — in this instance, there are two deaths — the woman, whether she's aware of it or not, hungers for a strong male shoulder to lean on, and the man — although he may hate himself for it — starts looking for a replacement for his lost love."

"It's not like that here, Doc," Pick said.

"You're on goddamned thin ice, Pick, in a situation like this. If you don't want to hurt the woman, keep your distance. If you don't want to get kicked in the balls again — this widow is not your late girl-friend — keep your distance."

"How did you hear about my late girl-friend?"

"In my first transoceanic telephone call," McGrory said. "Your father told me. They're sending her body back, too, and he thought I should know."

"Were you going to tell me about that, McGrory?"

Dr. McGrory chose to ignore the question.

"If you're going to be going on pass the day after tomorrow," Dr. McGrory said as he took his notebook from his shirt pocket, "you'll have to have a uniform. I'll give you an authorization for the officers' sales store, and to prove what a really good guy I am, I'll call the manager — a Jewish boy named Francis Xavier O'Malley — and tell him you're a friend of mine, and really need the uniform tailored by tomorrow at seventeen hundred."

"Were you going to tell me about Jeanette's body, McGrory?"

"That was then, no. This is now, and I just did. They're going to have a formal — what the hell is the word? — 'reception 'ceremony' for it at North Island Naval Air Station in three, four days."

"And am I going to get to go to this 're-ception ceremony'?"

"That depends on how you behave when you bury the lady's husband," Dr. Mc-Grory said.

He tore a page from his notebook and handed it to Pick.

"Give that to O'Malley," he said. "And don't let them cut the material too much when they take it in. I have every hope that you'll soon be a little heavier."

Pick chuckled. "I didn't think about that," he said. "I guess I'm now a 42-Skel-etal, right?"

"Something like that. I also am enter-taining boyish hopes that when we're through burying people, you'll understand that I really am trying to be a friend, and that you'll start talking to me."

"Life is funny, McGrory," Pick said. "The one thing you can be sure of is that you can't predict the future."

XVII

[One]
8023d Transportation Company (Depot, Forward)
Wonsan, North Korea
1335 31 October 1950

"You can look at it now, sir," First Sergeant Jackson J. Jamison said to Captain Francis P. MacNamara. "It's just about done, and I think we have the finest crapper in Wonsan."

"Well, let's have a look at it," MacNamara said, and left his tent and followed Jamison past a long line of three-quarter-ton trucks to the edifice to which Jamison had made reference.

It sat on a small rise in the compound close to — but not too close to; MacNamara had selected the site himself — the men's tents. It had a wooden frame, to which canvas had been nailed.

There was a door at each end, for ventilation. Inside was a four-holer of smooth, unpainted wood. There was a sort of center pole, a sturdy six-by-six timber, to which a box had been nailed. The box held a dozen rolls of toilet paper, half a dozen spray cans of DDT, which would both kill the flies and sort of serve as a deodorant, and a box of candles.

MacNamara walked to the rear of the structure and examined his personally de-signed waste-disposal system. This con-sisted of cut-in-half fifty-five-gallon fuel barrels to which handles had been welded. A wooden shelf structure permitted the half-barrels to be slid under the holes in the four-holer. They would be changed twice a day.

Five minutes later, just as Captain MacNamara decided he was *very* pleased with the latrine he had designed and or-dered constructed for his men, First Ser-geant Jamison touched his arm and directed his attention to the line of three-quarter trucks down which they had re-cently walked.

A jeep was now coming down the line. Standing up in the front seat was Colonel T. Howard Kennedy, the X Corps Trans-portation Officer.

Captain MacNamara had three thoughts.

He's looking for me. I wonder what he wants?

Who does he think he is? Patton?

If I handle the sonofabitch right, he might be helpful in me getting to stay on active duty when the war is over, as it looks like it's going to be any day now.

MacNamara said, "Damn good job, First Sergeant. Tell the men."

"Yes, sir."

MacNamara then hurried around to the front of the latrine, and saluted crisply as Colonel Kennedy drove up.

"You weren't in your office, Mac-Namara," Colonel Kennedy said, more of an accusation than an observation.

"I was having a look at the new latrine, sir. Perhaps the colonel would like to have a look?"

Kennedy gave him a strange look.

"Perhaps some other time, Mac-Namara," Colonel Kennedy said.

"Yes, sir. I realize the colonel's a busy man."

"You have no idea how busy," Kennedy agreed, then turned to the business at hand. "MacNamara, I want you, right now, to start moving your vehicles up around Hamhung. You're too far south to do anybody any good here."

"Yes, sir. Where in Hamhung would you like me to set up, sir?"

"Anyplace you can do your job, Captain," Colonel Kennedy said, somewhat abruptly. "But start moving now. Not after supper, not tomorrow morning — now."

"Yes, sir," MacNamara said.

Colonel Kennedy looked at him for a

moment, then said: "It's important that we get your vehicles north, MacNamara. X Corps is attacking north, and we'll be moving rapidly. If you have any trouble, let me know. Can you think of any problems right now?"

"Yes, sir."

"Well?"

"Drivers, sir," MacNamara replied.

"What about drivers?"

"Sir, I have right at six hundred vehicles to move. I have four officers and one hundred thirty-seven men — I have eight in hospital — and with just that many men, I'll have to make a lot of trips. Four, at least."

"You know, I didn't think about drivers," Colonel Kennedy confessed. "Let me get back to you, MacNamara. In the meantime, get off the dime."

"Yes, sir."

An hour later, Colonel Kennedy returned.

"We're going to kill two birds with one stone, MacNamara," he said, sounding pleased with himself. "Maybe more than two."

"Yes, sir?"

"The 7th Infantry Division Replacement Company has to be moved to Hamhung, too. Tents, equipment, and men. Instead of having them moved by a Transportation

Truck Company, *you're* going to move them."

"Yes, sir."

"They have about three hundred replacements waiting assignment," he said. "I figure one in two of them should be able to drive a truck, and just about all of them should be able to drive a jeep."

"Yes, sir."

"That should give you all the drivers you need. Hie thee over to the Reple-Deple, MacNamara, they'll be expecting you."

"Yes, sir."

"Time is of the essence, MacNamara. Time is of the essence."

"Yes, sir."

Captain Roscoe T. Quigley, Adjutant General's Corps, who commanded the 7th Infantry Division Replacement Company, had quickly informed Captain MacNamara that he wasn't exactly happy with his orders from Colonel Kennedy, which he described as "verbal and vague in the extreme."

"I don't even know where I am to set up in Hamhung," he said, almost wistfully.

The moment he laid eyes on Captain Roscoe T. Quigley, AGC, a tall and slender officer with a pencil-line mustache, MacNamara had decided that Quigley (a) would much prefer to be in a heated office somewhere carefully checking Daily Morning Reports for prohibited strikeovers than where he was, trying to keep warm and dry in a leaking, dirt-floored tent, with the responsibility for feeding and housing three hundred–plus soldiers and (b) that Quigley, like most AGC officers in his experience, would be a real pain in the ass if he didn't quickly understand who was giving the orders.

"I think I know what we should do, Captain Quigley," MacNamara had said, firmly.

"What's that?"

"You and I will lead the advance party," MacNamara said. "A small convoy — say, no more than twenty six-by-sixes . . ."

"That's a *small* convoy?"

"We have six hundred vehicles to move. Yes, Quigley, I'd say twenty against six hundred is a small convoy. Wouldn't you?"

"I had no idea there were that many vehicles."

"You and I — taking with us two of my officers and, say, forty of my men, and as many of your officers and men as you think you'll need — will go to Hamhung, reconnoiter the area, locate suitable areas for your replacement depot and my unit, and start setting up. Then you and I, having learned the route and the problems encountered on it, will bring enough noncoms back here, where they will set up convoys of the others. In the meantime, while you and I are up north, I will have my first sergeant run what I suppose you could call a driver's school for the drivers. You have any problems with that?"

"When had you . . . uh . . . planned to . . . uh . . . *launch* your convoy?"

"In an hour," MacNamara said.

"You mean today?"

"Colonel Kennedy told me, Quigley, that time is of the essence," MacNamara said. "You can do what you like, of course, but I'm going to start for Hamhung in an hour."

"Oh, I'll go with you, of course, Captain MacNamara," Captain Quigley said. "But I was wondering about an escort, I guess is what I mean."

"What do you mean by an escort?"

"I think we have to consider the possibility that we may encounter the enemy on the road."

"I doubt it," MacNamara said. "If there were enemy forces in the area, I'm sure Colonel Kennedy would have told me. Anyway, we're going to have, say, at least five men on each truck, times twenty trucks, which means we'll have at least a hundred men. That ought to be enough to defend ourselves."

"Well, I'll get right on it, of course, but it will take some time to issue ammunition to . . . What did you say, one hundred men?"

"They have weapons but no ammunition?"

"You wouldn't believe the incidents that happen when the men in the replacement stream have access to live ammunition," Captain Quigley said. "It's like the O.K. Corral."

"Well, they better have live ammo now," MacNamara said. "A full combat load."

"You're right, of course," Quigley said.

"I'll be back in an hour," MacNamara said.

[Two]
The Director's Office
East Building, The CIA Complex
2430 E Street
Washington, D.C.
1615 31 October 1950

"May I come in, General?" Major General Roger J. Buchanan, USA, Ret'd., inquired of Walter Bedell Smith after he had been standing for two minutes — it seemed longer — in the open door, waiting for Smith to look up from what he was reading.

Smith lifted his eyes to the door and made a waving motion with his hand.

"Sure, Roger," Smith said. "What have you got?"

General Buchanan had worked for Smith through most of the time Smith had been General of the Army Dwight David Eisenhower's Chief of Staff at Supreme Headquarters, Allied Expeditionary Force in Europe, and had come to work for Smith shortly after Smith had been named Director of the Central Intelligence Agency.

"An urgent Eyes Only The Director from General Pickering," Buchanan said, walking to the desk and laying a manila folder on Smith's desk. Smith opened it. It was a thin sheaf of paper, each sheet bearing stamps reading TOP SECRET and EYES ONLY THE DIRECTOR at the top and bottom.

Smith picked up the sheet and started to read it, then looked at Buchanan.

"You haven't read this, right?" he asked.

"Of course not, General," Buchanan said. "It's classified Top Secret, Eyes Only The Director."

They both chuckled. It was a private joke. They both knew that it was impossible to transmit an Eyes Only message that would be seen only by the eyes of the addressee. It had to be seen by the cryptographer (and probably, since this was a high-level message, by the officer supervising the cryptographer) when it was dispatched, and then by the cryptographer at the receiving end (and again, more than likely by his superior). And then, after it had been delivered — in this case, to the director's office — it had to be read by the Director's Executive Assistant (General Buchanan), who had to know everything the director knew.

About the only use Smith and Buchanan thought the Eyes Only classification had was that Eyes Only messages — if they weren't immediately shredded and burned — had their own filing cabinet. Which also meant that the officer in charge of classified documents had to read it to know where to file it, or what it was he was shredding and burning.

Smith bent slightly over his desk and began to read the message.

TOP SECRET
URGENT

TOKYO 1605 30 OCTOBER 1950
FROM DEPUTY DIRECTOR FOR ASIA

TO (EYES ONLY) DIRECTOR, CIA, WASHINGTON

DEAR MR. DIRECTOR,

ATTACHED HERETO IS A MESSAGE I RECEIVED TWO HOURS AGO FROM MAJOR

MAJOR KENNETH R. MCCOY, USMCR, PRESENTLY IN KOREA. I ATTACH GREAT IMPORTANCE TO IT FOR SEVERAL REASONS:

1. IT IS THE FIRST TIME MCCOY HAS FLATLY STATED THAT SUBSTANTIAL CHINESE COMMUNIST FORCES ARE ALREADY IN NORTH KOREA. HERETOFORE, HE HAS MADE IT CLEAR THAT HE HAS HAD NO HARD INTELLIGENCE TO BACK HIS BELIEF THAT THIS IS THE CASE. I CONSIDER IT GERMANE TO POINT OUT THAT MCCOY SPEAKS CANTONESE FLUENTLY AND IS A HIGHLY SKILLED INTERROGATOR. THERE IS NO POSSIBILITY THAT HE DID NOT UNDERSTAND, OR MISCONSTRUED, WHAT WAS SAID TO HIM BY THE CHINESE PRISONERS.

2. I ATTACH GREAT IMPORTANCE TO THE POSSIBILITY MCCOY SUGGESTS THAT THE PRISONERS ARE IN EFFECT MESSENGERS SENT TO MAKE IT CLEAR THAT CHINESE MILITARY FORCES WILL ENTER THE CONFLICT IF EIGHTH ARMY AND X CORPS CONTINUE TO ADVANCE TOWARD THE MANCHURIAN AND SOVIET BORDERS.

3. I HAVE JUST CONFERRED WITH MAJOR GENERAL CHARLES WILLOUGHBY, GENERAL

MACARTHUR'S INTELLIGENCE OFFICER.
WITHOUT MAKING REFERENCE TO MAJOR
MCCOY'S MESSAGE, I ASKED GENERAL
WILLOUGHBY IF HE HAS HAD ANY NEW
INTELLIGENCE WHICH HAS GIVEN HIM
CAUSE TO RECONSIDER HIS BELIEF THAT
THE ENTRY OF THE CHINESE INTO THE
CONFLICT IS HIGHLY UNLIKELY, AND EVEN
IF THERE WAS SUCH INTERVENTION, IT
COULD BE EASILY DEALT WITH BY EIGHTH
ARMY AND X CORPS. GENERAL
WILLOUGHBY STATED HE HAS HAD NO
INDICATION WHATEVER THAT ANY CHINESE
FORCES HAVE CROSSED INTO NORTH
KOREA FROM MANCHURIA, AND HE
THEREFORE HAS HAD NO REASON TO
RECONSIDER HIS POSITION.

RESPECTFULLY SUBMITTED,

FLEMING PICKERING, DEPUTY DIRECTOR
FOR ASIA

ONE ATTACHMENT, TOP SECRET URGENT
MSG FISHBASE 1125 30 OCTOBER 1950
TO DEP DIR FOR ASIA

TOP SECRET

"Very interesting," Smith said, raising
his eyes to General Buchanan.
"He's putting a lot of weight on the judg-

ments of a pretty junior officer, isn't he?"

"From what I hear, a rather unusual 'pretty junior officer,'" Smith said. "The President is taken with him, I know that."

"What are you going to do, General?"

Smith pointed to a red telephone on his desk.

"Get on there, Roger," Smith ordered, "and ask when the President can see me."

"Yes, sir."

Buchanan picked up the handset and was about to push Button Two, which would cause the telephone in the outer office of the President's office in Blair House to ring, when, with a sudden movement, Walter Bedell Smith reached over and pressed the switch in the base of the telephone, halting the call.

Buchanan looked at him in surprise.

"Roger," Smith said, "the Director would like to see the President, not General Smith."

"Whatever you say, sir," General Buchanan said.

"These are white shirts and multicolored neckties we have on," Smith said. "And there are no epaulets with stars on them on our shoulders. We're going to have to keep that in mind. Starting with you. You can call me anything but 'General.'"

"Certainly, Your Holiness," Buchanan said.

Smith chuckled and took his finger off

the telephone switch. Buchanan pushed Button Two.

"This is Roger Buchanan of the Director's office," he said. "Director Smith would like to see the President as soon as possible."

Smith mimed clapping his hands and mouthed, "Very good, *Mr.* Buchanan."

Buchanan smiled at him, then said "Thank you" into the telephone. Then he covered the microphone with his hand. "He's there, Mr. Director. She's going to ask him."

Less than thirty seconds later, Buchanan said, "Yes, sir, he is. Hold one, Mr. President."

He handed the phone to Smith.

"Good afternoon, Mr. President," Smith said into the phone, then listened for a moment and added, "I'm glad to hear that, sir. I would like his opinion of what I want to show you. I'll leave directly. Thank you, Mr. President."

He put the phone in its cradle.

"General Howe is with the President," Smith said. "Fresh from the Far East."

He pushed himself out of his chair and walked quickly toward his office door.

Buchanan picked up the red telephone and pushed Button Nine.

"This is Gen . . . this is Roger Buchanan. The Director's car at the door — now," he ordered.

[Three]
The President's Office
Blair House
Pennsylvania Avenue
Washington, D.C.
1655 31 October 1950

"That was quick, Mr. Smith," Harry S Truman said to Walter Bedell Smith.

Smith looked around the room and saw there was no one in it but the President and Major General Ralph Howe, NGUS, who was in civilian clothing. That pleased him. That meant that the President would not, out of courtesy, show Pickering's Eyes Only to any one of a number of people around him who really didn't have to — shouldn't — see it.

"I came as quickly as I could manage, Mr. President," Smith said.

"I think I should say this," Truman said as he shook his hand. "I wasn't trying to be distant, formal, when I called you 'Mister.' I'm just not comfortable with 'Beetle.' It sounds disrespectful."

"Mr. President, you can call me anything you'd like to call me."

"How about 'Smith'? Would that be all right? Or even 'Smitty'?"

"Either would be fine, Mr. President," Smith said.

"Maybe 'Smitty' goes a little too far the

other way," Truman said. "*Smith,* you remember General Howe, don't you?"

"Yes, sir. Of course. Welcome home, General."

"Thank you," Howe said.

"When you called, Smith, I was just about to send Ralph over to see you. I have ordered him to repeat to you some of the unkind things he's been telling me about Douglas the First, Emperor of Japan, and his Royal Court."

"I'll be interested to hear them, sir. At your convenience, General."

"What Ralph tells you is to go no farther," Truman said. "Especially not across the Potomac to the Pentagon."

"I understand, Mr. President," Smith said.

"What have you got for me?" Truman asked.

"An Eyes Only from General Pickering," Smith said.

He started, somewhat awkwardly, to try to open his briefcase.

"That would be a lot easier if you were sitting down," Truman said.

"Thank you, Mr. President," Smith said, and found a place on a small couch.

"Are you a drinking man, Smith?" the President asked. "Or is it a little early for you?"

Smith hesitated, and finally said, "I take

a drink from time to time, sir."

"Ralph and I are about to have a very stiff Jack Daniel's," the President said. "Is that all right, or would you like something else?"

"Jack Daniel's would be fine, sir, thank you."

Howe got out of his chair and walked to the door.

"Charley, get us three Jack Daniel's — better make that a bottle — and ice, et cetera," he ordered, then came back in time to carry the envelope Smith had finally gotten out of his briefcase to the President.

Truman opened the envelope, took out the contents, and then pushed himself far back in his red leather judge's chair to read it. He did so carefully, put the papers back in the manila folder, and then, just as Charley Rogers, also in civilian clothing, came into the office trailed by a white-jacketed steward, threw the folder on his desk and said angrily, "Sonofabitch!"

"Mr. President?" Charley Rogers asked.

"Not you, Charley," Truman said. He pointed to the manila folder. "Hand that to your boss, and then sit down and have a drink with us."

Rogers moved to comply as the steward poured the drinks.

"That'll be all, when you finish, thank

you," Truman said to the steward. "Leave the bottle."

The steward quickly finished what he was doing and left the room.

"Charley, do you know Director Smith?" Truman asked.

"No, sir."

"This is Charley Rogers," the President said. "Master Sergeant Charley Rogers. He and I go as far back as General Howe and myself." He paused, then added, "One vote the other way, and it would more than likely be General Rogers and Master Sergeant Howe."

"Sir?" Smith asked, confused.

"When we mobilized for the First War," Truman said, "we elected our officers. Did you know that?"

"I think I heard something about that, sir," Smith said.

"I got my commission, captain, and command of Battery B that way. I was elected to it," Truman said. "Ralph got his the same way. He beat Charley by one vote . . ."

"True," Howe said.

". . . and Charley didn't want to be a second lieutenant . . ."

"Also true," Rogers said, chuckling. "I still don't."

". . . so he became First Sergeant," Truman finished. "I've often thought electing officers is a pretty good way to get them."

Rogers and Smith shook hands.

"Well, Ralph?" the President asked. "What do you think of that message?"

"Mr. President," Howe said, "from what Pickering says, and knowing McCoy as well as I do, I'd say you can take this to the bank."

"Unfortunately, it's not as simple as taking it to the bank," Truman said. "It has to go to the Pentagon. And that opens a whole new can of worms. There's a lot of pressure on me to relieve Douglas MacArthur. If they see this, that'll give them one more argument that he's — how do I say this? — *past his prime.* And should go. Ralph tells me that he's a military genius, and Pickering agrees with him."

"General Howe . . ." Smith began, then stopped to look at the President for permission to go on. Truman nodded. "You said you place credence in this major's intelligence?"

"That's right, I do."

"It doesn't surprise you at all that he seems to have intelligence that refutes what we're hearing from General MacArthur?"

"The only thing that surprised me . . . What do I call you? 'General'?"

"Not 'General,' please," Smith said. "I really don't mind 'Beetle.' "

"Okay, Beetle. The only thing that surprised me — and now that I think about, it didn't really surprise me — was that the Killer was back in Korea. Charley and I saw him just before we left Seoul to come home. General Almond told me he took a pretty good hit."

"What did you say, Ralph?" the President asked. " 'Took a pretty good hit'? What do you mean?"

"The Killer? Is that what they call him?" Smith asked, chuckling.

"His friends can," Howe said. "Charley and I are in that category."

" 'Took a hit,' Ralph?" the President pursued. "Back in Korea from where?"

"The Navy Hospital in Sasebo," Howe said. "He was in North Korea, way up where the Russian, Manchurian, and North Korean borders come together, listening to Soviet Army radio traffic. On his way out, he got hit."

"You didn't tell me that, Ralph," the President said.

"I didn't think it was important. All he heard was routine stuff. Not enough to be able to say the Russians won't come in, but enough to make him think they probably won't."

"Goddamn it, Ralph," the President said. "I meant about him getting hit. How badly?"

"Apparently not badly enough to keep him from going back to Korea," Howe said.

"Presumably he had General Pickering's okay?"

"Mr. President," Charley Rogers said, "if the Killer thought he should be in Korea, he'd go if he had to crawl, and I don't think General Pickering would try to stop him." He paused, then added: "He wasn't crawling, sir. He was limping, and you could tell he was in some pain, but —"

"Sonofabitch," the President said.

"You sound as if you're angry with *him*, Har . . . Mr. President," Howe said. "Don't shoot the messenger."

"My *displeasure*, General, is with Emperor Douglas the First, and this deaf, dumb, and blind intelligence officer of his, not Major McCoy," the President said. "And my *displeasure* is such that, knowing myself, I know that whatever decision I make right now I'll regret later."

"You have time, sir," Smith said. "McCoy's message said he was going to insert observation teams to verify what the prisoners told him. It'll be twenty-odd hours before we get that report, probably."

"Yeah," the President said, then grunted. "When I heard what he did to rescue Pickering's son, I told General Bradley I wanted him decorated. With the Silver

Star. Did that happen?"

"I understand General MacArthur . . . at least intended . . . to make the presentation himself," Rogers said. "McCoy didn't say anything about it. He wouldn't."

"Goddamn it, I was decorating him, not the goddamn Emperor!" Truman exploded. "Give him another medal. Give him a . . . Legion of Merit. That's for senior officers, isn't it? He's been functioning like a senior officer — give him a senior officer's medal!"

The President saw the look on Rogers's face.

"You find that amusing, Charley?" Truman challenged. "Why is that amusing?"

"I'm afraid to tell you, sir," Rogers said.

"What's so goddamn funny, Charley?" the President said, and there was menace in his tone.

"The thing is, sir," Rogers said carefully, "that enlisted men, like me, and junior officers, like Major McCoy, who are close to the men, consider the Legion of Merit to be the brass's good-conduct medal. If they don't get social disease for six consecutive months, they get the Legion of Merit."

Howe laughed. Truman glowered at him.

Then Truman laughed.

"I never heard that before," he said, shaking his head. "Did you, Smith?"

"Yes, sir, Mr. President," Smith said.

"My wife told me, when I was given the Legion of Merit."

That produced a hearty laugh from the President.

"Well, then, to hell with the Legion of Merit for McCoy," the President said. "Give him something else. Give him another Silver Star." He paused. "Will you relay my wishes to the Pentagon for me, Smith? Right now, I don't want to talk to anybody over there."

"Yes, sir, of course."

"And while you're at it," the President ordered, "find out if Pickering's boy got the Navy Cross I ordered for him. If he doesn't have it already, find out why."

"Yes, Mr. President."

"You can tell me tomorrow when you come back here to tell me what McCoy's men have learned about Red Chinese troop dispositions."

"Yes, sir."

The President extended his empty glass to Charley Rogers and said, as much to himself as to the men in the room, "If I relieve MacArthur now because he's indulging this intelligence officer of his and is not taking the proper action, and McCoy is wrong, and the Chinese don't come in, every Republican in the country is going to say I cheated him out of his victory at the last moment for political reasons. And that's exactly what it will look like."

No one said anything.

Charley Rogers handed him a fresh drink.

The President took it and leaned against his desk, and stirred the ice cubes thoughtfully with his index finger.

Then he smiled.

"Six months without VD, huh?" he chuckled. "I wonder if I should tell Bess about that one?"

"I wouldn't, Har . . . Mr. President," Howe said.

"Hell, I couldn't," the President said. "If I did, Bess would immediately start to examine the ribbons of every general she saw, and God help the poor general who didn't have a Legion of Merit." He laughed, then raised his glass to Rogers. "Thank you very much, Charley. I needed a laugh."

[Four]
The House
Seoul, South Korea
1655 1 November 1950

"All of my life, Major McCoy," Lieutenant Colonel J. D. Vandenburg, USA, greeted Major K. R. McCoy, USMCR, as McCoy walked into the dining room, "I was told that Marines, whatever the situation, are models of military sartorial splendor. I have to tell you, you are shattering that illusion."

McCoy was wearing black pajamas, U.S. Army combat boots, a fur-collared Army zippered flight jacket, and a huge black fur cap, which he took off as he smiled at Vandenburg.

"I really like the hat," Vandenburg said.

"I took it away from a Chinese officer —"

"You're sure he was a *Chinese* officer?" Vandenburg interrupted.

"I am sure he was a *Chinese* officer," McCoy said. "He told me he got it in Russia. I believed that because he spoke pretty good Russian. I'm going to give it to my wife. I think it's Persian lamb. I thought maybe she could make a muff out of it. Or a purse, maybe."

Vandenburg picked up the hat and examined it.

"Or wear it as a hat," he said. "That's very nice. Only senior officers would get such finery."

"He admitted to being a lieutenant colonel," McCoy said. "I suspect he's more than that."

"I was fascinated with your idea that the first Chinese you interrogated were messengers. . . ."

"Can we talk about that after I get something to eat?" McCoy asked as he took off his flight jacket. "I haven't had anything to

eat since breakfast, and that was cold powdered eggs."

"Sorry, I didn't think. You want something to drink?"

"I'd like a stiff shot of scotch, and then a
cup — several cups — of hot coffee."

McCoy walked to the door to the kitchen
and spoke with the housekeeper, who told
him there was cold chicken and cold pork,
but that it would take only a minute to
heat it up."

"Heat it up, please," McCoy said, "but
get me some coffee right now, please."

When he turned around, Vandenburg
had put a bottle of Famous Grouse and a
glass on the table.

"You want ice? Water?" he asked.

"This is medicinal, not social," McCoy
said. "Straight is fine."

"Against the cold? Or do you hurt?"

McCoy lowered himself carefully into a
chair, then splashed two inches of whiskey
into the glass, picked it up, and drank
about half.

He exhaled audibly, then said: "Both. If
I keep moving, I'm fine. But when I sit
with my knees bent — as I have just been
doing in the L-19 — it gets stiff, and then
it hurts when I move. If I don't move and
get cold — and it was cold as hell up in
the L-19 — it's worse."

"You probably should still be in the hospital in Sasebo," Vandenburg said.

"If I knew where I could lay my hands on somebody who speaks Russian and Cantonese and knows what questions to ask, that's where I would be."

The housekeeper appeared with a silver coffeepot and a cup and saucer. When she had half-filled the cup, McCoy told her to stop and poured the rest of the scotch in with the coffee.

He took a sip.

"You were telling me about the colonel with the hat," Vandenburg said.

"Let's do this like the professionals we're supposed to be," McCoy said. "We have a map?"

Vandenburg nodded, pointed to half a dozen maps rolled up and standing in a corner of the room, and then went and got one.

"Northeast Korea, right?"

"Better bring one of the northwest, too," McCoy said.

McCoy took a healthy sip from his coffee cup and then stood up as Vandenburg laid a map of northeast Korea on the table and anchored it in place with whiskey glasses.

"The first Chinese I talked to were captured here," McCoy said, using his finger as a pointer, "southeast of the Chosin Reservoir. The positions he gave me of

ChiCom forces here, and here, and here, all checked out."

"Interesting," Vandenburg said.

"One of the reasons I came here was to get confirmation to General Pickering as soon as I could," McCoy said.

"And the other reason — reasons?"

"I thought if you had turned up the same sort of intel, it probably should go in the same report," McCoy said. "I have the feeling there are only two senior people who don't think I'm a nutcase on the loose. Pickering and Almond."

"Almond believes you?" Vandenburg asked.

McCoy nodded. Then he asked, "Have you got anything that would back me up?"

"A hell of a lot of rumors and unconfirmed sightings, but nothing solid, I'm afraid. Just before you came in, I got a report that the 24th Division — they're on the west coast, past Chongju, almost to the Yalu — has taken some Chinese prisoners, but it was too late for me to go up there today. I'm going to go at first light."

"I have to send my report tonight," McCoy said.

Vandenburg nodded his understanding.

"The colonel with the hat was captured here," McCoy said, pointing again at the map, "thirty miles east of the eastern shore of the Chosin Reservoir. Same scenario as before, except this guy was wearing an officer's uniform, and I didn't have to 'discover' that he was an officer. But he said and did the same things. The Chinese are coming in with overwhelming force, which they intend to use when X Corps is stretched out making a dash for the border. And he gave me troop dispositions. I hope I can check those out tonight, but I'm going to be very surprised if they don't check out."

"If they do, that would support your idea that they're sending us a message, right?"

"I think it would," McCoy said. "What the hell else could it mean?"

The housekeeper came into the dining room carrying a plate of roast pork, rice, and gravy.

"I should be noble and ignore that," McCoy said, "and go upstairs and send the report. But I'm hungry, and I don't want to climb all those goddamn stairs."

"I'll get a typewriter," Vandenburg said. "You can dictate it to me while you eat." He saw the look on McCoy's face. "I'm actually a very good typist. I used to be a CIC agent; a typewriter to a CIC agent is like a rifle to a Marine."

"I wasn't asking —"

"I know, Killer," Vandenburg said, and walked out of the dining room.

★ ★ ★

"Well, Major McCoy," Vandenburg said, handing McCoy the sheets of paper he had just pulled from the typewriter, "can this old soldier type, or can he type?"

McCoy took the papers and read them.

TOP SECRET

OPERATIONAL IMMEDIATE

SEOUL >ENTER TIME DATE HERE
EYES ONLY BRIG GEN FLEMING PICKERING
TOKYO

1. REFERENCE MY MESSAGE FROM
FISHBASE 30 OCTOBER 1950:
QUESTIONING OF THREE EXFILTRATED
STAY-BEHIND TEAMS THIS DATE
CONFIRMED IN EVERY SIGNIFICANT DETAIL
THE CHICOM TROOP DISPOSITIONS
FURNISHED THE UNDERSIGNED BY
CHICOM PRISONERS YESTERDAY.

2. ADDITIONALLY, ONE OF THE TEAMS
CAPTURED CHICOM CAPTAIN WON SON
HI, WHO WAS EXFILTRATED WITH THEM
AND INTERROGATED BY THE UNDERSIGNED.
DESPITE CONSIDERABLE PRESSURE HE
REFUSED TO SAY ANYTHING ABOUT HIS
UNIT, ORDERS, OR ANYTHING ELSE.
HOWEVER, HIS IDENTITY DOCUMENTS

865

AND A LETTER FROM HIS MOTHER, CAPTURED WITH HIM, ESTABLISHED THAT HIS UNIT WAS THE 2077TH RECONNAISSANCE COMPANY, 42D FIELD ARMY. AT THE TIME OF HIS CAPTURE HI AND THREE NONCOMS WERE RECONNOITERING CREST OF HILL LINE WHERE TEAM HAD BEEN INSERTED. NONCOMS DIED IN ENGAGEMENT.

3. REGRET TO INFORM YOU THAT ONE OF THE FOUR TEAMS INSERTED WAS APPARENTLY DISCOVERED BY CHICOM FORCES, AND MUST BE CONSIDERED MISSING IN ACTION, POSSIBLY CAPTURED, BUT PROBABLY KIA. CREW OF EXTRACTION AIRCRAFT REPORTED SIGNS OF HEAVY ENGAGEMENT, AND WERE THEMSELVES DRIVEN FROM AREA BY SMALL ARMS FIRE. ZIMMERMAN IS SENDING SEPARATELY FROM FISHBASE NAMES OF THOSE LOST AND OTHER DETAILS.

4. AT APPROXIMATELY 1400 HOURS THIS DATE, UNDERSIGNED INTERROGATED TWO CHICOM OFFICER PRISONERS, LIEUTENANT COLONEL KEY HOW AND CAPTAIN LEE SOU, CAPTURED BY ROK 502D INFANTRY IN VICINITY OF KUDONG, APPROXIMATELY 30 MILES EAST OF EASTERN SHORE OF CHOSIN RESERVOIR. EXCEPT THAT THESE

OFFICERS MADE NO EFFORT TO CONCEAL THEIR OFFICER STATUS, IT WAS ESSENTIALLY A REPEAT OF THE POW INTERROGATION THE UNDERSIGNED MADE YESTERDAY. CHICOM FORCES WILL NOT ATTACK US FORCES UNTIL THEIR LINES ARE OVEREXTENDED BETWEEN HAMHUNG AND BORDER, WHEN QUOTE ANNIHILATION WILL BE ASSURED ENDQUOTE.

5. FOUR TO SIX STAY-BEHIND TEAMS WILL BE INSERTED AT DUSK TODAY, DEPENDING ON WEATHER CONDITIONS, AND A REPORT OF THEIR FINDINGS WILL BE FURNISHED AS EARLY TOMORROW AS POSSIBLE.

6. IN VIEW OF THE FOREGOING, THE UNDERSIGNED BELIEVES
A. THERE IS NO LONGER ANY REASON TO QUESTION THE PRESENCE OF SUBSTANTIAL CHICOM FORCES IN NORTH KOREA PREPARED TO ENTER THE WAR WHENEVER THAT DECISION IS MADE.
B. THAT THE CAPTURE OF A SECOND GROUP OF SENIOR CHICOM OFFICERS WHO MAKE ESSENTIALLY THE SAME STATEMENT REGARDING CHICOM INTENTIONS REINFORCES THE

THE POSSIBILITY THAT THEY ARE IN EFFECT MESSENGERS HOPING TO HAVE PLANS TO ADVANCE TO THE YALU RECONSIDERED OR CANCELED.

7. THE UNDERSIGNED HAS CONFERRED WITH STATION CHIEF SEOUL, WHO SAYS HE HAS NOTHING CONCRETE TO CONFIRM OR QUESTION THE CONCLUSIONS DRAWN BY THE UNDERSIGNED.

K.R. MCCOY
MAJOR, USMCR

ADDITION: DESPITE PARAGRAPH 7 ABOVE THE UNDERSIGNED WHOLEHEARTEDLY CONCURS WITH MAJOR MCCOY'S ANALYSIS OF THE SITUATION, AND EXPECTS WITHIN A MATTER OF DAYS TO HAVE HARD INTELLIGENCE CONFIRMING MCCOY'S ANALYSIS.

J. D. VANDENBURG, LTCOL, INF
STATION CHIEF, SEOUL

TOP SECRET

"Well, you can type," McCoy said. "But what's that 'addition' that I didn't dictate or, for that matter, ask for?"

"Well, Major, you don't have any choice. I outrank you. It stays in."

McCoy looked at him.

"Killer, you're a bright guy, figure it out for yourself," Vandenburg said. "If that got to Washington without my addition, some chair-warming sonofabitch who's never been closer to the Orient than Big Wang's One Hung Low Chinese Buffet and Take-Out is going to say, 'Hey, he sent this from Seoul. What about Vandenburg? We really should know what Vandenburg thinks. If Vandenburg didn't say anything, he probably thinks McCoy is as full of shit as a Christmas turkey, and we have to judge this accordingly.' Now they know what I think."

"Thank you."

"My pleasure. Now we're going to put you to bed. Does your leg need a fresh bandage? Before I was a CIC agent, I was a Boy Scout. I know all about bandages."

"I find that hard to believe. You being a Boy Scout, I mean."

Vandenburg raised his right hand, three fingers extended, as a Boy Scout does when swearing an oath.

"You can trust me, Killer. I'm in the CIA," he said solemnly.

Major Malcolm S. Pickering, USMCR, was standing in front of the mirror in the bathroom when Lieutenant Patrick McGrory, MC, USN, pushed open the wide door and entered the room.

Pick had just concluded that he looked like hell. The uniform tunic hung loosely from his shoulders, which he had more or less expected. But he hadn't thought that he might have problems with the shirt until he'd stood before the mirror, buttoned the collar button, and begun to knot the field scarf. Then he'd seen that the shirt collar was an inch — maybe two inches — too big for the skinny neck rising from his shoulders. He realized why: Without thinking, he'd bought shirts in 'his' size, which meant they were far too large for him in his walking skeleton condition.

It was too late to do anything about it.

He turned and looked at McGrory.

"Good morning, Doctor," he said. "And how is my favorite leprechaun feeling today?"

"I'm impressed," McGrory said. "That's an impressive array of fruit salad."

870

Pick gave him the finger.

"I mean it," McGrory said. "I was impressed when I saw the list of your medals General Dawkins sent over —"

"What?"

"I said I was impressed with the list of your medals when General Dawkins sent it over —"

"What the hell was that all about?"

"General Dawkins called the hospital commander and said that he wanted to make sure you had a uniform, as they are about to pin another medal on you —"

"Oh, shit. That was a mistake. With its typical efficiency, the Crotch put my name on somebody else's citation."

"— and that he was sending his driver over," McGrory went on, "with an official list of your medals so that you would have them on your uniform when they took your picture when they pinned the medal on you. The hospital commander summoned me, handed me the list, and told me to take care of it. Which I did, by telling Francis Xavier O'Malley I was sending him a list of ribbons which he was to make up when getting you your uniform. And as I was saying before you so rudely interrupted me, I was impressed with the list, but am even more impressed now that I can see them all on your manly breast."

"Manly chicken breast," Pick said. "Or chickenly man breast?"

McGrory chuckled.

"I did notice your collar seems a wee bit roomy," McGrory said. "But for the record, you have gained eleven pounds while in my loving care. You'll get it all back, Pick. You lost a hell of a lot of weight, pal. It won't come back overnight."

"The O Club had the effrontery to serve me rice with my pork chops last night," Pick said. "I will never eat rice again in my life."

"Is that how you made it, on rice?"

"We are back to my terrible ordeal, are we? Okay. I'll give you that much. Yes, rice was a staple of my diet during my terrible ordeal. Are you now happy?"

"The longest journey begins with the first step," McGrory said solemnly. "I think Confucius said that."

"I hate to break off this fascinating conversation," Pick said, "but I told Mrs. Mitchell I'd be waiting for her in the lobby" — he looked at his wristwatch — "in six minutes."

"She's not coming," McGrory said.

The wristwatch, a battered pilot's chronometer, had a new alligator strap. It had been a strange experience watching the salesgirl in the Ship's Store replace the old one, which had surprisingly held up all the

way in Korea. He had remembered sometimes passing the time at night watching
the radium-tipped sweep second hand
gradually losing its luminescence, and
when it had — it had usually taken about
forty minutes — holding the watch to his
ear for the sound of its ticking. It had been
comforting, proof that there was more to
the world than human-feces-fertilized rice
paddies, dirt roads, and thatch-roofed
stone hootches. And unpleasant people
trying to kill you.

He heard what McGrory said.

"What do you mean, she's not coming?"

"She called and said she was sorry, but
coming here was impossible, and would
you mind taking a cab? I guess you were
in the shower. You didn't answer your
phone."

"So what happens now? I thought I had
to be placed in the care of a responsible
person?"

*So I don't have to go to the funeral. Great.
I didn't want to go anyway, and McGrory
probably told her he was sorry, but the policy
is that nutcakes can't be released except in the
company of a responsible person, so I'm off the
hook.*

So why am I so disappointed?

McGrory took out his pocket notebook,
tore off a sheet, and handed it to Pick.

"You get in a taxi and go to Mrs. Mitchell's apartment. That's the address."

"All by myself?"

"Yeah, against my better judgment, all by yourself."

"Why against your better judgment? What do you think I'm going to do?"

"I have already told you what I'm worried about," McGrory said. "In my experience, putting together two people — especially two people of different sexes — who are both suffering from an emotional trauma is a prescription for disaster."

"But you don't want to play God?"

"I hope I'm wrong."

"I think you can relax, Doc," Pick said. "The last thing I'm going to do is fuck up a nice lady like that."

"Good," McGrory said. "I was going to say, 'Have a nice time,' but you're going to a funeral, aren't you?"

[Eight]
Apartment 12-D, "Ocean View"
1005 Ocean Drive
San Diego, California
0955 2 November 1950

The Ocean View apartment building was a large, curved structure overlooking the Pacific Ocean. When Pick got out of the taxi, he saw a Marine Corps staff car and a Cadillac limousine parked in the curving drive-way, and a black wreath hanging from the nameplate on the right side of the double doors. That surprised him.

Maybe the owner's patriotic. Or maybe just a nice guy. Or maybe he knew Mitchell.

When he had walked down the hospital corridor to the elevator, and then out through the lobby, he had felt what, for lack of a better term, he thought of as "funny in the feet." He felt that way now, but he understood what it was. He had figured it out in the taxi. He was wearing shoes for the first time since he'd put on flight boots the morning he'd flown off the *Badoeng Strait* for the last time.

Even after he had been promoted to Category II and permitted to take his meals in the Officers' Club, he'd worn slippers.

The doorman was a short, plump Mexican who directed him to the bank of elevators on the right of the lobby.

He walked down the corridor to 12-D, which also had a black wreath on the door, pushed the button, and heard chimes.

A young woman in a black dress and wearing a veiled hat opened the door to him and smiled a little uneasily.

"My name is Pickering. Mrs. Mitchell expects me."

"I'm Dianne Welch," the young woman said. "Al's wife."

Okay. Now I know who you are. I don't know an Al Welch, but you expect me to. That makes you a Marine officer's wife. The sorority has gathered to do good for a member of the sisterhood now a widow.

I really don't want to be here. I really don't belong here.

"Babs is in the living room with the family," Dianne Welch said. "Down the corridor and straight ahead."

I wish there was some way I could turn around and get out of here.

What did she say, "with the family"? What family? I thought Babs . . . Mrs. Mitchell . . . said both their families were in Kansas? No, Arkansas.

Shit!

At the threshold to the living room, whose windows overlooked the Pacific, Pick was intercepted by a Marine captain, a pilot. He saw Mrs. Mitchell standing with two middle-aged women and a middle-aged man by the window. The room wasn't very large, and it was crowded, mostly with young Marine officers' wives and a few Marine officers.

Not many.

Of course not. Their husbands are off on what the Crotch euphemistically calls a Far East Deployment.

"Major Pickering?" the captain asked.

"Right."

"I was getting a little worried," the captain said.

"About what?"

"We're about to leave for Saint Paul's, sir, and you —"

"I'm here."

"Yes, sir. Sir, I'm Captain Kane. I'm the coordinating officer."

"Okay."

"Sir, you are to ride in the limousine with the widow, and at grave site, you are to sit next to Mrs. Mitchell."

"Who decided that?"

"Mrs. Mitchell, sir."

"Okay. Well, I suppose I had best pay my respects, hadn't I?"

"Yes, sir. She's over by the window with Captain Mitchell's parents and —"

"I see her. Thank you," Pick said.

He walked across the room toward Mrs. Mitchell, who smiled faintly when she saw him. She was dressed very much like the officer's wife at the door, in a simple black dress with a veiled black hat.

"Oh, I'm so glad to see you," Mrs. Mitchell said. "I'm sorry I couldn't pick you up. . . ."

"Not a problem," Pick said.

"This is Dick's mother and father," Mrs. Mitchell said. "And my mother. This is Major Pickering, who was on the *Badoeng Strait* with Dick."

Hands were shaken all around.

"Babs tells me you're in the hospital," Mr. Mitchell said.

"Yes, sir."

Dick Mitchell's mother looked at him as if she didn't like him.

What's that all about?

She thinks I'm fooling around with Babs . . . Mrs. Mitchell?

Or how come I'm back alive from the Badoeng Strait *and Dick isn't?*

"Babs didn't say why," Mrs. Mitchell's mother said.

She obviously didn't want to say "Neuro-Psychiatric Ward."

"It's sort of an extensive physical checkup."

"Really. Were you ill?"

"Pick was shot down and spent three months evading capture," Babs said.

Pick. Not Major Pickering.

"I read about that," Mr. Mitchell said. " 'Marine Pilot Rescued After Three Months.' Was that you?"

"I don't know what you read, sir."

"That sort of thing happen often?" Mr. Mitchell asked.

"No, sir. I don't think it does."

Captain Kane walked up to them.

"If it's convenient, Mrs. Mitchell, it's that time," he said.

"Anything you say," Babs said.

Kane gestured toward the door.

"You're to ride with us in the limousine," Babs Mitchell said.

"So I understand."

"I need to talk to you for a minute," Babs Mitchell said, and added, to the others, "You go ahead. We'll catch up."

That did it. Now Mama has her proof that we're fooling around. And Bab . . . Mrs. Mitchell is so naive, she doesn't even see that.

She took his arm and led him into a corridor. The door at the end was open. It was a bedroom, the bed covered with women's coats.

"I'm sorry about this," Babs Mitchell said to him. She was standing close to him, and he could smell both her perfume and her breath, which smelled like Sen-Sen.

"Sorry about what?"

"When I called them to tell them about the funeral, to invite them, they didn't say anything about coming. They told me I was making a mistake I would remember all my life —"

"He was your husband, for Christ's sake!" Pick blurted, and then quickly added, "Sorry."

"— and that was it. And then they just showed up last night. Right after Captain Whatsisname and a representative of the Officers' Wives Association showed up to tell me how they were going to help out today."

"What are you apologizing for?" Pick asked. "I don't understand."

"I thought I would call up and tell you, but the truth is I guess I really wanted you to be here."

And what did the good Dr. McGrory have to say about that? "The woman, whether she's aware of it or not, hungers for a strong male shoulder to lean on."

"I'm glad you did," Pick said.

Am I just being polite, chivalrous? Or what? For Christ's sake, what?

"I think we'd better go," Pick said.

Leaving unsaid, Or your mother-in-law, and maybe your mother, too, will really think there's something going on between us.

The rear of the Cadillac limousine provided upholstered seating for three across the backseat, and two jump seats.

Mr. Mitchell was in the jump seat, the women on the bench, leaving space for Babs on the bench and Pick on the other jump seat.

From which location, when he sat down, he was unable to be unaware of her knees and the lace hem of her slip.

Black. Black is the color of mourning. Also of sexy feminine underwear. What's the connection there? McGrory probably has a theory.

"I hope Pick — Major Pickering — won't be offended when I tell you this," Babs Mitchell said as they were rolling through San Diego. "But he's just experienced a terrible loss himself."

"Is that so?" Mother Mitchell asked.

"His fiancée was in a plane crash in Korea the day he was rescued," Babs Mitchell said.

Why is she telling them this?

Because she has finally picked up on Mother Mitchell's — or her mother's — suspicions that I am the reason she doesn't want to go home to Kan . . . Arkansas. That's why, stupid.

"Oh, how awful!" Bab's mother said, sounding sincere.

"She was on an Air Force medical supply aircraft that crashed," Pick said.

"A nurse?"

"No, ma'am, she was a war correspondent."

"Jeanette Priestman," Babs Mitchell said. "Of the *Chicago* . . . what?"

"*Tribune*," Pick said. "The *Chicago Tribune*. And it's Priestly, not Priestman."

"Sorry," Babs Mitchell said.

"Don't be silly."

"My son and his wife, Major Pickering," Mr. Mitchell said, "I still don't really understand why, recently became Episcopalians. The funeral service will be an

Episcopal service. Are you familiar with —"

"Yes, sir," Pick said. "I was even an altar boy once."

"Were you really?"

He's pleased. He doesn't think I'm trying to get — or have already been — in his son's widow's pants.

"Yes, sir, I was. And before that I sang in the choir of a church also called Saint Paul's."

"Really?"

"Yes, sir."

I think I just made the first goal for Protestant Episcopal Christian virtues.

Hell, make sure!

"Jeanette's body is being returned later this week," Pick said. "So I suppose you could say that Babs and I are trying to support each other. . . ."

Unless, of course, you are aware of the McGrory theory concerning two people of opposite sexes who have both experienced an emotional trauma.

There was a Cadillac hearse outside St. Paul's Church, through the windows of which a flag-draped casket was visible. And a flower car. And several more Marine-green staff cars. And half a platoon of Marines, in dress blues. Two-thirds of them were carrying Garands, and the others were apparently pallbearers.

A function normally performed by one's brother officers.

But they're off on a Far East Deployment and thus unavailable.

Mrs. Babs Mitchell took Major Malcolm Pickering's arm as they followed Mr. and Mrs. Mitchell and Babs's mother down the aisle of the church toward a reserved pew near the altar.

As Major Pickering dropped to the kneeling bench —

So you haven't done this in years.

So maybe you're a little hypocritical.

So what? The point of the exercise is to convince Mr. and Mrs. Mitchell, Babs's mother, and of course Mrs. Babs Mitchell herself that you are not only a fine Marine Corps officer and gentleman, but a Christian gentleman who wouldn't even think of nailing Mrs. Babs Mitchell.

— he saw sitting directly across the aisle from him, in dress blues, Brigadier General Clyde W. Dawkins, USMC. Beside him was Mrs. Dawkins, looking like a slightly older version of the officers' wives who had been in Babs's — *Mrs. Mitchell's* — apartment.

Both looked at him. Mrs. Dawkins smiled. He smiled back.

Marines carried the casket in and set it on a catafalque in the aisle.

The ceremony began.

It was, Pick thought, mercifully brief.

The Marines carried the casket back down the aisle.

Captain Kane came to the pew and indicated that it was now time for him to lead the widow back down the aisle and out of the church.

Mrs. Mitchell took his arm, and he did so.

She didn't cry. But that doesn't mean she's not all torn up.

How do I know that?

Does it matter? I do.

On the slow drive to the cemetery, Mr. Mitchell said, "I was surprised the ceremony was so short."

Well, that's the way we Whiskey-palians do it. Wham, bam, thank you, ma'am, and out of the church and into the ground.

"That's what Dick liked about the Episcopal church," Mrs. Babs Mitchell said. "The . . . I guess the word is 'liturgy.' I thought it was a beautiful ceremony. And Dick would have loved it when they sang 'The Marines' Hymn' as a hymn."

The two squads of Marines who would fire the salute were already lined up, standing at parade rest.

Mrs. Mitchell took Major Pickering's

arm and he led her from the limousine to a line of folding chairs set up under a tent.

The pallbearers carried the casket from the hearse and began to set it down on the casket-lowering machine.

"Oh, God," Mrs. Babs Mitchell said softly. "I guess this is really it. Oh, Dick!"

When Pick looked down at her, tears were rolling down her cheeks and she had a handkerchief to her mouth, trying to hold back the sobs.

Without thinking about it, Pick put his arm around her shoulders.

Then she gave in to the sobs.

Pick gave her a comforting squeeze.

She took a deep breath, exhaled audibly, took the handkerchief from her mouth, and looked up at him.

"Thank you," she said. "I'll be all right."

He removed his arm from her shoulders.

The priest took up his position at the head of the casket and began the graveside service.

You're going to like this even less, Mr. Mitchell. This usually takes about two minutes, tops.

In the limousine on the way back to the Ocean View, Mrs. Babs Mitchell did not cry. She sat across from Pick with the folded flag in her lap, stroking it with her finger tips.

She had cried three times during the graveside ceremony. First when General Dawkins, on behalf of a grateful nation, handed her the folded flag.

Then she had cried when the bugler played taps.

I felt a little weepy then myself.

And she had cried when the firing squad did their little ballet, which had put Major Pickering in the probably prohibited-by-regulation position of holding a weeping female closely with his left arm while he saluted with his right. Every time there had been the crack of twenty blank cartridges going off simultaneously, Mrs. Babs Mitchell had cringed, and he could feel her bosom pressing against him.

On the curved driveway outside the Ocean View, Major Pickering told Mrs. Babs Mitchell that he was sorry but he was going to have to get back to the hospital.

"Are you all right?"

"I'm fine. But my pass is about to expire."

"Thank you for coming," Mrs. Babs Mitchell said.

"It was an honor."

"No, I mean it," she said. "Thank you."

She stood on her toes and kissed him on the cheek, and he felt again the pressure of her bosom against him.

"I'll come to see you," she said. "All right?"

"That would be very nice."

Now, why the fuck did I say that?

You're a highly skilled liar with a good imagination.

Why couldn't you come up with something clever that would cut this off once and for good right now?

He shook hands with Mrs. Babs Mitchell's mother and Captain Mitchell's parents, and turned and walked down the curved driveway toward a taxi stand without looking back.

XVIII

[One]
The President's Office
Blair House
Pennsylvania Avenue
Washington, D.C.
1900 2 November 1950

"Who's this Lieutenant Colonel . . . Vandenburg?" the President of the United States asked after reading McCoy's message.

"He's the officer the Pentagon sent to see if General Dean could be rescued," Major General Ralph Howe said. "I suggested that he be transferred to the CIA to keep him out of Willoughby's hands."

"I remember now. It says here he's the Seoul station chief," Truman said.

"After I got your message about him, Mr. President," Walter Bedell Smith said, "I told General Bradley that was your desire. He placed him on indefinite duty with the CIA, and I so notified General Pickering. I can only suppose General Pickering designated him as Seoul station chief."

"Good man?"

"General Bradley thought he was the best man for that job," Smith said. "I mean, trying to get General Dean back."

"Ralph?"

"First-class man, Mr. President. I understand why he and the Killer get along so well."

"So well that he'd going along with . . . I'm not going to call that young man 'Killer' . . . *McCoy* because they're pals?"

"No, sir," Howe said firmly. "He would not."

"Vandenburg's the fellow who stole General Walker's airplane, right?"

"Mr. President, I said nothing of the kind," Howe said, smiling. "But I admit that he's probably justifiably high on the list of suspects."

"Huh," the President snorted. "Well, you say he's a good man, and he goes along with McCoy all the way. Where does that leave us?"

"I think there is no longer any question that there are substantial numbers of Red Chinese in Korea, Mr. President," Howe said.

"I never really doubted that. What about this business about the Chinese sending us a message?"

"I don't know, sir. I'd bet on McCoy."

"Okay. Let's take that as a given. So what do we do about it?"

"First thing this morning, Mr. President," Smith said, "I checked with the Pentagon. There was nothing in the overnight messages from the Dai Ichi Building suggesting that the Supreme Command has changed its mind about the Red Chinese coming in."

"That makes things difficult, doesn't it?" Truman said. "I find myself in the position of agreeing with a major — and a lieutenant colonel — and disagreeing with a five-star general who Ralph, General Pickering, and ninety percent of the American people think is a military genius."

"Mr. President, may I make a suggestion?"

"I'm wide open for suggestions."

"You could have the Army urgent-message General MacArthur saying they have intelligence suggesting there has been a substantial movement of ChiCom forces to the border and probably across it. And what does General MacArthur think?"

"Why not just send him a message saying the CIA has interrogated four senior Chinese Communist officers?" Truman asked. Then he added: "Don't bother to answer that. I can't do that, because they know who the CIA people there are, and we're right back to me telling a five-star military genius he's wrong."

"I think Beetle's idea is a good one, Mr.

President," General Howe said.

Truman looked directly at him for perhaps thirty seconds.

"Okay," he said finally. "That's what we'll do. But I want you to write the message, Ralph."

"Why me, Mr. President?"

"Because, of the three of us, you're the only one who really knows Emperor Douglas the First. I don't think we had an hour together on Wake Island. And God only knows what kind of a message he'd get from the Pentagon if Smith just told them I wanted a message sent. Either it would be mostly an apology for questioning his genius, or it would be designed to get a response they know would make me mad. What I want him to do when he gets the message is personally think it over, and not just buck it down to General Willoughby. You know how to phrase it to make him do that."

"Okay. Good thinking," Howe said thoughtfully.

"And when you two have finished writing it, I want you, Smith, to take it to the Pentagon, give it to General Bradley, and tell him I want it sent as-is and right now."

"He's not going to like that, Harry . . . Mr. President," Howe said.

"He doesn't have to like it. I'm not sure

about some of the others, but I am absolutely sure General Bradley knows who is Commander-in-Chief," Truman said.

"Will there be anything else, Mr. President?" Howe asked.

"Yes," the President said. "Get me the names of those Marines who are missing, the 'stay-behinds' who got caught. When this is over, I want to write their families."

"That's very generous of you, Mr. President —" Smith began.

" 'Generous' is not the word," Truman interrupted him.

"I was about to say, sir, it is generous of you to find the time."

"Abraham Lincoln did it when he was living across the street," Truman said. "And as bad as things are, things were worse for him when he did it."

"Yes, sir," Smith said.

"I'll get the names and addresses of the next of kin, Mr. President," Smith said.

"And that reminds me," the President said. "What about the Navy Cross for Pickering's son?"

"The commandant assures me, Mr. President, that the decoration will be awarded within the next forty-eight hours. And he told me that yesterday. He may have it already."

"Okay. Thank you."

[Two]
8023d Transportation Company
  (Depot, Forward)
Hamhung, North Korea
1235 2 November 1950

The maps Captain Francis P. MacNamara had obtained from the X Corps Engineer — not without difficulty; maps were in short supply — showed that it was approximately sixty miles by highway from Wonsan to Hamhung, and a few miles farther, no highway, to Hungnam, which was on the Sea of Japan.

The problem was that this was Korea, where a highway was any two-lane paved road, and the definition of "paved" was loose. It often meant that it was paved with a thin layer of gravel. Furthermore, the road — there was only one "highway" — had not been built to withstand the traffic now moving up it, in terms of either weight or numbers.

The United States X Corps was on the move. The order had been issued to advance to the Chinese border. That meant not only the American 7th Infantry Division and 1st Marine Division, and the four ROK Divisions, which were "up front," but the mind-boggling support and logistical train needed to support it.

It wasn't simply a question of supplying

the attacking divisions with food, fuel, and ammunition, or even also moving their supporting tactical units, the separate tank and artillery battalions, and so on — and their food, fuel, and ammunition — but the nonfighting units had also been ordered moved out of Wonsan. These ranged from Mobile Army Surgical Hospitals to Quartermaster Ration Depots, Ordnance Ammunition Supply Points, down to smaller units such as Water Purification Platoons, Shower Points, and a Mobile Dental Surgical Detachment.

Into this mix, all trying to move up the same winding, crumbling, narrow two-lane "highway," Colonel T. Howard Kennedy, the X Corps Transportation Officer, had added Captain MacNamara's 8023d Transportation Company (Depot, Forward) and the Replacement Company of the 7th United States Infantry Division.

It was worse than anything MacNamara had seen in France in World War II, and when he first got into the line of moving vehicles, he had used his experience in France to predict that it would take six hours to move the sixty miles. It took eighteen.

Not all of that time — in fact very little — was spent on the move. Most of it was spent stopped, as units, or individual vehicles, with a higher priority passed them on the left lane. The basic rule of thumb was that medical supplies went first, then ammunition, then food.

Overworked, and thus sometimes snarling, military policemen guided high-priority convoys onto the left lane, past stopped convoys with lesser priorities.

The first military police officer Captain MacNamara encountered had asked him for his movement priority, which would then be painted on the lead vehicle for the edification of military police along the route.

"Verbal orders of the X Corps Transportation Officer," MacNamara had replied, with as much assurance as he could muster. "The colonel said, 'Time is of the essence.'"

The MP officer, also a captain, had smiled at him.

"Good try, Captain," he said, and dabbed a blue paint circle on the windshield of MacNamara's jeep. Within an hour or so, MacNamara understood that the blue circle indicated a priority way down on the list.

Several times MacNamara seriously considered replacing the blue circle with a yellow one. Yellow seemed to represent the priority immediately after ration trucks, and there was an assortment of paint in one of the mobile workshops he had included in the first convoy, but he decided against it. For one thing, it didn't seem right, and for another, he didn't want another letter of reprimand in his service record, which he would get, sure as Christ made little green apples, if he was caught.

He wondered how long it was going to take him to return from wherever he was going in the Hamhung-Hungnam area to Wonsan. The southbound lane, so to speak, of the highway was usually crowded with northbound vehicles with a priority. Only a few vehicles were passing him going south.

He wondered if maybe he could somehow get a message to the officers he had left behind, telling them to saddle up and get moving as soon as they could because he would not be returning. In the end, he decided against this, too. It was his responsibility to go back and set things up, and he would.

Sixteen and a half hours after MacNamara had left Wonsan, he was again stopped in the right lane as priority convoys passed him in the left. Another MP officer, this one a lieutenant, came southward down the shoulder of the road in a jeep.

"Where are you headed, Captain?"

"Hamhung, Hungnam," MacNamara replied.

"Which?"

"I don't know. I have to find somewhere to set up — on the highway, preferably. I'm a vehicle replacement outfit. And I've got the advance party of the 7th Repple-Depple with me. They need a place too."

"When I come back, say, in thirty minutes or so, you — just you — follow me. The turn off to Hamhung's about five miles up the road. You can find a place, or places, to set up while the rest of your convoy is still on the highway."

MacNamara had little trouble finding a suitable area for the 8023d. It was about half a mile in on the turnoff to Hamhung. The only thing wrong with it was that it was terraced, which would seem to indicate that it had once been a rice paddy, or paddies.

It was dry now, and obviously hadn't been a rice paddy for some years. That left the question in his mind: *How long would human shit contaminate a rice paddy?*

He had no idea. But it didn't matter. He had seen enough of the area to know that the terrain was either rocky hills or flat areas that either were or once had been a rice paddy. He thought the one he had chosen didn't smell all that rotten, but on the other hand, he had smelled so many rotten things since arriving in the Land of the Morning Calm that he suspected his sniffer had been overwhelmed.

He consoled himself with the thought that it was now getting chilly — it had been as cold as a witch's teat in the jeep overnight — and one of the prerogatives of being a Transportation Depot commander was being able to tell your noncom in charge of the Radiator Repair Section to rig a heater for your jeep, and that would keep the smell down.

He set up a temporary headquarters in one of the mobile service vans he had thoughtfully included in the convoy. Nature called, and he didn't think it would wait until the men dug a quick latrine, so he went up the hill a little and dropped his trousers behind a large boulder.

The wind coming off the hill was surprisingly unpleasant on the cheeks of his ass, and he thought that about the first thing the men were going to do when they finished laying the perimeter barbed wire was build another latrine like the one he had just finished building in Wonsan.

Jesus! If I can get through to Wonsan on a landline, I can tell Lieutenant Wright to just put the sonofabitch on the back of a tank retriever. I'll have to tell Wright to cover it with a tarpaulin so people won't know what it is. But that would save a lot of work.

As soon as I finish my dump, I'm going to see if I can find a phone. There's no telling how long it'll take to get the X Corps Signal

Company to lay a couple of lines in here.

He heard a sound he hadn't heard since those CIA guys dropped in on the 8023d in Inchon. *Fluckata-fluckata-fluckata.*

He looked up and around and, as the *fluckata-fluckata-fluckata fluckata-fluckata-fluckata* sound grew louder, located it in the sky.

It was flying over the road in the direction of Hungnam.

It was painted black. He wondered if it was one of the two he had seen at Inchon. He wondered what the hell it was doing.

Jesus, if I could get my hands on one of those, I'd have that goddamn latrine up here tonight!

[Three]
**Office of the Commanding General
Headquarters X United States Corps
  (Forward)
Wonsan, North Korea
1245 2 November 1950**

The black H-19A fluttered to the ground fifty yards from a collection of vehicles of all descriptions parked in a somewhat random pattern outside a two-story brick building that had, before the war, housed a regional secondary school. The downwash from the rotor blades blew leaves all over the area as the helicopter touched down.

There was much activity as Engineers, Signal Corps personnel, and other technicians set up the X Corps headquarters. As Major Alex Donald, USA — very carefully, to make sure he didn't run into cables strung between telephone poles — set the H-19A down, Major K. R. McCoy, USMCR, saw two flags, their poles set in what looked like artillery shell casings, in front of a van, a 6 x 6 truck onto which was mounted a square boxlike structure.

Such vehicles usually housed either communications gear or the machines required for some sort of maintenance function, but were sometimes used as mobile offices. That was obviously the case here. The flags hung limply on their staffs, but McCoy could see that one of them was the blue and white X Corps flag, and the other was solid red with white stars. That meant the van was occupied for the moment by the X Corps Commander, until the support troops working frantically in and around the school building could get his office and command post set up there.

The moment the H-19A touched down, McCoy unstrapped himself and climbed down from the cockpit. The Big Black Bird had attracted the attention of a lot of people in the area, more than a few of whom noticed that the guy getting out of the helicopter — a Marine officer — seemed to be in some discomfort. A few even wondered why, but their primary interest was in the helicopter itself.

How come the goddamn jarheads have a big machine like that, and The General himself has only a couple of lousy H-13s?

There were two MPs, armed with Thompson submachine guns, guarding access to the general's van, and McCoy had to wait until they verified his story that he was Major McCoy, and General Almond expected him. But finally he was passed, and walked to the van, stood on the lower step of the folding steps to the van, and rapped on the door with his knuckles.

After a moment, Captain Al Haig pushed the door outward, saw McCoy, and waved him inside. McCoy carefully hoisted himself into the van.

It was simply furnished. There were three identical desks. A master sergeant sat at one of the desks along the wall, using a typewriter. An identical desk sitting next to the master sergeant's desk — it had four field telephones on it — was obviously Captain Haig's. Major General Edward M. Almond sat at the third desk, all the way inside the van and facing the door. It held two field telephones and the leather map case Almond always carried with him.

"Major McCoy, sir," Haig said.

McCoy saluted.

"You wanted to see me, sir?" he asked.

"What happened to your pajamas?" Almond asked.

"I've been interrogating prisoners, sir," McCoy said. "They seem to be more impressed with a Marine than by someone in pajamas."

Almond chuckled, and shook his head as he opened the long flap of his leather map case, came out with a sheet of paper, and handed it wordlessly to McCoy.

TOP SECRET

URGENT

SUPREME HEADQUARTERS UNITED
NATIONS COMMAND TOKYO
0730 31 OCTOBER 1950

EYES ONLY COMMANDING GENERAL
X CORPS

PERSONAL MESSAGE FROM GENARMY
MACARTHUR TO MAJGEN ALMOND BEGINS

MY DEAR NED,

I HAVE CAREFULLY CONSIDERED YOUR
URGENT OF 1015 30 OCTOBER.

GENERAL WILLOUGHBY, WHO HAS ABSOLUTELY NO INTELLIGENCE DATA WHICH EVEN SUGGESTS THERE ARE CHINESE COMMUNIST FORCES OF ANY SIGNIFICANCE IN NORTH KOREA, THEREFORE BELIEVES THE SIZE OF THE CHINESE FORCE, IF INDEED IT WAS A CHINESE FORCE, WHICH ATTACKED THE INFANTRY REGIMENT OF THE 3RD ROK DIVISION 29 OCTOBER, WAS NOT AS LARGE AS REPORTED TO YOU.

HE POINTS OUT THAT MAJGEN LEE DO WAS SHORT MONTHS AGO A LIEUTENANT COLONEL, MAY NOT HAVE PROVEN CAPABLE OF COMMANDING A DIVISION-SIZE FORCE, AND WHEN HIS DIVISION FAILED TO REPEL WHAT WILLOUGHBY FEELS WAS PROBABLY A REGIMENTAL-SIZE ATTACK, AT MOST, EXAGGERATED THE ATTACKING STRENGTH TO JUSTIFY HIS LOSS OF THE BATTLE.

HOWEVER, SINCE YOU OBVIOUSLY FEEL SO STRONGLY ABOUT THIS, AND BECAUSE OF MY OWN PROFOUND FAITH IN YOUR JUDGMENT AND BATTLEFIELD SKILL, I HAVE DIRECTED WILLOUGHBY TO PROCEED TO YOUR HEADQUARTERS TO CONFER WITH YOU AND SEE FOR HIMSELF.

> THE BATAAN IS BEING PREPARED FOR THE FLIGHT AS THIS IS WRITTEN.
>
> VICTORY IS WITHIN OUR GRASP, MY DEAR NED.
>
> WITH PERSONAL REGARDS,
>
> MACARTHUR
> GENERAL OF THE ARMY
> SUPREME COMMANDER
>
> END PERSONAL MESSAGE FROM GENARMY MACARTHUR TO MAJGEN ALMOND
>
> TOP SECRET

McCoy muttered "Jesus Christ!" and raised his eyes to General Almond.

Almond put up his hand to silence him.

"Jerry," he called. "Do not list Major McCoy's visit in the diary, and go deaf. You understand?"

"Can't hear you, sir," the master sergeant said.

"He's sending Willoughby here?" McCoy asked.

"General Willoughby visited Wonsan yesterday," Almond said. "And stayed there long enough — probably forty-five minutes — to see and hear enough so that he could get on the *Bataan* and return to

Tokyo to assure General MacArthur that he has nothing to worry about; there are no ChiCom forces in North Korea to speak of."

"What do we have to do to convince that sonofabitch?" McCoy exploded.

"It's a good thing Sergeant Youngman is deaf," Almond said. "Otherwise he would be shocked at such vulgar and disrespectful language coming from a Marine officer."

"Sorry, sir."

"However much justified," Almond said. "McCoy, did you . . . uh . . . send the intelligence I had the feeling you were going to send?"

"Yes, sir. And I said when I had further confirmation from my stay-behinds, I would send it, and I sent that confirmation. This time it was a lieutenant colonel with the same message."

"I thought you probably had," Almond said.

"Sonofabitch!" McCoy said, and put his hand to his forehead and wiped it.

"You just staggered, McCoy," Almond said. "Are you all right? Jerry, get Major McCoy a chair."

Master Sergeant Youngman jumped to carry his chair to McCoy.

McCoy eased himself into it.

"Thank you, Sergeant," he said.

"Can I get you anything, McCoy?" Captain Haig asked.

McCoy raised his head and looked at him.

"I honest to God could use a drink," he said.

Almond pulled open a desk drawer and came out with a bottle of Old Forrester bourbon.

"Is this a good idea?" Almond asked. "You look feverish. Do you have a fever?"

He didn't wait for an answer, but instead came around the desk and put his fingers to McCoy's forehead.

"You have a fever," he announced. "Is this whiskey a good idea?"

"I'll be all right, sir," McCoy said.

Almond signaled Haig to hand over the glass Haig had in his hand. He poured whiskey into it and McCoy drank it down.

"Thank you," he said. He looked at Almond. "I had a bad early morning, sir."

"Did you?"

"We were exfiltrating stay-behinds," he said. "One of the teams was overrun. We brought the bodies back with us."

"I'm sorry to hear that."

"They were . . . uh . . . pretty badly mutilated," McCoy said softly. "And we didn't think to take ponchos with us. So . . . uh . . . the reason I'm not in my pajamas is . . . uh . . . that they really needed to be washed."

"How many men?" Almond asked softly.

"Four, sir. It was their first time out — they were some of the Marines that you borrowed to guard the hangar at Kimpo, and who I asked to volunteer for this stay-behind exercise."

He held his hand to his head for a moment.

"And that sonofabitch says there are no Chinese? Who does he think is running the ridges, looking for my stay-behinds? The North Koreans? They left their dead behind, too, so that there could be no question who did the . . . goddamn fucking butchery."

"Take it easy, Major," Almond said.

"Sorry, sir," McCoy said.

"You want some more of this?" Almond said, touching the bottle of Old Forrester.

McCoy looked at the bottle and then at Almond, and then reached for the bottle.

"I should say, 'No, thank you, sir,' " he said. "But with one more drink in me, maybe I'll have the courage to offer a really off-the-wall suggestion."

"What?" Almond asked.

McCoy tossed down another drink and shook his head, as if to clear it.

"If you dismiss this out of hand, sir," he said, "I'll understand."

"Dismiss what?"

"Why don't we march some prisoners into the goddamn Dai Ichi Building? Twenty, twenty-five ordinary Chinese Red Army soldiers, right into Willoughby's office."

"Christ," Haig said disparagingly.

"Could you get the *Bataan* back here?" McCoy pursued.

Almond looked at McCoy for a long moment.

"I suppose I could get an Air Force plane," McCoy said. "But that would take time, and if this is going to happen, it has to happen now. And if I used the *Bataan*, it would mean you were involved, and proof that I hadn't borrowed the Chinese from Chiang Kai-shek."

Almond didn't say anything at all.

"Sir, my orders state that I am to get any assistance I need from any military organization," McCoy said.

"Such as the X United States Corps?" Almond asked.

"Yes, sir. I don't have the orders with me. But you've seen them, sir."

"What I think you need, McCoy . . ." Haig began, and stopped when Almond raised his hand.

"You do have some imaginative ideas, don't you, Major McCoy?" Almond asked thoughtfully. "And you try to cover all the possibilities, don't you? I suppose that's very useful in your line of work."

"General, if I hadn't proposed that, I'd have regretted it, really regretted it, later," McCoy said. He turned to Haig. "And that wasn't the booze speaking, Al. I owed it to those Marines I brought back in pieces this morning."

"I understand," Haig said. "I wasn't —"

"Jerry," General Almond interrupted him. "Get your pad."

"Yes, sir."

Master Sergeant Youngman went quickly to his desk and returned with a stenographer's notebook. "Ready, sir," he said.

"Classification, Top Secret, Priority, Operational Immediate. To Supreme Headquarters, UNC, Tokyo. Unless the Supreme Commander personally, repeat personally, rescinds this order, the *Bataan* will be immediately, repeat immediately, dispatched to Hamhung. I will be advised of departure time and ETA. The signature block, Jerry, is Edward M. Almond, Major General, USA, Chief of Staff, Supreme Headquarters, United Nations Command."

"Jesus," Master Sergeant Youngman said softly.

"Take it over to the comm center and get it out right now," Almond said.

"Yes, sir."

[Four]
Haneda Airfield
Tokyo, Japan
2130 2 November 1950

Brigadier General Fleming Pickering, USMCR, wishing he had thought to wear his raincoat, stood in the cold drizzle until he was sure the four-engine airplane landing was indeed the *Bataan*. Then he got in the front seat of the Buick.

He was not in a very good mood. For one thing, he wasn't sure that McCoy was even going to be on the airplane.

When he had — five hours before, in desperation — telephoned General Douglas MacArthur and asked for his assistance in finding McCoy, MacArthur had asked why.

"May I ask why you need him here so urgently? And frankly, I'm a bit surprised to hear that he has recovered sufficiently from his wounds to be in Korea at all."

"Mrs. McCoy called me from Tokyo General an hour ago, sir. She felt it best to be in a hospital —"

"She's having the baby?"

"Possibly, sir. They don't know if this is another false alarm or not, but . . . if she delivers, the child would be a month, maybe five weeks, premature, so they're hoping for the false alarm. I'm at the hospital now. I just spoke with her physician,

910

and he said it would benefit her — perhaps keep her from delivering now — if her husband could be with her. And if something goes wrong . . . Sir, I thought it over carefully before asking. I think McCoy is entitled to a little extra consideration."

"I quite agree. A splendid young officer. I'll get an urgent off immediately to General Almond, asking him to locate him, and making sure he has a space on the *Bataan*."

"Sir? What about the *Bataan*?"

"General Almond ordered the *Bataan* to Korea. I don't know why, but I suspect he wishes to bring his disagreement with General Willoughby about the possibility of the Chinese entering the war to me personally. Anyway, the *Bataan* is there, and it can bring Major McCoy when it returns here."

"Sir, has there . . . I realize this line is not secure, sir . . . been any change in General Willoughby's position on that matter?"

"No. And that's the source of the friction between Willoughby and Almond. Between you and me, Fleming, I sent Willoughby over there to placate Almond. Apparently, it wasn't enough, and he wants to plead his case in person. Almond has dug in his heels like a mule, frankly."

"Yes, sir. General, I very much appreciate your courtesy to me in what really is a personal matter."

"That's what friends are for, Fleming," MacArthur said, "if I may coin a phrase. I'll tell Jean about Mrs. McCoy, of course. I'm sure she will want to call on her."

A telephone call five minutes before to the hospital had reported there was no change in Mrs. McCoy's condition, and Pickering tried to console himself with that knowledge.

He was more than a little annoyed with McCoy for a number of reasons, based on what he had learned when he finally got through to Fishbase looking for him.

Zimmerman had told him he didn't know where he was exactly.

"When he brought the bodies back from the exfiltration this morning, General . . . Did you get that message, sir?"

"There were KIA?"

"Four, sir. The Chinks apparently did a real job on them. To send us a message, the Killer said."

"Define 'real job' for me, Zimmerman."

"Well, sir, it looks like they tortured them before they killed them, and then they cut up the bodies pretty badly. It wasn't pretty. The Killer was pretty upset."

"Did I understand you correctly, Zimmerman? McCoy made the run in the H-19 to extract the teams?"

"That's 'exfiltrate,' sir," Zimmerman had courteously corrected him. "Yes, sir. He was on one of the Big Black Birds, and I was on the other."

"I expressly ordered him not to go on infiltration missions," Pickering had said. "And I thought you were aware of that."

"Sir," Zimmerman said uncomfortably, "what the Killer said you said we couldn't do was stay behind ourselves."

"I'll discuss that with him when I see him," Pickering had said. "But — and this is in the nature of an order, Ernie, so pay attention — if you see McCoy before I do, you are to relay to him my orders that neither of you are to make extraction runs anymore under any conditions. Is there anything about that you don't understand?"

"Yes, sir, there is."

"What's that?"

"I understand about the Killer, sir. He's really in shitty shape. But I'm fine, sir. Why can't I go?"

"Ernie McCoy is in the hospital again —"

"Oh, shit!"

"— and if I can locate him, he's coming to Japan. That leaves you in charge, and I can't risk losing you. Okay? No further questions?"

"No, sir."

"I'll let you know what happens with Mrs. McCoy," Pickering said.

"That's the *Bataan*," Pickering said to

Captain George F. Hart, USMCR, who was in the backseat, and Master Sergeant Paul T. Keller, USA, who was behind the wheel.

"I saw it out the window, General," Hart said innocently.

"Meaning I didn't have to stand out there and get rained on?" Pickering snapped.

"Now that I think of it, General . . ."

Keller chuckled.

"I don't know why I put up with either one of you," Pickering said.

"Maybe because we're lovable, sir?" Hart asked.

"I'm going to really give McCoy hell — if he's on that airplane — and I will be highly annoyed if either of you acts as if it's funny," Pickering said.

"General . . ." Hart said.

"What?"

"Nothing, sir."

"Out with it, goddamn it, George!"

"General, you've told me — Christ, I don't know how many times — never to give an order you know won't be obeyed."

"And I should have known McCoy was not going to obey that order? Is that what you're saying?"

"General, you asked me," Hart said.

"Here it comes," Keller said, pointing out the window, as the *Bataan* turned off the taxiway and approached the tarmac in front of the hangar.

"You two stay in the car," Pickering ordered. "If McCoy is on the *Bataan*, I'm going to take him under the wing and bite off a large chunk of his ass, and I don't want an audience."

Ground crewmen rolled up movable steps to the rear door of the airplane. Pickering got out of the front seat and walked toward it.

The *Bataan*'s door opened and four military policemen, wearing steel helmets and other battlefield accoutrements, and carrying Thompson submachine guns, came down the stairs and quickly assumed positions facing the stairs.

What the hell is going on here?

McCoy appeared at the door, a Thompson hanging from his shoulder. He looked around the area, then started down the stairs. Then he saw General Pickering. He smiled and raised his hand in salute.

That smile's not going to do you a goddamn bit of good, McCoy!

Your ass is mine. You won't forget this ass-chewing for the rest of your life.

Pickering marched coldly toward the stairs.

He watched McCoy start down the stairs again, saw him slip, or stagger, saw him grab the railing, and then fall. He ended up sprawled on his stomach at the foot of the stairs.

Two of the MPs rushed to help him.

"Back where you were!" McCoy snapped, and tried to push himself up. And fell back down again.

Pickering rushed to him. He heard two car door slams, which told him that Hart and Keller had seen what happened, and were coming.

"You all right, Ken?" Pickering heard himself asking with concern.

There goes the goddamned ass-chewing.

"Let me sit here a second, sir," McCoy said. "I'll be all right."

"What the hell happened?"

"I guess I got a little dizzy, sir," McCoy said.

"Keller wants you to do it again, Killer," Hart said as he came up. "All he saw was the crash landing." And then he saw McCoy's face. "Jesus Christ! Did you break something?"

"No," McCoy said. "I don't think I did my fucking leg any good, but I don't think anything's broken." He looked up at Pickering. "If you'll take the Thompson, sir, these two can get me on my feet."

Pickering took the submachine gun.

Hart went behind McCoy, wrapped his arms around his middle, and with no apparent effort hoisted him erect.

"You're sure nothing's broken?" he asked.

"I would know," McCoy said. But he didn't protest when Hart grasped his right upper arm firmly, and motioned for Keller to do the same thing with the left one.

There was the sound of sirens, and moments later, four Military Police jeeps came onto the tarmac from behind the hangar.

"Well," McCoy said. "I'm glad nothing was really wrong. They took their sweet time getting here."

"What's going on?" Pickering asked.

"I had the pilot tell the tower to send MP jeeps here," McCoy explained.

Four MPs, one of them a lieutenant, all in sharply creased olive-drab Class A uniforms, with white leather accoutrements and plastic covers on their brimmed caps against the rain, rushed up.

"What's going on here?" the lieutenant demanded, and belatedly recognizing the star on Pickering's collar points and epaulets, added as he saluted, "Sir? Good evening, sir."

"I'm going to need a forty-passenger bus," McCoy said. "And an MP escort to the Dai Ichi Building," McCoy said.

"What for, Ken?" Pickering asked softly.

"To transport thirty-two Red Chinese prisoners of war, sir. They were captured this morning. I understand General Willoughby doesn't think the Chinese are in the war. If this doesn't convince him, I don't know what will."

The lieutenant looked at General Pickering. "Sir, I don't know —"

"It looks simple enough to me, Lieutenant," Pickering said. "You heard the major. Get a bus, and get it right now."

By the time the bus arrived, so had a half-dozen more Military Police jeeps, plus a jeep with the logotype of *Stars and Stripes* painted beneath the windshield, and carrying three men whose uniforms bore WAR CORRESPONDENT insignia. Everybody had a camera.

"What's going on here?" several of them demanded at once.

"We're about to unload some Red Chinese prisoners of war," Pickering said, "who will be transported to the Dai Ichi Building for interrogation by General Willoughby."

That produced a flood of questions — including "Who are you?" — all of which Pickering ignored.

"Lieutenant," Pickering said to the MP lieutenant. "Permit the press to take pictures as the prisoners are taken off the airplane. The Geneva Convention prohibits the interview of prisoners without their permission, and I'm sure that permission will not be forthcoming. So keep them away from the prisoners. And keep the press here when the bus leaves."

"Sir, I don't know who you are," the lieutenant said.

"That's not important," Pickering said. "I'm a general officer, and you're a lieutenant. All right?"

"Yes, sir."

"I will need a ride in one of your jeeps," Pickering said.

"Yes, sir."

"General," McCoy said. "I want to go to the Dai Ichi Building."

"Hart and Keller are going to take you to the hospital, Major, and I don't want any argument. I'll meet you there."

"I really would like to see the prisoners go into the Dai Ichi Building, sir."

"Even if I told you Ernie's back in the hospital?" Pickering asked.

McCoy's face showed his stunned reaction, but he didn't say anything.

Pickering took pity on him.

"She's all right, Ken. It's probably another false alarm."

"Then there's no real reason I couldn't go to the Dai Ichi Building, is there, sir?"

Pickering looked at him for a long moment.

"I guess you've earned that, McCoy," Pickering said. "Lieutenant, I won't need that ride. Why don't you start off-loading the prisoners?"

"Yes, sir," the lieutenant said.

"George, bring the car around for Major McCoy," Pickering ordered, then climbed the stairs up to the *Bataan* after the lieutenant.

[Five]
Room 39A, Neuro-Psychiatric Ward
U.S. Naval Hospital
San Diego, California
1430 2 November 1950

In Tokyo, and in Korea, it was the middle of the night, and it was raining, a cold, steady drizzle. Halfway around the world, in San Diego, California, it was midafternoon on what Brigadier General Clyde W. Dawkins somewhat grumpily thought of as "another goddamn perfect Southern California day."

In the back of his mind, there had been a faint, perhaps somewhat disloyal, hope that there would suddenly develop a thunderstorm of such proportions that a full-scale retreat parade would be out of the question. His last check of the weather, just before he got in his staff car at Camp Pendleton, had completely dashed that hope. The weather was perfect and it was going to stay that way.

Major Malcolm S. Pickering, USMCR,

was not in his room when he pushed open the door and marched in.

The nurse on duty in the ward said, "General, if you had asked me, I could have told you he's in the Officers' Club."

General Dawkins turned to Captain Arthur McGowan, his aide-de-camp.

"Go fetch him, Art. Bring him up here to his room," he ordered.

Major Pickering appeared in his room ten minutes later, smiling happily.

"May the major express his deep appreciation for the general's very timely interruption?" he asked.

"What the hell are you talking about?"

Major Pickering reached into the pocket of his hospital bathrobe and brought forth a very thick wad of twenty-dollar bills, which he waved happily.

"Straight poker," he said. "I was on a roll. I would never have been allowed to walk away from that table with everybody's money had this splendid young officer" — he pointed at Captain McGowan — "not marched into the Ping-Pong room and announced, 'General Dawkins's compliments, Major. The general desires to see you at your earliest convenience.'"

Dawkins smiled and shook his head.

"Art, give us a minute alone, will you?" Dawkins said.

Pick waited until McGowan had left the room, then asked, "Why do I think I'm not going to like this?"

"Sit down, Pick, and don't open your mouth until I give you permission. That's an order. Say, 'Aye, aye, sir.' "

"Aye, aye, sir," Pick said, and sat down in the folding chair.

"At 1700 hours this date, there will be a retreat parade at Camp Pendleton . . ."

"Yes, sir?" Pick asked.

Dawkins held up his index finger, indicating he really wanted silence.

". . . in which," Dawkins went on, "approximately a regiment of Marines stationed at Camp Pendleton, plus approximately a heavy company — about six boot platoons — of new Marines who are graduating from the Marine Corps Recruit Depot, San Diego, as we speak, plus a company-sized group of Marines from Marine Corps Air Station Miramar, will participate. Additionally, there will be a flyover by fighter aircraft from Miramar and from Marine Corps Air Station El Toro.

"The purpose of this exercise is to present, under appropriate circumstances, various decorations to members of the Marine Corps. Fifteen decorations, in all, will be presented, ranging upward in prestige from the Purple Heart to the Navy Cross, which, as you know, is the nation's second-highest medal for valor. We are sure the recruits, now Marines, will be inspired to see all the heroes in the flesh."

He stopped, looked at Pick, and raised his index finger again.

"The reason for the Marines from Miramar and the flyover by planes from El Toro and Miramar is because the Navy Cross is to be awarded to one of their own."

He stopped.

"You may speak, Major Pickering," he said.

"You are not talking about me," Pick said.

"I am talking about you. My adjutant will read aloud, for the edification of all concerned, the citation I showed you a couple of days ago."

"But, Dawk, I told you that wasn't my citation!"

"Under the present circumstances, Major, I think it would be best if you addressed me as 'General Dawkins.' "

"Aye, aye, sir. But it's bullshit, and you know it."

"I attempted, Major, to raise your doubts about the wording of the citation to the commandant," Dawkins said. "The commandant called me personally. He said that he had just had a visit from the Director of the Central Intelligence Agency, who used to be an Army four-star, and who told him the President of the United States had asked him to find out if the Navy Cross he had ordered for you had been awarded, and if not, why not, and if not, when would it be. The wording of the citation was not open for discussion."

"It's bullshit," Pick repeated. "I won't take it."

"It may be bullshit, but you will take it, and you will not make any comment now, or in the future, to anyone, including me, that will in any way suggest that there is something wrong with the wording of the citation, or that you did not do what the citation says you did." Dawkins paused. "Say, 'Aye, aye, sir.'"

"General, 'Aye, aye, sir' means I understand and will comply with the order. I'm not sure I can do that."

"Yes, goddamn you, Pick, you will. You're a Marine officer, and you will take an order. Say, 'Aye, aye, sir.'"

"Jesus Christ!"

"You can — and knowing you as I do, you're entirely capable of — doing something this afternoon to protect what you think is your honor. 'I cannot, in good conscience, accept this . . .' or something similar. If you do that, you will be pissing on the Marine Corps, insulting a lot of good Marines, and personally embarrassing me. Your call, Pick. But you will get into a uniform, and you will get in the car that will carry you out to Pendleton, and you will line up with the others to be decorated, or so help me Christ, I'll have you court-martialed."

Dawkins pushed himself abruptly out of the chrome, plastic-upholstered armchair and headed for the door.

"General!" Picked called after him.

Dawkins turned.

"I really don't give a shit about getting court-martialed," Pick said. "But for you, Dawk, because of . . . If you think it's important that I . . . Aye, aye, sir."

Dawkins looked at him for a moment, then nodded.

"Okay," he said. "Thank you. Now tit for tat: So far as deserving the Navy Cross is concerned, I put you in for the Navy Cross on Guadalcanal. Before I put Billy Dunn in for his. They said we could have only one — I never understood that, but that's what they said — and they decided it should go to Billy, because he was the squadron commander. I protested as loudly as I could, and was told to butt out. I've always felt you deserved it more than he does."

"Jesus Christ!" Pick said.

"And if you want, you can tell Billy I

told you that, and on my word as a Marine officer, I'll confirm it. Or you can be a good Marine officer and keep that between us."

"Yes, sir," Pick said.

"See you on the parade ground, Major," Dawkins said, and pushed the door with his hand to swing it open. It didn't, and he pushed harder, and this time it swung outward.

Captain McGowan was standing there. Mrs. Babs Mitchell was standing behind him.

"I beg your pardon, Mrs. Mitchell," General Dawkins said, holding open the door. "Please come in. I was just leaving."

"Am I interrupting anything?" Mrs. Babs Mitchell asked.

"No, you're not," Dawkins said. "We have concluded our business. Good afternoon, ma'am."

Mrs. Babs Mitchell entered the room. General Dawkins went through the door and it swung closed after him.

"Was it all right that I came without calling first?" Babs Mitchell asked.

No. Jesus Christ, those eyes!

"Of course. The general got me out of a poker game at just the right time."

"Excuse me?"

"I was playing poker at the club," Pick said, and pulled the thick wad of bills from

926

his bathrobe pocket. "And I was way ahead, and wanted to quit, but couldn't think of a way to."

Jesus Christ, I'm babbling!

"Oh," she said, obviously confused. Then she asked, "You won all that money?"

"Yes, ma'am," he said. "How are you doing?"

"Fine," she said. "How about you?"

I'm just trying to sort out that I'm going to get a Navy Cross I absolutely don't deserve but have to take for the good of the Corps, but that's all right, because I didn't get the Navy Cross Billy Dunn got, even though I deserved it more than he did.

And when I saw you, my heart jumped.

In addition to which, I learned, just before I went to the club to play poker so that I wouldn't have to think about it, that Jeanette's body is already here. A day early. Flown to the States, probably because of Dad, as cargo in a Lockheed Constellation of Trans-Global Airways. Too late to reschedule the welcoming ceremony, of course, so that will be held tomorrow, as per schedule. And I have absolutely no idea how I'm going to handle that.

Aside from that, everything's just hunky-dory.

"I'm fine."

"You look a little funny, Pick," Babs said. "Are you sure?"

When she looks at me that way . . .

"I'm fine."

The door swung inward, and General Dawkins walked back in.

"Excuse me," he said.

"Is it too much to hope there's been a change in the schedule?" Pick asked.

"There may be," Dawkins said. "Depending on Mrs. Mitchell."

"I don't understand," Babs said.

"Mrs. Mitchell, Captain McGowan tells me that you haven't received your husband's decorations," Dawkins said.

"I told . . . whatever his name is, the next-of-kin officer, that I would prefer to get them later, that I wasn't up to two ceremonies, the funeral, and that," she said.

"If you don't like this idea, just say no. I assure you I'll understand," Dawkins said. "This afternoon, there is going to be a retreat parade at Camp Pendleton, during which a number of Marines are to be decorated —"

"Oh, I don't think so, General," Babs interrupted.

"— including Major Pickering," Dawkins went on, "who will receive the Navy Cross."

Babs looked at Pick.

Oh, Christ, don't look at me that way!

"Why didn't you tell me?" she asked.

"He didn't know until I told him just now," Dawkins said.

"What are you proposing, General Dawkins?" Babs Mitchell asked. "That I get Dick's medals at the parade?"

"Yes, ma'am. That's just what I am suggesting."

"Thank you, but no, thank you," she said.

"I understand," Dawkins said.

"Pick, what do you think?" Babs asked, looking into his eyes. "Wouldn't I be out of place?"

I really wish you wouldn't turn to me for advice, Mrs. Mitchell, he thought. *I'm the last sonofabitch in the world who should be offering advice to you.*

"No. No, you wouldn't be out of place. You're entitled to Dick's medals. And getting them at a retreat parade would be something you'd remember the rest of your life."

She exhaled audibly.

"Maybe you're right," Babs said, and turned to Dawkins. "All right, General. What do I have to do?"

"I'm going to send an officer to escort Major Pickering," Dawkins said. "Would you like him to pick you up, too, and take you out to Pendleton?"

She thought a moment.

"Yes. That would probably be best. What time?"

"The retreat parade starts at 1700, which means you'd have to leave San Diego at, say, 1600."

She looked at her watch. "That doesn't give me much time to dress. Simple black dress, hat, and gloves?"

"Spoken like a true Marine officer's wife," Dawkins said. And then heard what he had said. "That was intended to be a compliment, Mrs. Dawkins."

"And I took it as one," Babs Mitchell said. "That's what I was, until recently — a Marine officer's wife."

She put her hand on Pick's arm. The warmth of her fingers immediately went through the thin hospital bathrobe.

You really have absolutely no idea what you're doing to me, do you?

"I'll see you in a little while," she said. "I'm relying on you to get me through this. The escort officer will pick you up first, and then me, right?"

"I think that would be best," General Dawkins said.

When she took her hand from Pick's arm and headed for the door, Captain McGowan pushed it open and held it open as she passed through it, and then General Dawkins followed. Then he went through it and it swung shut.

Major Pickering stared at it for a long time, until he realized he was holding his arm where Mrs. Babs Mitchell had held it.

Then he said, "Shit!" and went to his bedside table and took out a bottle of Listerine mouthwash, which he had had the foresight to fill with scotch in the Officers' Club, and took a long pull, and then another.

[Six]
The Parade Ground
Marine Corps Base Camp Joseph H.
Pendleton, California
1710 2 November 1950

Brigadier General Clyde W. Dawkins, USMC, rose from his chair in the reviewing stand and walked to the lectern at the forward edge. He tapped the microphone with his finger, which caused the loudspeakers mounted on poles to pop loudly.

"Ladies and gentlemen, distinguished guests, Marines," General Dawkins began. "Two of the officers to be decorated today recently flew together off the aircraft carrier USS *Badoeng Strait*. One of them is here only in spirit. His decorations will be accepted by his widow."

There was a sudden, rapidly-growing-in-volume roar of aircraft engines.

Three Corsairs in a V formation appeared low in the sky, and then three more, and then three more.

They flew no more than five hundred feet above the parade ground and then began to pull up. The center Corsair in the third V applied FULL MILITARY EMERGENCY POWER, increased the angle of his climb, and changed course to the right, left the formation, and disappeared into the sky.

General Dawkins again addressed the parade.

"Marines to be decorated, front and center!" he barked.

The band began to play "The Marines' Hymn."

[Seven]
The Ocean View Apartments
1005 Ocean Drive
San Diego, California
1850 2 November 1950

"Would you like to come in for a minute, Pick?" Mrs. Babs Mitchell asked as the Marine-green Chevrolet pulled into the driveway.

I would gladly sell my soul to Satan, or whoever else would have it, to go up there with you and never come out.

"Thanks, but no thanks. I'm a little weary. Call me?"

"Of course."

The escort officer walked Mrs. Mitchell to the lobby, watched through the glass door until she got on the elevator, and then walked back to the staff car and got in beside Major Pickering.

"You all right, sir?"

"No. But I will be just as soon as we get to the bar in the Coronado Beach Hotel and I have a pick-me-up. Or three."

"Sir, my orders are to make sure you make it safely back to the hospital."

"Screw your orders," Pick said. "If General Dawkins finds out — and I can see no reason why he should — I'll take the heat. Sergeant, the Coronado Beach Hotel."

"Aye, aye, sir," the sergeant driving said.

[Eight]
Air Cargo Terminal
Trans-Global Airways
Lindbergh Field
San Diego, California
2025 2 November 1950

"I'm not sure about this, ma'am," the assistant station manager said to Mrs. Babs Mitchell. "He said I wasn't to let anybody in here."

"It's all right," Babs said. "We're friends."

"If you say so," the assistant station manager said, and put his key to the lock

933

in the metal door in the hangar door.

Babs stepped through it.

There were lights in the hangar, but they were mounted high against the roof, and the hangar was crowded with pallets of air freight waiting for shipment — most of it, she saw, addressed to "Transportation Officer, 1st MarDiv, Korea" — and it was some time before she saw him.

He was standing with his hands on his hips — looking oddly belligerent — before a coffin shipping case in a far corner of the hangar.

She watched for more than a minute, and he didn't move.

She didn't want him to hear her coming across the gritty concrete, so, standing on one leg at a time, she took off her shoes before she walked to him.

And he didn't sense her presence — which surprised her — until she touched his arm.

"Hey, Pick," she said. "How are you doing?"

"How the hell did you find me?"

"Well, I was worried about you, so I went to the hospital and you weren't in your room, and you weren't in the Officers' Club, and then I remembered hearing on the radio that her . . . her . . ."

"Jeanette's body?"

"Yeah. *Jeanette's body* would be formally

received, or whatever they said, in the morning. And I thought that maybe it had come in early, and you might be out here. So I called up and asked for you, and he said you weren't here, but I could tell he was lying, so I came out. Wrong move?"

"What made you think I'd be out here?"

"I just knew. I know how you think."

Jesus Christ, I hope not.

He didn't reply.

"I'm surprised they let you in. You really don't work for Trans-Global anymore, do you? I mean, you're on military leave, right?"

"I own the airline," Pick said. "That probably had something to do with the station manager letting me in."

"You own the airline like I'm Marilyn Monroe."

Jesus Christ, she doesn't know!

"I slipped him twenty bucks from my poker winnings," Pick said.

Jesus, I can smell her.

"What happened to your shoes? Blister?" he asked.

"No. I didn't want to startle you, so I took them off. How you doing?"

"After twenty, thirty minutes of solemn contemplation, I decided that Jeanette is not really inside this Container, Human Remains," Pick said. "So it doesn't really matter that it's not covered with the flag."

"There'll be a flag tomorrow, won't there?"

"Probably. I don't know. I don't care. I'm not going. I said good-bye to her twice, once over there, and I'm doing it again now. Have just finished doing it, now."

She took his hand with both of hers.

You don't really want to do that, Mrs. Babs Mitchell. My high moral character is weakened in direct proportion to the amount of imbibed booze. The needle on the Moral Scruples Remaining indicator is already in the red.

"I'm sorry, Pick."

"You shouldn't be. Despite popular legend to the contrary, the real bastards of this world do get what is coming to them. Or don't get what they would really like to have."

"I'm not sure I follow that."

"That's probably because I am just a wee bit tiddly."

"I noticed," she said matter-of-factly. "If you're really finished, I'll take you home."

By that, obviously, you mean home to room 39A in the loony ward.

"I thought I'd catch a cab and go back to the Coronado Beach," he said. "But I will take a ride as far as the passenger terminal, where I can catch a cab."

"Why there?"

"Because that's where the cabstand is."

"I meant the Coronado Beach Hotel?"

"Because I have an apartment there, where I can have a few drinks in private, and thus not disgrace my officer's uniform by being shitfaced in a public establishment, or run afoul of the hospital O Club regulations."

"You have an apartment there?"

"Yeah, I have an apartment there."

"If you're ready, I'll take you there."

"That would be a very bad idea," he said. "As a matter of fact, I will not, thank you just the same, take a ride to the passenger terminal."

"Why would that be a very bad idea?"

"Because I'm having a hell of a hard time keeping from putting my arms around you while standing in front of Jeanette's casket, and I know goddamn well what would happen in your car. Much less my apartment."

She looked into his eyes.

"Okay. Now you know," Pick said. "That's the kind of a prick I am. And the sooner you get away from me, and the farther away you get, the better."

"Okay. I'm warned," she said. "Let's go."

"Didn't you hear what I said?"

"I heard you."

"But you don't believe me? Is that it?"

"I had a couple of drinks before I went looking for you," Babs said. "Time to think very seriously about the dangers of someone like myself being desperate for another man in my life, of someone like you being especially vulnerable to someone like me."

"And?"

"I had another drink and went looking for you."

"Jesus, Babs!" he said softly.

"The drinks I had are wearing off, so if we're going to do this, you'd better get another couple in me pretty soon."

"I don't think you know what you're saying," he said.

"Yeah, I do. Why not, Pick? Who are we going to hurt?"

"The last thing in the world I want to do is hurt you, add to your problems," Pick said.

"I know," she said. She put her hand on his cheek. "Likewise. Who knows? Maybe we can solve each other's problems. It seems to me worth trying. What has either one of us got to lose?"

"Jesus H. Christ!"

"Come on, let's go," she said, and took his hand and led him away from the Container, Human Remains. Halfway to the hangar door, he freed his hand and put his arm around her shoulder. Six steps farther, he stopped, put both arms around her, and kissed her.

[Nine]
Apartment A
The P&FE/Trans-Global Suite
Coronado Beach Hotel
San Diego, California
0830 3 November 1950

"I think this is what your friend Dr. McGrory would call 'postcoital depression,' " Babs Mitchell said to Pick Pickering.

They were having a room-service breakfast; both were wearing hotel-furnished terry-cloth robes. The robe concealed all the curvature of her body.

It doesn't matter. I can see her face. Even without makeup, she's beautiful.

Okay. Here it comes. You knew goddamn well it would.

"Now that I've thought it over . . ."

"Something bothering you?"

"I had too much to drink last night," she said. "You must think I'm really a slut."

"No I don't," he said.

"You don't?"

"I don't."

"I wish I could believe that."

"Believe it."

"Oh, God, what have we done?"

After a moment, Pick solemnly said, "If that question was addressed to the Deity, I'm sorry to have to tell you He's not available at the moment. But — as one of His favorite people on this particular planet — I feel confident in telling you that when He finally gets around to answering your query, He will say something like 'Nothing wrong.' Or 'Good for you.'"

"'One of His favorite people'?" Babs parroted incredulously.

"I have the proof," Pick said. "He put us together, didn't he? Just when we really needed each other. Would He have done that if He didn't like us?"

"Oh, God, I'd like to believe that."

"I told you, He's not available at the moment. But you can believe it."

She stood, walked around the room-service cart, and put her arms around his neck from behind.

"Oh, God, I really hope this works," she said.

"For the third time, I'm sorry to have to tell —"

"I'm going to have to stop saying that, aren't I?"

"I don't know. He'll probably wonder why you stopped talking to Him."

She pulled on his ears, and he twisted in his chair, and somehow his face wound up inside her bathrobe. And then, somehow, the bathrobe became completely unfastened and fell from her shoulders.

He had just picked her up and thrown her over his shoulder and announced, "Me Tarzan, you Jane! We go make whoopee-whoopee, okay?" when the door chimes sounded.

"Come back next year," Pick called loudly.

"It's Captain McGowan, sir."

"Oh, shit," Pick said softly. Then he raised his voice. "Be right with you, Art."

He carried Babs into the bedroom, dumped her unceremoniously on the bed, and went to answer the door.

"Got a message for you, sir," Captain McGowan said.

"From General Dawkins?"

"No, sir. From Japan." He handed it to him, then said, "Sir, when you go back to the hospital . . . The general told them he'd asked you to spend the night, and didn't think he had to ask their permission. They were about to send the Shore Patrol looking for you."

"My compliments to the general, Captain, and please relay my appreciation for his understanding of the situation."

"Yes, sir, I'll do that. Good morning, sir."

Pick tore open the envelope.

```
UNCLASSIFIED
URGENT

OFFICE OF THE CIA DEPUTY DIRECTOR FOR
ASIA TOKYO

0305 3NOVEMBER1950 TOKYO TIME

TO MAJOR MALCOLM S. PICKERING, USMCR
DETACHMENT OF PATIENTS
US NAVAL HOSPITAL SAN DIEGO

VIA BRIG GEN C W DAWKINS, USMC CAMP
PENDLETON, CALIFORNIA

PERSONAL MESSAGE FROM DDCIA TOKYO
TO MAJ PICKERING BEGINS

MAJOR AND MRS KENNETH R. MCCOY,
USMCR, ANNOUNCE THE BIRTH OF THEIR
SON, PICKERING KENNETH MCCOY, IN
TOKYO JAPAN AT 0215 3NOVEMBER1950.
MOTHER AND CHILD ARE DOING WELL.

END PERSONAL MESSAGE FROM DDCIA
TOKYO
```

Pick went to the bedroom door.

"What was that all about?"

"One more proof that He likes me, sweetheart," Pick said, and sat on the edge of the bed and handed her the message.

*Christ, she doesn't even know who the Killer
and Ernie are.*

She handed it back to him.

"Friends of yours?" Babs asked.

"Yeah. You'll like them," Pick said.

"If you're happy," Babs said, "I'm
happy."

Afterword

I was an X Corps sergeant/combat correspondent in Korea shortly after the events fictionally chronicled in this book took place. As such, I was able to read the official version of what happened in the X Corps and 1st Marine Division After Action Reports.

What follows are the facts as we now know them, from our own sources and from those of the Communist Chinese, more than half a century after the conflict.

On 3 November 1950, Major General Charles Willoughby announced to the press that there "possibly" were from 16,500 to a maximum of 34,000 Red Chinese soldiers in Korea.

There were, in fact, 180,000 Chinese soldiers facing the Eighth United States Army on the west of Korea, and about 120,000 facing the X United States Corps in the east. They had begun crossing the Yalu River and entering North Korea in October 1950, each carrying a personal weapon, eighty rounds of ammunition, sometimes three or four "stick" hand grenades, and a week's supply of rations, dried fish, rice, and tea. There were some machine guns and some mortars, all hand-carried.

They moved in at night, halting two hours before daybreak to prepare camouflaged positions. They then slept through the day. Anyone seen moving was shot on the spot, and his body hastily concealed from American aerial observation.

Red Chinese and American historians are generally agreed that the first battle of the Chinese intervention was the attack by the Communists' 124th Division on the 3d ROK Division, which was then advancing near the Chosin Reservoir. The 3d ROK retreated thirty miles south. The 7th Marines counterattacked, killing more than 1,500 Chinese and virtually destroying the 124th Division in a three-day battle.

The Chinese pulled back to plan, and it was decided then that the primary mission of their Ninth Army Group would be the destruction of the U.S. 1st Marine Division.

Misinterpreting this inactivity of the Chinese — and still grossly underestimating the size of the enemy forces — General of the Army Douglas MacArthur ordered X Corps and Eighth Army to stage attacks designed to, as MacArthur said, "end the war by Christmas."

The attacks didn't.

On Friday, 25 November 1950, preceded by a heavy and lengthy artillery barrage, General Walton Walker's Eighth Army began its march to the Yalu.

Initially, there was very little resistance. But on the night of 25–26 November 1950, the Chinese struck with overwhelming force. By morning, they had broken through Walker's lines, and the Eighth Army's right flank was exposed. The Turkish Brigade was sent to plug the hole, and was virtually destroyed.

By nightfall, Walker had ordered the beginning of what has been called the longest retreat in the history of the U.S. Army: 275 miles in six weeks, during which the Eighth Army suffered 10,000 casualties.

In the east, on 27 November 1950, Major General Edward M. Almond's X Corps — about 100,000 men, including the 1st Marine Division — began to strike for the Yalu.

The 1st Marine Division commander, Major General "Howling Mad" Smith — who openly disliked his orders from Almond and MacArthur but had nevertheless begun to comply with them — positioned about 7,000 Marines to lead the fight.

They were unaware that three Red Chinese divisions, about 30,000 men, were in the mountains on either side of the Yudam-ni Valley, ready to attack, and that the rest of the Chinese Ninth Army Group was moving to cut the main supply route in many places once that attack began.

Nor had they heard about the beating the Eighth Army had taken the day before, and was taking as their attack began.

General Smith's 5th and 7th Marines had some initial success, destroying one Red Chinese division and mauling another. But by the end of the second day, the Chinese plan to chop up the main supply route was also meeting success.

And on the Chosin Reservoir's east shore, the Chinese, in division strength, for all practical purposes wiped out the hopelessly outnumbered 7th Infantry Division's 31st Regimental Combat Team, including a reinforcement by just over a thousand men of the 1st Battalion, 32d Infantry (Task Force Faith, so named for its commander, Lieutenant Colonel Don Carlos Faith).

On 30 November, General Almond ordered General Smith to withdraw, and thus began the thirteen-day retreat in sub-zero temperatures from Yudam-ni to Hungnam, which deservedly has become Marine legend:

To move down the one-lane road, it was first necessary for the Marines to clear the Chinese from the ridges on each side of the valley.

The Marines did so, one ridgeline after another.

Marine Aviation flew close ground support missions whenever the weather permitted.

Marine Artillery provided what support it could.

For nine days, over the thirty miles from Yudam-ni to Chinghung-ni, where the 3d U.S. Army Infantry Division had established a line, the Marines were in constant combat with ten Chinese Communist divisions.

It was during this period that General O. P. Smith was quoted as saying, "Retreat, hell! We're just attacking in another direction!" — although there is some doubt about the attribution.

The first "Retreat, hell!" comment came in France during World War I, when orders were issued for the Marines to retreat. "Retreat, hell! We just got here!" one said. The line was already part of Marine legend by 1950, and somebody certainly must have said it at the Chosin Reservoir.

During this period, too, the legendary Marine Colonel Lewis B. "Chesty" Puller, who was then commanding the 1st Marines, did say something near the Chosin Reservoir about which there is no question:

"Don't you forget that you're 1st

Marines! Not all the Communists in hell can overrun you!"

The Marines came out, bringing with them their weapons, their vehicles, their wounded, most of their dead, and a substantial number of Army soldiers they had rescued from certain capture or death.

The 1st Marine Division had suffered 718 Killed in Action, 3,508 Wounded in Action, and 7,313 "noncombat" casualties due to frostbite. There were 192 Marines Missing in Action.

Fourteen Marines were named Medal of Honor recipients.

The Marine Corps estimates 25,000 Chinese were killed and another 12,500 were wounded. The U.S. Army estimates there were 30,000 Chinese KIA and another 30,000 Chinese were frostbitten.

On Christmas Eve, 1950, the 1st Marine Division, with the rest of the X United States Corps, was evacuated by sea from Hamhung. X Corps took with it more than 100,000 Korean refugees. The only thing they left for the enemy were some engineering bridge timbers.

On Christmas Eve, 1950, Lieutenant General Walton H. Walker was killed in a jeep accident. Lieutenant General Matthew B. Ridgway was named to replace him.

On 11 April 1951, President Truman sent, through ordinary Army channels, a message to General of the Army Douglas MacArthur, which read:

"I deeply regret that it becomes my duty as President and Commander-in-Chief of the United States Military Forces to replace you as Supreme Commander."

General Ridgway was named to replace him.

After he came home, was promoted, and retired, I had the unique privilege of coming to know Lieutenant General Edward M. Almond and of having him talk to me — usually in his basement office in his home — at length about his role in the Korean campaign, and his relationships with General of the Army Douglas MacArthur and other members of the Supreme Commander's staff.

One day, when I — and if memory serves, my twelve-year old Boy Scout son Bill — arrived for lunch at General Almond's gracious hillside home in Anniston, Alabama, he met me at the door and handed me a letter he said he had just received.

General Almond was then well into his seventies, but his eyes were still a brilliant blue, and when I looked at him, I thought I saw the beginnings of tears.

The letter was on Marine Corps General Officer's stationery. There were three red stars at the top.

The letter was from Lieutenant General Lewis B. Puller, USMC.

It began:

My Dear General Almond,

On the occasion of my retirement from the United States Marine Corps, I felt duty bound to write to you to tell you that you were the finest combat commander under whom I was ever privileged to serve.

There was more to the letter, now long forgotten, but I shall never forget those opening lines, or General Almond's reaction to them.

W. E. B. Griffin
Pilar, Buenos Aires Province,
Argentina
6 August 2003